HARVEST AMERICAN
Writing

MERRY MEN

BY CAROLYN CHUTE
The Beans of Egypt, Maine
Letourneau's Used Auto Parts
Merry Men

Carolyn Chute

MERRY MEN

A Harvest Book

Harcourt Brace & Company

San Diego   New York   London

Requests for permission to make copies of any
part of the work should be mailed to:
Permissions Department,
Harcourt Brace & Company, 6277 Sea Harbor Drive,
Orlando, Florida 32887-6777.

"The Clearing of the Land: An Epitaph" by Larry Levis from
Widening Spell of the Leaves. Printed by permission.

"Plovdiv/Stone Ridge, NY" by Yuri Mikail Vidov Karageorge from
Sadness in Ardor. Printed by permission.

"Morning Train" adapted and arranged by Elena Mezzetti.
© 1963 (renewed) Pepamar Music Corp. All rights reserved.
Used by permission.

Library of Congress Cataloging-in-Publication Data
Chute, Carolyn.
Merry men/Carolyn Chute.
p.   cm.
ISBN 0-15-159270-5
ISBN 0-15-600191-8 (pbk.)
1. Country life—Maine—Fiction.   I. Title.
PS3553.H87M47   1994
813'.54—dc20   93-11028

The text was set in Stempel Garamond.

Designed by Lydia D'moch

Printed in the United States of America

First Harvest edition 1995
C D E

Dedication

Please let me honor here all the farmers who still work the land themselves, who are not agribusinessmen or agri-businesswomen, but *farmers*, who know family and community interdependence . . . America's last vestiges of freedom.

And honor to all those millions who were born to be farmers, as they have been for thousands of years, but because of modern "education," Big Business, and Mechanization they cannot be and will never know their true gift but are instead herded into welfare lines, prisons, or the slavery of Big Business . . . may they find it—the gift—in another life, another world.

Acknowledgments

Thank you, Jane Gelfman, world's best agent, and Cork Smith, world's best editor.

Thanks also to the MacDowell Colony (three thanks), the John Simon Guggenheim Memorial Foundation, and the Thornton Wilder Fellowship. And to the Maynard-Bluelight-Cedric-Chatterley-Pen-in-Hand Foundation.

Cynthia Poirier, Charles Perakis, D.O., and the good people of Gorham Public Safety . . . thank you for saving my life . . . I hope you never regret it.

For moral support and technical advice, a thousand thank-yous to the following in this haphazard order: Bill Langley, Skip Perry, Mary Howell Perkins, Danny Pierce, Stan Jordan, Lucy Jordan, Arlan Norton, Don Hall, Ruth Stone, Ellen Wilbur, David Gregory, Dana and Sandi Hamlin, George and Geoffrey and Gerard Garrett, Madison Smartt Bell, Frank Collins, Lawrence Naumoff, Blair Folts, Tim Wooten, David White, Bondella Sironen, Ken Rosen, Richard and Ruth Smith and family, Jim Chiros, Florence Connell, Owen and Margie Penny, C. C. and Lib Penny, Richard Anderson, M.D., Wee Gee Tarr, Edie Clark, Joannah Bowie, Annie Penny, Alicia Rouverol, Alix Kates Shulman, Sandy Ives, Peter Pfeiffer, John Sieswerda, Guy and Betty Gosselin, Elmer Walker, Ed Gallant, Richard Dillard, Gerry Griffith, Kathleen Poirier, Carol Metcalf, Rick Libby, Ruth Austin, Jeanne and John Matthew, Leaf Seligman, Brandon Bowie, Annie Evans, Sanford Phippen, Gladys Hasty Carroll, Elisabeth Ogilvie, Jonathan Treitel, and Carol Gallagher.

Joseph Ray Penny, Michael Chute, Denise Giardina, Lucy Poulin and all the good people at H.O.M.E., Leo Kimball, and the Elizabeths Dodge and Moore—you quiet heroes, real-life heroes—you save the day. Thank you.

Thank you, Toto "Wildman" Chute. Forever and ever.

A Partial Cast of Characters

Author's note: There are many characters in this book, many more than identified here in this list. Only a few characters are central. The rest are walk-ons, like the people you see only to say "Hi" to in the P.O. or at public suppers and fiftieth wedding anniversaries. Please do not struggle to keep everyone straight. Just get into the story, and the characters who are meant to be in the foreground will make themselves apparent.

Barrington, Edmund   Husband of Mary Fogg, father (by Mary Fogg) of Lloyd Barrington and (by Bett Johnson) of Forest Johnson, Jr.

Barrington, Gramp (Gramp B.)   Paternal grandfather of Lloyd Barrington, father of Edmund Barrington

Barrington, Lloyd   Son of Mary Fogg and Edmund Barrington; grandson of Gramp Fogg and Gramp B. (Barrington); half brother of Forest Johnson, Jr.; nephew or great-nephew (on his mother's side) of Unks Walty, Roger, Stan, Howe, Douglas, and Jim; cousin of Carroll Plummer

Curry, Phoebe and William   Parents of Gwen Curry Doyle

DiBias, Anneka   Daughter of Francine Soule and George DiBias, granddaughter of Merlin and Dottie Soule

Doyle, Gwen Curry   Neighbor of Lloyd Barrington; daughter of Phoebe and William Curry; twin sister of Dennis Curry; sister of Will, Lawrence, and Guy Curry

Fogg, Gramp   Maternal grandfather of Lloyd Barrington, father of Mary Fogg Barrington

Johnson, Bett   Wife of Forest Johnson, Sr.; mother (by Edmund Barrington) of Forest Johnson, Jr.

Johnson, Forest, Jr.   Half brother of Lloyd Barrington; nominal son of Bett Johnson and Forest Johnson, Sr.; actual son of Bett Johnson and Edmund Barrington; husband of Peggy Johnson; father of Linda and Jeff Johnson

Johnson, Forest (F. D.), Sr.   Husband of Bett Johnson, nominal father of Forest Johnson, Jr.

Johnson, Jeff   Son of Peggy and Forest Johnson, Jr.

Johnson, Linda   Daughter of Peggy and Forest Johnson, Jr.

Johnson, Peggy   Wife of Forest Johnson, Jr.; mother of Linda and Jeff Johnson

Plummer, Carroll   Cousin of Lloyd Barrington, son of Grace Fogg Plummer (Lloyd's mother's sister)

Soule, Dottie and Merlin   Neighbors of Lloyd Barrington, parents of the sixteen Soule sisters: Alberta, Brenda, Cassandra, Faye, Francine, Gail, Kim, Lydia, Marcia, Pam, Robin, Sherry, Tammy, Tina, Wendy, and a sixteenth daughter whose name never appears in this story

Soule, Sherry   Daughter of Merlin and Dottie Soule; sister of the fifteen other Soule daughters

Prologue

The breaking waves dash'd high
On a stern and rock-bound coast,
And the woods against a stormy sky
Their giant branches toss'd.

—Felicia Dorothea Hemans
"The Landing of the Pilgrim Fathers in New England"

IT WAS a poor piece of land but they made it feed them . . . potatoes and certain beans . . . and there were deer and in time, apples. But especially deer. The man was a Fitzgerald. He and his sons would string up a half dozen dressed-out deer near the shedway and head back out for more. And the wife had no daughters and she was delicately built and odd and fell often into naps although she never died of any of them . . . and she fell into weeping at times . . . and she was swept away by angers and swept off by fears . . . and she spoke of the wish for death . . . but she never died of this wish. She did the work of many women and she was kindhearted. The dogs hung around the door as much for her baby talk for them as for her tossing out bones and gristle.

An Indian woman started coming along the road every day while the husband and sons were in the fields or on a hunt, an Indian woman who seemed to come from nowhere and carried nothing. She would come and stand at the door and the dogs would sniff and make low growls around and around her and she would raise her fist at them. The woman of the house knew what the Indian woman wanted.

So the woman of the house would split up some biscuit wood on the block beside the stove and feed a nice fire, and she would start some flour with lard. And all the while, the other woman's dark eyes blazed at the wife through the tiny window of the door and this wife of the house gave away the biscuits as much out of fear as generosity.

The Indian woman's eyes never softened with gratefulness. And when the hot biscuits were held out to her, she would always grab them and turn away and the dogs would follow her back to her disappearing point, vexing her, and jabbing her with their noses in the folds of her skirt. The Indian woman was a secret the wife kept, for she was so afraid of the Indian woman that she couldn't speak of her to her husband.

In time there are no secrets between wife and husband and the husband was furious to hear of all the "wasted flour and lard."

The next midmorning the Indian woman's figure appeared and the dogs hurried up the road to do their work of vexation and jabbing.

Off in the cleared field to the right was another figure . . . the husband raising his rifle to his shoulder . . . CRACK!!! . . . and the Indian woman imploded, became only what seemed like the pile of her dress in the road.

The husband hurried for a look.

The sons arrived. One son came back up to the homeplace for a shovel.

The wife then lay down on the bed in the low-pitched corner of the little house . . . afraid . . . for there is always something to fear.

The Law

A generation of men is like a generation of leaves.

—*Homer*
The Iliad

1 THE CONSTABLE, Erroll Anderson, hunches a bit. He shivers. He is never dressed right for these emergencies. He beams his flashlight onto one of the truck doors which has printed on it: FOREST JOHNSON, SR., & SON. BACKHOE & DOZING. SAND & LOAM. EGYPT, MAINE. 625-8693. He makes this light dance in a frisky way, but the expression on his face remains coplike and earnest. The lettering on the door jiggles and bounces, then slides away. "So," says he.

Forest Johnson, Jr., is leaning hard into the fender of one of the trucks, arms crossed over his jacket. "Take a guess," says Forest, Jr.

The constable shrugs.

"Take another guess," Forest, Jr., says.

"Hard to guess," says the constable, his frozen breath chunky, broken like small sailing ships rolling out and away.

"The possibilities are limitless," says Forest, Jr., with reverence.

"Ah . . . he's taken all your Craftsmans and put them in your wife's silverware drawer and put all your wife's silverware in your tool chests." The constable says this without chuckling. It is said with earnestness.

Forest Johnson, Jr., shifts his weight, but keeps his shoulder to the fender of the truck, eyes on the constable's face. He is waiting for another guess, but it remains a silent, nearly melancholy moment.

2 | Another day, another emergency.

The constable's jeep has a new ping in the engine, but there's still guts left in the old gal. She makes the long steep tarred drive without much trouble. There's the State. Double blue lights. Antennas long and feely. Parked by a rose arbor.

Another state cruiser pulling up the drive beside the constable, antennas wagging. The sun is breaking clear of the trees over along Bond Road. This is the Maxwell residence. How rich? Nobody knows. Nobody knows anything about the Maxwells. They are off-limits people. You never see them at the IGA or the PO. It's a wonder how they get from home to wherever they go to without ever being seen. Though of course they are seen, just unrecognizable, a blur of a face behind the windshield of an unrecognizable car. Perhaps a different car every time? A different route? A different time of day?

The constable veers the jeep off to the side of the drive, lets the state cop pass. The constable sees down over the embankment of the once greener-than-nature lawn to the depths of frostburned goldenrod and witchgrass, glinty, dewy . . . there a dark Mercedes. It is not smashed up or stripped. It just looks uncomfortable there.

People stand around the white arbor, some in work clothes, some in their fall-months' leisures. And the cops dressed straight-creased, gray-blue and edgy. Light pops and glints from their buttons and badges. On the hot top, where the Mercedes might be parked if it weren't in the field, is an open casket, a fairly embellished hardwood beauty. Inside the casket is an individual wearing a suit of dress clothes.

A sharp-edged businessman's voice says, "I consider this a threat."

The constable, Erroll Anderson, nods to Bob, one of the state cops he knows, but otherwise he just stands there with nothing to say. He glimpses about with his froggishly round eyes at the mashed grass and weeds leading down to the Mercedes, then back to the face in the casket . . . more unsettling than a real dead face, a very well-done papier-mâché or clay is what it looks like, with very wide-open, very human-looking glass eyes. The shirt is a bold red-and-white stripe. Pliant under one gloved hand, a cardboard pirate's hat.

The constable, Erroll Anderson, would like to mention that the pirate's face looks just like the face of the man who is angrily gesticulating to the cop, that man with the sharp-edged voice of business, Maxwell himself, no doubt. Whoever made the pirate did quite a job, the constable marvels. He has a desire to reach out and feel the pirate's face and to see if the slightly graying hair is human or horse.

Another state cruiser arrives and then the sheriff's brown car, its radio sputtering. More metal and gleam and officialness, more fuss.

The constable is thinking how lights deter crime and considers his lecture on this that he gives a lot of complainants these days. But from every high place of this massive residence of glass and odd-angled gables are security lamps. Surely even hidden cameras and sudden buzzers, wails and bells . . . security being a kind of life-style here.

3 | The constable, Erroll Anderson, hunches a bit, freezing to the bone. His breath is shaky white tatters falling away. "So," says he. It's his fifth emergency at the Johnsons' in only a few days.

They rise grinning to the mad flicker of the constable's flashlight. Fourteen trucks. Also flickering is the half word, the deep breath, the two men moving through the predawn. Their boots crunch. Along the deathly silent line are the grilles facing out and the rigging of plows and their rams, cables, hoses, two V-plows, several wing plows.

Forest Johnson, Jr., now snaps his flashlight onto a patch of light snow and what looks like a wide-open lead-color rose.

The constable squats for a close look with his own light. He clears his throat and his bowling jacket gives a little bluish ripple. "So," says he. His froggishly round eyes are, as ever, earnest. Earnestness is in the air. For it is known among them in Egypt, Maine, who know all, that the older Forest is up there in his bed in the Johnson house dying. Dying of oldness.

Old Forest, Sr. "F.D." You just never see F.D. around anymore.

And now here we are, it has come to this, Forest, Jr., with a bit of gray at the temples.

Forest, Jr., is swishing his light over more mangled shapes. Chiseled smashed fuel caps. Once perfectly round. Once locked. All cast upon the snow. One from each truck.

Forest Johnson, Jr., directs his viselike bitter line of a smile at the constable. Looks like Forest, Jr., thinks there's something about the constable that is insubstantial and silly. Forest, Jr.'s frozen breath bunches and bounces around his face so now there's no face. When his face reappears, it's just this dark sovereignty of eyes behind steel-rimmed glasses and a fierce close shave. It is only with words of many *S*'s or *Z*'s that something of his teeth shows . . . and there, the tooth that is blue-gray and skewer shaped. Odd for a man who isn't too poor to get it fixed. But, as those in town who know these things know, the Johnsons are not in the kind of business where you need a nice, big smile.

Forest says, "Everything is empty . . . even the backhoe. Even Peggy's car. If I'd had a lawn mower out here with a half a cup of gas in it, he'd have gotten that, too." He steadies himself against the iron flank of the low-bed.

The constable glances at Forest's boots, that usual quickie blushing way people look at Forest's boots. It is legendary, the once-public-spectacle of his once-imploded feet, the rods and twigs look of the broken feet. Everybody that was outside the old bank that day looked. Everyone in passing. So many people. And so much blood. The yellow bulldozer was blood. And the clapboard wall of the bank was blood. And the ambulance driver was blood. And the chunked-up sidewalk was blood. That much blood makes you a celebrity in Egypt. Blood becomes your middle name.

And what do his feet look like now? Everyone knows someone who knows someone or who himself claims he has seen the feet.

Forest smiles on and on, his thin appraising smile, says, "Like if you're going to do a thing, you want to be the best you can be. Right?"

Now the constable squints at the center of Forest's dark jacket.

Forest grimaces. "I imagine that's how *he* looks at it, too. Like for instance . . . you, Erroll, wouldn't want to be anything less than a great constable, a sort of a Nobel-Prize–winning constable. So it is with him. He wants to be the best, world's best motherfucking royal pain in the ass . . . and god bless him . . . he is." Then comes half chuckle, half groan. "Don't see much for tracks here, do you?"

The constable swooshes light in all directions, stops at a tough grouping of plantain leaf. "I'll be honest with you, Forest. If this were murder, something like that would be done. Fingerprints. Tracks. Samples of all varieties of things. Labeled plastic bags. Guys working around here as dainty as archaeologists. I mean *nobody* is capable of leaving no tracks at all. There's something here. Impressions. State boys would investigate the living hell out of this area. In twelve hours, they'd know where everybody on Rummery Road was last night and what brand of fabric softener they use in their socks. I mean . . . you know . . . like baby-rape-death or mutilation-mother-murder. *Any* murder. Armed robbery with a dead cashier behind the counter." He looks up to the despondent gray spot along the spiky black top of the mountain . . . dawn. "Between you and me," he says softly. "If it 'twas the gov'nor had his wristwatch stolen or some billionaire oil baron's ashtray taken from the back of his limo, *then* people get excited. But you and I . . . ordinary guys . . . our troubles are cheap." He almost chuckles. Instead he sighs. "Although, you know of the Maxwells . . . have the helicopter and all those antique cars. Built that place up on Bond Road?"

Forest's expression shows neither recognition nor puzzlement.

Constable says, "He hit them, too. Maxwell was pissed and got a lot of them scrambling over there . . . but . . . I guess the State boys weren't able to find anything. We all just have to hang in there, you know? Best to catch him at it . . . or with the stolen property on him. We'll watch him close for a few more hours . . . his place . . . his in-laws' place . . . his buddies. But you know, Forest, we're always watching him. He's one of our favorite pastimes. He's . . . he's a very weird dude . . . I . . ." The constable cocks his head as if hearing creepy movie music. "Eventually we'll get him, Forest. Eventually . . . but . . ." He sniggers. "You see . . . most of what he does is . . . pranks. Tricks. They just don't add up to much. It's just not worth it to the State to set up a major investigation over it . . . most police effort today is on drugs, not . . . not . . ." He leans close to Forest and jams his flashlight under his own jaw and ghoulishly rasps, "Sommmmmmmme-times our friend makes thinnnnggggs *appear.*"

Forest snorts. He leans away from the low-bed and gives a brutalized fuel cap a little affectionate stroke with one of his boot heels.

The constable gets a quickie glimpse of the boot.

Forest says huskily, "So when I kill him, you can do something with *my* tracks, okay?"

Erroll squares his shoulders, blue satin waves of his bowling jacket moving in and out of place. "Don't joke like that in front of me, okay?" He beams his flashlight into Forest's face, then lowers the light. There's a breeze now, small of force, but big with cold. Erroll starts up a little teeth chattering and dances from foot to foot. "It's been proven, Forest, that light deters crime. I'm surprised your insurance company isn't all over you about getting yourself lights. A couple of mercury lamps . . . one here . . . one over there . . . well worth the money . . . get your money back in six months for what he won't steal from you."

Forest's dark eyes get small, more tightly focused behind his wire glasses, scrutinizing the constable so hard there's almost a cross-eyedness. His voice softens. "So he can see better what he's stealing, right?" He looks up into the black sky, eyes blinking wildly. "Forget it, Erroll. I like the no-lights method . . . because *he* won't see me when I lay low for him with my thirty-ott-six."

The constable's little dance picks up momentum. He looks yearningly in the direction of his jeep parked near Johnson's house across the lot. He wonders, "You going to wait around here every night for the next two or three weeks, maybe two or three *months* . . . all night, every night? I doubt it." He steals another glimpse of his jeep.

Forest Johnson smiles. "Sure I'm going to." His voice is the kind of voice some men have that goes softly hoarse on certain words, so that his voice, like frozen breath, gets tattered and shredded, then again whole. "You don't get it, do you? I'm really into it now . . . the beauty of it. It's a damn beautiful thing. Romantic in a way."

4 | When the constable is finally alone in his jeep, he runs the motor for heat while he marks his report sheet. From out of nowhere a candy cellophane hops onto his bowling jacket in a friendly way. He brushes it hard but now it hops to the opposite cuff. He considers how he has always been an honest man, a nice man. But how gray and vague and flexing the wide world is. Inside the jeep, the heat builds and the ride home is solemn, but toasty.

Super Tree Man

They have perhaps a year or two
Left of this
Before history begins to edit them into
Something without smoke or flies, something
Beyond all recognition.

—*Larry Levis*
"The Clearing of the Land: An Epitaph"

1 | LLOYD HAS NEVER seen this little girl before. Never. Till now. This thick-legged girl sitting on top of the kitchen table, bare but for terry underpants. Lloyd tries to find familiarness in her face. Unk Roger has said she's Lloyd's "own cousin." "Own cousins," Lloyd knows, are the kind you're supposed to visit more often than this . . . or at least see them walking around at a wedding . . . or the IGA. He flashes his eyes on each face here, then flashes his eyes away, crazed with wonder and fear.

A red-haired woman rinses a washrag in a pan of bloody water . . . squeezes . . . then slops the rag once again on the scratches shaped in V's and willy-nillies on the little girl's legs, the washrag looking like a good-feeling thing, crawling into place around each ankle, adrift up and down the legs. The woman's fingers are like shafts of light, so thin, maybe weightless. The little girl stares at the woman's hands. The child is blue-white and long. Long bodied, eyes rounded in the poor light.

Through the open doorway looking out, you can see their deep-water yard. Rain coming up to the door. And off across the openness, power lines with their high wires . . . peat and ledge and juniper and blackberry and sumac, all the awful stuff. Nothing to make you shady. And close to the door, a logging truck like the wall of another building. And all over all of this is the kiss-kiss of rain. And Unk Roger is in the doorway looking out, wearing his black lace-up boots. He stands like a guard. When his face shows, he is wearing his high-and-mighty look. And the woman's face has gotten high-and-mighty, this probably being because you have a certain thing, a certain "look" that runs in the family. Lloyd has figured this must be so . . . like in a family you have big bones or little bones. But besides this there's something going on . . . a twinkle in the woman's green eyes . . . a little joke going on here. Jokes are always going on when you are age eight and three-quarters . . . jokes above your head . . . jokes not on you but *without* you. In the place where the red-haired woman's teeth once were, between the hard ridges of her gums, there's a cigarette, which is not lit yet. It jiggles, blue-white as the little girl and perfect in its unsmoked condition.

There's no place to sit here. Just one upholstered chair with an old man in it. There's barely room to stand. Lloyd sees that his father, Edmund's, crotch is against the table. His father, Edmund, . . . a man too dark to show much of a flush. And yet Edmund's face is aflame. Bothered. Edmund's dark eyes seem to find something about the woman's house-dress.

Now Lloyd's father, Edmund, pulls a blue bandanna from his overalls pocket, draws it across the back of his neck. Lloyd hopes his father might do something next that will let Lloyd in on the secret joke of all this.

Old man in the chair. Has a white pearly lumpiness to his fore-head and one temple. But Lloyd has seen worse than that. Just another chain saw story. They all start with, "I was workin' over to blah blah blah . . ." You hear Clayton and Rick tell theirs. You hear Hazen's. And that other guy at the store . . . guy with one hand. Another and another. Foye is the name of these people here. Lloyd's dead mother's people. She has so many people, which also includes Gramp Fogg and the unks. All her people. Every road you take, there's somebody to wave to and blow the horn. Or else you got to stop the truck and talk a million years to someone standing by their mailbox. Usually boring. But these . . . the Foyes . . . they are making a fire on his father's face.

The woman says, "You boys come to see the transmission?" and her cigarette frisks up and down on each and every word.

"Yup," says Unk Roger by the door a little testily. He doesn't even turn around.

What they have on the drainboard is four nice pies, painfully swollen, exuding winey-black from the fluted edges and from the fork marks of their high meridians. The sweet right heat of them mixes with the bad odor of tomcatness although there's no tomcat in sight . . . and some odor coming out of the father, Edmund, . . . not just his usual woods, cattle, and work . . . but something like alarm . . . but not alarm . . . something other.

The woman says, "Too late. A feller was here last night . . . paid cash."

"Zat so," says Edmund, his eyes on the middle of the woman.

Lloyd sees his father's shoulders thickening, flexing, the throat working its undulating big timbre around a thought. Lloyd leans his weight onto his palms on the table to lift himself up for a handstand sort of thing he is known for doing on everybody's furniture and at school at times when he himself least expects it, which sometimes causes furniture to flip. He swings his legs to and fro. The bloody water in the pan sloshes out some.

"Stop," says Edmund deeply, but very, very soft.

Old man in the chair turns his coffee mug around and around. Coffee mug on his knee. No place else to put it. *Very* small house.

"You need a boat?" the woman asks Edmund. "We got a boat that might be for sale. You want to look at it?" Her eyes make tight little bee circlings around Edmund's face, then stop outright. Eyes into eyes. The stare is held.

"No thanks!" snorts Unk Roger from the door, still facing out, staring into the warm rain.

Lloyd crosses his arms to hide his fat-boy breasts.

"Know these boys, Emery?" the woman asks the old man.

"Yep," says the old man, looking up from his coffee mug, nods into Edmund's eyes and then toward the back of Unk Roger's head . . . but not to Lloyd . . . Lloyd not part of the tangled, weary old past.

The little girl has purple hands.

Unk Roger says, "Ready, Ed?"

Edmund says, "In a minute."

Unk Roger now has disappeared from the doorway. There's just the sucking sounds of his boots in the black mud, somewhere between the towers of darkened forklift pallets, some long low cars, big water with boards crossing to the clothesline, little water in puddles shaped like feet. And the logging truck, huge, huge. House, eensie-weensie.

The father, Edmund's, eyes drift to the little girl's purple fingers curled around the black-painted rim of the washbasin. "Blackberry-picking champ of the world, eh?" says he. His voice strange, thick, like caught in the middle of a swallow.

The woman says, "She learned her lesson this time." Then she cocks her head, squints out into the dooryard. "Sure you don't need a boat?"

"Not me," says Edmund, a smile flickering across his face.

The woman's mouth stiffens around the cigarette, like drawing smoke, though there's no smoke. She lets the washrag slide into the dark water and says, "Okay. Done." She hauls the little girl over the table edge to the floor. The table thumps and sways as the little girl goes under. Lloyd wants to see where she went, but he would have to stoop and put his face down there in the darkness.

The woman strikes a kitchen match, keeping her back to Edmund and Lloyd as she lights up. They don't see her face for a whole minute. She just smokes and smokes the long while. "You wouldn't like a nice cat, would you?" she says at last, turning.

"Not me," chuckles Edmund Barrington, his eyes blacker, wider now. And hers . . . full of sport. Tosses her red hair, shoots out her smoke craftily over one shoulder. "Double paws," she says deeply.

"Good for him," says Edmund with a grin.

2 | On the way home the pie has a special place in the toolbox on the flatbed. It's a pie the red-haired woman gave Edmund. There she wanted to sell him stuff so bad, doesn't sell anything, just winds up one less pie. When Lloyd says, "I'm going to eat the *whole* thing!" for about the fifth time, Unk Roger says, "Talk about something else."

Lloyd asks, "Why?"

Unk Roger watches the fields pass.

Edmund Barrington keeps reaching to fool with the wipers . . . letting them slash a half minute . . . then twists them off for a half minute . . . then back on for a half minute . . .

Neither Edmund's work shirt sleeve nor Unk Roger's T-shirt sleeve seems to get much flutter from the open windows. This is because Edmund drives slow. Always very, very slow. Even without pies.

"Why, Unk? Why?"

Unk Roger sighs. "Because sometimes you harp on a thing till it grates on me. Okay?"

Lloyd thinks about the pie. He can still smell the smell of the little Foye house on himself and in the air of the truck, mixing with the sweet air of other people's mowed fields, mowed lawns, and the sky of pale rain not dropped yet, and the leaky gas tank smell, and the brake fluid smell, and the cow smell of the flatbed.

Unk Roger glares at Edmund's hand, which is giving the wipers another twist.

Lloyd says, "The thing I'm not supposed to talk about . . . I bet you I could eat it and never be hungry for a week."

Unk Roger sighs, takes off his black-frame glasses, cleans them on one knee of his work pants.

Edmund grips the wheel now, like the truck is careening at eighty miles per hour. And Lloyd can hear the hairs in his nose, which means his mouth is shut too tight.

Now Lloyd wonders dreamily, "Guess how many blackberries might be in the thing I'm not supposed to talk about. A million?"

No answer. Both men deadly silent.

"Probably a million," Lloyd answers himself.

3 | Unk Walty uses a Phillips in one hand, a claw hammer in the other. He has given the white swollen lips many blows, but they don't budge.

Unk Walty, like all Dougherties and Foggs, has an inherited muscularity, the small-waisted, tensed-with-power look of a weightlifter, though he never fusses for it, never thinks about proteins, never works out. It's just a thing that all Dougherties and Foggs have . . . bodies of the gods. And yet there's something about Unk Walty that makes it clear that the ice is the boss, Unk Walty the slave.

Lloyd says, "If you wait, it'll just melt."

Unk Walty sets the Phillips on the table, then uses both hands on the hammer. THWONK! THWONK! CHINK! CHINKA-THWONK!!!

Lloyd says, "Want me to get a bar, Unk?"

Walty replies with a gasp, "Not yet . . . but that's a thought."

When the first slab lets go, it makes the whole house boom.

"Atta go," mutters Gramp B. from one of the far-off back rooms as the ice is flying into pieces over the linoleum, east, west, north, and south in the big kitchen. Unk Walty takes a quick little bow.

Lloyd grapples the largest ice chunk from the floor, embraces it to his bare chest. He laughs crazily. It squirms to get away. "LOOK, UNK! LOOK!"

Unk Walty whacks at the remaining ice with the Phillips and hammer.

"LOOK, UNK!" shrieks Lloyd, dancing with the ice, pushing between his uncle and the refrigerator. "LOOK! LOOK! Feels good! LOOK!"

Rivers of sweat run out of Unk Walty's dark hair. Another hunk of ice lets go, strikes the linoleum, skids, one piece off to the left disappears under the table.

Lloyd nudges Unk Walty's bare elbow with the ice. "LOOK, UNK! Feels good, doesn't it!"

Unk Walty takes a folded white handkerchief from his trousers, wipes his face and neck, staring with gravity into the refrigerator. "I'd like to have gotten a picture of that . . . you know . . . a Before and After."

Lloyd kisses the ice chunk. Dances around. "Look! Unk . . . this is nice for a hot day . . . feels GOOD!" Kiss. Kiss.

Unk Walty says, "I'm *looking*, Lloyd . . . but dear, PLEEZE don't put your mouth on it like that. It's probably germy."

4 | Next day it's another visit to Foyes'. The rain has stopped but the air is thick and makes skin feel worse than lapped candy. This time it's Lloyd and his father in the truck alone. No pissed-offish Unk Roger. So Lloyd gets to ride with his arm out in the air and he is wearing the blue Civil War kepi Unk Stan found in the Wilkinsons' barn in the part that didn't burn. When Lloyd wears the kepi, he keeps the visor low

to make shade and secretness over his face. His expression is expression-less, like you are supposed to be when you are in a war.

The vast truck with loading clam is gone from Foyes' dooryard. It's just the little brown house there in the puddles and mosquitoes and all the piles of stuff the lady likes to sell. No trees. The sunny stickyishness of the day is terrible here without trees.

Edmund goes right through the water to the door. There are more boards laid out there to walk on, but ol' Edmund just sloshes out around them. The door isn't a door now, just a doorway, the door taken off the hinges. Some repair in the works it looks like.

Lloyd, hurrying up behind his father, catches sight of the little girl in the kitchen alone wearing nothing at all. If it were him, Lloyd thinks, and he were caught with no clothes, he would hide or at least grab some-thing to hold in front of him.

Edmund asks the girl, "Where's your mother?"

"SHE *SEEN* YOU COMIN'!" The girl laughs like the funniness of this will kill her.

Edmund bellers, "IRENE!!!! HEY! YOU AROUND!!!?"

There are more pies. The blackberries around here must grow in a most wonderful way.

"Wait here, Lloyd," says Edmund and he disappears around the side of the house.

Hot yard. Hot kitchen. Heat that squeezes. This whole visit feels like a big hot mouth.

Lloyd pulls his kepi lower and steps over the doorsill and looks around. His kepi visor gets in the way of his view of the little girl's face. All he sees is the neck down.

The girl moves deftly like a blade into the narrow space between the table and the Coleman cooler and Sunday papers in a tower against the wall. With her palms on the table, she hoists up, the table rocking madly . . . then one heel, then the next thump the floor. She ducks away. Lloyd swears she took one of the pies but it's all so darkish and hard to see here . . . corners and underneaths all mysteries chock-full.

There on the doorsill, Lloyd does an about-face and now has his back to the room like Unk Roger did yesterday. He wonders where his father has gone. Probably to take a piss behind the house. Or to find the red-haired woman and act weird some more. Lloyd listens. But all there is to hear is miles and miles of creaking zinging tall-grass bugs down the power line cut between the two mountains. He pretends to be a soldier at attention, keeping an eye out for enemies. He pretends he has one of those old-timey rifled muskets and a bayonet for poking the guys who are on the other side in the wrong army. He tries to imagine how he looks to a car passing . . . if one were to pass. He imagines he has a beard and wounds all over him . . . none of them hurt a bit . . . but blood and guts are all over the place in soft butcherish piles. He just keeps his eyes straight ahead, chin raised, chest out. And he imagines that he's not fat.

His father takes forever. Why? Why? Why?

He wonders if there will be a pie to bring home this time. He says as if to himself, "Looks like plenty of pie here."

How he sweats! Everything in the air sticks to him. Every dust speck. Every pollenish thing. And the old beautiful-bad smell of this house. Slowly he turns and sinks to a squat. Under the table it's like a little room . . . a striped, stained bed pillow with stained white cat in a loose sprawl on it. The cat's tongue goes in and out of its head like a dog's. There's too many dolls and stuffed animals, way too many, all shoulder-to-shoulder and wearing real people jewelry and winter caps. Saucers and bowls in all the laps. Enough blackberry pie to go around with some left in the pie plate. The little girl right there on the floor. A lot of sand on the floor.

Keeping his kepi low, Lloyd gets a good long study of between the little girl's legs, which is nothing like he imagined. It is just a simple thing. Like a smile. He raises his chin and finds her eyes fixed on him. She has such a look of peace.

He asks, "You live under here?"

She asks, "Why are you so fat?"

It moves up his back and neck slow. An icy rage. He narrows his eyes, which makes her eyes widen. He makes a fist close to her face. "Because I *kill*," says he.

She jerks her head back.

He feels better.

5 | Unk Walty tapes Lloyd's poem on the refrigerator so everybody walking by can get a little culture. Unk Walty says Lloyd is going to be a great artist. It runs in the family, says Unk Walty. The poem goes like this:

LIFE

by Lloyd S. Barrington   age 8¾

A winter day is a pretty glass thing to look at. Like a nice
    rock you pick out.
A summer day is a dead fish. Pretty bad. But sum peepil like it.

6 | Lloyd works the Scotch tape, putting up a new poem. "This one's
better, Unk. I got more stuff in it."

LIFE

by Lloyd S. Barrington   age 8¾

Winter is like walking threw a dimond.
Summer is like walking threw an old fish bol nobuddy has
    changed for ages the kind that you get fish all ovr
    along the top sucking and poop is ther of fish that
    looks like littel sausiges. Prety bad unlest you like it.

Unk Walty steps up to the refrigerator and squints at the new poem. He
says, "What did you do with that other one, Lloyd?"

"I mushed it."

"Well, get it and fluff it out. They are *both* good!"

"Well, it's scrunched pretty bad," says Lloyd with a scowl, patting
and pressing it out on the table. "And there's rips."

Unk Walty moans. He snatches the paper from Lloyd and grips it to
his heart. "Next time you go scrunching up another one, you check with
me first."

Lloyd says he will.

7 | Lloyd sees rat poison on the seat of the truck. Cartoon of a dead
rat, X'd out eyes. Unk Roger is fiddling with fuses under the dash,
head screwed around on his neck in a way that looks like torture.

"Hi," says Lloyd, leaning with crossed arms onto the open passenger's
window. "Unk Walty says for you to fix the flag . . . weld it or somethin'.
That's what he says to tell you." Lloyd is wearing the enormous straw
hat with the long limp straw fringes his cousin Carroll Plummer won at
Old Orchard Beach but never wears. Hard for Lloyd to get his head all
the way in the window with so many wavering straw fringes.

"What flag?" wonders Unk Roger a little nastily. Sweat running rivers out of his eyes. Fumbles one of the fuses. It bounces off one lens of his eyeglasses, lands in and among the tools and boots on the truck floor.

"On the mailbox," snickers Lloyd. "You think I meant the kind at school?"

"Right," groans his uncle, untwists his head, goes on a search for the fuse.

Lloyd says, "Unk Walty says for me to help you."

Unk Roger gives a snort. "Nice of him. But first go back and tell him I've been out straight all day and STILL AM and if, if, IF I get time, I'll go look at it."

"Okeydokey," says Lloyd.

Roger finds the fuse. Fondles it. Says, "So where's your father? Over there at Foyes' puttin' the pickle to Irene?"

Lloyd giggles. "Pickle!"

Unk Roger stands up, pulls his black-frame glasses off, arranges them with care next to the rat poison. He says a little bit whisperishly, "I see another black eye or tooth through the lip in your father's future." He blinks his eyes open and shut fast about six times and grins. "*That* is what I see."

"Nawwwwwwww," groans Lloyd.

Roger pulls up the front of his T-shirt, pushes his face into it, wipes his forehead, cheeks, neck.

"I made a new poem, Unk. This one is better but Unk Walty says to keep both. You going to have time to read it?"

Unk Roger says through the soaking weave of his T-shirt, "I'll read it when I come in. I'll read it first thing. I promise." Roger's bared belly is dark hair, deep navel, forceful, dark thundercloud of a belly. Wears his belt buckle on the side. Unk Walty says Roger thinks he's a "cool cat."

8 | It is hard to keep the pencil sharp when the jackknife isn't very sharp either. The new point doesn't seem improved. He smoodges the pencil along with anguish. And his tongue angles around at the corners of his mouth.

LADIES
by Lloyd S. Barrington   *age 8¾*

Ladies give peepil nice pies.
Then you give them a pickl. Thats the way. I would give

both kinds. Unk Walty says we have an overload.
Might as well give her a bunch. Pickles you get in the
sweet flavor and little seeds but sum dill. I dont know
about Dad how manny he brot. Ladies like nice plates
to keep in the closit. They have a blue world you can
look in to. Litil bridge. Litil house. Trees.
Nice and shady. You eat on these plates its a big deal.
Ladies have hare. Men its short. Ladies ladies ladies!

9 | This night, as nearly always, his father comes to bed only a few
minutes after Lloyd does. This house . . . there's not much TV
watching here. Not like you see with other people sitting up, sitting
around. Not here. All the unks, Gramp B., and Gramp Fogg, and Edmund
putting in such long days. Work. Work. Work. Work. Cattle, woods,
sawmill, cemeteries . . . all the long days. Weekends as well. Saturdays,
Sundays. It's never long after supper that the lights go out. And in the
dusk of Junes and Julys before the lavender skies have a star, they are all
down on their beds.

Heavy-duty sons-a-bitches. He's heard them called that . . . all of
them. And he's heard them called Republicans. Heard it said that Unk
Stan once crushed a Revereware saucepan in his hand. Could do it again.
Either hand. Even Unk Walty, though he seems too nice. But it's good
he can crush a thing if he had to.

Lloyd takes up his mother's side of the bed nowadays. His mother.
He was eight years old when she finally died and now he is still eight
years old. In a few days after they put her in the cemetery, Edmund
invited him to his bed. The bed is not a Hollywood bed, the latest thing,
but there's a puffed comforter from one of the catalogs. And on the wall
peacocks made of metal. And for each side of the bed a lamp made like
a Colonial person . . . man on his father's side . . . Lloyd gets the lady
with the lace umbrella.

Lloyd knows his father's silence. The silence that isn't sleep. The
silence that is something else. The man never tosses, nor gets up to pace.
He doesn't move. But after time, nearer morning, Edmund Barrington
will make his terrible dark fall into sleep. By four A.M. when he gets
up . . . always ahead of the others, moving from room to room in his
heavy boots, pulling the chains to lights, his dark ravenous eyes moving
in his head, moving over the others at the breakfast table, his tightly

honed-down scrutinization of each face . . . he is refreshed. His appetite is good. Hot cereal or pancakes. Gobs of butter. No one would know it to look at him that his night was a bad one. Only Lloyd.

Tonight as Edmund's head with its close-cropped black hair ventures to its pillow, Lloyd says as he always does, "Good night. Sweet dreams."

"Ayup," says Edmund as he always does.

10 At Moody's Variety & Lunch, there's no ever sneaking in. No matter how good you are as a quiet person somewhere else, Moody's screen door all but screams your name. Jingle bells. Chrome bells. Brass bells. And bonging cowbells. And the bang of the door itself. And then that softening, chuckling, hush small golden tinkle at the very end.

Jeannie Moody at the register gives the boy a nod. Bare-chested fat boy. Dungarees cinched around the belly with something . . . could be horse harness. Then there's his green cotton work cap, a perfect fit against the short dignified fringe of his dark brown hair. He has just come in out of the bright street. He has come here on a tractor, alone like a small man. His arms and face are tanned roughly, but the belly and broad back are a sweet sweet baby-white. Behind him, beyond the screen door, Rummery Road buzzes with heat, pounds and rattles with trucks from the sandpit and from town, their pewy blue stink mixing and swirling, hanging low. And a deafening hot pop-popping of the idling tractor that the boy has left with one big tire on the curb.

He is a boy with one green eye, one eye mostly brown.

The understanding the lunch-counter guys have is that a young boy is always fair game. They wink amongst each other. One swivels all the way around. "Hey! Whatcha doing with Ed Barrington's tractor. D'ja steal it?"

"No." The boy barely moves his lips. In his hand there's a smudged paper. In the corner of his eye, the heckling gleam of wristwatches and eyeglasses, the convergence of a rolled up sleeve with a bottle of Fanta grape moving toward a mouth, an ear getting scratched, shoulders squared, swiveling synchronized stools, more of them turning to face him on.

Now he steps up to the bulletin wall with his splay-footed fat-boy walk.

"He looks like the stealin' type to me," one of them rasps.

"A highwayman if there ever was."

"They got a way about 'em."

Silence, but for hot coffee sucked through a pair of lips and menthol smoke dispelled through teeth. Ketchup . . . GLOINK. And the white road heat and traffic beyond the screen door steadily keening . . .

"So you swear you didn't steal it?" one of them wonders at last.

The boy doesn't answer, but no answer is worse than the wrong answer. Five or six snorts and one outright HAWWW HAWW make this clear.

"Somebody ought to get the constable. Ray, go get the law on down here. Hurry. This guy is bad news. Another ten minutes, Ed will never lay eyes on his John Deere again."

"T'will be sold on the streets of New York City." This is a voice of a low and contented timbre at the far right end of the horseshoe counter.

Jeannie Moody at the register, leaning on her elbows, warns them, "You guys just shut up and eat."

"AWWWWWWWWWW!"

"Oooooooooo-eee!"

"Mean Jeanne!"

A drop of sweat rolls down the fat boy's bare back. There before him is Moody's bulletin wall thick with trade. Some things tacked, others taped. FOR SALE: Evinrude 6-horse. Like-new Zenith TV. FOR SALE: Come-along and chains, tires, hubs. Baby bunnies, very cute. Color photo of a ranch house with breezeway and garage . . . FOR SALE BY OWNER, TWO ACRES, ARTESIAN WELL. Black-and-white photo of a Palomino horse. Free kittens. Found beagle. Lost dog, black . . . comes to "Blackie." 1956 Rambler wagon. 1949 PLYMOUTH . . . good for parts . . . make an offer. Finish carpentry . . . call Chet Flint evenings.

The boy does some rearranging of the cards, notes, and tacks until his own sheet of paper is in place.

Silence, but for the bubbling of the cooler, but for one man swallowing his soda the wrong way, choking. Silence now. The thunder of their eyes on the boy's hand. He turns for the door.

"Bet he's makin' a damn good deal on that tractor," a voice whispers. "That's what he's puttin' the ad up for. *The tractor!!*"

Chuckles and snorts.

"Hurry, Ray . . . get the law on the phone before it's too late."

"Naw . . . I wanna see how much a good deal he's giving on a hot tractor."

"You ain't got a single ounce of trustworthy decency in you. I guess I'd better find the constable and maybe he can handcuff you, too!"

Chuckles.

"Better hurry," Jeannie Moody says disgustedly. "Handcuff that one first . . . long overdue."

"Awww . . . you'd miss me too much!"

"Ha!" Jeannie snorts.

The boy is out the door now, the bells clanging, bonging, jangling, and the final whispery tinkle, everyone straining to the far left to see through the screen the fat boy mounting the tractor.

"Never mind the constable. Time's running out! What we need here is a citizen's arrest!" the man named Ray clamors, dropping from his stool, taking long-legged exaggerated steps around a frazzled wicker rocker. Many rockers. Some knock into others, a chain reaction of happily creaking empty rockers.

Several men rush at the door. Through the screen they chorus, "CITIZEN'S ARREST!" and "STOP HIM! HELP! HELP!"

Jeannie Moody sighs, "Somebody oughta turn a hose on you guys."

The guy named Ray grips the door latch and gives the door a big shake, sets the bells bonging and jangling again. Then, "Jesus! Pretty some slick with a tractor. Lookit him go."

"Well," says one of them. "I know one thing . . . he's pretty serious lookin' when you plague him. Picture of his old man."

"Shame," says another.

Couple of snickers.

"Lotta kids are the picture of Ed." Roll of the eyes.

More snickers.

Somebody wonders, "What's that about a guy once that used to sell the Brooklyn Bridge to people?"

"Coffee, Jeanie! I need a refill!"

Over at the bulletin wall three men have converged, one with his work cap over his heart and a very grave expression on his face. Another gives the change and keys in his pocket a slow suspenseful jingle.

The boy's paper partly covers a church rummage sale notice. The handwriting of the boy is drowsy-looking, done in smoodgy pencil. The paper reads:

> ARE YOU TREELESS? DO YOU NEED SHADE BAD? A THING
> PRETTY TO LOOK AT THREW THE WINDOWE. NICE FOR
> BIRDS. CALL: 3347 FOR YOUR FREE TREE GARINTEET TO BE
> A HUGE GREAT TREE AFTER A WILE. YOU CAN HAVE AS
> MANY TREES AS YOU WANT. SIX ARE GOOD. IN A ROW.
> JUST CALL UP AND SUPER TREE MAN WILL BE THEIR IN A
> FLASH TO SAVE THE DAY. IF YOU DOANT BELEIV IT YOU
> ARE WRONG. JUST MAKE UP YOUR DECITION IF ITS OAK
> YOU LIK OR MAPIL BEETCH OR PINE OR CHRISTMAS
> TREES HONBEAMS HEMLOK ELM ASH BIRCH I CAN GET
> SOME APPLE TREES BUT NOT SO EASY. ON BIRCH I
> WOULDNTE GO FOR GRAY IF I WAS YOU NOT POPLES
> EATHER BUT JUST THEY GROW FAST BUT MOST PEEPIL
> SAY NO ON THES. OAKS AND MAPILS AND BEECH ARE
> BEST FOR YOU TO GET SHADY. YOURS TRULY SUPER
> TREE MAN.

"What's it say?" one of them back at the lunch counter wonders. The guy named Ray says deeply, "Try 'n' guess."

11 | "Hello?"
"I am calling fer dee super tree mannn." Fake accent. Teenage cracks in the voice. "I'm calling from the Sahara Desert and I need a VERRRRY big . . . VERRRRRRY VERRRRRRRRRRRRY big order real quick. Hoooooeeeeeee-heee-hheeeeeee-heeeeeeeee! . . . Click." Dial tone.

Unk Walty comes back to the table to clear off from supper. One of the unks is left still picking over one of the chickens. This is one of the unks that doesn't live here anymore but comes around after his shift to find food.

Unk Walty wipes down the cleared end of the table, looks up, and sees the other man staring at him. Unk Walty says matter-of-factly, "It was nobody. Maybe just some lightning striking the wires somewhere."

12 | The meal is beef. Yesterday's leftover biscuits. String beans fixed with cream. Pickles of both kinds.

A blue, black, and white butterfly has gotten into the house with the opening door, tumbles up and down the screen of the door with its wish to get back out. It is a house of only men. The widowers and the never-marrieds. None divorced. Some coughing. Some gagging. The need to spit is great with Unk Douglas and Unk Howe and Gramp Fogg, the three cigar smokers. No cigarettes. All cigars.

Edmund Barrington is stationed at the kitchen sink, the rest of them done with handwashing, ready at the table, waiting, eyes on their empty plates. Seems like they might go on ahead without Edmund, but they don't go on ahead without him. Unk Roger fiddles with his fork, but that's the extent of it.

Unk Walty has a kettle of squash peelings on the floor between his feet, works a black-bladed knife over the lumpy face of a hubbard, Unk Walty's face always bright with welcome to see them coming in from their day. Wearing his cloth slippers, it's a sign he's just had his bath while supper was on low heat. "Must've been a stinker of a day in the woods today, Ed?"

"Yes 'twas," says Edmund.

Unk Walty looks out at the yard full of parked trucks, which are just checkered shadows through the screen door. He turns toward the table. "Who was it, Rodge . . . your science teacher wasn't it? . . . said sweat cools?"

"Yep," says Roger. "Sweat cools."

"Zat right?" says Edmund, squirting pink dish soap into one palm.

"Big science!" titters Unk Walty, then drops his head forward over the chunk of hubbard laid out on his knees, back to his business.

Edmund snorts, "Well, one might as well piss all over one's self to feel refreshed." The water pipes thump as he runs cold water over his forearms, over the black maps of pine pitch, and then the hands. He rubs water into his dark crew cut, the erect ears, the grimacing neck muscles. He even wets his shirt, splashes a little extra down inside his collar like a woman giving herself a little extra helping of Chanel.

Unk Walty sets the squash preparations aside. Makes a row of tin and glass pie plates on the sideboard. All eyes of the men waiting at the table watch Walty's hands . . . hands that make all pies possible . . . not just the old standby kinds of pies . . . but pies beyond one's wildest imagination.

"Where's Lloyd?" Edmund asks, feeling for a striped towel.

"Oh!" Unk Walty seems surprised by this inquiry. He flutters his eyes slightly. "He's on a mission." He returns to his chair, folds his hands in his lap, slides his eyes to the left.

Gramp Fogg laughs nervously. "This some joke?"

"What?" Edmund frowns. "What's this?"

Walty is smiling his greatest most welcoming smile, smiling around at everyone. He says, "There's something wonderful about to happen. Somebody is on the way."

There's total silence from the other men. Unks Jim and Stan are especially blush-faced, the bright glare of their bifocals flashing back the ceiling light, keeping thoughts to themselves. Even the smokers . . . their gaggings, chokings, and snortings are all on hold.

Gramp B. speaks up. "Last thing I saw of the little cutter he was glurping down milk straight from the jar. He oughtn't forget a tumbler to keep his own personal goo off the jar."

The screen door wangs open and Lloyd bursts on the scene. "*Whooooooooooooooooooosh!*" He swerves for the refrigerator, seizing upon the milk jar.

"Super Tree Man!" crows Unk Walty. "Thank goodness you are here!"

Edmund turns to look, striped towel dangling.

Walty stands again, the tallest of the Foggs and Dougherties, way taller than any Barrington . . . an impressive sight. In middle age, no spread. Great head of dark hair but for a single searing white streak, hair that he doesn't part, just combs it straight back. Raging wild hair. He always has to fight to keep it on the edge of obedience, but always it fights back. He reaches, feels the material of Lloyd's Super Tree Man cape. "You got some kind of stain on it already!"

"But Unk! I've been diggin'!" Through the dark green mask, Lloyd's eyes glitter.

Edmund's eyes slide over his son's polo shirt with STM stitched across the chest, the bikini bathing trunks over green tights and heroic stance.

"Super Tree Man," growls Gramp B. from the far end of the table. "I don't get it. Are you supposed to be a tree?"

"No, Gramp!" Lloyd groans. "I save the day! I bring trees. I make the world nice!!"

There's the crunch and soft guiltyish slush-slush of someone beginning to eat, tired of waiting, going on ahead.

"Zat real satin?" wonders Unk Roger. He moves his eyes from the cape to Edmund who stands unmoving with the striped towel.

Walty gasps. "No-ho! That was Connie's bridesmaid gown. There was a lot of material in that gown! Good to put it to some good use . . . like . . . like helping a hero save the day." Unk Walty hides his mouth with his knuckles, eyes full of fun.

Edmund's eyes fix on Walty's eyes.

Walty stops smiling, draws his hand down.

One of the men leans onto the table for a strangling cough. Unk Stan. He paws around for a paper napkin to catch his cheekful of biscuit.

Lloyd struts, pivots to make the cape flare, eyes glittering in the holes of his mask. He throws his arms forward into flying position. He bounces on the balls of his feet. He announces, "I've helped *five* treeless people today. Saved the day." Now he struts again, circling the kitchen floor, his cape brushing the leg of his father's overalls. He knows his father's eyes are on him, his father's eyes being the eyes of the whole wide world. And the gasoline and pine odors, odors of cattle, and his father's own gloamy odors pour over Lloyd like white light, like a kind of fame.

Unk Walty speaks in anger. "What's wrong, Ed?"

Lloyd stops moving.

Edmund squints at the platter of beef with Roger's right hand spread there, a hand like his own, hand for mastering tools and levers and beasts, hand for forcing his will over nature. Edmund says, without looking up from his brother-in-law's hand, "Let me get this straight, Lloyd. You have been running around in public with that rig on?"

Lloyd speaks to the wall he's staring at. "I thought . . ."

"You been *out there??*" Edmund jerks his thumb over his shoulder at the window of bright evening and too many butterflies.

"It's sewed nice," says Unk Jim.

"Yep," says Unk Stan, smiling nervously, then opens his smile for a forkful of meat.

"Yes, Walty," says Unk Howe. "You done a good job. Looks store-bought, don't it? Can't see where there's no flubs or nothin'."

Edmund's lip curls. He tosses the towel into the dish drainer, then walks his hunched bulllike walk to a chair, jerks it out from the table, sits.

Lloyd's cheeks show his shame.

Walty says, "Ed, he's only a child. Only a little boy."

Nobody looks at Lloyd to reaffirm this. Nobody looks at Walty or Edmund. They just eat, cheeks big with biscuits, everyone tired and hot, wishing Walty and Edmund would not bicker, for once, a quiet night . . .

Edmund reaches for the mashed potatoes and says, "Well, boys . . . suppose the weather's going to turn?"

13 | He sits on the bare mattress in his old room. It is still called "Lloyd's room," but it's the room of Lloyd *before* his mother's cancer. The before-cancer Lloyd . . . which is a lot like the before-cancer Edmund and the before-cancer Unk Walty and the before-cancer Gramp Fogg and the before-cancer Unk Roger and the before-cancer everybody . . . this before-cancer room where he keeps his stuff but never sleeps in the bed his mother said was called a "Hollywood bed" and "the latest thing." There's no footboard to a Hollywood bed, but a headboard made of plastic-covered stuffing, same as the "latest thing" kitchen chairs, which have a plastic covering of a red crushed-ice print while the bed is a cream color crushed-ice print. His mother and her catalogs! "You see, dear . . . this is the latest thing." She had been dying for years and years. There was always money for her to order a little something, to have a little joy. If Edmund didn't have the money for the order, her brothers would, or her father, or her father-in-law. Who could say no? She always turned the pages slowly, gave each page a hard study and a little pat. There'd be a catalog open on the kitchen table at all times, ready to go . . . like some people keep their Bible out . . . or the phone numbers of their friends.

Now Lloyd unknots the ties of the cape. He folds it and folds it and folds it into a tight square, then crosses the room to a bureau drawer to hide it. He listens to the house. Quiet between the contented tired coughs and snorts downstairs. And the silence of the outdoor heat beyond the window and the weighty silence of the hotter heat of this attic room. He sees in his memory the fat lady, one of the ladies he saved today with trees. He sees her dress of greens and yellows and the little specks that were bees. He hears her high yodelly voice. And there her face in her kitchen window as he set out the row of trees, his urging the trees out of their Dixie cups, giving them little sticks for support, and three loops of fishline. And on top of her house a big spotted cat with a red collar watched him. Although the cat and the fat lady were silent as he strode off down the sandy shoulder of the road toward home, his cape swirling, there were cheers and admiring whistles. Thousands. He laughs now, a little spit of a laugh to remember her, for the lady was indeed *fat* . . . much fatter than himself. Way too fat.

14 | His father has said he has a job for Lloyd. Now that his father has stopped the cattle truck on the edge of the Foyes' wet yard, Lloyd gets to hear what the job is.

"You set here at the wheel, but don't mess with the gears or pedals. Just keep your eyes on the crown of that road there. You watch and if you see the Ford with the clam coming or a fifty Plymouth . . . you know, the one with the rope . . . you lay on the horn. Okay?"

Lloyd says, "Okay."

"I don't mean 'beep beep.' I mean you use both hands until you see me come out in the dooryard. Okay?"

Lloyd looks over at the doorway of the little house and the red-haired woman is waiting with her hip cocked out on one side, her head cocked the other way. She wears a housedress of blue and pink flowers faded in a pretty way. No cigarette. Just her hands playing absently with a button. But the cigarette fingers are mustard gold. There's another little girl looks quite like the other little girl, only together you see one is bigger. Now Lloyd wonders if the two times he was here, maybe one was one of them, the next time it was the other.

His father backs away from the truck, his dark eyes on Lloyd, his spine like the hair trigger of an overcharged gun . . . ready, set . . .

His father turns away.

Lloyd watches the V of his father's overalls dead center of his back, then his father standing in the kitchen that's too small to sit down in, then realizes already he has taken his eyes from the crown of the road. Over the broad hood of the cattle truck, white-hot and black, Lloyd's eyes keep watch. He is wearing Unk Roger's old canvas fishing hat, little metal-rimmed holes for ventilation. And tied flies, which are still perky and could still trick a fish.

He glances back and there's the new Foye door. Shut. His father and the red-haired woman inside. The two girls outside. One girl has sneakers and plaid shorts. The other a sleeveless ripped dress, soggy patent leather shoes, no socks. Both have lots of nice hair fixed like ladies. Keeping on the far edge of the water, they wave to him. Little maidenly waves. He nods. Flashes his eyes back to the crest of the road. For what must be half an hour he doesn't let his eyes move from that road, even with the girls shrilling and squealing to get his attention. He resists. His will power is mighty.

He hears before he sees. If you didn't know, you'd think it was sleigh bells and something like grave deep-voiced chants of a thousand men . . . sort of Christmassy and beautiful and very grand. But Lloyd knows the sound of the chains of an empty logging truck beating upon metal, upon its metal stakes. And the roar of the engine in a big hurry. Even before the grille makes its terrible flash into the sun, he doesn't wait to see if it might be some other logging truck. He mashes his palms and chest to the wheel. The horn shimmies in his chest as if it is his own cry.

Now he sees it's *the* logging truck. No load, no bounty. Coming fast . . . expanding bigger and bigger and BIGGER . . . screams to a stop, grille to grille with the cattle truck so close all Lloyd can see of the driver now is his fingers gripping the wheel. Even as his father is in the dooryard, the horn still blares, radiating from his chest . . . his screaming heart . . . he can't stop it.

The driver drops from his truck. It's not the old guy Emery with the sawed head. It's a more medium-age guy. Walking toward Lloyd's father. A guy not much taller than Lloyd himself. Not as fat as Lloyd, but fat. Edmund Barrington is looking at Lloyd and the mouth is speaking but drowned by the steady horn that holds all sound in its rippling tides.

When Lloyd finally frees himself, lays his head back, it's so quiet. No one is talking. Just all the buzzing and zinging of the white fields and weedy ledges. He rolls his eyes away and hears his father saying, "Hey, Brad, howzit goin'?"

And then the other saying, "Okay. Okay."

Lloyd sees a baby tree beyond a scattering of plantain on sand. Just one tree. A miracle to have landed there. Frisky with life. He can tell even from here it's an ash. Someday it'll be big and it'll make the Foyes' shady.

15 On the seat between them rides another pie, this one wrapped in newspaper. They have come about a mile away from Foyes' . . . almost. Out of sight. His father's dark, dark eyes are fixed on the road ahead but his mouth is starting to look like he's chewing . . . and then the whole face goes snowy white. Edmund pulls the truck suddenly onto the shoulder, shoves open the door, leans out. Throws up.

Lloyd's mouth waters. In his jaws and glands and stomach he feels what Edmund feels. He opens his door. But his stomach won't let go. Just a lot of spit comes, everything on the verge and jerking.

His father shuts his door and rests his arm along the open window and gazes out across the twisting hills of hay and woods and fallow meadow through tears caused by his vomiting. He pulls a handkerchief from his overalls and swipes it over his mouth and then his nose which makes a great HONK!

Lloyd gives up and slams his door shut.

Edmund says, "It's better if you can get it out. There's nothing worse than having your stomach stuck in your neck." He chuckles softly. " 'Cept maybe our teeth punched out and our heads stuffed up our asses."

16 Unk Walty whispers, "Lloyd. I want you to see something. But wait here. Watch the clock. In exactly fifteen minutes, come up to my room and ask if I'm ready. I'll tell you to come in if I'm ready. Okay?"

"Yup," says Lloyd. He can tell Unk Walty is on top of the world. Something special for sure.

After fifteen minutes, he travels up the cluttered attic stairs, much more cluttered since CANCER. Nowadays things pile up on the stairs even though Unk Walty is neat and tries to keep up with it all. The stairs are just storage to everyone else, the unks not being as considerate to Walty as they had been to their sister. Their sister was dying. Walty is not dying.

"You ready, Unk?" Lloyd calls through the door.

"Come in!! Come in!!! COME INNNN!!!!" Unk Walty clamors.

Lloyd whaps the door open cop style.

Unk Walty is a cowboy. Every inch of him is pure white. White ten-gallon hat. White shirt with tassels long as shoestrings so pretty they make watery ripples spilling from the V of the chest, and above that a creamy white and wheat-color embroidery of flowering cacti, and birds with diamonds for eyes. Cuff links made with huge diamonds. Pants white satin. Very, very tight. Boots with tall heels. White suede, tooled with peach-color whorls and more jewels, twinkling in lavender, hot pink, and baby blue. Cowboy scarf knotted to one side of Unk Walty's brawny neck, a scarf so dazzling white, so gossamer, so long, so floaty!

Lloyd is speechless, blinking.

Unk Walty turns around once, then strikes a pose. "Well! What do you think?"

"Neat!" chirps Lloyd, stepping closer. "Are those *real* diamonds?"

Unk Walty lowers his eyes. "No. But sharp-looking all the same, huh?"

Lloyd's eyes glide over this amazing development.

"I've always wanted to be a cowboy that sings . . . if I could sing," Walty admits.

"You could *save* people," Lloyd says.

"Why, of course!" Unk Walty agrees.

"And ladies would love you."

"Everybody would love me. Wherever I'd go, people would half faint and say, 'MY GAWD!!! It can't BEEEEE!!! It's WALT FOGG!!! I can't believe my EYES!!!' They'd be after me with autograph books. Throwing me kisses." He sighs, overwhelmed.

"Would you ride bulls?"

"NEVER!!!"

Lloyd fingers the tassels that are slippery. They squiggle out through his fingers. "Come down and show Gramp Fogg."

Unk Walty exaggerates holding the door shut against the rest of the household, then says with sorrow, "None of them would understand. They are all so . . . so . . ." He sighs. "so . . . well, you know, . . . so *serious*."

Lloyd rolls his eyes toward the door. "I know."

17 | Carroll and Dana Plummer are the two cousins Lloyd would be least likely to pick to come spend a week here. But it's Lloyd's father and Unk Roger that's done the picking. Ten hours a day of hay and other hard work don't seem to reach the Plummer boys like it might someone else . . . the older one, Dana, expressionless, moving the hay up and over, up and over, the hay flashing, hissing . . . and the one named Carroll singing at the top of his lungs. Elvis songs. Not the way Elvis does them. For Carroll it's two or three lines, that's it. Bellered off-key. Same few lines over and over and over and over. Cigarette hanging from his mouth when it's only he and his brother and Lloyd working . . . one cigarette after another although Edmund and Roger and Gramp B. would throw a fit to have people smoking in the hay. Carroll Plummer eleven years old. Well, almost twelve.

They stop to pass the water jar. Warm water. Great choking gulps of it. They pass it up to Lloyd who straddles the tractor seat. Lloyd says, "Thanks," but the tractor's popping drone blanks out this soft word.

Such a spectacle these Plummer boys, sons of Lloyd's dead mother's sister. Pale hair, long bangs they have to keep shaking off to one side, dark-lashed yellowy green eyes, brand-new dungarees. All skin that shows is burned to the color of lions. Easy muscularity, that Dougherty blood. At peace with their bodies. The weight of the hay and the weight of the fainting heat is nothing to them. Only the hay matters. Each wagonload a crown of gold.

Lloyd passes the water jar down. Carroll grabs it to finish it off, but Dana grabs it from him. Lloyd laughs. Lloyd who is only eight and three quarters and fat, but as the unks all say, "a good man with the tractor." Lloyd's cap for today is his John Deere advertisement one. He wears it with the bill backwards just like Unk Howe likes to do. The last of the water has gone down Dana Plummer's throat. Then it's back into the swing of things, taking the tractor along the curve of piled rock, moving the hay higher on the load, heaping it to the sky.

18 | Ten hours in the fields and putting up hay in the barns doesn't reach the Plummer cousins at night either, doesn't knock them out like it does the others . . . supper, dessert, then bed for the others. Not the cousins . . . long into the late hours it's TV, TV, TV. Just the two of them in the dark parlor, sprawled out on the cool linoleum gazing into the gray fluttery TV world with Unk Roger's stuffed crow hunched there on top.

Lloyd, in the doorway, says, "Ain't you guys going to bed *ever?*"

Dana says, "Shut up."

Lloyd crouches down next to them. He can smell something like beer.

The show is creepy. It is a story about a guy named Cory who lives in future time. Sent to prison. Prison in the future is you get sent to another planet. A whole planet all by yourself. Nobody there but you. Rocks and desert. Weird music playing. Cory is sent there for *life*. But he's given a lady robot for company. The robot looks real. Real enough to kiss and stuff. Nobody else around. Just kiss kiss kiss. This robot is *nothing* like a square metal robot that flashes lights and talks in a metal voice.

"Are you guys drinking beeeer?" Lloyd asks.

"Shut up," Dana commands.

As Carroll watches the show he does a weird thing . . . hums very very softly to himself . . . the same Elvis song he's screamed all day. Thumps his foot. Then he pulls from a bunched blanket a beer, takes a swig, fussily arranges it back in the blanket.

Lloyd wonders where Dana has *his* beer hidden.

An official from Earth shows up with a pardon for Cory. Tells Cory he can come back to Earth with him! Pretty great news! Let's go! Cory is happy of course. Earth is better. Has trees. And probably Cory has a mother and father and relatives who have been crying for years . . . all jumping for joy now.

Cory and the robot look at each other with big love in their eyes.

Oh no, not her, explains the official. Robots don't go back. No room in the spacecraft. Sorry.

Cory says he can't leave her ever ever ever.

Don't be silly, says the official sternly. That's just a robot. He shoots the robot right in the face, blows her face off. Maybe Lloyd had started to think the robot really was a lady, but they just *said* she was a robot. Well, now he sees her face exploding into a bunch of wires. She falls down and her voice calling Cory's name gets creepy and deep like a dragging record. Sounds like a man. Then deeper than a man. Monster deep . . . then slower . . . then stops.

Lloyd sees Dana's hand reaching over to the blanket for the beer by Carroll's shoulder. So it's the same beer. They are sharing it. Then without a word, Dana passes the beer to Lloyd. Lloyd takes a sip, passes it back. "Which would you rather get?" Lloyd wonders. "Live on the weird planet with that robot? Or you go home and she dies?"

Carroll keeps humming softly, thonking his foot.

Dana says, "I would kill the official and take the robot back to Earth. I'd tell 'em on Earth a moonman musta ate the official. I wouldn't let that asshole do that to *my* girlfriend."

Lloyd looks at Dana's profile . . . so much to admire. Fifteen years old, almost sixteen. And the world by the tail.

19 | Nearly a week now of pitch-black swelter in the attic, hard wretched half-sleep, waking to Carroll Plummer's low humming. And sometimes Carroll paces. At least it sounds like pacing there in the next room, while at other times it sounds like he must be sitting on the edge of his cot, thonking his heel on the floor. How much work and heat and scary TV would it take to make him tired? How *much* can he stand?

20 | Edmund says as they ride along, "I have another job for you."

Lloyd is silent, fiddles with the door lock. Up. Down. Up. Down.

Edmund says, "Same job as before. Okay?"

Lloyd says, "Okay."

But it's a different place. Edmund parks the left wheels on a yard of tar. Pleasant Street. Mill houses, telephone poles and wires. No trees. What a world.

"A Dodge pickup . . . black with a blue passenger's door. You see it comin', you lay on the horn. But you can stop once you see me back out here. Okay?"

"Okay," says Lloyd.

But the stranger's pickup never comes. The sun moves from one set of roofs to the other. Trucks of other descriptions pass. A few cars. A swarm of bicycles. Some of the cars park across the street. In alleyways. Or parallel. A black-and-tan dog looks at Lloyd a while. Seems bored. Sniffs and wets some tires. Slumps in the middle of the street. Lloyd wonders if the dog is waiting for someone or just has nothing to do.

Eventually his father steps out from one of the doors. Has that same way of working his neck and shoulder muscles as at Foyes'. Same humpy bulllike walk. Same high flush. Only no pie.

21 |

DOGS

by Lloyd S. Barrington   age 8¾

Dogs in the street.

Dogs with feet.

Dogs in the air.

Dogs in your hair.

Dogs nice to you. Eveyware. Dogs. Help yourself. Theres
   plenty.

Dogs on the ochean. Sea sick. Sinking. Help! Help! Bring out
   a life saver.

Onse a yellow hungrie dog at my scool. Yoooooo
   hoooooo! Yoooooo! hoooooo!

Opin up the door. Opin up the door. Let one in.

Doggiedoggiedoggiedooroo dooroo.

22 | TrEES
by Lloyd S. Barrington   age 8¾

TrEes are good for you. Make you shady. Green for summer. Fall is best. Then they are like no clothes see there
arms in the sky everiething waving only Stil you cant tell
wich are girl trees but trees know.

   Under trees are ants busy.

   Trees dont move but their busy. If you are a tree you
get to be old way old. Unless you get sawed. This makes
them scream a little . . . eeeeeeeeeeeeeee. Wood is nise but
trees scream for you to have wood but you have to have it
and there are plenty more in the woods but not on PLEAS-
ANT STRRET where it is the worset place. No shade but
skinny lines. I would die. Dogs hate it. Everbodie hates it. A
tree would have to find a crack. But if I were a tree I would
look more to sumplase els. No hope. Just hard. Tar and
cars. Trees aRe best. Green is a good favrit color. What is
yors?

23 | Unk Walty has them ripping up newspapers, stirring wallpaper
paste in a kettle. It's the cousins from Bridgton . . . Aunt Margaret's . . . all very cute but Walty calls them "evil savages." The kitchen
has its usual cigar smell pouring out of the walls and woodwork. But also
the new smell of wallpaper paste. And cold orange pudding pie. Pudding
pies are the kinds Walty always makes when the little kids come. The
youngest of the cousins wears print sneakers and his dungarees cut short.
He says softly, "Poo."

Walty says deeply, "My offer still holds. The outhouse is still very much there."

The kid shakes his head slowly, looks down.

"Well, go out by the side of the house then and squat in the grass. Jesus Christ."

The kid doesn't seem to hear this, just keeps his head down.

"Come on, Allen! You gotta do it," one of the little girls insists, drags him through the door to the shedway. Out in the shedway there's screams and banging around. The girl reappears gasping. "He won't do it! What a wicked baby!"

"So you left him out there in the pantry to feel things?" Walty demands.

Unk Roger, Lloyd, and Dana Plummer come in from spraying the orchard and carry on them the dizzying killer smell. No Carroll Plummer. Some sort of trouble with Carroll. Carroll's gone home on foot.

Unk Walty is working his thumbs into the gray mash of his creation, the indentations, delicate creases, and folds of it. The little cousins have all made round blobs, trying to copy Unk Walty . . . but there's no comparison . . . only Unk Walty is the real "artiste."

"Kiddies at play," says Dana with a snicker and a toss of his pale bangs.

Unk Walty says nothing to this.

The littlest cousin appears from the shedway gripping a huge green boot. "More," he says, pointing back at the open door.

Unk Walty takes a deep anguished breath. "*That* is Grammy Fogg's. PUT IT BACK." He takes more gray mash from the bowl and works it over his creation.

Unk Roger is drinking water from a tumbler, standing by the sink to refill another time. As he drinks, he groans into the glass. This makes the small cousins titter and teehee.

Walty snaps, "You kids better hurry up with your sculptures. Your mother will be here in ten minutes and that's the *end* of my commitment."

The littlest cousin, having returned the boot, comes up behind Dana Plummer and touches the back of his jeans. "Poo," he says softly.

Dana turns, looks down, puzzled. He forces his blond damp bangs off to one side with the flat of his hand and grins. "What?"

Unk Walty snarls, "He's scared of the outhouse."

"Do it in your pants," Dana tells the kid.

Unk Walty winces. "If he does, he's going to carry it with him till his mother gets here. And he will be tethered to a tree in the meanwhile."

Dana says, "Look, Allen. I'll give you this many pennies if you go poop in the outhouse. I'll go out with you. And I'll give you the money the minute you're done going."

The kid looks at the pennies arranged on the older boy's palm.

"It's not *that* bad of an outhouse," Walty sniffs indignantly. "It's the way people have been doing it for thousands of years."

Dana leads the little boy out through the shedway, both of them straight as soldiers.

Lloyd comes to stand close to Unk Walty, watches the man's hands on the mysterious gray shape. "What is it, Unk?" he wonders.

Unk Walty winks at Lloyd.

Edmund comes down from upstairs dressed in his best plaid shirt . . . red and green . . . and green work pants . . . kind of heavy-dressed as usual for such hot bad weather. In fact, he looks a little Christmassy. He says to Lloyd, "I need you to come along. Okay?"

Lloyd says, "Okay."

"Go get a shirt on, couldja? We might be a little late."

Through the shoulders and elbows of those standing around, Lloyd glimpses his father's close-set dark eyes staring at him. Lloyd swallows hard. A bit of nausea coming on, and clenching throat, the pride in and fear of these things that he knows, their confidences, their trust.

24 | MY COUSINS
by Lloyd S. Barrington   age 8¾

If you make a pie for littil cousins som lands on the floor.
If you make a pie for big cousins they eat ALL of it but say wat eles Im still starvd.
My uncil hates it wen they are here for him to babysit but about Wensday he makes a million plans like the plan he has to make a pupet show or walk to the cemitary or pat rabbits at the Lockes. He HATES rabbits becase they coud rip you but he goes becase Cathy and Dee Dee and Timmy and Allen do like them A LOT.

----

25 | DEMOCRATS
by Lloyd S. Barrington   age 8¾

Democrats are stupid.

Democrats want to spent. republcans never spentd. They save.

They make a contry nise. If you want to live hear be a re-publecan otherwis go live in Rusha were its cold also salt minds. Its were you work.

Must be weerd.

26 |

A new day comes like an unspent shiny coin. His father steers the truck up the long drive to the old Spiller place off Graves Falls Road. This is the Chevy, dump body and ram, sides boarded up solidly.

Edmund blows the horn.

Nobody home. No car in the yard. Striped canvas seats in a circle under the maples. Also a green striped awning contraption like an open-sided tent making a long shade over tables that look made of redwood, tables end to end.

"Rich types," says Edmund. "Go give their buzzer a few mashes, would'ja?"

Lloyd sails out of the truck, hefts himself up over the long lawn and stone steps while his father waits, arm stretched out along the open window. Lloyd hurries back to the idling truck with a note. He comes up to his father's side of the truck, gasping for breath, and because he's wearing his Civil War kepi today, it means he must keep his straight-faced war look at all times. He says from a corner of his mouth, "Here's a note from their door."

Edmund snatches the note, mushes it, tosses it to the floor. He steps out of the truck. Lloyd hurries behind him, watches him work the chained pins out of the tailgate, then Edmund walks his bulllike humpy walk, returning to the cab. Lloyd watches the dump body rising, the manure tumbling in clumps onto the grass next to the stonework bank of rho-dodendrons. Edmund jerks the truck forward a time or two to loosen what clings to the bed. Up across the infinite lawn, sprinklers rotate, swinging the sun-glistening water in wide arcs like fairy glitter . . . *shwit shwit shwit shwit* . . .

As the dump body drops back in place, Lloyd hops aboard beside his father. Edmund seesaws the truck, facing it out, ready to roll.

A Chrysler swings soundlessly from the road up the long drive.

Edmund starts the truck rolling forward, but then he brakes it. The Chrysler seems to take up as much of the driveway as the truck. The driver waves wildly. She leaps out. What she is wearing looks to Lloyd like a safari costume . . . khaki shorts and shirt with epaulets. Only there's no safari helmet. Instead just hair in a dark glossy flip. This is unlike most ladies who would tell you the style is pin curls or permed curls. "Excuse me! Excuse me!" she shouts. She hurries up to Edmund's open window. "I can't *believe* you just did that, Mr. Barrington! Didn't you find my note on the door?!!"

Lloyd tries not to let his eyes give away the note's balled-up condition on the truck floor.

The woman's eyes drift the length of the truck, eyes bearing down smooth as a paintbrush. Then she says in a deeper and very quiet voice, "I'll pay you as soon as you move the fertilizer to where I asked you to put it . . . on the bare earth over there near the vegetable garden. Would you move it now, please?"

The Chrysler is, with its hanging-open door completely blocking the truck's way out over the strip of pavement.

The woman's little mouth is lightly pinkly lipsticked and smiling . . . little mouth . . . little firm smile. Edmund bares his teeth. She bares hers. She is an older lady, but nice teeth all the same. Edmund sneers. His teeth are nice, too . . . a little yellowed . . . but very solid. And his eyes are tightening on her face, a stone-cold dark scrutiny . . . a siege.

"Well?" says she.

He tears the shift into reverse. The truck lurches backwards up onto the blue-green lawn. He works the clutch and gears deftly, the rear duals kicking out whole carpets of turf.

A mile down the road, he pulls off onto the shoulder, his hands on the wheel shaking. Lloyd figures his father is stopping to vomit again. But Edmund just stares into space. Flies come to Edmund's cheek. First two flies, then a third. Then one for his forehead. The hands have dropped down onto the thighs of his overalls, are spread open there, relaxed.

Lloyd stares openmouthed at this which his father is doing. It's a special thing not everyone can do . . . this tricking your blood into quietness. It is like a turtle goes under the mud and sleeps . . . a thing like on the edge of death . . . a thing that is terrible to look at . . . kind of scary . . . if you didn't know how nice it is.

27 | Constable out by the barn with Edmund. Constable in his newish Ford Galaxy . . . white. Taillights big around as plates. Blue cop bubble on the dash. Edmund leaning there with his back to a white fender, looking down at the circle he is drawing in the dirt with the heel of his boot. Constable says Edmund has to pay for the wrecked grass. Constable says, otherwise court. Might as well pacify the lady. Might as well. Edmund turns, leans over the hood onto his forearms to think, working his hands together, weaving the fingers, listening as the constable's voice floats out into the evening. No moon. No stars. Just the soft low-wattage look of the windows of the farmhouse and a little bit of day still thick and creamy on the mountain across the road. And mosquitoes. One lands on the top of the deputy's left ear . . . whap! Deputy flicks the dead mosquito away.

Herefords grouping up near the gate. Each eye of each animal is like a planet, so much reflected there. Up along the roadway bugs whirr and buzz more sweet than Edmund can stand. A light going out upstairs. Gramp B. hitting the hay . . . his own father just sixty years old. You catch up eventually it seems.

Edmund Barrington working his jaw, thinking. You look close, you don't see much of a fighter.

28 | ### RICH
by Lloyd S. Barrington   age 8¾
Rich peepil are mean. They make their eyes small. You see them you get a shiver. Everybdy haTes them. Do you hate them? You better.

29 | Lloyd watches the cards whirrrr and snap. It's the first cold night of late summer. A lot of frozen breath and blowing into hands. Lloyd watches the cards as if he knew the meaning of all the players' moans and catcalls and cussing. When they burst out into laughter over a play, he laughs along.

"Jeeee-zusssss! I can see my breath!" Dickie Nichols wails, Dickie

Nichols who lives here, but there seems to be some problem about his getting into the house.

Here in the garage it has everything but a car in it. Stuff in neat piles, moths around the light bulb.

"Dickie. When she going to let us in?" the dealer asks. Dealer is a young guy with a work shirt that reads WICKS WELL DRILLING, EGYPT, MAINE across the back in copper-color embroidery.

"Ain't," Dickie says. "She's madder'n hell at something which I don't know what it is and I'm going to *payyyyyyyy*, don'tcha see? If I can guess what she's pissed about, it wouldn't go so hard on me. But till I guess the answer, I can't know what I'm apologizin' for so I can't apologize so here we are."

"Go," says Edmund, nodding toward the cards in Dickie Nichols's hand.

"How many you want, Dickie?" asks the well driller.

"Two," says Dickie, wrinkling his nose, pushing two cards from his hand facedown in front of him.

Another young guy, very young, very drunk, eases his head back against the concrete wall, shuts his eyes. At peace.

Lloyd rocks his stool around, jiggles his legs. His legs have the tired willies. But he doesn't think about home. Being with his father is all that matters. Never without a hat, he wears his father's cast-off green crusher . . . added to his collection just this week. His father's new green crusher is out on the truck seat. Has a blue jay feather in the band. Lloyd's crusher has a red chicken feather.

"Me and the pony and the dog all on Joycie's shit list, don'tcha see?" Dickie says, sulking.

There are haw haws and snorts. Lloyd doesn't get it, but he laughs along.

He looks from face to face, trying to understand . . . faces leaning close, breathing out frostiness. So many faces . . . all familiar. One guy wears a coon tail pinned to a cowboy hat. Also a very thin child-sized bareheaded big-eyed young-looking pimply guy wearing a military jacket. He looks about seventeen years old, but Lloyd knows this is the father of one of his school friends, David. Across the table is George Nee from High Road. And Jimmy Sanborn who seems to have gotten weirdly thin.

"It's the doghouse for ol' Dickie," says a guy Lloyd recognizes from Moody's store . . . one of the Moody brothers . . . or cousins . . . he gets them mixed up. This guy wears so many gun and fishing sportsman patches up and down both arms of his plaid jacket, it gives him the look of *government* . . . some official State-of-Maine outdoors expert . . . or warden. He has one eye that's whitish blue, which Lloyd decides is worse than Lloyd's own mismatched eyes. The blue-white eye of the Moody guy looks like a marble. Looks blind. But he seems to do okay with the other. "Tight in the doghouse, Dickie." The Moody chuckles, laying out four cards facedown.

"I smell an ace," murmurs Dickie, easing into a deeper and deeper sulk.

Moody shows his ace.

"I'll say it's a tight fit!" chortles the well driller. "With the pony and the dog in there with him!"

Laugh. Laugh. Laugh. Laugh. Laugh. And Lloyd laughs along.

The well driller deals the Moody four cards.

"The dog don't have a doghouse," Dickie says. "He's in the house by the goddam stove."

Howls of laughter. Lloyd howls, too.

They joke about other things. And laugh more and more savagely. Reaching for more beers down by their feet under the table. The coon-tail hat guy gathers up some sawdust on the floor around Dickie's table saw and packs it into the open mouth of the very young, very drunk guy. The young guy spits out the sawdust, murmurs, "Don't" in his sleep, then slips off his seat into the lap of the well driller. Well driller eases him down among the feet. Face on the cement.

"Nite! Nite!" crows the coon-tail hat guy.

They all laugh like hell.

Edmund's dark eyes are red as fire in the white parts, and his laughs have become great bellers.

The ᶜ rds, snap-snap.

There's winning.

There's losing.

"Jesus! What's it 'bout thirty degrees tonight?" someone whines. Shiver. Shiver.

"Crisp," observes another.

Dickie Nichols looks hot . . . wet-faced . . . red cheeks. But he is always this way. A nervous wreck. High-strung. Even though he's a big guy, his voice is always a high bantam roosterlike yodel. He is losing at every hand now. Losing bad. As the Moody with the white-blue eye lays out his full house, there's roars of painful disbelief from weirdly thin Jimmy Sanborn and the coon-tail hat guy. Dickie Nichols just lays his face on his arms.

"If you wanna win it back, Dickeroo, it's your house, your land, and your car!" Moody says villainously, twisting a make-believe very villainous moustache.

"I'm depressed," Dickie laments. "When I'm depressed, I don't play so well. And I don't get good cards. Ain't you guys' balls froze? I'm ready to quit."

"You *gotta* quit!" hoots the well driller. "You're OUT!!"

"And I wouldn't take the gift of your car, Dickie," says Moody somberly. "I hate Fords."

The cards go around, the pot piled with one-dollar bills.

An oldish man, dressed only in a dirty T-shirt and work pants, searches all his pockets for money. He has tattoos up and down both arms, so poorly made so long ago, they have spread and faded into black blobs. Seems he, too, is running out of money. But not as low as Dickie Nichols. A bill shows up at last.

Dickie snarls, "I don't have to quit. This is *my* place. I charge you all rent for your asses on these chairs. That gives me some free games."

"No way, Nichols. Sorry. No deal," says Moody.

Dickie stands up, swaying, pointing at Moody with his beer. Dickie smiles, his eyes a slitted gray. In an almost ballerinalike slow motion, he twists around to feel the back pockets of his pants. "Anybody got something to write on? Louie, toss me that pen."

The well driller pitches him a ball-point which hits his chest, drops to the floor. Lloyd reaches for the pen, puts it in Dickie's hand.

On a bit of paper Dickie spells out a single word: WIFE.

"Right, Dickie. Ha! Ha!" says the white-eyed Moody, shaking his head. "Good try."

Dickie says. "You fucker, give me a hand! Or get out of my garage."

Moody deals him a hand, shaking and shaking his head with an indulgent half smile.

"I'll take his wife," says the coon-tail hat guy.

Dickie hunches down on his lawn chair, eyes boring into the face of each man as they consider their plays.

Edmund wins this one.

"Well, well," says Dickie. "What a coincidence! Kinda neat the way that worked out."

Edmund collects the bills, folds them with care. Leaves the paper that says WIFE on the table.

"Okaaaaaaaaay," says Dickie. "You get the grand prize, Eddie. You get my wife."

Edmund stands. "Time to go," says he. There's nothing unusual about this. Edmund so seldom comes around to play and when he does, he always leaves early, especially right after he's won a hand or two. Hit-and-run. That's his style.

Dickie stands up lightning-bolt straight. He's such a big guy with graying quills of hair around the sides, bald on top . . . the angle of the gray quilled hair . . . like a gauge . . . shows how charged he is. He heads out through the breezeway.

The well driller says, "Jesus . . . ain't Dickie a ticket tonight?"

Edmund says deeply, "I've got to get my boy home."

"Awww. It's only ten-thirty," complains the oldish man with the tattoos.

"The kid looks more wide awake than anyone else here," says Moody.

"Come on, Ed," the coon-tail hat guy urges. "Stay and see what Dickie has in mind. I'm curious as hell. What a comedy."

They can hear pounding. It's Dickie's fist on the locked kitchen door. Then his shrill voice, "Let me in! I'm not kidding! Open the christly door!"

Moody leans toward this, cups his ear. Shakes his head. "Crazy bastard," he says softly.

A splintering and crack of wood.

All the guys look deeply into each other's eyes.

"I need another beer," Moody sighs, pushes to his feet, and disappears out through the garage's side door to where he has his stash hidden.

Lloyd is alert to the alertness of his father, attuned to every muscle and hair. His father gives Lloyd's shoulder a gentle squeeze, says, "Gotta get the boy to bed."

Lloyd moves as his father moves, a little bit of a stumble over the garage stuff that takes up most of the floor.

Something slams inside the ranch house beyond the breezeway.

The well driller says solemnly, "Dickie gets a few beers into him and he's gone Neanderthal."

Couple of nervous chuckles.

"I'm dealing another hand, you guys," says Moody on his return with a fresh beer.

Then the soft slap-slap of cards.

Feet coming along the breezeway. The breezeway door, the new modern hollow kind, opens easy. It's Dickie. Got his wife. She wears baggy pajamas. Her hair has lost its curl. Face mashed from heavy sleep. When Dickie gives her a shove in Edmund Barrington's direction, her huge breasts roll around under her pajamas. Long-limbed woman, long fingers, no rings. Hard lines around her mouth. But the pajamas look cloud soft. And so it is with her, all that's meant to be soft on a woman looks extra soft.

Dickie is out of breath. He says in a strangled voice, "Here she is, Eddie! You win her!"

Edmund sinks to straddle the chrome-legged chair, shakes his head, sort of smiling.

The oldish guy in T-shirt says sadly, "Dick. You go a little too far with a thing."

"SHUT THE FUCK UP!!!" Dickie screams. "Who the fuck are you, Billy?"

Guy in the T-shirt gets up fast from the table, tries to get around them to the door, but can't quite make it clear of Dickie's elbow and Edmund's right boot, and Lloyd who is hovering. But another guy makes it out the door . . . the well driller . . . he's had enough.

Edmund starts to stand again, but Dickie leans in his face and says in a terrible whisper, "Here, Barrington! Take your prize. I want to *see* you fuck her. Okay?"

Edmund says, "I'm leaving."

"Why? Ain't she pretty enough? Ain't she showing enough skin? Want a better look? Want her barer?" Dickie rocks her from side to side, tries to shake the pajama bottoms free, but they are bunched, caught against his belt. Now the woman's eyes are squinched shut. Outside the well driller's truck starts hard, a long *yoing yoing yoing yoing yoing*, slow to fire.

Edmund says, "She's pretty as any. Leave her be."

"WHAT!!!" Dickie screams. "WHAT'S THAT???" He gives his wife three great shakings so the breasts under the pajama fabric wag against Edmund's face.

Edmund slides his chair back. He stands. "Leave her be," Edmund says softly.

"I'm leaving," says the oldish guy in the T-shirt. "This ain't a nice place." He shoves past, out into the night.

Dickie forces his eyes to widen in feigned astonishment. "Why, Ed! Shame on you! Don't play like it don't come easy to you. Fearless widower who seemed to us all like a widower *before* you was a widower . . . if you get my meaning. God-DAMMMMM!" He laughs high, a shrieking. He gives his wife another rocking and sway . . . like his intent is to soothe, but what he's doing is working the woman closer to Edmund, a motion at a time.

Now Edmund and Joyce Nichols are eye to eye.

Dickie giggles. "Give 'er a real look, Eddie. Don't she look familiar? Doesn't this prize look . . . like . . . like somebody you remember from the not very distant past . . . like, say, three summers ago?" Dickie snickers a private snicker to himself. "The summer I was out on the road so much . . . remember? 'Snot a secret you been pokin' it to her in secret . . . 'less it's a secret to you 'cause you are confused. *I* would be confused if I hung mine out as much as you do yours. *I* might get them all mixed up, too. Like with Doris Roche. Or Bett Johnson. Or . . . Gloria what's-her-face . . . and all them Harris women. I'd be so mixed-up, my eyes'd cross." Dickie gazes at the few remaining faces, crosses his eyes, keeps them crossed a long moment showing them how confused a man like Edmund Barrington should look. Now he mashes his cheek to his wife's cheek so the two faces up close are what Edmund sees, one grinning with eyes crossed, the other face with eyes shut, mouth trembling. "This one is Joyce Nichols," Dickie explains. "Ooops! How would you know? I mean, she probably does look different than the way she looked when you last saw her. She wasn't as dressed up as this, was she, Eddie? Lemme see here . . ." He jostles her off to the left, working at the pajama top . . . the wife beginning to cry, to fight back. But one breast bulges free of the pajamas, wags about as Dickie works the next button almost daintily to free the other breast.

The coon-tail hat guy groans. "Why can't we all win her?" he suggests, standing up fast, knocking into the table. Empty beer bottles roll off, smash on the cement.

Dickie persists. "Okay now, Ed. Does she look like how she was when you saw her or you gotta see more to jog your memory?"

"More," the coon-tail hat guy says hoarsely.

Joyce gets Dickie by a fistful of his quilly hair, pulls hard. Looks like she's pulling some out. Dickie knocks her hand away. "Come on, Ed . . . take your prize. Do it here. Now. Be brave. None of this sneaky-snakey-creepin' in the shadows shit. Show us you ain't afraid to take Joycie the honest way. Come on, you cocksuckin' son-of-a-bitch . . . you won her fair 'n' square this time!"

Joyce sees the close-together dark eyes, the scrutiny of Edmund's eyes on her face.

Dickie gives his wife a shove.

Edmund opens his arms, seems to embrace her . . . seems like passion.

But then the wife is jerked back again and Dickie seizes Edmund by the front of his plaid going-out shirt. Edmund's head smacks the cement wall. Dickie hisses, "You goddam asshole! You think I MEANT it?!!!! I was just *joking!* JOKINGGGGGGGG! A little joke. You fucker, I'm going to break you."

Clutching her pajama top together, the woman sobs her husband's name over and over, over and over.

Lloyd cries, too.

The coon-tail hat guy says to the others, "Game's over, looks like." And he strides out.

Dickie steps back to gather himself up for the punch. Like you aim the ax for the chopping block, he wants his fist to go through Edmund's face and brains to the wall.

But where *is* Edmund's face? Vanished. Dickie blinks around. Edmund has gotten away. But Lloyd is still there bawling.

Joyce, still gripping her pajama top together with one hand, pitches a headless plaster lawn duck at Dickie, but the thing sails past him, between the faces of two other poker players, smashes upon the cement wall.

Dickie grins. "Ain't that the cutest thing? Joycie, you just gotta learn to pitch overhand. Quit throwin' like a girl." That's the last thing Lloyd hears as he takes off running down the crushed rock driveway to where his father's truck *was* parked . . . but is gone . . . Now he sees it down on the road beyond a thickness of sumac . . . parked there . . . waiting. He runs and runs for that truck, too scared to be heartbroken yet. Too scared to figure out which thing about this night weighs heaviest on his mind.

30 | Lloyd seldom climbs trees. Being fat, climbing is not so easy. He can climb a thing if he has to, but it's not a thing he would just go and do out of friskiness like his cousins and his friends might. If his father wants him up in the mow, he goes. If his father wants him to get up into the cattle truck and throw out a rope, he does. But trees . . . he stands alone today under the old maple that makes spots of shade that run like bright water over the ground when the breeze picks up. And overhead a thousand whispers. Spots of shade on Lloyd. He is wearing his pirate hat . . . not a great pirate hat . . . mostly cardboard. At his side, lashed to his dungarees, is his sword. Being a pirate, it's okay with his father. When his father sees him striding around with his sword and pirate hat, it's okay. Once Edmund even said, "Yo mates."

Also his father doesn't mind his Civil War kepi or the World War II helmet or the Davy Crockett hat or the cardboard king crown.

31 | DISHES
by Lloyd S. Barrington   age 8¾

My mother loved thes dishes very prety.

A blue world you look into.

Hold one stedy and look hard and in you go.

Litle bridge for you.

A dish round like the world.

Prety trim around it.

Unk Walty says you call them Blue Willows. The name of
the kind of plates.

You put them out on spechil days. Visits.

Peepil who come from Massichusets places like that. Thats
Aunt Bert.

None have broke but onse I seen a crak. I wontd say who
did it but his frist name begins with C.

Ha ha try to gues.

Also nise to look threw is colord windowes.

32 | SCHOOL
by Lloyd S. Barrington   *age 8¾*

School is weerd. You sit for hours. But it is the law that you
    do it.

33 | POKER
by Lloyd S. Barrington   *age 8¾*

Playing poker it maks peepil crazy. Doant do it.

34 | RATS
by Lloyd S. Barrington   *age 8¾*

Rat poyson is very mean.

Rats have feelings just on the other side insid and on there
    skin.

Stomacks blowing up is mean.

There was a guy callt pie piper. Rats liked his music so
    much they jumped in the water and dide.

Why dosnut somebody figur a way to make them just
    leave.

35 | VISITS
by Lloyd S. Barrington   *age 8¾*

Unk Walty and me we visititd Mrs. Cooper and her sister.

Unk Walty has a lot of people we visit to bring stuff Very
    old.

Mrs. Cooper's sister is very old almost a hunred and
    rememrs.

We brot them som green beans, summer sqash, jam,
    cream and 2 pies one was apple one was green toma-
    toes horribil but the ladies said oh my you are the
    angel!

Unk Walty liks you to say this angel stuff I can tell you.
    Also Unk brot them som very old pikchurs to keep of
    them selvs as litle girls when they were litle girls these
    Grammy Fogg kept. Then for a litle minut Mrs. Cooper

and her old sister and Unk Walty cried. I almos did but held on.

36 | Nancy Bucknell is coming for supper.
"Must be serious," says Gramp Fogg.

Unk Walty rolls his eyes.

Unk Howe says lots of young women drive cars these days. Too bad Nancy Bucknell wasn't one of them.

Gramp Fogg says, "I'm afraid I don't agree with you on that, Howie."

Unk Stan says Nancy Bucknell is some relation to Moodys two or three times removed.

Unk Walty rolls his eyes.

The unks hash over some of the Moody gossip, recent and past.

Unk Jim looks at the clock and says Ed must be bringing her the long way and blushes at this thought.

Unk Walty is making a nice roast. Makes a big to-do with every kind of vegetable and a nice yellow cake with lemon frosting. But he is very quiet. Not much to say. A lot on his mind with everything bubbling at once.

Lloyd is stooped over the wastebasket making his pencil sharp with a jackknife. "Chickadees come next," he says. "I've never seen a poem about a chickadee. Have you?"

Nobody replies to this. Just silence. Unk Walty says at last, "Don't ask these guys, Lloyd."

"There's a song 'Bye Bye Blackbird,' " says Gramp Fogg, watching the road from his chair by the window. He sings a little of "Bye Bye Blackbird," remembers most of it.

Edmund's pickup pulls in and Gramp Fogg pushes his glasses against his eyes, leans forward trying not to miss anything.

Edmund comes in. Dress-up plaid shirt. Dark cotton work pants. Looking spiffy.

Where's Nancy, they all ask.

"Roger is showing her the calf," says Edmund. Now his eyes catch sight of the Blue Willows on the table. He steps up to Walty, who is stirring the kettles. Edmund's voice cracks. "What's this!"

"What's what?"

Edmund points.

Unk Walty sees the finger pointing at the Blue Willows.

Edmund says, "What made you think you could do this? Were you thinking with your toe?"

Gramp Fogg sighs. "This ain't no time to fight. Your lady friend is coming up the path."

Edmund muckles onto one of Walty's great sinewy forearms, Unk Walty a head taller, lean as a boxer, proportioned like Mr. America, like MR. UNIVERSE, rearing back, cringing. "It's a special occasion!" he insists croakily.

Edmund shoves Unk Walty who is backing, backing all the way into the nearest bedroom. There's the view of Edmund, but Walty's around the corner.

Nancy and Unk Roger come into the kitchen. Nancy has regular brown hair in the regular tight pin curl, regular blue-frame glasses, with a smile like she's glad to be here.

Unk Walty steps out from the back bedroom door first, nods hello to Nancy, then picks up the Blue Willows easy-careful into a stack, tears in his eyes.

Edmund returns.

Nancy looks into Edmund's eyes. Crossing the linoleum toward him, one of her shoes squeaks like a mouse.

37 | RAT ELECTRIC CHAIRS
by Lloyd S. Barrington   age 8¾

I thout of a way. It is my invenshion but you can hav it. I invendt it but only in my mind now no real thing I made. You have to be good electrishin to fix one ok. Here is how. It is a box with litle door. Rat goes in. Door slams. Rat dosntd suffer AT ALL. It happens so fast. Big zap. Electrisity comes and kills him but so fast. Then you candt get the door open till you unplug it becuss you mit forget and open the door and put you hand in and that be the end of you to. Out with the rat. Worst thing is if its a mother rat with baby rats wating. That is the only problam. But in a wile Ile think of something else. Anything is better than poysin and traps that doant always kill but sqish there feet. It is very important to be nise in this world but you look all around and you doant see many peepil tryng to figur things out. Peepil just go around like goofs doing all the old stuff that is awfill. A rat electric chair isnt so hard no body couldndt have made one back in the beginning of rats. It is going to take me som time on how to figur out how to be electrishun. Any Body can have my idia NOW. Pleaes hurry. Stop the suffering.

38 | Two days of heavy rain. Unk Walty keeps the sewing machine on a steady roll. "Feeling artistic," he tells Lloyd.

Suppers are quiet. Just the clink of forks and a lot of cigar smoke. Nobody says much about Nancy Bucknell. Nor the Blue Willows. Just weather.

Tonight Gramp Fogg helps Unk Walty pick up the table. Edmund gets himself an apple from the cellar, shines it on his shirt front awhile, staring at Unk Walty's back from across the kitchen. Unk Walty begins to slam the pans and silverware around. Gramp Fogg lights a cigar. Unk Walty turns, eyes on the apple in Edmund's hand, sniggers, "Well, if I had a brick up my ass like you do, Edmund, I'd have to take a little laxative, too . . ." This ends with Walty's voice shaking, on the verge of weeping.

Edmund smiles a slow wide smile, his fierce teeth bared. He passes Walty and goes straight for the parlor which is always cool and woody-smelling and private. But there's a man back-to in a straight-back chair. Jumps the hell out of Edmund. There's something not quite right about the stranger. An aura of death about him . . . motionless—absolute. Edmund circles around to face the visitor. Not a muscle moves of the shoulders under the white, white shirt nor the neck, which wears a long silky scarf. Tall cowboy hat. Edmund's eyes widen on the stranger's face, then down to the tall-heeled white boots that are tooled and jeweled. Such tight satinish white pants!

Edmund sees Walty has come to the parlor doorway, drying a fistful of forks.

Says Edmund, "Walt, you are a weird man."

"Thank you," says Walty, managing a small bow.

39 | "Unk, it looks just like real. Kinda creepy," says Lloyd in a voice like prayer.

"Those are glass eyes from that taxidermist Stan uses. Butchie Taylor . . . he was very nice about getting me some. But the rest . . . all done by the hands of Michelangelo here." He takes one of his quickie bows.

Lloyd feels the nose. "But didn't you have to look in the mirror?"

"A little, yes."

"It's creepy. It's like you . . . if you were . . . *dead*." Lloyd lowers his eyes, then flashes them onto Walty.

Walty says, "But Lloyd, dear, . . . art is not life . . . it's the *illusion* of life!"

Lloyd stares at the papier-mâché face. "You are right, Unk. You *are* an artist. Real. But . . . sometimes artists do paintings."

Unk Walty laughs, a little tsk tsk of derision through his teeth. "Paintings. Too silly. What I want is to make . . . make people's hearts jump . . . to feel a *presence!*"

Lloyd says, "You could probably sell this man for millions."

"*What!*" Unk Walty holds his forehead. "Sell my soul?????"

---

40 | MY FATHER
by Lloyd S. Barrington   age 8¾
(for secret coleckshion)

Last night my father cried in the night time.
You wouldndt know if you were not me right there.
But he cried kind of loude so mabe you would.
It was becus he was mad abot the dishes how wat a rat
    Unk Walty was.
And then it was the cowboy. That was the straw.
                    He fights all the time with Unk
                    Walty.
Gramp Fogg says thers a clash.
My father asked how Iv been doing. I said fine.
He said losing Mama is a hard thing to get ovr.
People stay in the air a long time he said. You can feel
    them werever you go.
He said hE wants to die. Mabe he was joking. He joks
    sometims.

---

41 | Three men in the cab of the cattle truck. And one boy. Truly his
father's son these days. His father's shadow.

Ninety degrees in the cab. The necks of the men run like rivers. Heat, a sort of grief.

They ride by filling stations. Little stores. Traffic piles up behind them . . . the fast-driving people . . . giving Edmund Barrington the horn . . . the jaws of the fast drivers set, eyes popping.

The fast drivers pass the cattle truck. Even on hills. Even curves. They glare over at Edmund Barrington's profile as they pass, speed being righteous.

Seems each car that passes makes the truck cab hotter, but nobody suggests stopping for sodas. For sodas you would use "spending money."

You seldom see the Barrington or Fogg men's *regular* money in plain view. Certainly not "spending money." When you see the little purse of bills being removed from Gramp B's overalls, for instance, it is something you look away from.

Lloyd would never whine, "Gimme this" or "I want that, pleeeeeeeeeeeeeeeze!" Lloyd knows sodas are out there in the world. Deep in the gurgling cold water of the coolers. Some red. Some pale green. Some orange. They are there in the world to admire. Like sunsets.

The rain comes all at once on the roof and windshield like fists of hundreds of furious men. Next thunder and lightning. The worst kind. The kind that seems like it rips. Edmund steers the truck to the far right, into the blind gray wall of rain. The two Herefords in the open back of the truck don't complain.

"Rotary comin' up, Ed," says Gramp B.

Lightning on both sides of the cattle truck, snapping, shrieking, cracking, booming . . . lightning that looks like white nerves. And on both sides, fast-driving cars . . . giving Edmund the horn. Edmund steers two-handed, keeps his silence.

"See. It's coming up there. It's Route 28 we want. Keep left," Gramp B. advises.

Out of the solid black rain, road signs leap out. Edmund hunches over the wheel. Road signs with words and numbers that shift and strain like constellations of the universe, merging with the dark shine of other people's fenders between the slash of wipers.

Very hot for Gramp B. to hold Lloyd on his lap. And the big squeeze on both sides. Roger on one side, door on the other. Temperature inside the truck rising.

Everything seen through the windshield, the rain erases. Then the wipers erase the rain. But more rain pounds down to replace it. Taillights all going in a mad rush into the Y's and O's of the traffic rotary. Edmund gives the truck a hard right swing. There's a big banging in the back. Cattle trying to keep their footing.

"Thought we was going to Suncook," snorts Gramp B. peering past Unk Roger's silent profile, Roger in the middle, feet on the tranny hump, knees high, eyes straight ahead.

Edmund swings the truck into the lot of a filling station, makes a slow chugging lugging-down circle around, gets the truck aimed out, then stops. Again the steers, caught off guard, are banging around.

"Thought we was goin' to Suncook," says Gramp B. "See Route 28 over there?"

Edmund has nothing to say.

Lloyd feels Gramp B.'s thigh tighten under him. They all study the traffic circle through the slash of wipers and mean fists of dark rain . . . the hot glaze of their sweaty faces . . . the old understanding that Edmund and traffic rotaries don't mix.

"All you had to do, Ed . . . was make a left," Gramp B. nags on.

There's a dried carnation swinging from the choke, flower from Edmund's dead wife's grave. Tied there by Unk Roger, Roger being the brother who was closest to her in age. The kinds of grief are so many.

"I shoulda drove," says Gramp B.

42 | OLD PEEPIL
by Lloyd S. Barrinqton   aqe 8¾

Old peepil are very brokin down in all places. Cant hear
   you. You have to yell.
Som hear so you yell and they look at you funny. You got
   to find out wich ones.
Old peepil wait for you to com vist even to fix there clock
   to new time or sweep or even just talk abot there legs
   hurt. You never know what.
Old peepil very brokin but also very nise acep ones that
   are quiet and look mean but Unk says thats just a
   look.
Som in good shape but like you to sit at the table and hear
   abot there sisters stomach. Ones thing is his foot.
You cant forget them.

You say oh I better get ovr there and see old Bertie and his
sister or Mrs. Rice.
You cant forget them Unk Walty says.
They hav no hope unlest you are there.

43 Another day. A cooler day. Feels good. Riding with his father
and cousin Carroll Plummer. All three keeping an eye out for
Leroy MacKenzie's new place. Going to check out a good deal Leroy has
on a compressor. A dog steps out into the road and Edmund stomps the
brake. "Jesus!" he yells, pulls the truck off onto the shoulder.

Edmund bails out, swinging the door wide. He looks back up the
road. It's a dog with a lot of white hair between the toes. Like between
the toes are explosions. The dog is nuts, circling around and around in a
lopsided way . . . into the road, back onto the shoulder and back, sniffing
the pavement, then making a little skip over to the right, back onto the
sand. Edmund walks to the dog, Lloyd hurrying behind him . . . hurrying,
splayfooted fat boy, never graceful. Edmund hefts the dog up into his
arms, starts on foot back along the road where they've just driven from.

Lloyd panting, arms swinging, asks, "What happened?"

His father neither slows nor hastens. The dog's plumey white tail
hangs down over the hip of his overalls. Such a big dog, and yet neither
does she struggle nor Edmund tire.

Lloyd looks back, sees Carroll leaning against the truck sneaking a
smoke.

The dog has the spotted legs and black-and-white face of its breed,
but the eyes . . . one is bulging pink, the other bulging filmy white.

"What happened?" Lloyd insists.

Edmund says, "Old guy up here mentally retarded. Can't take care
of himself. Can't take care of his dog."

"What's wrong with her eyes, Dad?"

"Blind. She shouldn't be out loose. But she's out loose as you see.
Someday she'll get hit. I should stop and go back and get my rifle out of
the truck." He lowers the dog to the sand gently. She stands there un-
steadily, the head drifting to one side. "Yessir, I should go back to the
truck for my gun and take care of this problem *now*."

The dog starts stepping along again in its small perpetual circle.

Edmund snorts with disgust. "Think I should go back for my rifle,
Lloyd? I'll leave it up to you. What would you do?"

54

Lloyd shrugs mightily. He can't speak. His mismatched eyes search his father's face for the answer, for there must be a right or wrong answer to this . . . a little quiz . . . a little joke.

The dog makes a somewhat wider circle, then stands on the crown, panting hard, swaying its head toward the high weedy bank.

"Lloyd. Tell me. What's this old dog remind you of?"

"I don't know," Lloyd answers, squinting suspiciously.

"Sure you do!" His father blinks his eyes in a crazed unseeing way. "It's somebody you know very well and ain't worth a shit."

Lloyd thinks of all the people he knows very well. He shrugs. "I don't know."

Edmund grins fiercely, his dark eyes terrible and teasing. "It's a puzzle, isn't it, how some people get along in this world, how they manage to go so long?"

Lloyd squints. "I suppose."

"I want for you to go back and get my rifle from behind the seat. The shells are in the glove box. Then . . . I'll shoot this old dog." He is looking at the dog tiredly, then looks up and grins. "Then . . . the next right thing would be for some good-hearted person to shoot me."

Lloyd frowns.

Edmund makes a rush for the dog, scoops her up in his arms again, heads down the road to the old farmplace where she lives . . . Lloyd following a little distance back . . . stopping to throw a rock into a backed-up culvert . . . stopping to inspect an eroded piece of Coke bottle . . . looking preoccupied and composed in his canvas fishing hat with the tied flies around the brim.

44 | SPITER
by Lloyd S. Barrington   age 8¾

If you are litle enouf a spiter rolls you up to eat later on.
Spiter spiter big and gray.
You woud be so hidious a feeling.
No face for spiters creepy just legs and suckers to suck out
    yore middles.
Dana my ~~cusin~~ cousin thinks spiters are funy catches them
    for his room for living in jars. Onse he had a BIG one
    on his neck and didnte even feel it he says. Carroll

smashis them but I wish a spiter big as a house woud
give Carroll a big surpris. Ha! Ha! you woud see me
laufing most.

45 | EYES
by Lloyd S. Barrington   *age 8¾*

Most peepil hav regula eyes.

I hav one eye Unk Stan says its hazel Unk Walty says no
it's GREEN.

The other one has big things in it in the green part which
are brown.

Looks weerd.

Mama said it was Irish blood. Yukk.

If I wantd to get it out ther is nothing I can do but go
arund with blood in my eye forvre and hav ever body
ask me abot it. Wats that? Wats that?

If I tell them they say GROSSSSSS! Most peepils eyes doant
got blood mine   are a mess.

You ever seen a rabbit with pink eyes? Pink eyes all buaeti-
full and pink.

If you have eyes both the same color be lucky its not mine.

Up in the woods where we throw stuff Unk Roger and
Gramp B. put our cows head and other stuff. Then the
eyes rotted out. Without eyes she couldntd see you
looking.

You ever see some lamas? BIG eyes. You wodntd beleev
how prety.

Unk Walty took me to see them. And we got to go on
rides.

Unk Walty gets sick on some rides. We had to skip all
those. But then one ride I got sick. Unk Walty is nise
abot it didntd laufh like som would ~~laufh~~ laugh. Dana
Plummer woould laugh. And call you a pussy.

Back to eyes. You woud HATE my eyes if you had to hav
them.

———

56

46 | Another visit from Nancy. This time one of her girlfriends has dropped her off. They can hear her tooting "Shave and a Haircut, Two Bits" which means Nancy's friends might be the fun type. They can hear Nancy giggling out in the yard, a little visit to the calf. This time there is Gramp Fogg there to show her. But first Gramp Fogg is probably telling her all of his bull and cow jokes except for the dirty ones.

But something is wrong with this visit. Supper is nowhere near ready. No signs that supper will ever be ready. Unk Walty is in some kind of papier-mâché frenzy. Heads. Half-finished heads. Finished heads minus only the glass eyes, paint, and hair. Others in *very* early head stages. Wallpaper paste smell. But no roast or chowder smells. No pie smells.

Lloyd gulps from the milk jar, screws the lid back on, gasps, "She's almost in here . . . should be any second, Unk."

Unk Walty says, "You mean Nancy?"

"Yuh. She's out around the door rock practically. Think she'll be hungry?"

"Why, of course, she'll be *starved*," Unk Walty says huskily, raising one eyebrow, patting more gray mash into the hollow cheek of a head.

Unk Douglas roams out from the living room, rubbing his eyes, working some congestion around in his chest. Squints at the clock. "Where's supper, Walt? What we going to eat? Those?" He looks at a completed head that's in the approximate spot where his plate usually goes.

"You lay a finger on my masterpieces, you'll be sorry!" warns Unk Walty.

The screen door rattles, Nancy's gently polite but quirky little way of knocking.

"Come innnnnnn!" Unk Walty yodels. "Unless you're selling something!"

Nancy steps in and looks about her with a little nervous smile. "I'm selling patent medicine," she jokes, sets a bottle of dark, almost black wine on the table. Everyone watches Nancy's fingers release the bottle's neck. What kind of woman is this Nancy? To look at her you'd hardly tell her from dozens of other women. The blue-frame glasses. The dress with a little belt. But the jazzy horn blowing and the wine make the unks shift uncomfortably in their seats.

"It's so good to see you all," Nancy says.

"Well," sighs Unk Walty. "There seems to be a problem with the gentleman . . . *you know who* . . . he's indisposed."

"No, I'm not." Edmund's voice speaks from the back hallway.

Unk Walty laughs. "He always bounces right back."

Nancy helps herself to a wooden chair, keeping her knees together in a ladylike way. She is watching Unk Walty's hands work the gray mash expertly over the skull shape of newspaper strips and wire. She smiles at this as mightily as Unk Stan is frowning.

Lloyd says, "Unk makes people. You want to see the cowboy in the parlor?"

"NO! NO!" Unk Walty snaps. "Not yet. On one of your future visits . . . okay? I'll show them all together. It's a complete project, you see. It wouldn't be good to see only part. To an artist, that's as bad as being naked in public."

Nancy smiles, says, "Oh, I understand! It'll be so nice to see it when it's all done." She is looking toward the sound of Edmund's boots creaking the hallway floor. He seems to be dallying. Nancy gets up off her chair.

Walty says, "I'm not the only artist in the family, Nancy, dear. Go over to the refrigerator and see Lloyd's poems."

Nancy turns toward the refrigerator and pulls the magnet from a poem, holds the poem to the light of the near window. She smiles as she reads it, glancing up, trying to make out Edmund's form in the dark hall. "My! This is wonderful, Lloyd." She steps over to Lloyd and pulls him against her for a hug . . . a kind of headlock hug . . . another shocking thing about Nancy . . . Nancy very strong for a ladylike lady.

Lloyd asks, "Which one is it?"

"About turkeys," she says close to his ear.

Unk Walty says, "Lloyd has poems on every subject."

Edmund sidles into the kitchen, not looking at Nancy square in the face, but she can see anyway that something has happened to his face.

"Oh!" she cries and hurries over to him. "What's happened, Ed?"

Edmund says, "Oh . . . the tractor. Damn machines."

Walty snorts.

Unk Stan tries to turn away before anyone can see his smile.

Edmund sinks into a chair, keeping his eyes away from Nancy's inspection. "Stitches, too," she says, sitting in the next chair, eye level now. "Why didn't you call me?" She pats his hand. "My gosh, will your vision be all right? Your eye wasn't injured was it?"

Edmund says, "It looks worse than it is."

"Nothing wrong with Ed's *eye*," says Unk Walty. "It's not his *eye* that brings pain."

Edmund turns and glares at Unk Walty with his one good eye. Even the eye that's just a slit in a vivid purple bulge communicates threat.

"When's supper?" wonders Unk Jim at the shedway door, tipping his striped railroad cap to Nancy.

Unk Walty says, "My! Yes! Where is that ol' supper?"

Edmund leans back wearily in the straight chair, legs apart, both eyes closed.

"Well," Nancy wonders, smiling shyly. "Would you all mind if I cooked something up? I can rustle up something . . . maybe something cool, keep the kitchen from heating up. I'll work with whatever you have. I bet I can make up a little something nice."

Unk Walty says, "In due time, I'll start the meal. I'm running late as you can see, but if you abandon work like this, it dries out on you. I'm almost done. Heavens. You people act like savages! Drooling! Frothing!"

Gramp Fogg ambles in from the shedway, cigar of hugest dimensions in his teeth, finds his seat at the table, stares down at where his plate should be.

Nancy beams. "I brought a present." She reaches across the table, pulls the wine bottle into Edmund's view.

He says, "Open her up. Let's get started."

"Good idea!" she rejoices, bounding from her seat. "Where's the corkscrew?"

"None *here*," Walty declares, his back still turned away. "Never've had a use for one."

"Well, a wood screw and pair of pliers will do just as well," Gramp Fogg suggests, getting to his feet. "Want I should go out for a look, Nancy?"

"Oh, please don't go to any trouble. We could save this for another time."

"No trouble t'all," says Gramp Fogg, takes his work cap from the peg, clamps it on with a look of great purpose, exits through the shedway.

"How sweet of him," Nancy says, smiling around the room.

Gramp B. now arrives at the table, looks disgustedly at Edmund's latest black eye, and then at the papier-mâché heads.

Lloyd says, "Unk Walty, these heads are bald, but they all look like ladies."

Unk Walty sighs. "I don't want anyone looking at my work till it's done . . . *Pleeeeeeeze*. It's like having everyone see you naked. I hate it!"

Now everyone squints at the head nearest them. Edmund whitens as he recognizes something. He lowers his face into his hands.

Nancy says, "While we're waiting, why doesn't Lloyd read us his poem?"

Lloyd perks up. "I'll read my new one!" He pulls a piece of very smoodged paper from a pile by the bread box. "You really want to hear it?"

"Oh, yes!" Nancy cries out. "Such an artistic family! You are all so lucky."

"Okay," Lloyd says. He reads painfully slow, but with a clear almost booming voice and a flush of elation: "YOU LOOK IN THE EYEBALL OF A STEER IT IS VERY PRETTY AND WET THERE . . . BIG AND ROUND WITH YOUR OWN FACE LOOKIN' OUT REAL SMALL BUT YOUR NOSE LOOKS BIG. STEERS DON'T MIND YOU LOOKING IN THEIR EYEBALLS. THEY ARE NEVER REAL BUSY."

Nancy applauds. Unk Stan and Unk Jim clap and whistle. Gramp B. nods.

Unk Roger opens the screen door, his high laced-up black boots creaking the floor. He finds a peg for his cap, looks at the table for his supper, sees no supper, passes out of the kitchen without a word or much eye contact.

"Ed," Nancy says, placing her hand on his shoulder. "You must be so proud."

Walty snorts. "Ed *never* reads Lloyd's poems." After a long silence, "Nor his papers from school . . . which are all Excellents."

Nancy looks at Edmund. "Of COURSE he does. You read his poems, don't you, Ed?"

"I just don't know what to say about them. I read 'em. I'm just not a motor mouth about it . . . where's the damn wine opener?" He looks toward the shedway door where Gramp Fogg went.

"Not *everybody* likes reading," Lloyd explains. "Some people . . . just don't! It isn't a big deal. You guys are just making it a big deal and it isn't. Dad don't *have* to read my poems. I like reading them out like this anyways. And anyways I don't want *any*body reading them any-more!" He charges at the refrigerator, yanks poems off, crumples them to his chest. "Anyways, they're not done. Makes me feel . . . naked!"

Edmund's unswollen good eye fixes hard on his son's face, the single dark eye with its reflection of light in the middle, and Lloyd's darker eye looking back, utterly perceptive.

47 |

STEERS SHOT
by Lloyd S. Barrington   *age 8¾*

Dontd feel sorry for steers to die.
Dad says you got to die somtime better to die on a nise
    day wen you arnt an old reck or
canser all in you.
Dad says steers happens very fast doesndt it. I say yes.
    Prety fast.
He says one minit a nise day next minit heaven.
Town Clerk lady Mrs. Springer says animals dontd go to
    heaven.
Dad says that a bunch of shit.
He says Mrs. Springer isnt geting into heaven.
Dad says he is sick of all peepils foolish ideas he says ack-
    shually no body knows.
He says dontd worry it will turn out nise for ever body
    anything has to be better than this shitty stupid life.

48 | What a day! The worst this summer. Humidity trickling off the refrigerator, off the walls. Nothing is nice to touch.

She flushes with irritation that someone hasn't remembered how she says she can't answer doors. It is such a hardship for her to cross a room. Yet as she hears the pounding continue, there's the lovely yodel of her high voice, "Yoooooo-hooooo! Come in! I say come right innnnnnn!"

He finds her in her upholstered chair in her kitchen as before. A very very huge woman . . . woman cumulus . . . maybe three hundred pounds. Close by are the heaps of her necessary things: aspirins, cardboard box of felt Christmas stockings that she is sewing, boxes of birthday cards to pick from, calendar, alarm clock, Thermos of tea. A large globe. This is for purposes of settling arguments in case some arise in discussions concerning continents and countries. Postcard collection. Photo albums. Towers of photo albums. Radio. TV. Phone. These things make walls around her chair. Radio, TV, and phone are quiet.

He appears in the space between the supper table, which is the open end in the teetering walls of her "necessary things," he, so stodgy and severe looking . . . and heroic looking . . . even without his green mask and cape. She looks him over. He looks her over. When this moment of appraisal is over with, she speaks in her yodelly voice. "So you are here."

"Yep," says he. "I'm just one of your ol' ordinary neighbors for a visit. You like visits?"

"Yoooooo are my best naaaaaybor!" she yodels. She points toward the cluttered supper table with its two old wooden chairs, one painted white, one painted dark green. "Have a seat. Do pull yourself up a seat, dear." Her eyes glitter on him.

He picks the dark green, positions it to face her, flumps onto it with his fat-boy "arrumph!"

"You are just who I wanted to talk to," says she. "I was hoping you'd know where that nice feller, Super Tree is."

"Super Tree *Man*," he corrects her.

"Yes . . . well, where *is* he?"

"Gone," says he.

"Oh, dear. I'm sorry to hear that." She sighs woefully. "My son-in-law was over with the tractor to cut my fields and he always does my lawn there, too. You see? Out there. He sweeps around over here a couple times in the summer to keep down the blackberry bushes and . . ." She shivers at a horrible thought. *"Sumac."*

He laughs, little spitty-sounding small manly laugh.

She heaves herself around in her chair and faces the glowing window as she tells him the rest. "So he did it . . . and the little maples were . . . murdered." She sighs.

He is trying not to let her notice him noticing her huge bare bluish legs with the dimples deep as belly buttons. Again today she is wearing the dress he likes. He can see in its flowery print the tiny bees as he also quietly absorbs this whole kitchen, the little things all around that make a home a home.

She says, "I have a treat for you." It is no easy thing, her straining onto her feet, then scuffing heavily to a cupboard. She unwraps from wax paper a half a French horn.

He sees that on her feet are blue felt slippers stretched wide. He sees that in front of her chair, worn down to the black tar base of the linoleum, are two feet shapes . . . like a ghost of her sitting there even when she's not.

He says "Thank you" for the French horn, which he eats, even laps the wax paper. He visits with her for the rest of the afternoon, their chairs close. One of the discussions is about tornados and what they are strong enough to pick up. One especially long discussion they have is about all the worst possible malfunctions of stomachs.

49 | The splintery boards of the attic floor talk under Edmund's boots as he steps into the bedroom, pulling the swollen door shut. He sits on the edge of the bed and stares across at the gable window, at the gray light of an August night.

Eyes wide on the V of Edmund's overalls, Lloyd wonders and wonders and wonders. His father bows his head. It's not prayer. Edmund is not the praying kind. It's more of a moment of dread, like the bed is not a good place.

Now Edmund pulls off his boots and socks and overalls and drives his legs into the bedcovers, stretching full length to begin his long fight for sleep.

The gray evening fades awfully slowly.

Strangled thin help-helps! like mice caught by cats . . . sound terrible . . . but it is only the flying squirrels in ordinary conversation as they swing down, down, down out of the white oaks, going from one white oak to the other, white-bellied, black-eyed characters. Over the years they have always made Lloyd uneasy.

Edmund sweats hard into the sheet under him and the top sheet, which is really a flannel summer blanket, old and a little oily, and like these walls, sweat of the generations of Foggs and Dougherties, a hundred years of mothers and fathers, a hundred breathless summers and creepy squirrel cries, all gone . . . honed down to one man, Edmund Barrington alone in his tenderness. And the son, alone in his. Two heads like two planets afloat in the immeasurable galaxies.

Lloyd knows the moment when his father's stony awakeness enters stony sleep.

The moment has come. Lloyd rises . . . an inch . . . then another inch, slipping out from the covers . . . each long slow movement of his fat self preplanned, expertly executed, studded by the terrible squeaks of the night squirrels. Each black moment reels him out another inch from the bed. When the floor starts to giggle under his weight, he leans cleverly to the left or right. Between these steps, he listens for Edmund to speak his name.

But once he is out of his father's hearing, out of his father's range of grip, out into the night, out along the sandy shoulder of the road, his cape flickering behind him, he is speedy. And very, very light. A fat boy by day, maybe so. But tonight and many nights to come, he's a thing of glory.

50 | You would never notice them unless there were a breeze to waggle their leaves, which might then catch your eye . . . a dozen baby maple trees in a long row . . . the spires of early morning sun seeking, making fragile stick shadows beyond each. If they make it, in thirty years, the fat lady's yard will be in deep cool splendorous shade.

51 | A black-and-tan bored-looking dog, sort of houndish, steps from the collapsed porch of a mill house at 22 Pleasant Street, raises his muzzle to the morning air . . . sniffing . . . something suspicious . . . since there are no secrets to dogs . . . dogs seeing the unseeable. His paws take him along over to the first suspicious thing, a baby tree, its seven leaves a little droopy. The wee sapling is trussed up with gray fishline and little sticks. The dog, with purpose, raises his hind leg and marks the tree. Then with purpose, he moves to the next, gives it an arduous sniffing . . . *sees,* then marks that one, too. Then onto the next and the next, the whole even-numbered side of Pleasant Street. Now back down the odd-numbered side. Each baby tree sniffed, *seen,* and marked. He is as thorough as a good surgeon. He leaves none unattended to. Plods back to his tarred alley, collapses with satisfaction to give his private self a little wash. There's thumping around and clatter inside the houses as people are waking. Two oil trucks come to life out behind Allen's Oil.

52 | The men come in from the day. Edmund at the sink. Unk Walty in his slippers, heaping potato salad into two Tupperware bowls . . . his special recipe potato salad. There are materials in that salad nobody else would think to put in a potato salad. At the Friends of the Olde Towne House supper, they all declare Walt Fogg's potato salad is the "world's best." But here at home there's no praise, no complaints, either. It is just forked into mouths with everything else and that's that.

Now Unk Walty is turning, smiling his smile of welcome. "Well, well . . . howdy!"

Unk Roger finds his place at the table, rubs his knees. "I'm getting old," he says.

"Ha!" Gramp Fogg snorts. "That's growin' pains."

"So!" Unk Walty says cheerily. "Nancy called and says she's going to be about a half hour late. But I told her that was fine . . . that the chicken ain't quite dead yet."

Unk Roger shakes his head. This is his way of laughing.

"I thought we was having deer meat," Unk Stan says.

"He was just pulling her leg," Unk Roger says, now shaking his head at how Unk Stan missed this joke.

From his place at the table Gramp B.'s eyes widen suddenly on something he sees through the parlor door.

Walty hums, tosses a mashed lemon rind into the garbage plate.

Gramp B. notices that all the women sitting in the parlor, at least the ones he can see the faces of from his place at the table, are women he's seen around town. Some he could name. Only instead of the modern rigs women wear these days, these women are wearing beautiful woven hats with big brims, small felt hats with velvet bows, bonnets with fabric daisies and peonies. Beautifully sewn blouses. Lacey to the throat, fastened there with a brooch or pearllike button. Long skirts. Gloved hands and little ladylike feet in old-timey shoes. And there's the cowboy. Only now the cowboy has had his head switched. Under the huge white ten-gallon hat is *Edmund's* face. Gramp B.'s eyes slide over to Edmund his son, the real Edmund, Edmund at the sink lathering up his hands and forearms. Then Gramp B. looks down at his own hands, then back to the parlor doorway. It is plain these are all women Edmund has *experienced* over the years . . . been unfaithful to his dying wife for . . . has had broken teeth, broken nose, broken wrist, black eyes, half-unhinged jaws, and smashed windshields for . . . terrible phone calls in the night because of . . . and gunfire. All lovers of Edmund Barrington . . . except for one woman, the one most directly facing the open door . . . Mary Barrington, Edmund's dead wife, a lace-edged hankie in her hand, raised to dab the tear that's in her eye. Gramp B. braces himself. Roger is leaning to his left now. He sees through the doorway what Gramp B. is looking at. He rolls his eyes toward Edmund, then to Walty. This is a bad scene. Roger is readying himself, opens and closes his hands on the table, every nerve along both arms jumping.

Walty hums, shakes a little pepper on the strips of deer meat, plops them into the hot salted pans.

Lloyd shuffles in from the shedway, shuts the door behind him with the heel of his sneaker. He is wearing a new cap. Says RED SOX. Lloyd not the sports type at all, though he *looks* like a damn good catcher.

"Where's Nancy?" he wonders.

"Late," replies Unk Douglas whose back is to the parlor door so he doesn't look worried yet.

Edmund turns from the sink, short black hair wetted together. His recently smashed-up eye has smoothed out into a regular eye again. Just a tinge of yellow-green. He has put in a big day, messing with a truck transmission, mowing cemeteries for the town, two small ones and the big one over on Rummery Road. Cutting out saplings up behind the field. Fixed a pump. Repaired a quarter of a mile of fence. He steps toward the table, then sees the white worried looks of his father and brother-in-law.

Lloyd says, "What kinda pie's that, Unk?"

Walty says cheerily, "Lemon Supreme. And that other one is a creamy date layered thing with graham-cracker crust I made just for you."

"MMMMMMMMM. I love dates," says Lloyd.

Edmund stares at his father and Roger, his own body getting braced like theirs though he doesn't know yet what for. Next he turns, *sees*. He steps out around the set table to the parlor door, stands with his hands at his sides, looking in. Then he just very gently and tiredly rests his head against the doorframe.

53 | Lloyd settles onto the bed easy. He gives himself a whole minute to do this, to be sure not to creak the bed. He's running late this time. It's almost dawn.

His father's voice is sudden, gives him a jump. "Where you been?"

"To the outhouse," Lloyd replies.

"To . . . the . . . out . . . house," his father repeats to make it clear.

"Yup."

Long silence.

Edmund says, "You must have something bad going on in your digestive tract to be workin' on it for five hours."

Lloyd is silent, sitting board straight on the edge of the bed.
Edmund is silent.

The pale light comes orchid color and silky, light that is both tired
and tireless. It churns across the room and lights up Edmund's eyes that
are dark and Lloyd's that are one green, one green splotched with brown.

54 | East Egypt. Main Street. Midmorning traffic, mostly trucks slow-
ing at the bridge. Stephanie Foster and Diane Sargent out walking.
Stephanie's baby in the buggy. Diane has her baby by the hand. The walk
is slow-going.

"Lookit that little tree with the string," Stephanie says, pointing.

"Well! I almost stepped on it!" Diane complains.

"There's another one."

The two young women squint up along the sidewalk.

"There's some more . . . see? See there?"

"Kind of little, aren't they? They'll never make it."

"Maybe it's a new fast-growin' rugged type."

"They must have planted them pretty early this morning. I was out
here after supper last night and I didn't see them *then*."

"Well, you could've missed them. You don't see the darn things unless
you're lookin' straight down."

"Mmm. Pretty shrimpy."

"Do they really expect them to make it with all these gorillas we got
around here like Pete and Donnie and what's-his-face?"

"Well, don't give them any ideas. They'd be runnin' them down on
purpose."

"Who puts trees out, anyways? The Town or the State?"

"Maybe the Audubon Society."

"Nah . . . I think they're birds."

"Probably the State. The State, I'll bet."

They move on, baby buggy wheels squeaking duskily. They pass
another little tree. And another. Diane's baby squats, grabs one. "No,
no, Michael. *Nice* the tree. Nice it." She kneels down and steers his hand
for a little gentle pat-pat of the tree. "See?"

"Hard to picture them making it," Stephanie says with a sigh.

"Maybe a couple will. It'll look nice. In the old days they always had
trees. People are just so mental these days. All they want is wide streets.

You look at all the old pictures of this street. It was all trees. Both sides. Things were pretty then."

"Pete and them will probably annihilate these. What assholes."

"You can say that again."

"If I see anybody messin' with these trees, I'm calling the Town."

"State maybe."

"Whoever."

55 | Another night. Another mission. He knows the feel of the dark, how it unfolds and smooths out, the September fields creaking with song, the long roads pulling him into nothingness. His polo shirt and tights fit him a little loosely these days. The bikini bathing suit needs a pin. His legs are hard and thrumming. He sees what nobody sees. He hears the old trees along the roads talking deeply and the young ones that make their sweet sopranos. His sneakers cause no sound. The feed sack of baby trees and trowel swing abruptly, but also silent. Up ahead a thing humps across the road, leaps for the culvert, scrambles up and over the stone wall. In the kindly darkness, he has nothing to wonder. In the dark he knows everything about life. The big picture. He knows that life put him here on earth to make people shady.

Special Recipe
Blackberry Pie

A WOMAN and her daughter together on a Sunday night in a kitchen in Egypt, Maine. Overhead frosted glass light fixture. Freshly swept floor. Spider plant in the window over the sink. Open doorway beyond which there is gently clucking electronic group laughter . . . now shrieks of dismay . . . now wild laughter. Daughter's T-shirt shows a fat striped cat wearing sneakers.

"Where's that yellow bowl, Mum?"

"Right in here behind this."

"Oh, yuh . . ."

"Go get your berries and let's see again what we got to work with."

"Hmm . . ."

"Listen! If we're going to get this done, we've got to have the TV off. I'm not going to be talking to the side of your face."

"Mum, I can do both. I'm not a one-track person."

"Well I am!" The mother goes into the living room and the electronic group laughter becomes sudden silence.

Daughter gets the brown bag of blackberries, pushes the refrigerator door shut with her elbow, wears an expression of supreme tolerance for this, the intolerable.

The mother takes the bag, peers in, pokes around among the berries. "What smells like bacon?"

"What a nose! Jeepers . . . you should work for the cops. You are close. This bag we brought the stuff back from Hukki Lau in. Ham-fried rice. Guess it kinda seeped in."

"These are pretty pitiful lookin' but I guess we can make do."

"Well, we picked 'em Thursday. They've been settin'."

"Well, these will be fine. There's more than four cups here. The rest we can throw into pancakes or something. So really all we have to do is mix 'em up with the flour and 'bout a half cup of sugar. Your grammy Foye always used white . . . but I make about a fourth cup of it brown. She also made the pie higher. Great big pie . . . twice as many berries, but like I say, we had berries coming out of our ears in them days . . . because of the power line. I remember feeding blackberry pie to my dolls and bears."

"We got some *red* raspberries down to Westbrook . . . around the parking lot of Dad's work. But there weren't enough to make something out of. We just ate 'em." She watches her mother's hands spooning flour into a glass cup.

"Well, you be careful eating things around parking lots . . . some old drunk pissing on 'em . . . might have AIDS. You've got to be careful these days."

"Mum . . . that's not how you get AIDS." Daughter rolls her eyes.

"Well, even regular piss . . . nothing I'd want in my mouth."

The daughter tsks. "So what else do we put in this pie?"

"Salt and a little orange rind if you have it around. Your grammy Foye never used orange rind. It's something I heard about and tried and it adds a nice little tang."

Daughter watches her mother's hands cutting in the shortening, crumbling it with fingers and palms. And now she takes a turn . . . fingers and palms . . . delicately, feeling the relationship with flour that is as the finest heart-to-heart talk.

Daughter says, "So you really got this recipe all changed around."

"Not really. It's pretty nearly the same. I always put a dab of butter on top of the berries before the top crust goes on. That's exactly like Grammy used to do. And the flour's the same and all that. This is really the same pie."

Riches

The deeper the sorrow, the less tongue it has.

—The Talmud

1 | THE MOTHER PHOEBE spreads her right hand on the fender of the housekeeper's station wagon, her eyes fixed on something in the barn.

Twelve-year-old Gwen appears behind her, Gwen appearing or reappearing? . . . as into her breathless walks in the woods she *disappears*, humping along, arms folded across her narrow chest . . . then the usual is that she'll disappear again . . . to her room? The secret secret life of Gwen Curry.

But now here she is . . . near.

Phoebe, the mother, pushes away from the station wagon and wonders, "What's Daddy's car doing here?"

Gwen, breathless from her hurry, chokes out, "What?" then sees for herself the Buick inside the barn, the long low dark panorama of it, and there along the slanted barn floor is her father's slightly clenched hand . . . luster-faced wristwatch with its fine second hand sweeping . . . light blue stripe cuff, button in the buttonhole, looking smart. "It's . . . OH! OH, NO!!" the girl shrills.

Suddenly the mother, Phoebe, is smoking. The two smoking fingers are there in a to-and-fro blurry sequence, as there has also been the sequence of white summer mornings, white skies, white fields . . . and Phoebe all in white, white definitely being Phoebe's color. There is Phoebe over the years and years, summer after summer, a chain of Phoebes, white paper doll Phoebes, one stepping from the next, crisp middies, jerseys, boat necks, sweaters, blouses with a ruff, pedal pushers and shorts, skirts and sheaths, robes . . . white terry, off-white terry . . . the ongoing ruthless pale fleet . . . all moving toward this moment, this open barn door with the eyes of the Buick's taillights watching. And there, her husband, Dr. William Curry, spread-eagle on the plank floor.

The girl, Gwen, is stepping into the barn. This morning Gwen had imagined her father at his office. There was nowhere else to imagine him, his narrow-shouldered stoop as he did his good work, his "sainted work" as Phoebe, her mother, always calls it . . . his "gift to humanity" as Phoebe also always calls it. He had left the house right after breakfast, hadn't he? But no, plain as day, he is stretched out here in the barn on his stomach.

Phoebe's two smoking fingers work the cigarette in and out of her lips.

Gwen steps closer, partly into the barn's gloom, while her left pants leg and sneaker still remain a step behind in the fiery daylight.

"Sleeping," explains Phoebe's little mouth pinched around the cigarette. Cigarette is jerked out of her mouth. "SLEEEEEPING! Aren't you, William! Pretending to be asleep. GET UP!"

Gwen knows this is not sleep. Even if it were, her father never sleeps in the day. He never even looks sleepy. Beat. The housekeeper Doris always says he looks "beat." But he's ever-moving, coming, going, the noiseless heroic visage of his Buick sliding in and out of the trees, the quick scuffing step of his high-polish brown shoe.

The daughter, Gwen, goes over to him now, her big narrow sneakers slapping along. She stoops, gives his shoulder a nudge with her knuckles. From high places in the cluttered loft, through the daylight cracks in the barn walls, light comes down, light that is ointmenty, swollen, and orange, light that seems to have an odor. "He acts funny," she whispers.

"Playing a joke," says Phoebe in a matching whisper.

"Daddy! Stop playing a *joke!*" Gwen coaxes. She sees down his collar and to where his wrists strain out of his tight perma-prest cuffs. His head is averted on his neck, cheek easy against the gravelly plank floor, that same surrender with which his cheek goes to the pillowcase of rosettes or the crochet-edged ivory pillowcase or the blue or stripe up there in the high-ceilinged tulip-papered bedroom of the house at the end of one of his long "sainted" days. His eyes aren't open now. But they aren't closed. What shows of his pupils is greenish black and paralyzed, enameled terrible eyes. His glasses are gone. Somewhere. Where? Where? Where? "STOP PLAYING A JOKE!!!" Gwen shrieks. Gwen knows this is not a joke. Not sleep. Maybe a joke. Maybe sleep. Maybe not? Maybe? Everything sliding out of focus, yellow and perky with stars. Everything sudden and razor-edged. What? What? "Mother! He's scaring me!!"

Phoebe, the mother, moves into the barn. She grows darker the deeper inside she passes. Her mouth with its bright lipstick is set in its endearing lopsided way, beauteous Phoebe, with the Patti Page hair, now eclipsed, her cigarette vanished from the small silvery hand. She says, "Gwen, give him another little poke there."

Gwen shakes her head hard.

Phoebe sighs. "All you have to do is push him with your foot." She giggles. "You don't have to use your hand."

"You do it," Gwen tells her.

Phoebe's little dressy moccasin. White with a little white leather tie. Sweet peach-color beads. A tsk tsk of a moccasin. Within it the sassy little foot. Phoebe raising this foot, and sweet-fit moccasin, its sweet adorable ways. Gwen watches her mother's foot and moccasin give her father's shoulder a push.

2 | Now the mother Phoebe slides the barn door shut using both hands and a bit of shoulder . . . "Unh!"

3 | What is it hanging there? A human heart. Cantaloupe-sized. A plastic model for disassembling to see the valves. Hangs over the kitchen table. Was it one of the brothers who put it there? Or Phoebe in collusion with one of the brothers, a kind of cute joke? Suspended by such fine string, it surely hovers.

It has always been there. Maybe nobody strung it up there. Maybe it *does* hover, because the Curry kitchen table and Curry kitchen is just the place for all things working against gravity . . . all things great and sassy. All things of diverging possibilities. You can only guess. It is hard to remember the kitchen before the heart was hung.

The housekeeper Doris and young Dennis Curry are paused to consider Mickey Mantle's future. Dennis is leaning against the refrigerator, scratching under his shirt, his hair gobbed together from too much riding around with open car windows. The housekeeper Doris is serious, absolutely reverent about Mickey Mantle. Dennis has no reverence, only big laughs . . . and braces that give his big laughs a black tortured look.

Phoebe steps in from the high noon to this kitchen of no gravity, place of guesswork, slanted cool room where no food is cooking, no food seems to have ever been, plastic heart jarring slightly to the slam of the door . . . she says cheerily, "Well, Doris! I won't need you for the big search. Guy promised he'd do it and he knows best where all that stuff is. Some of it he's picking up for his apartment. So I told him to go ahead. That would be Wednesday. So plan to wax that day instead. Okay?"

Doris says fine.

Gwen hangs back in the doorway.

Dennis says, "I'm starved."

Phoebe speaks from her fire red lipsticked little mouth and white Patti Page hair, gray eyes lowered on a chair nobody ever sits in. "Well, as soon as Guy and Daddy come in, I'm making sandwiches for all of us as fast as I can get to it. It wouldn't be right not to wait for Guy . . . and Daddy, too . . . all because of one starving person." She gives Dennis's shoulder a squeeze. "My growing *boy*."

The daughter, Gwen, still by the doorway seems to be trying to cover her face with her forearm. Her shoulder thumps once against the wall.

"What's the matter with *her*?" Dennis wonders, one corner of his dark irreverent mouth flickering with fun.

The housekeeper Doris turns to look. "Oh, dear. What's the matter, Gwen?" She takes a step toward her.

"Nothing's the matter!" Phoebe says sharply.

The housekeeper freezes just short of reaching the girl.

Phoebe has turned to dig butter knives from a drawer.

The daughter, Gwen, hurries from the kitchen of cool white faces, blazing mouths, intermittent eyes, to the long hallway, up the stairs to the hot narrow other hallway, the row of closed doors, one with a radio thrumming softly beyond it, then on into her room where she sits on the bed, breathless. There's a flash on the wall. She sees down through the window. It's one of the Armstrongs' gardeners opening his truck door for his lunchbox. Lunch. Lunchtime. Always the same time gardeners eat their lunch. The Currys have no gardeners. No garden. Phoebe Curry calls the Armstrongs' gardeners "Farmer Browns." She has called the housekeeper Doris a "Farmer Brown," too. Once Dennis told Doris, "Mother calls you a Farmer Brown. You call her a Farmer Brown, don't you, Mother?" Phoebe said that that was ridiculous. And where did he ever pick up that expression? Then Dennis had chuckled deeply, he and Phoebe each looking away from each other's faces in the terribleness of the moment.

Now here in Gwen's room . . . alone . . . dark honeycomb look of the walls, overlaid with printmaker's type cases with their one-inch and two-inch rectangular recessions made just right for every tiny glass or ceramic creature . . . the collection of figures which began before memory. Begun by whom? Gwen never asks. Nobody adds anything to the collection now. So many vacant openings are left . . . tantalizing for a child who would want to fashion a tiny world. What Gwen has pushed into some of the openings are acorns, a dried lima bean, sea glass, pretty rocks, plain rocks, very sciency unpleasant-looking rocks.

Then there's the bare wall against her bed. Chalky to touch. A color one might associate with chlorine. Like warm smelly indoor pools and athletes.

There are books. But neither Gwen nor Dennis turned out to be much for readers. Just school assignments. No disappearing into one's room with a "good book" as Phoebe does, sometimes for many days straight. What does Gwen do when *she* disappears if not read, listen to the radio or hi-fi? What does she do in the woods?

Here and now she weeps. But it is not a wet weeping. More of a running away of the muscles, jaws, throat, forehead muscles all willy-nilly, and on the edge of her bed she is rocking ever so slightly. Gwen cradling Gwen. She knows she looks foolish. But with the door closed, you can do anything. Privacy is important.

———

4 | The mother Phoebe is fixing sandwiches . . . cold cuts, pimiento spread, peanut butter and marshmallow, peanut butter and jam. Potato chips. Pickles. Saturday food, she has always called it. Woven placemats on the round table's edge, spaced like numerals of a clock. Placemats are stained. One looks like it's been chewed. Here come the plates. Clunk. She leaves them in a stack there. The table is blond, reflects the blue and blond summer light of the windows. She takes a plate and does up a sandwich on it. All ready. Plate for William, the father, who everyone is expecting home early for his "Saturday food" . . . Saturdays being only half days at the office. Cold bean sandwich. His trademark. Nobody else here can stomach cold beans. As Phoebe now sloshes together a nice fruit punch, nobody can glimpse her face. She has made a turban with a flowered scarf to keep her pageboy off her neck as the day gets warmer. The back of her neck is sweet like a girl's.

Guy has come home for more stuff for his apartment, but seems settled in here as ever, his chair sideways at the table, the *New York Times* folded into a chunk on his thigh. Cigarette smoking itself on the rim of his plate. Guy doesn't have the large head, broad face of Phoebe or Dennis who looks like Phoebe. Guy Curry is beaked and narrow-jawed, some signs of past acne. The eyes are large and pale blue . . . eyes that belong in a large head, large face. Hair a little long. Shoulders a little stooped. Rings on two fingers of each hand, high-school ring, college ring, fraternity, and decorative . . . baggy sweater, jeans, sneakers, no socks. *No socks.*

Dennis drums his fingers on the table, picks a plate from the stack, looks at it as if the sandwich he is wishing for is hidden in the leafy pattern there. Now he fans himself with the plate. The air being fanned gives the hanging cantaloupe-sized heart a little neurotic twitch.

Phoebe places the pitcher on the table, red punch slapping the sides of the glass. Lemon slices and maraschino cherries diving and bobbing merrily, full of the devil. Fun fruits. Phoebe's hands shake. But only slightly. She sets out a platter of sandwiches. She says brightly, "Dig in now!!" as if to thousands of guests.

"Where's Gwen?" Guy wonders, eyes still fixed on the *New York Times,* cigarette still smoking itself out on the plate rim.

Dennis snorts then whispers just to himself, "Throwing a fit."

"What?" Guy asks, jerking his chair around, impatient with this, his being excluded from something.

Phoebe settles into her chair with a sigh. "Eat! Please! You are all making me nervous. Your vulture act is what I'm used to." She rams the bowl of potato chips toward the older son. He says thank you and picks a sandwich, piles a few chips on.

Dennis opens sandwiches to see what's inside them.

Guy asks, "You okay, Mother?"

"Why? Was there supposed to be a problem? Fallen trees? High winds? Rabid rats?" She giggles, pushing a potato chip into her teeth, settling and resettling herself on the chair.

Dennis says to himself with a kind of admiration, "Rabid rats."

Phoebe selects a peanut butter and marshmallow sandwich.

A truck grunts past on the road. Phoebe's eyes jerk to the window. She lights a cigarette, quickly shakes the ash. In her lovely hand, the cigarette is wandlike, breezy, fairy-tale clever, brewing with power.

Guy glowers at Phoebe's peanut butter sandwich, sees it ooze, untouched.

Phoebe is inspecting the stones of her many rings, taps her ash again into the plaid beanbag ashtray. She smokes. Dreamy slow motion. To let smoke out, she pops her lips slightly. This makes smoke ride like gray kisses across a beam of the afternoon sun. She taps her ash again. Actually she smashes the ash. She looks down at her long fingernails, inspecting them for flaws. "Everything okay in Boston?" she asks.

"Wonderful," says Guy, not looking up from his reading. His cigarette is in his fingers now, but still hasn't reached his mouth. He looks up now directly into his mother's eyes. "Where'd you say Gwen is?"

Phoebe examines her nails more intently.

Dennis says, "Upstairs," then smiles meaningfully.

Guy looks up at the heat register that opens up on the floor of Gwen's room.

Phoebe stirs her cigarette butt around in the ashtray, considers her sandwich. "Mmmmm. What a nice day. Nice lunch." She tucks a little of her blond hair back into her turban.

"Dad's late," Guy says absently.

"Oh . . . some emergency at the hospital!" Phoebe says and bares a bright smile.

Dennis's stormy eyes seem fixed on something that has nothing to do with this room. Practically his whole sandwich is in his left cheek. Big bulging cheek. Glittering braces. And yet, such a beautiful boy. All that sexy, cowlicky, vagabond hair. The full fine nose. The full fine lips. Even grown women . . . his teachers at the academy, flush to speak the name Dennis Curry.

Phoebe bites off a bit of sandwich. She chews, works it around and around in her mouth like gum.

Dennis is noticing that his mother's mouth doesn't swallow. He is watching when she spits in her plate. He contemplates the kinked-up orangy thing. "Yeck!" says he.

"What's wrong with your sandwich?" Guy asks.

"Nothing's wrong with it!" Phoebe says cheerily. "Why would there be anything wrong with it?"

"It's kind of piggy to spit in your plate," Dennis tells her. "Not very ladylike. Kind of sickening actually."

"Well, just don't look at my plate. Keep your eyes on your own plate. My goodness!" she crows and fires up another cigarette with a little silvery *zzzzzt*-snap of her lighter.

5 A white Triumph convertible reels up under the low maples by the kitchen door. Radio full blast . . . a song about love . . . the singing voice seems tired, ready to yawn. Now the D.J. exclaims that that was Bobby Vintonnnn!!!!! Everything disc jockeys tell you has big emergency to it.

No need to open the Triumph's doors. Just tumble long-leggedly out and over. This Lawrence, this next oldest son, good humored spring to his walk, still a little too playful for law school? Too silly? Too offhand, man of fun? But the flawless grades, mind like a razor . . . this other self carried like a rock and pitched hard. Lawrence Curry. Reaches for a bakery box on the seat. Always remembers a little something for his mother. Gallops for the house. He is drawing his lips off his teeth as though he is pretending to be a horse. Piled outside the door and just inside the door are cartons and paper bags of the brother Guy's things headed for his apartment in Boston. Lawrence asks Guy if he needs help "loading the barge" and "Where's Dennis?"

Guy says Dennis is carrying down the last two armloads.

Lawrence looks around the kitchen, eyes twinkling. He doesn't note the dangling plastic heart. Seems the rest of the kitchen is enough to amuse him completely. His eyes also twinkle on his brother Guy's socklessness.

Lawrence himself would *never* be without socks, while Guy who is Mr. Serious . . . no socks.

"Anybody need a cruller?" Lawrence wonders. Shakes the bakery box to the tune of the Bobby Vinton song still winding sleepily in his head. "Where's Mother and Dad?"

"I don't know," Guy grumbles, pushing out through the door with a heaped wicker laundry basket and a suitcase. Lots of grunting. He calls back, "I don't know anything anymore."

Dennis appears with a bunched roll of shirts and sweaters under each arm, shaking hair out of his eyes.

Lawrence says, "Want a cruller?"

"Why is it always crullers?" Dennis whines. "The world makes jelly donuts, too!"

"Mother likes crullers."

"So get assorted."

"Say, where *is* everybody? Mother reading?"

"I guess."

Dennis goes out as Guy comes back in. Guy heads for the crullers box. Lawrence stuffs one whole cruller into his mouth, tosses Guy one, then, gripping one in each hand, garbles, "I haven't had any dinner yet. I need nourishment if I'm going to be a moving man."

Guy sees through the window that a long light color car has materialized behind the Triumph. He says, "Someone's here."

A rap on the door.

"YEP?" Lawrence calls out.

Door opens. Tall man with white sea captain's beard and thin hair, but eyes, startlingly black-lashed and young, steps into the kitchen.

Behind the stranger, Dennis is reappearing, breathless. Aluminum door shuts itself, breathless.

The stranger moves toward Lawrence and takes his hand, and with the other hand reaches to squeeze Dennis's shoulder. "I have some trouble here." Even as he speaks, even as he has not released Lawrence's hand, red ambulance lights swipe through the gray dusk, coming closer along the row of trees. "Your mother has asked me to tell you that your father has passed away. She didn't have the heart to tell you herself. She's a very softhearted woman as you know. I'm so sorry to have to be the one to tell you. It is a loss to me, too . . . a finer man nowhere . . . none better . . . a *young* man. I'm sorry."

Dennis croaks, "So where *is* everybody?" He squints out through the window at the revolving red lights.

"Your mother tells us your father is in the barn," the stranger replies. "And your—"

Lawrence and Guy bound out through the door.

Dennis starts for the door. "Is my mother out there?"

"No," the stranger says evenly, but warmly. "She's with Marcia. They went out for a while. Your mother is actually doing quite well. You mustn't worry . . ."

"Who's Marcia?" Dennis asks. Testily. Eyes glimmery. Hand on the door.

"My wife. I'm sorry. You were really young the last time we met. I shouldn't have assumed. I'm Harry Pelm," puts his hand out for a shake.

Above them through the heat grate, Gwen listens.

Dennis grasps the stranger's hand, but keeps his face turned away.

"I'm sorry," Harry Pelm says, his dark-lashed eyes wide with discomfort and poise. He releases Dennis's hand.

The two of them head out for the barn, the aluminum screen door sucking itself shut behind them.

6 | Where did the platter of cupcakes go? This early morning there were cupcakes. Then Gwen never saw them again. They had been on the counter almost directly below the heat grate. Gwen had watched her father's long fingers closing up on one to admire it . . . but did he eat it?

She can't recall. It didn't matter then. She hadn't listened for the muffledness of his voice with the cupcake and words mixing around together because she would have never supposed anything then. Now the "supposes" are everywhere like dive-bombing birds and hollow screeches.

The cupcakes were pale with pale frosting laid thickly on each. The frosting was almost green. An undeclared green. Perhaps flavored mint. Mint was rising in the air up through the heat grate. And there were Phoebe's yellow cigarette odors and the housekeeper Doris's Chock Full o' Nuts on perk.

"These look good, Pheeb," Gwen heard her father say. She tries now to remember if he said anything after that. But all there was was Phoebe's singing out, "Tootle-ooo!" the way she does when the "good doctor" is turning toward the little back hall to leave.

How Phoebe HATES cooking! She *never* makes desserts. Never does roasts. Nothing like that. It's hard to predict what the evening meal will be. Sometimes it has been a really nice effort, a few chops with canned peas and the brand of bread that isn't "batter whipped," doesn't help "build children's bones nine ways" . . . none of those. It would be one of the nicer brands.

But then other nights no food smells were on the air when the good doctor stepped through the door. But he never complained. After a while, he'd just fix himself a sandwich.

Sometimes Phoebe was into her tricks. William would whip off the lid of the silver server and there was a roll of toilet paper. Or a light bulb. Or B & M Baked Beans still in the can. It seemed there may have been a message behind these tricks . . . something between Phoebe and the good doctor . . . but with Phoebe and all the boys shrieking, it did seem to be just plain fun.

Gwen sometimes laughed, too. But sometimes not. She would glance at Phoebe who was pointing at William. "Fell for that one!" Phoebe would chortle, looking directly through her cigarette smoke at William and around at each howling son . . . all laughing . . . around the man the circle of wet mouths and pink snouts wheezing open and shut, the stranglehold obscene.

William would flush. But he wouldn't give up either . . . kept wearing his small saintly smile.

7 | Phoebe watches her daughter making toast. Gwen, tall. Hair, brown with a side part. A single barrette. This summer Gwen will not wear shorts. She won't let anyone see her legs bare. Nor her arms. You only get to see her forearms. No upper arms. No underarms.

There's the question of where did her sleeveless blouses go? Those her grandmother sent up from Connecticut. Where are they? Behind a big rock? Thrown in a bush? Is this what she does on her long walks? Her disappearances? Throws away expensive attractive clothing that poor Farmer Browns would give their eyeteeth for?

Gwen *could* present herself as someone they could all be proud of. But no. She walks around with her arms folded over herself and humped, humping along. Corduroys bag out from her long legs. Big shirts opened out over the hips like tarps. And there's the thump of her big sneakers over the floors of this kitchen! The terrible terrible sound of her step.

And to think GranMom Sheehy has this idea Gwen should take ballet!!!

The phone clamors.

"Guy! Answer that, would you?" Phoebe pleads, white-faced, hushed.

Guy picks the phone from its cradle and speaks clearly, keeps his back to the room.

The daughter, Gwen, sets her plate out and there's the margarine ready while the toaster does its work.

Phoebe hangs onto Guy's clear words, his accent still Connecticut, though they left Connecticut when he was a toddler. It seems he has come to sound *more* Connecticut than less, a thing he has achieved, worked hard for . . . like the academy and college awards, and now his engineering work, the companies and connections in Boston, New York, and overseas. He has even already had his hand in politics. He goes in a dozen directions and in the middle is this voice, impersonal, yet obliging, clean, midrange, a little nasal. She tries to figure who he's speaking with. She guesses Mrs. Armstrong the neighbor with the gardens and army of gardeners or Dr. Varney . . . but she eliminates those because of something in Guy's voice. She guesses again.

Gwen opens cupboard doors, finds the platter in its usual place. Wheat print. Clean as a whistle. Gwen narrows her eyes. Had he eaten ALL the cupcakes? A dozen at least. There's no end to this guesswork.

"Who is it, Guy?" Phoebe ventures.

Guy is nodding at the caller's words, covers his other ear with a hand.

Phoebe starts a cigarette, gives it four desperate, noisy, brutal sucks, then she flounces her cigarette hand, a sexy movie star gesture. "Who is it, Guy?" she persists. "Is it GranMom?"

Guy turns to face Phoebe and whispers, "Yesssss. You want to talk with her?"

Phoebe backs away, shakes her head, says, "Tell her Winslow is doing the eulogy. She'll like that. She likes Winslow. Ask her if she remembers Winslow."

He puts a palm up. "I can't hear you both talking at once." He chuckles. He listens, listens. He sighs, looks deeply into Phoebe's gaze. "Mother. She wants to know if she should come sooner than to-night . . . it would . . . be . . . easier if . . ." He listens to more words coming from the phone. "Mother," he says to Phoebe. "She would prefer to talk to you directly."

Phoebe backs away. "Just tell her to come when she can for gosh sakes."

"Come when you can," he says into the phone, then listens hard to the response while Phoebe says, "Tell her what the funeral director said about your father . . . about the funeral director's little boy having that puffed arm that time."

Guy covers his ear.

Gwen is humped over her toast now, spreading margarine on.

Phoebe urges Guy to tell GranMom about the flowers from Gerrity's.

He tells about the flowers from Gerrity's.

In time the phone call is done. Guy has excused himself. The pipes to the upstairs bath now whistle and shake in the walls. And now Phoebe is alone in the kitchen with the daughter, Gwen. Gwen in all her bagginess and overcoveredness. Gwen making another piece of toast. Phoebe stares out the back window. Purple and yellow patches of the Armstrongs' garden show through the low hanging trees between the two properties. Phoebe smokes slow and easy, the smoke loose and cloudlike. Phoebe can't bear to look at Gwen's billowing shirt, long bony jaw gnashing toast, but she hears it, the terrible sounds of the toast.

8 | Noontime. There's no meal. There's no one converging. There's only coming and going. Car doors slamming, cars sliding away. There's order. There's appointments. There's plans. A grand design. All the decisions to be made for the funeral. The visitation BEFORE the funeral. The burial. But for the *table* nothing. There's no Phoebe and her children breaking bread. Food? You find it. You slap a little of this or that on a cracker. There's more bakery boxes opened on the table. You open a bottle of root beer, stand around and chug it down. Now Phoebe has gone to her room to read. And the others fall away into other parts of the house or out to hose down a car.

And now for a while it is only the sound of the piano, its serious questions, the long melodies at the high end of each scale . . . Lawrence, who, of all of them with their years of lessons, is the only one who plays for the joy of it . . . for relief . . . to give his fingers something to sink into, head tipped to the side, eyes closed. Funny-guy Lawrence is not always funny. "Woodland Sketches." The notes thin as ice and air and sun as if Lawrence could be a young man scaled down to a pollen speck.

How do we grieve here in this house? How do we give each other comfort? Is there comfort? Yes, comfort, the absence of shrieking laughter?

9 | Well, so she wasn't reading after all. With her flashing pale hair, she bursts into the kitchen with a woven beach bag of gladioli heavy against her hip. White shorts a little grubby now. Young Dennis coming down from his room sees. Phoebe knows that Dennis knows where she got the glads but that it's not really stealing like crooks steal, but charmingly mischievous. Phoebe fetches the largest porcelain vase from the shelving along the cellar stairs, arranges the glads that are dewy and rambunctious. She stands back to judge her work. Applauds herself. Dennis grimaces then fades from her view as she maneuvers the great wagging bouquet through the living-room door straight to the piano, one gladiolus beating Lawrence's head and shoulder. The music stops. He stands up quickly from the stool. "Excuse me!" Phoebe sings out.

The midnight surface of the piano plays back the reverse image of the glads. And on Lawrence's face the color glows. "They're pretty, Mother. Who sent them?"

Phoebe lowers her beauteous great gray eyes. "Don't ever, ever tell, will you, Lawrence? The Armstrongs wouldn't understand!" She stretches tall, up on her toes and whispers through cupped hands into his ear. "Your mother has been naughty."

10 | Gwen has let the company in the front door, and now Phoebe pushes around her, shrilling, "Oh! Jim! Mary!" then bursts into tears.

The woman hugs Phoebe, pats her shoulder awhile.

"Such a terrible time!" Phoebe cries out, then searches for her Kleenexes among the big pockets of her white middy and slash pockets of her crisp blue-cuffed shorts.

Young Will and his wife, Skipper, who arrived late last night shamble down from their upstairs bedroom, leading their kids to the TV room, then quickly reappear. They are dressed in matching striped leisure jerseys, matching white bell bottoms. Young Will asks Phoebe if she'll take charge of the kids for the rest of the afternoon while he and Skipper do some necessary shopping.

Phoebe freezes, blinks at young Will and giggles. "Oh! No . . . please!

Take them with you!" She makes a nut-hardness of her tissue. "I just can't imagine having them today."

Will says softly, "They are easy, Mother. Have you seen them jumping off chairs?"

Phoebe giggles, glances at the guests who are still hovering in the middle of the rug. "No! Gosh, no. But I'd just rather not."

The guests' eyes grope around the room, avoiding the faces of the Currys. There! A blaze of gladioli! Beneath it the piano's dark surface simmers. The guests stray off toward it, then find two matching chairs by the fireplace. One chair blocks a sunny window, which makes the man in pale blue summer dress-shirt look headless.

Young Will is shaking his head, grinning at the company. "But, Mother, you raised five kids of your own."

"Let me introduce you before this terribly embarrassing moment goes on any longer . . ." Phoebe turns away from her son.

The man stands, thrusts his hand out as Phoebe says urgently, "Dr. York. This is my eldest son, William, Jr. . . . well, now it's just William without the junior. And this is Will's wife, Sharon. And this is Mrs. York . . ."

The woman nods from her chair. She is a trim shatterproof-looking gal, hair smoldering gray, straight cut. Matching tea-color and navy from ears to purse to toes. The man is not so sound. He is flown-apart . . . head burst by the sun boring in from the west. And now his hands are gone. Just a floating wedding band.

"And my daughter, Gwen," Phoebe adds.

Gwen says, "Hi," then holds herself, shoulders humped, her hands unavailable for shaking.

Phoebe bats her eyes.

"Please call us Mary and Jim," the woman insists.

Young Will says, "We've met before."

"Yessss. We have," says the doctor, smiling broadly. "Many moons ago."

"It's good to see you both again," says Will. "So nice of you to think of my mother. It means a lot."

"Yes," says the doctor.

"Of course," says the wife.

"We can stay for only a moment," the doctor tells Phoebe, returning to the chair, but only on the edge of it . . . not getting too settled. "We wanted you to know that we are only a phone call away if you need us for anything. We have been deeply saddened by the news. We will be at the funeral service, of course."

Phoebe tries to sit on the divan. But it seems the divan pushes her off. She circles a bit, working her hands in her big pockets.

Young Will crosses the rug to the woman and man for more hand-shakes, the man rising halfway from the seat. Young Will says, "It was really good seeing you again, Mrs. York and Dr. York . . . Mary and Jim." This young Will Curry bears little resemblance to his father. This son, short, small face, small-featured, pudgy. Striped jersey doesn't hide pudgy. His aspect at first glance is unthreatening, all this pudginess and stripyness. But the eyes. Inquiring, dark, and direct. Eyes that could make one feel silently interrogated, while his singsongy voice plays out formal pleasantries.

"Yes," Mrs. York agrees. "I just wish it were better circumstances. Again, we are terribly sorry about your father's death."

"Thank you," young Will says.

Phoebe watches her son and his wife retreat from the living room. Phoebe, hands deep in the pockets of her middy, turns and says, "It's not going to be easy . . . this life without my husband. And his poor patients! It's just awful. He wasn't some bum dying! Some ditchdigger! Some Farmer Brown!" She circles the vivid design of the Oriental rug, her footsteps making soft breath. She sinks to the divan, is pushed back up, crosses to the window that overlooks the long slope of hemlocks to the next road that winds up into the hills. "Life is strange, isn't it?" she muses.

The woman and man nod.

". . . a valuable pediatrician snuffed from the face of the earth!!" She turns, smiling tragically, hands folded. She sees the hall doorway is empty. Gwen vanished. Gwen phased out.

"Only fifty-one years old!" Phoebe is almost yelling.

The doctor says, "Well, we will all miss him. He always took time for everyone. And by the way, Dr. Kane and the people from pediatrics send their condolences. Jack will be writing you later on if he doesn't make it to the funeral service." The guests both rise from their seats. They take a few steps.

Phoebe lunges at them. "I will really miss all the nice talks William and I always had about medicine!" she says.

The doctor takes Phoebe's hands in both of his.

Phoebe's fingers maneuver to get a big grip. Seems if these people leave she will die.

11 | Phoebe helps herself to some of the housekeeper's special perk. From the den down the hall is the tootling and hilarious explosions of cartoons on the big TV.

Daughter-in-law Skipper's voice has a worried squeak to it. "We don't *need* to leave them here, Will. You shouldn't keep pushing your mother." Two red spots are fixed on Skipper's cheeks. Tiny Skipper. She has smile lines and frown lines so you know she's not a kid.

Young Will says, "I just thought she'd like this rare opportunity to spend time with her grandchildren . . . you know she hasn't seen them in six months. And she's not all alone here. Gwen can help. And Doris is around. And we've got the playhouse out back . . . big field . . . a million toys. They aren't bad kids. I just thought it was natural that Mother would want to fuss over the kids like your mom does . . . read to them . . . do *Play-Doh* . . ."

Phoebe shrieks. "That was below the belt, Will!! I don't know about Skipper's parents, but I've just lost my husband!" Her eyes blur with tears.

"Never mind," says Will, his dark eyes blazing.

"No!" Phoebe hoots. "Don't take them. PLEEEEZ! You are right. They're being good. It's only for a couple of hours, for gosh sakes. I need to get my mind off Dad. That's exactly what I need! THANK YOU!"

12 | Through the grate, life is like a memory. Already faded. Already sketchy. Nice and private.

It isn't spying because they know she's there. Sometimes when it's quiet there's the slisk skisk of her breathing against the iron.

In the short time young Will and Skipper are gone, Phoebe has new names for Ricky and Kathy, calls them Poncho and Sally. There's a water fight out in the yard. They fill their tin lemonade tumblers at the hose. And then Phoebe points the hose directly at Ricky leaving him choking, too stunned to cry at first. For a full minute Phoebe locks both of them out. She looks out at them through the window, pointing and miming great belly laughs. They both cry, then scream, dazed, staggering around the vast yard.

"ONLY KIDDING!!!!" Phoebe sings out from the now open door.

There's the bakery boxes to rummage through. Only one big iced cookie left. Phoebe stuffs it into her mouth. Plenty of crullers. Have a cruller. The kids look at the crullers. It's clear that they've never had crullers before. "Crawlers," says Ricky in a low exhausted voice.

The housekeeper returns from running some errands. Makes trips into the house with grocery bags.

Phoebe says, "Let's lock *her* out!"

The kids are all for it.

Now Ricky, who is not yet three, poops himself.

Phoebe snorts, "Well *this* is a job for Doris, not I. That's what house-keepers are for! But first let's go find what your mother has done with your spares."

"What's a spares?" Kathy asks.

Phoebe snarls, "You ask too many questions."

They trudge up the stairs, down the hall, passing Gwen's door with much commotion. Gwen never fears that the door will open. Unlike the mothers of Gwen's academy friends, Phoebe has always been good about doors . . . never barges in, in fact, almost *never* crosses that threshold.

Then there's stomping and voices past her door again, the voice of little Kathy asking another question.

Downstairs Doris has gotten into the house through the front door . . . just in time as Phoebe calls from the stairs, "Yooo hoooo, DoRRRRis! I have a job for you. It's a beaut!"

13 | Now the Shipleys have arrived. Kids from a mile across the back road, kids Phoebe encourages to hang out when she's in that special mood, kids she calls "little white trashes" and "farmers in the dell." She never lets them in the house. But on nice days, Phoebe and the Shipleys keep all the patio chairs full, Phoebe egging them on to tell her the most "trashy secrets of their dismal lives."

Now there's the shrills of Kathy and Ricky who are wound up and acting out, the Shipleys' big dog barking, and the stink of Phoebe's smoke rising up to the second-story screens, beating about Gwen's room.

Phoebe is lining all the kids up to see who is the tallest. "Well, Ricky is tallest really because he's only three. For three, he's tallest. You are seven years old, Bruce. Jeepers! What a shrimp for seven!!!"

There are surly Shipley swearwords. Big argument now. Phoebe orders the Shipleys to all go home now or she'll call the state police.

Gwen lies on her bed with a paperback book about a girl who has fallen off her horse and is afraid to ride again . . . or something like that. Gwen can't keep her mind on the story. But she falls ever more deeply into the illustrations, most of which are soft and ethereal, but for the musculature of the horse, which is dense.

Phoebe and Ricky and Kathy are in the kitchen now gasping for breath. "Made it," Phoebe crows. There's the clamping of the lock. "In a while they'll go away. They always do once you ignore them."

14 | A memory. Maybe it's not a memory to be counted on. Sometimes you can't trust memory. It's a thing that changes, one thing stepping out of another, memories of memories, cheap and floaty, poorly made. Maybe it was only a dream. Far enough back in time, *everything* rots into sepia and dusty rose. It was Dennis, her twin. Always Dennis she remembers best. Sometimes a little bit of Guy. But Guy and the others are most usually on that outer grayer edge of recollection, merging into one layered face . . . these older brothers all one brother. But in this memory Dennis is the one. He came running through bleary rooms . . . a doorway . . . brown walls, a honeyed banister with a globe lamp . . . globe lamp almost tipping over as he fell into it . . . giggling hysterically. Running. He was running but Phoebe, their mother, had called it "dancing." He leapt and spun . . . but mostly it was plain running. He was nude. *That* was his dancing. Phoebe cheers. Her hands clapppclappp-clapppclapppclapp!

The housekeeper. Not Doris then. It was *a* housekeeper, part of the chain, housekeepers over the years, the layered face . . . eyeless . . . lipless. Seems the housekeeper said "oh, dear" like soft pain.

"What's the matter!!" Phoebe turned on the woman, a little mean snap to her question. "Haven't you seen a beautiful boy before?"

Dennis and Gwen were how old then . . . Four? Five? Three? Two and a half? Gwen cried out, "Mother! See!" Hurrying with her buttons and shoelaces . . . pulling out of sleeves . . . feeling cool, feeling bare. "MOTHER! LOOK!" she had pleaded.

Phoebe's applause stopped as she turned and recognized the little girl, Gwen, the daughter—the daughter, the other twin, but not an *alike* twin, no.

Now Phoebe's voice is a thick low warning to Gwen. "Don't you *ever* let me see you do that."

But Dennis danced on and on and on with all his long height, fading dusty rose and straining taller through the dances of time and that part of him loose and vivid, the penis, the tumbling raglike dance of it, the mixing memory into dream of it, thickened by the many days and years of his many dances. "Dance!!" Phoebe's face would get its high red flush as she applauded. The housekeeper's bubble face . . . POP! . . . gone.

Dennis dancing.

How many times did he dance?

And Phoebe singing a song . . . something to dance to.

15 But did he eat it? She can't recall. They were pale with pale frosting laid thickly on each. The frosting. Was it green? A green not quite. What was that smell in the air, other than her mother's morning cigarette, other than the housekeeper's coffee going full boil? Gwen had seen her father's hand reaching. She was out flat on her belly in her pajamas. A long girl in pajamas, nearly thirteen years old, the toes of each foot clasped to the other. It was only yesterday, now already thinned to memory. "These look good, Pheeb," he had said. Then he was gone.

16 Evenings of past and recent time. It would be around seven-thirty. TV room. In the fireplace a mean little fire popping. Dennis stretched out. Bare feet. Messy hair. Dennis's cocky rugged vagabond look. A couple of ice-cream bowls and some tumblers around. The couch is often his evening territory. TV on low. Dennis smiling a little into the kindly smiling face of the TV.

"BEDTIME, GWEN!!!" Phoebe would sing out, Phoebe standing by the TV room door, usually standing, rarely sitting . . . except during her long disappearances in her room with "a good book." In the TV doorway, she smokes, feet apart. Her challenger stance. Gwen, in time, came to avoid her mother's face, Phoebe smiling that haha-nahnah smile.

It would actually be bedtime for both Gwen and Dennis. After all, they are twins. But "BEDTIME, GWEN!!" is how it has always went.

Next Dennis will say, "I gotta see the rest of this."

And Phoebe will say, "William! Tell them about bed, would you? You know I can't handle them."

And their father would look up from his reading and say, "Bed, kids."

And Dennis, "I gotta see the rest of this."

And the fireplace would snap and squeal.

Gwen gets up from her cross-legged position on the rug and goes.

One time when she was leaving, something struck her back. Hard as a shoe. Her mother and Dennis both tee-heed. But the father was silent.

17 | Memories. One for each day, one day pulled from the other. The daughter, Gwen, in bed. The mother, Phoebe, will be singing down under the heat grate, slamming cupboard doors, stomping around. Her singing is of itself wildly pretty, but as it goes louder and louder, it's too loud to be tuneful, just a screech. Now and then Phoebe drops a pan or can opener . . . or objects unknown . . . Gwen can only guess. Even stepping from bed and squatting over the heat grate, the view of the kitchen is only the square of floor and counter directly below . . . the rest, even as it happens, is no better than dream or memory. It is best to stay lying on the bed. It is best not to let the mother hear the scuff of a bare foot or a floorboard creaking or Gwen's uneven breathing. It is best to *seem* unaffected. Every night into the girl's earliest remembering, the mother had reached her through the night this way. A few times the father, William, had said, "Phoebe. How do you expect Gwen to sleep?"

So Phoebe sang louder. Show tunes. Pop tunes. Rock and roll. Television jingles. And once a shattery tinkling splat! A glass thrown into the sink?

And Gwen squeezes her pillow over whichever ear is up. On the blank wall against the bed, the pillow end, she had written one summer in pencil: MY MOTHER SHOULD BE DEAD. No one ever mentioned it but then again no one but housekeepers cross the threshold of Gwen's room. The whole family is very good about privacy. You don't ever see one of them barging in.

18 | How often does this happen? A car slows up at the house. A black car maybe. A light gray? Brown and cream two-tone. All these mixed in memory, this car slowing there below the trees. Phoebe's smoldering eyes. Hard, rueful, sea-breezy jubilance of her gray eyes. Eyes suddenly widen. Her chaise flips as she scuttles to her feet. Coppertone skids across the blue and brick patio stones. Through the pantryway entrance Phoebe making a mad dash. Gwen, only a baby, out of her wits, falling, getting up, falling again. In this memory it seems there's no one home. Just Gwen the daughter. Phoebe the mother. And a white rotting arbor of vines by the doorway, arbor which no longer exists . . . though it was never disassembled. It just vanished.

The car doesn't stop. It moves off into its sepia distances . . . silent. Memory is silent. Blanked. Wrecked. Partly dream. Therefore a lie.

Gwen catches up . . . "WAAAAAAAA!" Her unpretty wide-mouth wail. Gwen age two? Younger? Yes, younger. Older? Yes, all of these.

Phoebe is by a front window in the living room, her arms crossed, shoulders a little hunched, and when she turns from the window it isn't Phoebe's head . . . but something else . . . something unspeakable . . . something put there by the black-gray-brown cream car.

19 | Gwen, age ten? The brothers in periphery, the *vast* periphery of the table. Or wherever they would be. So many closed doors.

It was something about a patient who had come in with pain in her ears . . . just about Gwen's age, he had said, flashing Gwen his sad, amazed smile across breakfast, lunch, evening meal . . . seems it was breakfast. He told of the little girl's ear, what he found in the ear. He had that dark raised eyebrow above the plastic frame of his glasses to show you this was a most astounding thing.

The mother, Phoebe, wasn't listening. She was looking at her nails, her rings, the life lines of her hands.

Suddenly he had stopped and said, "Phoebe."

It was nothing new. Phoebe never listened when he got into one of his little rare chattery moods. And yet every time, as if what she was doing shocked him, he'd stop in midsentence. Then Phoebe would say, "What's that, William? Lint in your hair?" or "That second cup of coffee was too much for you, wasn't it?" And like that, it would be over. He would not resume.

Breakfast, lunch, dinner? All times blended, stirred, confused. And then there was the issue of lunch, which William called "dinnah" and the evening meal . . . William called it "suppah" . . . and Phoebe with narrowed eyes and curled lip correcting this to "dinner." And then sometimes with no food upon the table, a hand closing on some small cold piece of food, people standing about . . . Whose wrist dangling at eye level? Whose sneakers cross the floor? Who is leaving the room?

And the good doctor again with one of his little stories . . . interrupts himself to say with disappointment, "Phoebe."

"Oh! William. Don't go out with that sleeping crust in your left eye!" Phoebe says. "People will think you're a drunk who has slept in your car."

And Gwen had said, "Daddy? Do germs get germs? Smaller germs . . . you know. Do germs get *sick*?" She asked it around a cheekful of breakfast, hurriedly . . . so desperately she wanted him to feel better, to feel her concentration. The good doctor slid his dark eyes onto this question, giving it thought, his widening amazed eye now fixed on his daughter.

Phoebe guffawed. "Are you falling for that, Will!! The wily ways of a girlie-girlie trying to lure a man."

He said nothing to this, lowered his eyes to his plate . . . and had no answer for Gwen.

Did he believe Phoebe? Had he carried into the eternity of his death that lie? Too late now to tell him, "I just wanted to comfort you. I just wanted you not to hurt."

20 | Another memory. Phoebe the mother, Gwen the daughter. To-gether alone. The phone rings. Phoebe stops in the hall whispering the time-old question, "Who might that be?"

It rings again and again. Gwen only age two? Maybe three? She studies the terrible phone, black on the dark wood stand by the kitchen door by the hall. Ringing on and on. The two long rings that are the Currys' rings. The two long rings are the ones that speak the Currys' name.

Through smoldering memory-dream the black car passes down the road as the black phone rings.

Perhaps the doorknob of the nearest door shivers.

21 | Once . . . yes . . . this is another memory coming . . . once way back in the snowy frozen blank rooms, a pink lampshade pretty like a dancer's skirt. The TV room? Before TV, so it would be called "the den."

All this fizzy twitching geography of floors and furniture. And Gwen. And Dennis. And the mother. The conversation had taken a turn to why the Shipleys' dog humps peoples' legs.

With tinkly girlish giggles, Phoebe bent to whisper the details into the curved foreverness of Dennis's ear.

Dennis howled as though stung. Then he whispered up into his mother's ear.

And next a door closing at the end of the long trampled hall-runner rug.

And next, somehow, it is Gwen alone.

From the closed door now, more howls. Gagging howls. Tee-hees. Words into ears. Roars.

Gwen covers her ears.

22 | Recent memory. Eaves dripping rain.
"So what *makes* babies?" Colena Wentworth had asked.

And the health teacher Mrs. Roake had said in a quiet not-at-all-hysterical voice, "When you love someone very much and get married, then you have a baby . . . only then." And the class of girls became quiet as death. Nobody moved a muscle.

23 | An old memory, falling away into breezy altitudes. Dots of blue.
It had started off as one of those many rassles. Phoebe like a young pup in those days. Wrist rassle. Regular rassle. Tickling tournaments. Water fights an all-time favorite. Driving around in the field with one of her small foreign cars till she hit a rock, or one of *them* hit a rock . . . for it was often one of the boys at the wheel, Phoebe in the passenger seat shrieking "Faster! Faster! Sissy!!!" and tossing her hair and tossing her cigarette, everybody jerking left and right, bouncing . . . the car stuffed with riders . . . not all of them Phoebe's kids . . . but all of them kids.

Rassling could start during the evening meal. Big pig pile on the kitchen floor, a chair knocked into a skid. The good doctor would rub his eyes and go back to reading. He would turn a page. His chewing seemed to match the rhythms of written words.

But this rassle . . . this particular remembered rassle with the good doctor not at home had turned out queerly.

They circled Phoebe in the dining room, backed her up to the loaded plate rail. It would seem she could have won over them. They were all thin, hesitant children. None of them the vigorous creature that she was. Seems even one of her singing laughs could have stopped them. But no.

They took turns. One would run at her, yank her sleeve.

One of the oldest . . . which? . . . had said, "We are going to tie you. You are prisoner."

Phoebe shouted, "No. Not now. Get away!"

"Shut up, pig," Guy had said hoarsely. Guy, yes. Gwen remembers he was the one who said *pig*.

Phoebe made a deep sound, sounded like cackling . . . but it was with eyes brimmed full, wet, running over.

And then all of them pushed hard, a chugging machinery of thin wrists, arms, and elbows aligned.

Phoebe screamed. "PLEEEEEZ STOP!"

They pushed harder. And now some pulled.

She sank to the floor, hands covering her face.

The lovely old remembered wallpaper of that time seems evil here. The many opened needle beaks of the blue flickers among blue needle firs seem ghoulishly poised.

All the children backed off, standing as creatures in a forest, eyes flashing toward the door as if someone had walked in. But no one had intruded upon them in this place where the long dining room table was covered in jigsaw puzzle pieces. Only the sea captain's clock ticking.

Then young Will was crying. "Sorry. Mother! So sorrrreeeeeeeee . . . Mother!" He wept, patting her. He may have even tried to hug her. The others still silent. Young Will pleading, weeping, raging. "You okay? You okay?"

Phoebe had risen to her feet, smiling. "What's that on your elbow, Lawrence? You have something stuck there again. Is it another booger?" Silent Lawrence feels for the booger that isn't there, eyes down.

Young Will unrelenting, patting his mother, pawing, not a lot different from the attack moments before. "You okay? You okay, Mother?" he pleads. "You okay?"

Phoebe's voice, light as song. "Of course I'm okay, Will! Why wouldn't I be?" And she breezes out through into the kitchen to start lunch or the evening meal . . . there's no way to remember which.

24 | Recent memory, only months ago. Phoebe has invited Gwen into the big bedroom for a talk. This most deeply guarded inner sanctum, heart of the hive. The room is dark. Shades drawn in all four dormers as well as the mullions on the gable. And yet how bright the high double bed. How gay the wallpaper, tulips of crayon colors. Red and yellow, blue and green on white. Big framed wedding photo of Phoebe and the good doctor. A picture of Phoebe's brother George at the wheel of his yacht. And Phoebe's brother Ned in Mexico, a sand-colored world, Mexico. Ned, blond. And there's Phoebe's grandmother as a very little girl, white dress, white pet rabbit, gray lawn. No photos of the sainted doctor's family. But a framed map of Mars. The sainted doctor often speaks of the planets.

Phoebe tells Gwen there's been a "package" purchased especially for Gwen. Hidden in one of the back hall drawers. For when "it" happens, Gwen can go there secretly. Nobody has to know. Nobody will have any idea. Gwen can go to the package when it happens and get a pad whenever she needs it. As Phoebe speaks the word "pad" her nose wrinkles. She explains that the blood is not real blood. It's something "else." It's not a wound. Nothing to get in hysterics over. It's *nothing*. Her nose wrinkles. No one has to know. She explains that with plenty of soap and water, a good soak, no one will ever know. Phoebe has said all this as though someone were at the door listening now . . . or out on the roof clinging to a dormer.

Gwen doesn't have much to say about this.

Phoebe opens the door for Gwen to leave.

25 | Recent memories . . . you can trust them more, but like snapshots from film left on the dash of a car in summer, heat turning the dyes to hues of yellow, *any* memory is jaundiced, woozy, stained. Phoebe's pretty hands pouring coffee at breakfast. Her eyes flutter. Her smile is lush. For him. Her beloved sainted man. He is there chewing, chewing, chewing. His toast is on the plate with jam. He loves jam. Always great loads of jam. But such a bony man. The calories never show. His dark eyes are on his reading, one hand at the back of his neck. This is the position he is often frozen into when something he is reading has a grip on him. Something to do with medicine usually. But also politics. The universe. Birds.

Gwen moves toward the toaster. Last night it happened . . . the blood. She had made her quiet way to the back hall and the big blue box was there. She had managed to get the whole box to her room without getting caught by the others. She had managed everything. It had all gone smoothly.

Her father is chewing, lost in his fine print, his eyes running along the page. But Phoebe is smiling such a smile! Not showing her teeth at all. Not a grin. Just a little twisted bud of a smile, a scream of red lipstick, screaming eyes on the good doctor, savior of lives.

Gwen carries her plate of toast to the table.

Phoebe suddenly seems to be working against a sharp pain, the smile and her fluttering eyes tightening down against the pain. "What stinks?"

William looks up from his reading. "What?" He sniffs in one direction, then another. "I don't know. I don't seem to smell anything."

"Oh, yes," Phoebe insists, smiling more hugely within the hard red knot of her mouth. "It is pretty strong and getting stronger. Ikk!" She holds her nose. "I'll have to get out the air freshener," she says tiredly.

William looks up at the daughter, Gwen. "Do *you* smell anything?"

Gwen shrugs.

William shrugs.

Phoebe is up lightly on her feet, little feet, emergency feet, headed for the cupboard where the air fresheners stand, snatches the nearest can. Colonial Spice. She sprays and sprays and sprays. The air is turning yellow even as she sprays, turning to memory.

26 | The frosting. Was it green? Can she count on it? Was it flavored with mint, the mintiness rising through the heat grate? What color was his hand? Always such a pale hand. Was he dying already years before he died? Had Phoebe begun poisoning him way back? Just a little poison in the jam to get him used to the bitter taste? Then the cupcakes, the final dose . . . BLAM! But *would* Phoebe poison William? It wouldn't make sense. If the police arrived now to arrest Phoebe, saying poison was found in the good doctor's blood, wouldn't Gwen be surprised? Of course Phoebe didn't put poison in the cupcakes. Maybe there never were any cupcakes. Maybe it was just his keys on the counter he was reaching for and his words were some other words. But—oh yes oh yes oh yes—she *saw* the cupcakes. Oh god help me I saw the cupcakes! If only, she thinks, I could have found some crumbs for proof.

27 | GranMom Sheehy has taken over the cooking. As everyone knows, Phoebe's cooking lacks something. Out of GranMom's many satchels comes one of her cookbooks. A good brown smell seems to roll forth, even as the book lies spread and submissive as a dead moth on the vast flecked Formica counter. On nearly every page, greasy fingerprints and spots of tomato. And there, a hotness like stove heat is dispatched from GranMom Sheehy's fingers as she works them to do the hocus-pocus of measuring and dicing. Upon the bowl of spiced carrots, the moony-yellow butter winds down, and the steam flies up in a curl. Upon three platters herbed chops are laid one on top of the other, neat as books . . . but tender. The salad is a bravado of fruits and nuts and blond beans and scribbles of pasta on three greens. This is part of the legacy of GranMom Sheehy's father the great chef, world famous. "Bad cooking is only fear!" he used to exclaim as GranMom Sheehy recalls one of his many exclaimings. Yes, the chef was famous. But who in this room ever knew him?

Phoebe and Dennis hang out in the kitchen with GranMom. Dennis is waiting for a phone call from his friend who has a car . . . a much older boy. Dennis's popularity at the academy brings him "riches."

Out in the yard of misty bad weather, Skipper and young Will have returned from all-day errands and visits, taking forever to come inside. Walking, talking, hanging out near the playhouse with their kids.

Phoebe and Dennis shout at each other in Parisian French. GranMom Sheehy doesn't know any Parisian French.

Phoebe has her camera on the table, which GranMom requested on her arrival "to get some updating on the family albums" but all day Phoebe has insisted that the "right shot" hasn't been available.

"*Vas y. Apporte-moi ton caméra!*" Phoebe shouts.

Dennis disappears, reappears with his camera, a more serious model, settings and adjustments, lots of metal.

"*Eh bien.* Is it loaded, Roy!!!?" Phoebe shouts in "cowboy."

"Yes, Dale! It shooor is!" Dennis shouts back.

Phoebe leaps from her place at the table, cigarette hanging from her mouth, blond hair flapping out on the sides of her face. "DRAW!!!"

It's a camera shoot-out. Two simultaneous flashes of light.

Dennis staggers back, smashes into the refrigerator, cookie jar atop teetering. He grips his chest, slumps to the floor. "Aaaaa'm heeeeit!" he drawls.

GranMom Sheehy turns with floured fingers and looks sadly upon this moment. "A little respect," she insists in her gravelly, old-mannish voice.

Phoebe pivots. Three flashes left on her cube. BLAM. BLAM. BLAM. All three shots aimed at GranMom's feet in their little dressy navy blue pumps.

28 | Throughout the service, Phoebe Curry wears a smile of sleepy boredom and terrible alertness, her beautiful eyes fixed on the open casket behind the pastor who speaks of William Curry's achievements . . . service to humanity . . . enduring patience . . . and quirky shyness so many called charm.

The funeral home ushers have positioned Phoebe in the front row, of course, and next to her, Gwen, then the boys, Dennis and Guy, Lawrence with his new girlfriend, young Will with his wife, Skipper. Gwen is dressed in a navy blue sheath, dark dressy shoes, things her GranMom Sheehy helped her shop for yesterday. Also GranMom Sheehy bought her a hair trim, shorter at the nape than the sides . . . and a bit of rinse to give it red highlights. Feels to Gwen like a kind of disguise. Feels good.

Phoebe turns and whispers behind her hand to GranMom in the seat behind her, "It's *them*," and indicates the people across the aisle with a jerk of her head.

Gwen looks at "them," strangers . . . like most everyone at this service is no one she knows . . . but these strangers she remembers from last night at the visitation. They kept hanging around, keeping to themselves. "Like a pack of skulking wolves," Phoebe had at that time remarked. One or two of them had called Phoebe by name . . . her first name . . . not Mrs. Curry as most other strangers had. And these persons, the "wolves," had said how pretty everything was, how they'd never seen so many flowers. Banks of flowers were raised on three sides of William's casket, the corners of the alcove glutted by huge motionless blooms, wreaths, boughs, bows, and ribbons nearly blocking both doorways . . . flowers all up the side of one wall . . . flowers breathing, taking up all the air. Phoebe had agreed with the strangers that she, too, had never seen so many flowers, but that "surely they were *earned*."

Then the people, these "wolves," had looked into the casket, also with amazement, their eyes as wide as eyes can go for rather hard beetly eyes. They made no comments about William in the casket. No "I'm sorry"s nor "anything we can do to help"s. They just looked very hard at William dead. And then they left the visitation.

An hour later when Gwen and GranMom Sheehy left the visitation parlor out the back way, there they were, the skulking strangers. They hadn't really gone. They had been out in the parking lot the whole evening. They were grouped around two or three old cars and one pickup truck that had Maine plates. People with fear in their eyes. Certainly not any of the good doctor's colleagues who all share the poise of leopards. And certainly no friends of Phoebe's. Phoebe has no friends.

Maybe they are patients, Gwen had thought, turning to sneak another glance from across the parking lot. There were children among them. She expected GranMom Sheehy to make some comment from the side of her mouth after she and Gwen had gotten into the car. But GranMom had just sorted through her keys.

Now Gwen turns to watch the pastor's yellow teeth around the words of praise. The pastor, who drove up from Connecticut and is an old Sheehy family friend on GranFather Sheehy's side. Gwen thinks this pastor looks a little bit like her father, maybe just due to his age. The pastor has just now made a gesture with his hand, a gesture her father would make in reaching to snatch an intricacy from the air, a small word for a larger concept, any word for the impossible concept, on the edge of frustration.

Gwen feels William, the real one, fading. The real William Curry, Sr., in the casket sewed up into his finely strived charcoal suit, tie of mixed blues. His wristwatch ticking. From where Gwen sits, she sees only the body in profile, the face that looks like a rubber mask. They didn't get the mouth right. And they didn't get his dusky color right. William was *never* pink.

Gwen leans forward to uncross, recross her legs in this hard fold-up metal seat and there it is in a flash. The strangers are the Currys! Right there in the other half of the front row seats, seats of honor. Her father's people. Mother? Father? Sisters? She had sometimes wondered if he *had* a family. Once when she was very young she'd asked her father if he was an orphan. He had said no very gently as if filling her in on some unsettling fact of life. What made her know never to ask Phoebe the question? Now here they are. One of them, a young woman, has a baby across her knees. This person looks like Gwen!! And across the eyes of the others . . . there's that look young Will has when he's listening hard. And mixed in and among them are other traits she knows well, how astonishing! This mishmash, this miracle of genes. How well she knows them!! And the sleeping baby . . . Chinese? . . . Japanese? . . . Korean? Is the baby Adopted? Or is it that love story of love stories . . . exotic dark stranger with a bold claim on you and wide warm mouth? A gypsy maybe? The great unknown. And these people here now, alive and rustling, one stroking another's arm. And yes, weeping. In nearly every eye a single tear. A tear to each eye. That side of the room dazzles with the stars of their lighted tears.

And yet, *they* are dead. They never existed before now. And now only in the blink of an eye, soon to be gone forever. Gone again. Why? Who can she ask?

The pastor is speaking softer and softer, more somberly of the earliness of Dr. Curry's death.

Something grips Gwen's hand, Phoebe's small hand closing around Gwen's long fingers. Then tickling the hair around Gwen's ear, her mother's sorrow . . . "*What* are we going to do, Gwen?" Phoebe hangs on hard to Gwen's hand, Phoebe now weeping loudly, uncountable tears, shoulders convulsing, pale hair wagging, pressing her woozy perfumy dewy ripeness upon Gwen, crashing through that province of Gwen's own nerved-up secret self. Phoebe, the mother, sighing breathlessly. "Gwen! Gwen! What's going to become of us!!" A sob. "Gwen . . . oh, Gwen."

29 | GranMom Sheehy's turquoise scarf, sheer as a residue. But earrings chunky. Clip-ons. Her earlobes are durably thick. Like her voice. She wears a summerweight suit the color of eclair filling. And summerweight hose. Tan. This is going to be a visit to some of GranMom's old friends. A seashore visit. A "saltwater farm," she calls it.

"Dairy or truck?" a friend of Dennis's asks.

"It *used* to be farmed," GranMom Sheehy explains.

"No farmers. No farm," Dennis says deeply. His eyes and his friend's eyes meet. It is the Lothrup boy, square-jawed, "well-bred" looking, expensive-looking. But you know if Dennis takes to someone, they can't be a fortress of etiquette.

Gwen is hunched between the door and Dennis. There's plenty of room in the late Dr. William Curry's beautiful Buick, but Dennis has such a sprawl. GranMom drives. One-handed confidence. Her free hand plays with her scarf. She uses her rearview mirror and passes other cars like they are standing still. Her eyes keep to the road, mirrors, gauges. She has the square-shouldered buzzard-eyed yet offhanded demeanor of a jet pilot.

Phoebe hasn't washed her hair in three days. *The hair* is under her scarf of giant cream roses wrenched into turban shape. Little squiggles of blond there on her neck. The gaudy and the delicate in each other's violation. She sighs deeply. Then it is silent for a while but for the engine of the Buick, its deep-throated silky ease. So Phoebe hums a little, watches people's yards, yawns a huge tearful yawn, then, "Ho-hum."

There are medical journals and texts and letters still heaped on the floor under Gwen's feet. She has to keep her knees up a little more than feels good, but the solid shifting bulk of her father's life under her feet is a compensation.

Dennis leans close to Gwen's ear and breathes, "YELL-O JELL-O."

"Shut up," Gwen warns him.

Dennis tells the Lothrup boy, "She *hates* yellow Jell-O."

The Lothrup boy winks. "It's made with hooves."

"Yel-low hooves," Dennis enunciates, a bit of Vincent Price.

The two boys smile, eyes straight between the heads of GranMom Sheehy and Phoebe.

Gwen takes her knees into her hands, such long fingers, bony. Not at all voluptuous like Phoebe's, yet somehow gently alluring . . . obscene?

Dennis speaks close to Gwen's ear. He only whispers, but so close to her ear, it's a roar. "I SEE A MILE HIGH YELLOW JELL-O. YOU ARE INSIDE IT LIKE . . . YOU KNOW, LIKE FRUIT! LIKE A GRAPE. ONLY IT'S GWENNNNN. THE ONLY WAY YOU CAN GET OUT IS TO EAT YOUR WAY OUT!"

The Lothrup boy smiles indulgently, "Jell-O turns to water in your stomach. It's nothing but water really."

"*But*," Dennis adds ghoulishly, "yellow Jell-O is the MOST Jell-O. It will have my sister stuck like a fly."

Gwen simpers. "Funny."

Dennis gives Gwen's bicep a play squeeze.

Gwen pulls one of the books from the floor, a weighty text, and pretends to wonk Dennis with it.

Dennis cries out, "HELP! GWEN IS TRYING TO KILLLLL ME!!" He crosses his forearms over his head and hunkers down.

Phoebe says, "Gwen. Act your age."

Gwen positions the book on her knees and says, "I'm going to be a brain surgeon, and transplant the brain of a gorilla into Dennis's head so Dennis can think a whole new improved way."

The Lothrup boy chuckles.

Phoebe's cigarette lighter makes its urgent tsk tsk tsk.

"Hmmmm . . . let's see what's in here about brain transplants," Gwen says, flushing, feeling good. She flips a few pages. Words words words. Long arduous words like roads into a bewitched forest. She reaches for another heavy text from the pile. "Argh!" she gasps. "This one is heavy enough to knock you stone cold for the operation." She smiles.

"Anesthesia à la primitive," the Lothrup boy says gleamingly.

Phoebe sighs out a big smoke. "I've had all the bickering I can stand for one day." Her eyes sparkle with beginning tears. "I'm not my usual self. I've been through the funeral and burial of my husband. I've had three days with a house full of guests, some of them babies crying all night . . . the phone ringing off the wall . . . strangers, strangers, and some that I wish *were* strangers. What I really need is for my children to be polite to each other."

The Buick surges around a train of less speedy cars, GranMom Sheehy flicking the turn signal matter-of-factly. On and on, miles of GranMom Sheehy's mastery of the road.

Dennis leans against Gwen. "What I need is a little sleep. What's this thing in my way?"

Gwen swings the book, gives Dennis's left knee a thwonk which gives him a knee jerk. This has everybody in the backseat in crazy choking teenage laughter.

Phoebe bleats, "Mother! Please! Make them stop!"

GranMom Sheehy's guttural warning: "In another minute, Gwen and Dennis, we're going to leave you both out on the side of the road somewhere where you can become beggars."

"We would be adopted by kindly wolves," Dennis whispers.

The Lothrup boy titters then whispers to Dennis, "But the best thing is I'd get the whole backseat to myself. I could stretch out."

Dennis crosses his arms over his chest. "All because my mother is such a *baby*."

Gwen turns pages of the medical text.

Phoebe smokes with emergencyish hard pulls, watching the land flattening out, heading seaward. Tears in her eyes. Wind from the window dries them before they fall.

Dennis rests his foot against Gwen's right foot, her navy blue dress shoe, the shoes she wore today because Phoebe was in tears this morning when she saw Gwen's old gray splotchy sneakers, insisting that Gwen would shame the family . . . and with poor William in his grave, he couldn't defend himself against what people would say now, all of them talking about his daughter the "bum." And whatever happened to the newer pairs of sneakers? The white ones with the nice tapered toes. Where?

There's a long crushed rock drive and the Buick moving sulkily up, up, and up to a house with a veranda all the way around . . . dark green latticework, dark green trim and shutters . . . dark green everything against handsomely weathered gray shingles . . . weathered by the weather of the sea . . . the sea! the sea! . . . the immeasurable sea owned by these people and its weather owned by these people . . . all the grays and greens and weatherishness that money can buy. Steps, ledges, black iron sculptures of naked people, and there are stunted trees, mosses, and purple flowers . . . tended, intentional, inviolate.

GranMom Sheehy twists the key off. Closes her eyes, breathes deeply of the sea air, just like Phoebe takes in hungrily the drug of her last cigarette. Only a few yards away, the ocean roars, whooomps, and hisses.

"I'll just wait here till you're finished," Phoebe tells her mother.

GranMom Sheehy hoots, "GREAT! We came all this way and you are going to do this?"

"I'm not going in there with those people I don't know."

GranMom says, "My god. They are nice people, not savages. They are *gracious*, in fact. I never understand you, Phoebe. It will be hot in this car. Inside they have large overhead fans, cold drinks . . . rocking chairs, a lovely breeze up there on the veranda. Lovely people."

Phoebe holds her face, says into her fingers, "But I told you before we left I wasn't in the mood for all that phony smiling and yammer yammer yammer. I said for you to go alone. I *said* that."

"But then you promised you would *try*," GranMom Sheehy says softly.

"My husband has been dead for only five days and I'm supposed to be out on a holiday to the beach, right?"

"I'll feel rushed knowing you are out here in this hot car."

"Well, I'm sorry I'm such a bad person."

Dennis croaks, "Jesus, Mother! Quit acting like such a baby! It makes us all sick!" Now with one swing of the opening door, Dennis and his friend bolt away.

GranMom Sheehy looks back at Gwen. "Well, come on, Gwen. Leave her out here for her sweat bath. Let's go in and have iced tea and treats."

Gwen says. "Okay. In a minute, I'll find you, okay?"

Up above on a set of wooden walks Dennis and the Lothrup boy appear, leaning on the rail, looking out to the sea like two pirates . . . legs apart . . . youth which is smooth and razzed and scheming. And above them there's the American flag. There's wind up there where the boys and the flag are but not down here in this glinty parking area.

GranMom Sheehy strides up the first set of boardwalks and stairs.

Part of the house is stone with black metalwork around the many paned windows. There is leaded glass in one gable, cathedrallike. The image is of a milky purple phoenix rising from milky cool blue flames. "Looks like a mental hospital, doesn't it?" Phoebe says with a sneer.

"Yup," Gwen agrees.

Big dog bursts from the house, zigzagging down the set of walkways. Brown with a black stripe on its back. It is flung against the Buick as if by the hand of vindictive gods. Now the dog is mincing and goring the glossy surface with its claws.

"STOP!" Phoebe shrieks. "GET AWAY YOU IDIOT!!"

The dog lifts his lips. Growls low.

Phoebe climbs around, rolling windows up, flounces back into her seat with a defeated whimper as Gwen rolls up the windows in back.

Gwen's dark eyes are always so unreadable. They are not soft eyes. They are the unfeeling-looking eyes of someone who would flip the switch to the electric chair. They would never whisper of love. But it seems that such a whisper might be what her mother Phoebe needs right now.

Phoebe says, "Here we sit baking. We'll probably get sick. Your grandmother has no feelings for us. That's plain to see." She gives the horn a little tap, but it doesn't toot.

Gwen says softly, "Mother . . . if we run the car, we can use the air-conditioning. Let's do that."

Phoebe stares at the cuticles of her long nails, wiggles her fingers. "GranMom took the keys."

Gwen says, "You know Debbie at school? She has a dog that's kind of like that one. His name is Cain."

"That's nice," says Phoebe, watching the dog outside circling.

"Cain does tricks."

"Is that right?"

"Yes. He does one where he keeps a little rock on his nose if you put it there till you tell him okay!, then he flips the rock and catches it in his mouth. Then he brings you the rock and puts it in your hand. Kind of slimy though."

"That's funny!" Phoebe shrills. "A rock! Sounds like they're trying to make their dog look stupid . . . make him a fool."

"Debbie's mom told us they got Cain from the newspaper. He was abused and the humane society took him away. That's lucky for *him*."

"Yes. His lucky break."

Silence. The choking rubbery heat settles heavier and heavier.

Phoebe has got a cigarette going, nursing it hard. The smoke can't get out of the car. So it builds and builds fuzzing the faces of Phoebe and Gwen into dreaminess. "So what's Debbie's mother like?" Phoebe wonders.

"Oh . . . regular . . . nice . . . you know."

"Probably just in front of you. She probably talks about you the second you leave."

"I don't think she does that. Maybe. But I don't think so."

"I doubt she's perfect."

"She got run over by a car once . . . really awful."

"Really? She crippled?"

"No. She doesn't seem to be. But she had to have about a million operations on her back and . . . I think she said spleen."

"In about ten seconds my heart is going to stop from this heat," Phoebe moans, lips tightening on the cigarette. There's a trickle down one side of her neck.

"Wanna get out and just walk around?"

"No. That dog is vicious. We're trapped. You can tell he's vicious. He growled. You heard him."

"He didn't bite GranMom and Dennis and what's-his-puss."

"They probably let him out another door. In about two minutes my heart is going to stop. They'll have to have another funeral."

Gwen's dark dull eyes take on a little gleaminess. "Me, too. They'll have to have *three* funerals. They'll be sick of funerals. Maybe they'll just throw you and me into the same hole and call it good enough. And they'll use Dad's leftover flowers off his grave."

Phoebe snorts, blows smoke. "I wouldn't be a bit surprised."

30 | On the way home nobody talks the long miles, the miles and miles that pull the Buick back up into the hills, the roads closed in by trees, the curves dotted with white wooden posts and cable to keep people who drive fast like GranMom Sheehy from crashing down upon and among the tops of trees.

Gwen turns the pages of a medical book.

Dennis is snoring . . . just a feathery little half snore.

The Lothrup boy is quiet, but thinking.

In the book there is a dark-faced boy . . . it seems he's a boy . . . maybe a boyish man. Starved-looking. But he seems somehow reconciled to that. No shirt. And somehow reconciled to that. Did he *ever* have a shirt? In the first photo he has bubbles on his cheek.

Photo #2 his face has one normal eye, like the left eye of anyone. This eye seems to be settled on some ordinary thought. But the other eye is a hole of darkness, the face around this hole raised out like a squash.

The last photo is the same matter-of-fact reconciled-to body but there's no face. The head is many loaves of bread all seamed together and quaking, closed over the one eye and nearly closed over the last eye that still is down there at the bottom of the very long channel looking right at Gwen. *Leprosy, third phase*.

Gwen closes the book, closes her eyes. She will never be the same now. She will never enjoy two seconds of true bliss again. There will always be *him*. He has gotten into her through her eyes and that's that.

Every square inch of her skin. Ice. Every organ seized. All the pretty landscape flickering past in the blue-purples of late day are shrunken to a dot of light. There is only *him*.

31 | Gwen wants to go back to the way things were before the book. The front door in the unattended living room is the best way to get out. Out in the night, bugs shriek in the fields. Half-moon looks like a thing projected on a flat screen . . . a planetarium moon . . . dishonest but convincing.

The Buick is parked by the barn.

Now she thinks of a shovel. But where? *Is* there a shovel here at Currys'? It would be in the barn if there were one. Never mind.

She seizes the book from the backseat and runs through the high grasses beyond the patio. Along the treeline there's the stone wall she knows well. She digs at the ground first with her fingers, then with a stick, now a shard of rock. Poking and grasping, there's still not much of a hole. She considers ripping the book to shreds. But her hands don't have the power to open the book again ever. However, the power is great in her hands for ripping earth, loosening, scooping, wielding the rock and the stick.

She tries the book in the hole. She has lost her breath, chokes on the air that's thicker than dirt. Hurry! Hurry! She kicks dirt onto the book. Yes! Good enough. She gathers the dirt over it. A mound. Now a rock from the wall. Too large to heft. She rolls it into place. She would like to have burned the book. But there is no such thing as a secret fire. A roadside trash can on the way back home would have ended this sooner. But the bright day followed throughout the whole trip . . . stopping for ice creams . . . stopping to use restrooms. There *were* trash cans. And her heart raced with the urgency of these metal drums standing at the apex of all shuffling, needless motion . . . the vital drums. But there was no way to reach these drums. She had to act normal, like nothing was out of the ordinary. Whenever any of the others looked at her, they could never tell she had seen what she'd seen.

Now free of it, she will never see that face again. Never. Never. Never.

32 | Nobody sees Phoebe for two days. Not even at meals. It's not the same as a person who is not at home. Her presence balloons in and out of every room, dewy and lovely, singing its high notes, thundering silence.

Now and then there's the overhead creak of the floor and water pipes wheezing a half minute, then shut off. But silence once again. Phoebe with a good book. Phoebe is so often "lost in a good book." Well, you never *see* her lost in a book. She doesn't curl up in a chair in the TV room or living room. No reading at the kitchen table like William liked to do. Phoebe's reading is done mostly behind the bedroom door. Reading kind of like stealing. Or lying. Or murder. Or shame.

GranMom says "it" shouldn't be rewarded. "Don't plead with her," she advises. "It's a device. Ignore it."

Phoebe's children had never thought of it as a *device*, but ignoring it has always been the way.

33 | Eventually she emerges. Sleepy butterfly in a palest pink robe. "Need to wash my hair," she announces. She blinks as though the light from this kitchen's windows is acid. GranMom and the house-keeper Doris are arguing. The arguing subject today is the great fire of forty-seven, which wiped out whole towns in York County and Oxford County. "And that's why the trees of the Shapleigh Plains and Brownfield are all twisted and ugly," the housekeeper mourns. "They'll never be right again. You'll never see good wood come from it." GranMom says that's typical human self-aggrandizement. That humans think that nothing can flourish without human manipulation. That humans don't give enough credit to nature that nature can accomplish so much on its own. And that humans see only things in terms of one's meager lifetime. That one human lifetime is not forever.

"All I know is if you needed a ship's mast today, you'd not find one," says Doris, jamming the last dish in the drainer.

"Ships are made of metal today," says GranMom Sheehy with a thin smile.

"But if!" Doris laments.

"Ifs don't concern us," GranMom snaps back.

Phoebe seems enraptured by the plastic heart . . . red, blue arteries arched out from it like horns . . . there over the table forever and for-ever . . . voluptuous. A plastic heart for your kitchen! Such a kooky lovable fun frill. It *seems* she sees the heart. But it's really that she can't focus on how to begin to wash her hair.

She meanders.

She meanders the whole long day.

Finally while everyone else eats supper, the bathroom pipes thrum, hee and haw, and by bedtime Phoebe's hair is washed.

34 | GranMom Sheehy's Renault is packed to go. "Connecticut or bust!" she tells them in her barking near-baritone. She rinses out her teacup at the sink. Efficiency leaves nothing changed, no trace of itself in its wake, no mess.

Lawrence and Dennis check the oil of GranMom's Renault . . . Law-rence handling the stick and rag . . . Dennis sprawling into the open cavity of the car, staring past Lawrence at the house, at the door through which GranMom now briskly plunges. She looks no different dressed for travel than she does just hanging around the house here . . . white pumps, linen suit of wheaten, white bow at the neck . . . kind of George Washingtonish to match her George Washington face and hair and voice. Steadfast statesmanship.

Now she's behind the wheel, revving up.

Phoebe is dressed today, making the effort. She stands back from the car, going from foot to foot, hugging herself . . . a little chill this morning, her eyes fixed on her mother's face.

From the steps of the house Gwen gives GranMom a little wave. GranMom waves back. Then blows her a kiss. Gwen smiles.

"Well," says GranMom. "I'll call when I get back. Then we can go from there, seeing about what is best to be done with us all. We'll play it a day at a time for a while." She looks up at Lawrence whose sweater with high cuffed waist is more dressy than what he wore to the funeral. He is smiling, but his gray eyes are as sweet and sad as the overcast sky. "You," she says, pointing at his chest. "Check up here now and then and report to me. Use your judgment. I trust your judgment."

He nods.

Again Gwen waves from the door. GranMom blows her another kiss. GranMom will not look Phoebe in the eye. GranMom just revs the gas and feels the steering wheel, looks out across the lawn and hemlocks to the road below. She shifts into gear . . .

Phoebe runs at the car, screaming. "MAMA! Don't leave me here! Please! Don't leave me here alone!" Throws her head back. Covers her face with her ringed hands.

Lawrence moves toward Phoebe and reaches out

Phoebe leans her forehead against the Renault, her pale Patti Page hair falling forward.

The phone rings.

Phoebe jerks away from the car, head back again, now a howl of terror.

Lawrence says softly, "Mother . . . do you want me to stay for a few more days?"

"YESSSSSSSS!" she cries. "YESSSSSS! YESSSSSSS! YESSSSSSSSSSSS!"

35 Lawrence stays through the next day. But with the grandmother gone there's no gourmet meals. No *meals*. But how earnestly Phoebe sets out sandwich fixings.

Dennis goes off with friends old enough to drive . . . not his academy friends. These boys wear their hair in Beatle cuts, their collars turned up as if for bad weather no matter what the weather.

Gwen goes off on walks carrying the transistor radio GranMom bought her.

Lawrence sits at the piano, plays Bach and Brahms while Phoebe washes sandwich plates earnestly.

36 | There's a rousing little breeze. The trees talk in voices creaky and womanish. Lawrence is gone back to his life. The summer is moving away every hour like a dragon, oversized and ludicrous. These weeks have seemed as long as years. The meanwhile is memory. The house smells of the housekeeper's special perk and the stale furnace.

This week Phoebe has taken rolls and rolls of pictures. You bend over, she's right there to snap the flash. She gets Dennis and some of his friends with their mouths open or mouths full or mouths twisted into the palsy of a midword. There's one picture of the bathroom door shut. "This is a picture of Gwen," she explains to another carload of Dennis's friends stopping by to visit. And there is one of Gwen hunched over toast. Phoebe tapes her favorites to cupboard doors, walls, bread box, piano.

The Shipleys appear. It's as if Shipleys can smell a good mood in the air. Phoebe says cheerily, "None of you have had a ride in a big Buick, have you?" she gets a few shots of the Shipleys' dog humping Gwen's leg.

Shipleys look the Buick over and one asks, "Is this the car the guy died in?"

Phoebe shakes her head. Her hair is changing, more flossy, more flyaway . . . less like Patti Page . . . more like Marilyn Monroe. When she laughs, she runs her tongue over her lips. She is now wearing her lipstick whitish-pink. Has to be reapplied often. She has a stranglehold on the Shipleys, so bewitched are they by her flair.

Gwen heads out on one of her long walks, radio clutched to her chest.

Phoebe gets the Buick engine purring, then slides over on the seat and offers the wheel to the oldest Shipley called P.J. "Come on, chicken!" she dares him.

P.J. says huskily, "This ain't my first time."

"It's your first time with a Buick, I'll bet!" she sings out, lighting a cigarette, hunching down deep in the seat, feet up on the dash.

"Let's see the world, Captain!" Phoebe giggles, breathes out smoke, cigarette hand flouncing and flicking. "Slip off that hand brake and we're ready to roll."

P.J. can hardly see over the wheel but he has an experienced hotfoot, takes the Buick up the back way at a good clip.

Phoebe cackles.

In the backseat many Shipleys shove around a bit, but not much conversation.

The day is blue and bright. Delicious.

Shipleys' dog chases.

Phoebe sits up and leans out into the wind to get pictures of the scenery blurring past and the dog who is fading in the distance. Phoebe calls out: "LOSER!" Dog takes a shortcut across the small abandoned sandpit and reappears up ahead. Dog and Buick are again neck and neck for a while. Phoebe cackles.

"Turn around up here," Phoebe commands.

Shipleys not used to power brakes. When the brakes are hit, everyone is slammed forth . . . one cut lip . . . one bitten tongue . . . rubber S's screeched out onto the tar.

As all the Shipleys sit there dumbstruck in the car that's come to a stop broadside, Phoebe reaches over and gives P.J.'s right knee a little squeeze and says, "THAT is a Buick."

Heading back down the road, losing the dog again and passing the Curry house, who should they spy but Gwen trudging along with her radio. "Stop, P.J."

P.J. is friends with the power brakes now. The Buick sidles sweetly up alongside Gwen.

"Gwen!" Phoebe beckons. "Come with us. We're going to cruise."

Gwen's dark eyes slide over the panoramic Buick, and the panorama of Shipley faces, jammed together at every window. Shipleys with their Beatle cuts, chins high, lawlessness and enlightenment in their eyes. "Okay," she says and pulls open the door to sink in among them.

Phoebe directs P.J. to drive through the stone gapway and up the tractor road.

"This is Uncle Omar's," one of the Shipleys remarks as the Buick bounces along.

Something smacks against an axle.

Gwen watches the back of her mother's head.

Up along the treeline, Phoebe says, "Okay, Captain. Throw out the anchor here."

"You mean stop?"

"Correct."

Phoebe passes out cigarettes and everyone smokes. Some of the smaller baby Shipleys gag. But the older ones smoke with ease. Gwen slips her unlit cigarette into a pocket of her corduroys. With care. A kind of souvenir. Something delicate and temporary here. A kindness. She watches the back of her mother's head. Only the experienced smokers are smoking now. Contented slisking lips. Cow smell. And oils of human hair. Dungarees and plaid flannel shirts that make no sound rubbing together. Worn to softness, worn to silence. Girl Shipleys and boy Shipleys alike are not susceptible to fashion. But Gwen looks only at Phoebe anyway. She admires the way each hair falls against the other, how hair has the characteristics of water, the accumulated hairs invincible, a thing measured in fathoms and leagues if you were small enough to fall into it and sink.

37 | Another day. Another sweet treat of a day. Cold floors in the morning. Sun popping up from its hidey-hole in the hills. Fun in the air. The Shipleys show up early. Hang around the locked Buick, feeling it and leaning upon the fenders possessively.

"Where's Dennis?" Phoebe wonders of Gwen, but Gwen, munching toast, needn't answer. It's easy enough to guess where Dennis is. In bed. Out too late with his friends who wear their collars up.

The Shipleys suggest to Phoebe that for today's adventure, "We can all go over and spy on Uncle Omar's secret mother."

Phoebe is all for it.

Gwen stands in the kitchen door looking out, more toast in her cheek. Munching. Munching.

"Are you coming along, too?" Phoebe asks.

"If *you* drive," Gwen answers.

Phoebe glares at all the little Shipleys, then her eyes rest on Gwen. "Okay. So I'll drive. So you'll go?" Her now whisperish conspiratorial tone is putting its arms around Gwen.

So Phoebe drives the Buick, Gwen beside her, Shipleys packed in back, dog racing to keep up.

At the house of Shipleys' uncle, Phoebe eases the big car up into the weeds next to a telephone pole. Old farmplace. Too close to the road. No front lawn. Only the dirt where the uncle parks when he's home and one dying elm. Old trucks jam the side yards. Flatbeds and tank trucks on blocks. One has a smashed window, bees whizzing in and out. The doors of the trucks read: WICKS WELL DRILLING, EGYPT, MAINE, and phone number. Smell of horse. No sign of a mother.

"Nobody's seen her, but she *lives* here," a Shipley explains. "She keeps secret."

Phoebe looks titillated.

"Where's your uncle?" Gwen wonders, kicking into the sand.

"Out doin' a well prob'ly," a Shipley reports.

The dog shows up at last, gasping, drinks water from a hubcab, then throws himself down by the porch to pant and keep his eye on the Buick.

Gwen gives the windows of the house a hard study.

"He's rich," P.J. tells them in a voice that crackles with authority.

Phoebe snorts. "Rich smitch. This place is a dump." She snaps the camera four times at the refrigerator shelves leaning against the broken latticework of the long porch.

The group strolls behind the house. No horse. But more well-drilling equipment, mostly well-drilling equipment of the past . . . pretty much a History of Well-Drilling Outdoor Museum . . . and a yellowing vegetable garden that has forced its way up the hillside clear to the woods. And right here handy, a revolving clothesline hung with dark blue work shirts and socks. All clothes for a man. No clothes a secret mother would wear. And there by the barn, a hot looking army-green pile , . . fairly fresh . . . fairly horsey.

While fingering one of the blue shirts, Phoebe looks up at the windows of the house. "You are joking about the secret mother, aren't you?"

Gwen's heart pounds.

Shipleys all chortle at this. "No!" P.J. insists. "She's *in* there. You never see her. But she's in there."

Phoebe struts right up to one of the windows. From the back, in her tight white pants and special wiggle, anyone's guess would be Marilyn Monroe. She cups her eyes, trying to see in through the dark screens and old glass. "Well, just in case!" she chirrs, raising her camera from its neck strap. Inserting a bulb. FLASH! "There you go! We got her if she's sneaking around in there."

Shipleys look at each other solemnly.

Now Phoebe wiggles over to the garden's edge, pushes some leaves apart with the toe of her dressy moccasin. "Big squash," she breathes. She scooches down onto her knees, her rear up, snaps a few shots of the squash. "Squash portraits," she tells her audience.

She stands up, her camera swinging on its strap. Lights a cigarette, stands with one hand on hip, smoking hand raised, turning around and around slowly in delicious awe, eyeing the hoses on heaps of forklift pallets, heaps of tires, and a well-drilling rig that may have once been a great prize . . . now stripped of cables, a great old pounder . . . a kind of horizontal Eiffel Tower across the frame of its hoodless, engineless, wheelless truck.

"Gwen," Phoebe says in a quaking whisper. "I want one of those shirts with the writing on it."

The Shipleys look aghast, glance toward the windows of the house.

Gwen has no expression. There's no reading her hardened dark eyes. Phoebe flicks an ash. "Gwen . . . get me one of those shirts."

"Get it yourself," Gwen says in a low voice, eyes into her mother's eyes.

"Nobody will know," Phoebe says.

This makes Gwen smile, her eyes sweeping across the many Shipley faces, Shipley faces with all the deeper understandings of life. But the arms of her mother's desires once again close around her.

The Shipleys are one held breath. A girl Shipley says, "Omar is rich. He can buy a hundred more."

Gwen steps toward the clothesline. The writing on the shirt is penny-color. WICKS WELL DRILLING, EGYPT, MAINE. The writing is raised up, embroidery like in some old-fashioned hand and yet all business. Gwen's hand closes on the shirt. Now for the pins. She squeezes each one off and the shirt collapses into her hands.

SNAP! SNAP! SNAP! Her mother's camera. Her mother's fun. "Caught you in the act! Caught you in the act!" Phoebe chants.

Gwen turns, zeroes her blank eyes in on her mother while gripping the shirt to her chest, now dropping her face into the shirt's folds, into the good smell of a day's weather, into this new sweet silky hunger for more.

But the shirt is torn away from her by her mother's hand. Now Phoebe is wiggling and flouncing her way back to the car, the shirt a trophy over one arm. Phoebe doesn't look back. She just heads for the Buick. But

Gwen, hurrying to catch up, looks back. Is there really a secret mystery mother in that old place? Or is it just a story made up to scare people?

As Gwen slumps into the seat of the Buick, her eyes clearly readable to Shipleys, P.J. suggests, "You shoulda took more. There's plenty."

38 | It's the only way she can sleep. One pillow under her head. The other pillow on top. Her head in the middle. Phoebe there beneath the heat grate whistling theme songs to *Perry Mason* and *Lassie*. A dish explodes. Silverware crashes in the sink. And now Phoebe's operaish version of Campbell's soup . . . "Mmmmmm-mmmmm good, mmmmm good! . . ."

Gwen wonders. Maybe Phoebe isn't really targeting Gwen. Maybe when Phoebe does this, she's just *happy*. Maybe her happiness is just a little too glaring. An epic happiness. Maybe Gwen has misunderstood all these years. And here's Gwen, thirteen next week, the slow rocking of herself within the screech of her mother's happiness, Gwen cradling Gwen.

39 | At breakfast, Phoebe smokes faster and faster, paces a bit, watches the clock. Is she expecting someone? the housekeeper asks. No, Phoebe replies. But it's interesting how time can drag.

Gwen butters toast, raises an eye to her mother, and sees Phoebe staring at her.

What is the specialness between them? Perhaps the well driller's shirt, or the fact that the well driller's shirt has vanished with a *poof!* Last Gwen saw of the shirt it was over Phoebe's arm as all the little thieves hightailed it for the Buick. Gwen had supposed the next she saw of the shirt would be when Phoebe would become her little prankster self, perhaps having the Shipleys' dog wear it.

But instead it just seems never to have existed. The empty shirt. How outright Phoebe has cornered it, hoarded it, contained it, overpowered it, changed its course.

40 | Next week will be the academy. Long commutes by car pool, in and out of the new September darkness. Into the brick walls, brick sidewalks, and books. Portland. That other life.

Time is short now. Easy lazy time will soon be gone forever. Just study study study. There are times Gwen's grades are impeccable. But every other creation must fall away. Every simple gesture. There is nothing of these studies that touches her heart. It is only the sweet trancelike ease of it. And the prettiness of A's all in a row.

41 Tonight after sandwiches, she works her way along the shoulder of the road. No radio.

The moon is up, overly large and veiny.

She goes briskly, watching her step . . . a direct beeline to the tractor path that cuts up across the fields. The scummed-over pond tonight looks silver, hot, and solid. The grasses pull, ripple, and rise again. So fair. White as bleached weave. To her left the garden of the well driller. Too many tomatoes. Too fat. They have flopped to earth. They spasm. Rank now. Only garbage. And there is the sprawling farmplace of many connecting buildings. Well-drilling equipment. Well-drilling memorabilia! She laughs. She moves in secret toward this scene, stumbling along the garden's humpy stony edge. Secret, secret, secret. Gwen Curry, tall, terrible, chest muscles rigid, she is always secret. In moon or sun. Barely a tincture. The high grass sighs against her baggy pants legs.

The dark shirts are gone from the carousel clothesline. There are union suits there now. Upside down like three executed men. And yet, nothing like men. Not gorged enough. Too witless. Headless, boneless, footless. But what is death but witless?

In the well driller's house, only the kitchen windows are lighted, and there is a glow down in the grass around the foundation . . . a cellar window.

She watches all the windows for movement. No movement. Just the union suits swelling as the night moves. And how this silver night moves! Cold odors of mowed hayfields, husk and vine, all this harvest and the wild knee-high flower and seed and the heaving towers of fir and pine and oak.

She steps along, tensed for things in the high grass that might trip her. The bottoms of her sneakers are as nervous and clammy as two hands.

Now around the front of the house, she finds a pickup truck parked close to the porch, a truck that wasn't there the day of the shirt theft. Light from the kitchen windows passes lovingly onto the truck's grille, and onto one end of the porch. A rocking chair with one lighted arm. A golden path to this chair between shadowy stacks and towers: hydraulic hoses and bags of lime. A hundred-at-least empty soda bottles, beer bottles. Phone books? Hi-C cans. Snow shovel. And a smell. Sweet.

Her mind races, snaps, pops. She is not a thief. "I would bring your shirt back if I could!" she whispers. "I'll confess that I did it, and I'll say I'm sorry. I am nothing like you think!!"

She moves now to the side of the house and peers in through screen and glass, a kitchen stove like you see in history books, kind of pioneerish. It is black and vast and has lids. Everything about this kitchen has a little blackness to it, a little taint . . . a sootiness. Another stove by the sink . . . those iron spiders on top which mean that it is propane.

Bottle of shampoo on the side of the sink. Jackets and tools hung in ready muster at every corner, sack of dry cat food, a bushel basket of tough orangy summer squashes.

Small wooden table with its plastic flowered cloth wiped clean.

Where is the well driller? Where is the mother? This is just a sort of movie set. Can she trust her mind? This might not be real. Well, of course it's real! She is near to fainting. What are the possibilities of their faces? She imagines with a buoyant terror that they discover her. They kidnap her. Make her sit at the table. There are big deep kettles of pioneer food. The well driller is faceless. She can't quite conjure his face, but so many faces overlaid. He eats. Gwen and the secret mother watch this good thing of him eating, filling. She still can't imagine his face but his dressed body is vivid. Well driller shirt with penny-color writing. Pockets on the chest. Belt. Dungarees. Knees and feet spaced for the business of eating. After he sets his fork and knife down, he speaks. "Sleep." It is understood that Gwen will go with him into the unseen inner sanctum of his room and his bed. What next? She can't know. But it is something like being buried alive.

Over near the pioneer stove and chimney, past the jackets and gear and tools and boots, a light moves. The painted door is opening.

Gwen leaps back, runs. Just joking, just joking, just joking! I didn't really mean it! Bye! Tall grasses open up. She runs like hell.

42 | Returning from Portland from a day of buying school clothes, this benediction: Phoebe's little Saab humming prettily into the soaring manifolds of gold and purple of a September evening sky.

"Shopping! An exhausting ordeal." Phoebe groans. But there's nothing exhausted about Phoebe. Phoebe, full of life. Gwen and Phoebe in the front seats. Dennis in back, sprawled handily with the heaped goods.

Phoebe switches channels on the radio. Popular songs. Even the heart-wrenching songs give you a bouncy feel. Everyone in this car has a tapping foot. Dennis burps a big one. All day it's just Cokes, ice cream, burgers, malted milk balls, Bull's-eyes and Phoebe smoking faster, faster, faster. Phoebe taking pictures. Rampant. All up and down Congress Street, in one store and out the other. Spend! Spend! Spend! School clothes were the real mission. But anything goes. And Phoebe with her ready camera gets a shot of Gwen's feet showing under some louvered dressing-room doors. A picture of pigeons poking around a sewer. And then on the way out of the city, a picture of the traffic cop's gloved hand held up to stop their Saab for a blind man to cross. Picture of the blind man teetering on the curb.

Phoebe drives without headlights now into the indifferent dark gloam of Egypt roads. Risky. But who in this car cares? There is wildness in the world just waiting for you . . . hallelujah!

"Your mother is so cool!" Dennis's girlfriend Bethany had told him over the phone after meeting Phoebe last Friday.

"Yes," Dennis said gravely. "She's a regular bucking young filly."

Now another cigarette squeezed into Phoebe's little lips.

While in and among the low hanging trees the planet darkens to night; it is the sky that burns. Clouds piled straight up, straight ahead in a weird orangy atomic-bomb look.

Just before home, Phoebe cranks the wheel sharply left. This is something premeditated and frisksome. Something naughty.

Coming along toward the homeplace of the well driller Omar Wicks, she downshifts.

Every fiber of the girl Gwen is erect and feely. Hands clenched.

The yard of Omar Wicks is jammed with cars and vans and trucks of *guests* tonight. And converged around and upon the tailgates of those trucks parked along the road, there are many men. There's one man with his boot raised to rest on a back bumper. Others squatted. There are nearly a dozen blue shirts with the penny-color embroidered lettering. Many hands. Many beers. The gray mystery of their faces, dark spots for eyes. The gray insurmountability of certain bare forearms. The fortress of their togetherness against the unsettling solitariness of this small head-lightless oncoming car. The postures of the men tighten and bunch, re-volving to glance at who passes, to remark.

"Gwen!" Phoebe commands. Low and husky. "Find the camera and insert a flash, please."

Now the little car strains up the steepening grade, road narrowing, dropping now to washboard dirt. Phoebe brings the Saab to a grinding stop, backs around in the road middle, seesawing it. Cigarette dangles from her bottom lip.

"This is silly," Dennis says mournfully, slumps in the seat among the crinkling and munching of shopping bags.

Saab starts back down the hill.

Gwen finds the camera, works in a flashbulb. Hardly seeing. Mostly instinct.

Down, down, down and around the mountain, shimmying on the washboard, picking up speed now as the tires hit the tar. Big branch whomps the windshield. "Eeeeeeeee-yow!" Phoebe rejoices. More and more speed.

Up ahead the sky opens, turning maroon and yellow, swelling, re-arranging itself, while the fields rising steeply on both sides are soft and courtly.

All in one motion, Phoebe is raising her camera, jams the brakes, pulls on the headlights three times to splash the well driller's guests with hectic light, camera to the eye now, Saab swerving . . . FLASH! "HEL-LO!!" she hollers and gives the Saab the gas and all the men bark "HEY!" and raise their fists and beers.

"You whore." Dennis says this very low. But clear.

The Saab rounds the curve, swings to a near stop at the main road.

"Let me out," Dennis insists. "I'm walking home."

43 | This is what Gwen has overheard once: "When you miss your period, it means you're pregnant."

44 | At the academy in her new clothes, she hurries between classes to the most remote desk, lays down her burden of books. Her new clothes have such a beautiful fit. Can all the people here tell she is different? Ravaged. Eaten alive from the inside out. Is there a smell to pregnancy that certain people can smell but that she can't? *Can* they smell it? Is it getting worse? Soon they will turn to her with horror on their faces to see her so transformed. Soon. She feels her stomach routinely to see if it's rounded yet. But she's afraid to touch it for very long. And in the girls' room she checks for blood. Each time she checks, she nearly screams the words, "BLOOD, please!"

45 You don't see Phoebe but you know she's up there. She must come down for food after Dennis and Gwen leave with the Jacksons for school. Mr. Jackson doesn't ask why Phoebe hasn't taken her week's turn at car pooling. Perhaps she has called them on the phone for a little talk. Perhaps they are just being very kindly, knowing how Phoebe has been so recently widowed, and they're not expecting her to act right for a while. Perhaps they are mad. Gwen tries to read Mr. Jackson's face, but he just seems his ordinary jolly old self, complaining about Lyndon Johnson, keeping a nervous eye on his rearview mirror, jerking at the knot of his necktie as he passes cars.

Meanwhile Dennis says Phoebe is dead in her bed. He is eating a sandwich, shifting from foot to foot by the sink. He has been putting very little effort into his studies, as usual.

Gwen says "Maybe we should knock on her door." But she doesn't mean *we*. She is scared beyond action.

A voice is muttering . . . the TV in the TV room, talking to itself.

Dennis says, "Go ahead. Rattle her cage. But *I* like her better like this."

Gwen makes toast and takes it to her own room, stopping at the bathroom to check for blood. No blood. The blank void of no blood.

Now on her bed, she has trouble visualizing Phoebe's face. Her mother's face seems years ago.

And she cannot visualize a baby. She can only visualize a kind of steamy bloat. And what rotten luck to get pregnant without marriage and love! She is pregnant by *the men*. Like germs swirling through sneezes, so you are also showered by sperms. How crafty they are, these unseeable microscopic creatures exuded by men.

Pregnancy. So full of possibilities, the *many* ways. Gwen reconsiders every word. First the health teacher, who usually only talked about nutrition and first aid, answering Colena Wentworth's question about babies with "When you love someone very much and get married, then you have a baby . . . only then."

And "All you need is one sperm and you are instantly PREGO!" This Gwen overheard once somewhere.

The academy. Place of learning. Place of pride and achievement. She considers all the girls there, striding along, pushing at the sleeves of their sweaters, somehow immune, none of *them* turning out pregnant and there they all are at dances, pelvis to pelvis with boys!

Hours pass.

Toast lays forgotten.

Face cold. Body like ice. She tentatively touches her stomach. Slightly roundish?

The night of men, the air swirled and heaved, the colorific air roared with all dislocated hungers, eyes glittered. The solidarity of the raised fists and beers turned from shadow to red to hardness to grace. And Gwen hanging onto the dash for dear life saw in her mother's face, in her mother's flouncing little body there behind the wheel of the Saab, the clue to everything!

Passion. The conduit through which every unseen thing will rush.

46 It is in the hours following the news of the accident. One of the older boys dead. One better off dead. Ronnie Bartlett. Brian Sanborn. None of the names rings a bell. But Dennis. Light of this world.

Something is sour here. Something unnecessary and lax. Something yet to be known. First question. Second question. "Answer me, Phoebe . . ."

Shattered knees. Broken hands. Internal complications. Eyes closed. GranMom Sheehy's large beige purse on the raised bedside table.

Lawrence just arriving. Lawrence who is such a comic. Just the sight of him makes you smile, even now when smiling is out of order. You want to be buried in Lawrence's million past gestures . . . the puns and dry remarks . . . feigned bewilderments . . . jester truths.

GranMom Sheehy with many many questions. Phoebe cornered. Light of the big hospital window on the back of her fresh neck. Phoebe more than anything wants a smoke. No smoking around oxygen.

47 Whenever Gwen is home, she studies. It's a thing larger than she is . . . impeccable grades. It's the words enunciated by her mother in conjunction with Gwen's name. And school is so easy . . . the facts spelled out in front of you . . . unshifting like brick . . . nothing to guess. So easy. And throughout these hours, these days, these hard weeks, who else dares be loyal to Phoebe?

48 After the new year, Dennis is back at the academy. Dennis Curry at age thirteen, still flax-haired. Still high-voiced. But a hard long body, with an annoyed no-mercy, stiff-kneed piratelike walk. Makes him more appealing than ever. Everybody loves him. Teachers adjust his grades. Girls call him on the phone. Guys offer him drinks. He is not afraid. Only when he isn't drinking is he afraid. Only without the hourly cigarette. Only without girls whispering his name. But all these things are easy. So easy.

49 The blood comes . . . not suddenly like a scream . . . but faintly, just whispers. Then more and more. There had been no pregnancy at all. Just this misunderstanding. Something in the body that was jammed. Today the body says "Go!" Green light. It hums. She eats ravenously. Four bowls of Cheerios. Toast and jam. A grapefruit half with four handfuls of sugar. Some strawberries, half-thawed. She sings.

50 It is decided that the house will go up for sale. There will be a smaller, tighter nicely modern place near GranMom in Connecticut. A place simpler to maintain. And plenty of good private schools. Just down the block. None of this driving for an hour and a half to and from. Everything is accessible. The ballet, the opera, theater, good restaurants, great libraries, lectures of all kinds. "Vitality!" GranMom calls it.

And when they leave, the good doctor's body will remain buried in Maine. There's no sense disturbing the grave. "And he'll have that whole limp Casper Milquetoast Curry clan, which has been hanging out at his grave and wringing their hands. Those people are like buzzards!" GranMom's gravelly voice roars.

The Currys hanging out at William's grave? How does GranMom know these things? Who reports? Is she a kind of *headquarters* where policies are made, data is stored, and everything is reconciled? A beautiful well-oiled hum?

Gwen Curry watches her mother's face. Phoebe smokes, inspects her polished nails, her mind many miles away . . . already in Connecticut?

The foul play concerning William's death seems improbable now. Missing cupcakes have lost their power over Gwen. The missing well driller shirt. And sperms. They are nothing. It is the mirror now. She has trouble with mirrors. Daytime is okay. But once it's dark and if she is alone, mirrors shift slightly. The empty miles within each mirror offer countless possibilities. When she is alone, she hurries past mirrors, forcing her eyes straight ahead. The face in the mirror, which might be swollen like raised bread, wants Gwen to look. Or maybe it's no face, no head, just two prongs where blood had once gone in and out.

Of course this is ridiculous. Of course the face would be just Gwen's. But in the light of day, that's easy to say. Alone in her room evenings while with her studies, or stopping in the bathroom before bed, her mind has two truths . . . one of logic, one of the soul.

GranMom, Guy, and Lawrence arrange everything now, making calls to the realtors, lawyers, movers, drawing up lists while Phoebe blurts out a dozen thank-yous.

5

Into the Ages

1 | LLOYD is grown now. What does he know of us? Each day unfolding is like a puny star in the milky shape of the universe of his vision. It is a vision of himself running in the night through an unrecognized field. Perhaps it is all fields . . . all fields fallow. It is solid. It is not liquid. And yet as he runs, the grasses and sumacs rise, fall, bob and rock gently. And at times he sinks to his waist as you would in deep water.

Where has the corn gone? Where are the cabbages, strawberries, hay? Where are the new calves on their knees? Where are the backs of people bent at their work? The soil is fertile. But it is screaming weeping bawling land. Sirens, whistles, alarms, a crackling stench, and strobes of light burst from these oceanic waves of the fallow.

Arms now burst out of the earth. Arms much larger than would normally embrace you. Arms of a man? Woman? Or all arms made into this medley, this single pair. They are arms of reddish root, of great wood, of tuber. Earth's arms. And arms of the dead. And now a mouth is opening. Crying. "LLOYD! LLOYD!" He is scared witless.

2 | What she sees for the future takes some consideration. Oh, she supposes she will meet more people and they will fit into her life in quiet order. They step from the edges of dream and say hello. We will talk of our lives. We will enjoy the composition of a simple glass of Cabernet placed on a white windowsill, sun and ivy and a narrow border of clean ecru lace. For she has already learned to love old things. They are harmonious with Gwen's soul.

Progress

Roads of men. Roads between dolmens and towers
holding the feeling of warmth.
Roads through mountains and swamps to the place of birth.
Roads of caravans from all Easts to all Wests of all
those who live through us in a memory yet to be revealed.

—*Yuri Mikail Vidov Karageorge*
"Plovdiv/Stoneridge, NY"

1 | EVENING. A quiet few minutes at Moody's Variety & Lunch. Behind the register, Mrs. Laurie Gould gets up from her stool to kiss her dog. Laurie Gould loves to love-up that dog.

Forest Johnson, Jr., is also behind the counter, leans back in the creaky captain's chair, a chair with arms . . . dark bulky piece of furniture . . . sitting in it *does* make a person feel quite like a captain. Forest turns to look directly at Laurie, his dark eyes focusing on her wide, kind of wonderful mouth. Mrs. Laurie Gould. Purply flush. Purple pimple on the chin. Flash of blond hair, straight cut, folksinger style. She has cold-looking skin. Cool smile against the dull hum of the coolers and the vast and hollow half-minute since her last word. She has just surprised young Forest with a little bit of information. Mrs. Laurie Gould who seems much older than Forest though they are both just out of high school. And Laurie's young husband, Chucky, sitting on a short-legged stool in his work clothes, seems elderly. Seems he's seen a lot of long days. Seems nothing could surprise him. He is unwrapping a thing . . . a rubber bone . . . lowers it achingly slow to the floor and the dog with big boxy yellow head gives it a sniff and looks away.

Laurie taps her ash into the aluminum pie plate that is always handy. "Oops! Jeez. I'm sorry, Forest. I think I said something I shouldn't've." Taps another ash.

"I already had an idea on that," says he, spreading his hands on the counter, easing the chair legs down. He seems winded. "Don't worry about it," he assures her.

Laurie says, "I figured it was common knowledge." She opens her mouth for smoke to get out.

Two babies in their pen. Quiet babies. Just the hum of the coolers. No customers milling in the three short aisles. Nobody in the rockers by the stove. Nobody at the lunch counter. Suppertime in Egypt. Not many are far from their kitchens.

Laurie says, "I figured it would've got back to you by now . . . or . . . that your mother mighta told you."

Beef jerky display cartons. Slim Jims and extra spicy Slim Jims and Forest's eyes boring through the red and yellow print.

"Sometimes people figure these things out . . . they kind of . . . oh . . . you know . . . *sense* the truth," Laurie presses on.

"I *said* I knew, okay?" Forest sighs deeply, leans back to raise the chair legs again.

Laurie stoops. Kisses her husband, Chucky, on the ear. Laurie feeling frisky. Forest widens his eyes on her mouth, her mouth too bright, too violet in the store's new fluorescent lighting. Terrible mouth. Bore of a cannon. Eye of a storm. Bear trap. Sweet swirling smoke.

"Everybody knows," says Laurie peacefully. "I just sort've can't believe you didn't know it, Forest. Chucky, *you* knew about it, didn't you?"

Chucky says, "Yep."

Forest drops the front legs of the chair down hard. "I SAID I knew. Jesus. Don't get in a friggin' sweat."

"Well, *you* don't get in a sweat, Forest. Gosh, I didn't mean to start this. We was just talking along and poof!"

Old lady pushes through the glass door. Glass door more of a suppressed whoooosh these days . . . no bonging, clanking jangling bells . . . no tinkle at the end like a loved one's whisper.

Laurie plucks an evening paper from the stack, slaps it on the counter for her, knowing the old woman's wants, knowing the old woman's mind, knowing everyone's mind. When you work at Moody's Variety & Lunch, all of Egypt passes before your eyes sooner or later, over and over, over and over, over and over.

Old lady presses dimes into Laurie's hand. Laurie holds her cigarette away and leans across to kiss the lady's cheek. A big SMACKO. "Oh . . . you are my sweetest customer!" Laurie croons. Laurie's hair is young white. The lady's hair is old white. And Laurie is saying, "Now Mrs. Fickett! You take care!" Laurie's mouth that kisses hundreds, says to hundreds, "Take care!" And the hands that deftly make change to hundreds. Hands with authority. Mouth with authority. A kind of incumbency. You don't question these words of her mouth.

Forest looks out through the glass across the road to his home. Up on the little lawn there. House of brick. Fanlight over the front door. Foundation granite and fieldstone. An imposing slab of granite is the front step. Maple trees so old they have faces with pursed standoffish lips and squinty eyes.

The old lady is leaving, the glass swinging away, easing back.

There is something about one of young Forest's eyes. They are not crossed eyes. But they are not in accord. One eye gentle. One eye an ax.

Laurie dances out from behind the counter and jiggles a bag of M&M's over the babies. The babies rise up.

Forest's mouth tightens. Maybe it wasn't Bett. Laurie is mistaken. Not Bett with Edmund Barrington. Maybe Bett with *somebody*. But not Edmund Barrington. More likely it was a different Bett. A Betty. Betty Graffam. Or Betty Dyer. But not the Bett that is his mother.

His mother had warned him not to hang out so much at Moody's.

"Everybody hangs out at Moody's," his father, F.D., had insisted. "*I* hang out at Moody's. It's the hub!"

"Well, you aren't twenty years old," Bett had said. "With Forest . . . Laurie's husband might misunderstand."

Now this advice comes from some darker, cruddier place than Forest thought, not a mothering place, but a place of whispers where nothing is as it seems. He looks down at his hands, nothing like F.D.'s hands. F.D., pale elf. Forest, dark, almost yellowy skinned. Thick wrists. Before his eyes, the hands grow. Unfamiliar. Transformed now.

2 Another evening late in the week. After another day, which has followed another. Sky staying light later. And a sweet arduous thaw. It gives Forest Johnson, Jr., a big day to fill. He fills it. Working bare-handed now, bareheaded. Second transmission in one season in the same sand truck. A seized rod in another. He and F.D. and the crew watching the thaw, watching the roads rise and crumble like cake. A hundred and fifteen miles of Egypt roads. Frost heaves. Potholes. Flag it. Post it. The phone jangling on the desk out back. Pockets bristling with reminders. Reminders plastered everywhere. And in Forest's head, the voices. The town on his mind. You inherit the work. You inherit the town.

He steps to the doorway of the living room, which she still calls "the parlor," which is seldom heated, all the ducts shut and the old fireplace plugged. She loves this room. She often sits here alone. He is toweling off his hands. Greenish splats of hydraulic fluid prance down over his shirt front.

It is different in this room. No signs of the business. It is handmade divan scarves. Old fern-print rug in shades of gray and rose. Old wool sleigh blanket. No plants . . . but many ceramic animals with planter holes in their backs. Photo of her grandparents' farmplace in an ornate frame . . . not real gold . . . just golden. Photos with elms and horses and pale elfin farm people sitting on steps or standing in doors. In this room nothing "matches," therefore everything is right. Ceramics. A lot of ceramics. But not *way* too many. Not true tacky. Not over the line into plastic carnations! Nothing like that. Just sweetly overstocked, sweetly peculiar. Ladylike. Bett.

She is sitting now in the cool near-darkness looking out at the road and at the sky, sky that takes up the windows. Six-over-six panes. Sashed-open white cotton curtains. Sky is ivory and smoky blue-black. A breathtaking sky. Clouds that are discolored boulders hanging by some reverse gravity, some trick, some revised natural law. Some might be moved or spirited by this sight. How it ripples sinuously through the aged glass! This dying day. How the roofs of East Egypt horde down over the great bank, roofs rusted pinkish, some new and silver, some shingled black. And the river, black. And the river, silver. And the silver stack of the mill. Bett stares. But in her many years of staring, she has seldom seen a roof or sky. Her concerns remain most always within arm's reach. Her friends. Her sister. Her men: the two Forests. The perimeters of this respectable brick colonial. The slim volume of poetry on her lap. Her wristwatch with inscription. Her doctor's appointment next week. Getting the groceries. Remembering thumbtacks. This is how he finds her tonight. Bett.

She has her best coat on, gray with mock belt in back, her posture arrow straight. Her shoes tiny, made for tiny feet. Little buckles on the sides. Sweet. She is seated on the hassock waiting for one of them from the library's literary group to come by for her. As always she is ready to go before it is time. She glances at her watch, then back at the street. Her head, mother head, whole as a planet when Forest was very young. Every smile mattered, every urging, every praise tumbling from the huge mother head. Everything mattered. Now the head is horribly small. And hands veiny, paperish . . . disappearing.

He almost cries out. Little squeak in his neck.

She says without looking his way, "Hello, dear."

He is strangling but noiselessly. Strangling on his own tight throat muscles. "Going out?" he asks.

"Ayuh. It's my night, you know."

"Think they forgot you?" he teases.

"No, dear."

Her hair. Is it blond or white? It has always been the same. It could have changed from blond to white and who would know it? F.D. has always called her his champagne blond, his Jean Harlow, his Jayne Mansfield. A real joke, of course. She has such old lady ways for being only fifty. Decrepit sort of. Yet she's not ailing.

Forest narrows his eyes. He can't imagine her being pregnant with him . . . pregnant at all. It's as if *both* parents have all this time been a joke on him. Both impostors.

"Remember the time they forgot you?" he teases.

"They *never* forgot me!" she simpers. "Stop trying to plague me, Forest."

"They forgot you and picked up some other woman instead and she enjoyed herself."

She picks her dressy knitted cream color gloves from the chair arm behind her, spreads them on the knees of her dress, one empty glove to each knee like two hands. This is her way of being playful. "You stop it right now," she chides. "Go tend to yourself and tell Daddy there's that peach thing in the refrigerator when he comes in."

"I'm going to eat all the peach thing," says Forest.

"There's plenty for both," she says, turns her head toward the glow of Moody's Variety & Lunch, its beer lights, sandwiches-to-go lights and WonderBread sign all mixed into one gregarious patchwork reflected off her plastic-frame glasses.

He imagines balling up his damp towel and pitching it at the back of her head.

This is not a new feeling. This is not some symptom of Mrs. Laurie Gould's bit of information. This has been coming on.

The guys over to Moody's last week, reminiscing about the prior fall, their faces getting good color, they rub their palms.

One of them telling it, "Decided this was the special coon . . . this was *the* one. So I tell Larry . . . 'This is the one, ain't he?' And Larry says, 'This coon??? This coon??? Looks like a fucking bear. Sure he ain't a bear?' "

A few chuckles. They rub their hands.

"We had his dogs with us and Clayton's dogs and mine all going nuts around that pine. Pine it 'twas. But we say 'Sorry dogs, *this* one ain't yours. Sorrrreeeeee!' It 'twas a goddam special night. Course we was all shit-faced. Everything's special when you each got a couple-three six-packs in you!"

Lotta chuckles. Some HAWs.

"My little Ruger can do a dime on a cat's ass from here to the top of that mill stack . . . so 'taint nuthin' to pick off the front hands of a big bull coon in a twenty-foot pine tree. Took those hands . . . paws . . . whatever . . . right off cleeeeen . . . one shot to each. He sure let go!!!!"

Lotta chuckles. Hands rubbing together. Rockers paused.

"Goddam! Didn't that cutter let out a blat. Callin' us every cuss word in the book. Dogs are hot for him but Clayton and Larry're holding 'em back. Few kicks to that tailless bluetick bitch of Rick's don'tcha know . . . don't understand nuthin' less . . . ain't got but a pea for a brain, that one. Knock her over head over heels. And *then* some. Anyway, so my boy Rick's comin' in with the gasoline . . . our *special* request." Chuckle. "You'd think that coon woulda exploded when the match hit. Jesus! I never seen anything so funny in my life. 'Twas like a . . . one of those firecrackers that whips around. Clayton says to me 'GET OUTTA THE WAY!!!' We all jumped back. That flaming coon was everywhere!"

Forest's eyes move over the papered walls of his mother's parlor.

There's plaster under the paper, then the recently blown-in insulation, then boards, then brick. Dense. Seems impenetrable. And Bett alone there by the window in her gray coat.

3 | "Where are your people from?" he asks.

"Oh, everywhere," Meredith says with a toss of her right hand, then she names a bunch of cities . . . including Wichita, which he knew about. In school they had called her "the girl from Wichita." Now she tells him a little about the kids at the school she went to in her freshman year back in Daytona. Now it turns out as she talks along that she hadn't really lived in those cities. It was really some nearby towns, "the suburbs."

A peculiar habit to say you lived where you didn't live. It would be like saying you lived in Australia whereas you really lived in Mexico. Or like saying you lived in the clapboard house down by the PO when you really lived next door in the shingled one. But he keeps his silence, his eyes on the bumper of the pickup he's following too closely.

Now as she talks along it turns out she didn't live in Wichita, either. She is so beautiful and offhand, he couldn't stand it once. But now he's getting used to it. And sometimes it's apparent she resembles him. Though he is, at the marrow of his smoothness, still edgy, too steamy, quenchless, overtaxed. He asks, "Why did you say Wichita if it wasn't?"

"Well, we went there a lot. Dad's office was there and . . . oh . . . *everything* was there."

He glances up from the moving road, and his eyes screw tightly onto her face, his soft eye and his cruel eye, both very dark.

She sniggles delightedly. "And *because*, silly . . . you wouldn't know where I meant if I said Wellington."

But then he wouldn't know where Wichita was either. Well, Kansas, of course. But where is Kansas? Well, Midwest, of course . . . but it's not a thing you could picture. Why picture it? It bores him.

"What does your old man say about you letting me drive this?"

She smiles. "Nothing. Why?"

"He doesn't care?"

"It's my car, not his. Besides, you're a wonderful driver!" She pats his arm.

He shrugs dismissively.

Her car. Oldish Volvo. Mint shape. The only Volvo around. Exotic. In it, there's an otherworldly feeling. She has told him before that her folks brought it up from Atlanta. It was theirs since it was new. When they got their new Volvo they sold this one to her for a dollar. They always keep two Volvos. There's something wonderfully uneventful about a Volvo, according to her father.

"No salt on the roads in the South," Forest says with authority.

"I guess," she says, with a little amused smile.

And he is used to her tight sweaters now. This one is scarlet. He is used to all of this. Not dumbfounded like he was that day she settled into a desk in homeroom fresh from Wichita. Everyone was dumbfounded. The whole class stiffened as though it were cornered . . . as though it were one and she were many.

She is talking now about one of her best friends who is coming this summer on the bus.

"Which best friend?"

She is always telling of "my best friend." But it is never the same one. This one is Kathy from Daytona. "She studies art. I bet if I ask her she'll do a drawing of you in the nude . . . for me." She says this thoughtfully. "I would love to have a drawing like that. Would you pose for her, Forest? You have a beautiful body."

He shrugs. Seems he's distracted. But he's riveted, aroused. Aroused by this idea of himself naked for the artist, as though Meredith instead had just offered the chance for him to see this artist bared.

Now at Kool Kone he gets a banana boat for himself. All she wants is a vanilla cone. She had added that *she* wouldn't pose for an artist in a million years and pulled on the hem of her sweater to be sure it was all the way down in place. And she shifted in her seat. He looks down at the vanilla cone at the pay window as he counts out his change. Little curl on top. Sweet. It drives him nuts.

Meredith. How she had stood out among the dozens of Egypt area girls who were as familiar as sisters. Meredith unfamiliar. Her accent. Her nose. Huge funny beautiful nose and black mannish eyebrows and a long Italian last name. Part of her dark hair pulled back into a clip. Hair baby-fine as the magazine Breck girl's. Her accent . . . no, not Italian. Her accent a mix. All those cities that weren't what they were but were somewhere else. Everything very vague and boring and far-off. Best friends who are like the dead . . . always in past tense. Meredith unbounded . . . floating . . . long-bodied in the void of no homeland. No home! A kind of virginity. A kind of destitution. And he, Forest Johnson, Jr., is, wherever he goes, called by name. Famous sort of. Nearly everyone in Egypt is famous. Everyone knows everyone to the bone. He is struck with pity for Meredith. Struck with his own solidness . . . he a hero . . . she, this starveling.

The Kool Kone woman says he needs to give her six more cents.

He pales. He scrutinizes the change on the Formica. He counts out six more cents, all pennies.

Guys at Moody's say men use logic. Women are just emotion.

He knows who the Kool Kone woman is by her voice. Janet Merrill. Worked in the kitchen at school once. You see her around. "Thank you," she says.

"Yup," he says. He just can't bring himself to look her in the eye.

4 | The morning is black and it trembles with dump truck engines, while in and among these trucks are the scuffs and clangs and hoots of men.

Silhouetted against the fluorescence of one of the two open bays are three drivers hunched around the diminutive figure of F.D. Johnson, Sr. His gloved hands shout as much as his mouth does. His tight green cap stretches his eyes. And the gloves, as ever, are brand-new. He loves new gloves. He often lets the rest of himself go to fray, but his work gloves are never anything but fuzzy and soft and recent as new baby sleepers. "AND WHAT THE HELL HAPPENED TO FOURNIER'S JUNIPER BUSHES??!!" he yells. "We'll have to REPLACE THOSE! Jesus-God! They don't give them away, not those kind shaped like lampshades!" His pale eyes, watery from screaming, go red-purple from the braking taillights of a late-arriving driver, then back to pale. On his face is a look of fun.

Behind F.D., the son, Forest, is hauling a length of chain from the farthest bay. Young Forest flings the chain onto a low-bed. Then he reenters the bright bay. Now he strides again into the dark outdoors, squatting to check a tire on the rear axle of one of the smaller trucks.

F.D. cackles. "Just remember next time you see juniper bushes, we are not DINOSAURS!!" He stomps forward like a dinosaur trampling many juniper bushes. "WE ARE PROFESSIONALS! REMEMBER THAT! Even if none of us gives a fuck about juniper bushes personally, even if to you and me the damn things look like lampshades. REMEMBER the customer LOVES his juniper bushes and will call me up at ten o'clock at night in high emotion. So PLEEEEEEZ look at what your duals are backing onto. Be DAINTY!! Okay??"

Two more drivers have joined the group, their arms folded over their jackets and vests . . . one man fortyish, one in his fifties . . . both graying. They call out in unison over the din of revving trucks, "WEEEEEEEE PROMISE!!" And then everyone is having a hell of a laugh about juniper bushes. It doesn't take much to set these guys off. The new day is filled with dark relentless energy. It is common knowledge around these parts what a decent job you got if you can "get in with that Johnson outfit." Guys stick with F.D. for years, grow old and die, and would if they could, *still* keep kicking in the clutch for F.D., even after death.

5 | Another evening. Another handful of change. He turns from the Kool Kone order window with a banana boat and a vanilla cone, turns to the wide low panorama of the Kool Kone parking lot. He almost weeps. There is a bearded black buck goat standing on the hood of Meredith's Volvo.

Meredith leans out the passenger's window. "Shoo! Shoo!" She waves her hand. "Shoo!"

This shooing makes the goat feel nice. He gives a little nimblish leap into the air, body twisting in the middle, lands with all four hooves together as if on a silver dime. CLOINKA! Then he does a tap dance.

Kids in other cars shriek and point. "HEY, FOREST, BROUGHT YOUR GOAT, HUH!!!" and "HERE GOATY, GOATY!"

Meredith opens her door, places one foot down. A work boot laced to the top. Seems she will square things with this goat.

It is a goat big as a pony. He dances and dances, hooves cracking horribly against the Volvo's polish.

Kids in other cars going wild. Blowing horns. A weddingish blare. "P.U., JOHNSON WHAT STINKS?? HEY, JOHNSON!!!"

The goat has not had his horns burned off. They are ribbed, sweeping, iron-color, undulating, stretching forth feelingly into the green evening . . . effortless. His eyes are the usual horizontal goat eyes. Lusty. His eyes hold a humorous scheming view of Forest standing there with ice creams and paling face.

"Go on! Go away!" Meredith moans.

Goat lowers his head at her moans.

Meredith flings a ball-point pen, which just rattles against the fender, then plummets.

This makes the goat feel maniacal. He wags, boogies, tail spinning, leaps up to the roof of the car. Up there on top now with Meredith inside underneath. She rolls her eyes, falls back into her seat, covers her face. She is kind of laughing, laughing along with the kids in the next car.

He, the goat up there on the roof . . . you can tell he feels he's won something because now he goes into an even more frenzied, more high-stepping performance, bowing even, pleased, his bag flapping crazily . . . the horns of all cars all wailing at once. Kids yelling. "JOHNSON!! THAT YOOOOOOO WE SMELLLLL???"

Forest wants to yell back that bucks don't smell in spring . . . but it seems there is *something* in the air. Something unarguable.

6 | Forest gives the Granada the hotfoot, the Granada, his father's prize, pride, and joy. The color of heavy cream. Faster now. Bett doesn't complain. Instead she's telling him how the receptionist said her new spring coat "becomes" her.

Maybe she doesn't know he's driving fast, *faster*, bearing into the center of the road at each turn. She's probably not aware of anything outside the Granada. If you asked her "Where are we now?" if you *tested* her, she might not know the answer. She might give you one of her sweet disdainful sniff-sniffs that says it's not her job to know.

Now she is quiet. Staring straight ahead. Something in her thoughts makes her blush. Not an embarrassed blush. More a blush of deepest pleasure. This means she's reliving the doctor's office. She loves the doctor's office. Like some people like hitting the bars or dance halls. Or church.

Something about Bett seems less elderly today. Young. The extreme of young. In Forest's peripheral vision, it seems a well-behaved winsome little girl rides there. But even in his clouded periphery, the short tightly curled hair, which she calls her "set," and her blue pillbox hat . . . these are the apparatuses of a mother.

A school bus stops ahead. Forest sighs, hits the brake. Power brakes as creamy as the car's color. He eases the Granada up behind the bus and waits.

Bett doesn't see the school bus at all, he can tell. This bus that's so close it makes her face glimmer yellow! And the kids grinning down, giving each other rabbit ears. She is smiling onto a spot, somewhat short of the Granada's windshield. She tells Forest, "The doctor liked my collar pin. He said, 'Well, well, Elizabeth! What do you have here?' and I told him it 'twas a pearl collar pin, though of course he was just playing innocent. He knew this was real! He was just plaguing me, you know, the way he does. He says, 'Well, well, Elizabeth! What do you have here?' "

The bus and the Granada are moving along again.

"He said it 'twas *handsome*." Bett smiles into the yellow aura. Bus is close again. They have reached another stop.

Forest narrows his eyes on the two high-school guys that emerge and cross over to the mailbox that has gold stickum letters that spell out MOREY. The boys turn and look into his face. Forest is wearing one of his most icy sovereign expressions.

"I told him it was Mildred's . . . and he said Mildred had good taste. I said she certainly did . . . but even more . . . she was a generous dear soul. He agreed that fifty-three was too young to die."

The bus driver waves the Granada on. Forest mashes the gas. The Granada springs past, then on around through a curved tunnel of overhead pine, then back out into open space again.

The hillside fields are busy in the crisscrossing breezes. Shapes within shapes, gray and winter-killed against the new grasses that are a green fire. Forest watches the stone walls, utility poles, beer cans, and bunched up brown paper bags, a road sign with a squiggled arrow, his thoughts fixed on these things, these good and worldly things.

A pickup truck, red when it was new, now a flat color, put you to mind of a plastic cemetery rose. This comes toward him. Two heads are silhouetted in the cab. David Turnbull and King. David Turnbull, about six foot three. King, small. Yet King is always situated high. His head and David Turnbull's head nearly the same height. But Forest knows about the two upholstered chair cushions roped to the seat. Gives King the view he needs. Both King and David Turnbull keeping their eyes on the road, speculating on the vast business of life outside their vehicle.

They say David Turnbull is nearly completely tattooed under his biker clothes. David Turnbull, biker son of a biker father, probably a biker grandfather, perhaps that ancestral straight line going back to the Mayflower of Harleys. And now biker brothers. A biker sister they call Babe.

Biker stepfather. Biker bonfires at night. Party bikers. Pig roasts and disputes and bike burnings. All the biker uglinesses that go with the profession. Sometimes gone away for days. Gone to wherever bikers go to meet bikers of the world, to ride those hogs and iron horses low and thunderously over highways meshed into other highways. David Turnbull. Used to wear a Nazi helmet fixed with horns from a bull when he was sixteen. Wildest, meanest biker of them all, of all local bikers that is. But David Turnbull has been at the mill for four years now with only Sundays off and before that Vietnam. So the whole of that legend can't be true.

At the moment when the battered plastic-rose-color pickup and the Granada are juxtaposed, window to window, Forest sees King is wearing one of his Healthtex Playtog shirts. The one with the little footballs in the weave.

Bett declares, "You are thoughtful to take this time, dear. I know Dad needs you with the crew. But my-my, it's good to get that appointment over with. Thank you so much."

"You're welcome," says he and reaches for his sunglasses above the visor.

He has worn a dressy crew neck sweater over a dressy stripe shirt. For her. It means so much to her that he look this way in Bridgton at THE APPOINTMENT. Even the pants. He even wore these pants! It seems as he looks back on it now, the doctor was wearing the same. If she noticed that, it would be one of the high points of her week. Of her *life*.

The Granada steers so fluidly, he uses just two fingers of his right hand. His sunglasses reflect the blur of the Granada's speed, the low-slung telephone wires zigzagging up this mountain, up, up, up. At the fork, just before coming this back way into East Egypt, he swings the car onto the Shipley Mill Road, which is not the way home. Bett's eyes fall to his hand on the wheel. The road here circles back on itself nearly. A road of arduous rebounds. Now facing north again, going into higher country. The fields here steepen. Electric and barbed wire runs along on the right. Now the Granada swings into an opening, vast with sky, and the hills falling away down to the ponds, while off to the northwest, white and absolute, near and yet far, Mount Washington. The monstrous. The uncompromising. Where people don't die. They perish. Still white. Still winter.

Forest exclaims, "Pretty as a picture, huh, Mum?!!" He brakes the car so suddenly, she grabs for the dash. He pulls off onto the shoulder and gives a hard shove to the nosepiece of his sunglasses, which have slipped. He says, "My my my my my my my my. The view of views." The black hair lays on his neck. Hair so long it splits at the nape, flagrant against the collar of his dress shirt.

To the left edge of this razor-sharp vista of greater mountains and clear sky is a cape with its shedways and barns and gates. Farm equipment and old cars, heaped rock, muddy calf pens, tufts of weed, rock and weed, rock and weed, rock and weed. Rust. Shade trees in hard brown bud. Everything of a piece. Toad color and rust, terrible and yet pleasing. Five shaggy red cows with calves watch the Granada, ears cupped wide open, listening to the silvery hum of the motor. It is the home of Edmund Barrington and his people.

"My, my, my!" Forest nearly squeals. "Such a view! We are blessed to have such a view so close to home, aren't we?"

Bett is silent, staring at her small hands. She has become *aware* of the world outside the Granada, he can tell.

"It's something a person can't explain," he says softly. "Like a duckling gets fixed on a dog if the duckling hatches out and there's nobody around but the dog. So the duckling thinks the dog is Mumma. They say it's called 'imprinting.' Well, that's what this ol' town is to me . . . and all this *nature*. It's in me forever. It's probably the same with you. You just can't love another place. It's forever." His voice thickens on the word *forever*, a sound like pleading.

He pushes his sunglasses to the top of his head. "Now Meredith . . . that girl I've been taking out . . . her folks just move to a bunch of cities all the time. They never own their place. They just rent one so they can move without much work to it. Not me. I couldn't stand that kind of thing."

Bett looks at him briefly, then back to her small hands. "We should get going, Forest. I'm sure Daddy needs you."

His eye that is always fierce, even when the other is at ease, widens on her navy blue pumps, each pump with its little navy blue leatherette bow.

She stares at his hand on the wheel as if to will it into action.

"You mean, Mum, you don't like this view? Tourists would jump out of their cars with those cameras they got with lenses long as my

141

forearm and use up ten rolls of film on this . . . this super neat ol' work of nature. You should be ashamed! Taking so much for granted. These beautiful mountains. And there's Promise Lake, the narrow end that has the island on it . . . and the meadows and beaver bogs . . . all in one sweep. And there's where Dad got his buck two years ago, somewhere over on that ridge. Gosh, yes. Trees buddin' out . . ." His next three words are lost on his voice breaking.

She says, "Please."

Forest swallows, his eyes fixed on her face, his mouth tight against his teeth. Throughout all his praise of the view, his eyes have been only on her. His hand moves, flips the shift out of park, eases the Granada back up onto the pavement.

Bett says cheerfully, "We went up on Cog Railway when you were a baby. With Uncle Chet and Aunt Esther. You were fussy. Too little really. A few weeks old. We really shouldn't have gone. One man in the next seat from us says, 'Check and see if he has got a pin stuck in him.' That's what he said. I thought it was rude but your father and Chet laughed. 'Check and see if he has got a pin stuck in him.' That man just had a big mouth."

Forest has heard this story before, a recital actually. Every word the same. How many times has she told it? A hundred times? A thousand?

He says, "Yunh, I know."

"But you had colic. *Every* baby has colic."

He takes the Granada easier now over the twisting hills. The trees start to close in again. The sky is exhausted. Shrinking.

Cheerfully Bett tells him the doctor said her blood pressure was excellent. Cheerfully she repeats how he loved her collar pin and how she told him what a good soul Mildred was. Her knees give little jumps like something electric going on in there. She chirps, "Mildred was a dear soul. She even gave up her own bed to Nanna for four years and slept in a chair."

"I know, Mum. I was there."

"Oh, I know you were, dear. I'm just remembering aloud." She pats the arm of his dressy sweater.

In the rearview he sees the school bus rounding the curve, catching up. He gives the Granada just a little more gas, surging along the bends and dips as the school bus does, up and down around between the budding trees and NO TRESPASS signs and NO HUNTING, and stone walls, bashed mailboxes, pothole with its warning flag and the gray paste of a squirrel carcass on the crown of the road. A mile, then another mile, bending, dipping together with the bright bus in a choreography, lovely and deft. Till the bus's red flashing lights come to life again and the bus melts into the past.

He says, "We'll have to come this way again sometime, Mum. It's a little longer but well worth it. Nice."

7 | Midmorning of a day after another day. Stopping at the IGA for sodas and snacks. Forest and the new driver, Len Moore. Two dump trucks grille to grille outside in the fire lane. Illegal parking. Engines left idling. F.D. would have a bird to know it.

Len Moore, older than Forest, but a boy in the eyes of most. Happy, giggly. Gets the deli girl all charmed by the things he tells her. Leaning over the deli's high plexi, he whispers and coos. Len Moore . . . frizzed-out red hair, chin like a blade, big teeth. Teeth jump out at you. The deli girl calls him Flash. Len gives her his card. It's his used-car salesman card. The thing he does when he's not driving truck. And there's also his dog business. Raises Dobies. He's a man who never sleeps.

At the checkout Len Moore and Forest get squeezed between a lady with a loaded cart ahead and people behind who must be tourists. Tourists dressed in turquoise and white stripe, sporty socks and shoes, shifting from foot to foot, wondering what's holding things up. The tourists have wine and long bread in a carry basket. Nothing as hulking as the lady's paper towels, cat litter, and roasts being swung up onto the belt.

Len Moore tells the cashier her shoelace is untied.

"You can't *see* my shoe from there, Lenny," she retorts. Most people her age have not changed to calling him Len . . . or Flash.

What's holding things up, the turquoise-and-white tourists are wondering from behind. They don't speak this aloud. But their bodies lean hard toward the south.

Forest looks out through the big glass at the trucks, their idling motors keeping up enough noise to shimmy the air between all spoken words.

The lady up ahead is paying for her order with a check. Forest recognizes her from plowing down the Old Chase Boundary Road where she lives. He knows how in winter she covers her shrubberies with wooden structures like tables. Her husband is dead. Her kids are grown. Her groceries are enough to feed thousands. He sees she has celery sticking out there. And all those paper towels. Giant boxes of baking soda and cornstarch. Picture frames. Cotton rope. Her hair is puffed tall and dyed dark red. Forest looks bored. The cashier looks tired. The tourists look like they are about to throw their groceries at the walls. Only Len is smiling.

Lady is having help now wheeling it all away.

Cashier is reaching to price Len's sodas and Needhams.

Len says solemnly, "Whose Ford wagon's that out there? Somebody just sideswiped it."

Cashier says, "Lenny, you can't pull that one twice."

Len's huge teeth chop out at the air.

Len was a hero in Vietnam. Got medals. Hard to picture.

It is sudden. Like BANG! Only soundless. Len's tall teeth turning toward Forest and Len saying, "Jesus Christ! Anybody here smell goat?" Len looks around to see if anyone else notices. The tourists look pissed-off anyway, so there's no telling there. Two more people with loaded wagons have pulled up behind the tourists. Both familiar-looking women but nameless. Len beckons to the women between the two heads of the tourists. "Anybody back there smell *goat?*"

The two Egypt women cackle.

The tourists make no sound, even as the husband shifts the basket of wine and bread from one hand to the other.

"Wouldn't be any goats in the IGA, would there?" Len wonders gravely. He glances back up through the two visible aisles. "A goat could feasibly step on the automatic doormat and open the door, couldn't he?" He looks into the hard and soft scrutiny of Forest's dark eyes.

Now Len is telling the cashier about the special they had on television last night.

"Missed that one. I'll try to catch it when they rerun it," she tells him.

"They don't rerun specials," Len tells her. He presents her with one of his car salesman cards.

"I already have one of those somewhere," the cashier says, filling Len's free hand with silver change.

"Have another," Len says. "You never know when the need will strike."

Cashier accepts the card.

Len winks at Forest. "Come on, Billy . . . let's go." Len makes two fingers into horns on his own head, pivots, skips goatlike toward the automatic doors.

Forest places his soda and Twinkies on the belt, avoids the cashier's eyes. He knows without looking into them that the Kool Kone goat incident has reached her in some form or another. It has reached everywhere. But as she makes the motions of this sale, she says nothing. He glances back into the vicious glares of the tourists who, of course, have no inkling of the goat. Their eyes swirl in empty harmless space. Like marbles, they will roll away forever . . . earless, mouthless, never to remember.

8 | Alone in his bed in the room of sailboats wallpaper, Forest Johnson, Jr., tosses a sock to the floor. Sock he's used to clean the semen up with.

It has started to take charge of him, this one track of thought. Everything his eyes see takes on sexuality. Open doors. Deep armchairs. The snapping open of a paper bag. Sun and gasoline. The warm woods. His truck with a load of gravel clamoring downhill, jamming down along the gears. It need not be flesh. Just the white-hot-red future racing toward him. Everything swollen. Everything ten times its normal size. Every moment a possible surprise. Will you pose nude for my best friend? Wouldn't be any goats in the IGA, would there? Embarrassment that turns to goodly heat.

It is only at night that he is alone enough. Parked along the road somewhere anyone can come up on you in a sudden. No matter how secluded.

He imagines humping everything and everybody. People by the road. He imagines the people in their houses. Waiting. Ready. Before dropping from the high footing of his truck when he gets back to the shop, first he has to stall around, searching for change on the dash, trying to think of things that will cool him off so he can walk in front of people. By night he is nearly sick. The silent house. Its brickness. The high open rooms. The feeling. It is never finished. It is always renewed. By morning many socks, a few shirts. On and on until he has ravaged himself, a kind of self-rape. Sometimes he cries. His sorrow, a muffled croak! croak! into his fist. But then the sorrow burns back into rapture.

9 | At Moody's tonight the place is packed. Mrs. Laurie Gould has her hands full. Even with her kid brother helping, the line is long waiting for sandwiches-to-go . . . waiting for pizza . . . big night for pizza . . . and nobody makes pizza-to-go around here but Moody's. Special recipe. Hot. Crisp. Gobs of cheese. Pizza smell following you out the door. Even if you pick up only a jar of mayonnaise, you carry the Moody's pizza and Italian sandwich smell for many miles.

Old Andrew Moody not much help these days. Laurie's grandfather. He just hangs out, looking starved and whiskery. His many operations taking their toll. There's always new surgery coming up, unrelated to past surgeries. Nothing spreads. Each thing removed or rearranged leaves him clean as a whistle.

Most of the rocking chairs are full of old and oldish wise men. Some standing against the wall. Some squatted down, rocking a coffee cup on the knee. Not a lot of young guys here tonight. Albion Cole, neither young nor old, slumped on an inverted pail, smoking cigarettes that seem always to be short. Albion Cole who still keeps ALBION COLE & SONS on the doors of his logging trucks although two sons died in Vietnam, a third one made it home to die from a faulty hydraulic of one truck's loader. No sons now. A father who is no longer a father.

Everybody scrutinizes Forest Johnson, Jr., who is unwrapping an ice-cream sandwich. His second one.

"So what's this we hear 'bout you and old Spot Sklotsky's buck goat?" old Andrew wonders. "Big boxing match over on the lake I heard. You and Big Billy in the ring. They say he chased you a good mile. That so?"

All eyes on Forest.

"No," Forest answers. "That story is stretched. Nothing happened." Tonight Forest's black hair is wetted, fussed with.

"I heard you and some girl got your Dad's Granada wrecked . . . takin' a goat somewheres. That's what *I* heard," Ray Dyer snorts.

"No," Forest says, balling up the ice-cream bar's paper, gives it a toss to the kindling barrel. "Go over and look at the car if you want." He wears his sovereign, chilly expression, chin up, dark eyes fixed slightly to the left of Ray Dyer's face. Once they called Forest, Jr., a shy boy. But he's not shy. Never was. Something there to be confused with shyness. Shyness is a whole other thing.

"I heard it 'twas over to Kool Kone a goat got in the car and tried to eat the seats," Albion Cole says with an almost apologetic lowering of the eyes.

"No," Forest states clearly.

Everyone looking at Forest. A little bit of silence, but for Mrs. Laurie Gould chattering with somebody at the register, something about her dog's allergy. What else? Her dog. Whole world revolves around her dog and the two babies, which everyone calls "good babies."

Women are emotional. Men are logic. This is what the wise men here have said on other nights, on the many other nights of many other wisdoms.

Forest tonight is staying clear of Mrs. Laurie Gould.

Biker David Turnbull strolls in with King. King in the lead. King has a hard-core businesslike arrogance about him, wide chest and beady penetrating eyes of his terrier half, light step and levelheadedness of his poodle half. Blackish streaky fur bouncing along over his back and rear, a whiskered, massively eyebrowed little man of a dog. Ears sort of up, sort of not. He prances over to his favorite chair. His favorite chair is painted royal blue and has a thick tapestry seat. But somebody is in it. Ernest Bean, one of the younger guys. King sniffs Ernest's foot. "Howzit goin', King?" Ernest inquires, reaching down to pat King on the head.

King glances around, then flashes a look at Ernest's foot.

"Give him the chair for chrissakes!" booms Merlin Soule.

"Give him *your* chair, Merlin," Hal Wiley chortles.

"But he wants *that* chair," Merlin insists, pointing at Ernest.

Ernest leaps from the chair. "It's all yours, King!" Ernest throws out his hand in a fanfare-style introduction.

King hops up into the chair. It creaks to and fro, finally settles quietly, King sitting there facing the wood stove that has no fire in it just as the occupants of the other chairs face that stove. King is wearing his gray Bowdoin College T-shirt tonight. He has a collection of college shirts, but Bowdoin seems to be his favorite.

Young biker David Turnbull strolls over, peeling the cellophane from his Camels, stands behind King's rocker and smiles. Young biker David Turnbull dressed in full biker regalia.

"So," says Andrew Moody. "He know anything new tonight?" He jerks his thumb at King, but looks to David Turnbull's face for the answer.

"Ask him," David Turnbull says.

"What do you think of the Republicans, King?"

King looks away toward the window, bored.

Clarence Farrington shifts his weight in his rocker.

"King! Hey boy! Listen . . . what's that you say about the Republicans?" Albion Cole asks around his short cigarette, smoke unfurling on each syllable. Albion looks around grinning and a little perplexed. "Make him do it, Dave."

David Turnbull squats down beside the chair, all the biker leather creaking, the Harley-Davidson wing tips nearly plumb to the shoulder seams. King and David Turnbull look into each other's eyes a moment. "Listen, King. What do you think of the Republicans in Washington, D.C.?"

King lifts his lips, baring his teeth, and snarls a menacing low one.

A few of the men in the circle swing back into their rockers chortling, snickering. They never tire of King's opinion.

However, Clarence Farrington and Arch Vandermast and a few others look vexed.

"That ain't something new," Arch sneers. "That's the same old damn thing."

"Howzit you get him to do that, Dave?" wonders Ernest Bean. "I notice you put stress on the words *Washington, D.C.*, more than the other words. That some sorta trick clue?"

David Turnbull sets a fresh Camel on his lower lip. It sticks there as if by magnetic pull. "Well, of course, there's something to that. King doesn't care about little bullshit dipshit one-vote Republicans in the workaday world. King wouldn't mind Republicans as long as they stayed out of Washington. And . . . you know . . . he's not too cool on Southern agribusiness and Texas oil Democrats either. He's fucking sick of that whole pit of snakes."

This cracks up the few loyal King fans.

Clarence Farrington snarls, "Ask him what he thinks of Commies. How come you never ask him *that!*"

"Commies aren't here, Clarence," David says, his unlit cigarette bouncing. "King only worries about the immediate problem . . . not some notion."

Clarence scowls. "Well, you keep it up and they'll *be here*."

King stares up into David Turnbull's heavily haired-over face as the biker finally puts a match to his cigarette and inhales.

"He wants a cigarette," old Andrew Moody says. "Somebody get King a cigarette."

"No way!" David Turnbull says on a hard belch, rubs the front of his leather jacket, looks into King's eyes. "King's been hasslin' *me* to stop. He's been reading up on all that tars and nicotine stuff."

"King's a pretty clean guy," Ernest Bean observes.

"Well, in some ways," says David Turnbull. "But you don't want to leave him on his own 'round any cowflaps, rotten fish, or dead woodchucks."

Everyone studies King with gravity as if it were impossible to imagine.

F.D. Johnson, Sr., comes swinging in, dark blue work shirt opened to the white triangle of T-shirt, pale eyes merry. He winks at Laurie at the register, salutes his boy, Forest. All attention shifts. Lovable smart-aleck F.D. One of the world's few humans who can follow a good dog act.

10 | A few days. A few suppers. This supper blurring into the others, blurring into this plenitude, relied upon. Kitchen light overhead of a degree of brightness that never lies. F.D. eats like a horse. Off to his left is his cooled-off coffee, creamed nearly to white. Pulls it toward himself between swallows of stew and roll. Works everything around in his mouth, his whole mind rallying within his mouth . . . sorting the tastes . . . content. "Cookies in the air," he says with a sniff.

Bett says, "They came out awful." This is neither a wail nor a sulk. She says it with acceptance and great peace.

"You always say that," F.D. says inside a big yawn.

"Well, these are the worst," says Bett.

F.D.'s yawn makes his eyes run with tears. His yawns are as much a pleasure to him as his food.

Young Forest eats. No yawns of pleasure. No conversation. He just eats.

F.D. goes for thirds. He tells Forest about the planned "upgrading" of the Harlan Prouxl Road.

The partial upper plate in Bett's mouth makes her meal take time . . . and funny little noises, unnatural and awkward and puckery.

Young Forest lays his fork aside and swallows, clears his mouth. He announces, "Mum . . . don't bother to go in my room anymore . . . you know . . . for socks an' stuff. I can do my own laundry."

Bett swallows hard, blinking, says, "Oh, dear . . . that's all right. I don't mind."

"I'm not a kid, all right? Nobody needs to prowl in my room."

Eyes twinkling, F.D. has been looking hard at Forest's mouth especially on this speaking of the word *prowl*.

Young Forest pushes something off the edge of his plate a little too quickly. Like a person would do if he found a fly. But it's only gristle.

For a while there's no more talk, just silverware and chewing mouths at work.

F.D. finally pushes his plate away, feels for his pipe and book matches. Pouch of aromatic. He leans back, studying Forest as he walks the black briar around his teeth. He says, "What you got in there in that room of yours anyway? You sneakin' some beautiful babe up through the windows up there? Marilyn . . . I mean . . . excuse me . . . Meredith with the sweaters? 'Twould be hard considering the height of a Colonial roof . . . but possible. Rope or something. Big ladder. Bed sheets." He chuckles. "In that fairy tale the lady used her hair. *Your* hair ain't long enough yet."

Little, straight-backed Bett works her fork through her plate of stew, the table so small and Forest so close, he thinks he can smell the raw onion and chlorine bleach of her hands. And from her springtime print housedress there's still a hint of the morning's hot iron smell. Her silence is terrible.

Forest says into F.D.'s eyes, "Nothing in there but me . . . my space."

"Your room's a wreck," says F.D. Even as he speaks this insult, his expression and gestures are like a blessing given . . . packing the tobacco into the bowl, striking the match . . . then pointing toward the ceiling with his pipestem.

"Well, I'm moving out anyway . . . eventually. So you don't need to put up with me much longer."

"In the meantime, your room will crawl away." F.D. stares up at the ceiling, puffing, considering . . . visualizing. "I can hear things sometimes . . . little signals . . ."

Bett cries out, "Oh, Forest!" the name she uses for F.D. at such times. "It's not *that* bad."

"Yes 'tis," F.D. insists.

Bett says to the son, Forest, "Dear, you don't need to do laundry. Just pile it outside your door and I'll get it from there."

"I don't want somebody else to even handle my clothes. Wouldn't it embarrass you, Mum, if somebody was feeling *your* personal clothes?"

She smiles sadly. "But I've *always* done your clothes. I don't really think about it. I've just always done them. You are *part* of me . . . not some person off the street. You were my baby once."

F.D. giggles. "Well . . . there's also the matter of Forest's own personal saliva on that there dish, Mum. Therefore, seems he'd be offerin' to do dishes."

Forest says nothing.

F.D. speaks around his pipestem. "What's happening here is nature, I guess."

Bett beseeches, "Will you wash your clothes every few days and not let them pile up in there? That's all I ask . . . that you keep them going through regular and be sure to empty your pockets . . . especially paper . . . *especially* Kleenexes. They will wind up stuck all over everything. And please don't overdo the detergent . . . a little goes a long way . . . otherwise the suds . . ."

"I'm moving out anyway," Forest interrupts. "So it doesn't matter. I'll be gone. Nothing from me will mess up this house. Not even one tiny speck of dandruff. You won't have to worry."

"Where will you be going?" Bett wonders. "In town?"

"I haven't got a place yet. I just know I'm getting out of here."

Smoke rolls along over the plates and cups and silverware, white considerable balls of smoke, like what artillery made over battlefields of the past . . . mixing with the cookie smell and the bleach smell and the ironed dress smell, and the brown stew smell, the good smells of the good life.

11 It has been a long time, this King business. King isn't so young, though it's hard to tell the old-age gray in his beard from what always was. That gray of his schnauzer half. Forest recalls a few years ago, still in high school, he and some others fished the brook behind the mill, then followed it to the river and the locks to the mill parking lot. And there was King. Not the pink truck then. It was a Dodge . . . blue or black or both. With bad cab mounts. The thing listed. King was on his stack of chair cushions. He wore some other college shirt, not Bowdoin. Maybe Yale. King stared at one of the mill's doors. A buddy of Forest's stood at the truck window to block King's view. King just moved a bit to the left, keeping his eye on the mill, that door, that long bank of many-paned windows where machinery clattered and thrummed. There were treats all around on King's top cushion. Little bone shapes. The ones that come in colors. But King wasn't being sidetracked by those either. There was a bright manly anguish in his eyes. For perhaps King always believed that when David Turnbull was out of view, David Turnbull ceased to exist.

12 | A new day. Almost dawn. Headed along the broad upstairs hallway, F.D. passes the closed door of Forest's room and gives his usual good-morning rap of the knuckles and his usual "Rise and shine!"

A sign taped there now. Seems to have appeared in the night. Skull and crossbones like what's on packages of poison. The skull is drawn in black Flair pen . . . little cracks at the temples . . . a couple of teeth broken off. Sign reads: BOTHER THIS ROOM AND YOU WILL BE VERY SORRY.

F.D. chuckles good-naturedly. Seems he himself had done something similar years ago. Right in that very same room. His younger brothers always scouting for pennies he kept in a pile on his dresser. They'd even go into his pockets if pants were left over the bedrail. And of course, there were his magazines. Though nowadays they are of a variety to make a grown *man* faint, let alone bother Bett. Maybe the kid just wants to spare Bett. But more likely it's belligerence.

It is nothing new. Just the way it goes. Hormones. Experts tell you about it. All kids go through it. Some earlier. Some later. All parents take the blows. Nature. You can't get around nature. He swings around the high newel post and takes the steps down, two at a time, whistling.

13 | Alone in his bed in the room of sailboats wallpaper, Forest stares at the closed door. It is not just that he might get caught in the act. It's not just the piles of sticky socks and shirts. It's not that so much. No. It is just *them*, Bett and F.D. What must be protected from them is this space around him from his skin to the wall, that thin outer air, cool of the long night. There are times when he thinks if one of them ever touches him again, he would smack that hand away. Then now and again he wishes more than anything to be cradled. IT, whatever it is, jerks him from left to right . . . those deep ruddy howls of the men at Moody's . . . and F.D.'s crew talking from the corners of their mouths, walking from the knees, hunching like coyotes with their backs up.

It is the young girls that his imagination sees in all his waking and into sleep. They strive to the absolute blackest edges of his mind, their bodies jouncing, ripplish. Long legs flopping open like the legs of antelopes whose middles are being devoured. But through their narrow-eyed scrutiny and bitter smoke and buzzing fluorescent light, it is the Egypt wise men who have him by the balls.

14 Another supper. Young Forest is quiet, tired-looking. Bett urges him to go to bed early. He nods. Agreeable.

F.D. says, "What's this I hear about you and a couple of buck goats over on the lake?"

So, finally the story has come full circle, puffing and fluffing and bristling, to go on and on, down through the ages.

Forest gives F.D. a damning look.

F.D. eases back in his chair, splits open a dark muffin on its saucer. "It's just something I heard over at the salvage," says F.D. with a sigh. He just wants his boy to laugh with him. What would it take?

15 "Where are you?"

"I'm over to Patty's." Squawks and tee-hees. Definitely Patty's.

"Patty's crazy," says Forest.

Meredith whispers away from the phone. More squawking and giggles. Then, "Forest! Guess where we're driving to!"

"Wichita. I mean *near* Wichita," Forest replies grimly.

Giggles. Whispers. Giggles. "No, silly. We are going to Florida. It's break. We're all going."

"Tight squeeze in the old Volvo," says he.

"Forest? Can't you get some time off from your father . . . and . . . drive us down? It's just me and Donna and Judy. Patty can't go. So can you? Can you be our *prince?!!*"

He says slowly, "I'll know by tomorrow night, okay?"

"Is he there? Ask him now!"

"I don't have to ask him. I just have to make the time."

"You wouldn't believe the beaches down there . . . and with your skin, you'll be black! Don't forget, Forest, to bring summer clothes . . . not those Eskimo outfits and Paul Bunyan things you usually wear."

"Yep."

She gives the phone mouthpiece a big smooch.

He says, "Yep," then wishes to replace the "yep" with something else. What? A kiss? A dark sickness explodes in his gut. He guesses the best reply to Meredith's kiss would be something like "Yes, baby, gotcha" . . . but now he is totally silent and she says "Bye now" and he says "See ya later."

16 | Seems at the oddest times the biker David Turnbull has popped into Forest's mind. Often. There is something about the guy that is like a burr riding on your pants cuff. Or a dropped smashed cup, a wrong note, a window left open.

17 | She has made cookies for "my two men." Bett and her cookies. "Cookie genius," F.D. says with his relentless grin.

Forest breaks up a bunch of them into a bowl of milk. "These are pretty good." He holds one up into the direct line of F.D.'s gaze as if the cookie were a winning number.

Bett reaches to pat Forest's bare arm below his T-shirt sleeve, her temperature and his temperature the same, like two synchronized clocks, arriving at this warm high noon in the same split second, sweeping second hands rising. He lets her hand remain there with its little urgent grip. He tosses the cookie into the milk whole. Regards it. "It floats," he says nervously.

18 | Forest watches the smoke moving in tatters out of the darkness of Mrs. Laurie Gould's throat. Laurie Gould. Too much forehead . . . like her babies. Stick-out ears. The Verrill family trait mixed with Moody. If you're a Verrill or even part Verrill, you probably would look like a milk-anemic year-old baby till the day you die.

She asks him about Florida. He has nothing to tell about it, just how it took them two days and two nights to get there. He watches a customer sidling out from one of the short crampy aisles, stooping to fetch a magazine. Stranger wears a silky shirt and very long hair, frothing and blond, an extremely handsome square-jawed face. Not a biker. Not a hippie. A guy who thinks he's a rock star or something. The car outside the door is a Cadillac . . . this year's. There's a group of heads silhouetted, front seat and backseat. Maybe he *is* a rock star.

Laurie makes a face, reading Forest's mind. He reads her face, replies by smiling smirkily. Laurie smokes. She has nothing new lately to tell Forest. She fiddles with a ball-point pen. The coolers hum. The stranger thumbs through a magazine. By his foot are three six-packs of Canadian ale.

The first thing to start shaking is the air. Then it's the floor and legs of the stool and chair. Three Harleys rumbling to a stop at the four-way. One rider is David Turnbull, milk crate roped to the seat behind him. That's King's crate. King's yellow hooded sweat shirt is laced under the chin. Gives his head a bit of a point. Very small sweat shirt. All his clothes are about size 2. His eyebrows and graying moustaches flicker and flatten into the wind as the dressed-out Harley picks up speed and makes its godlike thunder past Moody's Variety & Lunch on its way to adventure and depravity.

Laurie sees what Forest is looking at. She says, "Little shithead growled at me. I picked him up to give him a little doggie smooch and he bore his teeth and growled. And so you know what David says to me? He says, 'Oh, he don't like people in his face.' " She twitches her nose.

"You shouldn't be all the time kissing dogs," Forest says grimly.

"Well, most dogs *like* love," she insists, spewing out smoke, then getting her sulky look. "But *that* one has illusions of grandeur."

He watches her force more smoke out between her strong large crowded cream-color teeth.

"You are too easy with your kisses," he says. And he grips her by the arms, her stool nearly tipping . . . gives her a hard, hard kiss . . . the kind that makes a purplish mouth more purplish.

She watches the back of his dark blue work shirt as he swings out around the counter, out through the glass door. She mashes her cigarette into the loaded pie plate and says "Hi" to the stranger who arranges many bills on the counter for the magazine and ale. And now change. The exact change. Then briskly he departs without a word as most strangers do.

19 | First hot night of the year. Big hubbub at the covered bridge.
      Forest and the new driver Len Moore show up in a pickup on the Egypt side of the river. Lettered on the truck's doors is FOREST JOHNSON, SR., & SON. BACKHOE & DOZING. SAND & LOAM. EGYPT, MAINE. 625-8693.

Bikers are hanging out along the guardrails. David Turnbull with his splotchy pickup and other bikers with their Harleys. No Hondas. No way. A few other trucks and cars on the shoulder by the woods. Radio whooping and bellering. Bikers leaning around David Turnbull's truck, jiggling a leg to the guitars, wagging heads to the drums. Someone groans "way to go" to the PLASH! of a kid cannonballing it off the bridge.

Len speaks solemnly. "There's Turnbull . . . the one that was in Nam. Only *he* got out early . . . before his time was up. Something *without* honor . . . something . . ." He rubs his chin. "I forgot now . . ." He whispers to himself. "*Something.*"

Once they've stepped out of the truck, Len Moore says to a kid with a fenderless bicycle, "We are here from the Town . . ." He winks at Forest. "Here on surveillance . . . making sure you brats aren't ripping more historic boards off the bridge."

"That's right. We're official," Forest says with his most dangerous-looking stare.

"You guys are only supposed to worry about the Egypt side," the kid retorts and spits on the pavement.

"We're official *everywhere*," says Len Moore. "Try us."

"We have powers of eminent domain," Forest says.

"We can confiscate your bike and your wallet . . . and everything in your pockets. Strip you clean," Len Moore says.

"And powers of extradition," Forest says.

"We can have you handcuffed and brought over to the Egypt side by state authority and keep you in a cell without windows till your trial."

The kid shrugs this off and disappears into the warm dark, into the bridge where the other kids are silently eavesdropping.

Forest and Len stride over to the motorcycles and the faded pink truck.

David Turnbull is not as bushy headed as a biker should be. Though the moustache is heavy, a disgorgement of sorts, the beard is trim. A bad short haircut. Like hair that's been scissored off by a poorly sighted old mother. The mill's personnel manager doesn't like long hair or big beards. But David Turnbull isn't going so far as to make it all real pretty for him. David Turnbull. Covered over every visible and much of his nonvisible skin below the neck with tattoos. One homemade one that says I DIED IN WANDA'S ARMS, though his wife's name is Kit. But the rest of the tattoos are pro. A real nicely done housefly big as a hand. A red maple leaf. And lots more . . . especially insects. No American flags. And no references to his time in Vietnam.

Other Turnbulls on hand tonight. Macky Turnbull and George Turnbull and Willie Turnbull, all full-blown bikers. In silhouette against headlights and lighted dashes, they all have heads like lions. Most Turnbulls are six foot two and over. A lot of hardware here. Chunky. A sobering sight.

Len Moore nods up at David Turnbull.

David Turnbull nods back.

Macky Turnbull offers Forest and Len Moore a couple of Budweisers. They accept.

Len Moore looks into the pink truck and sees King on his stack of sofa cushions. "That your dog?" Len wonders, pressing his unopened beer to the side of his neck and face to get a nice cooling.

"That's King," David Turnbull informs him. David Turnbull's arms are folded across his chest. Sleeveless unbuttoned denim vest. Tattoos in the night's shadows are undecipherable. Kind of ghastly. Like bloody abrasions. They leap to Len Moore's eye.

Len Moore asks, "What kind of dog's that anyway?"

"Twenty-one pound Schnoodle."

Len Moore snorts. "Well, he's okay. But myself, I like Dobies."

David Turnbull's eyes gleam with reflections and a good buzz. "Zat right?" says he.

"Where's his clothes?" Forest asks.

"He doesn't wear clothes in the heat," David Turnbull says quietly, swigs from his beer, smiles around at the other bikers, then adds, "Like Macky. Right, Macky?"

Macky haw-haws over this. Macky heavily layered, denim over denim and a short leather vest, visored leather cap, a sheathed knife almost to the side of his knee, tall boots . . . a single spur.

Len Moore pats King. Lounging on his cushions, King disregards Len Moore, just stares off toward the river, nose twitching peacefully . . . everything nice on the night air for King's nose.

David Turnbull unfolds the long thickly muscled splotched arms and says, "Want to see him do Wildman?"

Len Moore simpers. "Yeah. Get him to be a wildman." He rolls his eyes. He doesn't withdraw his hand and arm, but keeps his fingers rested lightly on the steering wheel.

David Turnbull speaks to King over Len Moore's shoulder. "King."

King turns his head, looks into David Turnbull's eyes.

"King, listen man." David pauses. "Be . . . Wild . . . Man . . ."

King flash-leaps to his feet, back and tail stiff as iron, lips pulled high. Fangs. Eyes slitted. Snarling. As King lunges, the snarl increases. King lunges again . . . all this so sudden, Len jerks his arm away, stumbles back. "Jesus Christ, you little twerp! Don't get too wild with me!" he says pissed-offishly. But King keeps making his lunges, snarling nonstop.

Bikers and associates of bikers chuckle peacefully and pleasantly.

David Turnbull says, "Okay, King. Rest."

King drops to his cushions, panting.

David Turnbull says, "Good man, King," reaches in to smooth out some of the ruffled hair on King's head.

Len Moore says angrily, "A dog like that . . . you should smack him. Put him in his place. I wouldn't put up with shit like that."

David Turnbull drinks from his beer, ignores this, turns toward his friends now.

King also ignores this, has gone back to a leisurely position on his cushions, head raised, sniffing the nice night.

Len moves on, his pale frizzed hair swirling around his head. Forest turns and leaves with him. Len is chortling. "Only one thing one of them's good for is to wet on your leg. A good Dobie would rip that puny thing's head off."

20 | Two kinds of baked beans. Bett's that are made with molasses. And those with brown sugar that Aunt Pauline brought. Aunt Pauline's beans have a paler juice.

Aunt Pauline and F.D. do all the talking. Both of them talk a blue streak. Sometimes they argue. Knowing the same stories, but she knowing them one way, he knowing them another way.

Bett wears one of her special dresses with little belt of matching rose-bud material. Bit of rose to her cheeks. It's not makeup. A flush is natural to her in the heat. Some would say her bejeweled pin at the throat is not a thing to wear with a pale summer dress. She gazes off toward the light of the low dining-room windows . . . this a dark room, nothing like the bright many-windowed kitchen. Here the only two windows are in the big grip of old lilacs gone rampant. Bett is smiling. Looking superior? Or content? Which is which?

Forest breaks open a swollen boiled hot dog with his fork. Suddenly he smells it . . . goat. He spits the beans and bread into his plate.

"Forest!" Bett squeals.

F.D. and Aunt Pauline cut off their conversation, eyes blinking on Forest.

Forest rises from his chair, eyes on Bett's face, one the gentle eye of the son, the other a stranger's.

F.D. asks, "Break a tooth?"

Forest says, "Excuse me," and walks with dignity from the room, out through the kitchen to the glassed-in back porch office. He knows it was only the new leather odor of Aunt Pauline's pocketbook so near him on the windowsill. He knew it before he rose from his chair. It was just that by then, every artery was on fire, pushing him. Now from the long wall of the office, heads of the deer all stare down at him. Ten heads. F.D.'s first ten bucks. No room for more. All that grandiose spiraling weaponry of eight and twelve points, once their claim to the highest laws of their world. Now just these sweet grandmotherly smiles. And eyes that need dusting.

Out on the back step Forest sits with chin in hand, digging a work boot heel around in the dirt. The silver-edged green evening is way too warm, but smells fresh . . . watery . . . clean. He sniffs his hands. They smell like butter and beans and mustard and fatty hot dog. These supper smells . . . more power over him than the embarrassment caused by the goat. These supper smells . . . mother smell . . . father smell. And all that in-between smell . . . smell of his own shirt and hair . . . not a buck goat exactly, but something like a buck goat would feel . . . full of pizzazz and stubbornness and fight . . . and the wish to overpower *them*.

21 He's in there. Water thundering. Doesn't hear her tap-tap on the bathroom door.

"PHONE!" Bett tries to be heard. Now she raps harder with her knuckles. "FORRRREST! TELEPHONE!!!"

Back at the phone, Bett asks, "Can Forest call you back, dear?"

Meredith says a soft yes.

22 Next night Meredith calls again.
This time Forest is handy.

Meredith says nothing about his not returning last night's call. She suggests driving down to Plum Island on the coming weekend. She has friends there. "Older than us. George is almost thirty! Brian and Carleen are even older than that. You just have to put up with a little bit of dull stuff till they get a few piña coladas in them . . . and later tequila. Then they are apt to do anything. Recite Shakespeare in funny voices . . . play tricks on the neighbors . . . and they like to sing."

He is quiet. But she's used to that. She's never known anyone so moody.

She says, "You'll love Plum Island. We can get some sun. They say the weekend will be good."

Forest says maybe.

"Say yes," she says prayerfully.

He says yes.

23 | Bett has her pale hair set in a wave that looks as solid as knuckles. Whenever she's just returned from the hairdresser, her posture is especially erect, her arms and hands move self-consciously. Supper is deer meat. Baked potatoes. String beans. Muffin. Orangy farm butter that Aunt Pauline brought on her recent visit.

F.D. is flushed, talky, gloinking cream into his coffee. "This one's your buck, Forest, ain't it?"

"Yes," Bett answers for him.

"It's gamier than my doe," F.D. observes.

Forest takes a gouge out of the oval of bright butter with his knife.

F.D. says, "Gamy is best. I like gamy. Otherwise might as well be eating a steer." F.D. savors the meat, eyes closed. Eyes pop open. His eyes look their bluest when he's feeling this merry. "Remember that feller up to Norridgewock . . . somewheres up that way . . . fired at what he thought was a deer's flag. 'Twas a little ghost a kid hung from a tree in his yard, made with a piece of sheet." F.D. shakes his head and giggles. "A guy as stupid as that ought to be hung by his acorns."

"Oh, stop," Bett chides.

F.D. grins, chomps into another thickness of meat.

Forest doesn't look up, but he's smiling into his plate.

F.D.'s voice rises an octave. And louder. Faster. "I tell people, you know . . . that my boy . . . he gets a deer *every* year. Usually within the first couple days. A deer a year since he was *twelve*. You don't see Thanksgiving roll around with him out trudging around keeping the family occasion held up. Between the two of us, Forest, you and I put some mighty fine meat on this table. Enough to keep us going all year. And plenty to give away!!"

Forest says, "Well . . . I've gotten pretty lucky."

Bett looks vaguely off through the windows to the quiet intersection by Moody's. A smile. It's hard to tell if she's smiling about this conversation or something concerning her "day." Maybe something the hairdresser said about Bett's hair or head.

"Don't be so christly modest!" shrieks F.D. "You're a damn good sharpshooter. It's second nature to you." He leans over his plate and seizes Forest by the upper arm and hisses, "Somewhere there is a guy settin' with his family tonight . . . eating a kid's *ghost*."

24 | It could be what they call the recurring dream only he's not asleep when the scene unfurls in blacks and whites and pinks, shivering across his eyelids. Alone in his bedroom of sailboats wallpaper, alone in the dark of too many midnights, he *sees*. The rape. It has fused to him like a tight glove, tight sleeve. She would have been alone one day when Edmund Barrington came around with some pretense to get inside this house. Edmund Barrington who is known for his affairs . . . his way with women. But Forest can't, in all his imaginings, imagine his mother with a lover, a passionate affair. A *permission*. He can't imagine her with anyone that way. She would not *reach* out. She would not be anything but that densely puny pink-cored high-ground hardwood that has taken root forever at the center of this house. Forest has begun to painstakingly wonder the ways Edmund Barrington could permeate this house and in some imaginings Edmund Barrington is at every window all at once. An army! Wouldn't it take an army????? Then the bulkhead. The back door, the front. KNOCK! KNOCK! KNOCK! HELLO! HELLO! Forest has gathered strength now to actually imagine the struggle. The black of the room. The white. His mother's legs. He imagines it hundreds of times even as it sickens and suffocates him. He starts to imagine it again. And again. For it is, above all else, a comfort.

25 | She is fourteen. She looks twelve. She smells of her parents' home, a lot of smokers. Not just her own two packs of Viceroys a day, but all the different brands of smoke of their household, gushing, glancing, mixing, tribal, ceremonious.

Her shirt and corduroys and Hush Puppies could be interchanged with her brothers'. She has never had long hair. She says her old man cuts it with scissors from the shed. DULLLL. They hold her down like a pig or calf to cut it, she explains. "I always fight 'em," she says. Once she got a poked eye. Her hair is dirty blond or brown depending on the light of day. Her eyes and skin are silver.

"Get you cleaned up" is what she says her old man says. "Save the principal the trouble." A lot of controversy over hair these days. Some say hair is wrong. Others say it's right. Principal says hair is "sloppy." And jeans are "sloppy." School needs tougher dress codes, the principal says. Kids say hair and jeans are "in." Christine's father has no opinions on jeans. But hair is for "whores and thieves and livestock," says he.

Christine loves Forest. Christine has loved Forest for a week and a half. She writes his name with a pen on her arm. She says when they get married, she will get some cats. Her father hates cats. She has always wanted a cat. "When a person is married, she can have as many cats as she wants," Christine tells Forest with a great guffaw and out comes the smoke . . . straightforward, no coquettish puffs and vespers. Forest pictures living with Christine and ten cats in holy matrimony. He likes to picture her old man's rage. He wonders if there's a state where you can still marry a fourteen year old.

F.D. has a little talk with Forest. "What happened to Meredith? The one that was *developed*?"

Forest says, "Home, I guess."

26 | Christine calls and asks for Forest. She has the deep and hearty voice of a young man.

"Forest, Senior, or Forest, Junior?" Bett inquires. She surmises this might be a customer of the business.

Christine laughs huskily. "Yoooo knowwww." She is trying to get Bett to shape up, to catch on. She holds out. No name. Just her throaty appeals to "fetch him off his perch."

But Bett holds out, too. She explains one Forest is outdoor, the other one indoor. Bett's voice shows no irritation. Just rock-hard resolve.

Christine says, "The big dark hunk."

Bett says, "You mean Forest, Junior, then."

When Forest reaches the phone he and Christine talk for over an hour. Christine rails about her old man. What a jerk, she says. He's kicking

Nicky out, she tells him. Nicky, the oldest brother, who when Forest has seen him around also looks like a twelve year old.

Christine says that when she and Forest get married, she will bring her younger brothers and sisters to live with them. Randy especially. Poor Randy. And she can fix Julie and Kathy's hair long and in bows. "My old man will shit a brick!" she hoots.

Forest holds the phone away during this hoot. He likes to imagine Christine's old man shitting a brick.

27 | Meredith calls. She says Plum Island turned out bad. He didn't miss anything. Almost nobody showed up. And it turned out to be too chilly to work on a tan. But there will be other times, she assures him. "We can go in a couple of months. They start renting that place in June for the whole summer."

He keeps quiet.

Now she is quiet, too. The line could be dead. She asks if his tan from Florida is fading.

He says he hasn't looked.

She says, "That just shows you how long it's been since I've seen you if your skin has had time to go back completely to what it was!"

He chuckles.

"Tans don't last long actually," she says softly.

He says that working outside he has probably got more tan which replaced and overlapped the old tan and it would be hard to sort out what part was from the trip and what part was from work.

She says it looks like her finals are all going to be easy this year. All essays. The kind you can bluff your way through.

He twirls the phone cord.

She asks if he heard about the P.O.W.'s on the news and he says yes.

"That's really terrible," she says sadly. "They will probably die. Maybe they are already dead." She says she hates to think about torture.

28 | Another night at the covered bridge. No bikers. Forest backs the pickup with deftness snug against the guardrail. Forest is plainly the oldest here tonight.

A lot of girlish giggling inside the bridge and the husky crowing of boys.

PLACK-SHHHHHH! Someone hits the water belly-down.

Beside Forest on the seat, Christine does a shrill two-finger whistle out the window. Someone inside the bridge whistles back. Then another. And another.

Christine can't get the door open against the guardrail. She hurries Forest with a shove, then bails out around him. He tells her irritably to take it easy. She pauses to get a sip from his beer. Then she's gone, received with cheers, shrieks, and groans into the depths of the bridge.

Trudging up into its arched open end, he sees there's a few more historical boards pried off to make a wider hatch for diving. There's a lot of girls here in bikinis and halter tops. Prints, polka dots, plain. None of them seem wet. And no wet hair. Just a lot of prancing, stretching, wriggling, elongated self-conscious sighs and breathlessness. A kid swishes past on a bicycle, smacks Forest's arm, hollers, "FIRE! CRACKERS! FOR! SALE! M-EIGHTIES and REGULARS!"

Forest is trying to locate Christine in the light that is only red-hot eyes of cigarettes and joints of marijuana and the shrinking brownish stubbly moon riding on the water below.

"What's that you got there, Louie?" one of the older boys asks the kid on the bicycle.

An older boy chuckles gruffly. "He's got contraband, John."

"Hey, Louie! Get over here! I want some!" orders the prospective customer.

Forest gulps some beer.

A guy from Promise Lake asks Forest, "Howzit goin'?"

Forest says, good.

The guy asks Forest if he's seen much of St. Pierre since he graduated.

Forest says, "No. Just around."

"Same here," says the guy. "What about Hines and Graffam?"

"Never see 'em."

"Me neither," says the guy. The guy smells wet and riverish. One of the few who hangs out here to *really* swim.

"Can this contraband be smoked?" the potential customer is wondering.

"Sure!" some older boys chorus.

Kid with the bicycle is feeling around in his saddlebags.

Lots of evil giggles and wild hysterics.

"Blanchard's gonna toke up fireworks. Get ready," someone warns.

Some of them are moving away. Plenty of room inside the bridge, lots of pitch black unclaimed territory.

"Toke it up!" someone urges.

The customer pays with a paper bill, then places the firecracker in his lips, fuse out. "Let's see here," he says. He lights it with a book match and the fuse hisses brightly. Everyone jumps away. Some pushing others. Ramming. A few shrieks. The customer gives his head a toss. The BANG! of white light is not far from his face, illuminating his big grin. Screams and nervous snickers from all directions. "Now that's what I call a buzz," the customer says.

"A regular lift-off!" bawls one of the others.

This cracks Forest up. He laughs along. Feeling good.

PLASH! Another diver doing a jackknife or something, maybe feet first. PLASH! PLASH! Dangerously close together. Everything dangerous. Dark. Exploding.

Now the headlights of a vehicle bearing down from the hill, slowing at the bridge.

"CAR!" someone yells.

Nobody moves much. Just a little space for the car to come through all that density of bared arms and legs and bikini'd rumps.

"GET OUT OF THE WAY, BRATS!" the driver of the car barks.

"SUCK MY COCK!" screams one of the older boys.

Kid on the bicycle says to Forest, "Give me the rest of your beer and I'll give you all the M-Eighties I got left."

Forest gives the kid his most imperious sneer, then turns to watch the car leaving at the other end of the tunnel, all the faces and bareness of bodies red, fading to pink as the taillights move on.

Somebody lands on Forest's back. He makes a grab at whoever it is, whips around, ready to fight. It's Christine. She says, "I need a sip!"

"Not many sips left," says he, breathing hard from his scare.

"One for me," she says and works the beer out of his grip.

Headlights moving fast from the Egypt side, maybe the same car coming back to make trouble. Christine pitches the empty out through the diving hatch into the river.

"CAR!" somebody shouts.

"Maybe it's the constable," a girl's voice says grimly.

"CONSTABLE! IT'S THE CONSTABLE!"

"Stop the constable," Christine says low.

"Ain't the constable!" cries someone from the far end.

Car speeding up.

Christine says gruffly and close to Forest's ear, "Watch."

Car getting faster, headlights explode onto the bridge, tires thumping, punching each broad board. Engine full of thunder.

"TRANS AM!" a boy yodels.

Kids flatten themselves against the bridge walls.

Christine announces, "Watch guys." Steps into the middle of the passage, throws her hand out traffic cop style. "STOP," she commands. Then she adds solemnly, "They usually do stop."

Trans Am bearing down, headlights full of thunder, engine full of light.

"DON'T CHRISTINE!" one of her dearest girlfriends gasps.

"My god!" another says faintly.

Screams.

Light fills all dark. In the middle of it there's Christine with her blousey wrinkled shorts and silver eyes.

Trans Am's brakes make a hyena screech. Trans Am fishtails, its rear fenders tapping one bridge wall, then the other . . . tunk! . . . clank! . . . kids running.

Trans Am's complete cessation of movement adjoins Christine's outstretched palm, a kind of rough kiss, gives the hand a little jostle there. Engine stalls.

Christine squints reproachfully at the windshield, at the place where a face would show if the glass weren't so tinted and it weren't night. There's no shout from the Trans Am's window. And nobody from the group of teenagers shouts obscenities at the Trans Am.

When Christine finally allows the Trans Am to proceed, Forest grabs her by the wrists and says in a fatherly way, "Don't ever wanna see you doin' that again."

29 | The moon is shrinking, the night less peopled, less astonishing.

Christine is alone with Forest in the truck that has lettering on the doors.

Christine sleepy.

Forest not sleepy.

Christine has smoked up all her cigarettes. The radio stations have faded and they mix. But Christine keeps wiggling the knob, trying to track down "something decent."

He makes his move.

She says, "What are you doing?"

He says, "Opening your shirt."

She clamps her hands over his. "No way, Ho-zay."

He says, "Why not?"

She laughs and says, "You are an animal."

He says, "I just want to love you."

She flutters her silvery eyes. "Horseshit . . . you call that lovin'?! I call that feelin'. Then comes fuckin'. You are an animal."

He feels like one of those eared cat balloons inflated with too much helium, skin thinned to bursting point. He takes her hands, both of her hands fitting into one of his.

She jerks her hands back. She spits. Wetness lands on his shirt front.

A split second for him to react with the heel of his hand to her collarbone, knocking her back against the door handle, back of her head flung to her left, thwonking the cab and his shouting, "QUIT THE SHIT!!"

"YOU quit the shit!!" she shouts. She grabs the sleeve of his work shirt and yanks. The seams screech open.

Forest lands on top of her with his forearm against her throat. He has never been so horny in his life. No suave flirtations nor pretty nuzzlings could ever occasion this diamond-hard glut.

But she, Christine, she's never been so boneless, scared, dispassioned. Her right hand appears. Greenish in this dashboard light. Sweet wrist. Fingers working a buck knife open.

Within seconds Forest is back behind the wheel wiping his hair back off his sweating face and temples. He starts the engine.

She holds the knife like this all the way home.

30 | When Christine calls, she always times it right. Seems she has a hidden camera here. It's when he lays his fork down after one of Bett's great pies. Or washes down the last cookie. Then the phone jangles on the wall and F.D., without looking up from his plate, says with amusement, "I wonder who that could be for?"

In hoarse desperation, Forest had told his father one night: "You look stupid."

Sometimes Christine talks about the wedding they will have and their life. She has it planned to the letter. She has already got some recipes stashed. Her aunt gave her one for a great blackberry pie using orange peels. "And I'll hunt up some pans," says she. Also she has names for the cats all ready to go. The first one will be Mike. "But if we have some kids before that, we ought to use Mike on a kid. I always liked the name Mike. Don't you?" Is this a kind of promise that she'll eventually leave her buck knife home?

Then some nights there isn't really a conversation, just Christine's smoking sounds and her hollering at her younger brothers and sisters and her gasping into the phone receiver, "This is such a friggin' madhouse!"

31 | Forest dreams of the blackberry pie she makes, her small dangerous hands making a tornado of the flour. Then the pie is done. Like in the nursery rhyme, something bursts out of it when she cuts into it . . . something like blackbirds . . . alive and noisy and smart-assed. And a sourish steam, like the abdomen of a deer being split open to November cold. But in the dream, he feels there's nothing unusual about this.

32 | Christine doesn't call for days.
He calls her but gets only deep-voiced toddlers who leave the phone receiver on the floor or something.

He drives past Christine's place, but the father's Plymouth is in the yard.

Forest lies in his bed in the room of sailboats wallpaper. It's the room F.D. had as a boy. And before F.D. it was one of F.D.'s mother's brothers who became a state legislator. Wallpaper for a child. It wears on Forest's nerves sometimes.

Tonight he thinks about roads. It seems that the well-being of Egypt roads gets heavier and heavier on his mind these days, the knowledge that winters will always come, the vast and indefatigable snows, deep as seas . . . to be pushed and rammed, cleared away again and again and again . . . to be done . . . and yet never done . . . always another snow, another mess requiring his vigilance. Then spring. Posting and flagging. Then summer. Patching and grading. Moving earth. Breaking ground for new homes. The backhoe's clasp more terrible than twenty men's, twenty men like Christine's father. Boulders, stumps, stone walls, red ledge, gray ledge, and clay, all of it flicked to one side with the pull and push of his own hands on the levers.

33 | The conversation at Moody's tonight is on "danger." "What is the most dangerous thing in the woods?" F.D. asks, eyes gleaming.

"Bear," says Ron Bean.

F.D. shakes his head.

Clarence Farrington and the other older wise men keep their silence, squinting at their hands.

"Yellow jackets," offers young Gary Moody.

"Wrong!" says F.D.

Forest stands against the bulletin wall smiling because he knows the answer, a previously "discussed" topic at the salvage yard two days ago and again "discussed" at the shop bays this morning. F.D. is really titillated by this special brand of danger, his voice especially chirpy.

"A woman!" F.D. at last reveals.

This cracks all the guys up.

"Didn't you fellas read about that gal up to Stacyville . . . Patten . . . somewhere up there? Gentleman was out deer hunting and she's lettin' her little doggie out to wet on a weed an' what not. 'Twas a black dog, kind of blended with his surroundings. Scottie dog, I think it 'twas. The kind you are supposed to keep in your *lap*."

Chuckles and snorts of disdain.

"Well, the doggie gets shot. Mistook for a deer . . . yard being full of trees. Honest mistake 'n' all. *Stupid*, but honest."

Albion Cole clears his throat. "Mistook for a *deer?*"

"Yes. Like I say . . . yard was full of trees. People had their house situated *in the woods*." F.D. is smiling, waiting for the appropriate silence from his audience.

Silence.

"So the dog's blown ta hell, but still yippin' and jerkin' . . . probably nerves. But the woman comes running out and *attacked* the feller and busted his jaw!"

Chuckles.

F.D.'s eyes sparkle. "She was only five foot two, it 'twas told in the article. Five foot two! And the guy was a six footer!"

"Five foot tooooo . . . eyeza bloooo . . . gootchie-gootchie-gooootchie goooo! . . . has anybod . . ." As Ray Dyer sings, all the wise men and young men wince with pain.

F.D. waits for silence, drumming the fingers of his right hand on his knee.

Silence at last.

F.D. continues. "So the gentleman takes this crazy lady to court. She got fined for harassment and assault. But they suspended all her jail time. Being a lady. Guess they take getting emotional into consideration."

A few guys make whining noises and whimpers, a couple of high squeaks . . . their combined impersonations of emotion.

F.D. waits for silence, then tells them, "But you see, she's been set loose. She's still out there. She busted a guy's jaw, but the law took pity on *her*."

"Maybe a *few* weeks of jail wouldn't hurt her," Ron Bean says softly. "Not life or anything . . . but something to show her the law ain't to be laughed at."

34 | The news at the covered bridge tonight is that Christine Weber is in the hospital beat up.

"It was Mr. Hartford!" shrills one of Christine's close cronies. "He confessed and had blood all over him."

Gasps.

"Who's Mr. Hartford?" wonders one of the younger kids.

"Teacher at school."

Forest remembers Mr. Hartford. He, of course, wants to kill Mr. Hartford.

"It was something *sexual*," one of Christine's cronies confides.

"Lovers' quarrel," sighs another girl.

"Mr. Hartford's in trouble. Because practically everybody knows the teachers aren't supposed to fool around with students."

"Maybe he'll get fired."

"He'll be sent to the MOON!" yells one of the guys Forest saw getting off the bus a few weeks back.

"He was nice . . . mostly," says another older kid reminiscently.

"Mostly he's a jerk," snarls another one. "Good to see him go."

Very near Forest stands one of Christine's friends. Bikini with a print of silver sea horses with strings that are tied in slim swingy bows on each hip. The bows hold everything together. A rig you'd never see Christine be caught in. The girl says, "Christine's mother told me she was in a coma but is out of it now. Her mother says the real bad thing is her eye. Several ligaments."

"*Severed* ligaments, dummy!" the other friend quickly corrects her.

"Without ligaments, your eye hangs out," one boy explains.

"Shut up, Mike," one girl commands. "You are grossin' me out."

"Pop-eye!" one of the youngest boys trills.

The bikers a few yards away are mellow tonight.

David Turnbull has let King out into the bushes by the woods. King sniffs everything, pisses all over everything, kicks up dirt. He does all the truck and car wheels. All the Harley wheels. David Turnbull watches every move King makes with a tender gaze.

Car coming toward the bridge from the Egypt side. David Turnbull snatches King up, gets a critical grip on him with one vast tattooed arm. King keeps his dignified expression no matter what. His heavy moustaches and eyebrows and the darkness around his deep-set eyes give him a wise sage look which is altogether different from his Wildman look which is also different from his distaste-for-Republicans-in-Washington-D.C. look.

Headlights arrive within heartbeats. The vehicle's tires thump along the boards. The bridge fills with light. It is the constable. He doesn't stop to lecture tonight. Some nights he does. Some nights he doesn't.

35 | Alone in his bed in the room of sailboats Forest Johnson, Jr., sobs.

36 | Forest catches sight of orange among the trees of the Moore Road cemetery between the two abandoned Hubbard farmplaces. Trees and cellar holes and dappled light. It's Lloyd Barrington's old flatbed truck.

Silver paint is peeling from the cemetery gate. Gate opened wide.

As Forest takes his own truck up along the edge of the stone wall, he sees there's an open grave to his left. Pile of dirt on burlap. Lloyd Barrington is in the cab of his truck with his hat low over his eyes. He looks asleep.

Forest parks close behind. He slaps his truck door shut, a door that reads: FOREST JOHNSON, SR., & SON. BACKHOE & DOZING. SAND & LOAM.

Lloyd Barrington doesn't look up, but Forest can tell he's not asleep for there's something languidly moving in his left cheek. The orange truck isn't all orange. There's one blue door. And a lot of Bondo. Windows down. Butterflies go in and out as they like. Also deerflies and cut flies. Mean flies.

Forest puts both hands on the door and looks down at the paperback opened wide on the crotch of Lloyd's dungarees. Without looking up, Lloyd turns a page and says, "Heigh ho there."

"Somebody died, huh?" Forest says.

Lloyd raises his eyes, one green, the other splotched with brown. The rest of his face is a raging mixed-color beard. He's a skinny-legged young man but otherwise solid and terrier-built. His face isn't fat, but once you've known him as a fat kid, what you see superimposed is fat. Very trampled green crusher hat like a lot of them in Egypt wear, but hair like nobody who wants to get along in Egypt wears . . . very thick, tied-back hippie hair. Lloyd says, "Dead. Always dead."

"I set myself up for that one, huh?" Forest says, a little pissed off.

Lloyd lays the paperback open on the seat to mark his place. Butterflies grope at the windshield. Butterflies in midair around Lloyd's crusher. There's something unnatural about so many butterflies congregated. Lloyd says, "Willa Phillips from over to Harlan Prouxl Road."

Forest blinks.

Lloyd says, "Lived with her daughter, you know. Knights."

Forest blinks again, says, "Pardon?"

Lloyd flicks his eyes toward the grave. "Willa Phillips."

Forest says, "Oh! Right. The dead one."

Lloyd says, "Diabetes. A lot of them wind up with that."

Forest moves from his left foot to his right, still leaning into the truck with his hands as if to keep the truck from escape.

Lloyd says, "So howzit goin' with the road biz?"

Forest says, "Busy. We're also getting ready to break ground on that subdivision on the Across Road and then that big place over past Lucky's. But first the sub. Twelve foundations. You wouldn't recognize the place . . . pretty much all cut off. Stripped."

"I saw what they did," Lloyd says. Lloyd's eyes slide to the left, quick little sneaky glances at Forest, sizing up this new close-up view of Forest Johnson. The dark blue uniform work shirt. Black hair combed with water. Combed nice. A little long. A little bit of rebellion there.

Happens to so many guys once you get out of school . . . gotta let go somehow, gotta let out, expand, go bananas . . . it feels so good.

They were never friends at school, though they were always in the same grade. Forest never had much to do with any of that gang of Lloyd's cousins, Dougherties or Foggs, Foyes, Beans, and Plummers. Not that they were a clique. Not aloof or whispery like cliques. It's just that their kinship was monstrous. So many! Spilling over. Unwieldy. They could accidentally trample you.

Forest can't remember that Lloyd was any honor student. No debate clubs or school plays. No student council. No varsity this or varsity that. No hanging around after the bell rang. And yet here he is today at twenty, Edmund Barrington's college man.

Sociology is his major they say. Whatever the hell that is.

Clarence Farrington and other Moody's wise men say it's when you study Russia. They say a suit and tie is what he should be wearing not those grave-diggin', shit-shovelin' clothes. In the Kremlin they expect a suit. "He's not about to get any votes here in America," Clarence has said disgustedly. "I'm certainly not going to vote for the goddam little Commie. Nobody's going to take him but the Kremlin. Well, as I always say . . . America, love it or leave it . . . and leave fast."

A few guys at Moody's say that why Lloyd dresses like a grave-digger and so forth is that those are his spy clothes. This is always sure to get Clarence or Arch Vandermast in a rile.

But so far Clarence stays cool. He just says quietly from one side of his mouth, "Ain't nothing sneaky 'bout draft dodgers, flag burners and hippies, which is what college is all about."

Arch often adds, as a point of interest, "Commies have been behind all that protestin' shit. FBI is finally gettin' on to that."

"Some hippies are just bikers," Howe Letourneau says.

"Well," F.D. Johnson sums things up, "there's all kinds of hippies just like there was all kinds of Indians."

And they all had a nice laugh over F.D.'s wisdom.

Now here in the sun-dappled cemetery, Lloyd gives what resides in his left cheek a few contented chews. "Waiting for the vault man," he tells Forest. "He's a little late."

Forest turns, fixes his dark-eyed circumspection onto the open grave.

Lloyd moves his own eyes, so weirdly colored, up and down the buttons of Forest's shirt.

Forest looks back at him a few seconds. Eyes look into eyes, miserably locked, embarrassed, but unable to pull away.

Now there's the growl of a rigged truck on the hill and the whistling of several doves flushed from the roadside. The doves resettle in the low limbs of the maples nearby. Forest pales at the sight of the vault truck. His voice is too soft on his next words so his words are lost. He chokes and repeats himself. "You ever hear this? You ever hear this what I heard? Your old man being my old man? You ever hear that?"

Lloyd moves what's in his left cheek to his right cheek and chews solemnly, eyes on the rigged vault truck as it heaves itself over the crest of the hill. He says, "That's what I heard. Yuh."

Forest says with a squeak, trying his best to keep his voice audible this time, "In the old days they'd have lynched him for doing what he did, you know."

Lloyd says, "Well, yuh, or make the woman wear a big red letter *A* on her dress."

Forest raises his voice as the vault truck roars up toward the open gate. "Well . . . that would be for adultery. But then there's rape."

Lloyd looks at Forest, smiles kind of friendlyish. "Big mystery, huh?"

Forest scowls.

"Besides," Lloyd says, looking into the side mirror at the vault truck easing through the gate, "nowadays we are not so puritanical, us citizens. We are nicer."

37 Alone again in his bed in the room of sailboats, Forest Johnson, Jr., sobs.

38 Bett says she always loved school when she was a girl.

F.D. says that's because Bett is an arithmetic whiz. School would come easy to a genius like Bett. You give her some figures to add, a column of two- and three-digit numbers, she runs them around in her head, whispers to herself, then tells you the correct answer with a little giggle. It's not like she's one of those human computers you hear about. Eight digits. Ten digits. All in a column as long as your arm. She's not like that. But still, it's impressive.

F.D. tests her regularly. He tries to stump her. Makes weird noises while she works the figures through her head. Noises like a karate yell or the call of a duck. Then he does her answer on paper to be sure. But there's no use trying to stump her. "I was always good in school," she will say.

This morning Forest comes down into the kitchen in his stocking feet. He's not the kind of young person you have to call three or four times to get out of bed. There's something emergencyish and firemanish about his love of road work and the excavating business.

He fetches a bowl and spoon and box of flakes. Jug of milk. He sets himself down at the breakfast table, white enamel table with black trim and scratches fine as hairs. There are leaves underneath, which you can pull out if you are a family larger than the Johnsons.

Bett's rocking chair is new. Fancy lathework. Gold stenciled grapes and foliage on a satin black finish. Bett can keep the whole household humming from that chair, her eyes on everything at once. Coffee popping black against the glass knob of the percolator. Gladys Hasty Carroll novel on her knee to finish by Thursday for her group. Baked beans in the oven to take to F.D.'s sister's Saturday. Clothes in the washer. Yeast rolls under a towel bulging over. Checkbook on top of a thickness of household bills. Upright iron heating up on the board . . . tink, tink, tink.

F.D. often says, "Organization and mathematics, you see. My wife, the genius!"

And Bett will say, "Oh, Forest. Stop." When Bett calls F.D. his real name, she says it with a voice lower than normal. Forest, the son, tries to understand. He's sure his father is joking about the genius stuff. But is it a joke *with* Bett, a kind of affection? Or a joke on Bett? Both man and wife are nervous in this . . . both giggling, both clench-jawed.

Forest realizes now that he's positioned himself uncomfortably close to his mother. He can look straight down at the words of the novel and the fine check of her housedress, which from across the room would look like a solid but pale blue.

Forest doesn't make conversation, just munches cereal, mashing the flakes into the milk with his spoon. It's one of those early summer mornings that starts off way too warm. By noon, who knows what you'll wind up with?

Two kitchen windows are up, robins chirruping all up and down Rummery Road.

A truck slows and Forest turns to see in the greenish dawn that it's a Nissen's truck with its parking lights still on. It moves expertly along the curbside at Moody's. Dozens of loaves of bread in that truck. Dozens of boxes of powdered doughnuts. Cookies, too. Some with fillings.

There was a kid at school whose father worked at Nissen's or Calderwood's in Portland. The kid said there were cookies on belts going in all directions. Cookies sometimes backing up. Broken cookies in heaps. And outside when the kid was riding away in the car with his mother after she dropped the father off there, the streets of the city smelled like cookies. It was like cookies were weather. The cookie smell was fat and warm street after street, on and on after each stop and turn. It was sweet for *miles!*

Even when Forest was only nine or ten and had no idea of what the future would hold, he thought that that was one of the nicest things he would ever hear of, that nothing else would come along to top it. And he was right. Nothing has come along.

39 And so on a Tuesday afternoon, Forest meets Peggy Clary at her parents' home in Bridgton. Leach field done, F.D. loading the backhoe onto the low-bed, Forest hanging out by the kitchen door, Peggy Clary just inside the door wearing a pale denim workshirt, jeans, and riding boots. Looks like a tornado couldn't make Peggy Clary budge from that doorsill.

40 Cars and trucks all grouped around, the flash of a side mirror as another door opens. The sky white with summer. A summer of good money, good deals. Land for a song. Old farms on the market for a song. New places in between those places, everywhere that the paper company doesn't own. Oh that paper company which is despised and loved . . . far-reaching. It won't let go. But what otherwise can be grabbed is grabbed. "Developed."

Here we have this "perfect spot on the knoll" . . . "old pasturing acreage" . . . "delicious view." That's what the new owners call it . . . "delicious view."

Backhoes and dozers hurtling against time. Delicious-view people don't like waiting for dreams. House and garage will be as big as a shopping plaza, the workers say . . . big grins . . . the impossibility possible . . . tell it around. Tell it at the PO. Tell it at the hardware. Tell it up and down the road. They say, "Big as a shopping plaza . . . house plans rolled out like a stair runner."

Forest works shirtless, his body browned, way browner than the Florida trip. The knoll has much rock from the ice age. And the following ages of earth unmovable, earth for all time. Rock. Face of God. With the easy clasp of the backhoe, the face of God is pulled away.

Easy as cake.

The cab of the backhoe jars and shivers, the diligent thrust, rocks bouncing away like rubber balls. And the motionless air of the glassed-in cab is to Forest's drizzling wet skin a kind of atonement.

The engine gurgles, grunts, the shovel goes for more . . . the layers going down . . . the black, the yellows and ores, pearly, and then more rock.

Forest knows, feels it in the hot slant of the sun, in his palms, wrists, and back, jiggling, jerked hard, this brotherhood with machinery, his backhoe and the backhoe operated by Len Moore mixing belches and roars with all the trucks and all the dozers. This good thing. This intercourse of robotized commotion, noise, and fuss. This progress.

In the Beginning
There Were Soules
(More Egypt History)

1 │ HOW IS IT Eben Hood died? Dropped in his field like a shot to the heart. Died with both hands on the plow and a face caught in that always good-natured red look of his. And they say, "Maybelle, ye should naugh' grieve. Be comforted that it 'twas quick! He never suffered." But the wife, Maybelle Hood, standing before the red ox with her goad and her sweating hair under the high hard noon couldn't speak, nor move from the spot. And the ox in his duty was also fast in his track but for the business of the tail at the business of the flies, all three, the wife, the man, and the ox seeming to be dead to the same dead heart.

———

2 | Bury him in the high field. All stones converge here, hauled from certain furrows . . . the red ox and the links of chain . . . all in servitude to one thing or another. Today it be death. You, Maybelle, and your neighbors bury him like a seed, deep in the dark. The wooden box his brothers and your brother make, soon to soften, pressing inward like a coat. Will his good hands reach the two hundred yards to this house? Praise be, yes! Sometimes the golden grasses, using his voice, will speak your name. "Maybelle." And the stone wall around his grave swells and recedes with the good intentions of the woodchuck. And sometimes the blue snow and the soil will be sweet with all those remembrances and his everlasting fertility singing in the spring of the year.

3 | She marries her mother's dead sister's husband, bony as his horse. And always he wears that little hat. And much loved among those in Egypt. He brings the baby that his first wife died by. He brings his bony horse. He is Ben Soule, cousin to Begins, cousin to Dougherties and Ezekiel MacBean. And all the stories you hear from any end of Egypt and the settlement have gone through the lips and three teeth of Ben Soule.

When he opened his hand to her, there they were! All one thousand bright hearts of the town.

He farms both his land and hers. He sells her ox. He prefers a horse, says he. She weeps.

But she watches him work from her place at the cradle. And her lust for the beauty of him working is so great that perhaps her pregnancies have come as much from her looking as by the bed.

Ben Soule.

4 | Meanwhile another Soule, a man whose wife died of poorly blood, a man who never remarried, now is in want of a wife to watch him die. Pox 'tis. You die in the fire of it. You die in its blister. And from you all your strength runs out in warm stinking rivers. It is the time for harvest. But who will harvest? His two eleven year olds who have started to live like wild dogs outdoors? Or these infants dressed in sacking, laying on this bed around their father, they in their own personal fires and blister. And one little child not sick yet. Jenny. Jumping, bouncing on this bed. The dying young father, mouth and eyes like hard bread, whispers "Stop." Jenny hears this, but doesn't like the word "stop."

The eleven year olds rally. They harness up the yellow horse, pile the pumpkins in the wagon. Somewhere down on Rummery Road there are town ladies with pumpkin pies in their eyes and coins in the folds of their aprons . . . "Even-steven" . . . God bless ye . . . nothing is owed.

5 There's no funeral for them that die of the pox. You don't touch pox! Fear screams a larger fire throughout the hills. The eleven year olds of Jonathan Soule dig the hole round because this is the shape he died in, curled around his dying infants.

So many watched for the pox after their pumpkin transactions. They remember passing on samples of pie. And this nice recipe. "Try this for a little cake. Cup of sugar, add in grease and cream it. Add two chicken eggs or one goose . . . salt . . . add four cups of flour, some soured milk and some of this pumpkin cooked and strained. Get your oven very hot. Now this little cake is very heavy. You can fill up your family so they would think they had eaten potatoes and roast!!"

Nobody died of the pumpkins. And nobody died of this recipe.

6 After the pox is gone for sure, the orphans of Jonathan Soule get a visit by their uncle Ben. He doesn't take off his hat in the house. He tells them there's plenty of room where he and his new wife, Maybelle, live and all their new babies. But there isn't room. He just says that. What else can he say?

The eleven year olds, now twelve, agree to go but little Jenny has to be lugged, and kicking. Ben sells their yellow horse. They watch steadily as the shaggy fat yellow horse is led away. It is a puzzlement that Ben sells a fat horse and keeps that bony wreck of a horse that's always been his. Eventually one orphan doesn't work out. Jenny. She is lugged kicking to Ben's dead wife's cousins who live in another town. They have no children. They say they'll take anything. They don't change her name. They leave her be. They don't pretend to people that she's their blood baby as most would do. They say, "Oh, no . . . she is not ours" as Jenny bullies the visitors' children and once even broke the preacher's spectacles.

Later she will marry another Soule, a cousin . . . third cousin once removed . . . and the Soules of today's Egypt can be traced directly back to this couple.

7 | And when Ben Soule dies, his children will bury him by the pines at his old place alongside his first wife. Maybelle will die and go to the high field with Eben Hood. And her sons and daughters by Eben Hood and her sons and daughters by Ben Soule will all live long and be buried in various high fields. And all the fields of Egypt will sing with these voices, sing to no one who would remember them. And the cleared pastures and gardens will be the inheritance. But what inheritance is song or field? Both things are fragile and easily smashed as a green fly. A green fly buzzing down through the ages, on its way, the way of the world.

Modern Day Soules,
Descendants of Jenny

1 | IT HAS COME TO THIS, the last night of the last fair, the long weeks of the many fairs when she has wanted him dead. It always comes to this, her walking briskly toward the arena where he stands. And he is always standing right where she pictured, his straw cowboy hat set back on his head in a cocky way . . . arrogance on his face, alive and well.

She, Dottie Soule, lingers very little at the other attractions, sheep muzzles pushing between planks. Sheep that seem to always know her. And there's shouts from neighbors and friends: "Hey Dottie!" and "Dot! How's the family?!" and "We just saw Merlin! Zat where you're headed?"

She stops at the biggest carrots. The biggest squash.

"Big squash," says one of her daughters.

"Wow!" another one nearly swoons.

"Bet it tastes like sawdust," Dottie snarls, swipes at her nose with a tissue from a pocket of her many shirts. Her nose is red and plugged tonight. Weeks of worry. Weeks of pissed-offness. Weeks of picturing Merlin on the go, spending money. Makes you more vulnerable to germs, they say.

"Here's the most perfect tomatoes," a daughter announces.

"Kind of wrinkled," another one notes.

"But *big*," the first one insists.

Dottie Soule looks over the heads of the girls to the whole glarishly lighted exhibition hall. With her back teeth she gnashes and smashes a cough drop. Mentholated. The TV ads promise it'll unplug your nose. She commands, "Let's move on! We ain't paralyzed, are we?"

The many girls go zigzagging ahead. They feel things. They can't get enough of feeling things. They beg for things. "Oh, can we get one of these trolls?!!!" Trolls without clothes, but lots of lavender, yellow, red, or blue stand-up hair. "You gotta be shittin' me," Dottie snarls.

They move on.

More greetings from neighbors and relations. Some say they've just seen Merlin at the pulling arena. They say he looks good. "I *bet* he looks good," Dottie sneers. "I bet he looks damn good."

Dottie Soule's glasses frames are blue-gray. This is meant to match her beautiful eyes. But the eyes are so embedded in the bifocal lenses. "Nice bones" has been said of her high cheeks by those few who remember her before-glasses self.

"Hey Dot!" a neighbor calls out.

"Hey Spence!" she hollers back.

Now glancing out through the exhibition hall's open end to the midway, she sees her oldest daughter's face and wild aureole of auburn hair. Sherry. Sherry and her husband, Lloyd, standing inside the glary light of a doughboy concession. Their child rides his shoulders, gripping his plenteous dark hippie hair. He hangs onto her by her ankles. The other child, the new one, is bundled in Sherry's arms. They don't see Dottie seeing them. The business at hand is doughboys and how to eat them with no hands.

Lloyd's hair. The trial of the family.

While Dottie's ponytail . . . well . . . it's a *tail*. Hard, tapered, supple appendage. Marsupialish. And the hair at her temples is pulled so tight, it makes her small Verrill ears stick out more. Ears not meant to be enhanced. But Verrill ears, so lodged in the genes, passed on down through the ages. So many other people in Egypt have them. Therefore, no one is ever taken aback.

Quilts. Mittens. Apple dolls. Popsicle-stick lamps. Birdhouses. Braided rugs. Fudge. A man with gray hair, gray suit giving out pamphlets on eternal life. "Are you the kind of man who would have a relationship with two big stupid horses?" Dottie asks him.

He looks not a bit alarmed over this. With his smooth smile, he asks her if she's discouraged with the way the world is going.

Dottie gives him a big wink, then lunges onward.

One of the small daughters announces, "Mumma! It's almost nine-thirty!"

2 | Her shoulders are squared against the wall. With so many shirts, you'd never know the true skinniness of Dottie Soule. She is not watching the arena but staring at the Kleenex in her hands, deep in thought.

When Merlin's team is announced in the lighthearted voice of the loudspeakers, Dottie raises her eyes, sees Merlin with one of his old fair-going pals and his new fair-going pal, young Carroll Plummer, hefting the doubletree. The team backs from the rail. She watches hard. These freaks, their formidable rocking weight, witlessly unaware of how silly and squirty men really are. How stupid a horse is not to see this. No sense of proportion. Rocket and Tommy, the giants, always dying to please Merlin Soule, who is nothing.

Dottie stares into the legs of the team blurred with motion into a pale butter of light.

Dottie feels for more cough drops. They are somewhere in one of the many pockets of her many shirts. Big search.

The team churns forward. BOOM BOOM BOOM BOOM BOOM BOOM Rocket and Tommy wheeling toward the drag. Their matched strides always chill her. Merlin with the traces. Merlin's posture board-straight. No strain. His power is absolute. And doesn't his fair hat ride nice. There's silence over the stands as Merlin Soule and his helpers back the team to the drag.

Silence in the stands but for some little kids yakking and Dottie's loud crunching on her cough drop. She gets a few irritated looks from the bench just below her. "Isn't this interesting!" she exclaims into their eyes.

With the doubletree linked to the drag now, Merlin's pals move away. Carroll Plummer, the young one, might be sober tonight. Might not be. Red chamois shirt tied around his waist. Hot work. Everything the guy *works* at he does deftly and it yields to him. It's life's leisure time that "fucks him up," they say. Carroll Plummer. One of the great mysteries.

It begins with Merlin's shout. This is the trick, you see. To *sound* bigger than a workhorse. And Rocket and Tommy dying to please. Dying to please him. DYING TO PLEASE HIM. They scramble forward. They hunch and hop against the weight of the impossible. On Rocket's yellow-brown rump come the hardest whacks, Merlin driving hard, Merlin yelling for more than they can give. And more. And more. They give it. Rocket swings his head. Neck muscles and hind leg muscles opening, closing like mouths. Pain or ecstasy? What difference?

They measure the pull.

Cheers.

"Another year, another pile of ribbons," Dottie says to the people on the bench below. "Ain't that the damnedest thing." She tsks, shakes her head. She smiles into their upturned faces. One of her blurred-behind-the-glasses eyes winks.

3 | Rocket and Tommy stand in the blue dark between the pulling arena and Number 4 Exhibition Hall while Merlin scooches on an upside-down bucket, his straw fair hat near. He grips the traces into his now slumped posture, to his thick middle, head a little bit bowed. Steam rises off the horses' backs, then the veil of this steam is pulled up into the small spotlight on a pole overhead. You would not know Merlin to be a winner if you saw him now. Light here is penitent. Nothing like *out there,* the crazy midway, the whirr of it, the tweedle-dee of it, the barks and trills. And it all goes around and around out there while in this soft dark outer limits Merlin is very still.

"Fair's hard on Merlin," Dottie snorts, moving toward him over the ground crisscrossed with electric cables.

He doesn't look up at her, just keeps his head hung.

The daughters have gone off with older sisters for their chance at doughboys and rides.

"You all right?" Dottie asks.

Rocket and Tommy shake their manes. The harness jangles, creaks, speaks.

Dottie replies to herself, "That's good. That's good to hear. I'm glad you're fine. Is that right? My, my. Good to hear it. Oh yuh? 'Twasn't anything really. Oh! Is that right. Yes, yes. My, my. Well, well."

She can only see the back of that close-cropped big neck . . . the familiar region of it. She sees he has chills.

She makes a quick swipe for the work shirt he has tossed nearby, drops it over his shoulders, "Fair's hard on Merlin," Dottie snorts, gives her plastic-frame glasses a little nudge with a knuckle as if to see him clearer.

"Shut up," says he, deeply, threateningly.

"Gettin' old," she says, unthreatened.

He remains silent, head hanging, and the horses' tails hang dead weight. No flies on this cold last blue night of the fair.

"Practically dead," she says. "You gave it everything you got. You look like you're ready to keel. Old ticker's lettin' you down. Feelin' any sort of symptoms? Time to take you out and leave you on an ice floe, I guess."

He says nothing in his own defense.

"So what do you got, you old fool? Buncha ribbons. Tear yourself up . . . don't eat right . . . just swillin' beer . . . neglectin' your family . . . wouldn't even recognize your new baby . . . nor either of your grandbabies, they've changed so much in the last few weeks. And here you are half dead . . . buncha ribbons."

He listens to it all. It is familiar, a reverberation coming down through the ages, not just all the fairs of his life, but all the fairs before his life. It is the *facts* of life. He rubs the back of his neck, rubs his close-cropped beauty of a head, shape of the skull showing like a missile, neck muscles still quite steely.

She says tearfully, which makes her nose more stuffed-up, "And for two days the pump was broke!"

"Shut up," he says very low, the just-before-you-pound-the-shit-out-of-somebody low.

She grabs his head, gives it a big squeeze against her shirts.

He gets to his feet. Bucket tips, clatters. The team jangles and jostles to the left. Merlin seizes Dottie by one skinny bicep.

"Yunh!" she gasps and falls forward.

The shirt she had laid over his shoulders drops, gets tangled with a foot.

Her glasses fly off into the night.

The other bucket tips and his fair hat churns away like a wheel.

All in a motion, Dottie muckles onto Merlin, around his middle. His one free arm gets her around her middle. His other hand manages the traces. But the traces are getting taut. Rocket and Tommy's eyes are showing a lot of white. They look to be on the verge of a nervous breakdown. Ready to bolt. Ready to fly. Like Billy Lord's matched whites behaved just before they trampled him to death. And Jim Sargent's team before it dragged a twitch of logs over his left leg. And old Hazen's team that took their empty scoot after them, splintering it a thousand times a thousand. Teams that are like trains. Like the unchained sea in chains, the unchained chained sea of *this* team all wrought down to the one free hand of Merlin Soule and there's Dottie twisting the thumb of his other hand. Horses shifting, dancy. Their heads jerk up, up, up. They grunt. They rumble. They snort. All over them their musculature hammers and boils. Merlin snaps Dottie's right arm behind her and Dottie goes to her knees. But her grip on Merlin's thumb is secure. Then there was the team that took the twitch of logs over Bert Curran's head. Rocket and Tommy moan with grief. How they hate this! How they always hate this . . . this goofing around, this Soule rassle, this Soule love.

"For Richer, for Poorer, in Sickness and in Health, to Love and to Cherish, Till . . ."

Well, I don't know but I've been told
Streets in Heaven paved in gold.
Keep your hand on that plow. Hold on.
Hold on! Hold on! . . .

The Devil, he has a slippery shoe
And if you don't watch out, he'll slip it on you.
Keep your hand on that plow. Hold on.
Hold on! Hold on! Keep your hand on that plow. Hold on.

—*Elaina Mezzetti,*
"Morning Train,"
as sung by Peter, Paul and Mary

1 | LLOYD BARRINGTON is home alone now, this rented house be-
tween Allen's Oil and Lucky's Bar and Grill. Pleasant Street.
Cereal bowl in the sink.
Cereal for breakfast.
Cereal for dinner.
Cereal for supper.
Two cribs in the bedroom. No babies. Along the wall are his hats
and caps on nails and brass hooks. More hats and caps than any one
person could need. As many hats and caps as you hear some rich women
have pairs of shoes. A week's worth of junk mail is jammed into the
curlicues of the aluminum storm door, in that big letter *D* that represents
the landlord's last name. Overhead the glass light fixture is not what you'd

call a cozy homey light. It pours down on the paperback book of essays that is open on the table. Lloyd's eyes are closed. Essays on agriculture and culture. No screaming face, half skull, half flesh. No vampire in the glowing windows of a many-gabled mansion. No spies wearing trench-coats. That is the other Lloyd you see turning the page of *Werewolf of the West*. That is the in-public-Lloyd. Lloyd when he's at Moody's Variety & Lunch or Letourneau's Used Auto Parts. The Lloyd that is there and about . . . looking like he's reading . . . but he's really listening to *you* . . . Lloyd turning the page to the epic of the man who through a scientist's error became a kind of walking onion who liked to kill and no one could stop him.

Here and now is the true Lloyd. The secret Lloyd. *America's Agriculture as a Culture: What Went Wrong?* On Lloyd's face a look of shock, of bloodless horror. The real reading material of the real Lloyd is the *real* horror.

He is age twenty-two. Big glut of beard. A real beard. Not a disguise. The public Lloyd and the true Lloyd . . . both hairy.

And such hair of the head! The way a lot of them do these days. Can't tell the boys from the girls these days, his in-laws say. And "College boy . . . ha!" they say. "Is that what college does for you? Gives you hair?"

Lloyd's hair. Thick as Sherry's used to be. *More* thick. More body. More surge. More highlights. Nothing like the heads of the in-laws . . . the brothers-in-law and boyfriends of Sherry's sisters . . . and the father-in-law. Merlin Soule.

Such heads! The rounded horizon of each skull so visible. Especially Merlin's. The missile shape of it. And in certain light, purpled and pumping like a heart.

For a long moment Lloyd brings the clear picture of Merlin Soule's skull to his mind's eye. The rightness of that skull. A kind of honesty. A kind of innocence. A kind of reasonableness. A kind of purity. A kind of cheer. A way, he, Lloyd Barrington, can never ever be.

2 | The city pounds, wails, buzzes, rattles. Nobody in this truck talking but Merlin . . . the BOOM BOOM BOOM of Merlin's voice. Loud. Though Sherry who is next to him doesn't seem fazed, her mouth fixed into the O of her new wonderlessness. Sherry in the middle. Lloyd on the outer edge.

Lloyd rides with his arm out the window, opening his hand into the air. Lloyd with the great streaky black-and-red beard over his dark green T-shirt. Lloyd's ponytail down the back of the T-shirt. Lloyd's hair the trial of the family, the worst thing to happen . . . until what happened to Sherry. He tries to account for some connection the Soules will make here between the bad thing of his hair and the bad thing that has happened to Sherry.

Merlin bellers, "JESUS! What they need fifty sawhorses and a flagman just to fix one friggin' manhole? Honest to Christ! Lookit 'em all standin' there! Honest to Christ!"

Windshields with unknowable faces converge. Car hoods and truck hoods bright with relentless sun, swinging left, swinging right, interlocking into lanes. Merlin steers, follows the downhill narrow streets leading away from the hospital, down, down, down. Driving one-handed. Driving with one knee cocked.

Lloyd knows. This is a contest Lloyd has lost. Something Lloyd has lost and Merlin has gained. Something between Merlin and Lloyd that must be owned. And Merlin now owns it. Owns the air around Sherry as he owns this pickup truck, his farm and herd, his 110 acres. Even on this truck seat this minute, Lloyd is losing. A sort of Grand Sweepstakes Final Elimination.

Merlin groans. "Now what's *this,* for crissakes! Some sorta new eyesore they're erectin'. Looks like a black oatmeal box!" Merlin squints over Sherry's bowed head to Lloyd, and Lloyd nods and says, "Yep, it does."

They ride along into the sun. Over an hour of hot road, hot glass, hot shoulder-to-shoulderness. Sherry has gone to leaning mash-faced into her father Merlin's upper arm now, making a goo there on his white dress shirt. Merlin twitches on his seat, shaking his head disgustedly as cars roar past him. "ATTA BOY! Goddam rush to nowhere!" he snorts.

Sherry gurgles.

Both men seem different after this gurgle. Merlin is quiet. And Lloyd an even more fantastic quiet. It's just the sound of the sweet-running truck down the last stretch into Egypt, along the river toward home.

Now by the road there's a sign with agriculture's generic cow picture and the words: MERLIN SOULE—REGISTERED HOLSTEINS. And there's the good smell of "the work" on the air.

In the dooryard Merlin backs the truck to the ell door, his forearm thrust out along the back of the seat the way he often does, Merlin and the truck together beautiful as silk . . . trucks, cattle, and horses . . . always the same . . . he puts them where they "ought go," a goddam right Yankee farmer. Gripping the shift now. Grimacing.

So many vehicles have appeared since this morning, parked in the glare. Too much metal, kettle hot. Blue grain silo, aluminum-roofed barns. Work rigs and equipment. Hot rods. Lloyd's own spotted many-colored truck. And three or four sedans unfamiliar. Looks like a funeral . . . which in a manner of speaking it is.

Merlin is bellering even before he's gotten his left foot out of the truck. "DOT! FRANCINE! GET THE DOOR!!"

Lloyd closely watches the pageant of Merlin's white dress shirt as he reaches up onto the truck seat to get a good grip on Sherry although it would be easier to get Sherry out from Lloyd's side. It doesn't matter. Merlin's way is the way now. Lloyd says nothing, stepping down into the high weeds on his side of the truck.

Soule sisters converge, some with their pale hair pinned up in summerish knots and twists, some with their hair down. They press around their father and touch Sherry as if to believe this is Sherry. Everyone feeling the BOOM BOOM BOOM of Merlin's orders in their chests. One sister backs away, digging her knuckles into her eyes and wailing as she has done every day since the surgery. Nobody has been taking this "well," but this sister, Francine, and Sherry were always close.

It seems as though Sherry leans across the steering wheel into Merlin's arms, the arms of her father . . . a tender recognition, a beholden. This is what it looks like. But it is not.

"Now, Daddy, *please* be careful of your back," one sister reminds him. All the sisters are advising at once, in the low and fluctuating timbres of Soule voices, of each one bullying all the others . . . all leaders, no followers.

A blue-and-black butterfly trembles on the dead center of Merlin's white dress shirt. And now one dances lightly on one of Sherry's half-open eyes.

Lloyd watches this and Merlin's thick-waisted, irascible, hunched walk blurring into the broad back and frame of Lloyd's own father. When Merlin's not dressed up like this, he could be Edmund Barrington's twin . . . overalls or uniform work pants and the scent of honest work. Whichever road you take here, whichever farmhouse you pick, knock on the door and Lloyd's father will answer that door. They are everywhere! All of them with their eyes level on you.

At the doorway to the Soules' kitchen where the screen is rusted to a reddish fog, two faces float low in one corner. Lloyd and Sherry's daughters. Still babies. Today they are pink-dress babies, fixed up nice as any magazine babies, fixed up nice for this special day.

Merlin carries Sherry like a bride.

The trees here that hem the sandy driveway and dooryard are elms. All dead. Like so many around town. Barkless and silver. More like giant slingshots. No shade here at Soules'. Everything buzzing and bright and infinite and deathless, even after death.

Sherry's hands are standoffish. There are round Band-Aids and a plastic hospital ID bracelet. Her freckles so familiar! "HEY! THE DOOR! WHO'S GETTIN' THE DOOR!" Merlin bellers.

More sisters come striding from the barns. And one son-in-law, Gary. Those that do most of the dairy work here with Merlin. Work for low pay and no pay. Work, a kind of love.

Eight-year-old Cassandra gets the door. And while in action, she gives the pink-dress babies a shove. And over they go. Both land on their plumped-out diaper-padded bottoms.

On the door rock Merlin turns slightly to work Sherry's loose legs around the doorframe.

The babies get to their feet as Merlin swings past with Sherry. One baby says gravely, "Dat's not Mumma."

Cassandra sneers, "Yess it izzzz . . . only she don't like you anymore."

Dottie Soule snaps Cassandra around by one wrist, backs her up to the wall, stares deeply into the sullen eyes and says in a low whisper, "*Do not.*"

Lloyd hangs back by Merlin's truck. He had carried Sherry when she *was* a bride, swept her from the seat of his own truck with ease. What a bride she was that day! And the far reach of her beribboned auburn braid, its swing like an open hand hungry for his thigh.

The pink-dress babies are gone from view now, churning, mixing, maneuvering among the other Soule children deep in the Soules' rooms. All Soule babies being beautiful with sweet complexions and fruit-color mouths, white walking shoes. Some are dressed in sailor suits. Others Osh-Koshes, dresses, pinafores, bloomers. A lot of hours at various sewing machines make up most of the Soule baby wardrobe. And Soule babies wear them well . . . maybe a little too self-consciously

Lloyd knows his babies are Soule babies now. Sage and Leighlah. At home here now. Swallowed. Gone.

3 | A day passes. Then another. Cars keep coming into the yard with casseroles and with people coming to get a look at Sherry. The sisters are jammed tight around Sherry's bed in deep chairs, fanning themselves, too hot to have clammy babies climbing all over them and yet clammy babies climb all over them. Phone rings. Phone rings. Phone rings.

Another day passes. More of the same.

But now in a week it is petering fast.

All Cassandra's life this has been the living room. The place where the TV is. Was. TV is gone now.

TV is moved to the kitchen. But the set-up of the kitchen chairs isn't right. And there's always the back of somebody's head in the way. Or a bottle of ketchup. Or the pussy willows.

In "Sherry's room" Cassandra slouches in one of the deep vinyl chairs, thumps her heel on the rug, stares at the chrome legs of the toilet. "Commode" they are calling it. But toilet is what it is. This is Cassandra's job. To guess when Sherry needs to "go" and to "help" her "go." The sisters and their mother, Dot, and Aunt Liz who is visiting today have promised to take turns . . . everyone putting in fifteen minutes. But they seem to have forgotten their turns. Cassandra thumps her foot, moves her eyes to the spot where the TV should be . . . now just a vivid blankness against the wall. Her eyes move to the drapes, their hard green synthesized gloss. She looks at everything but Sherry. Sherry in the bed. Needs rest, they say. But Sherry's half out of the bed, one leg lopping over the side.

Cassandra hollers out now and then. "YOU GUYS!!! COME HERE!! HURRY!!!"

And one of them yells back, "Just a minute!"

Minute? It's more like hours.

Sherry gurgles.

Cassandra grips the chair arms. It's getting darker outdoors. Cassandra doesn't move to put on the light.

Now another sound from Sherry's part of the room. A word? "MEEM."

"YOU GUYS! MY TURN IS OVER NOW!" Cassandra howls toward the kitchen door.

"In a minute," a sister calls back from the kitchen.

4 | He rubs the foot and he can tell she likes it because the foot pushes of its own accord into his hands. The foot *is* Sherry now. It is her harsh throaty commands and opinions. Sherry the bully. She bullied well. Bullied everyone but her sisters who you are always up against a brick wall with. Trying to get your own way with one of them, no hope, none of them give an inch . . . just one big furor. The Soule way.

The foot speaks to Lloyd. It says, "My dear one . . . my love . . . my husband. It is so good to be with you." This would be said in one of her sweet moods when he was doing things her way.

5 | Francine and Faye, Tina and Alberta, Pam and Brenda. They jam the doorway, jostling each other in quick flashes of blond and tawny hair, each trying to see into the dark room . . . to see what is going on there on Sherry's bed. They are unnaturally speechless. Their eyes are narrowed on Lloyd and on Sherry's bare foot. They exchange appalled looks. Francine crosses her arms, asks "How. Did. You. Get. In. Here. Lloyd?"

Lloyd pushes Sherry's foot under the covers. He stands up in his way that looks to people like he's old and stiff and achey. "No special way," says he. Something from his left cheek moves to the right. The tapered end of his beard flickers . . . or so it seems. He looks sad. Yet the suspicious eyes of the sisters flick over his dungarees for sign of something else.

One of the sisters quickly blurts out, "Well, it's probably not a good idea, Lloyd . . . to . . . hang around don't you think? Especially this late and it's getting LATE and nobody's really expecting you to have to help out, you've got all that work with your father and stuff and you know Sherry's not right anymore, you know it wouldn't be right. Right?"

Another sister butts in, "Sherry's obviously *helpless*."

"It's not a good idea to have him around," another says to another.

"It's asking for trouble," another agrees.

Lloyd says very softly, "Sherry's my wife."

All eyes bore into him.

"What—Did—You—Say?" Francine asks incredulously, but doesn't wait for an answer. "You are weird."

"Jesus," two or three of them whisper in unison.

They seem to want him out of this room and yet they block the door.

"Where's Cassandra?" one of them wonders.

Nobody knows.

"Lloyd," Francine says. "Any person would have to be . . . sick . . . you know . . . to . . . you know . . ."

He has always thought of himself as accommodating and kindly. He wants to please them as he always does . . . always giving in. Sick? He squints at this new image of himself.

And they are all looking at him, his sneakers so boyish with double-knots. Boyish, yes. Shy. Wholesome. Who could forget the fat boy who kept such a neat desk at school, fierce grip on his pencil, eyes on the teacher's face at all times. And the little poem he recited once after the teacher begged him. Then the teacher corrected his use of the word "was" with a plural "subject" and a lot of kids giggled themselves sick till the teacher asked for "manners, please." Some of them called him the Poetry Fatty after that . . . even after he thinned down.

Sweet, yes. Lloyd Barrington. Sweet.

But also something . . . something you sense but can't name, something about the guy that is cool-handed, that is foxy, scheming, creepy, sneaky.

6 | "What a little brat!" one of them shrieks.
They block the door. This is the way they deal with you when you don't cooperate . . . keep you from getting from one room to another, in or out of the house.

Cassandra demands, "Why can't *you* guys sleep with her!" She points at a couple of their faces. She tries to play offensive.

"We have our own places," Pam says. "We have to get home at night. And jobs. I know *I* can't get any more time off."

"You are the only one available," Pam insists.

Cassandra squats down, covers her head. "I'm not listening. Leave me alone."

"Cassandra . . ." One of them pokes her with a sandaled foot.

"I'm in there enough in the daytime!!" Cassandra wails. "What about

Wendy? And Robin? What about Lydia? I ain't the only one living here. What about Ma!"

"Stand up. You look stupid," Francine says.

"Sherry is creepy. I'm not even going in there in the daytime anymore. I'm quittin'. If you make me, I'll smash you."

"Nowadays kids are so violent," sighs Faye. "It's from all that TV."

"You stay with Sherry nights and we'll pay you ten dollars a week," Francine offers.

Faye snarls, "Jesus! There's no need of that, Frannie. We shouldn't have to *bribe* her." She swings down and gets a grip on Cassandra's blouse. "Cassandra. Get up, *now*."

"Cassandra. If Mumma asked you, would you do it then?" Alberta wonders.

Brenda says, "She'll do anything for Mum. Go get Mum."

7 | Sherry is on the bed. With the drapes closed the dark is complete. Cassandra is curled up in the farthest corner where the TV used to be. The edge of the rug is her pillow. But the sisters think the girl is in bed with Sherry. "It's just Sherry," they keep telling her. "Sherry wouldn't hurt a fly."

"Sherry is your own sister!" they remind her.

"Your own blood!" they remind her.

In the pitch dark it's hard to tell what Sherry is doing now. But it's plain that sleeping is not what she's doing. There's a thump, a jiggle. There's the weird wet sound of her open mouth.

In true terror, Cassandra stops breathing.

There's a cullomph! Sherry is on the floor now, too.

Both of them on the floor. Nobody in the bed.

Sounds like Sherry might be trying to get back in the bed. Or out the window. There's no telling. "Gror-meeem," says Sherry sorrowfully. There's a little more thumping, rustle of her gown. Then it seems she's given up. For the rest of the night neither Sherry nor Cassandra make a move.

8 | They have come to pick up a few of the children's things, they tell him. They don't wait for him to say "Come in" but push past him with their elbows and flashing blond manes of hair. Francine, pixie cut. Less hair but more elbow.

The two cribs in the bedroom are end to end. The rest of the room is the double bed with books and spiral notebooks stacked along one side, stacked with meticulousness. Books so appealing with their multicolored titled spines. A kind of neatness that's "not right for a man." The cribs are a mess, however, the deep orangy varnish of their rails representing cribs from another era . . . cribs from the Soule attic . . . cribs that were brought here to Pleasant Street for baby Leighlah and baby Sage . . . now heaped with pissy-smelling pink and yellow baby blankets, soured bottles, too many toys. "How did you ever have room for the kids with all this . . . stuff?" sister Brenda wonders, scowling.

Lloyd smiles a sort of stupid smile.

"How did the poor little things ever spread out?" wonders Pam.

Sister Francine asks, "What's this, Lloyd?" A paperback with a blue-white complexioned vampire working on a half-naked woman's throat. Blood drips from the lettering of the title. Another paperback with a wolf howling against a moon, which on second glance is really a round moon-colored screaming woman's face. Another paperback shows two cowboys shooting it out. The pages are sucked, curled from their once-sodden-with-baby-spit conditions. Some pages are ripped out, scrunched into balls mixed with the toys and sour bottles.

Lloyd says, "The little wenches've been over to my side of the room, have they?"

Francine lets the book drop to the floor, wipes the hand on the thigh of her jeans.

Also in the cribs are emergency candles. An egg beater. A roll of paper towels.

"Playing kitchen," Lloyd observes.

With two fingers, sister Brenda picks up another paperback, this one showing a detective with a snubnosed gun stalking someone. Detective's eyes gleam. Brenda snorts. "College know you read this shit?"

He shrugs.

Sister Alberta demands, "Didn't college teach you peace and all that hippie love 'n' stuff?"

"Yes, ma'am," says he.

"Why don't you read something more uplifting?" Pam wonders. "Like a *nice* story. I have a book that has a real nice story. I'll never get time to finish it. I can loan it to you. It's not got killing. Just love. You ought to read more nice things, Lloyd. Get your life together. Get a *nice* job. Something . . . oh you know . . . that has promise. Maybe you need some books with a nice lesson of life to learn. Maybe you could learn something. People are going to start thinking you are a sick man."

The great falls of his dark moustache give a jerk . . . a sort of amusement.

Faye, standing in the doorway with arms folded like a bouncer, her pale hair hung around her nearly to her ankles, a kind of perpetual bridal train, speaks into Lloyd's eyes. "I bet there's not one really wholesome scene in that kinda shitty readin' . . . like that one with the gun especially."

Lloyd's grin gets very sheepish. His odd mixed-color eyes lower down and among the women's feet . . . though now the eyes rise sharply to fix hard on Faye's face. He says, with a dismissive wave of one hand, "Love is for women." The hand drops to his side. "Murder is for men."

9 | Moody's Variety & Lunch at the four-way stop of Ginn and Rummery Roads. Since 1913. Used to be called Moody's Feeds, Hardware, Dry Goods & Groceries. Now nothing like it was then. Porch is gone. Pumps are gone. Glassy and modernized now. Even the bells on the door that so many remember . . . gone. And no slap of the screen door. Long gone is George Moody who wouldn't have put up with all this lingering you have here today, all these creaking chairs and wisdoms. In the days of George Moody, you would just do your business and go. George Moody had steel-rimmed glasses and the kind of gypsum, no-hinge face muscles that are incapable of a pleasant expression. He never said hello and he never said thank you. Certainly "have a nice day" would have torn something in his cheeks. And he *never* called a customer by name. And he never looked a person in the eye. It was impossible for the news of the town to get crossed over here.

Tonight the rockers at Moody's are creaking full-boil. The news is Charlie Shaw is dead.

Clarence Farrington says, "I known Charlie back when they had the farmplace over to Sweet Hill. His mother was a hunchback. You ever seen one of them?"

Albion Cole shakes his head gravely.

"Just in the movie," says Arch Vandermast.

Lloyd Barrington staring down into a paperback thick as a brick, turns a page.

Clarence says, "Ol' Charlie didn't last long after his wife died on him."

Ray Dyer says, "How come Charlie weren't no hunchback? Must not be a thing you take from your folks. None of them others was hunchbacks, either."

"I never saw her," Andrew Moody says croakily, breathlessly. Each of his surgeries takes so much out of him. This last surgery being the removal of some gland in his already wrung-looking neck. So many things missing from him, while his shaking and tremors increase. He's not much help at the register these days. But in this close circle of shared wisdoms, he is still handy, still honored. Every so often there's that great hitch in his breathing. Now and then his rocker gets very still and his head hangs over. It scares the others. All talk will stop. Then old Andrew will jerk upright, gusto in his eyes, shaking and tremors resumed.

"She kept to herself," Clarence recalls. "But I was goin' over there with my father to get chickens. She showed herself once 'n a while."

"Was it awful?" wonders Ray Dyer.

"Well . . . I didn't dare look direct. I didn't want it to look like I was gapin'. So it 'twas hard to get a look. I don't remember it 'twas quite like they make of it. I recall she had red hair. Carroty. 'Twas long like they used to wear it in those days, gobbed up in a little knot . . . like they did. Like Katharine Hepburn. She wore it like that. And I think in the face she kinda looked like Katharine Hepburn."

Lloyd Barrington turns a page, moves something cumbersome from his left cheek to his right. His paperback has a cover with a detective carrying a snubnose gun. The pages look as though some sort of weather has gotten to them. Seems like this is the same book he has had here before . . . months ago. But in between time there were others . . . the werewolf and the vampire and the Western saga . . . kind of interchanged. It would be hard to follow like that, one would think.

"You goin' to the funeral, Al?" Clarence wonders.

"Prob'ly ought," Albion replies.

"We're plannin' to," Andrew Moody gasps. "Millie mentioned it this mornin'."

Arch says, "That ol' place they lived at up ta Sweet Hill, I had family over there goin' back before Shaws settled up in there . . . but back on the old Boundary Road when you could get through with a wagon and certain automobiles. You ever been up there deer huntin', Ray?"

"Yep . . . been all over that part," says Ray, looking down at his hands.

Arch says, "My people were Hansons. And they were married into the Dressers who started the school."

Ray and Clarence and Albion nod.

Lloyd turns a page.

"Well, we went up there back right along when the paper company was buyin' up around here and there were still some of the old farmplaces standin'. Paper company burned all those along that side of the mountain that winter just before. 'Twas a Pike place down below. We took some lilac out of our family's place."

"Nice to have something from the old place like that," says Albion Cole.

"Yep," says Arch. "It took, too."

Ray and Clarence and Andrew and Albion nod.

Lloyd turns a page.

"I always have a way with stuff like that," Arch says. "Lilacs. And stuff like that. I just poke it in the ground and off it goes. I don't know why it 'tis."

"Lloyd, you know of any buryin' places up around Sweet Hill on the Bog Road side?" Clarence wonders.

Lloyd's crusher hat is low over his eyes for the privacy it gives him. Hat looks seriously trampled. Might've been green once. He raises his head and chews a minute. His eyes move gently upon Clarence's face . . . then dart away . . . shy, boyish. Doubtful he'd be feeling a lot of prestige from his father and himself being the Town's cemetery overseers. But they had all thought he'd be changed in college . . . acquire airs. And then leave. Be gone from the face of the earth like so many do. Some have even suggested that Lloyd may not really have gone to the university. Might be a hoax.

They all watch him tip his hat back a bit and look directly into thin air, consulting his "map" of the town, of those parts of the town that most concern him . . . the dead. He says, "I've heard about a couple of graves up there, but I haven't been able to find them."

"Well, we looked all over and we didn't see a sign of anything either," Arch admits.

Andrew says shakily, "They used to, at times, move people. Like them in the Cobb cemetery. There's nobody there. All you see is sinkholes. But they moved all them over to the big cemetery down to Cornish."

"There's one they left behind in that Cobb lot," Lloyd tells them. "A little girl. Smallpox. They wouldn't touch you if you had the pox. She's there so I've heard. There's also that guy over to Lynch Road where it comes in behind Lucien Letourneau . . . a Soule . . . you know the one that got buried with his kids. No marker. But we know thereabouts the spot. That was a case of smallpox, too, according to what I've heard."

Andrew frowns. Opens and closes his knotted hands. "Lloyd, you keep that other one up? That one of the little girl by herself?"

Lloyd says, "There's no trust and she's not a veteran. So it's not one the Town expects us to tend. But . . . I take the snippers in now and then and had Hadley do some blacksmithing on the gate. If you give these little yards a look like somebody cares, I think they get vandalized less."

"Poor little tyke," Andrew Moody says. "Up there in those woods all by herself."

10 | It is Sunday. He sits in the swelter of his truck cab waiting for the right moment to go in there and ask for a visit with his wife and little girls. He is, after all is said and done, a wimp. No match for them. How long might he sit here . . . an orange truck with a blue door, a red door and, now the latest, a Spam-colored fender . . . how long before they *see* him? Is it that they purposely ignore him? He listens to the heat of the fields, enjoys the hot cattle-smell from the open doors of the barns. He listens to the deep hot rooms of the Soule house, its low murmurs, its retorts and commands. The heat of another Sunday. The glare all around him of vehicles. Work rigs. Cars and trucks of the boyfriends of the sisters including the yellow jacked-up Merc of his cousin Carroll Plummer who lately is a friend of Merlin's, one of Merlin's many teamster pals, all of them bluff and brag, always talking fairs, grand sweepstakes, weighing, feeding, harness, vets . . . but mostly other teamsters. Teamster gossip. Then there's Rocket and Tommy, the new team named Rocket and Tommy like the old team. How many Rockets and Tommys? And always their working names "Rock!" and "T!" Rockets and Tommys all big as ships. Make the wrong move and you could wind up a wrenched, squashed mess. But ol' Merlin and Carroll just get energized by that possibility, it seems. Merlin and Carroll. The two matched heads, both of the voluntary baldness you call "gettin' a buzzer." The two missiles.

Hard to tell the difference between them when they're standing back-to. For it is said that true friends, like husband and wife, grow to look alike.

Lydia, one of the younger teenaged sisters who is wide-faced, wide-mouthed, and green-eyed, almost a twin to Lloyd's wife, Sherry, before her pregnancies, before she got her motherish look. Lydia. Long, red braid like a bell rope. The freckles. The prancing tiptoe walk that causes the braid to sway. Lydia, a tall girl, taller than Lloyd, most of the sisters being as tall or taller than their men.

Lydia is in the company of a neighbor girl, one of the Ficketts is Lloyd's guess. They appear at Lloyd's truck window and Lydia says, "*This* is Lloyd."

"*That's him?!*" the neighbor girl exclaims with disbelief. She peers into the truck at the white explosions on the knees of Lloyd's dungarees, the paperbacks on the seat . . . many paperbacks . . . burst-open and rifled-looking, weathered-looking. One shows a square-jawed spy in a trenchcoat and a barely clothed busty woman outside onion-domed government buildings. Lydia whispers into the neighbor girl's ear. The neighbor girl's eyes grow very wide. There's some whispering back and forth. Lloyd pulls on the visor of his khaki cloth work cap and says deeply, "The gnat that sings his summer song, poison get from Slander's tongue."

The neighbor girl squints at Lloyd's whiskery mouth incredulously.

"That's sick," Lydia says with curled lip.

"A popular notion these days," Lloyd says. He presses his knuckles to the dash. This day finds him with oozing blisters between his fingers and so much calamine it looks like he's wearing pretty pale pink gloves.

Lydia stoops, picks a cigarette butt from the sand, tosses it into Lloyd's beard. The two girls stride away, heading down to the paved road, looking back twice to see if he's watching them. He is. Lydia gives him the finger.

He presses each fist harder into the dash. Scratching poison ivy isn't allowed. Pressing is allowed. Seems like he's planning to drive each fist through the dash.

Now Cassandra, sulky and thin, muss-haired, one of the darker-haired Soules, appears in the dooryard from the direction of the near barn and calls up through the screened ell door, "SAGE! LEIGHLAH! YOUR FATHER IS HERE!"

The two faces of Lloyd's baby daughters come floating low into one corner of the reddish old screen.

Cassandra arranges a cinder block against the screen, now working a second one into place.

"Dah!" the youngest baby calls.

"Suffer," Cassandra says huskily.

The youngest baby claws at the screen to get out.

The older baby spits on the screen.

"You guys are going to run out of food soon," Cassandra informs them, collumphing a third cinder block against the door.

A third baby, youngest of Merlin and Dottie's, arrives at the screen, sucking her whole hand.

The older of Lloyd's daughters takes the doorframe into her hands and gives it a vicious shake against the hingework, and the hingework screels.

Cassandra dangles a baby shoe by its lacing. "Look what I found. It's mine now."

"MINE!" the older baby mourns.

The Soule hand-sucking baby begins to whine in sympathy.

The polish of this shoe is long gone. A shoe with special power over Lloyd's little daughter Sage. The shoe's silverish seams fan out like those on the palm of a hand, lines to read the future in, life lines, lines for travel, marriage, and business. The baby Sage smashes at the door. The two others fall to the floor in a screaming heap.

Lloyd swings the truck door open. A crackle of weeds and sand underfoot. He says, "Leave those kids alone." He moves menacingly toward Cassandra, his calamine-pink hands held out at his sides.

"Daddy!" the baby Sage wails, tries to claw her way through the screen.

"DAH!!" clamors baby Leighlah, pushing herself up on her feet.

Cassandra goes for another cinder block, ignoring Lloyd.

Lloyd says, "They have jail for bad girls."

She says, "Shut up" still grunting along backwards, working the block up onto the broad granite door rock.

Appearing now at the screen is Francine, hands on hips, her big bony shoulders squared. "Cassandra!" she booms. "Who is settin' with Sherry?"

"Mumma's in there, okay? Okay? Jeepers. You think I'm your slave. But I ain't."

Francine looks into Lloyd's eyes. "Hello, Lloyd."

The good essences of Sunday dinner that seemed to have been carried along on Francine, burst out the door, reach out to Lloyd . . . these good things that make up the world of his loss. Francine picks something linty from her summer blouse, flicks it away. Francine is now more Sherry than Sherry is. He almost weeps Francine's name. Now he can't imagine going into that room with Sherry, to the cold steel look of her surgically shaved bald head, nor to the abyss where words and emotion were once the great gush of her life.

He smiles crookedly, gives his khaki cap and his moustache a few nervous yanks. He squints off into the white humid distances that hide the hills, turns back and looks up through the rusted screen at Francine's smart-ass ha-ha expression. He blurts, "Hence, loathed Melancholy, Of Cerberus and blackest Midnight born. In Stygian cave forlorn, 'Mongst horrid shapes, and shrieks and sights unholy!" He pulls off his little khaki cap, bows his head showing the tight straight meticulous part of his long hair.

Francine has looked away from him, her cheeks in high color. Lloyd's tendency to lapse into these meaningless crazy verses among Soule women always embarrasses them. Stuns them, actually.

He turns, slapping his cap back into place, takes the meandering path between other cars and trucks to his own many-colors truck, the babies screaming, "MY DADDY GO!!!!!" and "DAAAAAAAAH!"

But the sisters will get out the tin mixing bowls and wooden spoon and spatulas . . . things babies love . . . things with which to make babies quickly forget.

11 | She thought it might work out to lay on the very edge of the bed, but the weight of Sherry next to her is still too close, too terrible. Terrible to hear Sherry's gargling, gurgling sleeping sounds. Terrible to hear Sherry's gargling, gurgling lying-awake sounds.

Francine trudges into the room to make sure Cassandra is really and actually *in* the bed. This *in*-the-bed the sisters insist upon. Hauling another bed into this room special for Cassandra is ridiculous, they say. Sherry is your own sister, they say. Your own blood.

Now Francine asks, "How's she doin'?" She points her flashlight around, points it in the corners of the room suspiciously although she already sees that Cassandra is *in* the bed.

Cassandra says in a dull voice, "Okay."

Francine asks how many times Sherry has had to pee.

Cassandra says, "I tried her on the toilet thing but she just sat there."

"The commode," Francine corrects her.

Cassandra moans into her pillow. "I've had too many turns!"

"Your own sister. You are a lazy little girl! For eight years old you act like eight *months* old!" Francine booms.

Cassandra stiffens as Sherry thrashes around under the covers. Sherry hisses through her teeth. The other end farts.

Cassandra is now deathly silent.

"Well!" says Francine cheerily. "I'm going home now. Just wanted to check in one last time."

"When you stayin' to take your ol' turn, Francine?" Cassandra demands.

"I don't *live* here, Cassandra. I take *my* turns when I can in the day."

"Why not Mumma? Where's all *her* turns?"

"Mumma's baby is practically due. She needs all the rest she can get."

"Maybe I'm having a baby, too," Cassandra offers.

Francine shuts the door. All the way out through the kitchen she laughs uncontrollably. Sounds like she's falling against the walls.

Now as the household settles down some, Cassandra listens to the night, a neighbor's car passing slow with something inside it clanking metal to metal . . . very broken . . . and an owl whoo-hoooooooooooooooo-awoooooooo-ing up behind the house. The darkness is total. Fiberglass drapes drawn across the screens. Not even a clock face to see by.

"Sssssssss . . . sweeeee . . . p . . . ka . . . sweeeeeep . . . Lloyd . . . eye . . . o!" Sherry's mouth says against the side of Cassandra's head. "Lloydmeeeem . . . meeeeeem! Peeeeeeeeen! Pleeeeeeeeeeeeep!"

Cassandra's eyes fill with tears. She knows without neurological expertise that this is a command, a plea. She can't go to her sleeping spot on the floor till Francine's car is gone. Francine, the meanest, most bossy sister since Sherry got the surgery. It used to be Sherry who was the worst. Lydia and Robin used to call her "Big Mean" and "Queen Beast."

12 | The sign by the road is cardboard and reads: 3-FAMILY YARD SALE. It's a big bad hot devil of a day. Soule sisters dressed light.

Cars all up and down the road on both shoulders; people from all over coming to pick and paw and exclaim how hot it is, some to discuss

Charlie Shaw's funeral. A lot of funeral talk around the Cousins' and Belangers' tables just as there's a lot of silver-haired people around the Cousins' and Belangers' tables. A lot of cordial remembrances. And a few sales.

The thunder increases too suddenly to be weather. There's the rise and fall of pistons pulling them nearer . . . Turnbulls and their wives and women, and Turnbull buddies. All on choppers. All Harleys. Mostly full dress Harleys. Chrome writhing and unbraiding. They pass the yard sale slowly, yard sale merchandise shaking and tinkling with this darksome vibration.

Down the road the choppers get turned around and come back.

"Hell's bells," sister Alberta says from the corner of her mouth.

One by one the Harleys shut down.

The Soule sisters on the chaise lounges stretch out their legs and stretch out their arms in self-conscious display.

Biker people spread out around the tables of the big sale. With biker people there's often a black T-shirt with *the wings* across the chest or back. A couple of them wear denim vests and shirts cut like vests worn over nothing but arduous tattoos. Macky Turnbull and Gordon Turnbull and George Turnbull. And there's David Turnbull's wife, Kit, here today. But no David Turnbull. No King. David Turnbull is the property of the mill these days . . . long hours . . . not many days off. "Man o' Wool" they call him.

More cars pulling off onto the shoulders, a flock of ladies with white and beige purses, a young couple with kids and a baby in a baby backpack. More ladies. Some tourists wearing white and turquoise tennis-type clothes and sunglasses.

The bikers wear sunglasses, too. Mirror ones. So across their eyes scenery and faces stretch and strain and flounder and slide away.

Even with the Harley engines shut down there seems to be too much nerve-rackingness. Something about biker eyes behind the mirror glasses secretly sliding over the yard sale merchandise puts the Cousins and Belangers on edge. Biker hands begin to feel the Cousins' carnival glass. Bikers moving in and among the old ladies with white and beige purses and among the little kids, everybody feeling the merchandise, hands reaching over other hands, a lot of excuse me's and soft hot throbbing sweaty-faced miserable smiles. Everyone being hot. Some people trickle. Some just look gummy. Nobody looks fresh.

And from here by the road, anyone looking up can view that hotter place, that truer hell. Past the house, beyond the barns and blue Harvestore silo, past pens and aluminum gates, some of the daughters of Merlin and Dottie Soule are humped over between rows of green string beans.

How is it decided on who gets to pick and put up green beans, and who gets to set out on chaise lounges and twirl their yellow hair?

Who would choose the string bean way?

Is there something about the string bean? Something more than meets the eye? Some special power to draw some people into two hundred yards of low bush? Some unseen fun? Some ecstasy? Some prize? What? At the end of each row, the pickers pivot, and continue squat-walking the next row, dragging the basket. Those flying hands! Hand over hand. The beans pile up, pile high. Why? Why? Why? Can't they find a better way? Less grit? Less squat?

A biker gives a box of old tools a careful study. A biker opens a jar of cat's eye marbles. An old lady pulls the chain of a lamp, feels the edge of the shade. Biker stoops to check out some paint-by-number pictures of a country lane . . . already painted. The Cousins and Belangers of the two high-priced tables have dropped out of the funeral conversation, eyes on the bikers, bikers feeling, feeling, feeling. Old lady with a purse is feeling the milk glass owl that a biker just set down. Bikers moving left and right. Bikers advancing. Bikers backing away, stepping around the baby backpack Dad. It's hard to keep a close watch on all these bikers at once. Bikers pushing their mirror sunglasses to the tops of their heads. Biker says the raccoon puppet here on the Soules' table would be nice for his niece. He makes the raccoon squinch Macky Turnbull's nose. Macky fits his hand into the Charlie Brown puppet and Charlie Brown gives the raccoon a little push. Raccoon and Charlie Brown waltz a moment. Another biker fitting his hand into a catcher's mitt. Kit Turnbull looking over old silverplated spoons. "Don't see many of these nice chowder spoons anymore. Or those butter knives. Nice and wide," she says in a soft gritty voice.

Eyes of Macky Turnbull and Gordon Turnbull glancing off the Soule sisters' flowered halter tops, cut-off jeans, and summer muumuus.

Bikers glance at Sherry, too . . . but in a different way.

Sherry who has plenty of sisters sharing the job of attending her today. Sherry with her bootcamp haircut, slack mouth, vague stare, and on her cheek a big brassy deerfly. Lots of sisters to deal with this fly problem. Seems the sisters aren't as fast as deerflies though. Deerflies are winning this battle over Sherry. Lots of bloody nicks on Sherry. But Sherry makes no complaint.

Sister Faye is getting playful. She has something hidden between her bare thighs . . . sort of like you'd hold a cold beer only *this* is a guessing game.

"A shamrock!" Cassandra shrieks.

"No shamrocks around here," sister Wendy informs her, rolling her eyes.

Cassandra frowns. "I *meant* four-leaf clover."

Faye raises a store-bought vegetable can, gives it a little shake, slips it back between her thighs. Couple of bikers see this. A couple of them smirk, but most of them look away quick. How truly bashful these bikers seem. How sweet. Bikers perhaps *seeming* sweet in relation to the Soule sisters, the married ones and the unmarried ones and the soon-to-be ready ones, Soules forever, working together, mobilized . . . the true GANG.

"Sounds like nails," Francine guesses.

"NO!" Faye booms. "It's not what's *in* the can. It's what's *on* the can."

Many many many eyes drift toward the can between Faye's thighs, just the rim of the can visible.

"Something *on* the can?" Robin wonders, squinting one eye. "Like you mean . . . like fingerprints?"

Faye snorts. Shakes her pale mane of hair. So much Soule hair here, the ranks of all their yellows, dirty blonds, strawberry, tawny, and tow. Faye doesn't lay an outright gaze upon the nearest biker, but it's plain to see she's crazy with the way he moves in the corner of her eye, a quick-moving small-built biker with a grimace indicating he owns many fierce unmet hungers. He is dark-haired with a little leather cap and a T-shirt that is green like a signal for *go*.

Another biker moves into her consideration now. This one has hair as blond as her own. But his has more curl. Fomenting. Cascading over the shoulders of his purple T-shirt, white Playboy bunny head in profile on the chest. His beard isn't much. Just a few hard-won reddish scribbles. Faye tremors slightly. Now another biker catches her eye . . .

Down the road at the farthest end of parked vehicles, a truck eases to a stop. Orange truck. Blue door. Red door. Yellow fender. Bondo spots. Chain saw and gas cans on the wooden bed.

Bikers sift through the Soules' jumble of kitchen utensils, yesteryear's tools, items that you'd guess were torture devices . . . thumb stretchers, fingernail pullers, eye jabbers, nipple twisters, and skin skinners.

With Faye so off guard, Cassandra pounces on her and rassles the can from her, the chaise lounge creaking ricketishly under them. Cassandra runs off with the can.

Sister Brenda bounds from her chaise, snatches the can from Cassandra and gives the can a big kiss. "It's HIM!!! It's HIM!! It's the jolly green giant. My honey." Brenda's silvery hair flashes and fumes around her red-and-blue halter top and long arms.

"Jolly green giant," Francine says matter-of-factly.

Faye moans. "That's right! At the peak of perfection! Ripe for the picking!!"

Francine shakes her head. "Jesus."

"You are sick," sister Pam says.

Jiggling one foot contentedly, sister Alberta explains, "If they put him on that can without that silly leaf suit, they'd sell a lot more vegetables."

The nearest biker gives his short-visored leather cap a sudden adjustment.

"Like hotcakes," Brenda adds, lifting her sunglasses to admire the vegetable can more directly.

Very pregnant sister Tina says, "There'd be no holding back the women of America." She twirls a thickness of her strawberry blond hair.

Sister Marcia takes calming puffs on her long menthol, speaks with her slow exhale. "Yuh, Mr. Grocer. Give me some diced carrots. Hurry up quick! Hubba, hubba."

All the sisters shriek and fling themselves around. Raucous as a gang of crows. One chaise flips over. Long legs with rubber thongs on the feet kick a table leg causing the merchandise to clank and tinkle and thud.

The blond biker tries out the crank on an ice-cream maker.

Another holds up the three-foot-tall framed picture of the Sermon on the Mount. "Three-D Jesus," he murmurs deeply to another biker who is balding on top, but plenty of beard. They each take a turn at wiggling the picture.

Sherry unattended now, but by flies. Sherry in one of her familiar summer tops, a pretty purple print. Bare freckled arms. Feet in new blond moccasins . . . the sherpa-lined soleless style . . . the kind not meant to walk far in.

You did not see Sherry here at the yard sale last year. Sherry the oldest sister, "Queen Beast," commanding officer of picking and canning, fastest picker, fastest at snapping beans, and you'd never find an imperfect seal by her hand. Sherry knew the secret of the loaded pantry is more tender than any silly whispered word of love.

Sister Brenda is back in her chaise, holds the vegetable can up.

Faye gasps. Covers her eyes. "GAWD! Don't torment me!"

Another carload arrives. One with a lot of kids. Kids go swarming and screaming toward the high-priced tables of glass and lace.

Cassandra circles Brenda's chaise, waiting for her chance to snatch the can again. Cassandra who loves a wild chase. Cassandra who likes to keep the pot stirred.

The crowd around the Soule tables thickens as a few more carloads arrive. Sister Pam makes change from the money jar. Sold: a coverless crockpot, some TV trays, and a Star Trek coloring book never used.

"I don't know if I could go to bed with a green guy," says Alberta.

"That's prejudiced!" Pam scolds.

"I like the green color myself," sighs Tina. "Wouldn't mind one bit havin' me a big green man."

Sold: Ashtray. Perry Como album. Two toasters. Bronze horse with chain reins. Four Merc hubs. Harry Belafonte album. Jar of buttons.

Sherry's head . . . not so blue-white and steely a head now as it was right after the surgery, and yet . . . her hair . . . it had been her glory once. How does a bald head differ from a bare ass?, she might have guffawed at one time had the subject arisen. Her face now shows no shame. Her face shows nothing. Around her head and face deerflies circle at the speed of light, sunlit like sapphires.

Sold: Set of tin canisters. Another Harry Belafonte album. Jar of cat's eye marbles. A couple of thumb stretchers, eye jabbers, nipple twisters.

A traffic jam in the road. Cars slowing, stopping, peering, slowing, moving on. Cars squeezing between cars on both shoulders. Cars parked for a quarter of a mile west.

Lloyd stands among the ladies and kids and bikers. He stands with his arms to his sides, eyes fixed on his wife's face.

Sold: A set of seat covers for a large sedan. Leopard print.

The chair they have put Sherry in is the oak mission rocker. It's not a chair anyone would pick to sit in. He sees her eyes can't focus on his face, but show some stammering recognition of his belt buckle. His T-shirt, white when it was new, is blotched with his work in the woods with Edmund this morning . . . pine, hemlock. As people rub past him, the smell of him is sweet and Christmassy.

Sherry squeezes one hand with the other. One eye is now clearly widening on his face, but her head eventually drops.

Is this shame he feels his own? Or something she confers to him? Or, yes, shared.

What would the sisters do if he tugged his bandanna from his pocket now and gallantly tied it on her head? A creased and sweaty bandanna. But still bright and fairly new. Red. He could flatten it a bit on the thigh of his dungarees with the palms of his hands. Hands with calamine and pine pitch in every crease. He could tie the bandanna around Sherry's head with the tails of the knot loose in a girlish way on the damp nape of her neck.

His fear. Enormous. The high yellowy humid glare of broad daylight enlarges every threat.

A Soule sister booms, "Jesus, Pammy! Don't sell those! I just took 'em off a few minutes to air my feet!"

Again Sherry raises an eye to him. COVER MY HEAD the eye screams. Pleads. Weeps. Eye loses its grip, drops away.

The crowd thins out between Lloyd and the table with Sherry there in the mission rocker. But he moves on, mixes in and among, then vanishes.

13 | Cassandra on the edge of the bed.
The voice at the back of her neck is choking and gibberish "Ack . . . nose . . . no . . . meem . . . mean . . . no! Neeenaneeee-nanneeeeeeeee . . . la . . . mean LA! . . ."

Cassandra whispers, "Shut up."

Voice says, "Smeeeeeeeee . . . ear hot . . . reeeeeeeeeed." Hand muckles the back of Cassandra's neck. The voice commands, "Bo . . . wank . . . Lloy!"

How come no one else gets Sherry's requests? How come it's only Cassandra?

"Lloy! Lloyg! Pleeeeeeeeek!" Sherry's maimed voice risen above its strategic whisper now settles back to silence. Sherry is listening to the household. Aware of her limits.

14 | Next day the yard sale is quieter. Leaner pickings.
Lloyd parks his truck across the tar road. He is loaded today with mowers, the push kind, weed whacker, pruners, saws, and gas can. Sunday. The Lord's day. Day of rest. All days the same in the graveyard biz. And any of his odd jobs. He keeps no schedule. No appointments. No wristwatch. No calendar. No true concept of the days of the week.

The Soule sisters in their chaises and the Cousins and Belangers at their high-priced tables watch Lloyd ease out from his truck, slam the door. He gives his striped railroad cap a little gentlemanly adjustment. Crosses the road. Such an old-mannish mosey. Today's T-shirt is a blatant all-out hippie tie-dyed turquoise-and-rose pink peace-sign threadbare shredded one-sleeve-missing mess. Mrs. Cousins murmurs a barely audible "Oh, dear."

Sherry is not among these sisters today. Neither is Cassandra and the pregnant one, Tina. Just the fit and ready ones, all of them smirking as if Sherry's absence means they've outsmarted Lloyd today, got one better on him.

"Heigh ho all," Lloyd greets them in his voice that always breaks into a raspy softness on a final word or syllable . . . in this case "all" is nearly lost.

"Hello, Lloyd," Francine says, crossing her arms over her T-shirt. Her T-shirt, unlike his, is fresh and palest pink with a smiley face, though the smiley face is hidden by her forearms.

The other sisters nod or pretend to ignore him. Kim is painting her nails. Alberta is watching for possible approaching cars from the west.

Lloyd paws through a box of Christmas balls and garlands. He opens a stained Betty Crocker cookbook, flips through MEATS, SALADS, BREADS, CASSEROLES, DESSERTS. He feels the ear of a man-sized shag teddybear. Hoists up the picture of Jesus, wiggles it to get the full effect. He can smell the sisters. About six bottles of Coppertone is what they smell like. Lloyd admires some toasters. Where would the Soules get six toasters? He pokes at a red dog collar. German shepherd size. Soules never had any dogs. Harry Belafonte records. An unopened can of surplus USDA luncheon meat that reads NOT TO BE SOLD.

He sidles over to the high-priced tables. Lace. Glass. Copper. Porcelain. Nothing like the Soule family's plastic and cheap tangled heap. Everything on the high-priced tables is arranged in such a pretty way. A kitty-cat needlepoint pillow. An antique quilt in browns and shades of cream . . . and soft birdlike blues. Nothing plastic here. Nothing Souleish.

The Cousins and Belangers are not sun people. They have patio umbrellas that make two nice spots of shade.

Mrs. Cousins says, "So, dear, you graduated at the university this spring?"

Lloyd answers with "Yes ma'am."

Mrs. Cousins stretches forward, closes her cool shady hand on his forearm. "So sorry about your wife, dear. Anything we can do, you let us know, won't you? Such a shame. My son had tumors in his brain, too. But his was cancer and we lost him. He was only thirty-six years old."

Lloyd, fiercely stricken, lowers his eyes. Through her hand on his arm he feels the whole trial. He smiles wearily, crookedly. He says softly, "The Moving Finger writes; and, having writ, / Moves on: nor all your Piety nor Wit / Shall lure it back to cancel half a Line, / Nor all your Tears wash out a Word of it. . . ."

Mrs. Cousins jerks her hand back. Both she and Mr. Cousins and the others behind the high-priced tables are shocked and discomfited.

Francine laments, "Come on, Lloyd! Talk English! Jesus!"

Faye calls over to the Cousins, "He doesn't say anything you can understand since college. Nobody can understand him. So don't feel bad. It's hippie lingo."

"He majored in Communism," Alberta tells on him.

"Not Communism, Alberta." sister Pam corrects her. "Socialism."

Lloyd's moustache flickers slightly, his spotted eyes suddenly merry.

Mrs. Belanger fans her paling face. A quite frantic little fanning. "I didn't know they taught such things at the college. I just don't believe that. Why would our government allow it?"

"He told *me* it was Sociology," sister Robin says.

Kim snickers. "I heard of a course called *Women and Social Change*. That must be about how to give operations to turn women into men, I'll bet. Hippies have made a mess out of colleges."

"Don't be dumb!" Faye scolds. "That's not a medical course. I hate it when you do that. Playing dumb."

Kim's laugh is a deep pleasurable cackle.

Faye says, "The real question is what *was* Lloyd's major? Try and pin him down on that and see where it goes . . ."

"I bet it was basket weaving and tofu!" Kim hoots.

All the sisters but Faye get a good howl over this.

Faye says, "Get serious, Kim."

After a moment of semisilence, sister Gail says, "He told *me* Psychology."

"He told Mum it was Social Welfare," Marcia tells them.

"Political Science!" insists Francine. "I remember him saying Political Science because we had that discussion about how politics is not science."

With a twinge of irritation, Brenda says, "I was *there* the night he said Social Welfare."

"You pick 'em like flowers," Lloyd says softly. "It's a nice place."

"Nice place!" Francine snorts. "Sex and drugs, right, Lloyd? LSD. And speed. And marijuana. That's what they do in college. Just a big good time!"

Mrs. Cousins closes her hand on Lloyd's forearm again, upon the black maps of pine pitch from early morning work at his unk Jim's sawmill, *before* the following hours repairing cemetery fence, and that being before finishing up the trimming of the big cemetery over on the river . . . where he got into more pine using his saw on fallen limbs. Big urgency in the lady's grip. She leans closer with her smell that is nothing like Lloyd's . . . and nothing like Coppertone . . . but the smell of whatever goes into her white hair to make it nice . . . the fussing and the fixing smell. The old sweet talc smells that further shape the losses of his life. She tightens her grip. Her eyes blue once, now less so. "I like a *good* boy," says she. "That's what *I* like."

Lloyd lowers his eyes. Lloyd sees the shadow move over the table of glass knickknacks and intricately patterned old chinaware. A shadow like weather but larger than what amount of weather can exist in a day. It is like you hear so many tell, of seeing your life before you in a flash. But what he sees isn't really images of himself of that future. What he sees is *them*. Just as he sees them out through his two eyes now, his own face unseeable. But he can see his hands, knees, and feet of the future. And he is not alone. There will always be *them* in their entirety.

At the university there was a drumming within the walls of the professors' mouths, their throats like hallways leading out and back again.

His pen always pushed along on its hard track, graphs, statistics, variables, control groups, evaluations, theories, discussions, proposals, laws . . . wonderment . . . his own tongue and the liquids there, jaws and inner ear squeaking and that hollow rushing like wind through rooms . . . his head cocked like a dog's . . . listening so hard . . . the truth is hard.

He saw the political science prof's hands making fists in his pockets as he paced to and fro, fretful, pressed, damaged in some way. Lloyd recalls his own hands heaped in a pile on his desk there. The sociology prof tells a joke. The class laughs.

Now Lloyd sees his own death cross the table of glinting glass and pretties. Not a shadow, but light.

His death is clearer to him than life.

He knows his death will be justified. And multiplied. *They* will die with him. Up and down the line, a thousandfold. The infinite mirrors.

He is not afraid because death isn't today. But he sees that every word and gesture, every intention of this world is leading up to that death, word by word, the magnanimous words, the many transactions, calculations, investments, buyouts, betrayals . . . like bricks cleaving to bricks, slowly amassing.

He raises his eyes to Mrs. Cousins's face, the shivery silk eddies and lines of her neck and mouth, the rimmed edges of her skull's eyeholes more pronounced than the last time he saw her. He says with a flustered grin, "I will."

15 | Dottie can't see much in this dark. If she remembered to put her glasses on, she would be able to make out at least the outlines of things in this kitchen. She protects her pregnant belly with one open hand, feels her way with the other hand. Feels with her toes.

It's with some of her toes she discovers Cassandra on the kitchen floor *outside* the closed door to the room where Sherry is kept.

Cassandra jerks beneath Dottie's feeling foot. Cassandra smacks the door with her hand. BAM! BAM! BAM!

Dottie asks, "What are you doing?!" Dottie backs up to the wall, snaps on the light. Cassandra is on her feet now. Little nightshirt. Long bare skinny legs. Big knee bones. Big bare feet. A Soule sister in that pup stage of life. Eyes very wide. "HELLO! MUMMA!" the child booms. "YOU! SURE! ARE! REALLY! HERE! PROBABLY! GOIN'! IN! TO! SEE! SHERRY! HUH?"

16 He parks behind his father's old Bonneville. His truck idles raggedly. Headlights are on, one beam aimed at his father's license plate . . . Maine, Vacationland . . . the other beam soaring to the upstairs window over the shedway. It is a house of only *two* men these days. The others laid low, long gone, passed on. And some who only used to stop by for suppers don't bother since Walty moved to Aspect Street a few years ago.

Just Edmund and Roger . . . still two bull-built heavy-duty sons-a-bitches in their fifties, still with hands that could crush a Revereware saucepan. Still with their appetites. Bad teeth don't dismay them. Whole platters of chicken, sheep, cow, pig, partridge, or moose. Near raw. Edmund Barrington and Roger Fogg, always looking out at you through the dark glare of their bifocals, gauging you, weighing you, worrying you. Dead reckoning. Still putting in long days, hot days, cold days. Work. Work. Work. It's never long after supper, the lights go out.

Sometimes their old friend Clayton comes around to help with butchering. To help mess with a tractor engine. Or to hay. Or to help eat out of their bloody plates. Clayton with the wrecked ears, ears that hang down. Never wears a shirt except when it's snowing. Old bunch of ribs and nubby spine and suspenders. And always some Band-Aids. A Band-Aid on his back or over a nipple. Band-Aid behind one hang-down ear. And white untanned gummy Band-Aid shapes where Band-Aids used to be. When Clayton comes around to help, he spends his nights on a cot in the kitchen, no blankets. He just curls up tight like a rat.

Lloyd studies each window. Not one light on. He lays hard on the horn. . . "BLAAAAAAAAAAAAAAAAAAAAAAAAAAAAAAAAAAAAAA-AAAAAA!!"

Lloyd and his father don't "speak" anymore. Even as they work together, which is nearly every day since Lloyd got done with college, they don't speak. They are seen together, side by side, two heads in a truck, or three when Unk Roger is along. But mostly it's just Lloyd and Edmund. Mowing graves. Digging graves. Setting flags for vets. Yarding pine on Bean land for Beans. Loading Christmas trees for Haskells. Sugaring. Running a motor up on block and tackle. Winching a truck out of the mud. Milling out hundreds of board feet at Unk Jim's. Side by side. No conversation. Sitting on the tailgate for a sandwich and Thermos of tea. Nothing but six inches between them. Six inches big as a mile. And it all has to do with HAIR.

Lloyd waits, then rams the horn again. "BLAAAAAAAAAAA-AAAAAAA!"

His father appears in the dark zone between the headlights, thin-haired, thick-waisted, eyeglasses jouncing with reflections. As he steps close to the open truck window, Edmund gags to clear his chest. Spits. Too many years of the unks' and the gramps' sidestream smoke. Edmund says in a word that's oddly deeply soft, "What?"

This is a breakthrough. This is the first word. The breaking of the ice. In some sense, a conversation.

Lloyd cuts the lights. No light now but for the greenly glowing dash. He shuts down the engine. There is now just the deafening shrill of tall-grass bugs, the cooling pings under the truck hood. And something thumps inside the house. A single thump. But between Lloyd and Edmund nothing . . . the single precious word fading fast.

The smell of his father's closeness. A smell much like his own. Woods and work and the good right mix of human and Hereford, that ancient brotherhood of men and cattle. But also Edmund possesses the scent of the inside of the house, beyond that screen door where Lloyd can't seem to get a foot into these days, not since HAIR. Not since his "goddam-commie-hippie-can't-tell-the-boys-from-the-girls look."

The house. The dim yearning sweet piled-up past includes a tweak of scent that is of Lloyd's mother. Dead for fourteen years. But forever the soft mustiness of her once livingness is guarded here. Her catalogs still somewhere here in piles, settling. Her dresses. Her blue china. Her candy and cigar boxes of photos and photo postcards of people you can only guess at. And her girlhood diary, which Lloyd knows contains passionate detailed daily installments of Minnie-Ha-Ha, her calico cat. The diary is wrapped in a light blue linen cloth. These things Edmund has always horded, unlike most people who eventually chuck everything out, who try to start anew, who try to heal. Instead Edmund Barrington wears the sweet decaying scent on him, this saga of his marriage at all times whispered.

Lloyd says, "So . . ." A pause. "How are you tonight, Dad?"

Edmund is of course pissed off with the horn-blowing-in-the-night routine. And probably a little puzzled. Edmund's fingers commence tapping the truck door near Lloyd's elbow. Lloyd can't see what's in Edmund's other hand, but he suspects it's the six-volt battery lantern kept bedside for emergencies.

Tall-grass bugs cheep and creak up and over the miles uncountable, orchestrated around the drumroll of Edmund's tapping fingers.

"So," says Lloyd.

The finger tapping stops.

No discussions these past months about Sherry's headaches and vision, the tests, the tumor, the surgery that cut Sherry's mind out. Edmund not asking; Lloyd not offering. Edmund hearing of Sherry in other ways. Could it be this hold-out is more Lloyd's than Edmund's? Or maybe even-steven. Or maybe a fiercely stubborn being exists between them, made up of the two?

The finger tapping stops.

Lloyd says, "I thought you might not mind I come back here to live . . . you know. I could give you the money I'm now forking over to the landlord. Seems silly for me to keep that house just for me. Clayton around?"

Edmund mutters, "No. He was. But now he's not."

"I want to come back awhile," Lloyd says.

"That so," Edmund says.

The shrieking of the bugs increases to a deafening roar.

"Can I?" Lloyd asks too softly.

Edmund's other hand appears with the battery lamp, snaps the white glare of it onto Lloyd's face, leaves it trained there a significant half minute, then snaps it off. "Still got that mess of hair," Edmund snorts. This of course means "no." His answer to Lloyd's request.

17 | Sister Pam, silverish hair piled high. Sister Alberta wearing her tawny hair in a twist. Hot in a car with so many babies. Babies are the most moist people.

"Stay outta them bags!" Pam commands, hearing a crinkle in the backseat. Not enough room in the trunk for all the groceries. Bags lined up on the floor. Babies lined up on the seat. Babies tired from shopping. Querulous hot looks in their eyes.

"Stuff has to be cooked first," sister Alberta tells the babies. The oldest baby, Sage, passes around bananas.

"What's going on back there?!" Pam snarls, reaches back over the seat, grabs a banana. "Jesus Christ! Do I have to pull over?!" She stops the car close to the curb by the PO. "Gimme them bananas! All of them! NOW!"

Lloyd on the sidewalk, messy T-shirt and a visored cap that reads JONESREDS across the front. Little cap. Big hair. Hair in a crisis. Hair in a tumble, beard nearly to his belt.

"ROLL UP THE WINDOWS!" Alberta commands. "Dad says don't let Lloyd around them kids."

Babies scream. Sage tries to pull down on the glass as it rises. "DADDY! DADDY! MY DADDY!"

"Let go!" Alberta loosens the fingers.

Leighlah, the younger baby, calls out, "DAH!" She climbs up onto Sage.

The third child, wee Soule sister, joins in on the struggle with booming voice, "DAH! DAH!"

Lloyd moves toward the car, raises a hand to the glass, eyes on the children. He speaks but is unheard.

Alberta says, "Get going, Pam! Spin outta here! Quick! Dad says don't let Lloyd around these kids unless he's around to keep an eye on things."

Pam scrinches up half her face. "What's Daddy's problem anyway? Lloyd ain't nuthin'. Lloyd never abuses no kids. If anything he lets them walk all over him . . ."

"*Some* guys snatch kids and take them to other states."

Pam gives the car the gas. "Jesus . . . Daddy's too paranoid about Lloyd."

"Maybe. Maybe not," Alberta says, crossing her arms.

Sage and Leighlah and the baby Soule sister all scream and kick. Sage stands on the seat, watching Lloyd grow smaller. "That wiz MY daddy," she insists.

"Sit down!" Alberta bellers, turning, pushing Sage into a "sit."

All three little girls have their buttercup yellow party dresses on. Earrings like pearls. Hair fixed with dried flowers. Eyes big. White baby shoes jab into the bags of groceries. Bananas, many loaves of bread, a cantaloupe, a box of tapioca. All crunching, popping, oozing. Baby mutiny.

18 | Another night, a cool one after many lumbering breathless hot ones. Tonight the night Dottie Soule's baby is due. Baby unmoving. Dottie's belly filled to the max. Packed solid as ever with Merlin's effortless and grand effusion.

Dottie is restless. Stairs cool under Dottie's bare feet. Going down to check on Cassandra and Sherry. Something a little unsettling. Something suspect. Tonight the dark is way darker than what is right. And Cassandra doesn't try to argue her way out of staying with Sherry now. Suddenly Cassandra is cheerily cooperative. Like Florence Nightingale.

Dottie wears her glasses this time. She moves along with stealth. But not enough stealth; she raps her leg on the solid oak mission rocker. "OWWW!"

She hears BAM! BAM! BAM! Three splinterish-sounding smacks on Sherry's door.

This time Dottie's switching on the light reveals Cassandra sitting Indian style with her back against the door. Wool blanket around her shoulders. Big man-sized wool socks bagging around her ankles. Eyes narrowed. The look not of a nurse but of a sentry.

Dottie narrows her eyes too. "What's up, Cassandra? Why are you outside the door again?"

Cassandra shrugs.

"Why do you hit the door like that?"

"Maybe a fly. I hit it."

Dottie squints very hard at the door. Then at Cassandra. "I'll take over for you. I can't sleep anyway. This baby feels like an avalanche."

Cassandra cracks up mightily over "avalanche." But as she laughs, she keeps her back to the door blocking the way.

"Go on, Cassandra," Dottie insists. "Your shift is over. Graveyard shift starts now."

Cassandra's eyes widen. "Why'd you say that? Graveyard."

"It's just another name for night shift. Like Uncle Rex at the mill. And Francine."

"Francine don't work at night, Mum."

"She started off nights."

Cassandra shouts, "WELL! I! GUESS! I'LL! GO! TO! MY! BED! UPSTAIRS! NOW! MUMMA! NOW! THAT! YOU'RE! HERE! GOOD! OL'! NIGHT!" She unbends, gathers her blanket as she stands, stomps heavily away.

Dottie puts her hand to the door. The woodenness. The porousness of old paint. She considers this door with its raging silence beyond.

———

19 | The summer has worn on and on, worn hard. Can't get rid of the heat. Faces like lard. Air like lard. Shirts and blouses that stick. The weight of humid heat being most heavy in the many attics all over Egypt. Attics like little hells. A window on the end of a gable, perhaps a dormer with flowery valances. And yet the thing prettiness can't disguise: ninety-five degrees downstairs, a hundred and ten degrees upstairs.

Cassandra lies on the floor between her bed and the open-stud wall listening to the sisters hunt for her. "CASSANDRA!" they call, opening and shutting doors downstairs. "CASSANDRA!! WHERE ARE YOOOOOOO!"

Out in the dooryard and barnyard, down along the tie-ups and pens, out among the cars and trucks, along the sandy shoulders of the road their calls are booming, coarse and lusty. "CASSANDRA!!" Up in the high field. Out across the low pasture. "CASSANDRA!" Big search.

The door to this room opens, this room that she shares with sisters Lydia and Wendy, the three beds made up in plaid summerweights. But it is neither Lydia nor Wendy who opens the door. It's *them*. The older more bullyish sisters. The ones that don't even live in this house anymore. "Cassandra." One of them is speaking to the empty-looking room. Another says, "Guess she's not in here."

Barefoot or rubber-thonged, long-boned. Swinging, slashing tails of hair. They heave themselves onto the door of the next room and the next, then the BOOM BOOM BOOM of them heading back to the kitchen. Headquarters.

After a few moments and a little miserable sigh, Cassandra pops her head up from her hiding place and sees into the blazing very green eyes of Francine standing with her hands on her hips in the open door. "SO!" says Francine. "AH-HA! Did you pass out or something, Cassandra?"

Another sister appears . . . stocking feet. Very very quiet on her feet. "GIRLS! WE FOUND HER! SHE'S UP HERE AFTER ALL! HIDING!"

Now on the stairs feet returning.

The room fills up fast. There is something. Like doctors gathering around with a big needle. Like thick legs of men gathered around a mutilated deeply worried creature in a leghold trap. Like in the movies of the old-time-God-days people getting ready to open the lion's door and toss someone in. Like bloodhounds and cops.

Cassandra collapses back into her flattened-out position behind the bed. "I'm sick. I need peace," she whimpers.

They pull her to her feet, set her on the edge of the bed. But not roughly. Not their usual neck-squeeze head holds. They are horribly and suspiciously *nice*. Sister Pam pats Cassandra's shoulder. "Dear, we want to have a talk with you."

Tina and Faye sit along the edge of the bed with her. Francine, Alberta, Robin, and Brenda stand with hands on hips before her, all of them with kindly expressions, and yet in the center of their overheated rocking-to-and-fro dimensions, Cassandra knows it when she sees it . . . power in cold blood.

"We have to ask you a *big question*, Cassandra," Francine begins.

Cassandra scowls, swings her feet. "What's that?"

"Well . . ." Pam hedges.

"You are the only person who might know the *big answer* to this big question, dear," Faye tells her.

Kim arrives at the doorway, exasperated, red. Her hair is in wet ringlets around her ears and a wet mash of hair on her forehead. She sees the sweet preplanned tender looks of the others and instantly transforms her expression to match. She sweetly murmurs, "Have you asked her yet?"

Faye speaks into Cassandra's eyes. "Men are nice in some ways . . . like Daddy, how he jokes around a lot and looks out for us. But there's this thing about men . . . some worse than others . . . that's *evil*."

Kim cries out, "Oh, Faye! Don't tell her it's evil! Gawd."

Faye glares at Kim, then her eyes fall back onto Cassandra, her expression adjusting back to its sweet mode, *beyond* sweet, beyond sugary, beyond honeyed . . . on into caramel . . . marmalade.

Cassandra snickers. "You guys are funny." Her mouth smiles, but her eyes search faces, these wide-cheekboned somewhat Nordic Soule faces that are, in photographs, strikingly beautiful but in real life have too much flex and fume, too much heckle. Too much.

Cassandra blurts out, "I *know* about sex if this is what this is about."

Sister Alberta crosses her arms under her breasts. "We aren't here to *tell* you anything, Cassandra. We are here to find something out." Sister Alberta is starting to look a little put off.

Sister Francine says softly, "Cassandra, dear, you know Sherry's not right. She's like a . . ."

"Vegetable," Cassandra says.

"Well, not *that* bad, but   "

"Stevie says 'vegetable'."

"Well, Stevie is mean to say that. I didn't know he was going around saying that," Francine sighs. The sisters exchange glances.

"He said *you* said it," Cassandra says into Francine's eyes.

All the sisters narrow their eyes on Francine.

Eyes blurring with tears, Francine says, "Sometimes I don't know *what* to say. This has been a terrible time! It's not important, for godsakes. What's important is Sherry is not like a regular woman. The tumor and operation have wrecked her brain! She's just a helpless baby! An infant who can't protect herself!" She wipes her tears with the inside of her wrist. "It's not right for somebody like Sherry to have sex. But *somebody* has been getting into Sherry's room and doing *it* to Sherry! We know because she's pregnant! Imagine! Jesus! A very very SICK man has done this! *Who* was in there with Sherry, Cassandra? Tell us!!"

"Maybe a burglar," says Cassandra quietly.

As if on cue, the newest Soule sister puts up a thin miserable wail from one of the rooms below.

"You know, don't you, Cassandra? You know!" Francine insists. Little bangs of her pixie cut are wet and darkening. Her face glassy.

"Cassandra. We *know* you *know*," Robin snarls. "So just tell us!" She swallows, trying to regain the sweet voice they all started with. "It's okay if you tell us."

Cassandra shrugs, fidgets with the cuff of her shorts. "If you know I know, then why do you keep askin' me if I know? It's dumb. Just go and know all of it you know and get out of my room. I need some peace."

"Cassandra," Faye says, patting her shoulder. "Was it Lloyd, dear?"

Cassandra scrinches her eyes shut and says exhaustedly, "If you already know what you know that I know and you know it's ol' Lloyd, why do you gotta do this and be a pain in the ol' neck!" She flops backward, covers her face with her forearm.

Every mouth a hard line. Every blouse and halter top and pair of shorts and cut-offs are soaking. Every throat and bosom trickles a little river. There is a grand, slightly squeamish silence for a moment as there is after every hard-won confession.

———

20 | By evening a good and right coolness at last settles in Egypt. And then the cool turns to cold.

The sisters and the mother, Dottie, watch Merlin bend around in his seat, gesturing to a man at the next table, a teamster they all recognize from past fairs. This is Merlin now, the before-Merlin-finds-out Merlin. The meal is baked beans. Three kinds of beans . . . pea, kidney, and yellow eye. Lopsided but tasty reheated biscuits. Biscuits whose beginnings were within eight different Egypt kitchens. And "butter" which isn't butter. And slimy sweet slaw. And pie. All nine kinds of Merlin's favorites, but you are only allowed to pick one piece at this supper. Big pan of beans coming down the line. No limit on beans. This is the before-Merlin-finds-out Merlin loading his plate, shooting the breeze, getting hepped up over certain fairs that are beginning, bragging on Rocket and Tommy, his babies big as ships.

It's the East Egypt Community Club's public supper. Water pipes sometimes bang under the floor, tickle the feet. Poor light at the windows. September. Dim and chill outside. Dim and chill inside. Not much for a stove here. Just the heat of cooking and heat left from the hot day. And the heat of the crowd. Big crowd. Too many. Too small a building for so many. Got to eat in rounds.

Some of the Soule girls and their boyfriends and boy husbands are still waiting in line, waiting beyond the ticket man's card table. They hoot and holler and wave to the seated Soules who wave back.

Sherry has a seat. It's her second time out in the world since the yard sale. Neighbors and such at the far end of the table and other tables either stare at Sherry or pretend there's nothing at all different.

Big K. Bean stalks out from the kitchen area and looks calculatingly among the tables. She and Mary Dresser have been steering newcomers to certain tables, giving old Art Heney a bit of a push for speed. There's a feeling here tonight of hurry-chew-swallow. Kitchen beyond the half wall is smoking, steaming, clanging, big shouts, splash of water . . . enough racket to seem like a ship being loaded . . . or the evacuation of a sinking one.

Now a string of people get the okay from the ticket man. He says, "Head in now" then "Whoa!" when there's enough.

K. Bean and Mary Dresser circle the tables watching plates. "Have more of that slaw, Mrs. Cramer. Eat up!" Elbows fly as the kitchenfolk move three more serving dishes of red hot dogs to the window of the half wall and from there to the tables.

Sherry's babies and the next-youngest Soule sister won't stay put in their seats. Blue-dress babies tonight. Fine as any magazine babies. Sweet complexions. Hair in bows. All three have blue bunny-rabbit earrings, ear-piercing of babies being the rage these days.

Big K. Bean warns, "Watch those little girls, somebody!" The sisters scoop up the babies. Babies wailing. Babies don't want to eat. Babies just want to run around and feel strangers' knees. Baby Leighlah reaches over Robin's shoulder, reaches out to the crowded room as if for a star. People at other tables laugh at the babies. They love the babies and various other babies coming and going here tonight. Babies a nice thing. Gives everybody's insides a goodly glow.

Carroll Plummer, Merlin's young friend, has come to the supper as planned, but can't get past the ticket man. Carroll Plummer has had a few drinks. When Carroll Plummer has had a few drinks, he thinks he can walk on water, swim through air, fly through walls. There's a little pushing and arguing out in the entry near the ticket man's table. "Quit it, Carroll!" one of the Soule girls commands.

"Meeeee and Bobbeeeeeee McGeeeeeeeeeeee," Carroll sings tonelessly, which means he has both hearing aids turned off.

Merlin lets K. Bean load his plate up with more biscuits.

"Butter," says he.

"Here's butter. Loads of butter. Good for your hair," she says and winks. K. Bean, one to joke. She is keeping her eyes sharp on everybody's coffee cups. "Dot, dear . . . you're getting low!" She swings the coffee pitcher to the right. A little splash to fill Dot Soule's cup.

"Thanks a million!" Dottie booms.

Dottie's and Merlin's new babe Tammy thrown over Tina's shoulder for a good pounding and big burp.

Tina and Stevie's new one asleep on sister Brenda's lap. This baby's name is Bert. Tammy has a little white bow taped to her peach fuzz. Bert has more hair but no bow.

People all around them eating faster and faster, trying not to talk, which is the curse of being in the first round. The curse of later rounds is that there might not be much food left. Either way you have your losses and gains.

There's a shout and Merlin turns around to the left in his seat to see Carroll falling back against a wall of the entry. Carroll looking sharp in his dark blue well driller's work shirt buttoned to the throat. But his eyes are just gray-pink blurs, his face a loose mask of drunkenness.

"Maybe you oughta get him out of here, Daddy!" Francine hisses.

"He'll calm down as soon as they let him through," Merlin says.

Now there's a chair shoved between Merlin and Francine. Another teamster, one they all know keeps his mother's farmplace over on Emma Story Road. Little guy with a rose to each cheek and a rotund middle. You'd swear this was Santa with a summer shave and late-summer clothes. He pushes some sort of schedule along the paper tablecloth, says with cheery solemnity, "What do you think of this here? You seen this one yet?"

Merlin squints down along the columns. "Ayuh . . . that's the way!" Both men grin.

A bowl of red hot dogs is shoved at Merlin from the left.

Somebody says sharply, "Pickles! Yes! Please!"

Somebody thrusts a server of pickles on down.

Not much of the lemon meringue pie left, somebody reports.

A couple of Soule girls and their girl chums and the Mexican girl who has been visiting neighbors are ushered to readied seats. One says close to Merlin's ear, "Daddy, they won't let Carroll in. He's acting like an asshole."

It is hard to see Dottie Soule's eyes now with the dim shapes of the windows riding on her glasses. She may be looking down at her hands. She has recently misplaced her wedding ring. It had gotten too big. It had grown. She looks so much like Cassandra tonight, her nine year old. Cassandra who is not here but over to Great Grand Nanna Soule's instead. The aiding-and-abetting Cassandra.

Tina's husband, Stevie, is wearing his baseball shirt, straddling his fold-up metal chair. He looks ready for a fight. Nothing to fight about yet. He only needs a reason for fighting to come along. Has a hard, hissing way of breathing through his nose.

Faye and Alberta have been taking turns feeding Sherry. Sherry who smells of pee. But nothing wet *shows*. Not with three thick old shirts pinned up under her dress. And there's the smell of mustard for she has clawed it from her plate into her lap. Faye swishes a paper napkin over

Sherry's fingers. Sherry's wedding ring gone. But unlike Dottie's, hers has not been misplaced. What would Sherry need a wedding ring for? Anyone would wonder. She'd probably eat it. Put it in her ear. God knows. Now there's mustard smeared along both her sleeves. Where is all this mustard coming from? And a splat of coleslaw. Nobody gave her any coleslaw. Faye wipes and wipes at the mess. A dozen balled-up paper napkins are by Sherry's plate now. Sherry's auburn hair is nearly grown to the same length as Francine's pixie cut. Sherry's eyes are fixed on a space just short of any actual object or face.

Outdoors at one of the windows beyond the Soule table, Carroll Plummer's face appears. His eyes seem to be focused on something just short of the actual thing, much like Sherry's. He can be heard through the glass singing out, "Yeah . . . just meee and Bobby MaGeeeeee . . . nnanan . . . yeaup yeup! . . . meeeeeee annnn . . . ." Flattens his face to the glass. Mashes his features. Mouth smears a wetness there.

The teamster with the schedule goes back to his own table, and Merlin eats the last of his slaw with his head bowed.

"Daddy!" Francine hisses. "I bet they call the constable on Carroll. He's really out of control."

"I'll go out in a minute," Merlin says.

"You better hurry. He's climbing up on the sill."

Merlin sighs. "The boy has a problem. I'm not his guardian."

"Daddy! You're his friend, I thought!" Francine narrows her eyes on Merlin's hand with its forkful of slaw.

"He is my friend," Merlin admits, nodding, agreeing, munching . . . shovels a forkful of pea beans into his mouth to work against the sweetness of the slaw. He raises his eyes and sees Carroll is gone from the window now. But nearly all the Soule sisters are glaring in dead silence in Merlin's direction.

Sherry grabs a handful of "butter" as a saucer of it comes her way, placed there by the hairnet lady from the kitchen.

Merlin says, "When I'm done eating my meal, I'll go out and have a little talk with him, okay?"

"*I'll* go talk to him," says Stevie steamily.

"No you won't!" says Tina. "You won't handle it right."

One of the other boy husbands, Greg, says with a big smile, "He'll handle it right." Keeps smiling fiercely.

Francine says to Merlin, "I think you should take him home in your truck . . . and give Mum his keys . . . then I'll take our car back. Just don't let Carroll go bombing around like that."

There's the sound of feet on the clubhouse roof. How did Carroll get on the roof? Merlin's eyes flick upward, then downward. "All right," says he.

Dottie appears suddenly at Merlin's left. She grips his shoulder. "Hey!"

"Hey what?"

She squats down next to him, looks up into his face. "Are you coming back home before midnight?"

He answers low and deep, "I don't know."

"Well, I have something I've needed to tell you all day but so much has been going on, I haven't been able to get you alone. It can't wait. It's bad, Merl."

"Jesus-God . . . you ain't pregnant again, are you!" he booms.

Everyone in the clubhouse skips a word, a breath, a heartbeat, leaving a space of silence . . . but for the jumping, hopping, and skipping on the roof above.

"No," Dottie says gravely. "But if you and I were playing that game Twenty Questions right now and you were real sharp at it, you might ask 'Is the person who is pregnant in this room? And is she the one with mustard all over herself?' "

21 It opens out of the darkness ahead like a yellow rose, Carroll Plummer's jacked-up Merc hot rod. Carroll Plummer who was mighty drunk when Lloyd saw him late this afternoon. But there seems to be some serious organization here, a clear thought-out plan. Stevie Foster's Chevy and Merlin's sweet-running black beauty of a truck. All three parked abreast. In a word, "roadblock."

Lloyd applies pressure to the brakes. Shovels clank against the wooden headboard.

Nobody gets out of the three vehicles facing him. Not yet. Just the row of three grilles . . . sort of grinning.

The night is quiet and frosty. Nothing like the sweat bath earlier today. The chirrings and creakings of insects in the tall grass has been silenced. Too quiet.

The driver's door to Merlin's truck opens wide and smooth, one foot down, then the other.

The other guys are fast. Throaty whispers. "Sick bastard needs his face smashed." This is Stevie talking. Stevie who wears no other kind of shirts but baseball, football, hockey, and hunter's blaze orange. Mostly baseball shirts. Baseball cap. Always talking "Ball." Talking baseball statistics. Baseball trivia. And this weekend's scores. Then the scores of all the other kinds of "Ball" . . . and all the trivia and statistics that go with those. Then his hunting talk. Winning. Losing. Nothing in the middle. No compromise.

Carroll Plummer hasn't spoken yet, just breathes floatish frozen white poofs. But Lloyd knows the sound of his cousin Carroll's drunkenness and the sounds of his sobering, which are even worse. Sobering up is when Carroll gets his most touchy.

Merlin walks into the spread of Lloyd's cockeyed headlights. Merlin carries a shotgun.

Since Lloyd doesn't have his door locked, they just open up. Carroll and Stevie get a grip on him, drag him out, slam the door. Lloyd in the middle pushed with ease to that door. "Sick bastard needs his face smashed," Stevie says again. Lloyd's eyes flick slightly to the right onto Merlin with the gun as if onto some far-off memory.

Carroll and Stevie knee into Lloyd's body, making a readjustment of his body to give his head a good smack against the cab. He is loose, pliant for them, doesn't make it hard for them. Another jerk and a shove, his head and the cab of his truck coming together for another smack, all in a single motion, and his arms outstretched, spread like a crucifixion.

"Bash him," Stevie says.

Merlin has nothing to say. Seems Merlin is past words. But he's moving fine with that shotgun. With Lloyd's arms held away from all soft parts of his body, the target is simple. The barrels of the shotgun are driven deep into his crotch. He bellers.

And tears run down into his beard. And perhaps a little begging? And throughout all this, Merlin has tears too, Merlin who is beyond words.

Carroll says croakingly, "Man . . . why'd you go and get Sherry like that? You made a big mistake . . . a *big* mistake. Merlin's out of his gourd. Ain'tcha, Merl?"

Merlin is beyond words.

Stevie wants to pull Lloyd forward again for another head-bashing, but Carroll's soberish-drunken weight leans upon Lloyd's left hip, thigh, hand, wrist, keeping Lloyd lodged in place.

Stevie says, "Goddam sneak. Nothing worse than a sneak."

Carroll murmurs something, maybe to Merlin. Hard to catch it.

"Pretty red fox," Stevie rasps, reaching to give Lloyd's dark and red-streaked beard a little sensuous tug. "Merl . . . what's that we did to that fox last summer? The *other* fox."

Merlin is beyond words. But the shotgun barrels remain fixed with eloquent pressure where he has put them. All over Merlin's face sweat has broken into hundreds of twinkly warts and tears of rage and fright . . . for it is a fearsome thing his trigger finger is considering.

Stevie wheedles. "Come on Merl! Give those triggers a squeeze. Give Lloyd a quickie fix here." And on Stevie's face the sweat twinkles. Sweat of triumph.

But Merlin. Wordless. Motionless. Merlin's face being the last thing Lloyd sees before the fists from both peripheries crash into his sight, making the night white and stinking and full of burning stomach-sick-deep-nerve pain and his own cries. With each blow to his face, he sinks farther down into a squat. The shotgun has been long gone, lifted away. No talk. Just their grunts as they do this work on him.

Then it all stops at once. Just as a little extra frosting on the cake, somebody tosses a fistful of sand into his face. And now warm beer pours on him. Or piss. With his nose blocked with blood, his eyes blinded, there's no way to make those certain fine distinctions.

22 | Edmund Barrington undresses in the dark by his bed. Without light, he knows where the bed is, where the near wall is. Nothing changes. He drops his overalls and shirts where he knows the straight-back chair beside the door is. There is about life in these hills these certainties. Beams, walls, a quilt, and the distance from these to the closed cattle gate, the distance between pruned Macowen and pruned Macowen, Cortlands, and Macs. The distance back again. These rhythms, these internal tides. He need not set a clock. The setting sun, the dawn, the repletion of the moon, the relinquished moon *are* Edmund Barrington.

Under the covers, he lies waiting. Darkness is not sleep. You can have eight hours of darkness, but sleep is the little fish hiding in the black water. You can only wait and wait.

He hears something in the corner of the room . . . not a mouse. He reaches for his six-volt battery lamp on the floor, snaps on its wide swath of light.

That's Lloyd sitting on the trunk over there. Lloyd's face bashed, the beard tangled with sticks and leaves and that way blood looks gummy when they open you up like that. Edmund quickly snaps the light off. Enough.

After a silence, Edmund wonders, "Wouldn't be you've been cozyin' up to somebody's woman, would it?"

Lloyd says thickly, "No." A pause, also thick. "I got this way by being faithful."

After a silence, "Honest to shit, izzat right?"

Lloyd says, "Yep."

Edmund sniffs indignantly at these ways of the world. He says in a wise and fatherly voice, "It's you be damned if you do and damned if you don't. That's what I always say."

Lloyd says, "I know. You are right." He will stay with his father tonight, curled alongside him on the double bed with his face and body hammering, buzzing, burning white-hot, his eyes and blocked breathing passages drying to something hard, turning to stone. Twice in the night Edmund reaches for the battery lamp, flashes the broad light onto Lloyd, sighs with relief over something imagined but not being so.

One night. Just one. Lloyd doesn't return the next night. He doesn't dare press his luck.

23 | It wasn't a planned party. But any time you get the Turnbulls together over at Madeline Rowe's, you've got a hell of a rumpus.

Now the morning light is lemon-white on the arms of chairs and the table edge. The floors chilled. Everyone sacked out on the floor. Late, late summer, hard, glorious, redeeming.

Macky Turnbull has him a woman under a blanket by Lloyd's foot. But the woman is turned away. A bare foot touching the wall.

David Turnbull's wife, Kit, wasn't here for this one. David Turnbull has King to sleep with. This is the way King and David Turnbull sleep: King's neck over David's neck. But King's eyes are wide open, keeping watch on the one bedroom that has a door. There's a whine beyond the door. Kaiser. King wants to kill Kaiser. It doesn't matter that Kaiser looks part great Dane, part panther. Whenever David Turnbull and King come around, King gets his stiff-tailed, stiff-legged, back-up shithead attitude.

Nothing like a fight has actually happened yet. But it could. So Kaiser spends time outdoors or behind the bedroom door. "We are protecting King from himself," Madeline always says.

Pinkish cat asleep in the red rocker by the woodbox. Cat's name, of course, is Pinkie. Then there's Atlas the cat. Cats are no problem. King's got no case against cats.

Over on the floor by the back door that goes out through a shedway there's a biker with frothy white-blond hair. Leather jacket with metal studs. Black denim pants. Boots. Straps. Buckles. Big knife. No blanket.

A few feet away, another blanketless biker. All leather and a classy silky bright-color scarf at the throat. When his hog's opened up on some straightaway, that scarf must snap and shimmy like blue fire.

Settled at the table, Lloyd says to Madeline, "You got any scissors?"

She has her back to him, standing at the sink in her robe. Bare feet set wide apart. He can tell she's that kind that thinks a cold floor against bare feet feels good. She dips tumblers and cups into a kettle of water warmed for rinse. Madeline Rowe. Big crazy black hair. Tooth missing in a place you wouldn't know of if she didn't like to show you . . . tooth lost in a who's-counting? tequila-drinking brawl with her man Reuben Bean. Madeline Rowe. David Turnbull's half sister. You want to know of the truths or the half-truths of David Turnbull or any Turnbull, you ask Madeline Rowe.

She paws and picks through four deep heaped drawers before a pair of scissors turns up. She's a little too quiet this morning. A little hungover. Quietness everywhere. Out on the porch a soft sensual little creak-creak. Rosie Bean, Reuben Bean's sister, giving Madeline's littlest girl a push on the porch swing.

Lloyd says it's time to get rid of some hair.

Madeline puts her strange slow dark-lashed yellowy eyes on Lloyd. She places the scissors in his hand.

"Where's your mirror?" he wonders.

"In the bedroom over the dresser . . . bedroom with Kaiser and the girls."

He twirls the scissors, cocks his head, grins sheepishly. His grin is *very* thick on bottom. His cheeks, eyes, and ears are bruised with a little bit of bright green, a *lot* of berry purple.

The creaking out on the porch stops and the door slips open. Little child peers across the sleeping guests to Lloyd who is straddling a straight-back chair, head bowed. Madeline is wrapping a bath towel around his neck.

Lloyd says in his voice that starts off deeply then always splutters off into raspy softness, "You don't have to be so civilized. A snappy hatchet job should take only a half minute of your time."

She keeps on fussing with the towel.

He says, "I'm turning a new leaf. No more hippie-Lloydie. No more high-fashion. I want to be just a nice plain guy. I don't want anybody looking at me anymore. I just want to slip through life . . ." He rambles on. Says a little something about the world of conformity.

In the near distance the whimpering and pacing of Kaiser keeps its spell over King whose eyes are like burning coals on that bedroom door.

Madeline Rowe's two hands envelop the circumference of Lloyd's thick auburn-streaked black hair.

The child, bottle of juice in one hand, scurries to the table. Her mouth ajar and wide eyes means she's never seen anything as green and purple and torn up as Lloyd's face in a while. Lloyd feels the pressure of cold metal as the scissors open and close on the back of his neck. One big clean *chomp*.

The little girl gasps.

Madeline Rowe holds up the ponytail of his hair trophy style. It is still tightened at the top with its elastic. Severed like an arm from Lloyd forever.

Lloyd says croakily, "More."

Madeline lays the tail on the table. The little girl stretches up to pat it with one hand, her baby bottle in the other hand.

Lloyd sees out the corner of one eye, the garden with sunflowers big as heads, burned by early frost. And a scarecrow wearing work clothes. Shirt has a name over the pocket. Part legend. Part real. He's seen it before on past visits. The name on the shirt which reads: REUBEN. Reuben, Madeline's man who is in prison. Lloyd at all times plagued by the vision of prison. He has read up on prisons. Prisons of the past. Prisons of today. Prisons of tomorrow. Basically prison is prison. A cage.

Madeline says, "There's this above your ears. How short you want this hatchet job anyways?"

"I'm not interested in bald. I just want regular hair, a regular life. I want to slip through life like an ant on his way, just hefting my load and moving forth with dignity and neighborly coexistence."

Madeline rolls her eyes.

He says slowly, "And . . . I want this beard off, too."

"You will look like somebody's sister," she says with a snort.

He says, "There are people who would say that the *me* of five minutes ago was looking like somebody's sister."

Madeline hands him the scissors. "Well, you know what they say, honey. It's damned if you do and damned if you don't."

He looks at her sharply, then says, "Right," rocking the scissors in his hand. "You got a razor?"

"Should," she says, pulls a washpan from under the sink. The razor is in a pink thingamajig for shaving legs. She presses it into his hand.

He says, "Madeline . . . you ever hear from Rubie?"

She says, "Sometimes," narrows her eyes on his face. "I thought you was going to cut off your whiskas."

He says, "Where's your mirror?"

She sighs. "You just want to feel like a pampered king."

King's ears flick, taking note of this reference, but his eyes stay fused to the bedroom door.

Madeline turns to ladle a bit of her warmed dishwater into the washpan, sets the pan on the table as Rosie Bean comes through the door, a cigarette between her fingers, says in her dark kind of steely voice, "Jesus. What's this? A sheep-shearing?"

Madeline leans toward Lloyd to recoup the scissors. What he feels at the sight of the bared wagging great breasts in the V of her robe he knows is good and right . . . and that what he feels for Sherry, which was once good and right, is now wrong . . . but there's something uneasy about what he feels now, too . . . as if everything you feel is always going to turn around on you.

Rosie takes the ponytail from the table and inspects it, her cigarette held aloft.

With the scissors, Madeline hacks at the beard.

Rosie says, "Cut easy-careful around that moustache. He should keep that. It's important to tell the men from the boys."

"He wants to be an ant," says Madeline.

Rosie flutters her eyes.

Madeline makes a lather of dish detergent. The cheap pink kind.

Rosie says, "With a nice big moustache like that, it gives you the look of Yosemite Sam . . . one of my all-time favorite guys." Rosie's cigarette smoke moves around the kitchen, a smoke that follows years of cigarettes smoked in this kitchen . . . perhaps including the last cigarette Reuben Bean smoked the day he was arrested. *If* he smoked. Lloyd never knew Rubie well. Just the legend. Madeline works the razor deftly. The baby girl is called Cookie. Hair that looks like a Japanese cut. She holds her bottle up, not sucking, just letting the big nipple linger in her teeth. Her eyes are golden brown like most Beans Lloyd has ever known. "Man's sore," she says around the nipple.

Madeline commands, "Step aside, Cookie. You are in the way." Madeline prances around and around Lloyd, eyes narrowed on her work.

Lloyd says, "Well, it's something all men think about probably. It's a thing you wonder about. Now and then."

"What's that?" wonders Rosie who is swiping at Cookie with the tail of Lloyd's hair. Cookie ducks and giggles, swings her bottle at the hair swordfight style.

"Jail," snorts Madeline.

Rosie flicks one hand. Dismissingly.

Madeline says, "Only assholes go to prison. You haven't got one asshole bone in your body, Lloyd. You are as nice a guy as they come."

"Well," Lloyd says softly. "It could happen to anyone really. Like a tax man comes to put you out of your home so you point a shotgun at him and tell him to fuck off. Or maybe . . ."

"Quit jawin'. I'm going to nick you if you don't hold still." Madeline sighs, dips the razor.

"Well, there's no end to the ways!" Lloyd says desperately.

Rosie says, "It's not really a good thing to dwell on. Work yourself up into a fit or something."

"Well, no. It's not like sports, is it?" He grins.

Madeline says, "Keep your face still *please* . . . unless you want to live life with only one lip."

"Sports?" Rosie is perplexed.

"Well, now *why* did I say that?" Lloyd simpers. He is getting racier and racier. Loud. He is not himself. He is being swept along on something. "*Everything's* like sports. So why did I just contradict myself like that?" He chuckles to himself, some private philosophical discussions he must carry on with himself alone so much over there in his little rented house. Both women exchange sadly amused looks. "Beats me," says Rosie.

Madeline pleads with Rosie, "Hold him still, would ya? He keeps wrenching around . . ."

Rosie warns, "Lloyd, if *I* have to hold you down, you will not be able to walk again. So just mind your *P*'s and *Q*'s for the lady."

Madeline scrapes away under Lloyd's chin. She says, "Lloyd, you should've got stitches on this mess. I don't think *that* one there is going to heal right the way it looks now. It's kind of gaping. You keep getting into fights like that, you should get yourself sewed up within a few hours . . . go to the emergency or something."

"It wasn't exactly a fight," he says solemnly.

Rosie swipes at Cookie again with the tail of hair. Cookie falls backward onto David Turnbull's boots. But there's no reflex there with David Turnbull whose drinks last night were hand over fist.

Madeline plunks the razor into the washpan. "All done! You've been terrible! You shoulda had ether! Jesus-God."

He stands from the chair, wiping his moustache with the sleeve of his shirt. He is not a tall man. His hands are large like hands of a tall man, hands as beefy and callused as any Bean man's, but his build is only medium-sized, ordinary. He makes a playful face at the baby, Cookie. She jerks her eyes away from him, arches her back, holds her bottle straight up, eyes on the ceiling, unfazed, transfixed, contented.

"Yosemite Sam!" Rosie crows and gives Lloyd a huge smooch on his cheek. "Now you need some six shooters. And where's that hat I seen you wear sometimes . . . the big one. Wear it over next time. What a riot."

Beyond the bedroom door there's the waking sounds of the older children.

Out through the window Lloyd sees the logging truck of Reuben Bean is slumped with its load going to moss. And beyond that the rise of the hills of Egypt.

Home.

It's not like you can promise to be "good." For even when you are being good, there's always that question . . . is it the law? And is everybody happy? Grief moves into his throat, hard, bricklike. The women see his look of panic but pretend they don't.

Cookie says, "Cup!"

"No," Madeline tells her.

"Do that again," Lloyd says to Rosie Bean.

She blows smoke off to one side, then sidles up to him and mashes a kiss to his mouth. "Then there's that other one you remind me of," she laughs, backing away, snapping her fingers. "Jeepers. What's it they call that thing? . . . uh . . . Wile E. Coyote! Always blowing up the Road-runner. Or pushing him off a cliff." She makes the two-fingers-rubbing shame sign at him. "Naughty you." Then she strides away, stepping over David Turnbull, King, and Macky Turnbull and his woman with the bare foot. Rosie disappears out the back way, leaving only smoke.

Lloyd thinks if he ever sees Reuben Bean again he'd never be able to meet the man's eyes. You could fall into eyes like that and there you'd be with the unspeakable truth. You'd be *there*.

"Thanks," he says to Madeline. "I can't see what I look like now but . . ."

"You're a trusting guy," she says, turning from him, already rinsing out the washpan with a plastic milk jug of water. She jerks her thumb toward the cupboard. "If you're hungry, Lloyd, get yourself some cereal. I'm not cooking for this crowd this morning. It's my only day off. You are all on your own."

24 | Black heat. Black night. Nearly dawn of another day. Song bugs have reawakened, miles and miles of them cheering madly. He rides the back roads slow, his left arm along the open window, his old Yankee Civil War kepi low over his eyes as if there were too much light. But there's no light other than the weak cockeyed headlights and the gray black hot fullness of this night, from which silver mailboxes with no names jump out at him.

And now and then a rotted limb splattered across half the road.

One of the headlights catches red eyes at nearly every curve. A coon. Another coon. A small nervous spotted cat. "Heigh ho," he softly says to each and he nods.

The other headlight washes over the low-hanging trees.

Warning sign says HILL.

The descent makes the engine bawl as he cuts back on the gears. Nearing the Soules' dairy sign, which shows a spotted cow, there's the feel of the hills closing in fast. Lloyd cuts the engine. Cuts the lights. The truck, in neutral, just rolls faster and faster. Quietly.

There's the Soules' one lighted window, a nonnegotiable utility gray floating on the black humbled reverie of the universe. Merlin Soule in his kitchen working on his coffee, getting set for the new day. The goddam right bulk of Merlin Soule. You can't really see him in there from this road. But you know he's there. He is in his place. Like Edmund in his kitchen. Like Madeline Rowe in hers. Mrs. Cousins and Mr. Cousins. Unk Walty and Morelli over on Aspect Street. And David Turnbull already at the mill, moving through the hot lanolin air. And Carroll Plummer, his cousin, putting on his well driller's shirt, humming maybe. And Stevie Foster and Tina with their new baby over to Noble Mountain. Another set of red eyes appears ahead. And the great good pines. Hills and sky. High and low. Holy.

He sees them all in their places.

Holy.

He sees them now, tomorrow, and yesterday, twisted in reddish veils of his pain, fear, and forgiveness.

25 | In the middle of supper, there's someone pulling into the yard. The kids run to a window. Madeline and a growling Kaiser meet him at the door. He is wearing his big-brimmed brown mountain hat for Rosie Bean, but Rosie isn't here. Rosie would get a scream over this hat.

"Well, well," says Madeline, leads the way back to the table. She's wearing a big stained and flapping work shirt, which means the cold storage is going hot guns these days, packing them in. Cortlands and Macs. And the old Macowens from the Across Road orchards. She has probably been home only a few minutes.

She digs out a plate for him.

Kaiser sniffs him for news of the outside world. Any word from King? No. No news is good news.

Madeline's two older girls watch Lloyd place his big hat on top of the gas fridge, out of reach of Cookie. He is *very* protective of his caps and hats. But Cookie is running for the bedroom that has no door, only a plastic shower curtain with a print of swans.

Madeline turns the lamp up. She says, "Close your eyes, Lloyd."

He does.

She scrapes half the macaroni and cheese from her plate onto his.

He feels something against his forearm, ticklish. Hair.

He opens his eyes. Cookie's face is solemn. She works it against his skin . . . looks like a dead weasel in the loamy kerosene light. But it's his old ponytail. She pushes it into his hand.

"Oh! That's weird," the oldest girl says. "She brought that out again."

"Thank you, dear," says Lloyd, "For the man who has everything."

Cookie feels one knee of his jeans. Kaiser's nose is stabbing at his other leg.

There's plenty of string beans. Madeline heaps string beans onto his plate. No bread. There's no sign of bread anywhere.

When Madeline is back in her seat, Kaiser moves away from Lloyd. But Cookie hangs on.

Madeline eats.

Lloyd looks into the testy uneven glare of the lamp as he eats. There's a striped towel going around to wipe hands on. He uses it to attend to his moustache whenever he suspects there's a gob hanging there.

Cookie pulls herself up into his lap, so he has to eat around her. On his lap she has a nice higher view of her sisters. She studies them solemnly. Lloyd brings his fork with string beans around Cookie's shoulder and fills his mouth.

No butter. Nor any stuff which seems like butter.

He gets his left arm around Cookie to keep her steady.

Cookie takes a string bean off his plate, mashes it into her mouth.

Madeline gives Kaiser a string bean in a secret secret way. Kaiser's tail whips the floor whenever Madeline looks his way.

Madeline says, "This ain't much of a meal, Lloyd. I don't get paid till next week. We've been working going on two weeks. Dick always used to hold back on us . . . but these new people are holding back longer. New owners." She rubs her eyes with both fists like a child. "You know . . . it was old Dick Emery's people before. Remember?"

Lloyd says, "Yep."

"These new guys are some company . . . out-of-state . . . la-dee-da. Everything's changed."

"Zat right?"

"They came around last week to announce themselves or something . . . mostly to look the place over, I guess. Nobody introduced themselves to *me*. Everything's changed. They got rules posted there this morn. Like 'docking' you on time. Danny says the rules come down from 'above.' He calls it 'above.' " She laughs. "Massachusetts is *south*."

Cookie leans back, tips her head back, looks up into Lloyd's face . . . both faces seeing the upside-down face of the other.

Madeline drops a string bean Kaiser's way.

The girls, Virginia and Florence, roam off from the table. One of them is whispering, *"He* never had a motorcycle. That wasn't him."

Lloyd looks over at the doorless cabinet by the woodbox. Cabinet bristles with rifles.

Madeline says. "If you see Macky, tell him he went off and left his projector here." She laughs deeply. Great billows of her black hair move against the rolled red bandanna she has bound it up with. "What do you think of those slides of his trip?"

Lloyd says, "All in all there were no surprises."

She says, "He takes a nice picture, though. Gets everybody in the middle. Some people can't do it. I always lose somebody's head."

The girls giggle from the doorless bedroom. They may be gone from this room but they're still tuned in.

Lloyd knows he should leave before long, let Madeline get some early sleep. But as Madeline pulls his plate away and Cookie starts up a warm snoring against the front of his shirt, he finds it hard to make the first move for the door. He is not pursuing Madeline Rowe . . . nor Rosie Bean. He is just here to be in the thick of his most fearsome nightmare. He is here to face it square on. To know what they know. To know the people closest to Reuben Bean. To know this thing to the bone.

26 | Next night during supper, the last of the kerosene is sucked up into the wick, the last flame melts red, crumbles along the wick, and Madeline says, "Shit" into the darkness.

"Shit," says Cookie.

"Where's the damn flashlight?" Madeline's voice speaks from some low place. "Who's been messing around under this sink?"

"Mumma, you had it out in the car, remember?" Florence says.

Kaiser growls low.

"Mumma, somebody's outside."

"Don't be foolish," says Madeline. "He growls at his own shadow. He growls at the wind." Yet Madeline gets to her feet, stands in the dark, eyes on the place in the darkness where the door is, a thousand hearts thumping all over her body.

Kaiser sniffs around the door and growls again . . . lower . . . longer . . . louder. Now he bellers, gives the door a couple of rakes with his paw.

"Somebody," Florence says softly.

"Where's Cookie?" Madeline whispers.

"Right here," says Virginia.

Madeline nears the door. No key for the door. The only enemy she ever knew was her man Reuben and he was always inside to start with. Madeline says, "You guys go to the back door in case you have to get out quick, okay?"

She waits for them to reach the back door, then fetches a rifle from the cabinet. She can't tell one from the other in the dark. She can't find the right ammunition in the dark. No matter. She just plans to point it and *look* well-defended. She opens the front door with her free hand. Kaiser skids across the porch, then bolts off into the night.

By the time Kaiser gets back from racing around, circling, and tracking along the narrow rutted road, Madeline has found the flashlight in the car and shines it on a paper bag on the porch. Farm butter wrapped in wax paper. Two loaves of store-bought bread. A clean jam jar with three twenty-dollar bills inside. Three faded graveyard-sized American flags with weathered-looking sticks with spear tops. Obviously for the kids.

Also with the money, a folded note. She opens it, reads the smoodgy penciled handwriting. *'Tis sweet to hear the watch-dog's honest bark Bay deep-mouth'd welcome as we draw near home; 'Tis sweet to know there is an eye will mark Our coming, and look brighter when we come.*

Her snort of laughter is more with relief than with immediate comprehension.

27 He heard a guy once telling about another guy who had been in prison for a year . . . some relation to Conners. The convicted guy had been growing and dealing reefer. The guy said that the Conners guy said that prison is a bright place. You can never get away from the light. Not shadowy like Lloyd had once pictured it. Shadowy would be better. There are many men. Many. Many. Many. It is like hanging in midair in a giant eye. "It ain't nothing like home," the guy had told the guy who told Lloyd. "Getting locked up is to punish you, but it depends on where you've been, right? To some it's not so bad, maybe."

No trees for miles. No stone walls and rocky streambeds. No mushrooms shaped like apple pies. No vinca around old foundations. No eating popcorn in your old truck. No deep sofas. No smudgy wallpaper. No sashed curtains. No good-looking women. No old motherish women. No babies. No little scrappy dogs. No string bean–eating big dogs.

No night.

It is fated. Lloyd *will* wind up "doing time." How can it be any other way? Every intention, every promise, every act of love leads him closer. And with all visions being one and the same, he sees that he will die there.

28 | She sees the headlights jerking along, coming off the old Across Road, making a sweeping left toward her. She makes up her mind that if *this* one asks her if she needs a ride, she'll say yes and then just happen to mention she's hungry. Since she's run away from home, time can be measured by three missed meals.

The car is not a "bomb," but nothing fancy either. It stops. Lloyd's voice from the backseat says, "Cassandra . . . where you headed, dear?"

She says a little too quickly, "Not home!"

The car is full of men. Scary-looking ones. Two guys get out. Looks like the Hell's Angels. But she knows it's just David Turnbull and Hilary Hubbard's brother what's-his-name, the Hubbards being some relation to Lloyd. This biker Hubbard has long foamy blond hair and on his left hand a gold skull ring. She slides into the front seat and David Turnbull gets inside beside her and positions a small dog on his lap. Dog wears a shirt with a print of balloons. The dog gives Cassandra's elbow a quick sniff, then looks back at the road ahead, dismissing her.

"What's his name?" she asks.

"Name's King," says David Turnbull.

Cassandra snorts. "Awful little King."

David Turnbull tips a beer into the place where his mouth is, somewhere thereabouts between the rambling black mass of his moustache and clipped beard.

Cassandra looks around back at Lloyd. His beard is gone. Has he been in a wreck? His face is swollen, split, and bruised. His bottom lip big as a banana.

She looks at David Turnbull whom she knows from seeing around, different from the other Turnbull bikers and biker buddies by the dog that's everywhere with him at all times. David Turnbull, tall. Tired face but a smooth neck. Sort of creepy . . . like a guy put together with pieces of people.

David Turnbull feels the stare. "So! How's the family?" he asks her.

"I don't know," says she.

"Well, how were they the last time you looked?" he asks her, straightening the cuff of King's balloon print shirt.

"Mean," says she.

"We can swing around over there, shan't we, ol' boy?" David Turnbull wonders of the driver. "Give her a ride to her place, huh?"

"No!" Cassandra gasps. "Never!"

"Well, I s'pose eventually," David Turnbull suggests.

"Never," says Cassandra.

The driver is another David you see around . . . David Moody, related to them at the store. It's the guy her father, Merlin, says went to college to be a minister. This is usually mentioned alongside the fact that Lloyd went to college to learn to be a communist hippie.

They keep riding along in the direction away from the Soule place, so it looks like she's gotten her way. She looks back at Lloyd. Lloyd is chewing, pushing something around in his teeth. She knows what it is, something disgusting. But nevertheless, it makes her hungrier than ever. She says thinly, "When are you guys going to have your supper?"

"We already had it," David Turnbull says. "Fried clams."

A little piteous squeak escapes Cassandra's neck.

David Turnbull says, "Here, have you a little sip. Won't hurt. Maybe help fill the pit." Passes the beer can her way.

She sniffs the beer. Pretty awful. Takes a swallow. Pretty awful. Takes another swallow. Passes it back. "Where are we going?" she wonders.

"To a birthday party," says the blond skull-ring brother of Hilary Hubbard . . . leather jacket, leather vest, leather cap. Breathing makes him creak.

Cassandra asks, "What kind of cake?"

"Didn't come out good," David Turnbull tells her.

The blond biker in back says, "It was supposed to be applesauce cake. That's what it was supposed to be."

"You guys made it?" Cassandra snickers.

The blond biker says, "I made a foundation for my old man's garage last weekend and it was a fucking lot easier."

"And softer, too," Lloyd adds. "We shouldn'ta stirred it so long maybe."

"Who knows?" the blond biker says mournfully.

After a few minutes of no talk, just the uniform shrills of the night bugs through the car's open windows, Cassandra says, "Daddy and Carroll took off."

Lloyd raises an eyebrow.

"You know. The usual."

Lloyd nods.

She says, "Mumma's very mad. You know. As usual."

Lloyd nods. His hat tonight is brown and big-brimmed. He looks like that cartoon outlaw, Yosemite Sam . . . the one with the temper, big pistols, moustache hanging to the ground. Lloyd's hippie look is gone. But this new look isn't going to make anyone happy either.

She says, "Mumma says it's not that he's gone. Good riddance! But he SPENDS."

"Right," says Lloyd, giving his outlaw moustache a few deep-thought pulls.

"Bet he gets jillions of ribbons and trophies," she says, a bit boastingly.

"Yuh," says Lloyd. "That's near certain."

For another long stretch, no talk, just the symphony of bugs and the minister's car engine lamenting the steeper hills. Cassandra considers the *evilness of men* which her sister Faye mentioned momentously the day of *the confession*. But it seems as they ride along here now in the small space of this car that what Cassandra feels is *starving*, but very, very safe.

The car slows down onto a short road with marsh on both sides, partridgeberry and alder bushes.

"Where's this?" Cassandra inquires, tapping her foot a little. A happiness has washed over her so big it gives her a couple of little knee jerks.

"Harvey's place. Old man," the David that is the minister tells her.

"Eighty-eight candles," says David that is the biker, pressing one pocket of his denim vest.

There's no light outside the house, no lights inside.

They all climb out of the car without hurry. Lloyd moves on ahead, seeming to know his way well through the blackness. He has a touch of a limp . . . probably something to do with the green-and-purple predicament of his face. She wonders why no one at her house has mentioned Lloyd got in an accident. But sometimes the worse things are, the more everything gets hush-hush. Perhaps with the wreck Lloyd was in there were other people and they all died, all squished, Lloyd spared.

From out of the darkness comes the single *thwonk* Lloyd gives the old man's door.

"Nobody's home, it looks like," Cassandra whispers.

"They're always home," says David Moody, the reverend.

They all collect around Lloyd on the sagging step as Lloyd turns the knob with care and the door sighs open. "Harvey. Jimmy. It's just us." Lloyd's voice, soft and low, and that little weird splutter at the end which he always has.

They all troop in.

Inside smells like burned toast. And it smells kerosenish and peoplish. The doorway is short, built for a time when most people were short as kids. Cassandra's eyes are wide but can't really make out the situation here.

The biker with the blond squiggly mass of hair and gold skull ring bursts out into song, "Happy birthday tooo yooo! Happy birthday toooo yooooo! Happy birrrrrrrrrrrth-daaaay deeer Harrrrrrrrrveeeeeeeeee! Happy birrrrrrrr-daaaaaay tooooooooo yoooooooooooo!"

A voice bellers, "WELL HOW AH YE! HOW AH YE! WELL, GOD BLESS YE . . . THERE YOU GO! COME RIGHT OVUH HEAH. GOD BLESS YE!"

Also there's snoring. Somewhere too near.

There's a dainty gnashing of glass against metal and the scrape of a match. Lloyd lights a lamp on the table.

Cassandra can see that the biker David has the whiskery dog under one arm, the dog looking from face to face in a creepily penetrating way.

She also notes that the Reverend David is kind of short. Broad-shouldered, barrel-chested, but awfully short . . . maybe because of being with the other David, the big biker. She also notes that the Reverend David isn't wearing a black thing with little white thing. He's dressed, instead, in a Wicks Well Drillers' shirt like Carroll Plummer wears. Everyone's job these days seems to be drilling wells. She considers this a moment.

From the shadows a hand grabs Cassandra, swings her around into a terrible crush, another hand pounds her back. "GAWD! AIN'T YOU SWEET!" informs the booming, bawling voice. "Ain't she a sweet one. Nice girl. GAWWWD." Bangs her back enough to knock her breath out. Big voice smells like popcorn.

"Now let go of her," says the blond biker. "Let her be, Harv. She wants some cake."

The old guy stands back now, grinning . . . no teeth. Wears a crusher hat like Lloyd usually wears. Suspenders. Very close but uneven shave. His eyes don't leave Cassandra. He looks her up and down, up and down, then giggles mischievously. "I like nice people. GAWD! Donchoo? You like nice people?" He rocks from foot to foot, his eyes eating her up.

"Yup," Cassandra says, a little self-conscious under the big greenish eyes eating her up.

David Turnbull starts poking candles into the rectangular frostingless cake, keeping a good grip on the whiskery dog with the penetrating eyes. Some of David Turnbull's tattoos show. One Cassandra thinks is especially neat is the gigantic housefly.

The blond biker says cheerily, "Hey, Harvey! Go wake Jimmy up! Hurry!"

Old guy stays put, just turns the top half of his thick body and bellers, "JIMMY!" He uses both hands to cup his mouth as if calling across the mountain although the snore is only a couple of steps away.

The snoring stops.

Harvey turns back to face his guests. "I like nice people," he insists. "God bless ye."

Lloyd asks softly, "How you been, Harvey? How's your knees?"

"Gooood," says Harvey. Now he chops both hands rapidly through the air. "You like deer? Guess WHAAAT! Like this!" He chops his hands some more. "They come overway like this . . . come through . . . like this . . . was whitetails. Must've been ten of them cutters! Like this!" His hands go chop chop chop. "Like this!" Now he hoots and throws his head back. His eyes fall onto Cassandra again. "You like deer?"

"Yup," says Cassandra.

"Have a seat," says Lloyd, pulling out a kitchen chair for her, a wooden tipsy chair as old as the house.

"YESSS. Set you down there!" hollers old Harvey.

Cassandra sees that although the person who was snoring hasn't spoken since Harvey called him, he is now sitting very wide awake on his cot at the edge of the lamplight.

"Jesus! This many candles is going to melt the cake," David Turnbull frets. With interest the dog watches David Turnbull's hand working the candles in a spiral away from the center of the cake. "Actually, we only have eighty candles here. They come in packs of twenty. So what the hell?"

"Who's counting?" the minister who is really a well driller chuckles.

Cassandra wishes they could just get on with eating the cake.

"You like birthdays?" old Harvey asks Cassandra, gives her shoulder a little easy pat.

"Yep," says Cassandra.

"I like 'em," he tells her happily. In his eyes the lamplight looks partyish and dancy.

"Now how old is it you say you are, Harvey?" the blond biker wonders.

"Oh . . . sixty-two," Harvey tells him, a bit of a naughty grin.

"How long you been sixty-two?" David Turnbull asks.

Old Harvey covers his face and giggles.

"Harvey! You know what happens to people who lie, don't you?" the blond biker asks.

This makes old Harvey really howl. "Yesss! I do!" And he pulls on his own nose. "Out like thaaaat," he says and throws his head back for more wild laughter. Now he goes to pull on Cassandra's nose but she jerks her head back fast.

"Whoops," the reverend says with a smile. "That was a close one." The reverend is blond but not with the curly frothy stuff that the biker has for hair. And no beard. Just a little end-of-the-day roughness. The reverend's hair is straight and streaky. Like The Beach Boys. His eyes large and light-lashed. Such a face. Such eyes. Eyes too big, too earnest. He looks so vulnerable.

The guy on the cot seems to look quite a lot like Harvey but not cheerful. He is melancholy. Bothered.

"Just think, Harvey," the blond biker says with genuine soft-spoken marvel. "Eighty-eight years ago you were a little gooey baby in this very house on this very day . . . eighty-eight years ago. Jeepers!"

There's the scratch of a match and the laborious one-by-one lighting of the candles. David Turnbull says solemnly, "There's a texture to this cake like nothing I've ever put a candle into before."

Blond biker says. "A good time for a little prayer." He looks over to the minister.

The Reverend David Moody says softly, "No time for prayer. When all those candles are lit, Harvey's going to need all the breath he can muster. And we may need breath to back him up."

The blond biker guffaws, causes all his leather to cheep and squeak. "Ol' Harv's got enough breath for twenty cakes. Don'tcha, Harv?"

"I DO!" Harvey booms. "I like twenty cakes!"

Candles are ready. Solid mass of flame in the shape of a cake.

"Harvey . . . hurry . . . blow!" David Turnbull shouts.

Harvey blows out the candles and spit flies.

David Turnbull looks into Lloyd's eyes. "Shit. I forgot that might happen."

Lloyd shakes his head, amused.

There's not much for plates. Most plates are gobbed into the dark sink. So the cake goes around plateless. Pieces of cake so rubbery and waxed-over that they sit like plates in the hand or on the knee.

Lloyd has to make a trip outside, returns wiping his surging outlaw moustache with a bandanna. Such is the inconvenience of chewing tobacco.

"Have some cake, Lloyd." David Turnbull turns around with King still under one arm, presents Lloyd with a sturdy square.

"Thanks," Lloyd says gravely.

The old guy on the cot looks at the square of cake on his knee, his expression unchanging. Now he gives the piece of cake a brutal twist and it lays in three firm equal pieces. His hands, like old Harvey's, are dirty, strong-looking, thick-nailed tools. Life-sustaining.

David Turnbull digs into a pocket of his jeans and offers King a little reddish bone-shaped dog cookie.

"Can't have King eating that cake, huh, Dave?" Lloyd chuckles.

"Wouldn't want something to happen to King with that cake inside him," the minister observes.

Harvey has found himself a chair and has pulled it directly in front of Cassandra so his knees nearly touch hers. His cake seems more fluffy than any that the others have. It flies about as he works it into his mouth, his eyes pinned to Cassandra's face. Once his mouth is loaded with cake, he reaches down and feels Cassandra's ankle. "I like them shoes," he says.

"I hate them. They look stupid," Cassandra retorts.

This makes Harvey have a true fit of laughter, cake springing out of his mouth, big hand slapping his thigh. "I like nice people," he says, reaching forward to cradle her face.

"Harvey, leave her be to eat her cake for godsakes," David Turnbull says.

"You're making the poor kid nervous," Lloyd explains. "Harvey, tell us some more about those deer you saw."

Harvey chops his hands through the air. "Like this they was!"

Cassandra says in the middle of this, "Don't worry. He don't bother me. I'm used to Sherry."

Lloyd turns away out of the light, sighs . . . a small private despair.

"Maybe those were the same deer we had hanging around over by the shop," says David Turnbull. "There really were quite a few. Kind of early for them to yard. A thing you would notice."

"Why that was for SHOOOOR!" Harvey booms, reaches to poke David Turnbull's knee. "They was. You know it!"

David Turnbull sees Cassandra reaching for three more squares of cake. "It's not a very tasty cake," he says softly. "You must be on the hungry side, huh?"

Cassandra shrugs, chews, swallows.

Now the cake is gone. Plenty of crumbs and chunks all around Harvey's feet. Looks like a whole cake has exploded there.

Lloyd goes out the door again and returns with his gift, an armload of last year's graveyard flags, some faded, some bright, some gnawed on the edges . . . but still quite nice.

"Why God bless ye!" Harvey rejoices, gives Lloyd a big kiss on the ear, Lloyd's big-brimmed hat flying off onto the table into the cake pan. "My gawd! Ain't them nice! Nice flags!"

Lloyd fussily brushes cake crumbs off his hat and reshapes it. He asks, "Where's those other flags I got you before, Harv? I thought you were collecting them?"

Harvey lowers his eyes, ashamed. Something has happened to his other flags. Lost track of. Left on the floor. Left outdoors. "Yahs . . . ahhh . . . he come here . . . big fella . . . BIG!" Harvey shows how big, flailing his arms about. "I was asleep I was. He sneeeeeked. I wouldn'ta knowed him. He skipped country."

"Right," says Lloyd.

Harvey keeps his eyes down.

The Reverend David Moody whispers to Cassandra, "His nose will be a mile long before we get out of here."

Cassandra laughs happily.

The biker David Turnbull presses something into Harvey's nearest hand. Harvey holds it up over his lap of flags, holds it toward the light. Opens it. Shuts it. A jackknife. He gets up, awkwardly clutching his flags, gives David Turnbull a manly swat on the shoulder, slides the knife into his rear pocket.

As they are leaving, Lloyd turns to Jimmy who is still on the cot and reminds him that his birthday won't be forgotten. "January thirtieth," Lloyd says. "Right?"

"That is right," the man agrees in a clear beautiful voice, clear like a trained speaker's voice, but for the accent of the old ones of this valley, its solid ancestral inflections. And as he has spoken, he keeps his same melancholy expression.

After a few of Harvey's lingering kisses on each guest's cheek or ear, they get out the door.

Out in the car, heading back over onto the main road, the minister with the Beach Boy hair and well driller's shirt says, "Let's get you back to your house, Cassandra."

"We wouldn't want your people on edge," says David Turnbull.

"Can't I just be here?" Cassandra says with a whimper.

"You've got to go home eventually," says David Turnbull, stroking King who is now curled on his lap.

"Who was those old guys?" Cassandra demands.

"Well, there's the retarded guy whose birthday it was. And his brother, the other one," David Turnbull explains.

"Can't I go stay there, maybe?"

The minister David and the biker David exchange glances.

Lloyd speaks from the backseat. "Something tells me, Cassandra, that you are in a searching mode."

Cassandra squinches her face. "What?"

"Well, there's some sort of rumble of discontent within your young breast," says he.

Cassandra says sharply, "You talk dirty."

There is a mile of silence but for the bugs in song and Lloyd spitting out the window once.

Cassandra sees the road they are taking is the one to her home. She looks from face to face with panic, sees the shadowy hand of David Turnbull giving King's floppy little ears a good rub.

The car chugs slowly up the drive, both Lloyd's eyes and Cassandra's eyes a little popping with apprehension as the glare of the ell door light fills the car. Lloyd's wrecked face seems especially colorific here. Lloyd sinks slightly lower in the seat, tugs on the big brim of his hat.

There are the dark shapes of the sisters at one of the kitchen windows.

"Well, I ain't goin' in." Cassandra crosses her arms across her chest. "You guys don't know what it's like."

Lloyd says deeply, "I knoweth."

King has risen now, his front feet on the dash, eyes scrutinizing the lighted house.

"They are very mean," Cassandra tells them.

Lloyd nods gravely.

It's not long before one of the sisters swings out through the screen door, arms akimbo, eyes narrowed on the car.

The minister steps out to shake her hand and to talk in a ministerly voice.

Other sisters and now the mother, Dottie, step out into the lighted dooryard, eyes narrowed on the car.

One of the sisters screams. Another screams. Screams of joy. "Cassandra! Cassandra!" they cry out. They lean into the car across the steering wheel, pulling on her, kissing. They paw and squeeze her. They groan. "My gawd, we thought you were dead! But here you are! Here you are!"

Lloyd slouches even lower in his seat. He wonders if they haven't recognized him or if, as often is the case, they are ignoring him.

He knows there's a reason for all this sisterly overly sweety-gooey niceness. He knows it might be the magic that happens when a minister of God is on hand. He knows behind their door it will be different. He watches the sisters and the mother, Dottie, ushering Cassandra along toward that door of the lighted house in a loud and cheerful leggy arm-swinging clump.

29 Coming into the little rented house on Pleasant Street, he squats down, unlaces his sneakers, stands them side by side against the mopboard with his work boots and winter boots. Walks around in his stocking feet. Floor is swept each morning. He likes a swept floor. His socks are red. Carried under his arm, his mail. A newsletter. No regular letters. Who would write him letters? He settles at the table with a bowl of Wheaties, munches as he reads. So much to read. In the world there's the printed word to fill a thousand lifetimes. It is best to be casual. Why make a race of it? You can never read the last word.

The stacks by his bed grow weekly into taller towers. The texts, workbooks, and novels from college . . . in their place of honor. And now more used, borrowed, found, bought. Books not cheap. Tolstoy, Genet, Steinbeck, Conrad, Orwell, Dostoyevsky, O'Connor, Babel, Mann, Poe. The newsletters and monthlies. The causes. The concerns. And a daily: *Christian Science Monitor,* with its effort toward truth. And here's *The Catholic Worker,* a different truth. And there are books on the Civil War years, the Industrial Revolution, the Reconstruction of the South, agriculture as a culture, automation, civil rights, economics, education. Sometimes he will hunker over one paragraph and dawdle on it for so long, eyes blinking, rubbing his forehead. The towers tower-tall, slightly leaning. So many towers. Like whores, they call his name.

Soule women say there's something a little yeck about a man being so neat. "I wouldn't want a man like that," Tina had told Sherry once.

And Sherry told Lloyd.

"Don't tell me what they say, Sherry," he had said to her in a rather ugly way. "It makes me *resent.*"

"They wanted to know if you fuss over crooked rugs like Auntie Mill used to." She laughed a deep taunting howl.

He glared out through the window through the bared arms of the maples along Pleasant Street . . . the sky a crisp, keen, unfurnished winter blue . . . and in the alleyways the dirty snow lay.

". . . and I fibbed a little and told them you did! You know, just to get 'em going. And it got 'em going all right!!" She tossed her wild auburn hair, her mouth open wide like the open screaming mouths on some of his horror novels and mysteries he keeps in his truck. She danced around and around him, sniggering. "No sense of humor! Loosen up, Lloyd-o. Where are those funny bones?" She poked him. "Zzzzzzzzzzzzzzt zzzzzzzzzzzzzzt!" Poking, pretending to be a bee, in this very kitchen, pregnant with their second child. Strapping noisy Sherry, making the clock sway on its nail.

30 | Another week. Another night. A strange sort of nightness. So much fierce light.

Out in the parking lot of the Fryeburg Fair, parking lot of over a thousand cars, the yellow Merc squeals up the outer lane. A group of people leap out of its way.

Two police cruisers pull in behind. Another glides up to face the Merc.

Cops get out. One shines a flashlight on the dented fender.

This has to do with the young man named Gary Kendricks down to Fryeburg Center whose body was just found in a tree because he was struck so hard and the driver of a car pulling out from the restaurant wrote down the last three numbers of this Mercury's registration. Seems we have a little red blood on Mr. Plummer's yellow paint here. "Seems you have amazing breath, Mr. Plummer. You ever taken this test before?"

Carroll Plummer has his hearing aids turned off, riding these roads in silence, in the silent roar. Their mouths move like fishes sucking for breath in bad water. The dark parts of their uniforms are black against the black night while the gleamy parts gleam in reflex to the gleaminess of the fair and against the contortions of gleaminess of over a thousand parked cars. Everything in pieces. But the parts add up.

31 | Dottie Soule's gray-blue-frame glasses steam up with gladness and pissed-offishness, moving a cough drop around with her tongue . . . the usual head cold brought on by the usual. She is nearing the pulling arena . . . the familiar moment . . . twenty-six years of fairs . . . twenty-six moments exactly like this. She almost runs.

"Wait up, Mumma!" her girls complain, detained by many elbows, handbags, people with big Smurfs, people eating gooey things or drinking with distraction from cups of Coke.

At the packed entry to the pulling arena, Dottie booms, "Well! WHAT DO WE HAVE HERE!" as if she has never seen such a place before. What a surprise! What a discovery!

All the teamsters, all the teams are against the closest rail.

Dottie leads her girls, the ones who are young enough to still hang out with her, to the top of the stands, zigzagging through the sea of faces, many strangers with red noses like Dottie's own. Bleary eyes. White breath. Cold drinks. Hot drinks. Babies. A Samoyed. A Pekingese. More Smurfs.

At the top of the stands, Dottie puts her back to the wall, crosses her arms across the front of her shirts and exclaims, "ISN'T THIS IN-TERESTING!"

Some faces smile.

There's eight teams along the rails and above them that solid sourish fog that is their breathing. Whenever a horse shifts ever so slightly, its harness jangles in sonata. And more white frostiness hurtles up heaven-enward.

There's Merlin's cousin's matched blacks with scarlet velvet panels on the harness and pewter hearts that spin.

Among the teams, the drivers are mostly men over forty. A lot of thick waists. A lot of graying hair. An old man's sport, it seems. Dottie's eyes slide over to Merlin. The back of his neck. In these few weeks of his absence she had forgotten how gray his is. She had pictured him differently. She leans forward, lets the cough drop fall from her mouth down into the dark well of space below the stands.

Lydia screams, "DADDY!!" and waves her arms.

Merlin and the man he stands with look up to the stands.

"Where's Carroll?" Cassandra wonders.

"Probably unconscious in one of the horse barns," Dottie says, pulls out a tissue for another bit of work on her nose.

"But Daddy *needs* him," says Cassandra.

Dottie narrows her eyes on Merlin. Although it is freezing, he wears only a T-shirt and work pants and the straw cowboy hat he's worn to half a lifetime of fairs and other teamster occasions. Hat is pretty ratty and darkened around the brim these days. Like his work boots. Ratty and dark, as everything he has let go to ruin in order to afford Rocket and Tommy's every need . . . and the Rocket and Tommy before these two and the Rocket and Tommy before the other two and all the Rockets and Tommys of his boyhood and the old teams of Merlin's father, teams with other names. Bob and Joe, was it? Dick and Duke? Jesus . . . how many fields of hay? How many sacks of grain? Vet bills? Time spent on mending harness? It'd be different if he used the horses to farm. But there's the tractor for that, which is a whole other dismal story. Dottie burps up the taste of eucalyptus.

"I bet Daddy's wondering where Carroll is, too," Wendy says. "He keeps looking around. See?"

"Don't worry about it," Dottie says gravely. "Dad knows plenty of guys droolin' to help him."

A dappled team wheels around toward the drag. There's that BOOM BOOM BOOM BOOM of each hoof . . . like dozens of dropped anvils.

Merlin watches this team with his hands on his hips. He smiles a little dismissive smile.

When the dapples lay into the harness and the drag lurches forward, the stands are silent as church. The pull is measured. There are cheers. But Merlin doesn't look worried. It looks like just another one of his finest hours about to unfold.

32 | They use their hands, elbows, knees, every means to bend him over the hood, though he's not fighting them. But it's something about his attitude. Sassy. They snap on the cuffs.

They are probably asking him questions. He can't be sure. He can't see their mouths. Everything seems far-off and Jell-Oish. Nice. Like in another life. Well, that is the way of drink. That is its purpose. All that is right is in your domain. All that is wrong is somewhere in that other veil, that other time.

He sings tonelessly, ". . . you men eat'choor ol' pork 'n' beans . . . I eat more chicken'n any man ever seeeeeeen . . . I'ma back dooooooor man . . ."

33 | Little church with a flat-top steeple. White with a green door. The door is nearly child-sized. The interior café-sized. Inside are beaverboard tables, folding chairs, salt and peppers. No pews. Beyond the cash register are the church women and men to cook your hot dogs, fries, onion rings, American chop suey, chowder, and chicken. It's about the only place at this fair where you can sit down while you eat. There is usually a line at the door, but this is the last hour of the fair, everything winding down, running out.

The bikers can tell the church women and men wish they'd leave. One especially straight-backed woman, young sort of, but with tightly curled hair and steely eyes, has an apron pocket that keeps jingling. Keys . . . the oh-so-subtle hint. All the women and men who volunteer here wear the same kind of apron. A butcher's apron. Utility. Nothing flowery. Nothing homey enough to make you want to linger. Also the heat seems to be shut off.

Among them at the table breathing frostily over their chicken wings and hot dogs, there's no David Turnbull. The church woman with the steely eyes had said, "No dogs allowed. Sorry."

"No dog, no Dave," David Turnbull had replied and now he and King sulk around outside waiting for the door to open now and then and a hand to pass out a buttered roll or french fries. Right now David's wife, Kit, goes to the door with two loaded hot dogs wrapped in napkins. Kit's deep gritty voice says, "Like you like 'em."

The church women and men eye these doings. Especially watchful is the youngish steely one. But as fierce as she appears, she is uneasy with how to handle bikers.

Macky Turnbull has a heinous way of laughing at the most incidental things. He laughs heinously at the way Lloyd Barrington sucks milk through a striped straw. He laughs heinously at one of the seascapes on the wall . . . a seascape with nothing in it but sea. He jounces heavily around on his folding chair, leather and hardware glinting, screaking. He favors one leg, keeps the knee straight. And on the end of this leg is the boot with a single spur.

Biker next to Macky looks dead. Both his eyes look glass. There's no food in front of him, just the bare table. It's hard to imagine what got him this far.

Beside the inanimate biker is his girlfriend who is dressed all in buff suede . . . more cowgirlish than bikerish . . . as if she belongs to another group and jumped fence. Her hair is bleached to brittle, teased up earlier in the day to a foot tall perhaps, then blown apart into chunks by the wind. She is lined and middle-aged, eyes accentuated with makeup and deep with certain knowledge. And about her round cheeks and slowly chewing mouth is a motherishness, a murmur of "Please pass that stuff" and a pat with her napkin to her lips. Her hands are plump. She wears no rings.

The door opens. Four people enter. Four blond women in stylish jackets and heavy shirts. Shoulder bags. Sneakers. One Smurf.

The steely-eyed church woman with the jangling apron pocket says, "We are no longer serving. Too late. Sorry." With these "normal-looking" new arrivals she is not too uneasy to be curt.

One of the normal-looking people says, "We're not eating. We just need to talk with these guys."

"We are locking the doors in five minutes, putting the lights off in ten," the steely pocket-jangling woman tells the normal ones.

Faye and Pam pull up chairs. Marcia and Brenda just stand. All are breathless and fiery-cheeked. There's been some hard hurry to get here.

"You've probably heard the news of what just happened!" Faye says between gasped breaths.

Bikers all looking like they haven't heard the news yet. Lloyd looking peeved, shoulders hunched, a little tired. His face is still bruised . . . but softly . . . a skin of yellow-green clouds. The cuts are no longer jellyish crusted leaky ellipses, but scarred smooth like shreds of red satin. And as if to match his face, he wears a maroon chamois shirt under an old sherpa-lined barn jacket. Sleeves of the jacket cut away. He's not got the true biker image, but he does fit in.

Faye pulls in closer to the table, her blond bridal-veil-length hair a little stringy from the long evening . . . but still wonderful hair.

A biker drops a cigarette. Sister Pam, with Smurf under one arm, stops the cigarette's rolling with her sneaker.

Faye says, "Well, Carroll Plummer was just arrested . . . hit 'n' run. *Killed* a guy down the road. Honest. We just heard."

Kit Turnbull who always smiles peacefully keeps smiling, for it is not really a smile of peace, just the natural way of her face. Her long fingers on the table and the slim silver wedding ring, even the wild wind ravaged tumble of crimpy black hair over her leather jacket convey this illusion of enviable peace.

"Looks like it's curtains for ol' Carroll," sighs a biker who wears an aviator cap with dangling straps. His beard is just squiggles of red-gold, so thin and few, you could count them in part of a minute. "Lloyd! Weren't he your brother-in-law?"

"Cousin," Faye answers for Lloyd.

"Jesus Christ. Poor ol' Carroll," says a biker who is bald on top, only a long fringe around the sides. His beard, however, triumphs . . . brown with silver gray. Stately. Metal-rimmed glasses. Upstate New York accent. "Poor ol' Carroll."

"Fuck," says another. "I wouldn't want to be in his shoes."

Macky Turnbull goes back to munching french fries. "I don't seem to recollect the guy."

The bald biker says, "He's over to Taylors' sometimes. Has the hearing aids."

Macky keeps munching, shrugs some.

Bald biker says, "1960 Merc . . . cherry. New paint. Yellow."

"Oh, yeah. Shit," says Macky.

"Someone saw his license number when it happened," Faye explains. "And a lot of people saw from a distance. So it isn't some mistaken identity."

Pam lowers the Smurf to its own feet, stretches her arms, gets a cigarette from her shoulder bag, says, "I knew it would happen."

From the direction of the cash register there's a savage jangling of keys.

"Prison ain't a pretty place," murmurs the guy with aviator cap and reddish beard squiggles. "I can tell you, man. It ain't the Holiday Inn."

Kit Turnbull keeps smiling peacefully even as she tidies up, scraping stuff from some dishes into others. Lots of wobbed-up napkins and chicken bones.

Biker with long blond hair and gold skull ring says, "That's bad about the dead guy. Ol' Carroll's gotta live with that."

The overhead fluorescent lights black out.

Kit carries some plates to the return window, navigating through the shadowy light that comes from the kitchen in back. Church men and women at the register say thanks.

"Better dead than to paralyze somebody," the bald biker says, standing up slowly, pulls a black knitted cap from his pocket. "Imagine if you were to paralyze someone . . . you know . . . right up to the neck. I wouldn't want to paralyze a guy." He smooths his cap on, unzips a pocket, produces a box of cigarettes.

"Well, dead is no consolation prize," says Macky Turnbull.

"Well, Plummer's got manslaughter and hit and run to live with," the blond skull-ring biker says.

"Plummer's going to have prison to live *in*," says the scriggle-bearded aviator-cap biker. "It ain't no Holiday Inn, man. Sheeeeeit! Ol' Plummer. He was just over to Gary's couple of weeks ago on top of the world. Now it's . . ." He hums a few bars of "Dragnet."

Marcia Soule says softly, "It's weird, ain't it?"

Keys jangle, lights flutter on, black out again, on again, flutter, and flit. Lights stay on. The dark was nicer.

Lloyd is very very very quiet.

"Well," says the aviator cap guy. "He could go up for parole if he stays cool. I've seen Plummer when he wasn't tanked and he's an okay guy."

"Yeah. He don't bother no one," says the blond biker. "I've known him all my life. He's my cousin, too . . . me and him and Lloyd."

"Deaf," says Kit Turnbull from where she stands, wrapping her throat in a yellow scarf.

"Not full deaf," the blond biker says.

"Well, the next thing to it," says the bald guy with cigarette bouncing on his bottom lip, beard shimmying.

Blond biker says, "He never could hold his beer 'n' booze. Just a few drinks and he'd go nuts."

Faye says, "He and Dad were friends. He logged with Daddy. And helped out in the milking and stuff. You couldn't get him to talk much when he was working . . . when he was . . . you know . . . not drinking. Then this running from fair to fair shit. I bet if it weren't for this fair shit, Carroll wouldn'ta got into this."

"He would, too!" Pam retorts. "He was such a banana."

Faye scowls. "Well, now Dad won't do nothing. Won't put up his bail. Won't even go in to see him. He says let Carroll's folks pay. But Carroll's folks are just about to lose their farmplace. You tell Daddy that, he just says that's *their* problem if they can't handle 'the business.' Carroll's folks don't have anything. And I can tell you another thing . . . neither does Carroll . . . that's for sure."

The aviator-cap biker again hums a few bars of "Dragnet."

There's the thick choking sound of someone vomiting. Lloyd sinks down out of sight, squatted now under the table. First a lot of wet vomiting. Then dry heaves. Then dryer heaves. Now a sound like suffocation.

All but the glassy-eyed biker jump up from their seats, faces paling.

Also paling are the faces of the church people.

Blond biker chuckles. "Before we come in here I seen three sausage sandwiches and two doughboys go down into Barrington. Then there was all that he ate here. Case of the piggin'-outs is what that is. Cured by startin' back on empty."

———

259

34 | On the wide wooden steps of his old farmplace, Marty Plummer, father of Carroll Plummer, finds an old blue canning jar. Against this shaded glass a bright red stripe is pressed from inside. He fetches up the jar, works the wires back. Inside is a small graveyard-sized American flag ripped from its stick. And there's cash. Many tens and twenties. And a note written smoodgily with heavy hand, that kind of handwriting that is actually printing. It reads: *By the rude bridge that arched the flood, Their flag to April's breeze unfurled, Here once the embattled farmers stood* . . .

"What the hell's this?" Marty asks himself, turning the note to examine the blank and wrinkly backside of it.

35 | There's the jerking of the mattress that means Sherry is changing her position. Cassandra holds her breath and listens for the voice of chopped-up words.

Cassandra holds stockstill and sure enough Sherry pushes her mouth hard against Cassandra's right cheekbone and says, "Meem" and then "Meemgrooo." It's actually a kind of cheery voice once you get used to it.

Cassandra reaches out into the dark and pats Sherry's thick, lengthening hair. Cassandra says, "Meem-groo you, too."

Now Sherry says some more stuff.

Now after a silence, Cassandra laments, "You know, Sherry . . . you know what happened? It's wicked. You know what I got this year?" Pause. "MRS. MOUNTAIN." Pause. "Once they moved her to sixth grade. Then they moved her to second grade . . . which was good cause I got to skip her. Goodie! . . . Looked like I had lucky stars. But guess what!! They put her back 'cause Mrs. Anthony went somewheres. I had Mrs. Anthony for only three weeks! Then there was the substitute man. He was funny. Then . . . BLAM . . . there's ol' Mrs. Mountain in our room last week. I coulda died."

Sherry groans, a groan of true sympathy. Sooner or later everybody winds up with Mrs. Mountain.

36 | Some of these old cemeteries . . . he needs to drive right through somebody's barnyard, past their dog on a chain, past their lawn chairs set in a circle. Some of the oldest burying places are up on the discontinued roads, in the thick of paper company land. But when you are graveyard man, you are bigger than the paper company . . . you are the *Town*. You are the *law*. You are master of the dead.

When he appears it is usually of a sudden and some will look up from their work or through a kitchen window and say matter-of-factly, "There he goes up to set flags." Or "Well, he's loaded with mowers today." Most of them know him by his Ford flatbed, though sometimes he drives his father's Powerwagon, and sometimes he and his father are in one truck in the company of one another. The old people know Lloyd like they know Edmund, all there is to know. There are no secrets among the living old. "There he goes," they say matter-of-factly. "Up to tend to the Perrys" or "Parsons" or "Webbs." There's not much more news to tell about the Barringtons. Most is history, part of those threads that bring all of Egypt together into this hard and swollen matrix.

Now in autumn he takes chain saw and pruners. The mowing is done. It's just a matter of keeping the forest back, the woods and bushes that would feast on the human dead. He has driven up the lane past the old Cobb place and entered into the black luxuriance of hemlocks, stonework gushing with vinca and its eternal purple flower. He parks to the gate so flush, the gate gives a jerk and a soft welcoming squeal.

He fills a cheek with a little tobacco, mashes the envelope back into the pocket of his faded hunting vest. Gets out of the truck achingly slow. Though he is only twenty-three now, he has these tired ways. Pulls pruners from under the seat. Lays them on the hood. Moseys back to the bed for the saw. The thing that moves around in his mouth is a thing of peace and calm.

He thinks about the Cobbs. He is only a boy . . . to be so obsessed with the encumberments of death and with the past, among his other obsessions somewhat related.

He pauses a few times, casting his eyes toward the nine marked graves, slate markers leaning to and fro like dark bad teeth. Others are just field-stones. He knows they often gave fieldstones to babies. He sees in his mind's eye the Cobb babies, swirled blue-pink bone within their skulls like mother-of-pearl. Babies, even in death, are radiant.

He believes the men sleep deepest. The hard life, they say. He need not witness the strain of their backs to know how these rocks were piled here. Oxen. The nerved-up great horse. Clang of chains. Mosquitoes on the back of the neck. Deerflies. Blackflies. Who could tell one from the other? Who can tell these men from horses in their shared lather . . . the hoots, the calls, the artistry of stone all in the honor of death.

Then a Cobb woman came uphill from "the place" and laid down a little vinca.

It seems the women can never be buried deeply enough, for they gush over you forever one way or the other . . . green with the little purple flower . . . she will never rest.

He carries the saw and pruners through the black iron gate and stands there studying his work and chewing.

There's the stump-thump of someone's hurried approach. He turns, sees the face of a woman, a stranger, her honey hair in a Cleopatra cut, her blazer black to suggest a matching with her corduroys which are charcoal gray. She has light makeup. An unfriendly expression. "Excuse me!" she calls once she's within earshot. "Excuse me!" as she rushes toward him. Though it's her eyes that slide over his truck, she behaves as though something nasty has gotten on her fingers. She presses them into the fabric of her corduroy pants. "Excuse me but *what* are you doing here?" Her accent and her tone belong to the people of blazers and Cleopatra-dos, that race of them from somewhere beyond imagination. He has *been through this moment before*.

He lowers his chain saw on a level cleft in the stone wall, holds the pruners against his thigh, and says softly, "Hi."

"I *asked* you what you are doing here? You have no business in here. This is private property."

He chews a little, looks off to the left of her head, squints a little. "I'm here to do some thinning today." He points out three saplings. "Especially those three little beeches growing out of Eben Cobb's chest there. And I notice a bit of a sag in the wall over there. I have a come-along for that, you see. And . . ."

"This is private property. Nobody here has asked to have this work done," she says evenly. Her eyes rake over him, his mashed and weathered once-orange felt crusher, his quilted vest also once-orange, his shirt and dungarees, his boots . . . his slightly scarred face. Her study of him is with open disgust. Or disdain. Disdain being more cultured than disgust. Disdain being something like disregard. She doesn't wipe her hand on her pants again, but the fingers flick.

He says, "You'll have to talk it over with the Town. Town might assist you with defining what your deed entitles you to and what it doesn't.

Town's your best bet. Town's who sent me here. Talk with them . . . with Harriet. Go give Harriet a call." He pulls at the great falls of his moustache. Dark, then auburn, then fading off to a lion color at the ends . . . everything about him not quite, everything fading into something other.

"This is private property. I don't need to call the Town about anything. I want you to get your car . . . truck . . . whatever it is . . . out of here. I didn't call for your services. Please leave. If I call anyone, it'll be my attorneys and the police."

"Constable," says he. "No police. 'Less you want the *state* police. But their barracks is an hour away. I'll be done by then. Try the constable. If he's at home. Try the bowling alley if he isn't. Or you could try the game warden. Nice feller. Sings in his church. He might be in church practicing. Try him there. But you could try the Town, too."

He spits something over the wall, then turns back to face her, puts his strange spotted eyes on her. Tips his crusher.

Now he turns with the pruning shears, squats, snaps a few popples at their bases. They flop over to the left. He hears the woman stamping back down the lane, considering her options to settle the "matter," which in the end are always many.

37 | He is hungry. He sits by the open window here on Pleasant Street and breaks open an orange. He arranges the peelings and seeds in a meticulous circular design on the painted wooden table . . . all by feel . . . for he has not yet switched on a lamp. There's just the broken, almost plaid light coming through the closest maple at the low window, the light of the nearest mill house keenly blue. It's the Chases who never shut off their TV, that pulsing bright heart of their home, now and then the blank black silhouette of a Chase passing across the glow. Lloyd watches intently. He strains to hear more of the voice that has just cried out "No!" Sometimes it's hard to tell if it's a Chase shouting or the TV.

All up and down Pleasant Street you see the dark shapes of certain women pausing at the TV, unable to sit for the TV, but needing to keep the thread of the story on their trips to and from the kitchen. And wouldn't these mothers' faces with that soft TV daze be forgiving if you interrupted them from their endless trek?

The orange is gone, nothing but a pattern of seeds and peels in the dark. And the glory of its odor that resembles nothing else.

He is now thinking about Rasputin . . . the monk . . . the great legend who in Lloyd's psychopathology class had been diagnosed as a sociopath.

Rasputin.

How the legend insists that even after he was poisoned and shot close range, he crawled after *them* up the stairs! Alas, he was kicked to death and hurled into the river on the kind of deep Russian night you would suppose. And therefore twice as dead? Maybe three times as dead. And *they* were relieved. But nevertheless decided to wait for good measure. And the deep Russian night was as you would suppose.

Then *they* went there with the means to break ice and there he was! His familiar hand raised out upon his chest in blessing to those who opened the ice.

Lloyd shifts in his chair, rubs his eyes. Sets his crusher hat on the table, rubs his hair. There's orange pulp caught in his back teeth. His tongue rassles it loose.

He is obsessed with the past. The greatest voice. His head is marching, munching, voices of the present weak and distant. The future crashes over the present like a wave. All time in one moment, all peoples converging. They traverse in poor order, mixed, piteous . . . dragging their contraptions, carting their dead. For there is *never* progress. Only fashion. Knots and weave. Leg irons. There are lessons, but no answers. Every question answered with a multitudinous scream. There the cotton gin. There the cave. The Greeks B.C. The Maine Bottle Bill. Last Christmas. The first Christmas. The American Civil War . . . war at its most. Most purple. Most bilious. The Milghram study. The Rosenthal effect. The Fall of Rome. The rise of the Third Reich. The Maine Mall. Chief Joseph's hands. Chief Joseph's hands hanging between his knees. War of Blair Mountain. Columbus lost. John the Baptist headless. The Ford. The Big Bang. Agriculture. Agribusiness. The FBI. Industry. Technology. The IRS. Lee Harvey Oswald. Mrs. Mountain and her tireless chalky hands, her terrible power. Ice Age. Freud. Slave ships. Hiroshima. The wheel. Black Thursday. Montezuma. Roosevelt's dog kicked out of a Portland hotel. Martin Luther King, Jr., speaking low . . . shouting . . . low . . . shouting. The accident of discovering fire. The Baby Boom. Jesse James. Polio shots. Vietnam. Cousin Dana Plummer saying the Navy is best. The Navy is *safe*. Homer. Women vote. The Gold Rush. Big rush. Rush, rush. Everyone rushing, yelling, pushing, screaming, dragging along, reaching, falling, weeping, squeezed into the hourglass . . . the past wide like the future . . . with Lloyd, just a medium-sized young man alone in the middle, alone in this kitchen with his face in his hands.

38 Joanne Foye turning forty. She knows the work of wool. She knows how the mill gets to be your parent with its big and pretty eye. Big hand to hang onto. For dear life. The mill. It is not a given. You stay on your toes. You stay awake. Always awake as *it* is awake, always with its eye on you. And you do the work of the mill, your piece which you do well. And fast. And over and over and over and over and you are the living, standing dead. And the looms clatter and the compressor thrums. Joanne Foye turning forty *is* the wool. She is the luxuriant hot sludge air trickling on the neck, the door next to the loading dock opening, closing since time beyond remembering, though she remembers the first time well, remembers it with a sparkle in her eye.

Gossip, joking, coffee. And wool.

Noise and wool.

Heat and wool.

Tall windows, light, and wool.

Twenty years.

And now this back pain like a knife. And the company doctor's little confusion . . . says there's nothing wrong with her back . . . that she must be thinking of it too much. Something perhaps concerning her *thinking*.

No cure.

So much missed work.

Now the chiropractor. Tells her there's pressure on the sciatic nerve. He tells her he'll fix her up fine . . . two visits a week . . . special machines for stretching and rubbing. And stay off your feet till the pain goes away.

Her friends say not to forget workman's comp. It'll help. Get yourself on that for a while.

The pain like a knife, like a white light, like a dark red torch. It finally subsides. Back into the mill again for the summer. Joanne Foye turning forty. She needs to show them. Needs to push. Joanne Foye at a kind of wondrous peak, fast and furious, scared. "Happy Birthday to You!" they sing at break. Cake and candles. Lots of turning-forty jokes. Hugs. So much to be thankful for.

Must have made the wrong move. The red-and-white light-and-dark pain is back on Friday.

More missed work, more rumbling rubbing chiropractic machines, more workman's comp.

In time, lots of time, lots of visits to the chiropractor, lots of workman's comp, pain subsides.

Back at the mill. Come to the office for a little talk. Bill who is the personnel manager pushing on ahead. Brad behind her, foreman of her shift. One of them closes the door. "Sit down," they say. The office is cool, gentle. Painted blue. The news they have is she, Joanne, is a thief.

"I am not a thief!"

"Yes, I'm afraid you are. We have proof. We have witnesses. See here what we found in your locker, Joanne."

Joanne Foye. Framed.

Coming home, son Bobby's stereo beating up the walls. Son Bobby says, "What's wrong?"

Son Christopher is too young to wonder.

Baby-sitter asks for her money.

39 | Days pass in gray beginning-ends. And fear.

Joanne Foye opening the tinny door of her trailer, finds seventy-three dollars in cash in a relish jar. Sun rising. Hills bristle gray. Frigid wind crackling in the trees, banging about. Almost rips the money from her hand. Trash bag there at her feet snapping, popping as though wind were inside it. But what is really inside are flags, the kind you see on veterans' graves. One has a stick. The wind grabs it and shakes it. Other flags in a damp clump. She carries these things inside and opens the two notes that are written in smoodgy print. *Here's to the red of it, There's not a thread of it, No, not a shred of it, In all the spread of it, From foot to head, For heroes bled for it, Precious blood shed for it, Bathing in red.*

The second note reads: *Your youngest boy might like the one on a stick to play with. The rest . . . use them as rags.*

Joanne Foye is a little annoyed, a little frightened. But the seventy-three dollars, without doubt, will come in handy.

40 | Lloyd has given up the rented house on Pleasant Street. Sometimes he hangs out at his father's house, reading by the kitchen stove or playing gin rummy with Roger. But he doesn't really settle in here.

He doesn't unpack anything, his many cardboard boxes of books, hats, caps. All that just stays in a damp heap in the barn.

Lloyd is restless. More and more restless. He will sometimes actually pace a circle even after long hours of work. And indeed, he *works*. Pruning apple trees in the sub-zero high winds of a hillside. Stacking two-by-sixes and two-by-twelves at Unk Jim's mill. Shoveling roofs. Watering cattle. Cleaning around the cattle in their stanchions. Plowing snow. Splitting firewood. Delivering firewood. All the labors of fall and winter that build up under your clothes a heat, a dull ache.

After everybody else here has fallen into their beds, Lloyd rides the roads slow. Or will visit the Turnbulls or others if they are up. Will visit Madeline Rowe. Or will sit in the plowed dooryard at his father's place, sit under the grayish domelight of his truck, motor running . . . reading the news. A lot of people say they've seen his Ford parked at some of the graveyard gates late night. Lloyd with his arms crossed over his chest, Lloyd staring, Lloyd chewing, Lloyd pulling on his outlaw moustache in a look of calculatingness. Some say there's something about the guy that's a little supernatural. But at Moody's Variety & Lunch the wise men say matter-of-factly, "Bullshit. Ain't nuthin' about it supernatural." What Lloyd Barrington is, they say, "is what you call *a bum*."

41 | Weeks pass in their symmetry. Months in their efficiency. Caleb Barrington is born.

42 | It is a hot one, one of those surprise heats in April. "Won't last." This is what the Egypt wise men all say.

Lloyd Barrington drives along the old Across Road, shuts down his lights, rolls along in neutral the last twenty yards, a glint of bluish moon on the truck's grille. He leaves the truck on the shoulder of the road and walks. He counts on the household of Soules to be asleep, and their sleep not to be fitful. With Caleb, Sherry's baby, waking for his bottle, there might be a sister on her toes. This, he has to consider.

The crunch of Lloyd's sneakers on gravel is lost to the little whining groans of the wind that has started up since midnight.

He knows the twist of the Soules' kitchen doors like he knows breathing. He works these doorknobs and hinges quieter than breathing, quieter than blood.

They have craftily moved her to a new room, the ell space upstairs that needs no guard. Sort of like the high tower where the princess was kept in old tales. Inaccessible, one would think.

Through the black rooms to the attic stairs, he keeps his left hand on a rear pocket to keep his keys quiet, the other hand a trembly proboscis, feeling along the stairwell wall. At the top of the stairs in a room with no door, Merlin and Dottie sleep. The little trick is to keep Merlin and Dottie's sleeping sighs regular. If a step creaks, he waits, listening, his eyes sweating with the heat, sweating with fear. But the night made black by the Soules' many fiberglass drapes is almost always faithful to him. His true enemy is the sunshine of a perfect day.

The *big* trick is to get around Merlin's hand if it's dangling from the bed. He must know if the hand is there, but without *really finding out*. The trick is to see the hand before he enters this space, and as always, Lloyd *sees*.

And yes, tonight the hand is there. The fabric of Lloyd's dungarees moves within atoms of the hand as he bears down to make his next step . . . three more steps to the low doorway that is Sherry's room . . . the room where she is safe from him . . . the room they must carry her up to every night.

He arrives. Big, bare, wooden room, vast with its woodenness, vast with bareness, vast with moon, the lovely many-paned blueness of the curtainless dormers facing the road, and the gable window that is nearly as crooked as a funhouse is. Bed, cardboard boxes, the chrome-legged "commode." Four more steps to the edge of Sherry's bed. His pant legs scratch together. He freezes, waits five whole unbroken minutes, swaying slightly with the nearby cadences of Merlin and Dottie's exhaustion.

A half step closer to the bed. The squares of moonlight on the plank floor through the sweatiness of his eyes look like raised pale beds, so it seems like a room of many beds, a ward of many Sherrys. Which one is real? All the beds squirm. He presses his knee to the actual bed, a low bed for she is known to fall out, a bed that smells like the sheets were dried indoors during this long past week of rain and humidity. And smells of piss, for as they say, she is "not right."

He removes the keys from his pocket, lays them in slow motion on the dresser there. Removes his change. Two quarters and a dime. All the money there is to his name.

A hand grips his pant leg. It is always the same. The ghosty, almost tuneful half whisper, "Lloy! Lloy!" Always the same. Everything in its place. Holy. Holy. Holy.

Preeminence

1 | MOODY'S VARIETY & LUNCH is thick with business this morning. Half of Egypt bringing in their kills all within the last half hour it seems. Even those who aren't having a deer tagged have such a hot flush and real emergency in their greetings. Most are just boys. Great blazing eyes. Radiant.

Around the barrel stove are the rockers newly painted in jazzy colors. Around the lunch counter are the stools. Everywhere, every seat, every space of the wall that's good for leaning against has been taken. Young men. Middle-aged men. Old men.

There's the ceremonious roaring arrival of a truck in the side lot. A high-up four-wheel-drive showboat of a truck. Glittering. Chrome in all possible places. Hubcaps to blind you. White roll bar and side rails made for drivers who *expect* to crash. Engine sounds like it could pick the truck up and fly. And bigger than life, one whitetail deer wired to the roll bar against the cab. It is arranged spread-eagle. It is split from rectum to chest, its tail, once snowy, now stained by its purple surrender.

The truck pitches to a stop. Both doors open at the same time. With ease. Two boys with sweet silly blotchy whiskers drop to the gravel.

Two more pickups arrive. One of them, grinding its gears, backs up to the weighing shed in a kind of big race.

Rifles in the gunracks. More rifles than there are pairs of hands.

A few men inside Moody's rise from the bright rockers, slide off the stools.

At the doorway, one calls, "Look at 'at. Little more dirt in the hoof, Duff, an you'd have him weighin' in two hundred. Sheeeit!"

At the register, Mary Moody is wondering, "Look like snow yet, Donnie?"

An old-faced guy with a young hard-waisted body and head-to-foot Day-Glo blaze orange replies, "We need something. Need a track."

"Come onnnnn!" Benny Knight clamors from where he is scooched on the windowsill. "You don't need snow to track, Donnie. Ain't you part Indian?"

Donnie chuckles.

Benny insists, "Can't you notice a bent twig and call it good enough?"

A few chuckles. A couple of hoots.

Two boys, standing waist-deep in the weak morning sun by the glass door, step aside as Tim Gowen enters. Tim Gowen and his boy. Boy about eight. Tim Gowen is small-built, fair. Tall rubber boots. His boots are the kind that you'd expect to clomp, but his stride is light and proud. The boy imitates the walk.

Tim has news. Found a lynx in one of his traps this morn.

A lot of ears perk up. There's a lot of leaning forward in the rockers.

"Big son-of-a-bitch," Tim says. " 'Tweren't no Here-pussy!-pussy!-Siamese-lap-cat." He illustrates the size of the cat, size of the cat's snarl, the cat's lunging. "Obviously the cat didn't have no idea about who was boss. He weren't going to get to do *that* too many more times, I'll tell ya."

Chuckles of understanding go up and around the counter, in and out of the rockers.

Another pickup swings into the lot. Three hunters who have arranged three bucks with heads swinging over the tailgate like dead outlaws being paraded down Main Street of a TV western town.

Tim Gowen tells how the cat almost hooked him in the pants leg with his free paw. He tells how this was the last straw, how he told his boy to go get a limb for a club. Tim Gowen shows how you show a lynx who's boss. Tim Gowen describes the paw that's crushed in the trap . . . and now the three paws that are "pulped." Tim Gowen tells how he said to his boy, "You want to ride him? I'll let you ride him before I put him down." No, the boy had said. He's still got teeth. "Well, let's smash out his mouth for you," Tim had said. "Not every day you get to ride a wildcat." So Tim Gowen tells how he got a bigger limb and smashed that lynx's mouth in and all that critter could do now was bang his head on you. But still the boy didn't want to ride the cat. So Tim Gowen had said to his boy, "What is it you scared of now? That cat *lookin'* at you? You don't like the way he's watchin' you with those scary eyes?" So Tim laughs at this and then explains how he took care of the eyes.

2 | In the office of Manpower Affairs in Portland, an appeals hearing takes place. Tribunal officer. Company reps. And someone wearing green work pants, two or three shirts layered for outdoor weather, November weather . . . though the temperature in this small room is nearly eighty. This man is in his forties as are the first three. But clearly he is not like them. He is *scared*.

He is here today because the company denies that they were ever late paying wages though he has testified that they were late with his pay many times. He couldn't live that way, he has testified . . . "I quit. Unemployment lady says it 'twas a good enough reason to quit. I didn't tell her no lies. She said getting paid late so much means I can collect."

Company wants the unemployment benefits to stop.

The man in the green pants and heavy shirts tells how he had worked for the former owner who was named Chip Hanson for fourteen years. "Then Chip couldn't keep up . . . sold to this company . . . corporation. These guys promised bonuses . . . promised vacations . . . promised raises nobody ever saw . . ."

The tribunal officer interrupts him. He says, "Mr. Gowen. Answer only the questions, please."

The man with the green pants and many shirts spreads his hands on his knees to keep his hands steady.

The tribunal officer and the company reps stare at the worker as he answers another question. Their chairs all face his. A tape recorder makes a soft brushing sound on a folding table. It seems the worker has trouble with speech, can't even say the word "forklift" clearly now. It's so easy to confuse him, to break him down.

Now and then one of the company men stretches his arms over his head in a gesture of confidence and ease.

The other one shows the tribunal officer a ledger of check receipts for proof that checks are always on time.

The worker looks at the flipping of ledger pages, then looks away.

Now the worker is saying yes for no and no for yes and half-finishing his sentences.

The tribunal officer says to the worker, "If you *were* paid late, like you say, Mr. Gowen, and you knew there was a chance of it happening *again*, why didn't you just save money aside for gasoline and food, instead of allowing yourself to run out like that? Did you not consider your actions irresponsible?"

The tape recorder whirrs pleasantly.

The worker has been listening, eyes on his hands. Seems like he's listening to a man speaking French or Spanish, which he does not understand.

"Mr. Gowen, please answer the question," the tribunal officer says.

The worker can't answer the question.

The tribunal officer and the company men glance into each others' eyes.

3 | Table of honor is the full length of the long, low platform.

Gwen enunciates a clear "No thank you" to the banquet waitress's offer to refill her water glass. She knows nothing of the waitress's face. She smiles that smile that comes out of her own face toward the easy laughter of the women seated at the table below. Inside her own face is where all life exists. The soul. The heart. As it is for us all. Is this the future Gwen Curry had seen for herself twenty years ago?

Her husband, Earl Doyle, is at her right.

At Earl's right a man talks low. The man calls someone "a prick," the name of that someone who is a prick being a name among thousands of names that have no meaning to her, while a thousand others bring a dull thud to her heart. Why the dull thud? her therapist had once asked. Flint-hard names. Names Earl speaks with ease. Some are in the news. With the therapist, she can't seem to home in on this feeling yet. Not that she is speechless. With the therapist she always chatters excessively.

She's not sure if Earl disapproves of her seeing the therapist. It's clear to her that he would never deem such "confessional discussions" as appropriate for himself. But he does not dictate her life. Nor does he *discuss* "life." She has told the therapist that she has translated some of his gestures into this: To display emotion you most certainly lose credibility and your judgment is questioned.

"It's not that Earl would deny that we all feel," she explained to the therapist. "And he's not saying *he* doesn't have emotions. I don't mean to make him sound terrible. Please . . . no . . . don't misunderstand me. Earl is a nice man. But . . . I guess Earl sees emotions as underwear." And she had giggled. And the therapist had wiggled his pencil, which is his way of laughing, she has come to realize.

Wherever she goes, whatever she feels, she knows she can get through it because the therapist's appointment is Thursday. Little bald unsmiling but warm man, wiggling his pencil. Little lifeline. When the appointment is over with, he'll give her hand a squeeze and say she is making progress, that a lot of hard work went into this session. Teamwork, he calls it.

Here now at her left and far left and out across the banquet room are corporate managers, so much top management . . . some middle management and sales, and those from the boards of directors from several concerns.

Somewhere near there's a conversation in hearty tones about lost luggage. Luggage having gone to London instead of Rhode Island. "Must have thought the tags said England instead of *New* England!" one of them laments. There are traces of high emotion here. For you see, the rules of appropriateness are complex.

"I don't ever take anything I can't carry on," another one of them says.

The tables are covered in cloth that drapes down nearly to their shoes. And the napkins are cloth. Not linen though. Some spongy impostor.

She gives Earl's forearm a little squeeze, then quickly but with a look of ease draws her hand back. Under her fingers the sincerity of the wool of his suit jacket tells her all is well. He is turning his head her way. He smiles. A warm smile.

She is exhausted. But not because of overlapping flights, missed flights, standbys and lost luggage. Earl's private plane eliminates all that. But the burbles!!! The proverbial leaf tossed on the tide!

There are no arguments here . . . no point-counterpoints. Everything is light. Light champagne. Light laughter. The seats aren't deep enough. There's a seaminess to this room. Some days it would give you a cheated feeling. Other days you are more forgiving.

The man at Earl's right has such a charming laugh. Even when he is calling people "pricks" and naming the flint-hard names, he seems so boyish and dear . . . warmth on the very *edge* of emotion. And this man is terribly handsome. And he has one of those plastic tabletop name tags that shows a recognizable name. William Carp. A name she's heard Earl discuss on the phone of his office. Sometimes Earl has called him "Mr. Manpower Affairs." And it's always with a dismissive gesture, as he does with so many . . . and yet to their faces, it's the first name always. Like you would a friend. "Bill."

The cup-shaped pastries with glops of creamed chicken were all the same a few moments ago, now changing, falling away as forkfuls are raised.

Across from Earl, an attorney she recognizes. "Jim." Earl toasts Jim with his champagne and Jim toasts Earl. Their eyes are like dark-ringed blue wide-open zeroes on each other's faces . . . that knack of staring *between* the eyes.

Meanwhile, "Mr. Manpower Affairs" with his charmingly devious laugh interrupts. Now again what he tells Earl is gruff and low. A secret? Something naughty?

Now the conversation of a table "off-stage" catches her attention. Three women discussing the entrapment of women by their houses, by family, by fears, by ignorance. Their voices are just an edge above the dull, steady low roar of the crowded banquet. And their silverware resonates truer than bells. One of them tells of a friend who finally divorced "the little worm" and was free to pursue a valuable career. They all have wristwatches. Authoritative crinkles around the eyes. Jackets in cottons and wools. No violets, no yellows. Nothing pink. Nothing fluffy. Their smiles are warm. But quick. Nothing lingers. Everything pulled faster and faster through the fierce conduit of C.E.O. time.

"Mr. Manpower Affairs" haw-haws at something Earl said, which she has missed. "Mr. Manpower Affairs" tilts his head.

She leans forward ever so slightly to see him beyond Earl's profile. He is turning his champagne glass around and around, hasn't touched his chicken. He finishes what she now realizes was a sort of story with a punch line. Chuckles go up and down the far right of the table. One or two deep snorts. Clinking of dishes.

Earl hasn't laughed at the story, but his eyes move in a signal of appreciation.

She tries not to appear drunk.

Are *they* drunk?

Her therapist has asked her if *she* feels she's an alcoholic. She always laughs. An alcoholic is someone who drinks alone, she told him. "I'm never alone."

But that was a lie . . . well, maybe a joke. What could be more solitary than her hours of work in her darkroom?

Now glasses of champagne are raised and lowered to the left and right of her. And out over the many tables . . . nearly a thousand present at this occasion . . . bottles uncorked with a poof or a bang . . . and ahhhs of satisfaction.

A thousand people being softened by degrees.

Gwen gives Earl's hand a squeeze. She sees that all the faces look appreciative now. Like Earl's face. Their faces mirroring his face. Earl Doyle in the place of honor as usual. Earl Doyle who is all. Mr. Diversity. Mr. Chairman of *every* board. Auto. Textiles. Broadcasting. Publishing. Energy. Pharmaceuticals. Film. Insurance. Agribusiness. Ice Cream. And a *very* concentrated interest in politics and education. Seeming serene, but really on constant alert, braced, ready, fit, fittest. The true conquistador.

Juxtaposed

THE FEET.

It's just one of those things. No one can be blamed. A juxtaposition. A fine crossed line. The thing . . . it has caught Forest's eye. But he sees it only as it is actually happening, when the fright is not even yet spangling at the ends of his fingers. He is just looking at it, this peculiar thing, this juxtaposition of him with *it*, this hazed morning, a Thursday, the high sun, the curtains on the bank manager's window, beige, the flagman, the bulldozer. Everything in position, moving toward the moment, moving inside these diesel-stinking roars.

The feet. No blame. He had kept his eye on the traffic coming off the narrow bridge, and on Feeney backing across with a load. And on the flagman with his sign up, and on the sun, and the bulldozer, and one of them with Castellucci Brothers walking with two sheets of plywood on his back and a power company meter reader's truck pulling away from the curbing over to Mertie's, the steel plates of the bulldozer's track, the wind and hissing sand, the wind grabbing and smashing and thumping and shaking, plywood man blown and stumbling, and the load Forest has come with, motor idling, across in Mertie's side lot, the spot of white, which is the macaroni man his daughter made, hanging in its chunky way from the visor of the truck's spotted windshield.

Between these many planes of noise, steel, and light, Forest is a warm and breakable fact of life, a system of nerves and bones, synapses, reflexes, now turned and backing toward the street, head turning from side to side, shouting, "OVER THERE!" and pointing toward his load. While F.D. is nodding, Forest turns away.

Forest is a rubbery burstable fact of life and in another twenty years, he will consider how all the years, the last twenty years of his life that have been spent in continuous but somewhat endurable pain have all impinged on this spot where he now stands between the bank and the narrow bridge and the mill and Mertie's Hardware and the sun and Fred Shaw on the bulldozer, and in this moment when he is still whole and healthy before he sees the peculiar wrongness of these things coming together.

12

Green

ACROSS THE AIRY HALL, she hears them in their council. One of them calls someone not present "an incompetent impotent little clerk," which causes chuckling. A briefcase is opened.

Earl isn't laughing but Gwen knows his look. His look that appreciates.

She is on her way out, tossing her short coat over her shoulders, snatching two camera cases. She has no time to get stuck in the usual introductions. They will think her steps going away toward the front door are Shelley's moving toward them with drinks.

The gentlemen are one voice, always familiar . . . echoes of Earl. One voice speaks out away from the rest, tells of the impending development of a "six-hundred horsepower tractor, which will operate remote control," tells of how many acres can be processed by "a single operator" . . .

She is glad to be out with the falling leaves. Her head is awhirl with images already photographed but yet to be put down into the chemicals and washes. She almost skips toward her car, which is not boxed in by the rental cars of the visitors. She starts her car and is off.

There is an image she plans to work with today. So far it is only four exposures on a contact sheet, the rest on that undeveloped third film. It is an image she has trouble with, mostly that too fine curve of light. She has worked on this project for months.

Meanwhile, she has been reading the book her therapist gave her. The authors explain that everyone is in an identity crisis . . . finding "one's self." Searching.

Her therapist said the shape of a lima bean is fetal, though she sees that he is shaped a little like a lima bean himself. He asked if she has considered that this lima bean photo project . . . this deep interest in lima beans . . . might mean she doesn't feel independent enough . . . that she needs more independence.

She told him that she has always liked the shapes of all vegetables and their vivid colors . . . "especially *carrots*" . . . and then she laughed her sweet hiccuppy laugh and said, "Maybe *that* means I need *more* of Earl, not less."

The therapist wiggled his pencil, almost smiled. He began to propose another thought, but she interrupted him. "What about all my tree prints! Oaks. I love oaks. I have photographed trees far more than vegetables." She lowers her eyes from his trained stare. "We shouldn't try to make something like this out of my work. It is art, not a disease."

But she, the artist, and he, the therapist, both specialists in their field, will never see eye to eye. Always on the surface. Never in tandem. In tandem? You can never really get that close to anyone, can you?

13

Red

THE FAIRS, the years, they interweave. Patchwork. Muddle. Dreadful and dear. Some things change. While some things will stay in place. Dottie Soule says with sore-throat huskiness, "Let's get ourselves situated on one of these rides." This year the tickets are blue. Dottie looks up at the red devil with his pitchfork. Twenty-foot-tall red devil. Pitchfork has skewered a screaming little man and holds him over flames.

Dottie's blue-frame glasses are no longer the fashion where even here in Maine, fashion has come at last. But hit or miss, there's still a lot of Dottie Soules around with their plastic-frame glasses, stoic oily little ponytails or tightly permed curls solid as knuckles. Immune. Unbending resisters. Deep as anchors in the waters of old ways.

Dottie's mouth twitches in concentration. "Sage . . . how many tickets for this ride?"

"Four," Sage tells her, then groans. "I'm not going in there. Not me."

"Me neither!" Tammy clamors.

"Nobody's going in with you, Ma," Stacy says, rolling her eyes.

"What do you suppose is in there?" Leighlah wonders. "Probably just a kind of funhouse, I'll bet."

Caleb. Looking distracted. Looking off.

Dottie's lenses glow toward each face. "What babies," she says grimly. She feels into her shirt pockets for another long tail of blue tickets, snaps off a few for the guy who has his hand out for them.

"Devil's Den," says Leighlah softly.

"I'm hungry," says Caleb. "I'll be back in a while."

"Caleb's headed for the trough," Sage says. "Oink. Oink."

The guy who operates the Devil's Den looks a little like the red devil. Long face. Ears, very tall. Dottie gives him a wink and hops leggily into one of the red dented buggies. Her face and rattail of hair look suddenly full of purpose—invincible . . . her mission, an important one. The guy bears his weight onto the lever and the girls watch their mother-grandmother disappear into the Devil's Den.

Inside Leighlah's neck, a whimper.

"That ride ain't nuthin'," Sage says with a snort. "It's just a baby ride. The worst rides are those." She points out the revolving rockets and giant bullet shapes in a train that are worse than any roller coaster, jerking, spinning in all directions around the roller coaster track. And in them, human faces, yeowling or quietly pale, blurred. Captive.

The girls sit on the edge of the platform facing away from the entrance into which Dottie and the train of empty red buggies have disappeared.

The Devil's Den operator stares off down the midway with a vague otherworldly expression.

"Caleb's just prowling," says Leighlah.

"Probably hoping he sees Junie Greenlaw," says Sage.

Leighlah smirks. "She hates his guts."

"He's just dying to spend all his money on those stupid games," Sage says.

"Viddie-oooo," says Leighlah, doing an imitation of caveman mentality.

"He's right over there. See?" Tammy points. "He's really eating."

"Oink!" Sage is relentless.

There's a clack-clack-clack and a rolling-around sound in the unknown depths of the Devil's Den behind them and sometimes a *whoooooooooosh!*, a bell bonging, a siren, and an ugly recorded heinous laugh.

Leighlah jiggles. Feet cold, face warm with high color.

All four girls watch what passes, legs of tall people, baby strollers, small dogs, lots of frozen breath, hands in pockets . . . everyone moving along as if pulled by this tide of harvest and fun, fear and victory, agitated peace.

"JEZUSS! I ALMOST WET MY GODDAM PANTS!" Dottie fusses cheerily, reappearing from the Devil's Den. Unchanged.

"George Washington Probably Slept Here."

I'm a lean dog, a keen dog, a wild dog, and lone;
I'm a rough dog, a tough dog, hunting on my own;
I'm a bad dog, a mad dog, teasing silly sheep;
I love to sit and bay the moon, to keep fat souls from sleep.

—*Irene R. MacLeod*
"Lone Dog"

1 | ROAR of the barrel stove. Coolers humming. Not many purchases tonight, just a lot of wisdoms and pizza-to-go smell. Tonight's wisdoms are on greyhound racing, Apache helicopters, ice fishing with old Charlie Shaw, wallpapering the right way, the ingredient they used to put in a Coke, the Philippines in the forties, aircraft carriers. And roads.

More rocking chairs these days to accommodate so much wisdom. Not long ago Louise Moody and her pal Dottie Soule painted them all in wild colors. Colors like Purple Ecstasy, Fandango, Canary, Blue Moon, Hawaiian Sunset, and Spring Beauty.

Tonight Louise Moody's boy is at the register. He helps out his mother whenever he can. But nowadays most people don't feel completely at ease with Louise Moody's boy, David. The *Reverend* David Moody who you never see in a church . . . who went to theology school but wound up a well driller. Tonight when there's no customers at the register, he comes over and stands by the creaking rockers and puts his hands on the back of Purple Ecstasy, which is unoccupied.

He does have about him the bearing of a man of God, leaning a little toward you on one foot as you speak, small strange smile, hands clasped like he's about to bless you, pronounce you man and wife or what all they learn to do in theology school. Always "please" and "thank you." Never a swearword. Always the proper thing. Dark blue work shirt that has WICKS WELL DRILLERS embroidered in copper-color thread across his broad back. A man greatly pronounced in the shoulders and chest for being short in height, just as Louise Moody, his mother, is short and bosomy. And his hair is noticeable. Streaky blond and straight down . . . his surfin' look. But never any surfin'. Eyes light and light-lashed. Nobody looks. It's hard to look into a minister's eyes directly. Even if, here he is, in his forties now, wife and kid, *but no church*.

The old wise men can't get enough heat, their configuration of dazzling rockers tensing and tightening closer to the stove.

Then there's this thing concerning the Reverend David Moody that is *very* bothersome. Something about the reverend that's not quite reverent . . . maybe not even quite legal. It is this that you notice over the days, weeks, years like the pattern on a snake. And over time the thing gets clear to you . . . this knowing by those in Egypt who know all . . . that the Reverend David Moody is in pretty thick with Lloyd Barrington. A bad, bad sign.

2 | Late October. Daylight mere as a vein. It comes from the night, strains along behind the black firs high at the shoulder of the mountain and low along the ridge of the sandpit. And in the foreground a different sort of light. The Johnsons' kitchen windows.

There's a grunt with silence all around it. Another grunt . . . an old Mack slow to start.

Peggy Johnson steps off the back door step of her home, crosses the gravel lot with a kind of stride that sets the dark spread of her gathered hair to flopping. It is plain to see that she is a woman who has spent much of her life with dominion over large beasts. Show horses. The dark, edgy, expensive kind. Dominion must be a flexible thing. For she was once a funny-faced young girl of twenty-three, whose "dowry" was four Arabian horses and a master's degree in business administration. No idea how to cook. No idea of how to raise children. Her parents had always been busy people. One a druggist. One a teacher of high school English. Dominion, leadership, administration. How do you channel it when married to a man like Forest Johnson, Jr.?

Now there's a nickering from the newish small barn to the far right of the old barn. While over by the shop doors, Peggy's husband is speaking in a low wavering voice with some of his crew.

Another two dump trucks come to life. They set the ground to trembling. V-8's. Two hundred horses each. Each and every truck is two hundred more horses. This is the bottom line, isn't it? Forest's *trucks*. Forest's *roads*. Forest's *business*. Makes a few long-legged prancing horses like Peggy's seem like a frivolty.

Peggy Johnson. Gray wool jacket zipped up to her chin. Chin always a little too high, the way of so many people who are short. Her smile shows perfect teeth, that unnatural, constructed, stagy look of teeth that have been "corrected" in youth. She pushes through the elbows and whirling frozen breaths of the crew and speaks. "Forest."

The racket of the trucks drowns out the word. But Forest can tell when his name is in the air. "Yuh, what?"

A backhoe driver steps away, his dark silhouette merging with those of the three drivers smoking in the nearest open bay. Most of the drivers wear Day-Glo blaze orange on some part of the body . . . hat . . . vest . . . gloves. Though nobody gets a Saturday off to hunt. Day-Glo blaze is more like a daydream when you work for Forest Johnson, Jr.

The dawn moves along now through the webbing of bared hardwoods, higher and higher, the kind of North Pole pale that comes with the North Pole feel of the air.

Peggy shouts, "Jeff just called! He's here in Egypt! If you want to see him, come back to the house when you can. He said he'd be here in about five minutes!"

Forest's steel-rimmed glasses fill now with white sunrise like a kind of sovereignty. He makes no reply to this news. His frozen breath is fast and vexed.

3 | The Camaro with the California plates swings down onto Rummery Road. The header is popping and barking. There's road dust and a crimp on the grille. But the paint is an unmarred tangerine, hotshot, showy.

It is turning up into the dooryard of the Johnsons' place, a colonial in a neighborhood of colonials and capes with dates instead of street numbers over the doors. Dates like 1799 and 1800 and 1806. Many have windowpanes that ripple. All of them have pale frost-killed lawns and fences or hedges like fences. The Johnsons' fence is a mix. Part white picket. Part wrought iron and granite post. The maple trees' limbs wag bare in the icy breeze, great-girthed manly trees. There are recessions in their bark you'd swear were grimacing faces. The Johnsons' colonial is smudgy brick. Grim. Its doors, its broad beveled cornerboards, eaves and window trim, are painted with a thick rind of what every hardware store calls Tile Green, thicker now than twenty years ago, the hurried unsanded layers of the years. Between the sashed white curtains is the black and blank look of the rooms. Each window identical to the next, multiplying the look of inside distances . . . of endless time. However, modern time gives itself away. There's Bett Johnson's turtle collection arranged in the kitchen windows. And on the front lawn there's a thing some call a Murgatroid, some call a "gazing globe." This one is ruby red. They are the rage these days.

The driver of the Camaro cuts the engine, stretches her long arms over her head and says with weary relief, "Well! Here we are at last! At the mansion!" She giggles. Like all her giggles, this one ends in a soft snort.

Beside her, her lover, with a short damp marijuana roach in a hairpin, chokes out his smoke too suddenly, says, "It's not a mansion."

Upon the ruby Murgatroid the image of the Johnson home bellies out, lusty and blushing. And the short front lawn is pink and convex.

"Well." The driver sighs. "It's a hunk of a place. George Washington probably slept here, right? Look at that fan-shaped thingy over the front door! Gawd. If I myself had grown up here, I'd be psyched and high as a jet right now. Not acting like an asshole like you."

4 | Too much dark, brass-latched furniture. Too many furniture scarves, which are too lacy and too white. Floors of narrow oak boards unscarred. Stashes of knickknacks at eye level. The smell of hot cookies moves through the rooms. Chocolate nut! Such a smell! Like two hundred years worth of cookie smell, thousands of thwanks of the oven door echoing the probable squeals of cookie-loving children. But otherwise, not much looks like kids ever existed here. It's not the place you'd expect a fun person like Jeff Johnson to have grown up in.

Noontime . . . long since the arrival of Jeff Johnson and his new California woman, Coti Pederson. And Eli. Eli who is Jeff's child by the other woman, his wife . . . Amy Johnson. Where *is* Amy Johnson? You can't get Jeff to answer that. Though Peggy and Nanna Bett have tried to make a go of it. Also some chitchat . . . like all the doin's around town here these days, the fields around the old farms checkered with new houses. And tar driveways. And houses that were never finished. The new, bigger high school. The bank that isn't called Maine National now. Peggy says maybe if the banks are going to change their names so often, they should just rent one of those signs on wheels that have the lighted shimmering arrow and the letters that can be conveniently rearranged. She is the only one who laughs at this. Now she asks what things are like in California. What part of California is he from these days? And how's the art world? And is he still painting those big flowers that aren't really supposed to be flowers? Or are you doing something like California scenes? She heard California is really pretty, not just the overpasses and parking garages and swimming pools and square houses that the TV world shows. Or commercial art . . . has he had a hand in that?

Jeff doesn't have much to say. Just a smile weirdly sweet and his dark eyes focused on some weirdly sweet thought to match. He nods a lot. He busts out into many giggles . . . giggles pouring from his mouth . . . his mouth which the new woman, Coti Pederson, immediately covers with her mouth . . . a kiss. Not just your hello or good-bye smooch. Not just enthusiasm. But kisses that push and ram, gush and squeak, lips screwing around like a lid on a jar.

The boy Eli, standing by the refrigerator, pulls the magnetic plastic pancake from the freezer door . . . fiddles with it, feeling the willful pull of it.

No sign of Forest.

Not much sign of Peggy now either. She seems to have disappeared . . . sometime during a kiss. Peggy out there on the porch office phone. Now and then out of the silence there's the clacking dial and Peggy's clearly accentuated doing-business voice talking salted sand . . . talking back-order on a new air compressor . . . then a date with the power company to lay 680 yards of underground cable. Then silence.

And Nanna Bett. Where'd she go? Somehow also vanished during a kiss.

Nobody around but Eli to show the art of kissing to, the art of bending over backwards with the other person adhered to your front and . . . uh! uh! . . . the sounds of passion.

The boy Eli asks Jeff, "Dad . . . when are we going?"

Jeff rolls his eyes.

The new woman, Coti Pederson, is restless, paces around and around the white-and-black enameled leaf table where Jeff now sits playing with the spotted-cow salt and pepper shakers. He peppers his left hand.

The boy Eli glowers. "Dad."

"WE JUST GOT HERE, ELI!" Jeff shouts. Then regaining his weird and distant smile, "You know, Eli . . . here in Maine, they give you awards for dumb questions. Someone's going to drive up in a minute with your trophy. The trophy is a statue of a stupid-looking kid with his tongue out about a foot and the tongue is solid gold."

Eli rolls his eyes. Eli is still wearing his Levi's jacket. His eyes in their dark lashes are pale, pale blue-green. From his mother, Amy, the vanished woman, he has inherited the unmistakable invincible Bean jawline, Bean nose. But from somewhere—who knows where?—he has inherited *fat*. Fat, mussed-haired, and rumpled, nothing like Jeff Johnson and Coti Pederson who both look California and glitterish.

5 Nanna Bett says this is as good a time as any to go upstairs and visit with Granpa F.D.

Nanna Bett is the first to reach the stairs, the kind of stairs with yards of polished rail and newel posts dark and hulking as upright bears.

"Well there!" Nanna Bett calls happily from the top. With a hand on one bearish newel post, she turns to look down at the faces catching up.

Eli reaches the top.

She clasps his shoulder. For a moment, her being small and he being quite tall for age seven, they are eye to eye.

Beyond the old lady's white hair is a window with white chenille drifting across like lazy snow. The hall wallpaper is white stripes and flowers. Hurrying around and down to the end of the hall, Nanna Bett stops at a door, turns a glass knob.

A high-ceilinged room. Many windows. A wheeled chrome-sided bed and deep armchairs for visiting. Not much heat up here.

Jeff Johnson says, "Howdy, Gramp. How're you feeling?"

The pantings of hard breathing are not from the bed, but from Jeff. All his fast breaths hang visibly white around his face. It always amazes him, his family's grip on a dollar, how they can stretch a dollar . . . *wring* a dollar. The temperature of this room is of a temperature more like that in a bulkhead where you'd keep potatoes and squashes for winter . . . not flesh . . . not a dying old man.

Nanna Bett pushes around Jeff and Eli and she gives the chrome side a hard shake. "Forest! It's Jeffrey! He's back! And the baby. The baby is all grown-up! You hear me?"

No response. No nothing. There's really not even a body there. Just a head and a lot of smooth flowing blankets of the solid colors new blankets are today . . . a mauve, a deeper mauve, and chocolate. One blanket is plugged into the wall. And other things are plugged into the bed and out of the bed. Plastic bags and bottles.

Coti Pederson's short dress is a red spot in the corner of Jeff Johnson's eye.

Nanna Bett hollers, "You hear me, Forest!" Now in a sigh and an embarrassed flash of her eyes on the visitors' faces, "I like to think he hears us. The doctor says you never can tell."

The boy Eli frowns at the two nipples in the blankets that must be the old man's feet. A little man. A very very very little man there.

Nanna Bett puts her hand on Jeff's arm. "You know, dear, a couple of months ago, Granpa would say words but he was confused. That's what the doctor called it. Confused. Confused is what the doctor called it. You know, Granpa would talk like he thought the room was full of men."

The boy Eli is watching the old woman's hand letting go of Jeff's arm.

"Brrrrrrrr," Coti says with a shiver, squeezing herself, and squeezing the knees of her long bare legs together.

"Not as toasty here as in Anaheim, huh?" Jeff says in a voice with a little edge to it.

Eli slides his eyes mockingly toward the red shape by the door.

With no voice, just her lips and teeth opening to form the message, Coti says to Jeff's face, "A-S-S-H-O-L-E." She turns and is now heard clumping with her high-heeled glamoury sandals down the stairs and away.

Jeff says, "Be right back, Nanna," then chases out into the hall, the boy hurrying to keep up, the stairway thundering, then doors slamming throughout the house.

6 | The Camaro parked outside the Johnsons' brick colonial has people sitting inside it. The Camaro is not arriving. The Camaro is not leaving. Its gas gauge reads nearly empty. No key in the switch. The car gives a little frisky jounce, then tips softly up and down to the vigorous waves of a kiss.

The boy, Eli Johnson, says, "Dad." The boy is with the brown paper bags and nylon travel satchels, loose, mashed, tumbled, ransacked-looking backseat. Under his feet a cream-color halter-top dress in a single agonized wrenched twist. Eli says, "*Dad*." Coti has disappeared somewhere below the headrests, below Eli's line of vision. His father's head and kissing mouth pushes down, down, down. "Dad," says Eli.

The smell of marijuana smokes of the past has a warm, live presence at all times in this car, a restful smell . . . the power of its odor multiplied by each waking hour of a day, multiplied by the days of a week, then multiplied by all the weeks and months of the ownership of this car by its present owner.

Coti squeals, "Stop that, J.J.! It hurts." Now the heads pop back up. Coti's hand with many rings and her wrist with three black voluptuous plastic big-as-bagel bracelets flops loosely over one shoulder of Jeff's sweater. Such a sweater! A nothing-you'd-normally-see-in-nature yellow. Certainly nothing-you'd-ever-see-on-a-Maine-man yellow. An electric-chair-full-voltage-last-thing-you-see-before-death yellow. A you-asked-for-it yellow. A bold flash. Unwieldy. Unlovable. A you-can't-be-serious yellow. A caution. A high risk. Not to be trusted. What is it? Faster, faster, faster, faster. Over-the-edge yellow. Just-another-day-in-Los-Angeles yellow. Now a kiss.

"Dad," says Eli. "Dad," says Eli. "Dad," says Eli. "Daaaaaaaaaad. Who's that lady?"

The kiss stops. The father, Jeff, sighs, wags his head from side to side. "What? What? What? What? What?"

"Who's the other lady?"

"Which other lady?"

There's a click-click and the restful smoke moves in a silvery whirl from the vicinity of Coti's head.

"The lady that's mad," Eli says.

"They are all mad," says Jeff, plucking the joint from Coti's fingers.

Now there's the deep grateful gulps of Jeff and Coti's smoking and the slamming of car doors and groans of engines over at Moody's Variety & Lunch.

"You think the new baby when he comes is going to want to visit here, too?" Eli asks.

Jeff tsks with irritation. "Jesus, Eli! How am I supposed to know? You think I have ESP?"

Eli says, "I think he won't want to visit here."

Coti giggle-snorts. "Stop doing that, J.J. It wrecks my dress."

Eli says, "Once I heard about a baby who was crying and the people didn't like him so they cut him up and left his arms and stuff in one of those green dumpsters." The marijuana smoke thickens and makes such a fuzzy silvery uncertainty around the two dark heads of the lovers. Coti takes the last small piece of joint into a bobby pin and then it's very quiet until Eli speaks. "Dad, I'm hungry."

"You better look after your wah-wah, Daddy," Coti simpers in a voice that's satisfied and jellylike and sexy.

Jeff sits up board-straight, sweater howlin'-yellow, turns to get a glimpse of Eli between the Camaro's high headrests. "You, Eli, are just trying to irritate the hell out of me. Why don't you curl up back there and take a nap and for *once* stop being a royal pest-pain in the royal ass!"

"How come we don't just go *in?*" Eli wonders. "Why are we out *here* but not making the car *go?*"

There's no answer to this.

"Dad, what if Mom has to have the baby right now? It was *supposed* to be that I was going to watch, remember!!! I bet I'm missing it. I just bet."

Jeff drums his fingers on the doorframe and watches Moody's Variety & Lunch in the Camaro's small sporty-sized sideview mirror.

Coti asks, "I thought your father was going to be around, J.J. Didn't your mother say something about him? Where is he?"

"Out fuckin' with his trucks. I knew it would be like this when we got here. I *knew* it." He watches Moody's getting busier and busier in the Camaro's side mirror, drums his fingers, sighs, adjusts his seat *way* back, now staring up at the Camaro ceiling.

Eli yeowls. "You are mashing me, Dad! What do you think I am back here? A piece of macaroni?"

Coti rolls her eyes, swipes an ash from one of her long, glossy golden legs.

Jeff seems on the verge of a whimper. "I don't know why we came all the hell the way back here to this."

Silence.

"The old man . . . Jesus. You wait. You'll see. He'll have plenty to say. A big fucking sermon. A big dragged-out fucking sermon. I can hear it now. I wish I'd never come back."

The boy Eli knees the back of his father's seat. "You guys just want to talk about them guys. *That*'s why we're sittin' out here. *I* know. *I* know." He chants, "*I* know. *I* know. *I* know. *I* know . . ."

"Shut up, Eli!" Jeff screams.

Coti giggle-snorts.

A light goes on in one of the upstairs rooms of the Johnsons' brick house and Jeff's eyes flash to it, his eyes, which are not the black-brown of his father's . . . but an off-brown, a brown that is like an attempt, an untruth, scant, depleted, a pittance. They are beautiful eyes, eyes that make a lot of women fall in love . . . but they are not the thing that Forest's eyes are . . . the *absolute*. He shuts his eyes. He pretends to sleep.

"Poor baby," Coti coos, patting the vivid yellow, the yellow like a scream, like a fright, the yellow that is a broken law sinking between her fingers as she coos and coos and rubs hard. In his pretend sleep he makes a little whistle through his teeth like how they sleep in cartoons and comedies and funny ads. Coti pretends to believe he is sleeping. "O, my love is having a dream," she whispers breathlessly.

Eli rolls his eyes, raises his knee, and gives his father's seat a great kick.

7 | It's suppertime and still no sign of Jeff Johnson's father.
Nanna Bett totters about, heating up the remains of Sunday's boiled dinner, sets the dining-room table with six brown-and-white patterned china plates and off-white linen napkins. The old candelabra is set low by its dimmer switch so it seems the whole room, like the plates, is

a sepia reminiscence fixed in time, a world very faded but with its integrity intact while Nanna Bett moves in and out with platters of food and fistfuls of silverware, Bett as organized and mathematical as ever, wearing under her print apron the same navy blue cardigan she was wearing six years ago, every button buttoned. The very same sweater! But it shows no wear. New, as if by her deliberateness, her mathematics, her TLC, Bett Johnson could bend the laws of nature.

Peggy had come out from the office to help Bett, Peggy in her big winter boots and the layers of wool socks that she wears over her pants legs. Peggy, like Bett, small-built . . . but those boots really *tromp*. At times she stands with her boots set far apart, hands on hips. She is not as Bett is, a *cute little person*. Peggy: little but big.

She had tried again to start up a bit of conversation with the guests. But the conversation wasn't much. Mostly Jeff and Coti slisking and sucking mouth to mouth.

Now Peggy is out with her horses: Victory, Bleak House, Mars, Monticello. High Priestess and Vassar. Between Peggy's little horse barn and the house, the wind sends leaves and sand flying. And the maples with disgruntled faces drop a couple of dead limbs. THWACK! and THWACK! The remaining limbs rattle and beat at the eaves. The early darkness is complete.

Headlights strike the kitchen walls. An engine's mutter is heard, a vehicle coming up into the yard close to the house. "Is that him, J.J.?" Coti wonders.

"No. It's not him," says Jeff. "It looks like one of his tenants that rents over the old barn."

Eli says, "Dad, where's their VCR?"

Jeff just shakes his head, rolls his eyes at this ultimate stupid question.

They hear the big boots come tromping back through the back way . . . little, big Peggy. Some silence, then the soft flipping of papers and filing folders out there on the porch office which shows through the open kitchen door. Pine paneling. Many panes of glass.

Another set of headlights, this engine geared low, hesitating at the place where a tree limb has dropped.

Coti says, "Maybe that's your dad."

Jeff looks out. Small snort. Shakes his head.

"Dad, if you find their Nintendo, we can do something besides nothing," Eli says deeply.

Nanna Bett hauls out more cookies from the oven. This time blond sugar cookies. Nanna Bett steps away from the stove and says, "Well, there!" then takes the butter that's been going soft since the noon meal from the small enamel table here in the kitchen, switches it for some cold, hard, white butter and totters full speed ahead with it into the dim dining room, then back again into the glare of the kitchen. She unbuttons two of her sweater buttons, gives herself a little pretend fanning and says, "Warm." She heads for the porch office, the kingdom of the many deer heads, the kingdom of Peggy's silence, and Bett is heard to murmur the word, "Supper."

Jeff and Coti get into kissing again. A *deeeeep* kiss with clasped tongues and grunting and rubbing and struggle. Coti's hair crackles with static. The couple has positioned itself in the center of one of the long low windows. What must it look like to people in their cars passing on Rummery Road or stepping with their groceries out of Moody's? Kind of like a movie screen with the snazzy California couple. Coti Pederson in her low-cut red dress that strains as she strains. She tosses her hair. Such hair! Hectic and black and popping with wee noisy stars. And handsome California Jeff, his hair short wet spikes on top, long preened frizzled curls over the nape of his YELLOW sweater.

Eli slouches at the table, his Levi's jacket hanging unbuttoned on either side of his big belly. He refuses to take the jacket off even though the kitchen is a roiling steamy cabbage-and-ham-smelling cookie-smelling eighty degrees. He says, "Dad."

Jeff flattens his hand on the cold window. He watches a car pass through his fingers.

"Dad," Eli persists.

Coti giggle-snorts, tosses her raspy black hair, parts her lips, licks them three times, the close-up-movie-screen-kind-of-glossy-lip-licking and half-closed eyes. "Oh, J.J. . . . pleeeeeeeez," she moans, giving Jeff a hard push backwards.

"*Dad.*"

Nanna Bett says, "Well, Eli . . . we are going to have a nice supply of cookies . . . there's . . ." She does some quickie calculating, staring at the overhead light, wiggling her fingers. "There's at least eight dozen . . . plus the three left from the two dozen we had at dinner." She swerves toward the small kitchen table where Eli presides . . . this beloved great-grandchild . . . born only twenty minutes from here, carried home to this house to so many laps he rarely needed his crib. The plan was Jeff and Amy and the baby would live here till Jeff graduated from college and could get a job . . . newborn Eli going around from lap to lap to lap. "Spoiling him to death!" Bett herself had complained with satisfaction.

Once when the child had gotten a good grip on one of great-grand-father F.D.'s fingers, F.D. had marveled that those were the hands of a future heavy-equipment man. "Can't you see him taking a load of sand across town now?" But Amy had said, "No way! He's got that grip from *my* side of the family. Nobody beats my father arm rassling," she had bragged somberly. "Try him sometime" she challenged, then laughed her husky, doleful Bean laugh.

Next there was damage. On all fours baby Eli had given the dining-room tablecloth a single powerful jerk and plates of food went into a few laps. "That there is the Bean grip!" F.D. had said with a great whoop. "The other grip is the Johnson grip . . . the one he plans to use to wheel them big two-ton babies around . . ."

And here Amy had interrupted to say that in her family the trucks were bigger. Her cousins all drove logs and chips. "Chips weigh TWENTY-SIX TONS." And F.D. gave Amy's right very-solid bicep a squeeze and she called him a "squirt" and everyone knew F.D. had become the happiest man in the world with Amy on hand to argue and tease with him through all the meals, while Forest, Jr., just kept a steady uncompromising narrowed eye on his daughter-in-law and it was plain to see that Amy and her people, the Beans and Spillers, were heavy on Forest's mind.

Then Eli's name for everybody was "Da!" or "Dadadadadada!" and everybody in all the rooms of the great house knew secretly that the beloved child was calling his or her name.

Then Eli mastered stairs, doorknobs, TV knobs, the refrigerator, and stove.

Then Jeff and Amy and the baby disappeared.

Everyone was stunned. F.D. had wept.

The call came two months later from Amy. "Jeff says to tell you we're all right. We're in California . . . Berkeley area . . ." No, Jeff didn't want to talk. "There's a lot of artists in California," Amy had told Peggy who had answered the phone that day. "Jeff wants to be with other artists. To get feedback 'n' stuff. This is what he wants."

Gone for six years.

Six years. Now and then a letter, always addressed to Ms. Elizabeth Johnson . . . RR2 Rummery Road . . . East Egypt, Maine. "Dear Nanna . . ." It would tell about Jeff's struggle in the art world. Two galleries had taken his work. One had a hundred people at the opening. He'd been doing some talks at high schools . . . not for pay . . . just to encourage kids. The only artists who get money are dead . . . ha ha. Jeff would put parentheses around the ha ha's. Or maybe he'd scribble a smiley face. He was wondering if she might give him a little loan. A hundred? Another time it was eight hundred dollars. Another time two thousand dollars. "Please don't tell the rest of them. I'm just so embarrassed. They wouldn't understand like you do." He'd sign it "Love, Jeff" or "Your grateful grandson, Jeff" or "In gratitude, Jeffrey."

She would send the money order and a little note from a common white unlined tablet: "Please send pictures of the baby and tell me how he's doing."

But never. No pictures. And no explanation or apologies for why there weren't.

Bett always sent Eli a birthday card with a five-dollar bill. Most times the cards came back. MOVED. NO FORWARDING stamped on them by various California PO's. Sometimes the cards didn't come back. But there was no word, no reply. It seemed those cards had just disappeared into the monstrous gravityless black universe of California.

Now Bett scrutinizes this new stodgy stranger, Eli . . . unfidgeting . . . unfriendly, actually. In his eyes the look of sovereignty and self-containment. Fat like an undercover television cop who, flanked by two flunkies in uniforms, kicks open a city apartment door to reveal a swarm of organized crime kingpins . . . or a murder in progress. There would be a cigar wiggling in one corner of the fat detective's mouth, in the otherwise stiff, unmovable, emotionless face. The other corner of the mouth would speak its merciless baritone: "A warrant for your arrest, pal . . ."

Out on the back-porch office there's the creak and rumble of the wheeled office chair. And now Peggy coming to supper. Tromp. Tromp. Tromp . . .

Jeff Johnson is now licking Coti Pederson's left ear. Then he licks the other ear. The earrings, each with four black plastic balls wag and clatter together. Jeff says, "Oh, God. This is embarrassing to Nanna . . . this that we're doing in front of her. Is this embarrassing to you, Nanna? If it is, we'll lay off."

Coti giggle-snorts and tries to pull away, but she's forced against Jeff's YELLOW sweater again, not by his hands, but by some invisible power within herself.

Jeff says, "This *is* embarrassing to Nanna. I know it is." He drops his head, laps Coti's bare throat and shoulders and the tops of her breasts that seem always to be striving to get free of the red vestlike dress. Coti's eyes jellyized in their passion. Her wild hair tossing. She licks her lips.

"We'll have to stop!" Jeff gasps. But he can't seem to stop. He tries to pull Coti up over his back now like a piggyback ride, but the long dark gold bare legs flailing and the flash of white panties makes it something else. Not a piggyback ride.

"Ooooooooooooooo . . . J.J. . . . pleeeeeeeeeeeeeeze! Why don't you get your mind on something else, J.J. Let's help your grandmother with the table, okay?"

But when she's back on her feet, she loses her senses again and starts up another kiss with Jeff, her inner-mouth having such pull that it seems like not only Jeff's lips but part of both sides of his face have disappeared into hers.

Expressionlessly, the boy watches these mouths.

Bett has come over to stand by him, looking down at his hands that are large for a seven year old but still heartbreakingly dimpled and babyish. Behind her glasses, her eyes are screwing up smaller and smaller, beckoning, fierce . . . seeing these dimples of Eli's hands . . . her wish to claim territory there. Eli Johnson home at last.

She reaches into her apron pocket for the tin tube of lip care, gives her chafed mouth a dab, smooths some into her loose cheeks, some into the cracked sores by her nails. The boy watches her do this . . . not outright . . . just some glances that seem dismissive and magisterial. He has a funny McDonald's fry smell and that pewy exhaust smell you would get from spending four or five days in a car that has holes in the floorboards and holes in the header pipe. And another pewy funny smell which Bett could not recognize in a million years . . . otherworldy, ashy, dark, and velvet. She snaps the cap back on the tube and says, "Eli, dear. I have clothes upstairs in my trunks that should fit you . . . mittens, caps, long underwear. A wool jacket. Wool socks. I'm just not sure we have any boots your size. But we could shop for those. This is for when you decide to go outdoors to play or to go see about Nanna Peg's horses or the trucks out at the shop . . . or anything you want to do outdoors. Cold weather's on the way."

His eyes move over her quickly, then he's back to watching one of his father's fingers tracing Coti's neckline.

And Bett says, "I have a cap that's especially nice. My sister's girl Donna knitted it. It's up on my bureau. I'll go up and get it for you after supper if you think you'd like it. You think you'd like a nice cap?"

Eli says, "Sure" with a cylindrical erect round *R* which is the California way of talking. But as if this were some disorder or dyslexia or sign of damage, Bett's small hand closes over one of his, her expression one of sadness and pity.

8 | When the back door jerks shut, all the little glass panes of the office windows rattle and strain and bulge outward like there's a pressure inside the house that might pop them. It is nine-forty P.M.

Coti whispers, "Is that him, J.J.? Is that your Dad?"

Jeff says, "Ayuh" in the way he likes to imitate Forest.

Coti giggles, tosses her hair, licks her lips, looks down across the front of herself, checking the many little black buttons of her short bright dress. "Why didn't we hear him drive in?" she wonders, still whispering.

"He came in the back way, across the lot. The shop's out there. There's two ways, three ways, actually. I'll show you tomorrow. We can walk out there. You want to sit up in the backhoe?" He is snorting with laughter at this even before she answers with just a squinching of her face. "This place is a regular amusement park," he tells her, rolling his eyes.

Out on the porch office Forest's voice is low and a little nasty. "What's the matter?"

Peggy replies with a single word, too soft a word for anyone in the kitchen to make heads or tails of.

In the glaring kitchen, cookies are in jars, and in waxed paper bundles and plastic freezer bags . . . in order. There's a sense they might even be numbered. There's a cookie getting gnashed up in the boy Eli's mouth. He seems so distant with the nannas, but has begun a real relationship with the cookies.

Nanna Bett is resting at last by one of the front kitchen windows now, tipped back in her thronelike stenciled black rocker. She has just returned from a visit upstairs with F.D. and the night nurse, the night nurse whom Bett dislikes. Before that, it was a small load of personal laundry on the short cycle . . . the washer thrumming out in the back pantry . . . and the whole house creaking and squeaking with her tiny hurried steps. Seems she had covered every square yard of every room. Over and over. Checking, watching, keeping order, retracing steps, feely, feely . . . like an ant.

Forest can be heard getting closer to the kitchen door, his walk easily distinguishable from the walk of others . . . a chuff-clump, chuff-clump, chuff-clump . . . and that chunk of keys he always wears from a belt loop jangling with each chuff-clump of his step. He pauses at the doorsill, one of his hands appearing first, seizing the doorjamb to hoist himself up.

Dark golden Coti Pederson in her high-heeled sandals is taller than Jeff. She is a towering, sleek broad-shouldered beauty, somehow both flat and full, her black hair in appealing disruption, her bare arms akimbo . . . Coti . . . a Los Angeles beautiful, too beautiful, great smoldery white smile, little doctored nose . . . Coti, whose looks would be okay on TV. But in this kitchen, her looks are an overdose. She pulls away from Jeff and flies at Forest, gets ahold of one of his hands, shaking, shaking, shaking that hand. "Well! Finally! So good to meet you! Yes! Yes! There you are, Mr. Johnson. My gosh, what a hand!"

Forest's hand has closed on her hand, but his eyes are on his son's face, the roundish lenses of his glasses steaming over from his entry into heat from windy cold, so that the dark eyes, one tightening in on itself with its astigmatism, are lost in their small matching fogs. "So what's up, Jeffrey?" he asks.

Coti is laughing breezy and beautiful, tossing her exotic hair, licking her lips. "What a *grip* your dad has, J.J.! A hand like a regular fossil or something. A real working man's hand . . . Jiminy Cricket . . . yes!" Her thumb is locked around Forest's thumb, though it's hard to tell which hand has mastery over the other, which one won't let go.

When it is finally finished, Forest jerks his glasses off, digs for a blue bandanna in a pocket of his wool pants, wipes and wipes the glasses lenses slowly.

"Dad," says Jeff. "I want you to meet Coti . . . Coti Pederson from Los Angeles."

Forest looks at Coti. "Yes," says he, his eyes lowering now to the job of wiping his glasses.

Jeff simply stands there, his yellow sweater thudding, drumming, exploding, going strong, his arms hanging at his sides over the black bushy-waisted California-style pants. The overhead kitchen light is unkindly and unbecoming to his wet glistening spiky hair . . . light not meant to co-operate with glamour but to fix and eat supper by. "I . . ." Jeff stammers, but he can't finish. So he laughs at himself, then clears his throat, starts again. "So how have things been here in the old Pine Tree State, Dad?"

Forest, now with his glasses back in place, goes to the table, pulls out a white painted chair, sits heavily, folds his arms over his chest. There is something more off-kilter about Forest's eyes than usual, maybe just a too well focused concentration, his mind having worked against some point of friction, past endurance. This is what you see. You seldom actually see him wince. His boots shifting will be the thing to catch your eye. Yes, pain. Whenever Jeff tries to picture his father's private thoughts on any subject, he sees only the agony of the crushed feet.

There is a painting Jeff finished two years ago. Oil on canvas. It is called *The Feet*. The painting is of one black-purple blossom with wide-open numerous folds, guarded and erect. And down between the folds into the more blank and inhospitable blackness you see what suggests a lure, a place you might travel to if you were small enough. Insect-sized. Jeff sold the painting for a couple of thousand dollars. But did anyone understand?

Juarez at the gallery had called him with, "These people want something purple . . ."

Jeff had gone nuts.

It had been one of a series, a dozen variations on this image. One was ten by twelve feet . . . the great shuddering purple-black bloom. He had told Amy and his circle of artist friends, "This is my father's mind."

Another one was "My father's left eye." He explained that his father's left eye was one thing, the right eye another.

His friends knew when to stay away from Jeff. Sometimes for weeks. For while he worked on that series, he was short with them and the Purple Madder, Mars Violet, Alizarin, blacks, Phthalo and Toluidine on his open palms was gore.

Forest shifts in his chair. This puts him with his back to the room, puts his back solidly toward Jeff. He leans forward, heaps his hands on the table, hands large for a medium-sized man. The child Eli stares openly at the hands there at rest, the raised-up jumble of veins . . . perhaps trying to see what Coti was talking about, what all the fuss was about, the idea of fossils for hands. Forest wears no jewelry but a watch. Unlike Jeff's hands which sport three rings including a pinkie ring. "All is usual in the Pine Tree State," Forest sighs. "It's what's been going on out on the highways and byways and freeways that concerns . . . uh . . . that bothers hell out of me. Like . . ." He cuts his own speech off with sudden silence.

Jeff stares at the red X of his father's suspenders, the hunched un-breakable barrier of Forest's back and waist, the waist thickened since Jeff last saw him . . . six years of big breakfasts, big suppers, creamy coffee . . . and in most ways, a nice life.

Coti looks down over herself again to check the look of her partially buttoned dress and the glossy golden bare sexiness of her long, long legs . . . toenails polished a coral tint.

Forest turns in his seat in time to catch the quick hand of his son reaching to tweak Coti's left breast, a small tense cone shape, which is the desirable mode of breasts these days. Fun breasts. Picture-perfect breasts. Big breasts might look too work-related. Too utility. Too moth-erish. In these times, breasts must be preserved forever in daughterishness. This is the last word in femininity. The new law of the land.

Jeff sees his father seeing his hand tweaking the last-word breast. Jeff, suddenly cocky, says, "Now look, Dad. This isn't going to be some sort of tribunal, is it?"

Forest chuckles.

Nanna Bett's big rocker faces the window. There are cars still pulling in and out of Moody's lot, even with Moody's closed early, the after-hours crowd still lingers on and on . . . wisdoms unstoppable. But Bett only looks at the short distance of her reflection on the wavery antique glass.

Little funny-faced Peggy appears in the doorway between porch office and kitchen, arms crossed over her chest, big boots set apart. Over the years she and Forest have grown to look alike in the dark exacting eyes and hardness around the mouth . . . though with Forest you rarely see his teeth, while with Peggy, smiles are always quick and frantic. But no smile now. Peggy looks on the verge of a wail of grief. She says, "Forest, ask Jeff where Amy is, would you? Just ask him where she is?"

"I didn't come all the way back here to fight," Jeff says.

Forest takes a blond cookie, lays it flat on the table with circumspection like a royal flush.

Coti crosses her arms across her red dress, shrinks back toward the wainscotted wall.

Forest turns in his seat to face Peggy and says, "*Is* there a real answer to that question . . . like a riddle? Or is it rhetorical?"

Jeff gives Coti a hard push toward the doorway to the front hall.

"Don't shove me, J.J.!" she hisses and jerks her bare golden shoulder away.

Jeff hurries past her. She follows. Eli is out of his seat, hurtling after them, all three headed upstairs, a lot of clumping and clunking of various-styled shoes. Now a little shouting overhead. And the slam of a door.

"Bett, did they tell *you* anything about Amy?" Peggy asks the back of the old woman's head.

The white head shakes no.

Peggy says, "I would love to get Eli off to one side. But to pump him for information would be putting him in the middle. Jeff and the girl whisper a lot. If we keep our ears sharp we might . . ." She closes her eyes and says wearily, "Why did he come back here if he doesn't want to *be* with us . . . you know . . . like . . . visit with us . . . talk and share . . . dear God. You know?"

Forest stands suddenly.

A car pulls out from Moody's and heads down Rummery Road toward town and, through the old glass, the car playfully wobbles.

Peggy sighs. "We already had our supper, Forest. We waited for you but it got late. Why don't you run over to the store and see if one of them would still fix you up a pizza. And we're out of Tylenols. I need Tylenols."

Bett turns in her rocker, enough so Forest can see her profile and small smile. "You'd be proud of Eli, dear. He's turned out to be such a little gentleman."

Peggy snorts. "Unresponsive is more like it."

"Shy," says Bett.

Forest shakes his head, looking amused, feels in a pocket for change, steadying himself with the other hand on the back of the chair, never able to put all his weight evenly on both feet.

Peggy says, "Bett, did you *overhear* them discussing any plans . . . you know . . . like they've come to Maine to *live?* Or is this an overnight?

I just can't get a picture of this. I mean . . . Jeff left . . . I mean, he *disappeared* six years ago as an artist . . . now he's *this*. When he's not stoned, when he's *between* smokes, he's Mr. Hollywood. I ask him what he's doing . . . you know . . . like you ask a person a normal question . . . 'What are you doing these days?' . . . you know . . . for work . . . and he acts like I just asked him when's the last time he did a bowel movement."

Bett, facing the dark window again, says to her reflection, "I thought they seemed full of plans. I think they have plans, Peggy."

"I'll bet," Peggy sneers. "And what plans might those be? . . . like between tongue-kisses, titty-feels, crotch-rubbing, and toke-ups out in the car. When did they show signs of these extensive plans?"

Forest grins, revealing the front tooth that is blue-gray with filling, not exactly the smile of a man of his "prosperity." "I hope you ladies can get this all solved by the time I get back." As he swings past his wife, he grips the doorframe with one hand and leans toward her, rolling his eyes toward the upstairs rooms where the guests reside. He whispers close to Peggy's hair. "You know what they used in the old days when vampires came around?" He pats the chest pocket of his dark work shirt. "Silver bullet."

It's just his little joke, Peggy knows. It's not a real threat. Even the threats Forest sometimes makes, the ones that aren't jokes . . . they come to nothing. He is, above all, a man of reason.

9 | Forest mashes the trigger. Without the usual thump-pump-pump of hooves and the splattering of leaves, this deer rises off the ground straight up and weightless like a deer out of a fairy tale, twisting into its gray and awful vanishing point. Everything gray. A trick of the eye? Everything moving, tree limbs knocking, mixed, brown against bright. Gone.

The bang of gunpowder has almost deafened his right ear.

A simultaneous shriek. "I'm hit!! God help mee!! PLEEEEEEZ!" Now a fading whine.

All this comes from several degrees left of where he fired. Yet the woods do often lie. As the seconds tick away in silence and his frozen breath stretches up, the possibility becomes plainer that his shot has found a human head. Human lung. Human spinal cord. Why now? Why when nearly every year of his life, even back in the times as a boy tromping these woods with F.D., he and F.D., matched stride for stride in a most earnest way, it was most always *one shot*, one deer, one simple complete action and it was done.

But now off to his left, downed leaves are slashing . . . another fading whine . . . stomp . . . stumble . . . stomp.

Forest calls, "Hey! Where are you? Listen! Tell me where you are! Keep talking to me, would ya? I'm coming!!"

Now nothing. Just the steely fullness of a cold white overcast day between bursts of Forest's breath, which yearn up, up, up into a tattered and thinning whiter white.

"For godsakes where *are* you?!!" he calls. He shambles toward hemlocks, nerve-rackingly black and reclusive low-limbed big girthed sons-a-bitches crowded along both sides of the stone wall. He recalls F.D. telling him all these stone walls in Egypt once divided cleared fields. All this was bright openness. You could see for miles. Mostly farms . . . farmers F.D. was related to or Bett was related to or practically related to. F.D. knew all. In F.D.'s head the map work of Egypt ancestry was feverish . . . cell upon cell, crosshatched and mazed, the families making up a thickened sustaining solid . . . a power. Unconquerable. And out from this came the stories and gossips, gossips which F.D. said "aren't gossip when people are dead." He then would giggle his high, shameless giggle because F.D. *loved* gossip of the dead *or* alive. Forest tolerated F.D.'s talk talk talk talk. It was the woods and the hunt that mattered. The inevitable kill, and F.D.'s whoop and little dance of victory. And F.D.'s merry eyes on Forest's face . . . Forest in F.D.'s regard.

Forest calls out again. "Are you all right? Please answer me!!" His voice is no voice on the word *right*, just a tremulous soft spot there, something his voice is known to do even in normal conversation. But now as he goes to call out again, the whole sentence is nearly lost.

There's a dry streambed between him and the high bank and stone wall, a lot of good flat, bare rocks like a little trafficless cobblestone lane. This stream is gorged and noisy only in spring when the snows of these mountains become run-off, mean and mindless, all headed downhill to East Egypt, to Promise Lake. He knows these things. This is his land. There can be no mysteries here. He listens. The silence is like thumbs in his ears. He looks for the easiest way over the stone wall, necessary for a man whose feet are not the way you'd picture feet to be.

Now just beyond the hemlocks, there's the slash-slash-crackle of leaves and brush and the thump of a stone rolling, like someone or some-thing digging itself down. He run-hops toward this, stumbling over an erupted beech root, almost falls on his face. The barrel of his rifle smacks against bark.

He sees her. A teenager he vaguely recognizes. Low income for sure. Miracle City, no doubt. He nearly sneers. Busty. Big-hipped. Big lips. Mouth purplish like a sore. Smacked by a hand? Or chapped by too much free run? Or chapped by indoors that feels like outdoors? Or from bad nutrition, eating shit food? So many poor these days. All of them look-ing familiar. He has probably held the door open for her at the PO or Laverdiere's, tipped his cap, said: "Gorgeous day" or "Cold enough for ya?" always the gentleman . . . Forest Johnson, Jr., . . . road commis-sioner, elected official; Kiwanis, Rod & Gun . . . everywhere he goes, people speak his name with neighborliness and respect.

Yes, this girl is familiar. A queer unsettling familiarity. It sits down all around him like a sudden, unpredicted, surprise first snow. She wears a puffed blue jacket, dark with use around the wrists and zipper. *Where* has he seen her before?????

The two thick pieces of her bright mouth move and at first he can't be sure in the shadow of the low-hanging hemlock limbs . . . but now it's plain. She's grinning at him.

The corner of Forest's mouth flickers and the hair on the back of his neck . . . it flickers. "You bitch," he says low.

She keeps grinning. Some of her white-blond hair is caught in a corner of her mouth and there's a half a leaf stuck to her cheek from her "fall." Her white-lashed eyes jerk to the left. He feels it then. The eyes of another person on him. He pivots. Surely. There's the shoulder and partly hidden face of another teenager who is skulking behind a triple-trunked hemlock. This girl wears a purple jacket. She has a long bony fierce expression, brown hair in cheap curly ripples to imitate fashion, like so many girls around town, distorted echoes of the glamoury heroines of their tele-visions. He almost laughs. Could there be more of these silly little gals clinging to trees, squatted behind rocks? He turns back to the first girl. His dark eyes move into their frantic astigmatized consideration of her. He gives the nosepiece of his metal-frame glasses a push. Now there's the rocking of the Weatherbee beneath its sling as he feels for it, keeping his eyes on her face. Her pale eyes widen as the sling slides down off his shoulder. He sort of, but not quite, is now pointing the muzzle at her smile. She knows who he is, who he is in this town, among those that are esteemed. He can tell by the way her vivid mouth seems on the verge of speaking his name.

"You want to die, Miss Smart-Ass," he snarls. "You girls play your games . . . they are suicide games. Stay the hell out of the woods!"

She has stopped smiling now, but in her gray eyes there's twinkles. Her eyes. Her only lovely particular other than that given loveliness of lovely humming youth.

Behind Forest the other girl squeals, "Get up, Anneka!"

Forest speaks to the girl on the ground, pale purply-mouthed Anneka.

"Some would say 'twould be your own fault if something of this firearm had wound up eating out a mess between your shoulder blades." True. True. Sportsmen's lobbyists and politicians and jurors rally around the guy who these days shoots people *in their own yards*. Mistaken identity, it is graciously called. And soon forgotten. Would they not have even quicker forgiveness for the hunter who shoots brats who play tricks, crossing the gray wooded line of November in their grimy blue and jam purple? . . . While he himself, in Day-Glo blaze orange from head to foot, is reflected in this girl's eyes as a kind of stunning power, a deserved bludgeoning. She raises her hand now to visor her lovely eyes from it.

"Big man out hunting," she says mockingly, her eyes fluttering up and down his height, now returning squarely upon the circles of his glasses, and it seems in a sickening flash that the kid is reading his mind. "Big man out being big man," she sniggers.

How much does she know? Does she know he's missed lunch, that his mouth is stinking from the gasses of an empty stomach? He flushes. He drops his gaze away. Why is she familiar?

Somewhere on another mountain a shot.

The voice of the girl behind him shrills, "Get up, Anneka! Let's go!"

In one hop, Forest pegs down one of the blond girl's ankles with his right boot, his right foot, which isn't a foot, and yet is more serviceable as a foot than the other one which is clownishly floppy. He grips a sapling, bears his whole weight hard on the girl. The other girl is running. Away or toward him. No telling which way. The tromping scuffle of her feet seems both closer and farther off.

There's a shot now on the hill across the old town road. A single reverberating handsome BOOM. He can picture the torn animal tumbling head over heels, kicking, perhaps bleating, perhaps only a paralyzed silence. Perhaps the black blood rag of its blown-apart jaw. Perhaps one of its knees explodes . . . which leaves the ripe bloom of its track for you to follow . . . panting . . . panting . . . the three-legged light step. Deer always quick to move, sometimes slow to die. When you catch up with your deer, he could be down, on his side, waiting for you. He will turn his eye on you. His eye calls you a name, a name you like. *You* call *him* a dumb bastard. Even when all other parts of him are dead, his eye still lives to watch you aim your rifle. You are twenty feet tall. You *win*.

Forest hears another shot. That finishing shot perhaps. His own trigger finger twitches with sympathy.

Something punches his back. A rock or a fist. Knocks the wind out of him, almost. He keeps his eyes on the girl under his foot. "Okay," he says softly. "Big man in the woods. You got it."

Another blow to his back, then the blomp-bm-bm-bm-bm of a rock rolling along toward him. Then another. And another. "Get up!" The rock-throwing girl howls. "Anneka! He's crazy!"

Now a punky stick.

Now a pummeling of acorns.

He bears harder with his weight onto the girl's gray sneaker and saggy sock. All this time she's kept her stare on his face. Her moving suddenly, knocking him back on his ass, is possible. An easy feat for a strapping young girl with a man who is crippled. But she just finally breaks her stare, bends onto her side, her back to him, even while her foot and ankle are twisted toward and under his boot.

An acorn pelts the back of his neck. Handfuls of leaves gobbed with ice splat the side of his face. Now some sailing sticks. His land. HIS land. This is happening on his own land! The girl behind him is shrieking, hunting up bigger rocks, longer sticks. And yet it's the girl under his foot, her back turned to him, that *bothers* him. His head rings with alarm.

He steps back, tipping his blaze orange plastic cap at the long-faced girl who is pitching a chunk of frozen moss at him. Piece of icy moss clanks against one lens of his glasses, burns his cheek.

"Settle down," he says in a fatherly tone. And now he smiles a fatherly smile, not showing his teeth.

It all ends fairly peacefully, his shambling in one direction, the two girls heading out toward the road, whispering and giggling. No harm done.

10 | Again Forest comes into the house late. He messes around out on the porch awhile, pulling off layers of clothes, tending his rifle. Then he shambles into the bright kitchen to find room in the refrigerator for a six-pack of Orange Crushes. With his back to the eyes that watch him, the **X** of his suspenders is the red and demanding focal point.

Jeff is buzzing. He stands with his foot on a chair, smiling around the room. When his father turns and faces him, Jeff avoids his eyes, saying "So . . ." He says "So . . ." a few times.

There seems to be more to what he's about to say, but he never finishes it. He just keeps looking around the kitchen, around and around and around, smiling, looking vaguely pleased.

Forest checks his watch with the clock over the gas stove. 10:51. He studies the boy, Eli, who is at the table. The boy has finally got his jacket off. The T-shirt is loose, floppy, long . . . probably Jeff's. It shows what looks like pre-Christianity horned beasts with electric guitars engulfed in flames. The beast faces have something quite like Jeff's expression. Rapture? There are words on the T-shirt. But they are lost in the folds. The boy's expression is nothing like rapture. His is the face of duty. Of unrest. A shepherd. His beautiful dark-lashed blue-green eyes are fixed on Jeff, always on Jeff.

Forest limps from the refrigerator to position himself by the sink, arms folded over his chest as if he were the guard of the sink.

Jeff's short-on-top spiky hairdo looks especially wet. And from his most recent toke-up with Coti in the Camaro in the dooryard, his eyelashes look wet and spiky, too. Before this visit, Forest has never seen Jeff so gaunt in the face before. Too gaunt in the face for the build of his face. Among them in Jeff's new life, the Los Angeles life, gauntness must be beautiful. And his smile presents more of his teeth than what looks comfortable. In the new life, the old Jeff Johnson smile must have been inadequate. Forest notices that Jeff isn't drinking from the brimming tumbler of water in his hand. Just has a big grip on it.

Coti is circulating the kitchen, same clonking high-heeled sandals as yesterday. But now instead of the red dress, it's some sort of calf-length pants of silver foillike material and a black loose sweater that hangs off one shoulder. Necklace and earrings of even larger bobbly objects than yesterday's. Dozens of silver bracelets. Her eyes are swollen, makeup smudged. It seems Forest has just walked into the middle of something other than a *kiss*.

"Mum's in bed," says Jeff. "She said to tell you."

"She shoulda made me guess." Forest chuckles, but his arms across the chest of his work shirt don't relax.

Coti's high heels wobble once as she passes Forest, but otherwise she's pretty expert at it, graceful and at home in such shoes. She speaks in a stuffy-nosed voice. "This patriotic wallpaper is really something!" She points out the little eagles, minutemen, and crossed muskets. Her hair tonight seems like more hair than last night, like some part of it might be a "piece" . . . the great flouncing black mass of scribbles and ringlets drawn up off her lovely long neck with a silver comb-clamp. Such hair seems to have been readied for a night out. To *where?*

Jeff says "Ayup," eyes gliding over to his father, then away. "Dad, you probably picked that wallpaper out. Right?"

Forest's lips go hard against his teeth. Then he says deeply, softly, fatherly, "You know I didn't."

Jeff giggles. "Just joshin'." He looks over at Coti's swollen face. "You see, Coti . . . Dad is . . . well . . . a kind of Captain America . . . you know . . . like Mr. Right . . . not as in correct . . . but as in *the* Right . . . like *way far* right . . . rightie right. But then again, he's right as in correct . . . absolutely correct. I mean it sincerely. He's a law-and-order man. Ask him about the electric chair. *Ask* him."

Coti shrugs, keeps admiring the kitchen, patting this and that . . . like she hasn't spent practically the entire last thirty-nine hours in this room. She admires a blue glass turtle from one window, then sets it back easy-careful.

Forest's eyes have come to rest on the table. A can of crayons. Something Nanna Bett keeps on hand for visits from kids. She keeps an orderly "special visits supply" in one of the highboy drawers in the front entry hall. Eli's fat dimply hands fiddle with the edge of the drawing he has finished. So he must have had his eyes off Jeff long enough to work those crayons awhile. Forest angles his head to see what the picture is of. Looks like a stick-cat on green grass and along the top is a narrow band of blue sky. The usual picture for a kid to draw. Nothing like the things Jeff used to draw as a kid . . . great swollen faces and shapes filling the page, spilling over, looking like something that might eventually grow to fill the room.

Coti picks up another turtle. This one looks like it's carved in soap. Made by a child. It is dried, cracked, soiled in its creases. In each of the four windows a parade of turtles. Some pottery, some glass, some metalwork. Lots of ceramics. Some that look like pottery are really plastic. Bett's collection is always a big hit with guests. Coti giggle-snorts, tosses her beautiful hair, comes circling back to Jeff, staring into his eyes, wriggling her hips just a bit . . . the silver-foil buttocks catching Forest's eye . . . something Forest has never before imagined possible in this house . . . pants of a cloth and fit that look like no pants at all . . . a kind of silver sculpture of a woman's hindquarters and thighs and so forth . . . a silver trophy . . . first prize. "Oooooooooooo," she sighs and slings her hip into Jeff's crotch. "I like to imagine you here in this house being a little boy . . . all those years you were a little boy."

Jeff is wincing from the punch of her hip.

She sings out, "Not much work to picture you a little boy!" She offers a little sideways in-collusion smile to Forest.

"Bitch!" Jeff says, grabs Coti by the hair, spills water on her.

She squeals. "Watch out, J.J.! Jesus Christ. Jesus. Jesus. *Jesus!* Get me a towel!"

Eli kicks a chair leg. A soft kick. Another soft kick . . . another . . . another.

Jeff says to Eli, "Act right." Then to Coti in more of a whimper, "Be nice, baby." He kisses Coti. He rocks her. Bends her. He uses the cuff of his jersey to wipe her bare shoulder dry. "You are all nice and dry now." He trails kisses down into the neckline of her black sweater.

"A towel, J.J.," she says, backing away. "Be serious, J.J.! I'm very wet. I need a towel. Get a towel and do it right."

Jeff reddens, passes the top of his right hand across his mouth. Everyone knows where the nearest towel is . . . little striped dish towels stacked behind the doors under the sink. Behind Forest. Forest who is staring deeply into Jeff's eyes, looking amused, creepily silent.

Jeff says, "You don't need a towel, Coti. It's not that bad. Don't act like a baby. I've had it. You've been like this all day."

"You didn't say that when you had your nice fuck," she says, eyes flashing to Forest, whose gleaming eyes move from Jeff's face to hers, his boots shifting slightly. Then he studies the boy Eli's dimpled hands. The boy looks so calm. Calmness or what? He has stopped kicking the chair leg now. He just seems mesmerized by the show.

Coti gathers the front of her sweater and squeezes some water from it. "Look at that!" she wails. "I'm telling you, J.J. You spilled half the glass on me!"

The tumbler, surely enough, stands half empty on the counter.

"You'll make it," says Jeff.

"Get me a towel," she says evenly.

Jeff shrugs.

"Get me a towel, NOW . . . or I've had it . . . I mean . . ." Her voice gets low. "I need the towel *now*."

Forest's eyes are steady on Jeff, keen on each of Jeff's limbs for signs of motion. Maybe Coti visualizes Forest making a quick move to the left, stooping for the towel, reaching to get the towel to Jeff, the kitchen bustling and scurrying with men fetching towels . . . but Forest does not move. There's just his eyes behind his metal-frame glasses watching with fascination and sad marvel this castration of his son.

There is a stack of bath towels and hand towels in the bathroom down the hall of course . . . the longer route. Jeff goes to get one there. Eli scrambles from his chair, crayons rolling over the tabletop, Eli hurrying after Jeff.

Coti sighs, sits down on one of the kitchen chairs directly under the light, her chin in one hand, face turned away from Forest. She watches through the old wobbly glass panes the lights going off over at Moody's. She knows Forest's eyes are steady upon her. There is something about this that is both terrible and fine.

11 | In the morning the trucks warming up in the lot beyond the house wrench Jeff Johnson awake.

His lover opens one dark glaring eye.

There's the clangs, bawls, and slamming truck doors, the mad rush before snow. The last leach bed. The last few culverts. Maybe a small house foundation. Most everything that you dig down for will play second fiddle soon to the vast indefatigable snows.

Among the paintings Jeff has stored with friends in California, there's one eleven-by-eleven-foot canvas titled *Wing Plow*. The painting appears to be of a dazzling warm white rose opened wide. The depths around the stamen are blue and melodious. Alluring. Come! Come inside.

Jeff sees Coti's face, her expression, which is no expression. So close to Jeff's face. Within inches. Her disappointment. Her boredom. Boredom not a thing so strong as revulsion. Boredom meaning empty.

A truck very near the house starts up with a beastly grunt-grunt.

Jeff says, "That's them . . . Dad's crew . . . everything's running today. Hear? That was seven and there's eight." He realizes how terribly prayerfully he says this.

"You're funny," Coti says wearily. "You are a funny person."

12 | Sharp and gleamy as a blade over the mountain behind the Johnsons' place. Sunrise. Now the first gunshots of the day. The season of the hunt.

Most of the trucks start with crampy lazy grunts. "Cold-blooded," F.D. had called it. But Forest, Jr., has no word for it. He seldom has the need to "discuss."

Forest comes limping from one lighted bay of the shop, his chunk of keys keeping the rhythm of his gait.

"Forest!" a lanky youth calls, while tugging on a pair of work gloves that don't quite conceal his long, long wrists. The door of his old Plymouth hangs open. Brian from Miracle City. Fired last Friday for taking too many days off. The frost is already sealing over the spot on his windshield, which is all he's had to see out through while driving here.

Forest pivots. "Yeah . . . what?" On each lens of Forest's glasses is the gray shuddering daub of the Plymouth's dome light.

The young man is scared shitless, as the expression goes. Gone into a rigor. He seems to be only a pair of hands in this fight to get his gloves on. He can't meet his boss's terrible gaze.

Forest doesn't step any closer to him, just stands in the center of the gray dark lot, wavering slightly in that way he always manages his balance. And drifting across his face and chest is the eerie stinking blue-white veil of exhaust of the dump trucks grunting and chuffing to life along the line.

Two drivers come trotting between Forest and the young Brian. Older men hired by F.D. years ago. Twin brothers with identical smiles but different jackets and caps. "Good great friggin' three degrees to you!" one calls out cheerily over the trembling uproar of the trucks.

Forest nods, pulls his black watch cap lower, then focuses on Brian again. Brian is about to ask for his job back. Forest knows. Just like Forest knows Brian once got his kids lobster claw cooking mitts from one of the ladies' craft shows. Two for each kid. Totalling six lobster claw cooking mitts at five dollars each. Because the kids had begged him. Had tantrums or whatever. This is so they could pretend they were lobsters. Monsters. Or something.

Brian spends his money in funny ways.

Forest also knows Brian has only one pair of work pants. Forest has always wondered how that works. What does Brian do while Brian's wife is washing *the* pants?

Also Forest knows Brian can't read or write. Brian just writes his name with a slow fretful hand, bearing hard. You see the blood disappear from his knuckles. Illiterate. So many guys are illiterate. Sooner or later it becomes apparent to one who is always on guard for it.

Forest moves his dark gaze over Brian's pants . . . *the* pair of pants . . . then to Brian's face. *One pair* of pants in a household of six five-dollar lobster claw cooking mitts! Surely Forest's hard black stare betrays some amusement over this trashy, sour-note, irresponsible family.

The young man, instead of getting the second work glove on, has pulled the first one off. Then loses it. It has flopped into the darkness where his feet are.

Another truck comes to life in a thunder.

Forest's eyes squint slightly.

The young Brian bends down for his glove and his voice from that dark region near his Plymouth's front left tire says, "I was thinking maybe you . . ."

Forest doesn't wait to hear this. He is already moving away toward the beep-beep-beep of a sanding rig that's backing into the empty shop bay. Waves his arms at another truck's side mirrors, one that's not starting. Swishes his gloved hands crisscross like a director stopping a running film.

13 | In the red gazing globe Coti and Jeff seem to be washing a blood-red Camaro that is bent like a boomerang. Makes Eli fall away with a big hog-snort of laughter. It is not as freezing a day as the other days, but not warm either. Yet Coti gallops around with bare legs and short, short striped dress and Jeff teases her with the hose, says he's going to spray her. She calls him an "asshole."

In the gazing globe Eli's teeth are little and vivacious and pink. A snazzy candy-colored tongue. Now a pinky beige school bus strains past, tailgated by a ruby-colored flatbed truck with four pinkly chromed snow-mobiles strapped on. Now more cars. All of them whipping around the beefsteak color road curve . . . everything gushing, flushed, and wonderfully indecent.

Eli mashes his lips to the ruby glass. The invincible log-sized candy-red lips kiss back.

14 So she phones Peggy. It often happens this way. The wife tells how her husband, Brian, had never missed a day of work since he started driving for Forest . . . nearly a year ago. It was only those four days last week.

Peggy says "I know it." Peggy is straining the phone cord as far as it'll go, her back arched, trying to reach the door, which hadn't quite shut when she hurried in. The slim knee-high riding boots and short jacket mean she has just finished two rigorous hours of lessons with her Saturday morning group of advanced riders. The high flush means she's enjoyed it.

"And he's a good driver. He's never had an accident. Even when we were in school and all the other guys drove like idiots, Brian never did that stuff . . ." The wife's voice rides along over this explanation like a hefty vessel on smooth seas. Usually the callers are breathless. Sometimes they almost yell. Usually it's the drivers themselves who call Peggy. But sometimes their wives. Every family has its spokesperson, Peggy has come to understand. When it's the driver himself, he'll start off low with great dignity. But Peggy must always say the same thing. "It's Forest you should be talking to. I really can't help. You have to talk to him yourself." But they all tell her the story anyway. Every detail. Trying to keep the tremble from the voice, just short of breaking down. And some do break down. Young men. Older men. When they ask for their job back, desperation is the common denominator. With the older men the story is longer with flashbacks to the times with F.D., how they had been right pals with F.D.

Most likely Forest will take Brian back. He usually takes them back. For all the firing and rehiring he does, you'd think maybe Forest fires these guys in a rage, then cools off. But it's nothing like rage. It is sometimes to get them to agree to lesser pay. Often less than minimum wage. No benefits. Under the table. And it is something in the cold black look of his defective eyes that toys with these people's lives. Like teasing. Like fun. She is perplexed. How villainous he's become. The Forest she married was not villainous.

15 At the oddest times, Forest will get a feeling that his right toes are being twisted, though he has no right toes. This morning the "toes" pester and taunt him and the gas pedal seems embroiled in flames.

Again the meteorologists' predictions of a storm have been wrong, the snow having gone out to sea. The morning is glittery and windy.

Bare. Leaves run over the road like hundreds of fast mice. Ginn Road narrows as it comes into the curve to a guardrailed bridge. "*His* roads," Peggy calls them. Said in a sad tone. Peggy, knowing the work of roads, the worry of roads, and so little money in the town's budget these days. But so much money to replace an exhausted part on a truck. Plow cutting edges used up like butter. But costing like gold. Forest does what he can do. Always his best. Certain selectmen sing his praises. He's always been shrewd with a dollar. Shrewder than old F.D. F.D. wasn't a spendthrift. But Forest, Jr., is *hard core*. And now *harder*. Shutting down. Closing in. The buck stops here, Peggy hears him say.

When did progress stop? Peggy would say she can almost put her finger on it. Even before it happened. It was in the air. In people's eyes. Perhaps it was the "progress" itself that looked too much like mutilation. That fierce glee of others scared Peggy. Now for summer contracts, no new houses. Just a few culverts, a leach field. Diddly-squat. But so much debt. "Forest's roads are all we have now," Forest heard her telling Bett a few weeks ago. And Bett had blinked twice and said, "There's one hundred fifteen miles of road in Egypt."

Today Forest wears blaze orange vest and cap, not the whole works like he would while out tracking. But enough to be ready in case a nice surprise appears alongside the road. Two rifles in the rack just in case. License in his wallet. And he watches the woods for sight of a white flag. Sometimes the twisting windy trees seem like a thousand running legs, white tails, tossing heads, bristling racks.

He is headed for the Foyes' to check out a drive shaft, rear end, and axles for a two-ton. He will not dicker. He will simply state his price. Foyes being desperate people.

Now as the pickup takes the hard curve, there in the middle of the road are three riders on three horses coming into his grille fast. "Christ!" he howls, slamming the brakes and downshifting, missing the first horse, fat-bellied, gray tail like a waterfall. And then the dark horse rearing up with its front hooves over his fender, too close for comfort. And there at the little bridge, a white-rumped Appaloosa, its rider staring into Forest's spotted windshield, the rider's wild white hair nearly invisible against the morning sun. It is *she*. The smart-ass girl who had mocked him in the woods. Still wearing that stained blue jacket, no gloves. And that white ice look of her skin. And the smoke of cold breath there tumbling from the purplish open parts of her mouth. Forest mashes the horn, knowing it'll freak the Appaloosa, and sure enough that nerved-up pretty horse nearly takes to the sky.

Now, truck moving on, he watches his side mirror trying to pick out the Appaloosa from the rest, but the whole jiggling reflection of trees and sun quickly slides away.

Could she ruin him? She has so much to tell. All his violations. She could make a good story of the man in the woods. And always with her little witnesses, her bodyguards, her familiars. And now, surely, yes she will ruin him. He feels a raciness like twenty coffees. Indeed. Yes. Tonight. Tomorrow. Cops. Social workers. Lawyers. But he'll deny it, of course. He clearly sees her colorific mouth speaking his name in a whirl of frozen breath. "Forest . . . yep . . . that's him. Forest Johnson." And the narrow-faced friend will shriek, "Oh yes oh yes oh yes!"

He looks to his side mirror again and again . . . a blur of trees and stone walls . . . and "his" road.

He remembers something. Her name. Anneka . . . oh, yes.

16 | Forest Johnson, Sr., . . . just an openmouthed head on a pillow. Quartz heater in the corner to keep the nurses warm. The nurses have started up serious overlapping . . . twenty-four hours of nurses . . . expensive. But with F.D.'s vital signs being what they are and Bett's refusal to "ship him to a nursing home," the remains must remain.

The day nurse, arriving for her shift, shivers, says to the night nurse just leaving, "Brrrrrrrr! It's *cold* out there, Darlene!"

"Can't be any colder than in *here*," the night nurse whispers.

The day nurse laughs heartily and says, "Cheap on heat," as she steps around Bett Johnson's feet. Always the misconception that Bett Johnson must be hard of hearing. Now the night nurse descends the stairs, squishy sneaker sounds, which Bett hears. Bett hears almost everything within the walls of this house.

"GOOD MORNING, ELIZABETH!" the day nurse shouts.

"Good morning," says Bett in an ordinary voice, sighs, then stretches her legs to look down at her new Hush Puppies.

The nurse shakes one chrome side of the bed. "GOOD MORNING, FOREST!" she hollers cheerily to the head on the pillow. She feels around under the blankets for his right hand, takes the pulse. The nurse wears a charcoal gray cardigan just like Bett's dark blue one. And, like Bett, a tight evenly crisped white perm. And both the nurse and Bett wear big-frame glasses with curved bows, the very latest in eyewear, nothing like the old things Forest, Jr., wears. Glasses that F.D. used to kid Forest about. Said they looked like somebody found them in an old trunk. Said they made Forest look just like Franklin D. Roosevelt and Harry S Truman. Then F.D. would howl like a banshee over this revelation. And Bett had snapped, "Everyone wore glasses like that in those days. Not just *those* people." Then F.D. referred to them as "hippie glasses." And Bett, indignant, had said, "Forest is no hippie!" Eventually it was plain that F.D. wasn't really teasing Forest. He was teasing *Bett.*

Now there's the sucking sound of the nurse getting F.D.'s blood pressure. She leaves his hand on top of the covers and settles into the chair next to Bett.

The nurse notices Bett's new Hush Puppies. "WELL, THERE! LOOK WHAT YOU HAVE, ELIZABETH!" she shouts. "AREN'T THOSE NICE!" The nurse has Hush Puppies, too. But a darker shade from wear. "WHERE'D YOU GET THEM?!!"

"Peggy took me to the mall for a . . ."

"THAT'S NICE, ELIZABETH!" shouts the nurse.

Jeff comes in wearing his dress suede jacket like he's about to go out.

Bett takes a manila envelope from the windowsill the moment she sees him.

The nurse is straightening the pillows of her deep chair, getting settled with a book from her woven satchel. Hardcover with a dust jacket: *Garden Delights.*

Bett picks five- and ten-dollar bills from the envelope, flattens them one by one onto the palm of Jeff's hand.

Jeff says, "That should cover it, Nanna."

"Oh, but let's be sure," says she, arranging another ten prettily on top of the others in his hand.

The nurse raises her eyes to this money transfer.

Bett sees the salmon-and-black stripe sweater showing there inside Jeff's unzipped jacket. She gives it a little feel and playful tug. "I like that," she says. "It's so hard to get a man to dress up. You look like such a gentleman now."

His eyes slide to the head on the pillow, then he says softly like you would if a sleeping baby were near, "Guess I'll go get this taken care of while it's still early in the day. These muffler shops get pretty busy."

"Do you have an appointment?" Bett wonders.

"Oh . . . I will," says Jeff, stepping away. "Thank you, Nanna. This helps *a lot*." Shutting the door gently.

17 There are hours at a stretch with Bett and the nurse sitting in their deep chairs. There's the flop-flop-flop of the nurse speeding through one of her many magazines or home-bettering books. And there's F.D.'s head and hand there motionless on the high bed. But it just so happens the nurse will hop up now and then and shout, "EXCUSE ME A MOMENT, ELIZABETH!! I NEED TO USE YOUR BATHROOM! MIND HOLDING THE FORT A FEW SECS?!!"

And then it just so happens that Bett is alone with F.D.'s head and hand and the pretty light of the windows and the tink-tink-tink-hmmmmmmmmm of the quartz heater at work and the CHANGGG! of the clock in the downstairs hall and the deepness of the old upholstered chair so deep for her that her knees stick up.

And once this really happened. There on the rose-color blanket F.D.'s hand stirred. The fingers folded together, thumb under. The hand rose up looking rapt as the head of a snake. Snake was looking directly into Bett's face. Snake swayed saucily. Teasing.

18 In the early morning the trucks warming up in the lot beyond the house had jerked Eli awake. But he was not charmed by their snorts and grunts, their thunder. The sound of them, the look of them whenever they are pointed out to him by anyone is unspeakably terrible. In Anaheim, California, trucks were just trucks. Big deal. But here trucks have a grip on this house, these people . . . these weird people . . . this fuss. *When* will he and his father and Coti be on their way home? Every moment there's the dark unsettling visage of himself being grabbed and locked inside one of the trucks with . . . the unspeakable thing.

Only when every last working truck has left the premises is there the soft little squawk of his bedroom door opening, and he, Eli, moving along with a look of great purpose and dignity to the door of where his father and Coti sleep. He says, "Dad."

No answer.

He squares his eye to the keyhole, sees the tormented blankets in a heap on the bed. An electric heater hums hot and red *close* to a bunched corner of their quilt. But no one there.

He appears in the kitchen. Square-shouldered. The bearing of an officer.

"Good morning, Eli." The two women speak in wolves' voices. These two women who Jeff keeps referring to as "the nannas" and "*your* nannas" . . . though until this trip, this prisonish terrible big brick wobble-window place with the wolf women and the trucks and HIM, the guy, the unspeakable . . . until this, Jeff had never used a word like Nanna. He spoke of "my people in Maine" or "my folks."

What Eli sometimes longed for was his mother Amy's people, for she had told him a million stories about them, said they were the best at everything . . . except for her uncle Reuben who beat up a game warden once . . . but she said even this with a kind of relish. And to her family she sent California postcards. And she called them on the phone and let Eli say "Hi" and answer questions about school and how old he was now. And he'd ask afterward if that was her uncle Reuben and Amy always said no, it was her father . . . Ernest. "Your Grampie."

But on the drive here Jeff and Coti told him this was not the Egypt, Maine, where Amy's folks lived. They were hundreds and hundreds of miles from that Egypt. Eli doesn't really want to visit them either. But maybe just get a look at them. What he wants is his mother and his cat and his video games. He feels like he might throw up now. Water runs in his mouth. His jaws weigh a ton. He answers, "Yup," though no question has been asked.

The two nannas hungrily study his dark hair flattened by sleep. One nanna offers him raspberry preserves on toast. The other offers him a visit to the barn to see her horses.

"Where's my dad?" he asks.

The nanna with dark brown hair and blue jeans and a million socks stands with her thumbs in her belt smiling funnyish.

The white white shaky nanna says, "He borrowed a little money. He was worried about his car. So they went down to get it fixed. Want some Wheaties? Or eggs?"

Eli moves toward one of the windows and looks down over the roofs and tall chimneys of the woolen mill and the river twinkling with early sun. And the bridges.

The thing about very very bad things happening is they sometimes happen when you don't know they're happening so there you are, not knowing if the bad thing is already happening yet or not.

19 It is a quiet evening at the Coldspot, which this time of year is called the Hotspot. "Hot," some might say, refers more to the fake fireplace with the electric log than any action that takes place here in this off-season.

Terri Dresser leans forward to get a closer look at Jeff Johnson's face in the dim light. "You're a new man, Jeff," she says.

This makes the Belanger sisters, Jessica and Miranda, tee-hee and Michael Labbe chokes on his beer. But Coti just keeps staring at the door which never opens . . . nobody arriving . . . nobody leaving . . . not much different here than back at the Johnsons' kitchen.

"I am shit-faced," Jeff snorts, tipping his beer to finish it off. He blinks. "This makes me my exact self. Right, Coti?" He gives a shoulder of Coti's tight baby blue sweater a little dainty pat. Coti is really something tonight . . . a rhinestone flower in her upswept hair, tall spike-heeled black boots, long black skirt tight like second skin, split nearly to the hip, black panty hose, dusky perfume, clear, black, angry eyes.

Once when Terri Dresser and Jeff had passed each other coming and going to the restrooms, Terri whispered, "Is Amy back, too?"

And Jeff had nearly spat, "That pig I'm not keeping track of."

Back at the table, there's another set-up of beers. Coti says, "I thought you said there was going to be a band, J.J."

Michael Labbe jerks a thumb toward the bar. "There *is*. That's them."

Coti looks over at the bar. A guy with styled hair, but otherwise a regular-looking Maine-type-plaid-shirt person. Another guy looks like Daniel Boone, head-to-toe buckskins. There's other guys at the bar, middle-aged men in work clothes and caps. And one very short guy with a business-lawyerish look.

Coti says, "Let me guess. The band is hiding *behind* the bar."

Michael Labbe grins. "Naw. It's Chris and Peter . . . there on the end. The guy in jeans. And him in the suede. Pete's inta black powder. He probably just came from a shoot." He looks down at his beer bashfully, then back into Coti's eyes. "This place must seem dead to you guys after what you're used to in California, huh?"

"Hey, Mike, . . . don't apologize!" Jeff says. "This is real nice. It's good to have a nice conversation with you guys. You couldn'ta updated me on all that happened over to Peachy's and everything if we had fifteen electric guitars and amps blattin' away. It's nice to have a good ol' conversation with your ol' friends." He burps.

320

Michael Labbe gives Jeff's arm a soft punch. "So true," says he.

"They do a great Talking Heads imitation," Terri Dresser tells them.

Jeff snorts at this. "Those two guys? Talking Heads is a whole buncha people."

"Well, they do it, don't they?" Terri insists and the sisters Jessica and Miranda nod eagerly.

"They do a little of everything," says Michael Labbe, glancing toward the little performance platform as if it weren't dark and bare.

"In the summers there's more people here," says Terri. "They really pack 'em in then. People from the camps an' stuff. A lot of summer people. People you've never seen before. And guess what!" She touches Coti's hand. "Once they had *Ernie Train* here . . . just before he died. I know he's country western but he's *big* and pretty much . . ."

Coti rolls her eyes. "Maybe we could go to Portland tonight." She looks at Jeff. "You said there were *clubs* in Portland."

Jeff says, "Yeah . . . let's go to Portland."

Terri wonders, "Are you guys going to stay here and live or is this just a visit?"

Jeff glances at Coti. "Well, a little bloodletting would be the ticket."

"Oh, shut up!" Coti snaps. "I'm sick of that." Coti isn't putting away much beer or marijuana tonight. She's staying clean. Alert.

"Bloodletting," says Michael Labbe, scratching his head. "That should be easy. Not as hard as most things."

Coti sighs. "*Pleeez*, J.J. Don't get onto this subject tonight." She peers off toward the bar, to the row of backs, then moves her eyes back to Michael Labbe's short beard and baseball cap, Michael Labbe being not much different from them at the bar, just younger. Then she looks at Jeff who is different.

J.J., the love of her life. How happy he made her this summer. He was just returning from an artists' colony where he had finished a series called *Winterworks* and he told her about life at the colony, all the gossip, which was very juicy, and the great food they had there and the famous composer who was there, though for Coti the name didn't ring a bell. But he told all his stories so wryly, his eyes wild and full of genius . . . his beautiful, beautiful eyes. All her friends at work said they shivered when he put his eyes on them.

Then his *Winterworks* series was chosen by a Los Angeles gallery and there would be a big opening where she could meet his artist friends.

Meanwhile, he took her to some clubs where they danced and he had verses of poetry memorized, which he whispered. And kisses. How many million kisses?

At the gallery opening she had worn her cream-white dress and he introduced her as "his muse" to all the people. And all his friends stood around her drinking a creamed punch in little cut-glass cups. The friends all seemed to look alike. Small chinned, straight coffee-stained teeth, glittering genius-looking eyes, nervous hands, wonderful collegiate accents speaking of the power of J.J.'s work. Oh, the depth and breadth of the work! Three paintings were sold for a couple thousand each!! And Jeff a little drunk that night but beautifully drunk . . . said his love for Coti frightened him, that he was dying from his wild dreams of her and after everyone at the opening had gone, all hundred or more people gone, and he was alone with her on the steps of the old gallery, he wept . . . joyous weeping. And he said he was about to embark on the greatest series of work in his life, a series of paintings of her. He said he was obsessed with her. He took her to more clubs. She knew he was married but she knew Amy was history. "Ol' Amy," he called his wife. But Coti he called "my goddess."

Now here in Egypt, Maine, Jeff says, "Coti, have another beer. It'll make you smile."

Coti smiles. "Let me finish this one first. I've got only one mouth."

The sisters Jessica and Miranda giggle shyly. It's plain they are awe-struck by Coti's presence . . . and Jeff who seems different since California.

Michael Labbe squints into his beer, says deeply, "Bloodletting."

"Don't get him going, please," Coti tells Michael Labbe. "If I have to listen to it some more, I'll puke."

Jeff pats Coti's hands and says, "I love you."

Coti says, "It is just that you have this insane obsession since we've been up here." Her eyes shine with tears.

The girls across the table look horrified.

"What insane obsession's that?" Terri Dresser wonders, returned from the restrooms, settling next to Coti in the booth.

Jeff says, "To explain my obsession would be to practice my obsession of talking about it . . . then Coti will . . ."

"Puke," says Michael Labbe. He pushes his baseball cap back on his head, leans toward Coti and says, "Look here. We are all on the edge of our seats wanting to know about this insane bloodletting obsession. We are all *very* curious. Aren't we?" He glances around at the simultaneous nods. "And you, Coti, are being the big roadblock between us and it."

Coti raises her chin, licks her lips, looks off toward the blank dark performance platform and sighs. "Well, don't worry about me puking. That was the wrong word. What I'll do if he starts on this *thing* of his is yawn . . . a very big yawn." Now she glances at the door. "J.J. . . . come on. Let's get going. How long does it take to get to Portland anyway?"

Jeff stands suddenly. He sways at first, but gets a grip on the back of the booth. "Headin' for the bright lights," he says with a grin. "Who wants to go along? My treat." He looks from face to face. It is plain to see that these few old friends in this soft dark light could be another kind of obsession . . . gods and goddesses in their own right. He gets a grip on one of Michael Labbe's forearms, tries to hoist him to his feet. Michael Labbe chuckling, "Okay . . . okay . . . okay . . ."

20 | It is dark, the darkest kind, but he knows the spotted white rump of an Appaloosa horse would burn through the dark, be seen, pretty as a face.

This is what they call Miracle City on Letourneau land, this place of the otherwise homeless, this place where he knows Anneka must live, for he saw that Appaloosa here months ago, too fancy-priced a horse to belong to someone living in Miracle City . . . any horse being too frivolous an expense for someone living here . . . sort of along the idea of six lobster claw cooking mitts bought by a man who owns one pair of pants.

He takes his pickup slow over frozen ruts, between and around the toys left in jumbles along this narrow dirt lane. And a metal dog leash. A soda can.

His headlights bounce across the trailers and campers and narrow particle-board camps. Camps between camps. More camps than ever. Thrown together in recent weeks in spite of the codes. In spite of the new bloodhoundlike code enforcement officer. Miracle City . . . in spite of everything.

Camps up above cling for dear life, every bit of usable land here is used.

Now the road forks, creeps back into the old part of Miracle City. So many cars on blocks or squatted low on their rims. Great tiered banks of split firewood, three times bigger than any of the camps. A couple of newish big-shot-looking four-wheel-drive pickups parked in the road, leaving little room to pass. Forest inches through. Such trucks. Roll bars and chrome. The kind young men show off in.

So many camp doors and windows snug to the edge of the lane. Like some village in a foreign land. These people with eyes that would stare you down as you pass. These people who rarely keep any rules of etiquette, only their own etiquette, which has nothing to do with Forest Johnson.

He sees the old Plymouth of Brian who tried to get his driving job back. On the downhill side of Brian's camp the windows have drapes. But the windows facing the hill have cotton curtains of a crisp pink ruffle.

More lighted windows. More toys.

Now out of the dark overhang of trees, a gutted deer swings out at him. One hoof clunks against the fender. Hanging the deer this way is no prank. Forest knows. It is pride. Someone's triumph.

Now more toys.

Eyes of a cat staring him down.

Frozen track of a horse.

But now at the end, no sign of the Appaloosa. He circles back, takes a left at the fork, circling, circling, humped over the wheel. It's many times around before he catches sight of it among the dark trees, the Appaloosa leaning in a restful way near a water tub. Forest shifts down, edging to a near-stop, his eyes making circles, memorizing things.

21 | Midmorning of the next day. They hear it. The unmistakable thum-p-thum-p-thum-p-thum-p of the Camaro pulling up into the dooryard. Eli hurries out to meet them. A little nasty argument out there . . . Eli railing them . . . Jeff in a high whine, railing back. Coti just hurrying along ahead . . . enters the kitchen . . . smiles at the two nannas with her most desperate flash of a smile, says, "Thank you so much for looking after Eli . . . we're really grateful." Then she is gone. Where? Upstairs of course.

Jeff is at the back door now, arms loaded with gifts for the nannas . . . Eli not with him . . . Eli hanging back outdoors . . . somewhere outside . . . yes, there he is standing by the Camaro with his back to the house.

Jeff is smiling. Spreads the gifts out on the table. Hallmark scented candles big around as forearms. One vanilla. One strawberry. One bay. And for each nanna, wrapped in cellophane, bouquets of dried statice and baby's breath. And a bakery cake. Jeff tells them, "There's crunchy stuff in the middle."

Both the nannas smile. Stunned. Reflexive. Wanting things to be good. Wanting happiness. Never really ready for the moment when the thing that happens is nothing like you've ever seen before. Like a flying saucer landing in the yard. Or the couch on the ceiling instead of the floor . . . or grass blue, sky green, music coming out of the sink, an ear for an eye, a talking nose . . . and the floor of this house trembling and tossing and everything flying off the shelves and floating from the cupboards while the power company meter spins and spins and the electric heater in the guest room up above, unbeknownst to those who care, has been running on high for over twenty-four hours with nobody there and the clock toc toc toc toc toc toc telling a time which means nothing.

22 | Coti is not going along on this little ride, Jeff tells Eli. "It's just us guys . . . you and me . . . we need to have a little talk."

Jeff warms up the Camaro, giving it the gas. The engine roars. An eager engine, raring to go. But the interior fills up quickly with exhaust. Eli narrows his eyes on his father's profile.

Jeff says, "I'll show you the back roads here, some of my old territory. You know I used to have a banana bike?"

Eli's thick girth shudders slightly. "A banana bike," he says with a deep chuckle.

"Right. It had a seat like . . . well . . . shaped like a banana. All the kids had 'em then."

Eli's face scrinches. "Weird."

"Well, it wasn't *exactly* like a banana . . . just sort of long and skinny and curved," Jeff tells him, looking over his shoulder, backing the Camaro down the driveway onto Rummery Road.

Now they are out on Ginn Road, the Camaro just rolling along, gripping the road. "I used to have a pony, too. And my sister had a pony. And we'd ride them while Nanna Peggy rode one of her horses and I could ride mine pretty good so I'd show off in front of the girls that Ma . . . you know, Nanna Peggy . . . was giving lessons to. Snooty older girls. Pony's name was Skip. Yep, old Skip. I never really got into horses though. Mostly girls like horses and guys like cars. I was into cars . . . sort of. Not tinkering like Granpa Forest. He likes engines. Me . . . I liked gettin' around. If I was between cars, I thumbed. Drove me crazy hanging around at the house. I had a lot of friends. Art teacher gave me special credits at school if I stayed after and worked on my 'masterpieces.' She and my parents all wanted me to do more art, less friends. So I'd keep 'em happy and do the art and then I'd do the friends. I just missed supper a lot. But those were good days. Keep your eyes peeled and I'll show you some of the real hot spots of Egypt."

"Where's the new header pipe you were supposed to get?" Eli asks gravely.

"They were too busy to touch it."

"When you get it, take me, okay? I'm not staying there with them again . . . okay?"

The exhaust of the Camaro is vexed and solid.

Jeff laughs. "Nanna Bett and Nanna Peggy beat you when we were gone?"

"You spent the money, didn't you?"

There's not much left of the day, just a cold trembly pink between the black bars of tree trunks along the ridge and leaves shuffling across the tar road.

"None of your business, Eli," Jeff says shortly. Jeff's magenta sweater is soft and tight-fitting like a leotard and has many little fashion buttons close together down the front. The permed curls of his dark hair lay over the back. This is not the way Jeff dressed and wore his hair until he met Coti Pederson. This is his Coti-Pederson-fun-at-the-clubs look. A year ago Jeff still had the artist look. Turtlenecks and jeans and sneakers. Little moustache. Splots of paint. A lot of white paint. Or purples, blacks, and reds. And a smell of linseed oil and the smell of the oils of his hair . . . dirty hair. Jeff had said artists caught in the muse can't fart around with the exterior concerns of shampoo.

Jeff says now, "Look out at the trees and scenery, why don't you? I'm going to show you some sights . . . some of my old haunts."

"Sights!" Eli laughs nastily. "Nothing but trees and a bunch of rocks."

"Maine's a good place."

"Stupid place."

The Camaro bears right at the fork. No road signs. No STOP. No YIELD. Just the jumble of woods against the dying despairing white and pink west.

More and more trees. Jeff humps over the wheel, watching the road hard. "I'll show you where they found a body once."

Eli shows no interest.

Another mile of trees, two or three newish ranch houses, then more trees. The night is coming on fast and as Jeff points out a farm where an old friend once lived, Eli snorts, "What a dump."

The exhaust from the holes in the floor is worse on the downhills. And there's one hell of a downhill ahead. Eli cups his hands around his mouth and nose, getting ready.

Jeff says, "So . . . what do you really think of the Johnsons? Nice people, huh? Nanna Bett and Nanna Peggy and ol' Forest . . . they really like you, I can tell."

The boy is choking, gripping his throat, eyes popping. "This car is worse than even before. It wasn't this bad before!"

Jeff says, "You can't find them any sweeter than Nanna Bett."

"My throat tickles!" Eli screams. "We are getting *poison*, you know. It's getting worse and worse. Soon we'll be dead. You shouldn'ta spended that money. I hate it when you do that. Mom says it's a com-pul-shon."

"Well, what do you think? The nannas and Forest would make nice parents to a little kid, wouldn't they?"

"This car is going to kill us." Eli groans.

"Roll your window down some more," Jeff says, his voice patient and somber.

Eli gives his window cranker a few jerks, then thrusts his head out into the icy night. The wind is noisy. Nice.

"I wouldn't go that far, Eli. You could get an earache that way," Jeff warns him.

The Camaro eases to a rolling stop, then easy easy easy pulls out onto the highway . . . not the usual fast showy way Jeff and Coti usually drive. This tonight is a new way.

Suppertime traffic is whizzing both ways. And trucks with logs, rocking on the crown like olden days ships. And trailer trucks of chips . . . screened vents along the top edges.

"Eli, I've got a question."

Eli keeps his eyes shut.

"Eli."

Headlights of cars coming out of the dark are like missiles and lasers. Eli opens his eyes and pretends it's a big war. He leans more and more of himself out into the night, shoots into the lights with his pretend laser gun. "Ptu! Ptu! Pit-chooooo! . . ."

"Eli, don't you think ol' Forest would make a nice dad? He's got a million trucks. I bet he'd give you rides if he was your dad. By the time I was thirteen I could swing one of those babies around the lot and down to the pit all by myself . . . and I could operate the loader . . . fill up the trucks with sand . . . or salted sand, you know . . . for sanding the roads. So I helped out in the big storms. Imagine! You always say you love trucks. In fact, I thought you were pretty crazy about trucks."

"ARMY trucks!" Eli screams, then goes back to blasting more enemy lights.

Jeff gets quiet, eyes glittery, close to tears. He turns the smoking rumbling Camaro up onto another back road.

Eli's ears are numb with cold and now there's no more oncoming headlights, just the narrowing crumbling pitch black roads going up, up, up, and around into the hills. Eli pulls his head in, gives the window a few reverse cranks, pretends to sleep.

"I am a fucked-up father." Jeff drives one-handed now, with his left hand covering half his face. "And your mother isn't any prize, either. You are going to turn out weird, you know?" He chuckles. "Well, *I* turned out weird . . . but I'm just that way because of being . . . you know . . . an artist. Artists are weird. But you are normal. You are a practical man. You and Forest could be partners . . . get rich. Jesus . . . you're just like him in every way."

Silence.

"Eli," Jeff persists. "What do you think would be the perfect mum and dad?"

The exhaust from the floor is voluptuous as the motor takes another downhill. Eli yanks his Levi's jacket over his face, coughs, gags.

"Eli?"

Eli slowly shows his face. In the dark of this car, with the carnivalish color of the Camaro's console lights, it seems Jeff's face *is* Forest's face, the two men having exchanged places in the blink of an eye. A trick of the horriblest kind.

"Eli, answer me," Jeff insists. "Wouldn't a regular guy like Forest be a better dad than some dipshit like me?"

Eli howls out, "For a father I want a GERM!!!!!!" Then he laughs, pushes hard with his feet, makes the seat buck crazily. He gives the dash a big kick.

"Eli, stop it," Jeff says in a low voice.

Eli keeps up his laughter. Then another blow to the dash.

Jeff pulls the car off onto the side of the road under a thickness of evergreens, rolls through some bushes that screel the fender. He leaves the motor idling, but snaps the headlights off. Nobody talks. Just the Camaro's low throaty bragging horsepower and devilish exhaust. The gas gauge reads nearly empty. Nobody passes. Nobody sees them parked there.

Eli says at last, "When are we going back to Anaheim? Mom must be wondering where we are. You haven't called her, have you? You think I don't know how to call long distance, but I'm going to find out and I'm going to call her and tell her about *this*." He rolls his eyes. "This is really stupid what you did. *And* Nanna Peggy told Nanna Bett not to give you any more money."

"Oh . . . so I suppose now they think that I lied about the muffler shop. The muffler shop really *was* too busy and wouldn't be able to squeeze us in till Thursday. I suppose they think I made that up!"

"When are we going to call Mom?" The boy's foot is raised and ready. "We call Mom on the phone right *now* and we go back to California tomorrow or I'll kick this whole car into a small smushed thing."

"Okay," says Jeff. "I promise. I'll talk to Coti tonight and see what she says."

"Never mind Coti," says Eli, then adds with a manly chuckle, "Let's leave her here with those guys and *she* can learn to drive the old stupid trucks."

23 | Before noon the wife of Brian Began calls Peggy. Peggy fingers the chipped rim of her tea mug as she listens. The wife doesn't tell how they are running out of food, though Peggy knows they must. The wife doesn't tell about expiring liability insurance. A child's painfully impacted tooth. Or the last light bulb in their house. The wife just asks if Peggy has heard about the big storm watch that is being reported. The wife's voice is low and controlled and unsettling like out of the dark a ghost story is told and you brace yourself for the sudden BOO! The wife reminds Peggy how Brian worked around the clock in storms, never a complaint. Now there's a peculiar rustling silence and Peggy wonders if the husband, Brian, has his ear to the phone alongside his wife's ear.

Peggy has seen this wife of Brian Began at the IGA, babies in the shopping cart, not much room for the food. The wife is an oldish-looking young girl with a vast rear end in stretchy butterscotch color pants or aqua print or stained pink ones, always the kind of colors that make a vast rear look vaster. Her hair stringy. Brown. Maybe there were glasses. Maybe not. But it seems there were. Yes, glasses. And those kids together in the cart. They glare at you. But amongst themselves is such a cozy-looking trust. Never fighting. And among them and with the wife, who would be lifting packages and cans from shelves, is the presence of Brian Began though he isn't there. They seem to . . . well . . . sort of advertise him . . . especially the kids. They wear his deep eyes.

Peggy asks the silent phone, "Has Brian talked with Forest yet?"

The wife says, "Yes . . . but Forest seemed . . . kind of busy."

Peggy says, "I don't really have any say in this. Forest is the one. I really don't. Maybe Brian could try him again . . . maybe at the end of the day. It's so confusing in the mornings. They've been trying to do so much this week, you know. So quiet all this summer. Then . . . bingo! . . . everybody's leach field is giving trouble . . . you know . . . everything comes in a rash." Peggy looks out at the bumper of the day nurse's Toyota parked close to the door.

Brian Began's wife's voice has more to say, getting softer, lower, closer to the phone, the terrible mesmerizing privacy of Brian Began's wife's voice pulling Peggy into it, deeper and deeper.

24 At Moody's Variety & Lunch tonight Brian Began warms his hands at the barrel stove while the wise men question him on how things are over to Miracle City and how're things with work and he tells them, "I never got back with Forest." Long-necked. Pale Ichabod Crane looks. Steely self-discipline. Those who know him well know of it.

And Albion Cole asks, "How's that you didn't? I would've thought he'd want you back . . . especially now."

And Brian Began says, "I ain't good enough for him . . . ain't royal enough."

Albion Cole sits squarely in Spring Beauty looking *very* alert.

Short, barrel-chested, Beach Boy blond Reverend well driller David Moody leans against the cluttered bulletin wall looking deep in thought. One of the reverend's kids has come along. Zachary Moody . . . who helps Gram Moody at the counter. Helps by climbing around and dropping things and saying "have a nice time" to customers, a thing confused with "have a nice day." Zachary has started to have a few freckles. Only a few saddled across the nose. But you can tell he's a kid who will eventually get the works.

The wise men are discussing the War on Drugs and how there's so many people on drugs these days . . . which you hear about on the TV evening news . . . people getting shot in the cities . . . "and those are always blacks or spics," Clarence Farrington says from his place in Purple Ecstasy. "Crack," he says with authority and a shake of the head. "Crack's worse than the rest. But then there's your heroin addicts and so forth all spreadin' AIDS. Some of them are white. Weirdos. Kill you in a minute to feed their habit. And then marijuana which is the worst . . . because . . ." He leans on his knees to share this secret. "A lotta people trying to make light of pot . . . saying it's nothing." His voice goes even softer. "Mark my words, they just want to get all the kids on it . . . and then you'll wake up one morning with one of your kids or grandkids standin' over you with a knife, saying he wants your wallet."

Zachary Moody rolls a can of Alpo under the shelves near the door to the returnables shed to set off the mousetrap. SNAP!!

Gram Louise Moody calls, "Zacharrrry!"

Clarence continues, "Back when the President was first elected, I saw where he suggested we have drug camps so we can put them all there for some *second thoughts.*"

"And some good old-fashioned discipline," Arch Vandermast adds with a snort. "Not enough discipline's their problem."

Clarence rocks back in Purple Ecstasy, stretches his feet toward the stove with cocky assurance. "I saw that about the camps way, way back when the President was first in office. But I haven't heard anything about it since. Probably the damn Congress thought it was too hard on 'em . . . or that whiny whimpering buncha sissies in that Civil Liberties outfit. So the drug problem just gets worse. So where *are* we going to put all them types? Gotta put 'em somewheres eventually. Can't let 'em just run around crazy. There are millions of 'em. *Millions.* Live in alleys. And they are costing you and me money. Our taxes wouldn't be so high if we could solve that problem once and for all. Clean those people up." He sighs. "The President's just being practical. Camps wouldn't cost us so much as all that stolen property that the druggies run off with to feed their habit. Camps would be . . . oh . . . along the lines of basic training. Good for 'em. Make 'em into men." He blinks his eyes with reminiscence and pride, then rocks to and fro a time or two. "Tents would be fairly cheap. Or those little temporary buildin's like for storage . . . or those tin hangar lookin' things they have in Alaska. You ever been to Alaska, Al?"

"No," Albion Cole replies quietly.

"Well, it's very educational. And you get a plane ride you won't forget. Those bush pilots are something. My boy . . . you know, Freddie, the one in real estate . . . he asked me along a few years back."

"Zat where you went, Clarence? I thought you were over to Russia," Ray Dyer teases from his place in Gladiola.

"Right. Me in Russia." Clarence shakes his head.

"Yeah, on some sorta secret mission . . . special spy stuff. It's always given me this idea of your having a double life."

"Yeah. Right. Me in Russia. Haha. No thanks. Buncha lunatics there. Not for me."

"Bet they're cheerin' over that. They're lucky. We *have* to have you."

"Haha. So anyway . . . we got a problem with these druggies. I say it's going to be the ruin of this country . . . all them goddam blacks and Mexicans, spics and Haitians and what not . . . sorry . . . I'm not prejudiced really. . . . But it's true. We've got to face facts."

Brian Began has strode down one of the short aisles, and is now circling back around.

"They shouldn't let them Democrats in Congress run them around like that," old Pete Bucknell in Canary pipes up. "They should put it to a vote of the people. I guarantee you put it to a vote of the people, with all of us fed up to our eyeballs, you'd see those camps approved and then they'd have to . . . you know, the Washington boys . . . would have to get off their asses and stop playin' patty-cake."

Brian Began arrives at the counter with a couple of cans of beans, pack of hot dogs and mumbles something softly to Louise.

Louise says, "We haven't given credit in a long time, Brian. I'm sorry. But it isn't out of meanness or nuthin'. It's just 'cause some people didn't make good on what they owed, you know." Her face goes red with embarrassment.

"My kids haven't had supper. It's just tonight. I'm hopin' to get work by Friday. I've checked in with some guys who might need some wood split but I can't find out till the end of the week."

"But can't you get welfare, Brian? They got welfare, you know."

"We got a little from the Town. Not much."

"You gone to the food stamps place?"

"Gas tank's empty," he says, perhaps a little testily.

Louise sniffs. "Well, I guess that's for women anyways . . . you know . . . them that's husbands run off . . . or . . . never had one."

"I figured instead of me spending a day hitchhiking on Route 25, trying to get to all these state people . . . I'd just spend time here lookin' for work." He looks at her levelly. "So . . . I've been doin' that."

Louise says, "I heard they might be hirin' down to KIKCO. I heard it from Butchie. Now there's a lead for ya. Somethin', you know . . . to do with makin' these little bitty things they put in electronics . . . rockets or somethin'. For the government. Nice job. Benefits and stuff."

Brian Began's back stiffens. "Yeah . . . okay."

"Have a nice time," says freckledy Zachary Moody as Brian turns to leave. The cans of beans and hot dog package are left on the counter.

Blond Reverend well driller David Moody seems so deep in thought, but blinks as the door shuts on a squishhhhh of air.

Arch Vandermast stands up and hurls another chunk of oak into the barrel stove, then turns his eyes on each of the old wise men's faces, jerks a thumb toward the door and says, "That Began kid . . . he ain't really tryin' too hard. I know at least six jobs he coulda got. He's just itchin' to get on the goddam dole. Mark my words. He'll get on it and stay on it."

Clarence Farrington sniffs, leans forward with forearms on knees, looks into the flickering damper holes of the stove. "Well, that's just another good reason to get some camps going. We could save us a few billion right there! They don't want to work . . . goddam 'em! Toss 'em in the camps with the goddam druggies. I'm sick of payin' their way. Don't want to work? Why should we get stuck with the load?"

"ZACHARRRRRAY! Get out of those Popsicles. You're lettin' all the cold air out. Come on now, dear. *Help* Gram. Get over here and *help* me! You want Daddy to take you home to bed?"

25 | The package of hot dogs is wrapped in a little graveyard flag and tucked into a one-gallon mayonnaise jar, lid screwed nice and tight since raccoons have been known to open lids. Two tall cans of beans. Two cans of raisin brown bread. Two cans of peaches. Inside the big jar with the flag-wrapped hot dogs, a note in smoodgy pencil reads: "*Better is a poor and wise youth than an old and foolish king, who will no longer*

*take advice, even though he had gone from prison to the throne or in his
own kingdom had been born poor. I saw all the living who move about
under the sun, as well as that youth, who was to stand in his place; there
was no end of all the people; he was over all of them. Yet those who come
later will not rejoice in him."*

There's no family at home inside the little particle-board camp. Probably Brian Began's mother-in-law has them over to supper. But so hard
a thing to ask of her too many times. Even asking with an unshaky voice
feels like begging.

Darkness gives dignity to these mysterious gifts. A dog comes along.
He sniffs them. A family of raccoons passes by a few yards away but they
don't think to check out this particular doorstep tonight. The gifts remain
in place and will be a surprise when the Began family returns at bedtime.
It'll make tomorrow a better day. Being able to visualize, to be certain
of your next supper, gives your whole day more zip.

26 | Six-thirty A.M. The trucks warming up out back make the floors
and walls tremble, a little tickling on the bottoms of Peggy's big
boots. Peggy stands here in the dark office watching the amber light
revolve. Spots and squares of light swing across her face, across the walls,
swing away, then back again. Snow is on the way. The official word.
They are rigging two more trucks with V-plows. There's only two more
trucks left to work the pit on the Harris job. They are giving it the big
push in these last hours, everybody showing up prompt this morning.
The new man, St. Martin, shows up early.

There's no dawn yet in this valley.

The yellow light swings across Peggy's face again, again, again. Her
hair is wet from her shower, makes her head look small and crafty and
otterlike.

Bett steps out onto this office porch from the kitchen, snaps on the
gooseneck lamp, which lights up the many accordion files along that wall
and the undersides of the deer heads. And Bett says, "So you brought
that gazing globe in, dear?"

Peggy spreads her feet farther apart, rocks on her heels, says, "What's
that?"

"You got that gazing globe in before the snow. That's good. 'Twas
on my mind."

Peggy looks over at Bett. "No, not me. I didn't bring it in."

"You didn't?"

Peggy says "No" and turns back to face the revolving light of the truck. It is the "new" used GMC Forest and the driver George DiBias went to pick up last night in Belfast. For the last fifteen minutes since the crew showed up, they've been fussing over the "new" truck, opening and lowering the hood, opening and lowering the hood. Nothing like a new machine to get guys twitterpated.

It's the first real investment in eight years. Parts to the 1970 Dodges, the Powerwagon, and the two-ton have vanished from the face of the earth. And some parts you can't jury-rig, weld on or wizard into existence no matter what. So . . . the "new" truck. Yellow. Beautiful and dear. Forest mortgaged to the teeth. Forest who hasn't eaten food for two days. Forest who is getting very, very quiet. And dirty . . . this morning no shower, no shave, no combing of the hair.

"Well, maybe Forest brought it in," Bett suggests. She squints out through the many-paned windows to the soft butter-colored squares of light they make on the lawn . . . and that spot of whiter paler mashed grass where the ruby red gazing globe would be if it were there. "You think Forest brought it in?" Bett wonders.

Peggy says, "I don't think so, Bett. He was gone all night after that truck. I'll go out to the shop in a couple minutes if you want. You sure it's not there?"

Bett says, "I'm sure, dear."

27 | Around nine o'clock the sky is dazzling with the look of promised snow, that unruffled, self-possessed, sweet, brimming calm that is so near explosion . . . on the verge.

The constable, Erroll Anderson, parks his jeep close to the house. He stands with one hand on the grayed picket fence that squares off that part of the little yard of two maples, leafless lilacs, browned tiger lily beds, and bumpy white lawn. Very small lawn . . . Johnsons using most of the unwooded part of their property for the business: the pit, the lot, the maintenance shop, the barn renovated into apartments, the horse stable and training ring and narrow strip of pasture that meets with the wood line uphill. And everywhere handy are the cutting edges, the various springs and hoses and clamps, the unpretty stuff of work.

Forest points out a spot on the little lawn. He takes his gloves off and leans against a maple and studies the *spot* then pushes the nosepiece of his glasses hard, glares over at Moody's Variety & Lunch and around the neighborhood while the constable mostly stares at his own jeep looking grim very grim. Both men look *so* grim. Much grimmer than men should look over one stolen gazing globe.

28 Next morning. Dawn is quickening beyond the black mountain, beyond the trucks that are hunched motionless in the frigid smoky shadows of themselves. The dawn is golden and clear. No snow yet. Another false alarm.

Most of the drivers converging in the open bay area are dressed in their blaze orange though none of them will be hunting . . . for there is no legal hunting on Sundays . . . and there is nothing but Sundays for you when you drive for Forest Johnson in the fall of the year. And when a shot is heard on the mountain, there's a feeling among the drivers that's tight and edgy . . . for among these drivers, these people of Egypt, the hunt is seen as a given. It is one's *right*.

And there are guns in the racks of many of the pickups parked along the edge of the lot . . . guns that won't be used . . . but can be admired by people along the way to and from this place. It's okay to drive around with them on Sunday and to wear the blaze. Parading is as important as the hunt itself. It is the thing that Forest Johnson, Jr., can't take away from you.

Down the line the great trucks come to life including the "new" GMC with its sweet clean synchronicity. The ground quakes. The dawn quakes. Exhaust and frozen "good morning"s and cigarette smoke churn up into a white and greater mix. A pickup bounces up the back way into the lot, guns in the rack, the thrum-bumpbump of hard rock music beating around inside the cab. As this truck makes its big sweep around to back in among the others, its headlights flood the legs of horses. Stirrups glow. There's a swirl of tails. And Forest, shambling across the lot from the house, sees that one horse has a white rump. Forest stops, spreads a gloved hand on the hood of Peggy's little car, staring and dry-mouthed. The rider of the Appaloosa is lost in swirls of exhaust, but it's easy to see that she and the others are converging around George DiBias . . . who was hired years ago by F.D. . . . George DiBias who is a whiz mechanic . . . who always smiles his gentle smile, keeps to his work . . . who rents one of the apartments over the barn . . . who married Francine Soule, woman with a loud laugh and many relations that visit routinely . . . and George has been married to Francine for close to twenty years . . . and they, George and Francine, have a kid . . . tow-haired girl.

Blood marches in Forest's temples louder than the trucks.

It is George DiBias's daughter, of course. This Anneka. All this time she has been HERE. One of the tenants. All along! Only a few yards from his table at supper! His bed at night. His morning showers. The horse . . . borrowed, of course, . . . the way girls do. Borrowed from some Miracle City friend.

His mind flashes back over the days with George. Back to the day of Anneka in the woods. George worked like hell with Forest these past weeks to bring those two Dodges back to life. Then two nights ago the long drive to Belfast to pick up the "new" GMC. George and Forest in the pickup. George talked about TV shows. Mostly TV movies. George is never much of a talker in the shop. All talk is in his hands, in the *clank* and *eeek* of tools. But in that cab . . . the intimacy of the cab . . . there was Forest's fearsome silence to fill. And Forest had never seen any of these TV shows. With reverence George told each and every scene. Then he got onto *old* TV shows. And *The Three Stooges*. Forest tossed his head back and snorted. Then something changed. Between Forest and George, as with so many, this with men, the fraternity of the yuck-yucks and yerk-yerks and arrrrrrruff-ruffs, the "See the clouds! See the clouds!" and Forest and George both in blessed relived hysteria.

No mention by George that his daughter had any "complaints."

Now Forest stares into the exhaust clearing up around her. Her back is to him. A homely knitted cap is settled over her crazy rabbit-white hair. Then as the horse, razzed by the good-feeling cold, jostles to the left and she is reining him back, she sees Forest staring and she stares back at him hard and unblinking. Then she's back into the silly chatter with the others ringed around George DiBias, something about "going to the moon!" and all the girls twitter over this and George shakes his head. And Forest recognizes one of the other girls, the rock and stick thrower, the "witness" from the woods. Forest knows her as much by her shrilling as by her long face and frame. "See ya later!" George calls to them as the three riders race their horses from the lot. And now the trucks are heading out, one by one.

Forest begins his shambling walk toward George DiBias to discuss today's work. The camshaft in the little Ford. And George, fat-faced and mild, is setting a match to a cigarette and waiting.

29 How many times in the last few months has he driven over the Burgess Road past the dam and the foundry, past the little ranch house that is painted lavender like an Easter egg? He knows how there's never a car in the yard, how the little lawn always mowed before had gone to seed this summer, how there's a white poodle, how the picture window is smudged from the white poodle who, having a good view from the back of the sofa, runs from end to end when you drive by. Sometimes the clothesline has sheets and clothes hung out. Sometimes the old lady and the white poodle are out by the mailbox, which is lavender like the house. She gets around with an aluminum walker. The poodle always lifts his leg on the hedge of high weeds along the shoulder of the road. Forest knows this scene to the last stalk of goldenrod . . . and never, *never* until this morning has he seen a red gazing globe there in that yard. Maybe it's a surprise to the old woman, too! Forest is well-acquainted with the legend . . . this disappearing, appearing, disappearing, reappearing trick.

He stomps the brake pedal and the sand truck's rear brake shoes sing their keening metal-to-metal. The great weight of sand rolls on and on along the shoulder of the road, finally stops. Now Forest backs the truck slowly, the engine grunting. This thing he must give some consideration to. He shuts off the radio, sits board straight at the wheel, giving the red gazing globe a hard study.

Rising high behind the lavender house is brutish Horne Hill, part bald-faced, ledge and juniper, the rest dark woods and young trees . . . young trees looking tensed as porcupine quills against the new snow. It is the first snow, amounting to nothing. Forest doesn't even call it snow. Just a festive feeling. Just a midmorning melt-off on these tar roads. But this early in the morning some greasiness, some fuss. And up in those hills, enough white to give a hunter a good track.

There are no other homes in sight. Just this one with the dog digging at the picture window nonstop, digging harder and harder while the sand truck stays parked across the road.

Forest lays on the horn with both hands.

Old lady appears, standing back from the window in the darkness of the room. She is probably trying to read what is printed in white lettering on the sand truck door. He *wants* her to see the name. It is his message to her. So then she can tell the son-of-a-bitch who gave her the red globe, that son-of-a-whorin'-sneaky-high-minded-pain-in-the-ass-lightsteppin' fox and his outlaw gang, that it's just a matter of time now.

For an instant, he considers removing his Weatherbee from the rack and leaving his message shattered in ruby shards on the old lady's lawn . . . like "Look here, asshole, this will be your head next. Leave my family alone!" But right behind the target is the broadside of the house. So instead he lays on the horn another half minute, watching the little dog going nuts and the old lady gripping her walker, motionless.

30 | Another morning with Coti and Jeff and the Camaro gone out for a while. Though you never know for how long. It could be hours. Or it could be days. But neither nanna seems to be around either . . . though he can pretty easily figure it . . . Nanna Bett sitting with the nurse by the man who is practically dead . . . and Nanna Peggy out brushing her fancy horses. He gets his Levi's jacket from the wall of hooks, steps out onto the door rock. All those other houses with their old fences and old trees, old wobbly windows. Don't *any* of these houses have Nintendos inside? Or *something???*

At the corner of the glassed-in porch office something catches his eye. A blue gazing globe. It's where the red gazing globe was before the burglar stole it. Only took the Johnsons a day to get another gazing globe while getting even *one* VCR seems out of the question.

He squints into the blue world, his face gorged with tall blue teeth. Blackish-blue lips. Now he stands back so his whole self and the sky and one wall of the house is seen in many great shades of blue. Four wee dump trucks. A bulldozer, very wee. A speck of a station wagon. The baby blue comb of a fence. And bitty antlike Nanna Peggy coming. He turns. Her eyes are wide on the blue ball and there's something in her expression. He steps back, feeling the evil wrongness of the blue ball.

31 | At Moody's there are two young mothers discussing the court trial of a man upstate who, while hunting, shot a young mother to death in her yard . . . thought her tasseled white hat was the tail of a deer.

They lean forward in the bright rocking chairs. One with an infant whose face is covered. The other uses a Kleenex to dab at her toddler's nose. Toddler with hooded snowsuit. Purplish cheeks. Chocolate mouth.

"Jury found him innocent."

"How can he be innocent if he admitted he killed her? That's not *innocent*. Maybe manslaughter, you know. Wasn't that what he was tried for? I wouldn't call it murder. But certainly it was manslaughter. He's not innocent of *that!*"

"They called it innocent."

"Ain't that weird."

"I saw pictures. Her little baby girl was blond. Looked just like Tracy from the angle they took it . . ."

When they realize Forest is there at the door, they lapse into a sudden silence as if Forest were the killer in the news.

Nobody at the lunch counter. Nobody at the register. Louise Moody out back clanking around with returnables, complaining to herself.

The young mothers are deathly silent.

Forest shakes open the evening paper. Real estate heavy on his mind these days. And the business section. And want ads. And of course, all the furor over the hunter on trial upstate. The whole paper pulling him down. A paper like lead. Everything suspect, tiresome, frightening. And he having too little food, too much coffee. Too many bills. Too little sleep. Too little time. And prices . . . shit . . . when did they stop promising to stop inflation? And what sleight of hand was it that made you forget that promise?

One of the occupied rocking chairs is canary yellow. The other purple. All the rockers are colors of jubilation, repainted in the days not long ago, when everyone was in that belief, in that frenzy of *spend, spend, spend.* The young mothers glance over at Forest and back at each other. The toddler pushes an aqua blue rocker into a red rocker. CLACK!

"Stop that, Tracy!" one of the mothers hisses. "Louise is going to come out and be mad."

Out back Louise Moody is having a bad time with those bottles and cans.

Forest rolls the paper up under his arm, leans on the counter for balance, finds change.

Louise hears the jangle of silver money, comes shuffling short-leggedly from the doorway at the back. Netted hair. Huge flowery-print bosom. Gaspingly, she gives the register a tap to open the drawer, takes Forest's change.

"Think it'll ever snow?" Louise wonders.

"Never," Forest says. "We're going to get crocuses."

This really tickles Louise. She laughs. She gasps. She shuts the drawer.

32 | The candelabrum slumps from the ceiling, its light enduring, its wiring questionable. Under the floor the pipes going to the kitchen thrum and shudder against Forest Johnson, Jr.,'s damaged feet. You can never tell when his pain visits him. He never mentions it. There's just his glasses pressed against his black and stoic eyes.

Jeff is talking about the possibilities of work around here. His voice and hands are a little too fast, his own dark eyes too terribly focused and glittery and clear in the way that makes you suddenly realize he might be wearing contacts. "Some job that involves people, you know . . . a job dealing with people!" he exclaims.

Coti says, "I would say definitely you are the people type, J.J." Then she giggle-snorts, licks her lips, takes little sexy gulps of air. Her sweater is long-sleeved but deeply V-necked and red. Red like what they used to say draws a bull.

Jeff is nearly shouting now. "Coti! I bet you could find something down to Portland pretty much like you were doing before. And you wouldn't mind the commute, baby. You like driving. There's loads of your kind of work down there at the hotels." He looks over at Peggy and then to Nanna Bett, skips Forest. "Coti was a cocktail waitress out in Cally." Jeff's knife and fork and spoon remain in their positions by his plate. His hands fly with his thoughts. "Just when we were leaving to come here, they were getting ready to switch her to hostess. Not as many tips. But it's nice work. Huh, baby?"

Eli says, "You guys . . . I heard a joke. When does a—"

"Don't interrupt, Eli!" Jeff hollers. "You can *wait* to tell one of your *jokes*. Jesus!"

Coti explains, "The hostess has to have a lot of clothes, though."

How slickly Forest is able to force a thickness of margarine across his biscuit while the circles of his glasses are directed at something else. What is it that he's looking at? That vacant spot on the tablecloth between Bett's left hand and Eli's elbow.

Jeff exclaims, "No problem! There's clothes in Maine!" He laughs. A real howl. An unnatural almost idiot sound.

Coti says, "You make everything sound so easy. You know it's not easy."

Coti can hardly keep her eyes off Forest. He has just showered and shaved and seems settled in his seat, almost content. For the past few years he has had this way of combing his hair with the part in the middle. And two short spread-out bangs at the front of the part. Like a man out of the late 1800s. And with those glasses. He's kind of . . . of a character! It is a thing that has caught Coti by surprise tonight, this thing with his hair. It is a nice thing. Kind of sweet.

Jeff says, "Here I am really psyched about this and all you do is bitch, bitch, bitch!"

SNAP!

Coti and Jeff both jump.

"What was *that?!*" Coti wonders, looking around at the china closet.

"Mousetrap," says Forest, scooping something yellow-green into his mouth. Another one of Peggy's recipes . . . what *she* calls "gourmet." What he has been known to call "lab formula."

Coti says, "Yugh . . . mousetrap," looking incredulously from face to face.

Jeff is now giving his meal a little poke. "What's this stuff, Ma?"

"Asparagus Astounding," says she, rolling up the sleeves of her blue plaid flannel. "It's got yogurt, mushrooms . . . a lot of turmeric . . . bread crumbs . . ."

Jeff interrupts. "My mother always has to do that, Coti, . . . tell you what's in it . . . *all* the ingredients."

Forest chuckles deeply. "Otherwise it's a mystery."

And Peggy says, "Why yes . . . you wouldn't want to eat a hidden rat tail, would you?"

Coti's eyes slide over to the china cabinet.

Bett laughs nervously. "Oh, Peggy! You say the darnedest things."

"Rat tail," Eli says happily.

Bett dabs her mouth with her napkin and says softly, "Goodness."

Eli gives Bett's elbow a little jab, cocks his head to see up into her lowered face. "Maybe rat *heads*," he says deeply.

Bett feigns a big shiver. "Oh *stop!*"

Coti smiles her lip-licking glossy smile at Forest. "Well, it's certainly nice to have you with us tonight, Mr. Johnson . . . Forest. It's the first real meal where we've all eaten together . . . like Christmas or something!"

Forest looks at Coti, reflection of red like two flags on his glasses. The margarine laid thickly on his biscuit is not the usual brand. It's something Peggy bought this afternoon . . . one of her experiments. It's as yellow as paint. He tears from the biscuit and chews lustily. "Yep, this is the way," he says.

"Well . . . don't expect the luxury of his presence very often, Coti!" Jeff says brightly. "Ol' Dad . . . work, work, work. Dad and his trucks. Dad and his backhoes and dozers. Dad and his bucket-loady-wiggle-wobble-Dr.-Seuss-Bean-Bog-pickers."

Coti covers her mouth and snickers.

Eli laughs out a little chunk of half-chewed mushroom, which lands on the tablecloth.

Forest says, "You can't make a business work while sitting on your ass."

"Right," says Jeff. "Dad has that memorized," he tells Coti close to her ear. But it's not a whisper.

"J.J., don't pick on your dad," Coti says. "I hate seeing that."

"You didn't mind it when you said what you said about him last night over to Greg and Sheila's."

Coti whitens, then reddens. "I never said anything about him I wouldn't say to his face!" she insists, on the verge of tears.

"What'd you say about me?" Forest asks, shifting in his chair to look more directly into her eyes.

Peggy shouts, "No more! This is very bad business, what we're doing."

"Confrontational," says Jeff. "Very healthy. What is sick is when people keep secrets."

Peggy says quickly, "Anybody who wants seconds on the casserole, there's a whole pan of it in the kitchen. And lots more biscuits."

"The biscuits are wonderful, dear," says Bett.

Peggy is starting to thank her but at the very same time, Jeff says, "So! What's this I hear about a prowler? Some trouble, huh?"

Bett says quickly, "Every now and then but no more than anywhere else."

Forest lays his fifth biscuit down carefully and straightens his back.

"You mean someone's been *prowling* around *this* house at night?" Coti tugs dramatically at the V-neck of her red sweater and at the chunky silver necklace of big suns, moons, and stars that lays in a heavy way upon her dark skin.

Bett insists, "There's no more crime here than other places."

"Well," says Forest. "Maybe there's no more crime around here if you count the whole community . . . but"—he smiles at his mother—"evil doin's seem to come to the Johnsons *more*. Crime types *love* the Johnsons. Burglars, prowlers, wizards, trolls, and all venomous sort seem to think the Johnsons are special people."

The phone rings. Peggy hurries to answer it.

Bett pats her white curls, brushes her lap, tidies her dress, and says, "You kids ignore Forest. He's just plaguing."

Eli says deeply, "Burglars wear masks."

"Right," Forest agrees. "You got it, Eli, my man."

Peggy returns, stands in the doorway with her thumbs hooked into the pockets of her jeans. "Phone for you, Forest. It's Harry Dyer."

Bett says, "Forest likes to pull a leg. This burglar thing is not as bad as he makes it out to be."

Forest stands, gets ahold of the backs of chairs, squeezing himself past the china closet and out of the dining room.

Eli turns to watch Forest go.

And Peggy says, "Dessert, anyone?"

33 | "Harry!" Forest hoots into the phone. He calls the contractors and all his longtime customers by their first names. Any of them will tell you Forest Johnson is as honest as they come, he'll treat you right. Even when some of the one-time customers who were having some sort of palace built called to nitpick, sometimes with innuendos about lawyers, Forest's voice never hardened. Always those softening modulations on certain words, seeming close to endearment. And now with the phone receiver tucked between shoulder and ear, talking state code requirements, buried cables, water tests, soils, he doodles on a folder with Peggy's red ball-point. A ladybug. A fish. A tree. A snowman.

34 | They meet up with each other in the upstairs hall. Forest with clipboard under one arm, gripping the banister. Eli outside Jeff and Coti's door just as that door has been shut in his face. Eli turns toward Forest. Forest asks, "So, what was the joke?"

"What?"

"The joke. You were going to tell that joke."

"Oh, yeah." Eli shuffles around a bit, squinting off to the left into memory. "This guy . . . see . . . there's this guy. He gets his clothes ripped, see? So he gets his wife to fix it and she sews it for him . . . but she only did see-saw."

Now Forest is the one squinting.

Silence.

"That's it?" Forest asks with a smile.

"Yep," says Eli with a smile.

There's something that's been lost in the telling. Forest chuckles, says, "Yes . . . that's pretty funny."

Eli says, "I know a whole lot more. I know at least . . . fifty." So he tells another. A pretty ruined knock-knock joke.

And Forest says, "That's pretty funny." Now Forest leans against the wall, opens and closes the clipboard's clamp. "You've probably seen *The Three Stooges*?"

"Yeahhhhh!" Eli brightens. "Woo-woo-woo-woo-woo-woo-woo-woo! Yerk! Yerk! Woyse goye, huh?" He stretches up on his toes. Pretends to twist and pound Forest's nose.

This really cracks Forest up.

35 | Lying next to Peggy in the dark, Forest says, "Woyse goye, huh? Yerk! Yerk! Yerk!"

And Peggy sighs. "Oh, Forest. Quit it. I always hated those guys."

36 | Anneka DiBias leans forward in the saddle, leans toward the many faces, and asks if they all heard the verdict on the trial of the guy who shot the woman wearing the white hat.

Everyone has heard. Yes. Yes.

"Now keep in mind, you guys, that the jury said he was innocent of *manslaughter* . . . that they didn't consider him reckless or anything."

"Like it wasn't *his* fault," says Mandy Dresser, astraddle the nearest bay horse, ". . . like it was *her* fault."

It is late day. Gray. That after-school kind of gray, slipping into dark by degrees. Sign on the brick PO wall says NO LOITERING. But this doesn't feel anything like loitering. This feels more like *purpose*. Feels like a wild fire. There's shouts of some people getting in and out of parked cars. These are those that want Anneka to shut up. Anneka gives them the bird and an exaggerated smile, eyes fluttering.

Now there's some women crossing the road from the mill. Heard about the fuss here. Some from the hardware store and bank. One or two men. But mostly women. Couple of Egypt's wise men near the PO door, arms across their chests, feet apart. One snorts, "Planning a little Tupperware party, I guess."

Anneka DiBias keeps on speechifying. With Anneka DiBias . . . it's always something. Known to some as the Hooky-Detention-Principal's-Office Queen. Ol' Anneka DiBias . . . ringleader. The shaggy borrowed Appaloosa horse is nerved up by the come and go of cars, nerved up by Anneka's shouting, nerved up, steamed up, tall ears attuned, lips flicking. Horse pulls to the left toward the other dark shaggy horses with their riders, riders all in jeans and high-topped double-laced sneakers. Some riders wear blaze orange vests. Some don't.

More women stepping from their cars. Girls. Mothers. Grandmothers.

Anneka cries out, "A mistake to be mad at this guy. I'm not mad at this guy! Are you mad at this guy???? Shouldn't be mad at this guy. Unhunh. He coulda been your brother! He coulda been my dad. Men are innocent lambs, you see. They just fall into these things. They don't use their heads! It's just all pure emotion and hormones! That guy was not a bad person! He was just out there doing what the *law* says is okay to do!! *Law* says it's okay so he does what the *law* says he can do! If the law says it's okay to piss in the post office lobby, well . . . he'd've done that, too . . ."

Chuckles and groans from the women.

The men who had been among them have vanished.

Wise men with arms crossed in the PO doorway smiling haughtily, shaking their heads.

Anneka doesn't stop to take a breath. "*Law* says it was the woman's fault. *Law* says if you aren't wearing head-to-foot blaze, you are likely to be a deer . . . a buck in fact . . . since that gentleman had, far as I know, a bucks-only-license. So the gentleman never even looked to see if the woman had antlers! *Law* says 'go shoot 'em up, fellers. It's your right!' *Law* says, 'Boys, those woods are *yours*. You can shoot up them woods even when them woods ain't actually woods anymore but yards and roads and playgrounds in the trees.' "

"Aw, shut up," says a woman with an armload of mail.

Anneka gives her the finger.

The woman gives Anneka the finger back, tosses her mail onto the dash of her car, drives away peeling her tires.

Another woman standing next to the wise men calls out, "Why don't you shut your trap, girlie, before you get yourself in big trouble. Nobody wants to hear that flap."

Egypt wise men shake their heads, looking pleased, looking greatly entertained.

Anneka persists, "What rights do *we* have? They say there's not as many people shot as there used to be. That's because nobody *dares* go out in the woods in October and November . . . and now December, too, because of that week of black powder. Jesus! Marcie, do you let your kids outdoors durin' those months?"

"Not much," says a soft-spoken woman standing with others along the fender of a silver-blue compact.

"You see! We don't get shot because we don't go out!"

"You talk stupid!" a woman who has crossed the street from the bank says with a snarl. She pretends to be headed into the PO, but keeps lingering.

Anneka yells to her, "*Who* is paying for this goddam blaze orange shit we gotta wear! They don't give it away! You *pay*. And according to law, it has to be so many degrees of brightness so by next year or the year after, it fades, and you've got to go blaze shopping again! Blaze vest, blaze gloves . . . and now the new law . . . blaze hat! It adds up! Why should *I* pay for some sportsman's sport? Why don't *he* pay? Like the state could send us all checks for blaze shopping out of the hunting license fees. You know, to be fair. You know, I'm not going to blame the guys. Like that guy that shot Courtney Gray and the one that shot that other one a couple years back and the kid over to New Hampshire . . . nope, I don't blame the poor bastard that thinks people are deer. He wants that trophy *real* bad so his buddies will think he's a real man. Ain't nuthin' worse than the burnin' need to be a real man. He's a victim, too! He's fucked! He's going through life fucked-up. All of them are. Them that got the red hots to get that trophy . . . and the ones that gotta live with dead people as the price. Don't any of you guys wonder why this is happening? Don't you wonder about this? I'm saying the LAW, our GOVERNMENT don't give a shit about those corpses *or* the killers. BECAUSE . . . it's money behind this and you know it! Guns, ammo, blaze vests, licenses! And those organization fuckers. Sportsman's groups. Most of those groups don't really care if hunters have a nice time out hunting or not. They just want that"—she rubs her fingers together—

"the dues. They want the dues coming in and they *loved* it when Courtney Gray got shot in her yard 'cause all the hunters was shittin' themselves and tremblin' and shiverin', scared they were going to lose their right to hunt in populated towns. I wonder how much food those poor suckers took from their kids' mouths in order to pay the organizations a little more to see this corpse get blamed for being in her own yard, being outside, being near trees, being DEAD!!!!!!"

A few women walk away, shaking their heads, sneering.

A young guy standing with thumbs in his belt shakes *his* head, glances over at the wise men by the PO door.

The wind churns down through the parking lot, slinging litter and leaves.

A woman wearing blaze jacket, tight blue-white curls, Rottweiler in the back of her pickup truck, leans against her truck fender and mutters, "Bet she likes a little meat on the table, don't she? How she thinks it gets there? Magic?"

But many in the group are nodding, agreeing with Anneka. Some women are quiet. Others have begun to all talk at the same time. Wet pavement clops with the hooves of restless horses. PO flag cracks like gunfire. And there go the cars and trucks of late day swinging off the narrow bridge into Egypt . . . and out of Egypt . . . and the thunderish shhhhhhhhhhhhh of the falls and the thrumm-bmmmm-bmmmmmm of the mill and more women and girls converging, and Anneka tells them she has "a plan."

37 | Bett counts the money onto the bureau first, mostly twenties, then presses them into Jeff's right palm.

Jeff says "I appreciate this, Nanna. I wouldn't have asked, but if Coti hadn't needed to get set for this job interview . . . and then getting the gas tank filled to get there and all that stuff, I would've had the money for the header still . . . but . . ."

"Is your appointment right off, dear?" Bett wonders.

"Well . . . no . . . it's one of those places where you just stop in."

"Being so busy as they are, you'd think they would have appointments," she says frowning.

"Well, I just feel so stupid about that other money. You must think I'm a jerk. You must think . . ."

"That's all right, dear. You're not a jerk." She squints at the bills left in her envelope. "Now Jeff, how much was that? Let's check to be sure. Count it out for me, would you?"

Jeff lays the bills on the bureau top and begins to count aloud.

The room here, like the rest of the house, has such handsome oak woodwork. These walls. Painted orange enamel. This room, "the spare," they always used to call it. This room here with the twin bed where Nanna Bett now sleeps alone. Used to be Christmas decorations. Trunks of off-season clothes. And the old spring rocking horse that his sister, Linda, and he had outgrown. If he were to do a painting of this room, he would title it *The Spare*, use an eight-by-eight canvas, entirely and solidly black with a wide-open orange poppy off in one corner, small as a star.

He counts along in his soft still-intact Maine accent . . . counts to the very last twenty-dollar bill.

And then Bett counts it again, her hands trembling, not with old age, but with her obsession with accuracy, which has become outrageous these days. On this third count, the total is the same.

38 | Jeff kneels, takes Eli's shoulders in a fatherly way, squeezing the shoulders, eyes level with Eli's eyes, says firmly, "Eli,   grown-ups *need* some private time together. Understand?"

Eli just stares at the dead center of Jeff's jersey.

Coti is also in the front hall with them, standing by the door in her short black fur jacket and jeans and her yellow-tinted sunglasses and that anguished glut of her beautiful black hair knotted high on the right side of her head with a purple silk lily as big as a hand. Her profile is outlined there against the sidelight panes she is looking out through. Long, long curved neck and chin like in the paintings by the old masters, that same pose struck by the goddesses and madonnas and nymphs in their pensive and yearning forever lives.

"Where are you going?" Eli asks Jeff sternly.

Jeff chortles. "You'd think I was a teenager!"

Eli's shoulder muscles and fat are too quiet against Jeff's palms. Eli asks again, more firmly, "Where. Are. You. Going?"

"You don't have to know all my business for godsakes!" Jeff whines. He releases the shoulders, stands up, brushes off the thighs of his dressy California pants. He snickers. "Jesus. Jesus. Jesus. Kids these days!"

Eli narrows his eyes. "You're going out to buy stuff, aren't you? Where are you getting so much money *now*? You borrow more money from *them?* You're going to spend it all on weirdness, and then we'll all die when the ol' exhaust thing kills us!"

Coti snorts, dark eyes and yellow sunglasses still aimed out at the empty street.

"When are we going back to California?" Eli demands. "You *said* to Mom we were just going to the beach! She must think we got drowned. *Then* you told me we'd only be here *two* days. I bet Mom's crying and the baby inside is probably crying. I miss Mom."

Coti turns around. The reflections on her sunglasses leave her expression unknown.

Jeff says, "Eli, I asked you not to harp about Mumma, didn't I?"

"This is a trick to control us," says Coti to the back of Jeff's head. "He will *not* control us."

"Don't talk about Mumma anymore," says Jeff. "You can think about her, but we don't want to hear it."

"Mom is probably thinking we are dead at the beach," Eli says.

"No, she doesn't," says Jeff.

"And you lied," says Eli.

Jeff sighs. "No, I didn't."

"I heard you. You think I didn't."

Jeff whitens. "So, you little bastard, you've been eavesdropping again. Lurking around and listening. So what are you trying to say you heard?"

Eli narrows his eyes. "Everything."

"Right."

"And you lie to Coti, too."

Coti gets rigid. Only the huge purple silk flower seems to have give.

Things have gotten very, very quiet around the corner in the kitchen where the night nurse and day nurse were having a chat moments ago.

Eli says, "And Smithereens is probably looking everywhere for me . . . like that one that walked a hundred miles looking for his people. Smithereens will probably get lost and starve."

"This is getting soooo stupid," Coti says. "I don't know why you fall for this stuff, J.J. Let's just *go.*"

Eli says, "If I come with you, I promise I won't do anything you hate. I promise I'll just sit there and hardly breathe and you can pretend I'm practically not there."

Coti sighs deeply, returns her gaze to the street.

"You aren't coming back, are you? You're going to be gone for days, huh?" Eli says gravely.

"What kind of guy do you think I am, Eli? Jeepers, we're just going out to do a couple of errands and to get some air and there has to be this scene first. Nanna Peggy and Nanna Bett like baby-sittin' you. Don't you like your own nannas?" he asks incredulously.

And Eli says firmly, arms crossed over his girth, "No."

39 | They explain that they were sent by their mothers to introduce themselves. "That house," one says, pointing. "That house," says the other, pointing the other way. They are both named Joshua. Together they hang out awhile, investigating stuff in the shed and lower rooms of the old barn. Then they lean against the fender of the day nurse's car.

Eli tells them about Smithereens.

He sees understanding in their eyes.

". . . and he was always mine. This was when I was in California where I really live . . . but when my father says we're coming here to visit . . . after he first said it was just the beach, but then he finally tells me we're coming here, I ask him can we go back and get Smithereens? They say no. If I had a laser gun, I'd point it at their heads and say, 'THE CAT IS GOING TOO. TURN BACK NOW OR YOU'LL GET ZAPPED!' He's really a neat cat. Stripes. Bit a baby once."

The two Joshuas are keen on every word . . . except for a kind of foot-to-foot shuffling urgency to tell about their own cats.

Now they all climb on back of a raised wheelless low-bed and run around there. They jump off. They climb back. They jump off. One of the Joshuas pushes Eli over the edge and Eli lays on the hard ground a few seconds, looking like he might be hurt. But now he is laughing. Wildly.

40 | It's fairly long into the day that Peggy sees the Camaro is in the driveway, but no Jeff, no Coti. Then at her desk doing some figuring in the accounts, her desk which faces the shorter wall of glass panes through which she can see the shedway to the old barn, she realizes her father-in-law's year-old silver-gray Ram Charger is missing. And Forest doesn't have it. He has the pickup. She asks Bett why the vehicle is missing. Bett's answer is a giggle and, "Don't plague me, Peggy."

"I'm not," Peggy tells her. "Did you give Jeff the keys?"

Bett says no.

They look for the keys in the front hallway cabinet drawer. Neatly vanished.

41 | It is the IGA parking lot. Cold wind rips at the manes and tails of the six dark horses and the one dark horse with the spotted rump. Rips at the sleeves and hair of the riders. And the laces of the riders' sneakers wag. Double laces and high-topped puffy sneakers being the rage with kids these days . . . they all got to have them. And the wind burns the riders' faces. Cheeks pink. Noses red.

Many people stop to talk with the riders. Mostly women. Some are pushing grocery carts. The rider of the Appaloosa writes down names. Everyone is intent on what is being said. Now and then someone points toward the nearest mountain or down the road. Beyond the farther, much taller mountain, a little pink trembly sun falls into the firs.

42 | Where's Jeff and Coti? Who knows? It's been two days. There's no bother to set up the dining room table. Kitchen table and the kitchen glare are good enough.

A little surprise. Forest comes in for supper though it looked like he wouldn't make it. Here he is. Peggy pushes her chair back and goes after an extra plate. Forest says they have finished all three leach fields and the Cooke job. There's both exhaustion and celebration in his eyes. He has grease on his suspenders. Splats of clay on his wool pants. He has missed a shave. He sinks into a seat, lays his glasses on the table, and holds his face a minute.

It's Bett's night to cook so nothing's burned, nothing's exotic or weird or fun, and everything comes out done exactly at the same time.

"That's pizza cheese on top," Bett tells Eli. "The kind that is stretchy. I used three whole packages thinking you might like it."

Eli nods.

Forest still has his face in his hands. He's very, very, very quiet.

The phone rings and Peggy leaves the table.

Forest drops his hands, slips his glasses back on, says "Yummm," draws the pan of American chop suey closer.

Eli's eyes have followed Peggy all the way to her disappearing point at the office doorway.

Forest says, "So, Eli, my man. Howzit goin'?"

Eli says a polite "Good," now watching Forest's hands poking around in the chop suey for extra chunks of hamburger.

The boy has a plastic dinosaur beside his plate. A loan from one of the Joshuas. It's Tyrannosaurus Rex. Stands tall as a milk pitcher. Takes up too much room on the little table. But nobody suggests removing it.

Forest's eyes behind his glasses are now most merry. He chews lustily, forks a heap of pickles onto his plate, reaches for bread.

The boy swallows at last, something he's had in his mouth unswallowable for a long moment.

Bett brushes crumbs from the table's edge into her tea saucer. She says in a most hearty and grandmotherly way, "Have more, Eli. That little bit wouldn't keep a bird alive." She pushes the plate of wheat bread toward him. Pushes the butter his way.

Eli looks hard at Forest and says, "You ever seen a laser gun before?"

Forest stops chewing, grins. "Nope. Never have." Annoyed by his beard stubble, he rubs his jaw against the shoulder of his dark work shirt.

Eli says, "If I had a laser gun, I'd use it all the time."

"You would?" Forest fills his mouth, then says around his mouthful, "What would a guy do with a laser gun?"

"In case somebody weird busted these windows and came in here . . . or sneaked in here, you know."

Forest jerks a thumb toward the office door. "I've got plenty of guns to deal with that. You want to stop a prowler, a nice thirty-ought-six will do just fine."

"Oh, Forest, don't." Bett sighs.

"You ever have anyone bust in here?" Eli wonders.

Forest narrows his eyes. "Eli, my man. This place is like the Alamo."

Eli repositions Tyrannosaurus Rex over beside his milk glass so that one of the creature's hands seems to have a grip on the rim. He says, "If somebody came in here . . . like *got* in here somehow and was kidnapping . . . like you know, tying us up, tying us in the mouth so we couldn't scream an' stuff . . . would you shoot them?"

"Damn right."

Bett giggles. "Oh, Forest . . . my goodness. You shouldn't tell him things like that. Let's talk about something nice."

Forest looks into her eyes. "Name something nice. Help get us started."

"This nice supper. We are fortunate to have this nice supper. There are people in other countries with nothing to eat."

Eli says, "I'm going to get a laser gun someday. Scientists are getting laser guns improved. They ZAP. You know . . . faster than the speed of light."

Forest hunkers across his plate, his face close to Eli's face. With his tongue he is pushing meat from his back teeth. He says, "Lead bullet will make a hole this big in the back of the head." He has spread his whole right hand in front of Eli's face.

Bett has lost track of the conversation, stretching her feet out to one side to see how well her new Hush Puppies are wearing, turning each foot one way and then the other.

Peggy returns to the kitchen, pulls out her chair. "I took the phone off the hook. Otherwise I'll collapse from hunger and will need to be fed through a tube."

"Who was it?" Forest asks.

"The Gowens. I told them you'd call them back about sevenish."

Forest, both cheeks now loaded with chop suey and bread, just nods.

43 The Marlin in Eli's hands drifts and wavers.

Forest says they have other guns for little fellers, that a nice Daisy would be the gun for Eli. Forest says he knows where he could get one if Eli were interested. Forest also says a gun that shoots a projectile of any kind is not a toy. He tells of three people he knows who lost eyes to close-range BBs. A gun is a tool . . . like a car or truck or backhoe. You have to always pay attention, learn the rules, and use your head. Forest says "a gun is a tool" a few times, but a thing keeps coming into his throat, a thing more like lust and unrelieved yearning.

He says, "My father . . . you know . . . Gramp F.D. upstairs there . . . he said in *his* time, deer season was bigger than Christmas . . . bigger than *anything*." He watches Eli's face for reaction. Eli is nodding, nodding . . . with politeness. His pale eyes in dark lashes, never warm, always flinty . . . now moving away from Forest's face to the Marlin, along the length of coated wood and blued metal.

Forest goes on, "You worked like hell all spring and summer and early fall breaking your ass to get food in, get the hay in, fill the woodshed, take care of what you had to do with your cattle and hogs . . . 'twas your last chance to patch up 'n' chink walls, chimney, roofs, and all. Everybody you knew was in this, getting the work up so they could get lickety-split out into the woods and orchards to hunt. Everyone you saw had him a rifle and was there like you were. 'Twas like you were all part of . . . this thing you knew was yours. It was there for you. Your reward. All together . . . you all had this reward. And there were so many deer then . . . they were everywhere. . . . All there just waitin' for you. And all the guys then, Dad says, were all muscled up from all that liftin' and pitchin' and squattin' and climbin' they'd done all summer and it 'twas like . . . like you were an army. And it was a high feelin' . . . better than Christmas. It 'twas like a . . . like . . . the peak of your life . . . 'cause you *were* in the peak of your life. You were strong as a horse and had a sharp eye. And that meat on the table proved it. And every fall for as long as you could bring down a deer, it 'twas the peak of your life."

Eli's grip on the rifle tightens. He aims it at each deer head along the wall, then lowers it. He says, "Yep, that's neat." But he doesn't look Forest in the eye. Eli is embarrassed. Because this feels kind of like one of those birds-'n'-bees talks. He aims the rifle again at the nearest deer head. And Forest is watching him. Forest's eyes are on him. Forest's eyes. One widening. One screwing down, tightening. Dark eyes. Old eyes. Guy of all those old, old ways. And here's Eli . . . Eli Johnson here . . . here in the here and now.

44 | A wedding? A party? A death? So many cars and pickups parked in the lot behind the Johnsons' brick colonial. And the door that reveals the stairway up to the DiBias apartment keeps opening and shutting as people hurry inside.

Up in the apartment it's standing room only. Young kids and babies zigzagging among legs. The young girls, mothers, and grandmothers don't all speak, but the voices that do speak are charged:

"She was in her own yard!"

"Her little girl, just walking age, was already inside the house. The mother had gone back out to get things out of the stroller."

"He . . . the *sportsman* was about four hundred feet or so between her house and her neighbors'. You see, there was about eight hundred feet between the houses. And it's okay, you see . . . it's okay by *law* to open fire with a rifle when you are in eight hundred feet of trees." This is Anneka speaking, Anneka aflame, Anneka ready.

"So in the eyes of the law, eight hundred feet is woods."

"Dear, in the eyes of *some*, eight hundred feet of trees constitutes *wilderness!*"

Chortles.

"That's because most guys these days don't want to get too far from 'civilization' or they'll get scared."

"They don't want to get too far from their VCR's, actually."

More chortles.

And a baby fussing.

"Anyway, because she had that white tassel hat on so close to the *wilderness*, the law says it was her own fault she was shot." Again Anneka, leaning from foot to foot, rubbing her white hair.

"There's one of those big lobbyists . . . big *sportsmen's* group, the one Erik got suckered into that sends him newsletters and you wouldn't believe how flaky they talk in those newsletters. The big guy of the organization says . . . now get this . . . listen to this . . . he says hunting isn't as dangerous as cross-country skiing and hiking!"

Groans and giggles.

"But listen . . . you know . . . I've never once, not *once* had a ski pole shot through my shoulder and lung by some skier four hundred feet away. And no hiking boots have come whizzing at me while I've been standing in my own yard or anybody's yard."

"I heard that same argument with Don's friends only they said tennis."

Howls.

"Watch that tennis racket sailing out of the woods . . . whoops! Wonk!"

Howls. Howls. Howls.

"Well, you see . . . the only thing *sportsmen* ever worry about is themselves, the *players* of the game."

"Of course."

"Any of you hear how they said it was that little gal's own fault because she was from out of state and didn't know she was supposed to wear blaze orange everywhere she goes during *the season*."

"During the *holy days*."

Couple of chuckles. Couple of amens.

And Anneka quiet now. Arms akimbo. Eyes moving from face to face watching this fire build.

"So what about that school bus that was shot at while it was going down the road?"

"And the people with the picture window!"

"Guess they should paint school buses blaze orange so it won't be the kiddies' own fault they almost got pasted."

"Yeah . . . right . . . yellow ain't bright enough."

"Blaze orange is the *legal* color. If it's not *blaze* orange, you haven't got *the* color."

"And don't forget, it has to be a certain *degree* of brightness of blaze. Read the law pamphlet there."

"How do you measure degrees of brightness?"

"Good question."

"Now the guy who shot the school bus. What in hell was he thinking?"

"Thought he had himself a big yellow buck."

"*Very* big buck."

"Well, maybe a buck driving a school bus full of little skippers."

Howls of laughter.

"But what I'm gettin' at is, the *law* says if it ain't blaze Day-Glo commercial orange, that special pricey orange, you are considered 'game' in their eyes . . . eyes of *the law*."

"The picture window people must've been from out of state, too. Or they'd have had themselves blaze orange drapes."

Snickers.

"HE PUSHED ME!!" a small child yells.

"Stop it, Justin!"

"I'm not from out of state. I was born here and my folks go way back and *I* forget sometimes and *I* don't think to wear my blaze every time I step out of the house."

"Jeepers . . . yes! I got all the way to the library yesterday and realized I forgot mine."

"Right. There's trees on the way to the library and then there's that big spruce in front of the library. Might be a big buck lurking in the shadows of that spruce."

Chuckles.

"A few years ago Michelle and I were sitting on that guardrail by the covered bridge and this guy comes roaring up, stops next to us in his Bronco or whatever . . . a thing like a Bronco. You know how guys like that all have to drive special *sportsmen-looking* vehicles. Anyway, there he is . . . this guy . . . older guy . . . whitish hair, grayish . . . whatever.

Has his window rolled down. He says, 'You girls seen a deer run this way?' Michelle and I thought it was a riot at the time, but now . . . it doesn't seem so funny. You know, when you get older and wiser, you change."

"I don't hang my clothes out anymore in deer season. You're bound to have some white dish towels or white socks or undies."

"Wouldn't want the old man's jockey shorts blasted."

Howls and high giggles which set off two babies crying.

"Chip doesn't wear underwear except in winter . . ."

"Oooo-la-la!"

"I'm going to be looking at Chip in a different way now."
Sniggering.

"Well, *lots* of guys don't wear underwear, Laurie!"

"Is that right? How izit you know this?"

A lot of whoops and ahhhs and promptings especially from the three Soule sisters leaning along the kitchen sink and drainboard.

"Well, it's just a commonly known fact."

Some solemn agreement here.

"Back to blaze orange, okay?" a less-fun person suggests. "There was a guy a few years back around the time Stacy was born. He was hunting and got shot. I can't remember if he died . . ."

"Maybe just paralyzed or blind."

"Right . . . anyway . . . what I remember is that he was wearing blaze. But the news guys said it in a way that sorta *said* it was his own fault he was shot because he wasn't wearing *enough* blaze . . . only cap and gloves. It seemed stupid to me at the time because no deer would be wearing *any* blaze . . . I mean the whole *thing* is stupid . . . a deer is a deer and a human is a human no matter what they're wearing if you are looking with BOTH eyes. Anyone who is that blind or that excited ain't fit to be loose with a *spoon* let alone a high-powered firearm. Like . . . I mean . . . with that mentality, how much blaze is enough?"

"Well, more than whatever it was you were wearing when you get shot."

"Right."

"Okay . . . so here's what it says in the law book on blaze. They call it 'hunter orange.' And this is what they say, '*HUNTER ORANGE means a daylight fluorescent orange color with a dominant wavelength between*

595 and 605 nanometers, excitation purity not less than 85% and luminance factor of not less than 40%.' "

Silence.

One big snort of laughter followed by many giggles and titters.

"Guess now we gotta purchase us some kinda special gauge to measure our brightness."

"Yuh, right . . . and if you're not bright enough . . . like your vest and hat get a little dirty or faded, you've got to buy new ones each year."

"Capitalist plot."

"I'm gettin' madder by the minute."

"You think legislators and the governor get a cut on the blaze orange gear biz?"

"There's no tellin' what they are all up to."

"So it's not the law that *nonhunters* wear blaze until you get killed or blinded and so forth, then suddenly, after the fact, it's the law, the rule of the game so to speak. Guys making the laws don't come right out and say, okay folks if you live near a tree, even if you don't hunt, it is the law you wear head to foot blaze Day-Glo orange. Because *that* would make a lot of people realize how bad this whole thing is and there'd be more fuss from the public, right? So instead, they just let somebody get picked off now and then and that's when it becomes *the law* indirectly. Know what I mean?"

"Yeah . . . if the law stated that everybody *had* to wear blaze from their toes to their eyeballs, it would hit home."

"Lotta fashion folks would be pissed."

"Yeah . . . and all those layers could be kinda hot on warm days."

"Especially while walking around your living room in front of your picture window."

Laughs.

"Seriously . . . why should we, the people, have to go through all this shit for a whole *month* just so a few guys can enjoy their sport?"

"More than a month, Deb. Don't forget that week for black powder in December. Everybody forgets that."

"Right. They keep expanding the season with all these new ways to bag their deer. Like bows and arrows and shit. Next it'll be spiked club season. Before you know it, it'll be the whole friggin' year!"

"That bow hunting is a real problem . . . those silly-looking spotted suits. You know. Camouflage. Jeepers! Lenny and I were coming back from New Hampshire one time last year and there were a pair of them walking along the road after sunset . . . *right in the road* and Lenny almost ran over one of them. Lenny says if you run over a hunter, you'd probably go to prison for the rest of your life."

Moans of miserable agreement.

"Anyway, why should we all go through this worry, keeping our kids in, our pets in . . . and even worry aside, even if it were just inconvenience, this is *major* inconvenience. Why? A *sport* isn't important enough for all this."

"The old days are over. There's too many houses now. Too much population."

"Population is way too big."

"If guys wanted to keep hunting, they shouldn't have made any kids. Kids grow up and need houses. More houses, less woods."

"And that tradition argument they have is a little weak. Guys say, 'We've always done it. It's part of our past. Our ancestry and all that.' So when guys in the South got laws passed saying you can't lynch black people anymore, you think those guys whined, 'Oh, but it's tradition! Me and Dad have always done it together. It's part of our heritage'?"

"You bet they did."

"And nowadays guns and hunting are *big business*."

"You can say *that* again! And their lobbies are wicked big."

"You ain't going ta see no changes no matter how many people get shot . . . 'less it 'twas the President or somethin'."

"You are so right. They'll just point to somebody who fell on their ski pole and say . . . see . . . there's less people being shot than those in ski accidents . . . or tennis elbow. And people seem satisfied with that kind of bullshit. Nobody questions it!"

"Makes you wonder 'bout the public's IQ."

"And then there's all this whimperin' about the right to bear arms. I don't care how many guns they bear. They can bear all the guns they want, one in every pocket, twenty rifles tied to their heads. I'm not suggestin' they take that right away . . . to *bear* 'em. What I want to see taken away is their right to shoot into the wind."

"Some people say just post your land. But that's a big joke."

"Right. It costs you money and then you gotta run around and tack all those signs up and measure between the signs. Imagine if you have a few acres, how much of your time is used for *their* little sports?"

"And what if you're really old, it's not so easy to get around doing all that climbing and hammering. And then all a guy has to do to *unpost* you is rip one sign down. Then all your work is for nothing."

"That's right. And anyway you could still get shot at by some asshole shooting from the land next to you that's not posted."

"Or while you're walking on the road or out on the paper company land. It's a friggin' war zone."

"Ahh yes . . . that's what these guys like about it. Kinda like playin' army. So okay . . . it's nature that makes guys want to play army . . . guys got the take-it-over win 'em feelin' in their blood . . . okay . . . but sometimes we have to be *practical,* too. Playing army isn't *PRACTICAL.*"

"I hate posting. It's just not . . . you know . . . friendly. NO TRES-PASSING. Sounds like a goddam yuppie."

"And signs all over the place are ugly."

"Posting means *nobody* is allowed on your land. But if you just want no hunting, you can't put up NO HUNTING signs . . . well, you can . . . but they don't have any legalness about 'em because the State owns the deer. The State owns all deer, even those walkin' on your land. Only the State can say who hunts and who doesn't. So you are stuck with posting NO TRESPASSING signs."

"Well, Dave and I have our land posted because of the sheep. We can't have people shooting our sheep."

"I . . . just . . . I can't imagine doing it. I'd be awake all night wondering if someone was ripping them down. It would turn into a worse aggravation."

"And like Patty says . . . posting makes us out like yuppies. You know how they act like they own the world. Yuppies want to keep *everybody* out."

"They just want to OWN."

"I hate that."

"That's *their* way of playin' army."

"I don't want anybody thinking I'm a friggin yuppie."

"What's a yuppie?"

"Jeepers, Carla, where you been?"

"Carla's on low pilot."

Snickers and an affectionate thump to Carla's shoulder.

"All I want is everybody to be happy."

"Robby hunts. He knows I came over here this afternoon and he thinks it's good we make a fuss."

"Kenny says the hunting organizations try to make out like hunters are all these wholesome type guys. But they're not. Kenny hunts, too, but whenever he's around a bunch of them, he says, the way those guys talk is *not* wholesome. He said most guys get their rocks off on a creature's suffering and love to hash it over afterward. He says they have no respect for creatures. He says they have an asshole attitude toward the deer . . . and an asshole attitude toward most people, especially ones they think are 'weak.' "

"Pete Sargent's dog was shot. The warden knew who did it. But he refused to tell Pete anything. Dog was on Pete's land, too . . . a very old dog. Could hardly stand. But the warden just didn't want to talk about it."

"So maybe even if the news guys *wanted* to report killed pets, there's no way for them to find out."

"And after a few more humans get shot, they'll make a law that head-to-foot blaze isn't enough. We'll be required to wear bullet-proof vests and helmets."

"Or that we should evacuate . . . rent a room in a hotel in a city somewhere for the duration."

"All for sports."

"Wholesome clean fun."

"Well, here's what Robby thinks. The law should state that there be no hunting in areas within two miles of a home, a school, or any building . . . or a road."

"Chip says a bullet can travel up to a mile and a half."

"Right. The lead starts to lose power by then and drop but it's still in motion."

"Some guys say that a bullet would never get that far in wooded areas because the trees would stop a bullet before it gets two miles. But listen close. From my bedroom window when the leaves are off, I can see Helen Greenlaw's yard light and we have almost a mile and a half of thick woods between us. I can see that light and light does not turn corners. Light would travel like a bullet, right? Maybe straighter. But basically the same."

"So even if there's really a deer, if they miss that deer, the bullet keeps going. So being careful that it's *really* a deer isn't enough."

"But they *aren't* careful! Here's how I figure it. Look at drivers. How many people go the speed limit, don't tailgate, and don't pass on hills, curves, and intersections?"

A grim silence.

"So there's your answer."

"So what do we do?"

"Well, this is why we're here. Anneka's got an idea. Anneka, tell 'em your idea. Wait till you all hear this. It's pretty wild."

And so it seems an open-and-shut case, blow after blow, this ax of hard facts, shrieks of reprisals, their buzzing strategies, only rags left of their fidelity. The ranks of Egypt's people are torn . . . irreparable after today.

Anneka leans in, her young, booming voice rushing on and on and the plan is a good one, they say. Yes, yes. Let's do it. Let's go!

45 | Their room is like all of the upstairs . . . cold. It is wallpapered in red. Not a restful color.

Cold red room.

Forest begins to unlace his boots.

Piled around Peggy's side of the bed are loaded accordion folders with dates printed in Magic Marker . . . dates going back . . . dates like Jan. to Dec. 1979. On top of her dresser are the remembrances of childhood. Large plastic horses with riders. Some fashioned after the TV westerns. Dale Evans. Roy Rogers. Others are out of history. And that one big bronze horse with its reins made of key chain through the holes on either side of its mouth. If you had put your hands in your mouth after playing with the bronze horse, the taste was bad. Today you might taste it just by looking, that bitter taste never far from memory.

On the red print wall are ribbons and framed photos of Peggy's real live horses of the past. Horses jumping hedges and rails . . . thoroughbred horses . . . with the rider dressed in a dark jacket and cap, dark hair . . . a thoroughbred-looking girl. The most recent photo shows Peggy with hand clasped to the halter of her terrible Mars. That photo also shows the fender of Peggy's brother's Audi, the Audi looking like some sort of blot or photographic mistake. Only the fine, trembling dark horses seem right in the company of Peggy Johnson.

In bed, Peggy waits.

Freed of its broad metal clip, her hair opens out in fingers on the pillow. It's not what you'd call thick hair. But always clean, brushed, dark brown, and bright like polish. Her gown. Lilac. She has called it her "new gown" for two years, for the years are fast, aren't they? And her old gowns were so ravaged by wear when the lilac one came into her life that it seemed a milestone of some kind.

Forest says, "Those silver things, Peg, . . . you know . . . on the cupcakes we just put in our stomachs. What are they made of?"

"Silver," says she.

Finished with unlacing his first boot, Forest lets it thwomp to the floor. "What are they really made of?"

Peggy rassles around a little under the covers to get into a position on her back, a position where she can watch him better. "You don't believe me? You want me to go down there and get the bottle for you? It says right on the bottle that the ingredients include silver."

"So inside me right now is silver."

"It says on the label that it's for decoration only, never eat it as candy. Probably if you ate ten bottles of them all in a sitting, you'd be doing the wrong thing. But all you had was a few."

He is silent.

Peggy stares at the nape of his neck with its dark hair cut straight across it. "Forest, is this another one of your creepy little comments on my cooking?"

He works to remove the prosthetic piece of leg and foot with its boot laced tightly to it. He says, "I'll never eat them again."

Peggy pushes herself up.

Now a rustle. He is tugging off a wool sock and there's the re-emergence of his only foot . . . a foot with just two toes.

Peggy watches the back of his neck. Even as he yanks his suspenders away, unbuckles the belt, pulls off shirts, it's always the back of the neck that is dearest . . . one of those throwbacks from school where you spent those encumbered million endless days in your desk and the closest living thing was the back of the boy's neck in front of you, that landscape of its hairs and spine nubs. Different boys at different times. It didn't matter. It was the nape of the neck that counted. Better than a face. Unconfronting.

Forest is sliding under the covers, folding his glasses with care. Peggy stares hard at him doing this simple thing, the hand reaching to position the glasses by his tumbler of water. Even if she is reading when he joins her for bed, she'll put the book up and watch him.

Forest says, "For the man who has everything, a pair of silver-lined kidneys." He cackles softly to himself. Then his voice deepens. "How much did the damn things cost?"

Peggy sighs.

Forest says, "Not like a new watch or anything, huh?"

Peggy smiles.

"Something we could hock maybe to help make a payment on this new truck? Or one of the insurances? Let's see . . . how many insurances do we keep? You see, I'm just keeping my eyes sharp for valuables to sell when things get tighter than they are now . . . Jesus, we're so tight now, Peg, . . . I just don't know where we're going."

Peggy switches off her little lamp. She knows all he is saying. She knows, she knows, she knows. Over the years in a marriage and business together, you are yoked, harnessed, twinned. She slides down into the covers and aligns her front to his back, moves her feet along the backs of his one ankle. Her toes are like fingers this way. Her feet are whole feet. Unlike his, her toes deft, clasping. Sometimes he says Peggy has monkey feet. It seems all daytimes that revolve around the perpetuation of big machinery, roads, phone, and paperwork speed toward this moment when each night there is this good thing with the feet. Peggy considers sometimes how when you looked at a boy's flawlessly tawny neck in school, you never dreamed . . . you just never imagined the way it would really be, the way in which a man would really need you.

46 | After four days of no Jeff, no Coti, and no reappearance of F.D.'s new Ram Charger, Peggy wonders about a barely audible humming noise coming from Jeff and Coti's room. She opens the door.

47 | Sometimes Peggy keeps secrets from Forest and Bett. Aren't secrets kind of like lies? Well, *white* lies. White secrets? Those tools used to spare those you love from pain.

Why does Forest have to know about the electric heater? Heater running on high for four days to keep a room warm that no one was in. Electric heat being like throwing dollar bills into the river! And the grille of that heater partly facing the bed and bunched quilt. Quilt was hot and stank of its near-burning point.

And even that about the room which wasn't dangerous edged toward danger. Everywhere, everything in twisted heaps. Clothes and food wrappers mixed. Soda cans. Pizza crusts. Glasses half full of spoiled milk. A room of garbage.

Peggy touched nothing but the electric heater. She carried it to the cellar, hid it behind the stairs.

The door to the room is closed now. No one has to know what she knows.

48 It's the fifth day since Jeff and Coti have been gone in the Ram Charger. Gone where?

"Trip to Mars," says Eli disgustedly.

The nannas don't reveal any of their guesses.

Nanna Bett takes cookies from the freezer so Eli and the Joshuas can have a nice time. All they talk about is the Joshuas' video games. And the video games Eli has back in California. Here at Johnsons' there are no video games.

49 It's late when Forest comes in from Kiwanis. He undresses by the bed in the dark and Peggy watches the solid silhouette of him against the light of a waxing moon.

To Forest the room smells a smidgen of Peggy's costly thoroughbred light-stepping horses. But perhaps the horses are just one of the many things weighing too heavy on Forest's mind.

Before he swings his legs under the covers, the phone by the bed rings. He snatches it, glaring at the lighted clock.

What he hears is stuffy-nosed crying, the kind of crying that means it's just a small part of a lot of crying. The only word he recognizes is his own name.

His voice speaks with a nasty edge. "What? What? What?"

Peggy raises her head so she won't miss what he's saying.

"I can't hear you," Forest says deeply. Is it Anneka? he wonders. Anneka *faking* tears to torment him? He is so sick of Anneka. She is in and out of his head all hours, cool as ice. She is up to something. Her whole existence on this earth is a major plan to destroy him. He is not a paranoid man. This is reality. A thing natural as a chick stepping from the egg.

The crying voice on the phone says, "Is Jeff there, Forest? Has he *been* there? He . . . he . . ." It is now recognizable to Forest . . . this, not Anneka DiBias . . . but the thick-necked voice of a Bean . . . Amy . . . Eli's mother.

Forest sighs.

Amy sniffs. "He took Eli almost three weeks ago and hasn't come back. You know how Jeff is . . . he kind of . . . you know . . . doesn't bother to let people know where he is. But this time he's got Eli! And it's right in the middle of school. First I thought maybe something had happened. Being during school like that. Now I'm wondering if he came back home with him to see you guys . . . Forest? Have you seen them?"

Forest doesn't answer.

"Forest? Are you there?"

"Yep."

"Have you heard from Jeff? Has he been in touch with you?"

"I don't know what I can do to help you, Amy."

There's a squeaking mashing noise, her crying resumed, perhaps into the knuckles of a hand. Now she hollers. "I knew it! I knew it! He's gone back up there, hasn't he? He's there, isn't he? The legal-aid guys said you were the first place to check . . . but I . . . I didn't believe that. I figured he was just over to some friends. These new friends of his. I've never met them. But you can just *imagine*. I called my folks tonight, too. But they said they hadn't seen anything of him over to your place. They haven't been over that way much. But then . . ." She snivels. "He *is* there, isn't he?"

Forest is silent. He is sitting on the edge of the bed, his one flesh foot against the cold floor, one fist on one bare knee. The fist opens, closes. Like giving blood.

Amy says huskily, "Jeff's planning something, isn't he? He's going for a divorce, isn't he? He's trying to get custody, huh? This isn't something I figured him for . . . but the legal-aid guys know everything people are apt to do that you'd never *dream* of."

Silence.

"I'm going to find a way up there and I'm going to *kill* Jeff if I get ahold of him . . . wring his friggin' neck."

Forest breathes into the phone to signal his impatience.

"I *will!*" Amy insists. "I'll wring his friggin' neck. He don't give a shit about Eli. You don't know what I've been through with Jeff! He's not normal. He . . ."

Forest hangs up.

Peggy says, "Was that Amy?"

"Correct."

"She's upset."

"Correct."

"She wasn't a perfect wife, but . . ."

"Correct."

50 They have not slept, yet there's difficulty in gauging the passing of time. Minutes? Hours? The gray moony light of the window seems unchanged.

Against Peggy's knees and ankles, there's the feel of Forest *waiting*, his body in a rigor mortis of waiting.

And then the phone rings as Peggy knows Forest knows it will ring. And they both know it is not Amy. Forest reaches, brings the phone to his ear. "Yes?"

"Forest. What's up?" Ernest Bean. Amy's father. Ernest Bean of many, many Beans who could all move on you like one single deft entity . . . something like a bulldozer does when it pulls you into itself by your feet.

Forest says, rising slowly back into his sitting position, "You need something?"

Ernest Bean says, "We'd like to have Eli over for a little visit. And my girl wants to talk with Eli on the phone 'n' see how he's doin'."

Forest says nothing. Peggy puts her hand out. Forest is trembling. This fear, this rage . . . it isn't something new. It is a thing that's like a map of roads and right-of-ways and streams and high and low elevations and boundaries and territories and covenants. A fear, a rage, a grief, a hatred turned inside out and around into infinity like two mirrors facing.

Forest's hatred for Forest.

Peggy jerks her hand back.

Forest is saying, "You want something, you go get yourself a lawyer. We aren't supposed to be talking." And he disconnects the phone. Sits there on the edge of the bed in the dark looking at the blue-gray window.

Peggy believes Ernest Bean's family wouldn't play tricks if Eli were to go over for a visit. Peggy thinks they are sincere. That they just want to see Eli and that Amy should talk with Eli and that Eli needs his mother's voice. Peggy believes there's enough of Eli to go around, that he's a big person, a grand guy. Peggy knows Forest knows the Beans can't afford a lawyer and that the legal-aid program in Maine is nearly busted . . . that the whole state government here is nearly busted. Peggy knows that the Johnsons are pretty well busted, that the Johnsons can't afford a lawyer either, but that Forest is counting on the fact that the Beans *think* the Johnsons can afford lawyers, that the Johnsons are financially set folks.

Against the gray light, Forest's bare shoulders, the musculature of the arms and thickened waist look ready for fight . . . a kind of fight to the death. Preordained, even as it is silly. But is, she knows, the way of the world.

51 | Coming into the bedroom midmorning, Peggy is startled to see Forest there. He is back-to. He doesn't turn to show her his face. He says simply, "It's gone . . . the lucky hundred-dollar bill. See?"

Peggy steps in closer.

Outdoors the rain is heavy. Warm rain. Weird hot rain in the cool heart of fall.

Peggy says, "Well, it's been a long time . . . maybe . . . you know . . . since you last looked. I hardly look at it anymore. It's probably been a while since *you* actually looked."

"Not really."

"You look at it a lot?"

"Yes."

They both stare at the frame which is blank now . . . black paper backing like a modern-art painting of doom.

Forest turns, has a big grin. "Have you been watching the news lately? Maybe it's the insurance companies . . . their new way of assured payment. Or maybe the utilities. Remote control cash suck-up machines. No need to ask for a rate hike. Just press the button to the cash sucker and whammo . . . whoooshhh!" He smacks one fist into the palm of the other hand, then drives the fisted hand forward like a rocket.

Peggy blinks.

52 | Tonight the road commissioner, Forest Johnson, leans his head back against the wall, eyelids lowered dreamily behind his glasses. Seems there's something lost and familiar in the buzzing fluorescent overhead lights of Town Hall. Forest Johnson, spanking-clean white shirt under his broad suspenders. Clean-shaven spanking-white face. He has come to talk about roads. But nobody of this finance committee tonight has gotten around to roads yet. They haven't even gotten around to any of their business yet. Just a lot of stewing over Miracle City as usual.

"So how *can* we get this problem squared away?" one committeeman wonders . . . big-jowled flush-faced fellow in a maroon alligator shirt. "How can we keep things looking halfway decent with all the riffraff we're dealing with here?" He shakes his head slowly, sadly.

"Are we talking junky-looking yards again?" a high-pitched-voiced, narrow-necked fellow pipes up. His reindeer sweater is homemade, done quite handsomely in browns and yellows. "'Cause I was drivin' up Rummery last week and I see that Johnson place is still a sight. Any of you gone past there lately?"

They all look over at Forest for a reaction.

One corner of his mouth flickers a smile.

"Well, that new GMC that's on the lot looks real sharp. I say it brings the valuation of the property up at least twenty thousand since it makes everything else there look more civilized."

Few chuckles.

"Yeah . . . but the old heaps are still there. Jesus, Johnson, . . . what're you doin' over there . . . collectin' 'em?"

A lot of delighted chuckles.

"He's got his mother bribin' our code man with cookies. That's what I heard."

"Shit! Is that all it takes?"

"Go to hell," Forest says with a snort.

A selectman, quiet so far, leans with forearms on the table. Spirals of sweet Borkum Riff. Spirals of sweet aftershave. Freckled bald head. Tolerant fatherly smile. "Okay. Okay. So what about Miracle City?"

"Barry says three more trailers and two more sheds or whatever you call them have gone up over there since . . . when was it Barry was over there? . . . August?"

A committeewoman, also with jowls, but also with a lot of hardwarishly clanking jewelry, replies breathlessly, "September twenty-third."

The freckle-headed selectman smiles. He looks more satisfied than worried.

A snowy haired older woman pores over paperwork, occasionally raises her eyes. Has little to say. There are also two older men in work uniforms, one on either end of the table. Finance committeemen for years, they are so comfortable here they sometimes fall asleep.

The big radiators along the wall start up a hissing and clanging.

Road Commissioner Forest Johnson closes his eyes. There's an un-opened root beer balanced on the left knee of his dress-up work pants, a kind of trick he often performs here at Town Hall when the talk goes on and on and on and on. He looks asleep too but for the can so deftly balanced. And the talk up and down the beaverboard table goes on and on and on and on.

"Things have gotten out of hand," a committeeman says.

"The problem isn't just Miracle City. It's all over town."

"Yeah . . . and if you don't believe it, take a gander up Seavey Road. And Barry's had nothing but complaints from Six Fields Estates and Silver Heights and The Village at Cold Rain Pond. You put in some decent homes, you can't expect those home owners to be happy with a mess like that on Seavey and all that up on Horne Hill bringing down their property values."

The town's newest selectman, very young, dark yellow hair combed wet, drinks water from a mug. He drinks a lot of water. He watches the others speak and nods respectfully.

Maroon alligator shirt guy says, "Some of these old properties've got quite an accumulation. Maybe they've got some goodies under all that shit."

"Buried treasure, huh?" chortles the reindeer sweater.

Many chuckles.

The young selectman says softly, "A lot of that stuff is used . . . you know for repairs. Or for trade. It's just the old way of life. It's just the way they live."

"Yeah," the reindeer sweater smirks. "We know."

"Yeah, but Mike, this isn't the Great Depression anymore. There's no *need* for it. It's not acceptable anymore. How do you get it through the heads of people like that?"

Forest Johnson's eyes open wide, glitter blackly up into the buzzing lights, as if he knows the wonderfully ironic punch line to this riddle. Or as if he knows of some mischief, like a firecracker under the folding chair of one of them here. Or a mouse.

"But where will it stop?" one of them wonders, wearily rubbing his eyes and face. "I'm referring now to Miracle City. I've given up on Seavey Road ages ago. What concerns me is if they get another beat-up trailer or particle-board shack going up every month over to Miracle City . . . that's twenty-four a year. It's like cancer. It's like cavities in your teeth!"

"Yeah . . . and some of those families aren't from here. Letourneau is bringing them in from other places now. Bunch from Lewiston, I heard. You want all the homeless riffraff from the whole country right here!? Jesus! Next he'll be bringing in boat people. And them from Ethiopia 'n' what not. What do we need to do to stop this guy? The National Guard? Our codes are nothing unless we can enforce them."

"There isn't much land left over at Letourneau's that's buildable anyway. Mostly just rock and ledge and swamp."

"You think a small thing like *no land* would faze them? They'll always find a way to squeeze in one more."

"Nowadays some people are pretty desperate," the new selectman insists.

"Desperate, my foot."

"It's just laziness."

"Or fussiness. Everybody wants a job with benefits, benefits, benefits. If they just take what they can get and work like hell, they'd lift themselves up."

The new selectman gets up to refill his mug with water from the fountain in the hall.

One of the old men in work uniform says with a sleepy grin, "Letourneau'll be puttin' up high rises before you know it."

Chuckle. Chuckle.

The bejowled bejeweled committeewoman speaks. "It wouldn't be half so bad if what they were doing were halfway attractive. But it's all so dumpy looking. That particle-board stuff." She rolls her eyes. "And sometimes no glass in their windows. Just plastic. Sheets of plastic. They might make cute little cottages with a little more effort and some imagination."

"Well, also it takes money," says the new selectman from the doorway, mug of water in hand. Nobody turns in their seats, but his voice is so soft there's a lot of one-eyed squinting among them.

"Money. Even when they get money, they spend it all wrong. Some of them *drink*. I say they *like* dumpy," guy in the maroon shirt insists.

"Well, dumpy looking is bad enough but there's the little problem of fire hazard as well," the reindeer sweater adds.

The new selectman, back in his seat now, caresses his water mug. Still speaking softly, but very clearly, "I heard an argument to that, that if the only alternative for some people is the street, then a hazardous shelter is safer than the street."

Bald freckled head is all that shows clearly from the sweet smoke as snorts of laughter come out around the pipestem. "But Mike, the marvelous thing about the street is that all streets lead *out of town*."

"I'd like to see all those shacks and trailers gone myself," says the bejowled bejeweled committeewoman. "Something nice put in there. A couple of respectable homes . . . homes with respectable valuation . . . and respectable people. Excuse me, Mike, if it seems heartless, but this is the real world we're living in."

New selectman says, "Some of those families have been around for years . . . you know . . . they are the grown kids of some people who farmed here and worked over to the mill for decades. It seems unfair that . . ."

Freckled-headed selectman interrupts with rolling eyes. "By *farmed* . . . do you mean that mess over on Canal Road . . . Dougherties and Foggs? And all that lot? You call those farmers? They can barely get out of their own way. And that Daniels outfit . . . some sorta tractor that looks like somethin' off the "Flintstones." I wouldn't buy a radish off of that crowd. Probably have to wipe the cowshit off of it before you ate the damn thing!"

"Well, now, Doug, . . . watch it . . ."

"Yeah, let's leave the farmers out of this for crissakes," the maroon alligator shirt man says, smiling broadly at the two old men in work uniforms at either end of the table.

"Well, I will for now, . . . but don't get me going on it again, 'cause I haven't a mite of pity for some of them. They just shouldn't be in the business if they don't know diddly-squat about business. I'm not talking about Hank and Giff here. These guys have their act together. You boys know I don't mean you."

The two old committeemen nod.

"You can't keep up, you fall by the wayside. That's life," the bejeweled bejowled committeewoman says. "I've got to agree with you, Doug. It sounds mean but a bleeding heart kills."

All eyes shift slightly to the profile of the young selectman at the words "bleeding heart." The radiator clangs suddenly. Hisses. A sort of scolding.

Road Commissioner Forest Johnson stretches his arms over his head. Now his wedding ring clanks against the root beer can as he seizes it and snaps off the tab.

The white-haired woman bends the corner of one typed sheet, sets it aside, folds her hands and speaks in a clear most official voice. "Are we ready to discuss the roadwork now? Forest has all the info tonight on the upgrading of Dustin Road up as far as Silver Heights and that Promise Lake estimate we asked for."

"Roads, roads, roads," says the freckled-headed selectman with a smile while the one in the reindeer sweater sings out, "The lonnnng and winding road thaaaat leeeads toooo yourrrrr dooooor!"

53 | In the night Peggy feels a hand tighten on her upper arm, Forest turning slowly to face her. He says in his voice that softens on certain syllables, "You keep your eye on Eli. Whatever you do, don't let him out of your sight."

54 | They come along the street with manful strides, just leaving one of the Joshuas' houses, two hours of Punch Out, Double Dragon, Tetris, and Top Gun. Though the nannas have suggested Eli stick around, stay within their view of him through the windows, he knows that if he had gone without video games much longer, he would have died.

"What're these green balls?" one of the Joshuas asks as they step to the edge of the Johnsons' yard.

"Neat," says the other.

Eli narrows his eyes on the eight green gazing globes standing in ruler straight parallel to the house. Gleaming greenly. A small alien army.

"Where's the red one you had? How many balls you guys got anyways?" a Joshua marvels.

Eli shrugs. "Maybe millions." He stands with his arms out from his wide girth, a little like getting ready for a gunfight, a fast draw. Seems these new green gazing globes might speak. They would say, "Okay, Johnson . . . it's you or us."

A Joshua giggles. "And where's the blue one? Didn't you have a blue one?"

Eli approaches the line of gazing globes cautiously. He sees many Elis. One swollen gluppy green Eli to each.

The Joshuas also step up to the gazing globes. One scooches, eyes level with the reflection of his face.

A Joshua confides, "My friends I told you about that went to Florida. They had a gold one. Gold is best."

The other Joshua says, "Maybe you guys can get a gold one, too. It looks like you guys collect 'em. *I'd* get gold next."

One Joshua says a little breathlessly, "Everything is very beautiful . . . green like it's summer."

"Yeah . . . 'cept the part that's bulging and hideous."

"Yeah. It's pretty neat."

55 | Near dark, Peggy heads for the barn, tugging on work gloves, chewing on a couple of fruit-flavored antacid tablets. Her breath bounces along after her, a chain of pretty paper dolls in the freezing air. She sees someone scooched in a mannish way in the open doorway to the stairs of one of the apartments in the large older barn. It's Anneka DiBias, daughter of one of the drivers. Anneka's had so much company these days. Whole gangs of girls and women coming and going. It is odd and discomfiting to see her alone squatted there, having pulled her bunchy knitted cap off, rubbing her nerved-up white hair, rubbing it, rubbing it . . . sort of apelike.

BANG! It's the slam of a high shoulder against wood within the newer barn. Mars. Whenever Mars senses Peggy's approach he tries to break the place apart. Lout. Oaf. No matter how classy a horse is, his love will always be rather goofballish.

Peggy's mouth still runs with the orangy antacid tablets. She gestures to the girl to come along. This is not the first time. Now and then the girl has joined her at this work of feeding and bedding down the horses, not much conversation, just the glurgles of water, the whispers of hay, just Anneka offering a little help. A strong-backed girl. Short-legged. Thick-hipped. The wide Nordic face. Face like snow. And there's the snow of her steady frozen breath jerking away. And there's the pale vigor of her hair, also jerking, working, reaching up. It is this image that Peggy has in so many ways dreamed of. In the days when the future was only imagined. When she was not even sure what her wishes were, though she knew she was busting with wishes, she wished for this, this kind of evening and that presence at her side.

The woman and the girl step along now and the orchid dusk within the open barn door is floating with the horses' big eyes, big shuddering necks, and rears. Big heat against the big cold.

Black Mars gives a low evil snort. BANG! Another blow to the boards of his box stall.

"Atta-go," Anneka praises, taking a pitchfork to a hay bale, breaks away its sections while Peggy snaps on the lights.

Some of Peggy's dark hair has worked loose from its barrette. Does this make Peggy look ravaged? She reaches for the side of Mars's halter. Takes it into her gloved fingers. Says in a low voice, "Cool it, mister." He rolls his eyes, snorts like a train, seems to be gathering himself up to jerk his head back, but does not. His frozen breath is most enormous. Peggy fills his water tub and those of the mares and the others. Water hoses always have to give you a little fight so you'll wind up wet and freezing and a little mad.

Although the woman and the girl seldom talk as they work, the girl's eyes always blaze with speech . . . wild plans. And Peggy wonders so much about her.

Sometimes when they are finished, they do talk some. They sit or stand leaning against the walls of tack, walls of recent show ribbons.

Tonight when Peggy asks about school, Anneka tells how she wrote a letter to the governor to complain about what he said in one of his speeches somewhere about forcing more homework on kids . . . about the idea that kids are not "*succeeding*" and more "*homework*" is the answer.

"What we need is not more HOMEWORK. We need more HOME," Anneka says, chuckling over this little bit of wit. Then she speaks into the empty darkness at her far right. "More home. Less school. School ain't a synonym for education. It's like saying mutton is a synonym for sheep."

Peggy's funny little face opens wide with one of her dazzling smiles. "Did the governor answer your letter?"

"Hah!" Anneka rolls her eyes. "A computer answers his letters. After I figured that out about the computer, I don't read the answers anymore. I give them to Mum to put her grocery lists on."

Peggy's smile is changeless. Like a portrait. Smiling, smiling, smiling. "You write the governor a lot?"

"Well, yeah . . . and the other bozos. All of them have computers probably . . . you know . . . like there's the computer that reads the letters, and the one that answers the letters." Anneka narrows her pale eyes. "No computer is here to do my homework though."

"Don't you get discouraged writing letters that . . . that . . . don't get read? What makes you keep doing it?" Peggy has stopped smiling, her eyes moving over Anneka's snowy face, snowy hands, the hands that write the dozens of letters sent out into the world that never listens.

Anneka chortles to herself, eyes on the box stall that is stacked with hay bales. "It's called the nuisance factor. *Bzzzzzzzzzzzzzzz.* Sometimes it's all you got. It's *all* you got. *Bzzzzzzzz.*" She makes her left forefinger like a fly landing on Peggy's jacket sleeve.

Peggy's arm jerks beneath the touch.

Huge silence.

Now there's some gloinks and varoooms of the good meal and good water moving through the big world of the nearest horse's stomach.

Peggy says, "Over the years it does seem they've come to expect a lot of schoolwork out of kids, especially homework, more than they used to."

Anneka says "Home—work" Each word is enclosed, strangled by emotion, on the verge of tears or mania or what? Anneka looks into Peggy's face. "Home—work. Get it?"

Peggy feels something of its meaning but not enough . . . she grasps for it . . . Get it? Get it? She is frightened of Anneka. Frightened *for* Anneka. Peggy says, "Well, guess I'll go in and burn some rice."

Anneka says, "You don't cook good? I figured you cooked good."

Peggy shrugs. "What's your cooking like? Are you a good cook?"

"Shit no."

Peggy says with a smile, "There's a knack to it, I guess."

56 | Outside at one corner of the shop, the larger backhoe . . . the eighteen-footer . . . the one that can take you eighteen feet deep. And George DiBias alongside the stretched-out boom, working a spanner wrench to loosen the cap from one chrome ram. And Forest turning away, Forest with the ram's rusty pins in one hand, Forest looking distracted.

George struggles with the weight of the loosened ram, grunting.

Forest sees kids zooming around the sandpit on four-wheelers and three-wheelers and dirt bikes.

School bus rumbles and screels to a stop out in front of the house and Anneka steps down from it. Late bus. The bus for kids who have extracurricular activities . . . or detention. Now the bus strains forward into a roll toward the four-way.

Forest sees Eli moseying from the house.

Anneka crosses the lot, tromping along in her felt-lined boots. She is not carrying books. She never carries much. She always looks as if she's just fallen from the sky, helpless bright nimbus of hair neglected, her only obligations being to some headquarters back in that other galaxy from which she was sent . . . big obligations, burning desires . . . but no homework.

Around and across the sandpit the four-wheelers and three-wheelers and dirt bikes snarl . . . wheelies and jumps and all those things to cause injuries and lawsuits that can break you, the landowner.

George, pulling the ram from the housing, gasping, face ablaze with fast blood, whispering, "Jesus, ain't she scored?" But Forest has lost interest in the work. He is keen only to activity *beyond* the shop.

Out in the middle of the lot, Anneka gives Eli a hot ball. He peels the paper off, gives it a toss. Anneka picks it up and seems to be giving Eli a lecture, waggling the cellophane before him. Eli looks embarrassed.

From somewhere behind Forest, George is saying sadly, "Crocus cloth can't do a thing for this bad a scorin'. I wouldn't even count on rechromin'. She's shot, don'tcha think?"

But Forest hears only the sound of brakes out on the road. Ernest Bean in his pickup.

Anneka says to Eli, "Some kids want to meet you."

Eli asks, "Who?"

Anneka names a bunch of names.

Eli asks if they have VCR's.

Anneka says they probably do, but "See those four-wheelers." She points to the rumpus in the sandpit. She tells him one of those kids has a snowmobile and a pet pig that will never get any bigger than a little dog. "Pig's name is Pete," she tells him.

The hot ball makes juice run in Eli's mouth.

Forest is shambling across the lot straight for Eli.

Truck right by the door of Moody's like Ernest Bean is going in for some shopping, but the truck door doesn't budge.

Anneka's peripheral vision begins to fill up with Forest.

"Eli," Forest says. "I need you to help me a minute."

"You like pigs?" Anneka asks Eli, the late sun seeming to slash her face and hair in half, half white blaze, half made cerulean blue by the deep shade of the house.

Forest's body now blocks all the sun.

Anneka's eyes shift.

Beyond Forest's shoulder in the near distance, there on the little spot of the Johnsons' frost-burned lawn, surrounded in grayed picket fence, wrought iron, and stone, is a single gazing globe. This one's a pretty shade of pink.

57 After the trucks have moved out in the morning and Peggy is at the sink rinsing out cereal bowls, the phone rings. She grasps for the receiver with a wet hand. It is Ernest Bean, speaking in that baritone many Bean men have. Says that he and the family would like to have Eli over for Thanksgiving. He asks if Peggy can see anything wrong with that? She says "No . . . well . . . no . . ." She has too many catches in her breath. Getting lightheaded. Leans back against the desk. She tells Ernest that he will have to speak with Forest, to call back tonight around seven . . . or out to the shop late afternoon. Ernest Bean seems to believe this is the wrong answer. He is silent. Waiting for the answer that makes sense. After a while, he says, "Nobody's seen him over to the school. You people got him in a private school? Waynflete or something?"

Peggy wishes she could find her businessperson's calm voice. But she bleats. "Pleeeze, Ernest! Please don't!"

58 At noon Peggy, Bett, and the boy eat chicken noodle soup and the boy tells his latest bad jokes, one from TV, one from the Joshuas. The nannas laugh their heads off. Nanna Bett drinks her tea with her little finger up.

Seems there's one of the nurses pulling into the back dooryard. A bit early for her shift. But as Peggy rises and looks out through the office door through the many little glass panes of the porch, she sees it's the pickup truck Forest described to watch out for. She says "excuse me" and pushes her chair back, pretending to be casual. She steps out into the office and sees Ernest Bean and his wife there on the high seat of their truck. The Beans. Grandparents to Eli like she and Forest are, grandparents with a heartache fixed like a stone in the chest . . . grandmother, grandfather . . . no more, no less. She watches the truck door ease open, Ernest Bean in a black-and-red wool shirt, blaze vest, jeans, boots, bare hands with an easy but heavy gait so much like Eli's. She backs away. She hurries to the kitchen, tells Eli to get up from the table very quickly and follow her upstairs for a little talk.

"A little talk?" he asks suspiciously, not moving.

"NOW!" Peggy hollers.

He rises and follows her.

She turns once to shout back to Bett, "Don't answer the door! Stay back from the door!"

Upstairs in Peggy's and Forest's room, Eli stands there, hands in his pockets.

Peggy smiles. "I . . . was . . . wanting to ask you what you've been wanting for Christmas. Something nice. VCR probably, huh?"

Eli frowns. He looks across the room at her with the bed between them.

Peggy's smile remains fixed and wide. "Maybe you'd like to make a list . . . you know . . . for Santa. I can give you a pad of paper and pencil. You can write down different things that Santa can pick from and then you won't know which of those things you'll be getting . . . so it'll be a surprise."

Eli's eyes slide to the phone on Forest's side of the bed. Then he looks into Peggy's eyes. "You guys act really weird here."

Peggy keeps smiling, smiling, smiling, unable to speak.

Eli says, "And you say you got burglars but nothing ever gets stole. Burglars *steal* stuff . . . money and TV's . . . stuff like that. You guys . . . have somethin' else. Ghosts. You ever seen a movie called *Polka-gyste?* Well . . . that might be what's here. It's very creepy here. You can get a minister like the one where the girl gets taken over and the minister made stuff come out of her mouth and then it was the devil or a ghost comes out. I think it's ministers that can help you get the polka-gyste, too. Once I saw . . ."

Phone rings.

Peggy pushes past Eli, seizes the phone.

"Peggy?" the caller asks. The caller is Amy.

Peggy kind of chokes. The room whirls through her tears.

"Peggy . . . I'm so glad it's you. I . . . just want to talk with Eli. Forest . . . he . . ." Amy sighs. "I don't know what's going on. I just wish someone would tell me something. I guess all I want is my baby. You know, it's the first Thanksgiving I won't have him with me? Peggy! I don't have *anybody* with me! Jeff and Eli were it! Now . . . I can't even *talk* to Eli. You'll let me talk to him, won't you? I'm his mother! Peggy?"

Peggy's silence.

"Where's Jeff?" Amy demands.

Peggy's silence.

"Does Eli ask for me?" Amy asks, softer, sweeter. Desperate restraint.

Peggy's silence.

"Peggy! How can you guys be so mean! Don't you think Eli needs his own mother? Peggy? Are you there?"

Peggy's silence.

"You know about the baby don't you? Did Jeff tell you I'm due in February? Did he tell you about that?"

Peggy lays the receiver back into its cradle gentle as a kiss. She keeps her face turned from Eli.

"Was that the ghost?" Eli asks a bit quaveringly.

Peggy sits on the bed. She looks down at the toes of her big felt-lined boots. "Something's very, very wrong," she whispers. She keeps looking at her boots. "Everything's just so mixed-up. You know, I have been proud of some things in my life. For instance, I believe I've always been a good daughter. I never gave my parents trouble. Stayed home. No sass. And I was an A student. I never resisted homework. Said please and thank you. The works. And I thought I was a pretty good mother . . . not perfect . . . but . . . good as any, I guess. Your father and his sister . . . you know . . . your aunt Linda we told you about . . . both had wholesome busy childhoods . . . they had every opportunity. And I think I'm a good daughter-in-law. Nanna Bett and I do very well under one roof . . . very, very well. And Gramp F.D. . . . before his strokes . . . we all got along, too. And as a wife. I am a good wife. I am a very good wife. I swear I'm a very good wife . . . and my heart is *filled* with Forest . . . and we have had a good life for so long . . . and we do for each other . . . and we've always worked together so well. But . . . *something* . . . is very, very wrong. It's starting to seem that none of us

are good people. I am not a good person. I am the worst. I am a very
bad person. I am *the worst*. It seems lately that we are falling apart . . .
not a family . . . nothing you could call a human family . . ." She still
stares at her boots, keeps her head down.

Eli releases a walloping manly sigh. He goes to the window and looks
down across the street. A guy is coming out of Moody's Variety & Lunch.
Has a soda and a box of donuts. Climbs up into a truck loaded with saw
logs. Shuts the door. Sits a minute in that truck. Young guy. Maybe
eighteen. Wearing blaze orange vest like everybody else around here.
Probably opening his donuts. Eli watches hard through the shadow of
the truck's side window . . . like deep ice.

59 | The constable, Erroll Anderson, hunches a bit. He shivers. He is
never dressed right for these "emergencies." He beams his flashlight onto one of the truck doors which has printed on it FOREST JOHNSON,
SR., & SON. BACKHOE & DOZING. SAND & LOAM. EGYPT, MAINE. 625-
8693. He makes this light dance in a frisky way, but the expression on
his face remains coplike and earnest.

The lettering on the door jiggles and bounces, then slides away. "So,"
says he.

Forest Johnson, Jr., is leaning hard into the fender of one of the
trucks, arms crossed over his jacket. "Take a guess," says Forest.

The constable shrugs.

"Take another guess," Forest says.

"Hard to guess," says the constable, his frozen breath rolling out and
away.

In time it's revealed that the plow hook-up on the "new" GMC has
vanished. "A great trick," Forest says evenly. "Not as cute as his colored
ball juggling . . . but magical all the same."

60 | Another night. Another sleight of hand. Constable Erroll An-
derson arrives to stand about with a flashlight, looking earnest.
This time it's the stolen-gasoline-mangled-gas-caps episode. Every vehicle
dry. "Light deters crime," the constable tells Forest. Deputy says big
lights are the way.

61 Insurance company voice speaks into Peggy's ear. It says BIG LIGHTS. The voice says big lights deter crime. The voice says to continue the coverage of this policy at the same "low rate," the Johnsons are required to have the lights installed. It is a standard requirement with all insurers for all small business policies. Peggy thinks in some ways this seems reasonable, though there's something . . . something about this voice on the phone . . . she can't quite pin down what it is . . . something she can't let herself think about. In the mail there's a recipe from her mother, cut from a magazine. She searches through the cupboards to be sure all the ingredients are on hand. And out in the back pantry there's enough potatoes to do up a double batch of the stuff. She hums to herself.

62 It is the few days that follow. Eddie Lane the electrician finishes up the installation of four security lamps. And as the suppertime dark settles in, the garish greenish purplish orangy extravaganza of brilliance smashes that dark.

At the supper table Forest says, "What's this?"

"It's made with squash," Peggy says. "And eggs and sherry."

"It looks delicious!" Bett chirps.

Forest chuckles, plops some of the substance on his plate, raises an eyebrow toward Eli. "Want some pumpkin goo goo?" he asks the boy.

Peggy says, "Forest . . . just for that . . . you are going to pay." She puts her tall smile in his direction.

Forest says, "Any meat in this, Peggy?"

Peggy says, "There will be in a minute."

Forest laughs with just his shoulders. His hair is combed with water, parted in the middle the way he does. His work shirt is rolled to the elbows. Peggy can't take her eyes off him, this striking man, the love of her life. He tastes the casserole. "Mmmm. What next?" he wonders. "Shrunken heads à la spinach."

Eli sniggles. He is used to this teasing. He kind of likes it. And he's noticed that since he's been here in Egypt, Peggy has never cooked the same thing twice. No repeats like with Nanna Bett. But with Peggy, you always have to guess what the meal is made of and you wait for Forest to ask and then after all the teasing, the meal is still a mystery in most ways. Supper is often the high point of the day. And fortunately Eli likes *all* food. He trusts food. Food is a good friend.

Peggy says, "Eddie was saying that lights are only part of security. He says . . ."

"Eddie was in here talking, huh?"

"For a few minutes."

"Eddie doesn't talk a few minutes. He talks for days."

"Well, he came in to run the wiring."

"I thought he used the bulkhead."

"He ran part of it up through the wall out back."

"He just wanted to get in here and talk," says Forest, drawing the bread plate toward him.

Eli understands this . . . the glint in Forest's eyes. This, like the food talk, is just play. In some very queer ways the Johnsons are playful people.

Peggy swallows a bit, clears her mouth. "Anyway, Eddie said they say it's best not to leave the doors to the house unlocked like we do."

Forest looks at her, his eyes blackening, vexed, pupils tight. "They?"

"The insurance companies," she replies.

He gives the nosepiece of his wire-frame glasses a push. "There's always someone of the family around here."

"Yes," Peggy agrees. "Yes, there is. But I'm thinking . . . you know . . . when . . . the day comes . . . you know . . . that F.D. passes away . . ." She keeps her eyes averted from Bett, but Bett is just fussing with her tea bag, arranging it on its little ceramic strawberry tea bag holder by her plate. Peggy sighs. "You know . . . when the nurses aren't—"

"This is our HOME!!" Forest rages. He rises taller in his seat. "You know . . . the family just coming and going in and out, living our lives!"

"Forest, I'm not saying it would be easy, but he was telling me about what some of the insurance companies have started . . ."

"Are you telling me that now the insurance companies can tell a man that he . . . not only has to have these very *expensive, irritatingly* bright . . . I mean BRIGHT-LIKE-ANOTHER-GODDAM-PLANET lights all over the place but he also has to get a key out every time he goes in and out the door, every time somebody in the family goes in and out the door so that what life would be like here would be like a *penitentiary?* And if we don't do it that way, *their* way, this insurance company will do some sneaky royal screw-over like not fork over the money when it's time to fork over the money on a claim. Right?!!! God almighty! I live up to my end of the deal. I've paid them *thousands* over the years and Dad has . . . and until *lately,* we've had not one single claim. In fact, what you're saying about locking up applies to people who haven't had any claims ever. I mean . . . you are talking about a kind of blanket rule they have, right? Ho! Ho! They want a person's money, but they want a promise in blood or something that you'll never want anything in return. And meanwhile, you creep around with lights and keys like in a goddam penitentiary!!"

Bett and Peggy are both looking wide-eyed at Forest.

Eli looks at his orangy casserole, which is quite good and tastes like cinnamon.

Forest leans toward Peggy and hisses, "The only thing these big lamps are going to do is keep the ol' light meter hot. It's just a racket. Probably the same stockholders own both enterprises."

Bett, gazing off toward the wallpaper of eagles and Revolutionary War soldiers, seems to be far from this conversation, seems to be deep in thought concerning the events of her day, perhaps a conversation she and one of the nurses had. But she says suddenly, "Eleanor Roosevelt said there's no such thing as security."

Peggy giggles. "Bett! I can't believe you'd ever give credence to something a Democrat said! I've always been under the impression . . ." Peggy can't finish. Her giggles have a hold on her.

Bett frowns. "Eleanor Roosevelt? Oh, she was just *married* to a Democrat."

"Bett! Eleanor Roosevelt was probably even *more* of a Democrat than her husband. You should read up on her if you're going to go around speaking in her behalf! You ought to know what you're talking about. Maybe your library group could research her sometime."

Forest watches Peggy's mouth hard.

Bett sighs. "We don't read politics. We read mostly Maine."

Forest grins. "No politics in Maine."

Peggy stands, takes the empty bread plate from the table.

Bett's eyes follow Peggy moving toward the counter.

Car pulls up close to the back door.

Tonight the plenteous food on the table seems dreamy . . . as with any oasis, there's a chance it's only a mirage.

Forest gets up from his chair. But Peggy already has the door and Forest, pivoting on his strongest foot, grips the back of Eli's chair.

Brian Began walks into the kitchen so ashen with fear he's almost blue.

Car drives away. Someone has dropped him off. The demise of his own car has many possibilities.

"Forest?"

"Yep?"

"I . . . was wondering . . . I heard your new driver didn't work out and I wanted you to know I'm still available."

Forest looks Brian up and down. Brian with the same pair of shrunken misshapen work gloves. Such long bony wrists. And the pants, *the* pants. Forest says, "Brian, let's get something straight here. You know I know about how you can't read 'n' write. It's a thing I just can't get out of my worries."

Brian says, "I'm a good driver. Reading has no effect."

"How'd you ever get your license? How? You got an uncle in the Registry? Or . . . is that a twin brother who got you the license and you impersonate him."

"I took the written test oral."

Forest looks aghast. "Jee-zuss! That makes me feel safe on the road . . . all these guys driving in my direction, can't read the signs, can't read the laws. That letting 'em do it oral. What do you think, Peg? Think it oughta be?"

Peggy standing behind Brian shrugs under Forest's bedeviled stare.

Brian says, "I memorize most signs. Most of them show a picture anyways. Or they're made a certain shape."

Forest turns, wiping his hands with a paper napkin. A little orangy casserole or butter on the fingers. Plops the balled-up napkin by his plate. He takes a wobbly step toward Brian. "If I had you as a driver again . . . it wouldn't rest easy with me to just hand you over the same pay as the rest. Wouldn't be fair. These other drivers deserve higher pay, wouldn't you say? Being safer . . ."

"I'm a safe driver," Brian says evenly. For a long moment Brian's eyes and the boy's eyes meet. Eli looks away first, his cheeks bulging with bread, working the bread.

Forest says, "Look at all those years my other drivers put into school learning to read while you fucked off . . ." Forest glances at his mother and says, "Excuse me." She seems unfazed, her fingers rearranging the position of her ceramic strawberry tea bag holder. "What did you do, Brian . . . quit school when you were ten and spend all those years watching cartoons and soap operas?"

"I got my diploma," Brian says. "I served my time." He almost smiles . . . a sort of twinkle in his eye lasting a half moment.

Eli stuffs lots and lots of bread into his mouth.

"Spare me!" Forest snorts. "A diploma!"

"I have a diploma," Brian says softly. "I put in my time."

"Tell you what. I'll take you on. Starting Monday morning. But there's no way I can pay you what I used to. You are a risk. You think I don't have to pay insurances? Well, let me tell you, buddy boy, I pay insurances up the ass. Insurances are starting to be the Lord God these days. And what would happen to my insurance rates if you were to run over somebody with a load of crushed rock?"

Brian's eyes are level into Forest's for a moment.

"And where's your license? Your Class B. You better have that. You still got that? Or'd you let that go during your little vacation?"

"I kept it up."

"Well, hallelujah," Forest says, shaking his head incredulously. "You comin' over Monday?"

Brian nods.

Forest says, "I'll want to see that license."

Brian says he'll bring it.

Forest says, "So is that it? You need anything else from me tonight?" He looks toward the door.

Brian turns to leave.

Peggy isn't standing behind Brian like she was. Where is Peggy?

63 | Pickup pulls off the shoulder, centers Brian Began in its headlights. Voice calls out. "Hey! Hop in!"

Brian Began climbs into the cab, slams the door. He looks to the face of the driver and sees it's Albion Cole. One of the regulars at Moody's and sometimes over at Letourneau's Used Auto Parts office. Albion Cole, one of the town's wise men . . . circulating wisdoms . . . Albion Cole, little gray-haired, gray-faced balding guy with a green cloth cap that hides the bald part. Used to smoke. Must have quit. Nowadays everybody quits, wanting to live *long* past their prime. Albion Cole of ALBION COLE & SONS . . . LOGGING & PULP . . . though there's no sons who work in the business . . . two dead in Vietnam, one broken in Maine is how the story goes.

Albion Cole has the radio on low . . . a talk show. Some of these wise men just can't get enough talk. The truck, fairly newish, takes the hills and curves slow and silky. Albion and Brian just listen to the talk show, a discussion on toxic waste dumps. And the truck pulls them into the night. Albion Cole need not ask where Brian Began is headed. He knows he's headed home. He need not ask where home is. Egypt's wise men know these things.

But now, nearing Miracle City, Albion speaks. "I wish I could hire you, Brian. I know you've been needing work. But as it is, I'm having to sell off two of my rigs and laying off my own cousin. It's a bad time."

"That's okay. I'm back with Forest," Brian says.

"Zat right?" Albion glances at Brian, a glance so fatherly and knowing, that Brian feels himself let go . . . every muscle softening, sleepy . . . he actually wonders if he's wet himself . . . but no . . . Jesus God no. He rubs his eyes hard. He tells Albion some things. Things about Forest's offer tonight, all about the "special pay." Brian tells it slowly . . . like you pull porcupine quills from a dog. Brian speaks of these things not in a whine or fit of nerves, but steadily into that powerful, greenly lit dark driver's side of the truck cab where the gray wise man sits, two hands on the wheel.

64 | Dump trucks all head for the pit across the shortcut in the back field. But the backhoe is being taken over to Hatch Road today to finish work there. Loaded onto the low-bed it moves through the pinkish greenish purplish orangy fierce light, moves jerkily and colossally across the kitchen windows, out onto Rummery Road, everything set to thunderous motion, charged with purpose.

The sky pales.

The security lamps snap off. The lights that need no hand on a switch. Lights that have eyes. Lights that have brains. No, they are not part of this Johnson enterprise. They are, these lights, thieves in their own right.

Peggy with the phone, talking business at her desk, sees the silvery Ram Charger whip across the many panes of the old porch.

Jeff and Coti are lighthearted as they enter. Laughing. Got themselves a box of live lobsters and again bouquets of dried flowers for each nanna. And other presents. A book for Nanna Bett . . . a glossy book of glossy photos of wildlife, fields, butterflies, and birch trees against rocky shores. For Peggy a silk scarf for her hair . . . blue, gold, and pink print . . . sketchy and rueful, sort of Japanese. Quite lovely.

"Think we can keep these lobsters in the bathtub till noon, Ma?!" Jeff is crowing. "There's just two. One for Coti and me so you don't have to make us any lunch. I know you guys aren't crazy about lobster. But Coti's never had herself a real ol' lobster!" Jeff and Coti look dreamily into each other's eyes.

From the office door where she stands, hands on hips, boots apart, Peggy says, "We don't hate lobster. We just find it to be costly."

"Well, we won't be having it every day either, Ma! But Coti should have it at least once. What do you think she should remember Maine by . . . maybe some moose meat? Dad still got some of Uncle Frank's moose in the freezer?" Jeff sniggers as though in the presence of adorable innocence.

Bett in her black rocker by the windows keeps blinking, rocking, rocking.

Peggy says evenly, "Some might call what you did, taking Granpa's Dodge, stealing."

Jeff looks stricken, then turns. "Nanna *gave* me permission! She gave me the *keys!!!*"

Peggy looks at Bett.

Bett whitens, doesn't speak.

Jeff smiles sadly. "It's all right, Nanna. Anybody your age is bound to flub up now and then. Nobody's going to be mad."

Coti smirks slightly. Her eyes are blasted red where the whites should be from nonstop marijuana and drink. "That's terrible, J.J.!" she gasps in her sexiest, gaspingest voice. "Don't make your grandmother feel bad. Let it go."

"Where's Eli?" Jeff asks.

"Out with your father and George in the shop," Peggy answers.

Jeff takes more presents from hissing plastic shopping bags. Boxes of peppermints. A pink ceramic hand mirror with matching brush and comb set. He spreads the gifts on the enamel table.

The morning brightens, dazzles. The sun is in white squares on the old oak floor. Jeff and Coti bop around the kitchen fixing their lunch. A transistor radio as big as a TV has magically manifested itself. Jeff pushes the sleeves of his new sweater up. The music bangs, shrills, shimmies. The nannas have disappeared.

Eli comes in from the shop. He is both majestic and sullen. Blackened hands. Smudges of black around his eyes and mouth. He gives Jeff and

Coti their usual lecture on irresponsibility. Then he gives them the low-down on what everybody said about them while they were gone. And he tells about the "polka-gyste." And he tells them all about how you clamp a heater hose to a radiator.

Jeff shows Eli the lobsters in the bathtub.

Eli says they look like giant scorpions. He asks if he can show them to the Joshuas when they get home from school.

Jeff says the lobsters will be history by then. When they return to the kitchen, Jeff explains how a lobster is going to be in Coti's stomach soon. And he gives Coti's stomach a sensual rubbing. And Coti gets breathless, licks her lips, stretches her arms, and pushes her chest against his shoulder.

Eli disappears.

65 | The school bus shudders to a stop and releases Anneka. Nothing in her hands of course. She strides powerfully up the drive.

Eli happens to be by the doorway of the DiBias apartment. Just happens to be.

And Forest happens not to be around. There's just the clangs of solitary George in the shop.

Eli asks Anneka if she can help him. He says he needs *help*.

Her great silvery eyes widen on him.

He says, "How is it you call long distance? Is it the 0 first or what? And are you supposed to use a thing called zip code?"

She asks, "Who you wanna call?"

He replies, "My mom."

She says, "Where's she at?"

He replies, "California."

She says, "Come upstairs with me. It ain't hard at all."

66 | The lobsters drop squealing and scraping to their boiled-alive deaths.

Coti makes a joke of it, but it seems that the execution bothers her.

The "lunch" is long over with when Peggy reappears to swivel the top off a big jar of mayonnaise. "Where's Eli?"

Coti is doing the dishes, jerking her hips to the blare of music from the new radio.

Jeff says, "He went out . . . probably back to the shop."

Peggy leaves the mayonnaise and goes to one of the kitchen windows and studies the yard. "Your father doesn't want him to roam around."

Jeff is wiping the table off with a dishrag, burps, stretches, looks content. "Ma . . . you guys give any thought to getting Eli enrolled in school?"

Peggy turns sideways, traces a finger along the woodwork of the window. "Isn't that something that you should decide? I mean . . . we don't even know if you're going to live here or if you're going back out west."

Coti and Jeff exchange glances. Jeff smiles at his mother. "Well, there's no problem about the school . . . you know . . . he might as well be in school. And . . . besides . . . I thought you guys would like to be the ones to sign him up. Make you feel young again. They'll think he's *yours!*"

Peggy shoves both hands into the pockets of her jeans, returns to the mayonnaise, pulls a glass bowl from the cupboard. She says without looking at Jeff, "You can't be as naive as you are sounding. Schools will require transfer papers from his other school . . . birth certificates . . . immunization records. You and Amy need to take care of that."

Coti puts the music up.

Jeff shouts over the music, "I just feel so sorry for Eli! You know how Maine schools are . . . you know. Poor state, poor schools! Poor town, *very* poor schools! Eli will wind up in what we used to call the ree-tard room! He'll be stigmatized! It'll smash his self-esteem! It's bad enough all this special ed shit they have everywhere. But here in this district . . . you know . . . Jesus . . . I remember Down's syndromers right in there in the same special ed room with kids that just had some little trouble! Makes you wonder if it's the administration that's retarded, doesn't it?"

Peggy shouts over the music, "What are you talking about!!?"

"His dyslexias!"

Peggy blinks. She turns on her heel and reaches to shut off the radio. "TALK to me, Jeff. Let's talk like grown-ups. What dyslexias?"

Jeff tosses the washrag into the sink from across the kitchen . . . a great aim . . . whizzes past Coti's elbow. Coti turns and glares.

Jeff rolls his eyes. "Well, looks like Coti's going to do the silent treatment on me for the next three days. She thinks lobsters *hurt.*"

"They *hurt,*" says Peggy. She goes over to Jeff, grabs him by a shoulder. "Jeff. I want to hear about Eli. This is serious."

Jeff shrugs. "Eli has learning disabilities that make it so he can't read and he can't write . . . just his first and last name." He holds up two fingers. "And he can't measure or assimilate new information fast . . . especially under stress. He even has trouble with telling time sometimes. He has bad days and good days. They told us that it's in the brain. Used to be they called kids lazy or stupid . . . still do in some schools. But they told us . . . you know . . . he isn't stupid. There's different ways to be smart. And you know what a little hotshot Eli is . . . he doesn't miss much. Oh . . . and another thing they said was that these things run in families. Well, there's nobody on our side like that . . . so it must have come through Amy and that bunch. Amy always said her father can't read shit . . . and Reuben never picked it up. That's what Amy's people call it . . . 'not picking it up.' " He looks at his own hands, turns one of his rings. "So it doesn't look good for old Eli."

67 | The room is cold without the electric heater. But there are plenty of blankets and quilts. So they stay under the blankets in bed or hunch on the bed's edge with blankets around them. They'd go ride around in the Camaro. In the Camaro you can crank the heat up good and hot. But the Camaro is low on gas. Need the gas for later on. And yes, the fumes. Fumes getting pretty rugged in the ol' Camaro. So they wait out time in the cold room, flipping through magazines, eating chips, or sleeping to the heady wail of electric guitars.

68 | Eli has been gone for hours. Peggy suggests they wait to put supper on the table. Jeff and Coti are gone again. This time in the Camaro. Who knows where to or for how long? Peggy says, no, Eli was not with them. She suggests calling the State Police barracks. Forest looks only at his hands. Bett lights one of the mint-scented candles that was a "present" from Jeff and Coti. Bett and Peggy carry food to the table. Bett's nicely crisped roasted chicken. Baked potatoes. Everything predictable. No scary surprises.

Forest leans back to let them reach across with the platters, and he watches the flame of the candle, a flame reflected in each lens of his glasses. Once everyone is seated, they begin to eat.

The back door screels open, shuts abruptly. Eli appears. Jacket un-buttoned. Face flushed. His pale eyes in dark lashes move from person to person.

Peggy has not told Forest about the dyslexias. Nor has she told Bett. She can't figure out how to begin.

Peggy considers how those pale eyes do not see the way she does. What do numbers and words look like to Eli? Like what? Swedish? Chinese? And how does the spoken word *sound* to him? Eli. Otherworldly being. The brain of . . . of . . . something other than herself . . . and yet he is part of her.

Forest puts his fork down. Puts his knife down. A mouthful of chicken swallowed in a hard gulp. "Well, well, well," says he.

Eli collapses into a chair, wiping his brow with a sleeve. He is charged.

"Where've you been?" Forest demands. "The nannas have been worried."

Eli looks at Bett, then Peggy.

Bett says quickly, "We knew he was all right. We knew he wasn't far. It's all right, Forest."

"No . . . it's not all right." He leans close to the boy. "You stay put. You hear me, Eli? You stay where we can keep an eye on you. It's a weird world out there. It's always been a weird world. But now it's even *weirder*. Ain't like it used to be in a small town. You just don't go trotting anywhere you like. Lotta weirdos out there."

Eli shrugs, flushing harder, eyes on his own hands, still blackened by his morning's work on the heater hose. The black. A kind of badge of triumph. A kind of A-plus. So much triumph today. For Eli, a good day all in all.

Forest puts his menacing grin with the bluish tooth and the others bunched around it very close to Eli's face. "You know, Eli . . . once . . ." He moves his grin and eyes in the direction of Bett. "You ever heard of rape, Eli?"

Peggy sighs.

"Forest!" squeals Bett. "What's ailin' you! Eli's just a little boy."

"Ah . . . yes . . . a little boy," Forest says. His grin is gone. His dark eyes with the pupils that don't match, one wide, one narrow, burn into Eli. "Eli, I'm asking you. You ever hear of rape?"

Eli shrugs.

"Once it 'twas women you heard of now and then who got raped," Forest says. "You didn't have to worry about boys. They could run around town without much trouble. Nowadays *boys* get raped, too." He eases back into his chair, head cocked, eyes still on the boy. "So . . . if you see a blue-and-white Ford pickup slow up . . . white toolbox on the back against the cab . . . and the guy . . . he's a big tall rugged-built guy with a red-and-black plaid wool shirt and four missing teeth and eyes . . . light brown eyes, black hair. This guy is going to grab you, Eli, and you'll wind up with a great big fat pecker up your ass."

Peggy smacks the table with the flat of one hand, rises out of her chair and screams, "FOREST! I HATE YOU!!"

69 She sees the State Police cruiser outside in the night. It hasn't got its blue lights churning. But its more than normal gleaminess distinguishes it from a citizen's car.

Peggy dresses fast. There's this brilliance of the security lamps that ensures that this bedroom will never know darkness again.

By the time she steps into the hall, she finds Forest sitting at the top of the stairs. Wears his jacket and a watch cap. Blaze gloves. His face is in his gloved hands.

"Forest! What's wrong!"

He rocks his face from side to side in the gloved hands.

She hurries over to him, sits on the step beside him. "Please uncover your face. Please talk to me. Tell me what happened!"

"I'm wiped out. Everything in the shop. Everything but the trucks. He took the engine crane. The welder. Compressor. Two of the Honda generators and extensions . . . the *new* ones of course. Transmission jack and jack stands. Every Craftsman but those on the floor. Axle jack. Even the fan . . . the one George runs in the summer. Batteries. Two Fisher plows. Tires. Rims. Everything. Almost everything but the oil spots on the floor. Looks like we moved out of the state! Clean and cute. He wiped me out, Peggy. No siphoning gasoline this time. No gazing globe tricks. Just a big plain fuckin' thievin' haul."

Peggy leans onto her knees. She has no words.

Forest says, "You know, it's funny, but . . . I'm getting pretty old an' fuzzy, I guess. Confused. I'm getting confused about which thief is working on me at which time."

70 At Moody's Variety & Lunch a reporter warms his hands over the barrel stove. Old wise men in the rockers and at the horseshoe counter give him the evil eye. Clarence Farrington in Pink Punch. Arch Vandermast in Pigeon Point. Younger men who are wearing the blaze are slouched along the bulletin wall, some smirky, some shy.

Reporter says, "Excuse me but would any of you know where I could learn a little more about this white-kerchief demonstration that's to take place here in your town this afternoon?"

Clarence Farrington leans forward with forearms on knees. His old spotted hands have crooked thumbs . . . no longer the hands of a hunter. His eyes small and gray and bleary . . . no longer the eyes of the hunter. And yet, by the pissed-off-angry spacing of his heavy boots, you know he still burns with the blood of a hunter. He says, "You mean the kid that's going to get herself shot, right?"

From under the arm of his nylon windbreaker, the reporter tugs a narrow, lined pad, scribbles on it while simultaneously laughing in a friendly fraternal manner. "And why's that?" he wonders.

"Because she's going out there in the woods looking for trouble!" bellers the old but still strapping, still bearlike Arch Vandermast. He looks among his many cronies for grins and winks.

The reporter scribbles. He grins and winks just like the grinning and winking of the wise men and the young men he is among. "You mean someone is going to . . . like take care of her? Give her what she deserves?"

Arch Vandermast says, "Nooooo, that's not what I said. You're puttin' words in my mouth. What I mean is . . . anybody going out into the woods this time of year without blaze orange is a damn fool or worse."

"Why's that?"

"Because she could be mistaken for an animal . . . her and those others with her . . . those others."

"Now why is that? Why would they be mistaken for animals . . . by that you mean *game* animals, right? Deer, right?"

"A white kerchief is going to look like a deer's ass," mutters one of the young men along the wall, his foot resting on an unopened carton of one dozen cans of Del Monte fruit cocktail. And all around him are the chuckles and titters of his friends' and neighbors' approval.

The reporter's eyebrows are raised as he scribbles the words of the young man.

Arch Vandermast says, "Now that guy . . . or anybody like him . . . who killed that woman upstate was sloppy. I'm not saying me or anyone else here would shoot without seeing what we're shootin' at. I'm not saying *I* would shoot some woman. But there are those who go out there and don't know what they're doing. It's just sloppiness. Most of your hunters are *not* sloppy."

"So you think the man the court acquitted should really have been found guilty of the manslaughter charges?"

"I'm not saying anything."

"But you think these women and kids going out today are in danger?"

Arch Vandermast shakes his head. "Noooo. You are trying to put words in my mouth."

71 | It is downtown East Egypt by the falls. It is windy. The long hair of certain young girls and women and the white scarves and handkerchiefs tied around their heads signal and beckon. Some wear white knitted caps. Some white mittens. Some are waving a strip of sheet. There are brown jackets among them. Chamois shirts in all the most quiet colors. One belted jacket of gray and tan tweed. *No blaze.* So many flashes of pale. Pale rides the wind. Pale is sailing along, spirited and insurgent . . . sassy.

A few homemade placards on sticks. HOW FAR WILL THEY GO WITH SPORTS? And IMPRISONED IN OUR HOMES FOR TWO MONTHS!! And MOTHERS FOR PREVENTION OF DEAD MOTHERS.

It is a quiet procession. Not much joking around. No chants. Kind of funeralish.

Two girls ride horseback. One of these riders wields a parade-style American flag strapped to the saddle.

Everyone else is on foot. Some grip the hands of toddlers. And there are babies in baby backpacks. Newborns in pouches.

The wind lifts the American flag, gives it a shake, then lets it settle.

With eyes squinted, you might swear this was a scene from history . . . a little mismatched out-of-uniform militia, headed out of the hills to meet the enemy.

Reporter pulls two cameras from the seat of his little car, snaps pictures at all angles. He squats on the pavement. He runs along.

Some passing trucks are loaded with logs. Some with pulp lengths. Some with chips. They snarl onto the bridge and turn out onto the highway. Cars. Vans. UPS. Telephone company truck with a bucket. A few shouts of support from rolled-down windows. Tooting horns. While other voices call out obscenities.

A car parks in a bad place by the bridge. And from it a man in a striped jersey leaps to snap pictures of the group as it moves toward him.

"Yes," one of the demonstrators responds to the first reporter's question. "We plan to do this every day till deer season is over, including their muzzleloader week."

"Are you a Maine native?"

"Yes, I am. Why?"

"A lot of people claim that it's only people from out of state who get shot, that you people in Maine know the rules. For instance, wearing the proper amount of hunters' orange and staying out of the woods."

"Who says that?" she pretends to wonder.

"Well . . . the sportsmen's organizations, for one . . ."

A woman with a small child in tow leans toward the reporter and says, "Mister, you have finally come to the right people for the absolute and *unemotional* truth."

"Remember!" one of them on horseback calls out. "Keep giving those white sheet strips a good shake!" She gives a strip of pale pink sheeting a wild wave. And in unison, nearly twenty flags of paleness answer hers.

The group steps along faster now as they make their way east on the shoulder of Rummery Road.

Now a van stops up ahead, far enough ahead to get a shoulder-mounted TV camera rolling, getting a close-up shot of one of the horseback riders, the one with the American flag . . . a girl with a puffy blue jacket and stained cuffs, white hair, face whiter yet. And anything that white is a sort of bull's-eye in this season of the hunt.

"We plan to start out every afternoon as soon as the kids are home from school," one mother explains to the microphone. "We'll meet here in town, then head out on one of the roads that goes up back, a different one each day. Then once we get to the woods, we all spread out . . . you know . . ." She smiles coyly. "Like deer."

72 | Saturday morning. Peggy and Anneka. Two figures astraddle two horses. Peggy's horses. Leggy horses. Arched necks. High stepping. Fluorescent blaze orange ribbons tied to their bridles. English saddles, weighing little. Leather sweet-soaped, soft as living skin. Everything floaty and desirable. Long purply shadows. Early by the clock. Long before any of Peggy's riding students are due to show up, dropped off by their parents. Time with students will be time spent with stipulation and obligation. Time with Anneka is something else.

Peggy has her Mars do some extra fancy stepping while young Anneka reins the other horse back and watches Mars's hooves thump the sawdust. Such a light step. A horse with feet of the fairies, eyes of the devil. And there's Peggy's posture, the vortex of all that equestrian ardor and clockwork of the hooves, Peggy the silent sweeping second hand.

"Some day I'll have a horse like Mars!" Anneka calls out . . . Anneka DiBias who will never own anything . . . always the borrowed horse . . . always the ill-fitting shoes or boots, makes her feet have a stuffed look, as they do now, jammed into the elegant stirrups. Now she takes the dark horse that is really Peggy's horse, Vassar, counterclockwise in the ring so that she and Peggy pass, smiling, pretending to tip top hats. Then Anneka reverses direction and the two riders walk the horses abreast and begin to talk in earnest about many things, all the things women or young girls talk about when they have come to that edge of closeness, discovering each other's lives.

And of course what it comes to at last is this simpering over the witlessness of men . . . the treachery of men . . . and men's secret sweetness. Anneka tells about Chris Shaw who she loves but how he doesn't love her but how Timmy Locklin loves her but she can't stand him.

Peggy tells Anneka about Forest. Tells things she has never told anyone before about Forest. She tells this young girl all the very truths of Forest.

Anneka says in a low voice, "Well, he doesn't seem that way to look at him."

And Peggy, all giggles, overflowing, tells more and more.

Now they do the ring in silence, just that pleasing squeak of saddles. Peggy says, "I have loved him all my life, even before that day. It's his eyes." What a stupid thing to have said, she marvels. What a stupid truth.

The girl says, "Well, yes . . . eyes are important," then tips her head . . . all those pale agitated nerves of her hair, and her expression suddenly sadly weary as though she herself might be caught in vivid memory of someone's eyes.

73 In their upstairs room Coti and Jeff sleep away the hours of cold in that cold wailing of electric guitars in this cold November daylight. Feet warm. Feet together under the covers.

74 | When Eli calls California again, Anneka's mother already has the number written out for him on a scrap of paper. She has drawn a heart with the number and "Eli's mother" written inside it.

75 | Sunday afternoon. Forest Johnson is taking the backhoe to Brownfield to have it ready for the job there Monday morning. Sunday or not. Forest Johnson takes no rest.

He is stopping the Mack and loaded low-bed along the road's shoulder between the entrance and exit of the IGA and pharmacy, leaves the engine idling. Makes his awkward way to the ground from the high seat. He has no purchases to consider here at the little shopping center. He hadn't a thought of stopping here until he rounded the curve from the bridge and saw there in the lot, between cars, three shaggy horses. Anneka on her borrowed Appaloosa managing the tethers of two riderless bays. Back-to in her puffy blue jacket, she has no idea he is coming her way, even with the chuff-clump chuff-clump of his boots on the dry tar . . . not till he is right there by her stirruped foot. She looks down, eyes widening on his face. She doesn't smile. And he doesn't smile either. Her white hair is combed with a part and barrettes, almost civilized. Kind of cute.

He is reaching now, placing his left hand on the shaggy white rump of the horse, its black spots there round as Oreos. Absurd. Merry-go-round horse. He spreads his fingers among the spots and says, "There's nothing nicer than a crazy young and flashy one. Is there?"

Anneka tightens her leg against the saddle. She glances quickly to the glass doors of the pharmacy.

He takes the bridle of the Appaloosa into his fingers. Horse jerks his head up, eyes rolling, tongue working against the bit. But Forest keeps his balance against the shoulder of the horse. Keeps his grip. The other horses churn a bit.

Anneka says in a level voice, "Let go or I'll give him a kick and drag you up and down this parkin' lot. Wanna try me?"

Forest keeps his shoulder to the shoulder of the horse, fingers locked around the bridle.

Anneka makes a sound with her throat and walls of her mouth like she is going to spit in his face.

"You are out of hand, Anneka," he says, smiling weakly as he lets go of the bridle.

Before the other girls return, he is back on the high seat of the Mack, pretending to study a clipboard of notes, but really his eyes are closed. And under the clipboard, against the tightening fabric of his wool pants, the sudden hard glut.

Every day, violated in some way. So many souls. All their needs, unjustified and justified, word upon word, deed upon deed, they steal. But now, how is it he has come to violate himself? His own body busy shaming him, like a mindless jutted-out fleshy bag of worms, like eyes involuntarily and so unprettily popping out from the face in violent death. The stupidness of his body! The shrewdness of his body. Forest's sex mightier than Forest. An army marching on without him to sneak up behind his back.

He jerks his glasses off and mashes the palms of his hands to his eyes, breathing in the gritty fluids of this truck cab. This beast. This traitor among all traitors. The machine that both cradles you and fucks you over. His palms come away from his eyes wet. He pushes his glasses back on and takes a look. The horses and young girls are gone. He watches people going in and out of the IGA and the pharmacy and the little auto parts store at the end. People stepping along, looking eager, grayed, squeezed. People he knows by name or sight. All of them shopping, shopping, shopping. What is all this shopping?

He slips the clipboard to the seat, pulls up the brake, shifts into gear.

76 | Early morning at Moody's Variety & Lunch. All rockers and swivel stools face the TV. The TV that Louise Moody keeps by the coffee pot and grill. TV with a screen the size of a slice of American cheese. The people on the screen are wee and busy. Little laughs. Little sales pitches. Little politicians telling little fibs and little blames and assurances and weee little promises on the morning news. In the evenings Louise usually carries the little TV over to the checkout. In the evenings there's the many little shows of little families with their miniature, unlikely, and quickly solved situations. Louise Moody will tell you her little TV is what keeps this enterprise going. For without TV to watch, there'd be nothing to listen to but the many wisdoms of the Egypt wise men . . . wisdoms which Louise Moody calls "bullshit."

But this is morning. The morning news is on again.

This moment all the wise men who are in the brightly painted rockers rise from these rockers, all rising at the same time, and those on the stools lean hard onto the horseshoe counter. There is suddenly no sound but the gentle hum of refrigeration and the dragonlike but distant chuggings of two chips trucks idling at the curb . . . and this wee TV news . . . *another* interview with the white-kerchief-flapping protesters, another close-up of the blond smart-ass DiBias kid on the spotted-ass horse and the American flag, and what looks on TV like *hundreds* of women and children, though the wise men know it is *not* hundreds . . . just some trick of the eye . . . or something . . . something maybe rigged. You can't trust anybody these days.

The Reverend well driller David Moody leaves the cash register where he's been helping his mother during this busy bacon, eggs, and black coffee hour. He comes up behind Clarence Farrington and places his hand on the old guy's shoulder but doesn't speak. Surely the store is as hushed as church.

The newscaster says the movement for nonhunters' rights is strengthening in Maine . . . Maine being one of the most fervid hunting states . . . the two factions have declared war. What they show of the group of women marching, spliced with the newscaster's comments, seems to take only about eight seconds. When it is over, the wise men and the young men groan and mutter. And there's some big ugly defiant burps.

"I wouldn't call that little group of *ladies* a *statewide* movement," snarls young Randy Belanger.

"They are making a lot out of nothing," tsks another young one. "There's more people killed skiing than hunting. You'd think that one woman killed up to Pittsfield was a massacre or something."

Big old bear-built Arch Vandermast turns to the Reverend well driller David Moody who is zipping up his jacket, heading for the door. Everyone knows Wicks has got a well that's down to five hundred feet over at Merlin Soule's place. Hoping to strike something wet soon. Yesterday they got into red ledge. Another guy of Omar Wicks's crew slides off his stool and joins David.

Arch says, "Reverend . . . don't you think all this damn hoo-ha with these women has to do with women's lib? Don't you think it's related to this feminist business?"

"Yeah!" Randy Belanger joins in. "Whose side are you on, Reverend? The sportsmen or the . . . *ladies?*"

The Reverend David Moody leans a little toward them on one foot, smiling his peculiar and private smile. His silky blond Beach Boy hair falls into his eyes, and he has to heave it to the side. He speaks. "Once back when I was young . . . in high school . . . when we were over to the Finley place picking potatoes, I came up that old tractor road they still had before Keely bought 'em out. I came out on the tar and there I was . . . scuffing along . . . just me . . ."

The wise men and young men are all looking like they've heard this story before.

". . . and I saw something which caught my eye . . . an odd thing going on in the grass across the road. It was two moles fighting. Two moles. Two big moles. At first I thought it was mating. But it wasn't. It was a battle. They were so mad, they didn't notice me even though I stood there pretty close. I never saw a mole-fight before." He shakes his head, eyes bright with the miracle. "After a time, they separated. And each went down a hole. The holes were about two feet apart. And you'd never know those two holes were there. But suddenly . . . zip! zip! . . . the moles had disappeared into those two holes." He rubs his hands together gently.

All eyes are steady, polite, and dutiful on the reverend's hands.

"Then they popped back out of the holes and went right back at it again. Mole-fight. So amazing. And I don't mean *voles* or *shrews*. These were . . . you know . . . the ones with the big claws. But mostly they were just a gray blur. Tearing into each other. They were so busy fighting each other, these two little guys, that they didn't . . . well . . . you see, it was this big thing fell like a rag out of the sky, just dropped like a rag on the moles. Cooper hawk. Snatched up both moles and flew away with them." He smiles sorrowfully, returns to the door, gives it a pull, and the other well driller and he leave together, door easing shut behind them.

The wise men and young men want to remark what a weird guy the reverend is now that the door is shut behind him. But they can't. Not with the reverend's mother here. They just try to take up where they left off . . . to get back on the subject again . . . to get back on track.

77 A supple motion in his peripheral vision. A feather step. Like a spy. Or a thief. Not even a leaf rustles. This brute of a buck merges with Forest Johnson's stare.

Silence.

The buck's frosty breath has gone from curlicues to something solid as curses. His nostrils, ears, and eyes flare. Seems he wants to scream at the pale planet of Forest's human face and Forest's black eyes behind the glass circles that estimate him. Yes, it seems the buck will yell. But in this slow half moment of time, he remains dreamily quiet.

The first actual sound is not the buck's next move, nor the gun going off, but is from Forest's beltline. A snort of hunger. It is as though something is tearing out through his shirts and jacket. Forest mashes the hair trigger. Again. Again.

The buck is already graying into a blur of motion. The hooves thump-pump-pump-pump, dancing sideways. Leaves explode, implode. The animal vanishes even before the rifle stock grabs Forest's shoulder, before the first bang of gunpowder, which deafens Forest's right ear for a time.

"FUCK!" Forest keeps the rifle raised, blinking his eyes as though maybe it is something with his vision, that maybe the buck really is still there. What is it about his vision he doubts more than ever?

And now as deer have that way of noiselessly merging with the woods, so does the corner of a large gray house *emerge*, a new house with a small flat bulldozed yard . . . directly in his line of fire.

He wants to swallow but there's a rigor there.

He always thought this was paper company land. Between his boots and those houses, he sees now the sudden drop fifty yards straight down to shallow water, big-hurry water.

So the houses are in New Hampshire.

Otherwise he would have known. He knows everything that happens in Egypt. Requests for building permits. Requests for subdivision. Appeals. Variances. He is among them that know. But all his knowledges are chopped off here at the stream. Beyond the stream, he knows not.

There is a wearisome magic about the way these new places have appeared in this region in the last few years. The building boom, they called it. Progress. Yes, progress. Five hammers for five weeks. Then bingo! . . . the Volvos and BMW's in the two-car garage, the lawn grassed. Even as he finally swallows, another house shudders and pulses into existence to his far right, a dark-stained reproduction saltbox with its small flat treeless machine-made landscape, its car-width ribbon of tar. He lowers his rifle, sets the safety.

What is there to believe anymore?

He watches for signs of life in and around the little yards, someone to come screaming, "You idiot!" Or just the cry, a keening somewhere beyond the black break in the window of a child's room.

But there is nothing out of the ordinary about these homes. And yet nothing normal. A continuing silence. Picture-perfect absence of life.

The water begins a soft mumbling. Or is it that he's just beginning to hear? He has the sudden awful sense that he is being watched. Hunted. He leans with his shoulder against a three-trunk red oak, narrows his eyes, and studies the spanking white towers of white birch across the stream.

There is no one watching him. There is no one there.

Even what looks like another hunter standing beside him is only his own blaze orange blazing there, reflected off the bark of the oaks.

78 Forest Johnson, Jr., stretches his arm along the windowsill. In the "old days," except for the glow from the floor register and the glow of the quartz heater by the nurse's armchair, and the beer sign of Moody's Variety & Lunch, there would be darkness. A terrestrial, restful, believable grayness. A reward for the hard business of morning, noon, and afternoon. But no more. The greeny pinky purplish orangy security lamps billow and seethe. They rule. And for what? Security? Has he not just been robbed of every tool and piece of equipment that could be carried off by a few men? He considers taking his Weatherbee and firing upon the lamps. Those lamps that don't seem to faze his wife and mother. The women almost coo over the light. It almost reaches his throat . . . a mocking imitation of their cheerful voices.

Until these lights, the visits he made here to F.D.'s room were a different thing. He'd come up and tell the evening nurse to go take a little break. And then he'd snap off her reading lamp and sit here in the dark. He'd listen to the sounds of his family down in the parlor. And the TV if Eli had that on. How dreamy these sounds are when heard through floors and walls. Like ghostly arms around you.

It is sometimes better . . . the love you share through walls.

And in that good old darkness, F.D.'s seemingly bodiless head would be unseen. Now in the light that shouts, Forest turns away to stare down at the parking lot over at Moody's.

Old F.D.'s breathing is easy and patient and forgiving. Almost a little giggly. Almost like his *voice* used to be. A high little-man's voice. Forest will never hear that voice again.

He tucks his shirt into his belt, adjusts his suspenders, closes his eyes, and waits. He is so satisfyingly thick-waisted these days, bullnecked and strong-looking . . . the way F.D. never was. He wonders if F.D. knows he's in the room visiting. He clears his throat deeply to let him know. But to really speak now and not get an answer! Forest would feel really silly.

He's glad there's no nurse here. No Bett. Nobody. Just himself and F.D. alone here in the depravity of this awful light, embarrassed together.

79 | Jeff is toned down today, wearing a dark mock-turtleneck, his hands bare of rings, dark eyes steady on his mother's hands as she moves her man three spaces.

"My gosh but this is depressing!" she giggles.

"It's supposed to be," Anneka explains, grasps the dice, rattles them close to her own ear, jerking herself back and forth a bit like the dice are Spanish maracas.

Bett blinks. "You tell me what this is all about and I'll play. I just don't see the point."

Jeff says, "You never figured out *regular* Monopoly, Nanna . . ."

"I certainly *did*," she scolds.

He leans into Bett and buries his face in the shoulder of her sweater.

She sputters in embarrassed delight. "Jeff! Sit up! Act right." She tries to get her composure back. She tugs down on each of her sweater sleeves.

Anneka rolls the dice. She says, "Now . . . see . . . dice aren't for moving your man. Dice are for shaking a number. And that number that you shake you draw that many emergency expense cards from the emergency expense pile. See? Meanwhile your man has to land on each and every space like the days of the week and each day has daily expenses and you pay those expenses too as you go along. See?" Her man is situated on the first day of the week which reads GROCERIES $90. But her dice show a TWO. So she fetches two emergency expense cards. "Wedding present, thirty dollars for this first emergency expense. And the second emergency expense is a busted tooth. Seventy-five dollars." She presses her forehead. "Now you see that after groceries and the wedding present, there's no way I can get the busted tooth fixed, so I need to draw a card from this other pile. Whenever you run out of money, you draw a HOW-YOU-FEEL card. Hmm. Let's see . . ." She reads the card. "This card says I feel *violent*."

Bett says, "I don't understand."

Peggy pushes her chair back, goes to twist the flame off under the tea water, pours water into a row of mismatched mugs and cups. One cup is brand-new, one of the presents Jeff and Coti bought. It shows a cockroach family in some complicated aspect of life, one of the roaches speaking his piece to the rest.

There's the rattle of the porch-office windowpanes as the back door closes and Anneka drops the dice into Coti's open hand. Coti's long nails are painted violet tonight to match her new violet ski sweater, worn with skintight black jerseyesque pants and knee-high black boots . . . not the *complete* ski look, but there's a cool weather *theme* there. Coti's man moves from day one to day two, which reads TELEPHONE BILL $45 just as Forest pulls himself up over the high threshold from the office, and she says, "I'm down to one dollar, not enough to pay the phone bill. *Plus* I've got these emergency expense cards. *Six* of them. This one says I'm out of light bulbs. Five dollars for two light bulbs."

"Draw a HOW-YOU-FEEL card," Anneka tells her.

"*Mood* cards," Jeff chortles.

Eli is jiggling and his chair jiggles and jumps around under him. He says, "Without light bulbs, it would feel DARK!"

Jeff squeezes Eli's shoulder. "What a wit."

Peggy, returning to her seat, says, "It's depressing . . . a depressing game. It . . . really bothers me . . . I mean . . . Anneka . . . the fact that you know all these things. It feels . . . real."

"Yes!" says Anneka cheerily. "It's the game where everyone loses."

Anneka and Forest's eyes meet. She has been expecting him. But it's plain to see he wasn't expecting to see her . . . not *inside* his home.

Coti reads the HOW-YOU-FEEL card. " 'I feel like an outsider.' That's what it says."

Jeff snorts. Shakes his head. "Jesus . . . this is really something. You thought it up all by yourself??!" He is looking hard at the girl's profile, her hair braided today into pigtails, pigtails so earnest, crooked and hard as little tree limbs. She answers, "Yep." Jeff shakes his head. "Amazing. How old are you?"

"Seventeen," she replies.

Forest in head-to-foot blaze orange shambles toward the front hall, his many keys rasping.

The girl Anneka rubs her pigtails. They fight back. Very springy pigtails. She says, "These HOW-YOU-FEEL cards are the most important part."

Peggy says a little nervously, "This game is . . . well, kind of an awareness lesson, isn't it, Anneka?"

Anneka moves her silvery eyes onto Peggy's face, Peggy looking on the verge of weeping . . . Anneka flushed and jubilant.

Eli shakes the dice. He tries to do it in the jazzy way Anneka had done it, but one flips into the air and clonks onto the oak floor.

"Way to go, Eli!" Anneka crows. She squeezes one of his biceps. He gets more and more jiggly, his chair almost ready for a kind of take-off. It's not hard to see he has a crush on Anneka DiBias.

Jeff says, "Eli, quit goofin' around."

Eli returns from fetching the dice and drops them easy-careful on the board. He shakes a double six which means twelve emergency expense cards for Eli. He draws the first card from the pile. He squints at it. He thumps one foot. Jeff leans his way, reads the card for him. "Toilet paper." Then Jeff laughs like a maniac over the idea of toilet paper being an emergency expense.

Eli says, "Shut up."

Jeff howls like a wolf.

Eli gives the emergency expense card pile a little pat as if to tame it.

Jeff has dropped his face onto crossed arms, his laughs sounding like sobs.

"Quit it, J.J.," Coti says angrily. "You are bumping the table and moving everything around."

"Where *did* Forest go?" Bett wonders. "He always used to like games years ago."

Jeff's face pops up, reddened and puffed from too much merriness. He narrows his eyes and says levelly, "He won't like *this* one."

"Nobody is supposed to like it," says Anneka. "It's the game where everybody loses."

"Yeah, but . . . I don't mean like you mean." He cups his hand over his mouth and whispers loudly, "He's *Mr.* Minimum Wage."

Peggy says softly, "Maybe this game would be good for your father."

Jeff leans back, arms crossed over his black jersey, big smile. "You all wanna hear a good minimum wage story about Dad. Well, last . . ."

"No!" says Peggy. "Not now. Please, Jeff. Behave."

He bows his head, dramatically shame-faced.

They make the next few moves quietly, the dice coming back around to the girl Anneka, who upon drawing another HOW-YOU-FEEL card says,

"This card reads 'I feel like getting drunk and driving around.' The rules are when you have two OUTLAWED FEELINGS cards like getting drunk and driving around together with this other one that says 'I feel like cheating on welfare,' you go to *jail*, go directly to *jail*, do not pass payday, do not collect your one hundred thirty-two dollars minimum wage pay for the week. *And* you stay in jail for the rest of the game. So . . . here I go." She puts her man in the matchbox glued to one corner of the board. It has JAIL written inside it in Magic Marker.

Coti says faintly, "This is really bleak. Games are supposed to be fun, you know."

Bett says, "Peggy, don't forget milk in my tea, dear."

Peggy says, "Bett, I've only made tea for you for over twenty years. I've got it memorized." Now she turns to call, "Forest! Can you hear me?!"

"He's in the parlor. I saw him," Jeff says.

"FOREST! COME HERE!" Peggy commands.

Eli winds up with his second OUTLAWED FEELINGS card, which Jeff reads aloud for him. " 'I feel like arguing with this asshole cop.' "

Anneka says, "JAIL!" and snatches up Eli's man and plops it into the matchbox beside her man.

Eli looks glazed. *Together* with Anneka in jail. He doesn't smile, though. He just jiggles and jounces his chair.

Peggy prepares the teas and coffees . . . Island Orange for Eli. It's what he calls "monkey tea" because of the monkeys on the box.

Jeff says, "Hey Eli. There's those monkeys . . . see over there . . . those monkeys on the tea box. That's Eli and his friends, Joshua and Joshua."

Eli says with slitted eyes, "It doesn't bother me when you say that."

Peggy says, "We don't want to get Anneka's game all gunked up with honey and milk. She's put a lot of work into making that game. So maybe we can take a break shortly and carry our teas and coffee into the parlor." She glances toward the parlor. It's not a room Forest is known to spend time in. And yet there he is, in there alone . . . like a trapped animal. Trapped by what?

Coti sulks, "I guess the game is over when we're all in jail, right?"

Anneka explains. "Well . . . depending on your combination of OUTLAWED FEELINGS cards. You might not get *just* jail. If you get certain feelings, you might get the electric chair."

Coti turns, looks out the window. "This is silly."

Jeff says, "Oh, what a pussy. Can't take life's punches. I think this is the neatest thing I've ever seen. Jesus Christ, where's Dad, ol' Baron of the Minimum Wage?"

Peggy disappears through the front hall doorway.

"Ma can't take it either," Jeff complains, moving his man to "enormous health insurance payment."

Coti glowers at Jeff. "See! You can never make it to the next payday before you're out of money or in some *mood* or in trouble. It's not really a game. It's . . . just some kind of joke."

Jeff looks like he's just got electrically zapped. "That's it!!!" He grips his temples. He turns to Anneka. "You! Gawd, do I love you!" He clutches his heart. "Lookit this little world you've created right from scratch . . . pure innocent imagination." He sighs. "A world here . . . where I can get to be in jail with all my friends and family!" He looks up to see Peggy giving Forest little pushes into the kitchen. Forest with blaze orange cap in his hands against his blaze orange entirety.

He leans upon chairs, working his way around the table to one window, looking out into the inflamed purple green orangy pink evening. And only a few hours ago this same Anneka DiBias was leading a march in and out of the woods up by the old depot, magnet for *more* TV cameras, *more* reporters. They are coming from everywhere now. Boston, Texas, New York, Chicago, Washington. He says without turning to face her, "Busy as a little bee, aren't you?"

Anneka squares her shoulders, rubbing her jaw manfully as if deeply lost in the next move of the game. She says to Coti, "One more expense and you'll get to be in jail with us."

Peggy says brightly, "Anneka! Explain to Forest how this game works. Forest, you listen now . . . it's called The Minimum Wage Game. Anneka made this game up all by herself . . . it's quite a thing . . . a lesson in life, Forest. Sit down here with us . . . pleeeze."

Forest turns, opens his hand over the game board, giving each of the remaining game pieces a little flick, knocking them to their sides. One skids to Jeff's lap.

Now Forest shambles back out through the porch office, bangs the outside door shut.

Peggy looks after him and sighs.

Jeff leans close to the girl's ear and whispers, "He doesn't like you. I can tell."

80 Anneka's mother says not to worry about the phone bill, that he can pay her back someday when he's rich. So he talks to his mother for nearly an hour. Amy, his mother, mostly raves about what a jerk Jeff is. Her voice is hearty and husky and she keeps switching the receiver from ear to ear. He asks if he can talk to Smithereens. He can hear something move across the receiver, like a sleeve reaching. Then Eli gets to talk with Smithereens for a minute. When his mother comes back on the phone, Eli asks, "Do you think he heard me?" Amy says, "He flattened his ears out. Prob'ly pissed off at that joke you've got for a father."

81 In the middle of the night that is never dark, Forest speaks. "She's trying to get you to join her little army, isn't she?"

Peggy answers wearily. "No . . . she's never mentioned it. She doesn't even tell me *she's* doing it. It's not one of our subjects of conversation."

"What *are* your subjects of conversation . . . besides her sly little board games?"

"We just talk . . . oh . . . you know . . . girl talk."

"Hard to imagine," says he. And then after a silence, "I guess she's honing in on you nice 'n' easy. Going to get you at the right time."

"Forest, she's just a kid. Needs a role model. Like kids do."

He snorts at this.

"Forest, you don't believe me, do you? You think I'm in cahoots with her and that I'm lying to you."

"No . . . I don't think you're lying, Peggy. I just think you underestimate her." He flips onto his back. He sighs. "She's no kid."

82 There's the grunts and grumbles of the trucks starting. And the tap, tap, tap of sleet on the window by the bed . . . sleet that only lasts a few moments before fusing back into rain. There's something so discomfiting the way winter won't really start this year. Jeff stares into the black, very round wide-open eyes of Coti Pederson staring at him across her pillow. Her breath is visible and frosty. Mixing with his.

"What are you thinking?" she asks.

"I'm not thinking. I'm having the king of headaches."

"Why do you always have headaches? It can't be a hangover this time."

"My head is full of carrion beetles," he says.

She turns her face away, wincing.

"I lied. I confess. I lied. I *was* thinking."

She covers her face.

One of the trucks comes chugging close to the house, next to the shedway that connects the house with the old barn, the barn of apartments. Probably George DiBias, stopping near his apartment door like he sometimes does. And up in that apartment, his big-mouthed wife, Francine . . . big slobbery kisses. Parents of the kid Anneka that made The Minimum Wage Game. Big-mouth love. Maybe ol' George might fall into Francine's mouth and nobody will find him. That whole Soule tribe could get you in a corner. Soule women always trying to sell you something, get you on the phone, tickets to a raffle, Egypt History Week, or some supper. Bake sales. You see them swinging along, long arms, long-legged women, big rears packed into pants, moving in pairs or a threesome down one aisle at the IGA. You get out of the way fast. Avoid eye contact. There's sure to be a raffle. Then there's their yard sales. And roadside strawberries. Roadside corn. Roadside apples. Everywhere you go you hear a Soule woman beckoning . . . calling someone's name. Maybe *your* name. Soule woman's hand grabbing you by the arm to say you look wonderful. Or that you look like hell. Soule women with their mouths wide open, arms open. Big Soule welcome.

Poor George. You hear a lot of Forest's drivers say it in George's absence. "Poor George. You marry one Soule, you marry 'em all."

Now the truck is shifted into gear, sputters and hisses, snarls away from here. And now there's just the plat-plat of rain on the windows.

"I *was* thinking. I was thinking about my father," says Jeff. "You are the one who asked. You are the one who pried into my privacy. My nice private brain. Okay?"

Coti sighs. "I obviously made a bad mistake. Forget I asked."

"I was thinking about my father, how he's like Adam."

Coti tsks.

He says, "You know . . . Adam of Adam and Eve." Jeff's voice gets low, has that kind of low, soft hysteria to it that Coti has come to witness more and more since they arrived here. "My father is a pure man. Enviable." Jeff's left foot jiggles frantically.

The sleet comes again, working thicker and thicker upon the windows and tree limbs . . . a live hiss.

Jeff says, "It started off all right. There we were, in Eden . . . you know . . . as in the Garden of Eden. Dad was pretty nice to me really. I mean *really*. You think I hate him, don't you, Coti? You think I hate Forest."

"You're nuts," she says.

"It's my fault. I do complain . . . but . . . it's because it was so close to working out, you know. It almost worked out!"

Coti is rigid.

"My father is innocent of the world's nuances . . . of the world of *big shit*. For instance, his ideas about the work ethic and success, heroes and villains. And royalty. His simplicity is enviable. His *patriotism!* He *believes* in white hats and black hats, no shit. He believes there are godlike powers . . . well, you know . . . big wheels in government and business with his welfare on their minds. Justice. Fairness. Liberty. He's always believed that. It's always been his religion, I guess. He's never been a rebel. He has faith in authority. And hell . . . you know . . . Dad's life isn't without suffering . . . hell no. He suffers. But *stoically*. Shit happens to him as you've seen with your own eyes . . . but he has faith that in the end, it'll all turn out . . . you know . . . he has faith in *America*. He is so pure. God, what a pure man!"

Coti presses her left foot against his to stop his jiggling.

Jeff says, "It would have worked out maybe . . . me and him . . . but for the fruit and the snake."

Coti shrieks into his face. "STOP IT!! NO MORE! Next is blood-letting, right??? We're going to go into that, right? It is getting SO MONOTONOUS, JEFF! I CAN'T STAND IT!!!" She grabs the alarm clock off the stand and throws it at him. It strikes his forehead with a metallic clack! . . . then drops into the blankets . . . and there's a lot of little clack-clack-clacks, which is the alarm going off. Coti swings her legs out from the covers. There's a nasty pink thumbprint-sized mark on Jeff's forehead.

Jeff's voice lowers into a deeper softer hysteria. "Education is the work of the devil! All that eye-opening stuff. The big fruits. Big fat apples. Venom of the snake! Once you've taken the bite, you can never go back! You are cast out!" Jeff sits up. The mark on his forehead is starting to swell brightly. He runs a finger down the nubs of Coti's spine. "Coti,

I'm just trying to work this through, baby. Help me! Please . . . just let me work this through. It's my *life!*"

The room is so cold. Much different than when the little heater was pumping out red warmth. Where did the heater go? *Why* did it go? Coti wonders this about the heater. But to Jeff its disappearance is a simple fact of life.

"Don't you ever think about where your life went wrong?" Jeff asks her. "Don't you ask *why?*"

She turns and looks at him, her riddle of beautiful dark hair tumbling off one shoulder. "You are nuts," she hisses.

"You are like him. That's it. You are like him . . . girl version of the same. Pure people. And Amy, too. So pure. All of you. The whole world . . . so pure. A world of buzzing bees. Just buzzing along, headed straight for the flower and back." He chuckles. "Jesus . . . I'd give anything to shrink back to the old me, take one of those trucks out into a storm, work like hell all night, see the world through one of those pocked windshields . . . 'America the Beautiful' . . . and what's that other one . . . you know . . . 'Oh Say Can You See By the Dawn's Early Light . . . Hope the Flag's Still Right There'!" He sighs. "But you can't go back after you et the fruit. You can't get back in through that little bitsy squirty narrow door." He moans. "Coti, baby . . . lay back down with me . . . Jesus . . . I love you I love you I love you I love you I love you."

"I never knew how weird you are."

"I'm sorry."

"And boring," she says. "The worst part of this whole trip is all these days going by and all we do is . . . you know . . . see your boring friends . . . sit at the table downstairs or hang out in this room, which is cold, and talk about your father. *Your father.* Jeff, *your father* isn't anything. He's just a guy!"

"Lay down with me, Coti. I promise to keep my promises. Just lay down and let's start the day over. Let's pretend we're asleep waking up all over again." He makes a pretend sleeping noise.

Outside the door, Eli's level voice speaks. "Dad."

83 Blue-and-white pickup truck eases in and out of this hard light of November, the hard ribs of sun and shadow. Maples touch like fingertips over Rummery Road . . . leafless now . . . everything pared to its body. Everything seemingly honest. The pickup turns in at Moody's

Variety & Lunch, idles in the side lot. Now it faces out, faces the brick colonial across the way. Nobody steps out of this truck to go into Moody's. After a time, the truck pulls out onto the road. The choppy November light closes in and around the truck like water. Truck returns several times this day. And the next. Sometimes there are two men in the cab. Sometimes one. Sometimes three. What is the plan? Everything moving toward the low flinty meridians of these short days, racing toward the quick dark. Maybe there is no plan. Just waiting. Desperation in sequences, getting hotter. Curses aimed at the Tile Green front door with the fanlight above it and the sidelights up and down. Curses upon each handsome brick.

84 | There had been a storm warning but the storm was reported to have gone out to sea. It is after midnight. But with a busted alarm clock, they can only *guess* at how much after midnight.

Coti says, "Now that we have no heat in here, I'd like to know what you're going to do about it . . . you know . . . now that it's freezing . . . *really* freezing."

Jeff laughs evilishly, his laugh ending in a little cry. Now his left foot jiggles . . . his hysteria always begins in his left foot.

"J.J., can't you ask them *where* they put the heater? It's *ours*, for godsakes. We bought it!"

Jeff shoves the blankets off himself and arches his bare chest into the frigid air.

Coti endures this with silence. Not even one of her disappointed sighs.

Jeff does something to his hair. Digging. Scratching. He reaches for the clock that's on the floor by his shoes and socks. He wings it against the wall. He flops back onto the bed, forearms over his eyes.

Coti tries to keep the covers in place around her, a fierce grip. Tonight's filmy gown's really a mint color. But in the lie of the security lights, it has an atomic-bombish dusky red glow.

Jeff sits up, hovers on the edge of the bed, staring at the dresser mirror with the familiar old photos crammed around the edges and the *unfamiliar* light bounding off the spotty surface.

Coti says huskily, "You weren't like this in Cally."

He shrugs.

She says, "You're crazy. I hate this place. Can't we just get the car fixed and go back in a few days. J.J. . . . please . . . I HATE it here. It's not working out."

"*California* is not working out." He stands, steps over clothes and shopping bags and the rubble of their long hours spent in this room. He goes to the wall, his parents in their bed beyond. He punches the wall hard.

There's a moment of silence. Then on the other side of the wall, an answering punch, the clatter of plaster tumbling down inside against the studs.

Jeff grins. "He answered me." Jeff punches the wall again.

Over there beyond the wall, his mother, Peggy, cries, "STOP!" But there it is . . . another fierce smack and clatter of plaster . . . his father's answer.

Jeff punches his side of the wall again.

Almost instantly a BANG! . . . like Forest must be using a piece of furniture over there.

And Peggy wailing and commanding, "FOREST! STOP! WHAT'S THE MATTER WITH YOU??? JEFF! YOU STOP—PLEASE! BOTH STOP!!"

Jeff lunges for the spare brass drapery rods leaning against the molding of the closet door. He turns with one in hand, swings hard like for a home run. Paper and plaster explode, skid and splatter over his bare feet.

A moment of silence. Then the answer comes. A savage blast, identical to his own.

Now Jeff is leaning a shoulder to the wall, breathing hard.

And on the other side of the wall, the father matches this pose, his shoulder against the wall, using his one foot for balance. Now Forest leans his forehead against the old red wallpaper that appears to be purple wallpaper in this lying light. And it is true, Forest is as naked as Jeff is, waiting, listening, catching his breath, getting second wind for more.

85 Jeff Johnson, last seen backing the Camaro out of the yard, is gone, gone for good, and he did not take Coti Pederson with him. Coti stays in the room upstairs. Peggy knocks on the closed door every few hours asking her if she'd like something to eat.

"No, thank you," replies Coti beyond the door.

"Are you cold? Wouldn't you like to come down and sit by the stove? Bett and I don't bite."

"I'm okay," says Coti. "Thanks for asking."

When earlier Peggy had asked through the door "Where did Jeff say he was going?" Coti had answered, "He didn't say." But he wouldn't be coming back, that's for sure. That's a sure thing. Coti knew that much for sure.

Later Peggy calls through the door again and asks Coti if she'd like to talk about going back to California. She says Forest is willing to help her out with the plane ticket.

Coti says that she'd rather go back in the Camaro, that the Camaro is hers. And she has a lot of clothes and "things" in the Camaro. She says she still owes payments on the Camaro. She says she has no idea where Jeff and the Camaro are but the bank owns the Camaro . . . bank in California. Her voice does not have a bitter edge to it, nor its usual sexy gaspiness. It just sounds straightforward and courteous.

86 | In the night a truck passes slow. Brakes rubbing their drums. Truck stops. But the solid, weathertight nonnegotiable brickness of the Johnson house sends its weird riddle of blindingly bright light rebounding from windshield and side mirrors. The truck moves on.

87 | Phone clamors near this bed. But Forest's fingers do not scramble to answer it. Who is calling? He considers the possibilities. Like a stampede of heavy animals, they visit this bed. On the fourth ring, Peggy raises up on an elbow. "Forest?"

"*No.*"

She eases back more deeply into the bedding.

The security light through the curtains and six-over-six panes hums upon their skin. Hums against their wide open eyes. And the phone shrills. And once again a truck approaches, idles awhile, then moves on.

88 | It seems F.D. has come to life to die. He is on his right side with his head thrown back, panting like a little overheated dog . . . harder, harder, harder. He has not had good teeth for ages, too stubborn to do right by his teeth, too reckless, too jokey. And now it shows . . . the shrunken mouth. It is clear it embarrasses Forest, Jr., that everyone here crammed in this room is watching the empty mouth and this bare business of dying.

They have come from a few towns north, F.D.'s sister's people. Some of Bett's people, too. Not a lot of people, but enough to make water gush through the pipes of this old house. Doors open. Doors click shut. A too cozy vigil in this room. Stripes of midmorning sun slash across the print stripes of Bett's sister's dress. The nurse reaches to lower a shade. Forest glares at her through his metal-framed old "Roosevelt" glasses, so she lets the shade pop back up out of her hand.

Bett's sister says, "Go get yourself a tonic at the store, Forest. Stretch your legs."

This strikes Forest funny . . . this thing an aunt will say to you no matter how old you get. He grins at her boyishly.

Old F.D.'s shoulders heave. Working hard. Straining inside the twisted pajama top.

A few more relatives crowd into the room. The nurse explains to the newcomers, "His vital signs are not good. It won't be long."

Forest flips through a heavy equipment magazine, finishes that. Flips through some *Readers' Digests*. Risks his way through a ladies' magazine.

Bett's back is a little hunched. Standing there, watching F.D. die.

Some of Bett's people have gone out to the hallway, standing along the balustrade, talking softly of another death in the family . . . comparing. That one was sudden . . . it's so different when it's sudden.

Quartz heater and an additional little whirring fan heater push a smidgen of warmth about.

Across the hall, beyond a closed door, Coti Pederson sleeps.

F.D. pants harder now. Powerfully.

Forest, Jr., stares into the nothingness of stripy sun and elbows, hardwood furniture, and peach wallpaper. With his steel-framed glasses, high-topped work boots so earnestly laced, shirt white . . . suspenders . . . green wool work pants, and that hair parted in the middle with the short pieces combed wetly to each side, he is like a man no longer living. Not a corpse. More like a glimpse of a man in his prime who lived in another era. Just a remembrance.

There's a whirring down in the kitchen. Someone running the blender.

"He's breathing faster, isn't he?" one of Bett's people observes.

"Yes, I think so," says the nurse. This is not one of the usual nurses, not the nurse that has the same hair and shoes as Bett nor the other one. The ones that always shout. This nurse has a plaid overshirt and jeans.

A kind of woodsy-looking nurse. She lays her hand on Bett's shoulder and says softly, "It won't be long now. He's doing his job. It's hard work."

F.D. tightens into a curl, his body squeezing smaller and smaller . . . efficient . . . practical. The nurse strokes F.D.'s thin hair. "Come on, Forest," she urges.

Everyone watches old Forest's elfin shape with its alarming power . . . pumping, pumping.

"Something's happening," says one of the young men with F.D.'s sister's people.

"Linda should be here," Bett's sister tells Peggy. "Couldn't she get a plane?"

Peggy says, "No. Linda couldn't make it." *Linda*, Peggy and Forest's daughter, their younger child. The success. The win. The independent self-assured. Nice job in New York. It's the kind of thing you are supposed to get to brag about. But sometimes there's this perplexing shame.

"And Jeff. Where's Jeff?"

Old F.D.'s breathing is in chunks now . . . long pause, long forceful breath, long pause, long forceful breath . . . on and on.

"My god," whispers F.D.'s sister. During F.D.'s pauses, she holds her own breath.

Forest stands, works his way around elbows and shoulders to the hall. He shambles down the hall to his and Peggy's cold room. He stretches out on the bed on top of the old olive-color tasseled spread.

The hoax is nearly over.

Maybe this very moment it is finished . . . F.D. dead . . . and Forest need not be the pretend son, the great fake. The junior. It is okay now that he looks in every way like Edmund Barrington. Peace flutters down on him. He crosses his arms over his chest and scrutinizes the old white-painted ceiling fixture that has no bulb in it. Long ago shorted-out.

89 | Another night with the sound of a pickup truck moving through it on the edge of dreams. And then the phone, which wakes him. He opens a hand on it, lets the vibration of the signals work against his palm like a small creature struggling.

90 | Another late night. Kiwanis. Good speaker. Good food. Forest gets home, pulls himself along up the stairway, his chunk of keys always strident. From the kitchen behind him come footsteps. Boots. The weight of a man. There's hurry. Forest grips the top newel post, turns.

Jeff's face is gaunter than the gaunt California look. And bearded. Not a real beard. Just a drunkard's beard. The kind that fills in the face out of spite. Forest backs up against the door to Bett's little room, studying Jeff's beard, the dark look of it, the dark blood of Edmund Barrington stealing down through the generations, blighting, creeping into this moment. "Where've you been?" Forest wonders in a casual sort of way.

Jeff groans, rubs his hair with both hands. "Right here," he says. "This side of the river."

Forest gives a quick once-over to the dark chamois shirt over the green work shirt. And there at the throat and wrists, the dimpled look of thermal underwear. "You look like a workin' man," he declares.

"Right," says Jeff, stepping around to press his back to the newel post. "Working."

"You got a new woman?" Forest wonders.

Jeff chuckles grimly. "Not exactly *new*. Just some backtracking." He chuckles again. "You know . . . one of these wholesome Maine women."

"How's that different from the California kind?" Forest marvels, feeling into his pocket for a bandanna, does some distracted-looking digging in his nose with it.

Jeff squints, slides his back a bit too far to the left of the newel post, regains his balance with a giggle. He says, "No difference in women really . . . no . . . nope . . . none. They are all the same, a chain . . . like McDonald's." He grins big.

Forest pockets the bandanna. "You know we buried Gramp yesterday, didn't you? Small town. News travels."

Jeff says, "No. I didn't know." He sighs, slips dangerously to the left of the newel post, but catches himself in time.

"So tell me. Where'ya workin' these days?" Forest wonders.

Jeff says, "Well . . ." He rubs his beard, his hair. He gives his eyes a good mashing with his palms. "I've decided to get the fuck out of the art biz."

"You are a changeable man . . . like . . . don't take this wrong . . . but like a lizard." Forest smiles his rare broad smile that reveals his bluish tooth. "So what are you doing these days, Jeffrey?"

"I just got sick of the old art world. So much bloodletting." Jeff grins *his* broadest grin.

Forest grins back.

Jeff's gaze slides from his father's face, down the shirtfront to the belt and batch of keys. "You know most people have to fight like hell to get vacation time. But in the art world, you've got to fight like hell to get *work time*. People always stopping by . . . thinking you're just home with nothing to do. So hard to concentrate . . . with everybody needing, needing, needing. And never having enough space. Walls that are never big enough. No place to store my work. Fighting for the right light. Scrambling for grants. Making out grants. Waiting to hear. Wondering. Trying to concentrate. Meanwhile, everybody needing, needing, needing. Banging on the door. And whatever image I had there coming down my right arm into that brush . . . pop! . . . it's lost." He grins.

Forest grins back.

Grin for grin. They are matched in ferocity.

Jeff says, "And there I am squeezed all up inside every brush-stroke . . . you know . . . this next brushstroke is going to be the most astonishing thing a human being ever painted or it's going to be just a big blot that'll turn my last three weeks work on that canvas into trash. And there's no repairing it!" He burps. He sways too far to the left. "Especially if you're using acrylics. Or if you're using waters . . . forget it! There it goes! Blop!" He sways, stumbles to the very edge of the stairs, swings backward out into space, grasps the newel post and neatly, almost with a dancer's grace, swings back into a casual slouch with his back to the post. "Thennnn the bloodletting when Jeffrey Johnson goes to deal with the high priestesses and high priests with the big nose holes at the galleries . . . *if* he, Jeffrey Johnson, can get past the recep-tionist . . . if if if Jeffrey Johnson knows the right people or had the right show at the right place the last time and the reviewers didn't have heartburn, *then* you might get past the receptionist and get to look up the nose holes of the high priest who gets to wipe the grease of his French cuisine lunch from his fingers onto my slides . . . and there I am, blood running like a river." He sees his father's eyes are, with their dark and blazing astigmatism, fixed onto his mouth as the word *river* fades.

"You spend my lucky hundred-dollar bill, Jeffrey?"

Jeff hoots, "You always do that to me! You always make me out like some kind of crook!"

"That's because you are . . . a goddam thief!"

"I am not a thief!"

"You are a thief!"

"I'm not!"

"Figured you needed to feed your need . . . your addiction," Forest says gravely.

There's the sound behind one of the doors like Peggy is dressing to come out. And at another door, Eli listening. And behind Forest, Bett's door with Bett listening. A whole household listening on the other sides of doors and walls.

Forest says, "It's also occurred to me that you might be buying drugs and selling to others of the need . . . like to stretch the dollar . . ."

"No dope for me!" Jeff says with a cackle. "Dad, I'm off that illegal terrible unpatriotic weedy stuff. No more for me! Just nice good ol' over-the-counter Jim and Jack. I'm doin' what's moral and right. Just say NO, I says. Just drink. Like the President, Dad."

Forest raises his chin.

Jeff glances from door to door down the wide hallway.

"Where's the sporty car, Jeffrey? The one with the bad exhaust that can't seem to find the sporty car repair shop. I didn't see it out in the dooryard. Your California woman claims it's hers. Now how's she going to get back to California without a car?"

Jeff snorts. "Give her a broom."

Forest almost smiles.

Jeff glances toward the door of the room where Coti is listening.

"So what are you doing now, Jeff? What's your new job?"

"Drinking, Dad. I'm a full-time drunk . . . eight hours a day and then some overtime. Except now 'cause I'm fresh out. So it's sort of like, you know . . . my day off."

Forest says, "I'm sorry." He starts to turn away, turn toward the door where Peggy is making more sounds. But Jeff leaps at him, seizes one arm.

The arm stiffens. Forest's face comes around fast. "What! What can I do for you?"

Jeff's breath is sour from his most recent bourbon. He is all breath. No answers.

Forest says, "What about your son?"

Jeff leans away, releases Forest's arm. "I'm giving him to you. I'll sign whatever papers your attorney conjures up. You want him? You want him, Dad?"

Forest flushes hard with his wanting.

Jeff crosses his arms, scratches his back on the newel post. Newel post creaks.

Forest says, "Don't you want to have a little talk with *him?* Maybe he ought to be clued in on this, huh? Out of courtesy or something?"

"I have. Clues. A lot of clues."

"Right. And what about Amy? She would have to sign off. And *she* is not going to do that."

Jeff snorts. "Amy is a Bean . . . remember. Low-dough. You think any judge is going to like Amy over you guys? And the only lawyers she's got out there or could get back here is *legal-aid*. None of that's worth shit these days. You guys got the bucks. I'd say, go for it."

Coti is now standing at the open door of her room. Very quiet, wearing a dark robe.

And the knob to Peggy's door twists . . . and Peggy is stepping into the hall.

And Jeff is saying, "Dad . . . I need work. I can go for my class B again. You know I can handle it. I *need* work. I got rent to pay. And you can use me. I know ol' Raymond is sick . . . right?"

Forest says, "Beg."

And Jeff says, "Pardon? What?"

And Forest says, "Beg."

And Peggy says, "Forest!"

And Coti is silent, courteously silent, barely present.

And behind Eli's door, no sound.

And behind Bett's door, nothing.

Jeff leans hard against Forest as if to embrace him, but slips down along his legs to the boots with the damaged feet within.

Peggy shrills, "Get up, Jeff!"

"But I'm begging," he says in a muffledness, mouth against Forest's wool pants.

Peggy cries out, "Enough!! Forest, enough!!!"

Jeff's hand strains up toward the keys on Forest's belt.

Forest kicks him.

Jeff walks backwards on his all-fours.

Forest kicks again.

Jeff covers his head.

Forest sinks down, gets a grip on Jeff's shirt and they both rise, teetering at the edge of the stairs . . . chunk of keys singing . . . Forest drives a fist into the soft hardness of his son's shoulder. And Jeff hits back. And down the long flight of carpeted stairs they scramble and thump and ram . . . and then Peggy is beating them apart with a broom . . . like two dogs . . . and it is over and done . . . one gone to the parlor breathing hard, the other gone out the back door.

And the phone rings.

And the security lights strain in at every window.

91 | Another day begins and ends.

Eli is set up with Bett's oatmeal carton of crayons in the glassed-in office, the room of sweet grandmotherish-faced deer heads. Forest has just come in from the shop, stands by the desk, sorting through mail . . . insurances, insurances, insurances, fuel bill, bank. The unpretty truths.

He turns and sees the boy staring at him, the great pale eyes in black lashes. Eli. He is scared of Forest. Since last night, what would it take to win his affections?

Forest leans toward him, peers down at what Eli has been drawing . . . but there's no drawing. Paper is blank. The kid is not artistic.

Forest picks an orange crayon from the carton, fills the paper with orange slashes, swirls, and zigzags. He stands back and cocks his head slightly. "Picture of hell," he says.

Eli keeps his eyes on the picture. No words. He is like the Eli of the first day on arrival from California. Cold-blooded.

Forest pokes the crayon back into the oatmeal carton with care. He smiles. "Hell is easy. Not so hard as most pictures." He pushes at his glasses, studies his picture and says "Ayuh" with satisfaction. He goes limping away into the other rooms of the house.

Eli's eyes move in among the crayon marks of the drawing. The picture is just a mess. Nothing you could call art in the "Art World." But the burning lines bewitch Eli. He looks a long while at them. He strokes them. He even drops his head and sniffs the paper.

92 | Anneka and her mother say they'll leave the room to give Eli privacy. He dials each number with painful care . . . interrupted twice by the electronic voice that jumps in there when you don't dial fast enough. He starts over again, a little shaky with the fear of getting the electronic voice again. But trying to dial faster only makes his mind blank. Each number completed without the *voice* is a gift. Then there's the ringing at the dark end of great distance, his mother germ-sized. Now her big HELLO.

This number with the area code in front of it and the number one in front of that. All his life it will have a place in his head. Like a brand on flesh. Like the only two words he can write. Eli and Johnson.

93 | It is not a thing she is used to . . . being alone here . . . *absolutely* alone. Coti gone forever on a plane. Eli with Bett over at Bett's sister's helping out at their craft shop. Forest at a selectmen's meeting. F.D. in the grave. It's not the kind of house meant for a person to be absolutely alone in. It seems to creak, crow, growl, and tease more when you're alone here. The small stone of her engagement ring twinkles madly from the security light pouring across the bedspread, engulfing her hand. Oh, her ring! That ring Forest spent so much on when he was so young.

The stairs outside her door give as though someone steps there. But nobody steps there tonight. She is alone.

Now a little cry in the eaves. Just wind.

Now the bedroom door opens.

Peggy rises up to sit in the pink appalling light or is it green or is it orange or is it purple? She sees the face that sees her face, neither one happy to see the other. There has been some mistake. He has made a bad mistake. It is said he doesn't make any mistakes. But somehow he has misjudged this house.

The set of the shoulders and arms is Forest. But the feet . . . feet in sneakers . . . whole feet, smooth-going feet . . . this is not Forest. Nor the hat. One of those green felt crushers like so many of the farmers and loggers around here wear. And the moustache spewing dark with gray, more gray since the last time she saw him around town. Of course she knows who he is. The legend. It's just that in this space, he is more so. Her throat is choked with fear and wonder. He is backing away, his eyes shyly averted . . . one light, one dark. The dark iris is like a hole in his eye. As if it echoes Forest's astigmatism, or Forest's bad eye echoes his.

That would depend on which man was born first, wouldn't it? . . . as to which was the echo of the other. But it is said that they have the same birthday! Born the same day to different mothers. Born the same hour? The same moment?

Now Peggy is unsure. Maybe his being here is not a mistake. Maybe it's his finest hour.

He eases the door closed.

He makes *no sound* leaving.

94 | Right away Forest discovers the missing guns . . . the complete horrific void in the gun cabinet out on the porch office. Now the only guns Forest has to his name are those two he carried tonight in his pickup. He and Peggy both sit at the little enamel supper table under the glare of the overhead kitchen fixture. All around them a creepy silence. It is midnight. Forest has taken his glasses off, laid them on the table. He leans onto his elbows, hands over his face. Eyes glitter through his fingers.

Peggy offers, "You want me to call the constable? Or the state police? Or somebody?"

He doesn't reply, but his eyes glitter more.

Do you want me to make you a sandwich . . . tea? Something?"

Between the fingers, the eyes. They stare at her without a flinch.

Peggy drums her fingers on the table, glances at Forest, then away. She is starting to feel scared . . . far more scared of Forest than of the thief.

95 | All day Wednesday, Peggy's people turn up, unpacking their rental cars of luggage, house gifts, and bakery pies.

"You look wonderful!" they all tell each other.

And yes, everyone looks terrific, hardly changed.

Catherine, the baby, who was only a few weeks old last year is now mobile. And she wears a white plastic lamb barrette in her hair.

The older kids swarm outside to meet Eli who has climbed up into the high seat of one of the old dismantled dump trucks. He looks purposeful and broad-shouldered as a man on the job.

"Over the river and through the woods!" Peggy's youngest brother Bryce sings out as he always loves to do. With a flourish, he unloads fruit baskets, imported wines, and various imported canned "treats" and then while he sort of hangs off Peggy and sings "When Irish Eyes are Smiling," their mother, Connie, tsks disgustedly and says, "You are only one-eighth Irish. It's hardly worth mentioning." But Bryce sings on and on, his voice a high thin screech. All of Peggy's family: such high sounds, tweeting and screeching, full of energy, and talk talk talk talk.

"Want to go see the horsies, sweetheart?" someone asks.

"Hor-see!" Baby points down the hallway.

Everyone laughs. So cute. So smart. "The pediatrician told us she's developing in the top ten percent range for her age," the baby's mother shrills.

Peggy gets Bett alone in the back pantry for a private little talk. Peggy shuts the door. She asks Bett at what point should they accept that Forest isn't going to get his deer this year? If they are to buy a turkey, it'll have to be soon. The stores may be closing early tonight.

The guests carry their luggage to the upstairs rooms assigned to them, including the two roughly finished attic rooms of the third floor. This is a full house for sure.

How the rooms of the second floor have changed in these last few days! No rental hospital bed and IV stand, no sleepy-looking nurse. No heaps of fast food wrappers and pastel teddy gowns, shopping bags, receipts, and grunting screeling hard rock on the radio. No crumbled plaster and fist-sized holes in the walls. Furniture is moved. Holes fixed. Floors swept. Air is aired.

Peggy's mother's springer spaniel, Buttons, needs a walk.

"Where should we put disposable diapers? Do you think they sort for recycling here?"

"Where's Eli? I have something for him."

The sharp-pitched screeching, tweeting voices rebound in and out of every high-ceilinged room.

Behind the pantry door, Bett and Peggy whisper. Peggy sighs, lays her head back against a calendar that has hung there since 1942. Shows a masted schooner on rough seas. December. A bad month of a bad year. Peggy looks at Bett and sees the same little twinkle in the eye that Peggy has in hers. Peggy says, "I'm going to go out and get the turkey now."

Bett nods.

"And then if Forest shows up at the last minute with a deer, I run like hell out the other door and bury the turkey, no questions asked."

———

96 Sister-in-law Madge , having first pick, saddles up Dolly, the new mare. Dolly is much taller than the other mares, as high at the shoulder as the stallion, Mars. This new horse. This beautiful gray. A royal queen! How grueling it was to work that money out of Forest! Peggy knows what's on the books. She *keeps* the books. She knows they are in trouble. And yet she literally wept for this horse. Why is it that even when you are a practical person, something will come along now and again that will make you crazy?

Peggy saddles up dark Vassar, who is a mind reader, who knows Peggy is tired, very, very tired, and so he won't joke and dance and carry on like the other horses surely would. Together the two women put their horses to a canter down over the first real hill, into a washout, then up and up and up through a dark channel of hemlock, hooves muffled upon the lane of hemlock spills like prayers of thankfulness. And yet the head-to-foot blaze orange the women wear and the blaze orange ribbons of the horses are not quiet.

Now as Peggy reins Vassar to a walk, she loses sight of her sister-in-law . . . but can hear the big horse's hooves striking stone up ahead and a neighbor's car passing out there on the paved Jordan Mill Road, a half mile away. So odd for Thanksgiving time, wearily warm. Like villainous breath. And way too warm to be comfortable in head-to-foot blaze orange quilted polyester. Peggy feels a wave of resentment. But toward who?

Vassar nickers to the big gray. And there's an answering nicker beyond the ledge, a small girlish nicker for so mountainous a horse, the beautiful gray, the royal queen.

Coming closer there's the rumpus of a logging crew on the back side of the hill . . . at least one skidder and the buzzes of two or three faraway saws. Now bringing Vassar at a hard run over the next hill, Peggy expects to catch sight of Madge and the big gray. But there's no sign of her. Just one roaring skidder heaving up over the ridge from the left. It crosses the trail before her with the thumps and crackles of its twitch. Vassar is uneasy. Peggy gives Vassar's shoulder a stroke of reassurance. Peggy can see something of a yellow-and-black plaid shirt inside the cage of the skidder but only the shadow of a face. And pounding through the warm air the diesel stink of machine, the sweet death perfume of harvest. Pounding . . . pounding . . . then down a grade and gone.

BLAZE ORANGE. There's sister-in-law Madge's legs and shoulders glowing as though she rides on air. The horse gray as stone. Gray as beech and sugar maple, blurred into nature. Peggy knees Vassar into a trot to catch up. "Hey!" Peggy sings out. "Let's follow the logging road back out and we can ride that pretty field!"

Madge says, "Yes! The red field!"

They turn back and pick along with care through the slash and mire where the skidder went.

Madge says, "It's too bad Linda's not coming again this year. How is she, anyway?"

"Oh . . . busy. She's not much for writing and she's taken after Forest . . . you know . . . cheapskate . . . so she doesn't call a whole lot."

"Well, it's expensive to live in New York."

"Yes . . . that's what she says."

Madge wonders, "I didn't see Forest around. Did you say he was working today?"

"No. He went out about four this morning to try and get his deer in time for . . . you know . . . tomorrow."

"Oh."

Peggy slows her horse nearly to a standstill as they commence down a washout. Madge takes the gray on ahead. Peggy watches the streaked mass of Dolly's tail nearly reaching the ground. How the other mares must gossip about this showy hussy!

Vassar stumbles. Just a little stumble. So much downhill, brush, rut, and rock.

At last when they come out into the field, the two horses and riders go abreast. Madge exclaims "Oh!" when she sees the backsides of the cul-de-sac of new homes. Silver Heights. And above that on the sunny ridge, The Village at Cold Rain Pond. More like titles to romance novels than neighbors.

Peggy sighs. "I forgot about those houses. I haven't been over this way for a couple of years."

Madge studies the houses with interest. "Look at that there. One of those big Japanese paper globe lanterns in that window. Looks nice with the plants and white wrought-iron furniture. Cozy deck."

"Mmmmmm."

Once out on the tar road, Madge says, "So Bett says Jeff and Amy won't be around for the meal tomorrow. Did they fly Eli up here?"

Peggy says quickly, "Both my Jeff and my Linda are pretty independent. They just . . . go and do." She seems a little stuck here, a little choked up.

Madge jumps to the rescue. "Well, you did a good job raising your kids. Spreading their wings is painful but normal. Kids who can't get out and take on the world are insecure! Both your kids have gone on to be successful! Don't knock it! Kids these days have a lot that's expected out of them. Parents who tie them down with their own wants and needs are being unfair. If Peter and Marietta and Sean wanted to live next door to me, I'd wonder what I'd done to screw them up! I really would!"

Peggy closes her eyes a moment to the jingle and squeak and clop-clop-clop of their procession along the tar road.

Madge insists, "Kids today have great opportunities. And you know that!"

Peggy frowns. "So what you're saying is we give birth to these . . . these children . . . have a relationship for eighteen years . . . then you kind of set them on a launching pad, light the fuse, and blow them away . . . like . . . rockets?"

"Peggy! Not rockets!" Madge laughs delightedly, the knotted-up-earflap blaze hunting cap Peggy has loaned her tipping rakishly on her honey-color flip-cut hair. "More like shooting stars. Call them shooting stars. Doesn't that feel much nicer?"

97 It is the A.M. of the next day. Thanksgiving. Predawn. Warm, beerlike sweetness in the air. Dark. Again Forest waits in the woods on the far east boundary of his land. A stone wall made flat here like a high seat. A tree to brace his back. So it has come to this siege. No birds. No squirrels. Nothing moves. And he has come to a point of neglect. Of obsession? A beard has filled in. A hunter's beard. Which resembles a drunkard's beard. Though some would say a hunter's beard is nobler. He has a fighting grip on the Weatherbee that he's laid across his thighs. The hunter's hands. Nobler than hands that compromise. His eyes see nothing in the blackness of the backside of this hill. He thinks of nothing but the shoulder, rib cage, forehead of a buck deer. The gray dawn expands beyond the crisscrossing of young oaks, dried blackberry, and slash. Dawn swollen, soft, cobwebby gray.

The earth turns.

He waits, not moving, not even to scratch the fierce itch near his nose.

Love. It is with the power of love that he raises the rifle and squeezes off two shots at the face with its starburst of morning sun between the antlers. The great buck bleats once as its jaw explodes into the smithereens of its face, purpled red, dangling bone, a strip of cheek fluttering like a couple of socks hung out to dry. The deer spins on a single hoof, romps to the left, white tail rippling. Forest fires into the shoulder . . . the shoulder . . . the shoulder. Now into the white. But the shoulder and zigzagging white ass remain intact, the white even whiter than before, legs and oak saplings crackling, breaking apart, treacherously lacing together . . . deer gone.

Forest rises from the stone wall . . . squinting . . . shambles toward the region where the blood should be and it is as it should be . . . a splat on the leaves . . . then another . . . then another. He follows. Veering as the red spottage veers. Here and there a frantic hoof's track driven deeply. The trail does a ragged circling back before its predictable lunge for higher ground. Forest heaves himself along, head bent. He reads the blood. It is like a chain. If he loses the trail, he finds it. He loses it. He finds it. At times he grasps saplings. Like oars. They push him up onto the steeper, higher ground, the mountain that is his own land, that he knows like the back of his hand. His rifle on its sling bears him backwards, pulls against the rise of the hill. But he can't be slowed. The stump of his footless leg hurts. He is tempted to crawl. Houndlike. He actually considers this.

98 | The day unfolds. Baby Catherine naps. Eli walks Nanna Connie's springer spaniel around with his plastic turquoise leash, lets him piss on truck tires. Nanna Connie's lips are thin and have red red lipstick and with her strong good teeth, she has such a good-to-see-you smile and her voice so screeching and sharp. She often lapses into baby talk. She uses this baby talk on everyone. This, Peggy has explained, is because her mother, Connie, taught high-school English for so many years.

The house smells of the turkey roasting slow . . . the terrible turkey . . . its footless legs jutted . . . its baldness . . . crisped like the face of a badly burned man.

Peggy's brother Bryce keeps everyone in stitches. It's hard to imagine him operating on eyes. How could he go all those hours in an operating room and not burst into song or crack a joke? When he holds his granddaughter Catherine, he looks into her eyes with such a goofball expression.

Except to hold the baby nobody sits much. They stand around with drinks. No one seems to stagger or disappear for a nap. Liquor just winds them up more . . . laughing, crowing, and heavy into trivia . . . Peggy's brother-in-law John a walking encyclopedia, a walking *Newsweek* . . . no small deed gets past him. And Peggy's sister Jolene rattles on endlessly in the jargon of her profession . . . no stopping for breath . . . no quiet bemusement, just one "whereas" and "whereupon" leading into the next . . . and with her funny, flirty little grin, you will always forgive her.

Peggy wonders about Forest. The meal is on the table. "Should we wait or should we go ahead and eat?"

They all vote to wait.

They go on with munching on nuts and pesto and runny cheeses and drink, drink, drink. And now they are onto the subject of outer space . . . the cost of keeping a satellite in space . . . the weight of a satellite . . . satellite legislation . . . who got the contracts for which parts and "Did you hear some groups are boycotting light bulbs?" This has to do with the fact that certain megacorporations make both light bulbs and aerospace parts.

The security lamps switch on, blaze in at every window.

Peggy's mother, Connie, checks her watch.

Peggy asks the question again, "Should we go ahead and eat?"

99 | He squats in the dark woods listening. As if the buck with the dangling jaw might call out his name.

He has lost his glasses. He imagines himself home, shaved, clean white shirt, his dressy striped suspenders, dining room table heaped, and in the air the scent of fried game. He imagines the deer heart sliced with onions on its brown print platter. The fresh heart. "Have some!" he would say, pushing the platter. "Pass it on! Try it! Get you a good slice there! Pass it on!" He imagines the hand of one of his in-laws taking from the plate. His in-laws. The eye surgeon. The lawyer or the engineer. Or the professor of geology. Or his father-in-law the pharmacist. His mother-in-law the English teacher. All of them in the pink from their liquor. Forest's black eyes would fix on each face, his soft eye and his cruel eye. "Get yourself a hunk of that steak," he'd say. And, "There's plenty of the heart left . . . dig in!" And Forest would square his shoulders and cut into the meat . . . his own musculature layered with the years . . . this Forest and all Forests past . . . heart layered over heart . . . another Thanksgiving the same as those before it. This year's deer heart pulled by his own hand from the chest of that deer.

But this year's heart mocks him. Veined, still thumping. Stolen from him . . . bounding ten feet a leap . . . headed for higher and higher ground.

100 He smells the turkey.

"Are you starving?! You must be?! Here . . . sit! Sit! We saved some of everything for you!" It's Peggy's mother, Connie, with her mouth red as fire. And Bett's old sister Millie quietly scraping turnip onto Forest's plate.

"You okay, Forest?" old Millie's old daughter asks.

Blaze polyester coveralls with shredded knees. Blaze jacket has ripped seams. Beard sturdily filling in, part black, part gray. Lip swollen. Welt on one cheekbone. Nails torn on one hand. Dried blood, his. Glasses gone. "Yep."

She pats his shoulder.

The family floats in and out of his poor focus. Faces round and pink as bonbons. And the sound from the parlor of jokes and world news and world trivia that gets especially shrill with after-dinner drinks.

One of the brothers' wives navigates through the blur from the hallway. Forest has met this one only once. Seems to be pregnant. Something there green and bulging. She tells Forest how much she still loves this house. She asks him what he knows of the history of this house. He turns his face slowly toward her and says softly, "I can tell you what happened in this house last Thursday."

She giggles. She clasps his shoulder. "You are so funny." She leans on his shoulder. He understands that the leaning may have something to do with all the great wines and the great scotch. She says, "I bet George Washington slept here, passing through on his way to hunt down Benedict Arnold."

"Benedict Arnold was actually one of the best officers the colonies had until certain complications entered in," says a voice somewhat to the left of the green smock, brother Chris who is part of every trivia conversation.

Another giggle from the sister-in-law. "We were just discussing the house . . . its history . . . and Forest was funnin' me. Right, Forest?"

"Right. I was." Forest smiles into the blur and whir of them all, then looks down, trying to bring what's on his plate into focus. The smells of colognes and perfumes close in on him from all directions. The sister-in-law releases his shoulder. The brother Chris vanishes.

Red lips of the mother-in-law say, "My goodness . . . I know you were hunting . . . but . . ."

Another brother has come to hover off to Forest's left. Says with a snicker, "Forest musta had a tangle with a yeti, eh, Forest?"

Forest smiles. "I spared him. I didn't think you'd like the taste."

This brother yeowls and slaps his forehead over this wonderous wit of Forest.

Forest listens to Peggy's voice off in the kitchen.

"You've already helped enough, Madge! Go sit down and enjoy yourself!" Peggy is getting closer into the range of pink faces. She says, "Forest" softly and lays something dark on his plate, then whizzes away back into the kitchen.

One of Peggy's brothers, the geology professor, steps from the parlor, says, "Hello, Forest. How are you?"

Forest can hear and smell coffee being poured, sees the line of reflection along the chrome pot and the cuff of a pastel shirt at the end of the gray cardigan sleeve. Forest asks how his plane ride went.

"Fine," says the geology professor. "And how are you?"

"All right," says Forest. "And how are you?"

"Fine. Fine!" The geology professor laughs, turns to the lowboy at his right and says, "Now what do we have here? Looks like lemon?"

Forest spears the dark meat with his fork. Deer meat. It alarms him. He almost rises from his chair. But this is just Peggy's kindness at work . . . a bit of deer steak from the freezer, left from last year's deer.

He chews, mixes some meat with potato and the lukewarm turnip.

Eli says, "Where's your glasses?"

Forest grunts. "I got sick of having people tell me I looked like Roosevelt."

Eli doesn't get it, keeps standing there like there should be more said.

Forest stops chewing. Narrows his eyes on Eli's face. "You been playing with a goat?"

Eli laughs. "Nope."

Forest puts no more food in his mouth. He waits a long moment, squinting away from Eli toward the movement of bleary figures in the kitchen. "So, Eli. What smells like a buck goat?" He looks back at Eli. One pupil gauging, one pupil loose and flaring.

Eli laughs. "This jacket, huh?"

Forest grips Eli's arm, pulls the boy close. "That's my jacket."

"Nanna said I could wear it! You weren't using it hardly . . . she *said*." Eli's voice contains a squeal of fear.

"I never used it to do any goat herding." Forest rises, steadies himself with a hand on the table. "Where've you been, Eli? Where the fuck you been?!!"

Peggy comes toward them nearly at a run.

Little dog barks from the parlor.

"Forest! What's the matter?!" Peggy demands.

"Why does that jacket smell like goat?!"

"*You* tell *me!* It's *yours*. When he put it on, it *had* that smell. I wasn't exactly keen on him using it . . . but . . ." She wrings her hands, lowers her voice. "I *thought* that . . . you know . . . he was . . . you know . . . bonding with you in some way to want to wear it . . . you know?"

Eli's breathing is heavier than his usual heavy fat-boy breathing.

Forest says, "Eli. *Where* did you find the goddam jacket?"

Peggy says evenly, "Down cellar. He and the kids were playing down there. Forest, pleeeez leave him alone. Make this right. Don't ruin this. Especially after what happened with you and Jeff. I . . . I think . . . I think this is fragile. You haven't got *that* many chances. He *loves* you, can't you tell? He *admires* you."

All the pink faces that haven't backed out of the dining room are quiet. Including Eli's face. Forest doesn't look at Eli. He pushes away from the table. Heading out through the back hall, his head strikes Bett's ceramic cow mobile . . . sets it to tinkling crazily.

Down cellar there are only two low wattage bulbs for light . . . but a *lot* of goat on the air. Shelves loaded with empty wire-top canning jars, voluminous tree-trunk-like ducts winding down into the old furnace. Broad hand-hewn beams above, too close to your head. You have to stoop in these old cellars, hunker along. The foundation is one visible wall of granite and fieldstone, the other walls swallowed by clutter and board partitions like stalls.

Where are the yellow eyes of the dancing goat? Had a goat been led in here? Shut in here? Not the *same* goat of course. But a look-alike black buck goat from *one who would remember*.

There is quiet upstairs. The family that isn't a family. Probably they are embarrassed.

Forest sees Peggy's face in smeary outline. "So . . . maybe . . . it wasn't the whole goat." He smiles boyishly. "The goat, you see. The *famous* goat."

Her bewilderment and dread make her silence monstrous.

Forest squints to see what her expression is. "The question is: *When* do you suppose our stalwart high-minded hero put the jacket there? The night he cleaned me out of my guns? Or . . . maybe today . . . maybe just before the kids came down here. I wore that jacket last spring and it did *not* smell like a goat then. Maybe it's not even the same jacket. Who knows? He is capable of all things. There could be a switch. A very funny man . . . like Bob Hope."

Now Forest squats. Over the dirt floor, no track. But of course, even if there were a track, he wouldn't be able to see it, and but of course there is *no* track. He says, almost choking, "You . . . sup-pose that night he . . . got . . . my guns wasn't the only time he's gotten inside . . . this house? Suppose there's been other times? I mean even besides this with the jacket? Suppose he's been coming and going freely?"

Peggy sighs. "Forest . . . for now . . . if we can just get through this with the family . . ."

He stands straight, gripping a stack of screens. "Fam-i-lee." He sneers. He pulls the door to the bulkhead open, hikes up the short steps.

Outside a cold hard downpour has begun. Each of a million droplets racing out of the darkness into the pinky orangy purple-green zone turning all to glitz.

In and among the parked cars Forest limps, Peggy follows. Here Forest keeps his remaining two guns. Truck never locked. An enticement? A dare? He jerks the Weatherbee from the top rack. He sniffs mightily of the air. Nothing that smells like goat. Everything washed by the colorific rain. He snaps the bolt back, pushes in five cartridges. Peggy watches him through the rain smashing into her eyes. He backs away from her, saying raspily, "He's here. When I came in, you see, I took note of his presence. He. Is. Here."

Her eyes widen on his mouth.

He says, "See? Over to the DiBiases."

Peggy sees he is pointing toward the apartment door, among the cars and trucks parked there . . . a red flatbed Ford with a tier of split hardwood across the back for weight.

Forest smiles. "See. It's *him*. He is visiting the DiBiases."

She glances up at the lighted upstairs windows of the renovated barn. She says, "So? He's some relation of theirs . . . of Francine's."

Forest plunges away from her, gripping door handles of the many vehicles, swinging around them with his rifle muzzle down, hunting for a place out of the horrid light. A place of NO LIGHT. A place to hide.

There is *nowhere* unlighted.

The rain smashes and smashes, twinkles and glitters, weights down the fabric of his clothes. There in a bright pinky green purply orange puddle he throws himself down, belly down, snaps off the safety, takes aim at the door that opens to the DiBiases' stairway.

Peggy leans into a car fender, buries her face in her arms.

Forest rocks over onto his side, gets the cross hairs on one of the security lights on the pole fifty yards away, the one that beams down on the line of dump trucks. Squeezes the trigger. BAMM! The light goes black.

Peggy bawls into her arms. "You wouldn't kill a person!"

"YESS I WILL," he bellows. "I *WILL* KILL! Kill my brother! Or my father! Or . . ." He wags the rifle muzzle toward the road . . . "My SON! Whichever son-of-a-bitch I lay eyes on first!"

BAMM! He fires upon another security lamp. Now darkness on two sides of the Johnson home.

Peggy lays back against the car, eyes wide open up into the pounding rain.

One of Peggy's brothers calls through the rain's roar. "WHAT IS IT?!! HEY!! WHAT'S OUT THERE?!!"

BAMM!

Another light poofs. Tinkles away. Gone.

The last light, positioned in the gable of the Johnson house, is not in a position to be fired upon. Forest sprawls on his back in the swirling water, eyes shut. Opens his eyes. Jerks at the bolt. Mashes in three more cartridges. Rolls back into position on one elbow with steady aim at the DiBiases' door.

Voices of Peggy's brothers hurrying through the rain.

Peggy calls to them. "GO BACK IN THE HOUSE, BRYCE!
CHRIS! PLEEEZE! GET INSIDE!"

"WHAT IS IT??? WHAT'S HE GOT OUT HERE??"

"PLEEEZ!" Peggy howls. "WE'LL BE IN IN A MINUTE!"

People come rattling down the stairs of the DiBiases' apartment. They
spread out among the cars. To Forest without glasses, each and every
blurry shape could be his brother.

The rain drives harder now, straight down. Could take your breath
away. Smother you.

Those around the apartment door and parked cars look out into the
night, some saying, "Who's shooting?"

Everyone seems so lighthearted. For who would believe the impossible?

Into the light of the open DiBias doorway, Lloyd Barrington steps
empty-handed, surveying the night. He pulls the door shut behind him.
This blocks the stairwell light. So now there's no clear silhouette of his
legs, chest, and head. Forest widens one eye to the scope, making a quick
guess that the cross hairs are on the center of the man's shirt. If he were
to open fire now, one after another, there'd be five chances to hit
him . . . at least get him down. Then what? Reload. Five more shots.
Reload again, five more.

But Forest is rolling onto his back, chest huffing, rifle at his side.
Paralyzed. He covers his face with an arm. He lays very still but for the
huffing and shaking of his chest.

Buck fever.

It's like that, you see. You have your chance, your big chance. But
all you do is fall apart.

101 Forest very quiet. Doesn't seem to be interested in getting into
dry clothes. Doesn't seem to notice Bryce's fingers pressing his
wrist for a pulse. Bryce asks for a thermometer but neither Bett nor Peggy
can find one. Bryce says never mind the thermometer. Forest stands up
suddenly, heads for the kitchen, leans upon the sink . . . drinks from
cupped hands.

Bryce offers to take Forest to the hospital. "Better safe than sorry."

Everyone agrees. Better safe than sorry.

They talk around Forest. Everyone talking. Forest drinking, leaning.
Bryce goes out to warm up the rental car.

Forest doesn't argue the hospital idea. He indicates only one thing. That he wants Eli to come.

Eli no longer wears the jacket that smells of goat. On the ride, he wears his old Levi's jacket. Peggy and Bryce take up the front seat. Eli and Forest in back.

The ride is long, Bryce driving *fast*. A fast ride always seems longer. Bryce is quiet. Everyone is quiet. Bryce passes a lot of cars.

Bryce passes a transport tractor trailer on a curve.

Forest says low and firm, "Slow down."

At the hospital, Forest asks the attendants if Eli can go into the curtained emergency area with him.

Peggy and Bryce wait out with the magazines and the people with bandaged hands, horrible coughs, and troubles you can't tell what to look at.

The nurse explains to Eli what Forest is in for . . . "a real breeze," nothing like it used to be when they used "cold goop" on your skin. She pretends to get cold willies. She giggles. Now it's "just these pre-jellied pads" and wires that she calls "leads," and Eli watches her handling the leads so slickly and breezily.

Now she works one of Forest's pants legs and long johns cuff away from his ankle, applies the pad and a wire. But when she tugs at the second pants leg, she is in for a surprise. She takes this, too, in a breezy way, asking Forest how long he's had a prosthesis.

Next more wires to the inside of the forearms and over Forest's chest. Forest on his back on the chrome table. Forest keeps his eyes on the ceiling. Eli keeps his eyes on the nurse's hands. The nurse's hands arranging the wires look familiar to Eli. Hands you could trust.

The nurse says, "See here, Eli, on this tracing . . . it's your dad's heart speaking. Like his heart writes a letter. Neat, huh?"

"He's not my father," says Eli evenly.

"Oh . . . is that right?" She is unflustered. "Well, you two look a *little* alike. Except . . . I can tell, Eli . . ." She can't seem to stop smiling. She is only a girl. Not much older than Anneka DiBias who Eli kind of loves, the kind of love you don't tell about. "I have an idea you like ice cream."

Eli says, "Why? You got ice cream here?"

She says ruefully, "Don't I wish." She pulls the graphed paper from the monitor, then rearranges the wires and pads. Starts up another tracing. "I love pistachio . . . you know . . green," she says.

Eli looks at Forest's chest with the wires in their new places. Some on hairy places. Some on bare parts. This private part of Forest shocks him. And in this fluorescent light, Forest's beard fuller by the minute . . . shocking.

The nurse takes the fluttering graphed sheets from the curtained area, then returns, begins to remove the wires and pads.

"Did the EKG say I'm dying?" Forest asks.

Eli's pale eyes widen on the nurse's mouth.

The nurse laughs as she lays all the wires aside. "You know what it says? It says you are going to be rich, travel widely, and meet a tall dark stranger."

102 | Peggy Johnson and Anneka DiBias push through the glass door of the pharmacy. The door that says OUT.

Between the parked cars and trucks and glittery bunches of shopping carts and through the bright wind, Peggy skips and spins and laughs. Walks backward. Anneka trudges with her beast of burden gait, which is so unpretty. Peggy gets several yards ahead. But they still talk back and forth over car roofs. They talk less of horses nowadays. They speak of everything. Heart and soul.

Of course there's this business of Forest's health . . . the thing that happened with the gun . . . has to do with his poor health. Forest now in bed, drugged and groggy. Peggy can't tell it enough . . . how the doctor called it "exhaustion." How she, Peggy, had thought there wasn't a real thing called exhaustion. But the doctor had said that's what it was. But the thing about Forest, Peggy had sighed, "is he's going to get more exhausted in bed than out working."

The wind smells of the mix of shopping center and the spiky gray mountain beyond. Peggy has one leg inside her little car, tossing the white pharmacy bag of Forest's "quiet pills" in the backseat. She realizes Anneka has stopped three parking spaces back. Anneka transfixed there behind a parked truck.

"What is it?" Peggy calls gaily.

"America Kicks Butt," Anneka says in a low voice.

Peggy smiles, settles in, pulls her door shut. She sees Anneka circling the truck. It's one of those trucks rigged to ride high. Roll bars and lots of chrome. Peggy inserts her car key. Warms the motor.

Now Anneka is pushing a shopping cart flush with the rear tire of the high truck. Now another cart. Now another. She surrounds the truck with carts. Now she drops to the seat beside Peggy.

Peggy shakes her head. "What if you got caught?"

"*I* wasn't caught. *I* caught *him!*" Anneka throws her head back and hoots, then stops abruptly, narrowing her eyes, smoothing back her hair.

"You're too hard on people, Anneka," Peggy says breathlessly as she checks for traffic, then takes the little car out onto the road toward home. She feels Anneka staring at her.

It's only a block before they are out of the mill houses and trade fronts to the old fallow pasturages and saplings and the river low on their right. Peggy says, "Anneka, you are a rebel in need of a cause!"

Anneka says softly, "Next time you got your butt near a mirror, check for bruises, okay?"

"What do you mean!" Peggy laughs nervously, almost chokes. She gets a more secure grip on the wheel.

"You haven't noticed anything . . . a little weird lately? Something?"

Peggy smiles sadly. "When I was in college, there were lots of kids doing their thing, protesting the Vietnam war . . . big demonstrations . . . bigger than those they have today. I wasn't much for protesting and carrying on. I wasn't part of that group. I had a few nice friends, and I studied hard. I majored in Business Administration. My mother was worried I'd get mixed-up in all that hippie stuff, drugs and protesting and free love. And she was afraid that the world had changed, that we'd all be swept away by demonstrations. But that was just the fashion. The thing to do. Around the time I was first married and was raising my family, all the protesters quieted down . . . got raising *their* families. They grew up! And protesting . . . well . . . it kind of went out of style. Kids these days . . ."

"Kids ain't *nothing* these days. We're just waitin' around fattening up . . . like beef." Anneka's silver eyes slide off toward the river, not waiting to see Peggy's reaction.

"Sometimes, Anneka . . . in the night I wake up to a car passing or the wind and you know what? I think of you. I think of you a lot. I picture that you are over there a few yards away in the apartment in your bed and you might be awake too. And I try to imagine what's on your mind. And I have such a terrible thing wash over me. I suspect that what you feel is . . . anger and despair . . . and darkness . . . and it worries me. Childhood is supposed to be a time for playfulness and innocence and wonder and . . . *opportunity.* Maybe sometime if you saw a doctor . . . a counselor . . . where you've not had some of the opportunities other kids have had . . . maybe a counselor could help you with finding yourself . . . getting on the right track . . . feeling more at peace with yourself."

Two young boys trek along the sandy shoulder of the road, both boys wearing blaze, both with rifles. Anneka mashes her face to the glass, giving her wide mouth a grisly ruined look and her nose spreads like a bathtub stopper.

With a grin, Anneka looks back over at Peggy. "I really love doing that."

Peggy sighs. "Some girls would want to look pretty for boys."

Anneka snorts with disgust. "America kicks butts, remember? Nobody's lookin' at faces."

As the little car pulls up into the yard, Peggy's voice switches to its more girlish mode. "You still want to come in and help me sort pictures? Or are you mad?"

Anneka says she'd like to do the pictures. But could they do them tomorrow . . . she has to meet some people at three o'clock.

Peggy scowls. "Is this your white scarves march? Hunting's just about over . . ."

"We plan to go to the last day and then there's the black powder season, which is especially dangerous since most nonhunters don't know about it. *In fact,* on TV and the radio they actually announce that hunting is over, just as the week of black powder season begins. So by our drawing attention to that, we could save a life."

Peggy just smiles and pulls the white pharmacy bag from the backseat. Between the house and the shop, a young girl on a bay horse appears. She leads a riderless Appaloosa. Roped to the back of the Appaloosa's saddle is a furled American flag.

Anneka trudges across the lot, hoists herself up into the saddle. Now she twists around to give the rolled flag a big kiss. Then she waves to Peggy.

Peggy waves back.

Anneka's kiss to the flag was not a mocking kiss. Nor worshipful. It seemed like just a kind of affection.

Peggy turns to go into the house.

103 In the morning Anneka shows up with a plastic-wrapped loaf of her squash bread. Anneka's hair, if she skips shampooing it a day, gets a look of thick pasta. It sure has this pasta look today.

Peggy stands in the doorway with her big boots apart, her fit-and-ready sentry look. But her "Come in!" is harsh and high. She seems too hungry for Anneka's company, like some old, old woman living alone with only plants.

Somewhere in the distance a school bus roars.

Anneka thrusts herself past Peggy, and once inside, turns and grins. "I'm here for the whole day! It's supposed to rain so we're calling off the march today. Guys don't hunt when it rains. Might make their blaze run. Or maybe *shrink!* I'd *love* to see that! I'd laugh like hell."

"But, Anneka, what about school? You seem to be missing a lot of days."

"I ain't missing shit. I learned to read before I started school. You know what school is? It's like spending thirteen years in a waiting room."

Peggy says, "This is more serious than you realize. Dropping out will be a mark on your life."

"Do I look like a desk person?"

With a bit of a quaver, Peggy presses, "Don't you have a guidance counselor at school? Someone you can talk to about your future? Your goals? And what you need to do to prepare? Anneka, what *is* your goal?"

Anneka grins. Big chunky teeth. The teeth bite down on each word. "I want to be a farmer's wife."

With Anneka in the door only a few moments, you see, it's never very long before they hit upon an arguable point. Then Anneka's silver eyes will swallow Peggy and Peggy will back off. It's a pattern that's been fixed between them. This, instead of a hello-hug.

"So, Peggy, where's this project we're about to tackle? I'm rarin' to go. I love old pi'tures. I bet you got some dandies! Probably one of George Washington when he slept here, huh?" She heads in through the office to the kitchen table, lays the squash bread there with a flourish. "Getchoo a chunk off of this bread. It tastes like a jack-o'-lantern. Old recipe of my Grammie Dot's. HEAVY DUTY. You eat this stuff, you don't need to eat again for twenty-four hours."

104 Peggy zips her wool jacket up to the throat, says, "This won't take long. I'm just dropping her off. You know pretty much which boxes have which years in them now. If you want to just put them from the 1940 through 1950 box into stacks that seem to go together, I'll label them when I get back." She leans over the coffee table to look at a four-by-six print of a row of young women ankle deep in a lake. She smiles. "You know where the bathroom is, and you know where Bett's cookies are . . . so make yourself at home."

It is the parlor. Always a little chilly. But Anneka in her heavy sweater is oblivious. She flips over a studio photo of a sailor and a small black-and-white taken with a flash of a kid in a bathtub. Anneka says in a villainous way, "I bet I could switch these with my Grammie Dot's pi'tures and you guys would never know the difference."

"Anneka!" Peggy laughs. "What a terrible thought . . . a weird thought . . . kinda like those stories of people getting their babies mixed up at the hospital."

"Don't worry. I won't do it."

"Forest might call to me while I'm gone. If he does, just yell up through that heat register there and tell him I'll be back soon. He is *supposed* to stay put up there. His 'quiet pills' have been working . . . so-so." She rocks her hand to show the look of so-so.

Anneka keeps her eyes on the photographs slipping in and out of her hands, one to one pile, three to another pile.

Peggy feels for the keys in her jacket pocket. It's not her style to carry a purse. As it is with Anneka also, no purse. They are in so many ways alike. Peggy yells out to the kitchen. "Ready, Bett?"

"Yes, I am, dear," Bett's creaky voice answers.

Peggy says, "So . . . if he calls me through the register, tell him I'll be back soon."

Now Anneka studies the metal grate in the ceiling. "That your room?"

Peggy says, "Yes. But nearly two hundred years ago John and Mary Remmick slept there. And then in the 1800s, William and Lizzie Grover slept there, F.D.'s grandfolks. Imagine that! William Grover was one of the first owners of the mill, you know."

"So they had slaves."

443

"Anneka! Of course not!" Peggy scolds.

Anneka runs her hands over her hair so hard it stretches her eyes to slits. She holds this eye-stretched look as she says, "Well . . . if you count the people working at that mill for peanuts. *That's* slavery. Nobody but slaves ever worked there. Even now. So this house has a long history of villains." Anneka lets her eyes snap back into shape. Picks up another photo. This one is a Christmas tree. Lot of shine. Lot of glow.

"See you shortly." Peggy heads out the back way with Bett.

Car makes a little whine, fades into a smaller whine, then gone.

Anneka studies certain photos hard. Others she flips into piles. A lot of pictures of Peggy and her brothers and sister who died. And the other sister who lived. The one that died . . . it was polio. No pictures of the polio part. But there's an obvious point where the sister named Vicky disappears. Peggy's mother has a black mouth. But in later color snapshots, the mouth turns out to be a dark and emboldened red.

Phone rings. Two phones. One ring coming from the porch office. The other from above.

Anneka hurries to get the porch-office phone so it won't wake up *the beast.* But too late. The ringing stops and he is calling out for Peggy in his oddly modulated voice. A voice hard and soft. He breaks words in half. Disembodied from him . . . a voice in the air . . . it has a grainy dark power.

He doesn't call again. Anneka crosses the rug. Under the heat register, she tries to see what's up there in that lair of evil kings. Seems kind of dark. "SHE AIN'T HOME! SHE'S GONE!" she calls with hands cupped around her mouth. "SHE'S GONE TO PARIS WITH A NICE MAN!" Chuckles to herself. "SHE SAYS SHE'S FED UP WITH THAT RED-NECK ASSHOLE SHE'S MARRIED TO, ESPECIALLY THE WAY HE TREATS PEOPLE WHO DRIVE FOR HIM! REMEMBER THE BONUSES YOU PROMISED ONE YEAR THAT YOU NEVER GAVE? AND THE PAID VACATION THAT YOU SWITCHED WITH ONE HOUR'S NOTICE TO BEING LAID OFF FOR A WEEK?! IT'S A LONNNNG LIST!! EVERY DAY YOU DO A NEW MEAN THING! WHAT A BAD DUDE YOU ARE, YOU OLD THING!"

He is silent up there. But of course he heard her. She can feel the whole great body of the house bristling.

105 The rain is dark. And it roars. It smashes from the gutters, trembles on the many glass panes. Peggy complains that driving back to pick up Bett "in this mess" is going to be a trial. She says Anneka is welcome to come along or keep on working on the boxes and bundles of photos.

"I guess I'll stay."

Peggy explains that Joshua Hart's mother is bringing the kids back from North Conway around four-thirty. "Don't let him into those marbled cookies. We are working on his weight."

"Okeydoke." Anneka pulls on an earlobe intently as she studies a photo of an old lady under sunflowers, which are face down on their stalks. Flowers, tall. Lady, short.

When the car's whiny little motor and the drumming rush of the rain merge, Anneka walks over to the heat register. She squints hard to make out shapes in the room of drawn shades. Something like brass latches of a dark-stained bureau.

She takes the stairs . . . hop, hop, hop. She rounds the newel post. Which door is which? All with stained oak woodwork. Glass knobs. One knob of white porcelain. But then there's a crooked door with a brass latch. A closet probably. She guesses the nearest glass knobbed door is *the one*. Mashes her mouth to the keyhole. Whispers, "Thisssssss is your conscience speaking. You've been bad, Forest. Bad man." She waits.

There's no reply from beyond the door. She takes a deep breath, speaks croakily, "I am the slavedriver of Rummery Road Past. I go way back. I made my fortune on the sweat and backaches of others. But now here I am . . . visiting you from helllllllll. It's been rough. I'm here to warn you, Forest, before it's too late for yooooooo. I hear you are practically dead. It's not too late for you to make your mind up right now to be nice to your guys . . . to give 'em a little reee-spect. A little raise maybe."

She opens the door. Just a crack. She sees one of those fuzzy synthetic blankets with a Xeroxed type picture of a tiger on it. Shades of brown and beige. Stripes. Big paws. The room is cold. Damp. Messy. Not cozy. Forest's work boots stick out at the bottom of the blanket. High-topped work boots. Laced tight. She can't see his face.

She closes the door easy, scoots back up the hall to where a lace bureau scarf covers a low antique cabinet. She lifts the little basket and stack of books. Tugs the scarf away. She stuffs one end of the scarf into the back of her jeans. Tramps heavily back to Forest's door.

At the keyhole, she whispers, "*And* another thing . . . another thing on your list of bad boy doin's . . . HUNTINGGGGGGG. Can you tell a deer from a woman? Hard to tell when you guys just shoot into the bushes! And there's other weirdness that comes over you in the woods. Unexplainable weirdness. REMEMMMBERRR! Bet you can't tell a deer from a woman—GUESS WHICH!!!" She gives the door a healthy shove. The door strikes solidness. It's him standing there, his eyes on her . . . black terrible eyes . . . no glasses. Just the high-voltage fixed look of pure rage. And a beard. White on the chin. Black on the jaws. And two parentheses of black around the mouth. Luciferish-looking. He has a grip on the near post of the bed. His weight is placed all on one foot.

Anneka says, "Peggy'll be back any minute . . . any sec. Need a glass of water or anything?" She makes a quick study of his work shirt and the faded red-and-black plaid vest. Green wool pants. Everything zipped. Buttoned to the last button. Ready. Like a man who fears the need for a fast exit. A strange way to rest, she thinks. He leans away from the bedpost, bearing weight onto the other wrecked foot. Anneka steps back to the hall carpet. Her lace scarf "tail" sashays there across her rear, trails the doorsill. He smiles at her. The Luciferish beard adjusts. He grabs. Swings her by the sleeve of her loose sweater into the room, then leans to shut the door with his back.

"I'll tell."

"You have a good reason to hate me," he says in his soft and hard voice. "Everybody hates winners."

She looks away from him, fixes her eyes low along the mopboard by the closet door. He keeps gripping her sweater, leaning into her for balance.

He knows that rape is not always a big struggle. That you can ease into it like you drive your plow wing into big snow to bank it high. And certain storms just swell like feathers.

He has Anneka by one hand. The fingers so easily gathered to his own hand, he can run his free hand through his hair and regard her. Anneka, this storm, her blinking silver eyes.

He locks her head to his chest so as not to see her eyes.

He says thickly, "I always wondered how those that don't belong here could . . . get in here . . . you know. I always wondered that."

Against his old pilled wool vest, her mouth has no sassy talk for him, no arguments.

After all, of these next few minutes there is nothing to be said. It has all been said down through the centuries like talk of tides, talk of time, war, and work. Just a couple of minutes of an hour pitched forward into a dim closed room. Just the facts of this life. Just the hard and hurtful mixing and messing of lives.

106 | *December 3, 1991*
| *Dear Governor,*

I have written you on many issues. This is the rape issue. I guess. But don't think you can decipher my handwriting. Okay? I'm not using my actual handwriting. Ha. Ha. Those other letters in my real handwriting I signed. And you always send one of those letters to me thanking me for my views. This time I'm anonymous. Okay? So you don't have to send me the letter thanking me for my views. Save your paper. Save a tree! I just want to tell you about the rape. I'm not telling anybody else. I figured you'd stay pretty calm. You always do. Ha! Ha! So he's doing the rape, this guy. I wasn't scared. Not really. I just thought HERE WE GO. I had mostly the idea of just getting through it. Just trying to stand it. Like in school. And even when he was pulling and yanking, I was thinking how school prepared me . . . you know, all those years of waiting through all those hours for the bell, how I stuck it out. He wasn't a real hurt type, not smotherish like some rapes I've heard of. Some are worse. There's the beat-up type and the gang rapes and so forth. But I'm not going to say this was a picnic, this rape. But I've had almost thirteen years of school. If I had to do one over again . . . school or rape, I'd pick rape. Rape only lasts about two minutes.

So maybe this is the school issue, not the rape issue. I always get stuck on the school issue. And I know you think all your dumb ideas about school are the last word. I don't know which issue this is. I'm feeling kind of crazy right now, I guess. I just wanted to ruin your day. Ha! Ha!

This is all for now. Yours truly,
Anonymous person.

107 The day passes. And the next day passes. Now this new day. He wishes Eli would come up to the room and talk with him. But Eli stays clear of the room. He never even hears Eli walk by the door, though he knows he must. Seems Eli must make a point of getting past the door soundlessly. He tells Peggy to suggest to Eli he'd like a visit. He finds it hard to look straight into Peggy's face. But when he gets a little glimpse, he sees nothing has changed. No indication that Anneka DiBias has let anything on to anyone. But Peggy is seldom around to talk to. Where is she? He is alone with the rising tick tick tick of the downstairs hall clock . . . innocence all around him while only *he* knows.

He calls the weather and stands at the curtain to peer at the sky. *When will it snow?*

The doctors have suggested a full week of quiet. But he is done. He throws the sedatives in the trash. He shaves. He finds Peggy in the office, has her drive him to his eye doctor where he orders new glasses, nothing like Roosevelt's.

108 He works in the shop with George DiBias. No one, not George or anyone can see Forest's face right now . . . his face, shoulders, and chest being under the old one-ton Powerwagon. Forest works a wrench to free the oil plug . . . then for the last turns of the threads, uses his hand. Warm oil lets go between his fingers and something in the truck's engine sighs, cooling down.

Somewhere over by the bench, George is humming something from TV. He is getting things together, ready to load the smaller bulldozer so he can set up over to Brownfield. There's nothing different about George today. George, father of Anneka. Anneka, the little whiz. The little wonder. If the police came to Forest with her complaint, he'd deny it of course. He'd say, "She's a girl with a cause, always making her statement. This must be her *feminist statement.*" And there'd be no proof the longer time passes. How many hours to wash proof away?

But why hasn't she told anyone? This kid with a mouth you can hear for miles, mouth of big ideas, mouth that calls you names in the woods and through doors. Why hasn't she told on him? Why? Why? Why? This hanging him by the heels by the cold wire noose of her silence is worse than all else.

He remembers. Up in the room with her. After ejaculation. Freight train and thunder gone. All vitality collapsed. Rising up on his knees, he thought he'd faint. He looked at her face. The silver eyes looked back. With each hour that has passed, he recalls. He brings it back and back and back like frantically flipping pages of a hard-to-understand book. Can he recall anything in her expression that revealed her embarrassment? Or disgust? What grace! This weird generosity. It is a power upon him.

He considers his chances of having her again. He begins to plan it, sending George off to drive sand for the Brownfield job, finding out which shift the mother, Francine, will have at the mill. There's only one door out of that apartment. Easy enough to block the girl's way out. Get her cornered in all their tasteless aqua blue shag and cheap upholstery. He imagines going into this living space of George and Francine, into their lives that are driving him crazy. Chafe his knees on their sandy floor, ramming Anneka, ramming, ramming, ramming.

Then forgiven.

109 Arch Vandermast, Egypt wise man, sitting closest to the stove in Pink Punch tonight, getting an eyeful of what's going on at the register. A fortyish woman paying for canned goods with food stamps. Once she is out, the glass door woozing shut behind her, he says to the wise man next to him, "There you go . . . another one."

A lot of wise men nod.

Arch Vandermast grips the arms of Pink Punch, shakes his head. "They are breaking America. They sit around and soak us taxpayers while we do all the work. If this country is in trouble, it's Congress and the damn State House not tough enough with these people. I say *get tough*. You work . . . or it's the army."

Wise man Albion Cole looks after the closed glass door, then back at Arch. There's a look in Albion Cole's eyes. Not a twinkle exactly. More like a beacon. A signal. A kind of Morse code. Like there's something with Albion Cole that's not quite in keeping. What is this town coming to when you can't tell your true loyal ones from those that might be turning . . . the worm turns . . . as the saying goes. Albion Cole. Man or worm?

Arch says deeply, "That's what I said, Al. *Army*. No job, you get a draft notice. Simple."

Clarence Farrington nods sagely.

Willie DeRoche turns to the very blond, very quiet Reverend well driller David Moody who is settled in Pigeon Point, a color of rest and calm. "What do you think, Reverend? What does the Bible say about food stamps? That's good as thievin', ain't it? Now how is it they took care of thieves in the Bible days?" He chuckles. "Nail 'em to the cross, right? Those Bible guys didn't pussyfoot around, did they, Reverend? We need a couple of those good ol' Bible-times guys in Congress to get this country turned around."

Albion Cole and the Reverend David Moody glance to one another.

David Moody, as ever, wears his well driller's shirt, which reads DAVE over the pocket in copper-color embroidery. Now he laces his fingers together between his thighs. Deep, deep in thought. He looks up toward the glass door and his voice is clear and quiet and soothing. Like the color of his rocking chair. "Once . . . back when I was in high school, my brother Herbie and the Plummer kids and I used to go over and pick for Finleys . . . when he got his first harvester . . . the one he towed with the tractor. Remember that?"

Clarence Farrington covers his eyes with a hand.

Arch Vandermast crosses his arms, readying himself for the long haul of this story they all know too well.

The Reverend has such a kindly but distracted smile. "Well I was coming back up the tractor path that used to come out on Finley Road on the New Hampshire side. I was supposed to meet my father for a ride home. I got out early for some reason. Anyway, I was alone. Very quiet pretty day. And there up ahead in the grass . . . I couldn't believe my eyes. I'd never seen anything like it . . ."

"Moles," says Willie DeRoche, eyes hard on the reverend's kindly, gently smiling mouth.

"Yes . . . two moles fighting."

A few of the wise men shift uncomfortably.

The reverend goes on. "Not mice. Not rats. Not shrews or voles. These were those gray moles . . . chubby-like, with big front feet and claws for digging. At first I thought they were mating. Kind of rough. You know . . . mating's rough. But after a while, it was obvious they were trying to do each other in . . . so mad you know . . . some problem in the daily lives of moles . . . some irksome thing. They were just this little whirring gray ball all aflip-flop." He pauses, looks sadly among all the faces.

Of course it's the mole story again . . . the story no one wants to hear.

"Well . . . all of a sudden . . . there it was . . . this thing just dropped like a grain sack over them. 'Twas a small hawk. Cooper hawk. Snatched up both moles. I couldn't help 'em out. Hawk flew off with both of them." Now the reverend rocks back into a comfy position, folds his arms across his broad chest.

There's never a punch line to this story. No little joke at the end, the thing the wise men wish for . . . those chuckles much needed to break the embarrassed tension.

"AMEN!" Arch Vandermast hoots.

And they all laugh like hell.

110 | Denise's Diner at noon. Clatter and clang of the quick lunch that isn't always quick. Forest Johnson has left the sanding truck a few yards down on the shoulder, not wanting to get boxed in. In front of him, a plate with a bagel, coffee half gone, folded newspaper, and a thickness of unopened mail.

They slide into the booth bench across the table from him. His eyes widen. It's Ernest Bean and Steve Bean. Big as bears. Layered in winter wools like himself. Ernest Bean's plaid wool jacket has a Ruger patch on the shoulder and white hairs all over like probably the family's old lame dog uses Ernest's clothes to sleep on when Ernest is out of them. First thing Ernest has to say is "How's the boy?"

Forest pushes his coffee mug around a bit. "Boy's doin' good."

The other man, blue-eyed Steve Bean, doesn't open his mouth, but stares. Hard. At Forest. A stare like a nasty grip.

Ernest says, "We'd really like to see him, you know . . . have him over." Ernest's eyes are not blue. His eyes are small, amber. Nose big. Mouth worn out. Too many teeth missing. Ernest not known for fighting like his brother Reuben. The story of Ernest's four missing teeth has probably no story to it at all. Just teeth gone by the wayside. No story to much of anything about Ernest. You know a work, meat, and TV man when you see one.

Forest turns his face, the daylight from the small curtained window dim and gray, two dim and gray smaller windows reflected on his new glasses.

Blue-eyed Steve Bean looks around, tips his cap to two guys hunkered on stools at the counter. He sees no waitress. He booms, "I'M FAMISHED!"

One of the men from the counter saunters over, bringing with him his coffee and a plate of sausages. Nothing but sausages. He slides in next to Forest. It's Artie Bean, Steve's brother. Dressed for the woods though he has nothing to do with the woods. It could never be cold in the carding room of the mill. "Morning all."

Steve tips his head sideways, calls out past Artie's shoulder, "Harriet!!! I'm hungry! Hurry!"

Guys in the next booth chuckle and haw and one says, "Quick! Throw him a biscuit." And surely a biscuit drops from above and bounces onto the table by Steve Bean's hand. A great rippling of hoots and cackles moves up and down the diner. None of this is *that* funny or new or surprising. Indeed, not. This teasing and goading and the clinking of dishes and the *blurp-blurp* of the coffee maker is just a script, worn from use, old and soft.

The waitress calls from the far end of the diner. "Put a lid on it, Steve! I've only got two hands and two sneakers!!"

Forest and Ernest Bean look into each other's faces . . . neither one friendly . . . both weary.

Artie Bean leans onto his forearms on the Formica tabletop. "You guys seen Nettle?"

"Nope," says Steve.

"He owes me fifteen bucks." Artie opens wide the fingers of his right hand, then shuts them tight. Then the other hand. A kind of exercise.

Steve snorts. "Good luck."

Waitress appears. Button-up blouse with a print of big, *very* big, almost wanton-looking yellow apples. "So . . . Steve . . ."

"Grilled cheese."

"Wheat or white?"

"Don't matter."

"Usual on coffee?"

"Yep."

"Ernest?"

"I ate."

"Artie and Forest . . . need any refills?"

Forest says, "Ah yes. And more cream, please." Forest looks hard at her bony ringed fingers with the pad. Now he looks up into Ernest's eyes. He says to Ernest, "I'll bring him over after supper. But I'll stay with him this time. He might be a little nervous. Save him some dessert. He's a real dessert man."

The waitress has hurried away.

Ernest nods. His eyes move over this new reasonable Forest Johnson. Now Ernest looks off toward the grill. "I wish I'd ordered something now," he admits softly.

"Here," says Artie Bean. He pushes the plate of jiggling frisky sausages across the table.

Ernest frowns. "No fork?"

Artie's face scrinches. "What *else* do you need, Your Majesty? Linen napkin to tuck in there . . ." He reaches and jabs two fingers into the space of his uncle's collar.

"Get outta there!" Ernest rears back, pushes the hand away.

"Any more food needed over there?" someone from the next booth calls.

Forest pushes his shoulders into the booth's upholstery. Closes his eyes. He hears something strike the table.

Now Artie is throwing whatever it is back. Seems he's made a bull's-eye . . . because they are all screaming "BULL'S-EYE!!!"

The feel of these men closed in around him is the vast unspeakable, actual truth.

He drinks from his replenished coffee, keeping his jaws and throat and chest in that position that signals gentleness, that signals surrender.

111 | February. The howls of the engines in these old rigs . . . seems they could rip your ears out. Forest has to shout. "MY FATHER USED TO LET ME STEER WHEN I WAS YOUR AGE!"

Eli looks at Forest's hands working the shifts. The tranny hump bristles with shifts. Forest lowers the wing, raises the wing. There's uphills. There's downhills. Forest shouts, "THEN I USED TO TAKE *YOUR* FATHER OUT WHEN HE WAS SMALL. HE LOVED STEERING!"

Eli looks at Forest's hands seizing upon a shift knob.

"YOU WANNA STEER, ELI?!!"

Eli shakes his head, no.

Into this forbidding roar of space between them, Forest calls, "IT WOULDN'T BE WHEN WE'RE DOING ROUGH PLACES LIKE

THIS . . . JUST A NICE STRAIGHTAWAY. YOU'D JUST SET ON MY LAP HERE. I WON'T LET ANYTHING HAPPEN. YOU JUST STEER. I'LL TAKE CARE OF THE REST!!"

Eli's pale exacting gaze slides to Forest's lap.

Forest asks, "GRANPA ERNEST HAD YOU DRIVING ANY LOGS AROUND TOWN LATELY? ANY SKIDDERS?!"

Eli shakes his head. "Skidder's broke."

Forest cocks his head. "WHAT'S THAT?"

"SKIDDER'S BROKE."

They ride along for twenty minutes of no talk, mesmerizing slant of snow and squalling engine and bouncy seat. So bouncy Eli conks his head on the cab roof once, but remains dignified, face turned to watch the snow move out from the plow wing below like a tidal wave . . . and the headlights . . . and the swing of the amber cab light.

Forest narrows his eyes, coming around into the stretch by Letourneau's salvage yard. The wind is getting up some gumption and throwing the snow back in the road on the side George DiBias had done probably fifteen minutes ago. But here on this side the snow gets blasted out and away from the farthest plow wing, the road behind them made right with the world . . . clean, cleansed, prevailed over.

Forest cocks his head, watching gauges, road, and roadside. Taking the grade now, the engine bawls. The plow wing's cutting edge beats and clatters this rough road. Cutting edges don't come cheap. What the cutting edge feels, so Forest feels in the flesh.

Heading down the level stretch of new homes and logged-off woods of the old Freetchie land, Forest sees Eli is still staring down from his side of the truck at the clattering plow, rams, and cables . . . the surge of it all. Like the rupture of sea over rock, the enduring watery properties of snow never fail to awe.

Forest shouts, "WHEN YOUR FATHER HAD HIS TURNS AT STEERING, HE PRETENDED TO BE IN AN AIRPLANE. WE WOULD TALK BACK AND FORTH LIKE PILOT TO CO-PILOT."

Eli keeps watching the plow wing banking snow, shrugs sort of listlessly. "NOT ME."

Forest looks back into the night. He sighs.

"IF I WERE STEERING," Eli explains. "I WOULDN'T PRETEND ANYTHING. I WOULD JUST DO IT . . . YOU KNOW . . .

I WOULD JUST PLOW IT. AND PEOPLE SEEING ME FROM THEIR WINDOWS WOULD THINK I WAS NEAT, I GUESS."

Forest jerks the shift to the far plow, raises the front plow easy, stops the truck with the truck's usual quarrelsome growl. He pats the wheel.

Eli edges over to him, working his legs and boots over the shifts. Forest really has to hee-haw to get Eli onto his lap up under the wheel, Eli not doing so well with his weight-losing these days. Forest shows him how to place his hands on the wheel. "WE'LL GO SLOW," Forest assures him, then lowers the wings one at a time, everything creaking, lugging, shivering, shaking, easing forward now into the diagonal windblown white shards. White shards, black shards. How can you steer into this disorder? It is blindness. So little sight of the road. It is just knowing these roads, knowing them from age six or eight . . . coming out of forever and going into forever.

So Eli steers. And beneath him along the backs of his legs there are Forest's legs, indiscernible from the force of the truck. Forest the almighty. Forest, the spire. Like them all who love Eli and who press on him these things they know. They close in around him and there's no getting out now. And this is good. For the powers of the night and the powers of the great truck are pitted here, two phantasms. neither one kindly. Eli hangs on for dear life.

15

Heart in Hands

ACROSS THE WAY, people are stepping out of rides that look like bullets.

Dottie Soule leads her flock of granddaughters to a concession. She orders doughboys.

"Well, if it isn't Dottie Soule!" Some old guy comes whooping out of the crowd. Gives Dottie's "muscle" a squeeze . . . the left arm . . . the skinnier one. "What are you doin' here, Dottie? Raisin' hell?!"

Dottie pulls the old man's cap down over his face.

"Whoaaa!" he laughs and ducks away.

Such dark, racy light. Everything surging and electric. Screams. And that low contented roar.

A van that has printed on it: BLOOD-PRESSURE MOBILE.

And there's a booth you can have your picture taken in, wearing costumes, hats, feathers.

Sign that reads WORLD'S SMALLEST HORSE.

Games that nearly nobody can win at . . . darts and bulletless rifles. Rings.

Quite a few kids pass with balloons on sticks. Plastic helium Ninja turtles. Kids looking sticky and salty with purple moustaches and gobbed hair, frozen breath, wild eyes. Quite a few kids in the Blood-Pressure Mobile. A man in a white jacket comes to the ramp, puts his hand up like a cop to stop the deluge. Dottie snarls to herself, "When *my* kids were little, they wanted to go to the city to X-ray their feet into Sears."

At the Four-H hall, Dottie buys a green bandanna with clovers on it and little *H*'s. "Turn around!" she commands one of her granddaughters. "Let me fix you up pretty, make you a ponytail . . . like mine."

The kid doesn't want a ponytail like her grandmother's. But she turns around anyway and against the nape of her neck Dottie Soule's hands go to work.

Triumph of the Beast

WE WILL NOT REST!

*—Placard of a protester
during the 1992 Los Angeles riots*

PART ONE

THE YOUNG GUYS hang back tonight along the wall and darkened lunch counter where it's less toasty. A few pairs of long legs in jeans. Sodas and juice drinks. Young guys have always got to have something in the hand. Gives a person a look of purpose. And young guys wear little smirks of pleasure for the old guys usually give you a good show.

The barrel stove roars.

Coolers hum.

Moody's Variety & Lunch. Sometimes it seems its wisdoms will implode it.

Old wise men can't get enough heat, their configuration of bright painted rockers tensing and tightening closer to the source.

One of the young guys who knows cars, knows a silver-gray BMW by the sound it makes slowing at the curb, by that gorgeous silver-gray sigh it makes, speaks. "Here she comes. It's the rich widow."

All conversation stops. "Rich widow, you say?"

"'Twas her car just stopping," says the young man.

Everyone watches the rich widow push through the glass door. Some squint one eye at the rich widow's high heels hammering along, jabbing along the painted hardwood floor.

Cigars are drawn.

Cigarette cellophanes crinkle.

Lighters clink.

Matches scratch.

The rich widow's hair is some ritzy business. You can assume she's paid a lot of money to have hair that looks like it's unintending to look that way. All those curly-o's and willowy-o's, streaked blond, streaked brown.

It is rumored that the rich widow has a hundred pair of shoes, a coat of the fur of every furbearer, maids galore, exotic pet cats with long necks and turquoise eyes, secret bodyguards never seen but never really far, private helicopter for trips out of state, and of course, she has houses in other states . . . mansions, of course . . . in warm states, of course. And a chalet in the Alps. It's rumored she's worth billions in investments, in all those ways rich people are rich, that kind of phantasm of wealth that is hardly taxed, maybe *never* taxed . . . computerized money . . . money played like a symphony . . . money that has nothing to do with a household and groceries and kids' school clothes . . . money that is bigger than life, a kind of planet of money tilting in and out of the stratosphere, humming, beeping, squeaking, sucking.

The widow jerks off her gray leather-palmed gloves a finger at a time.

The wise men are steeped in smoky silence.

The young men keep their pleased sneers. With his foot on a Calo cat food carton, one young guy stretches, cracks his knuckles, blows a kiss to the back of the widow's head. Then he blows a kiss at the glass door beyond which the silver-gray BMW is parked. This causes one small snigger from another young guy. But otherwise the whole place is muzzled.

Widow trots down one short aisle. She scans shelves. She gathers into the crook of an arm a box of colored pencils, very dusty. A jar of horse-radish. The last jar. From the coolers she chooses between two cheeses.

Around the farthest aisle she clacks along briskly. She arrives at the assemblage of rocking chairs, peers over the heads of the wise men to the wall. Wall bristles with notices, business cards, and so forth. She squints, trying to see through the cumulus of the many smokes. Or is it a squint caused by her displeasure with the smell here? The smell that is dense as a blur. The combined odors of nearly eighty years of Moody's patronage. Not just eighty years of feeds, hardware, general goods, chocolate, pizza, and newspapers, flies dead in the back window, mouse dead in the trap. Not just the patrons' mouths and open collars and wet boots and paper money and silver money and copper money of all those years here. But also of that which is beyond these walls. The suppers in kitchens. Stan-chioned cattle. Woods. Gasoline. The mill. How is it that the sweetness of home clings to some, while others it doesn't? The widow, it doesn't. However, she's not odorless. What is her smell?

It is plain the widow wants something from that bulletin board and the only way to get there is to cut right on through THEM.

Still no one speaks.

"Excuse me!" Her voice. High. All the consonants erect. Vowels peevish.

Albion Cole jerks his hand back as the fabric of the rich widow's rouge-color jacket brushes him. And in her wake is her odor.

Not that flowery powdery odor like that with women you are used to. Nor the woolen mill odor some women come home with. Nor of onion, dishpan, and that which goes along with the get-up-and-go of the body, mixed perhaps with the soured mistakes of a suckling child. The odor of the widow is not pink. Not yellow. It is black and white. Like a contract. Like a report. A mailgram. A FAX. A receipt for PAID IN FULL.

All the wise men and young men try to see around each other's heads to figure out what interests the widow at the bulletin wall.

A Polaroid of Barry Sargent's black Lab who has been missing since last summer? Name of "Spooky." Polaroid shows Spooky asleep by a table leg. Doesn't show much of Spooky's face. No, it's not Spooky's picture the widow is after.

Nor the COLOR TV & VCR FOR SALE CHEAP. MUST SELL.

Nor JESSICA GOULD TO BABYSIT AFTER SCHOOL. YOUR HOUSE OR MINE.

Nor SNOWPLOWING. CALL TED POPE AFTER 5.

Nor LINC BARTLETT FINISHED CARPENTRY.

Nor FREE KITTENS, ALL VERY CUTE & READY TO GO.

Nor YULETIDE CRAFT SALE COMING SOON.

Nor HOLLYBERRY EXTRAVAGANZA CHRISTMAS CRAFTS AND MORE. No. None of these.

Widow pulls a pen and lined pad from her shoulder bag, jots down a number.

Willie DeRoche's eyes widen on what she writes.

FIREWOOD, she writes. Then a phone number with lots of nines. And a name. LLOYD BARRINGTON.

Willie leans the other way now. Whispers to Albion Cole, "Load of firewood." Then adds in a deep somber whisper, "At the hands of the old fox."

The whisper is passed on, passed around and around. All eyes follow the widow's hand dropping the lined pad and pen into her shoulder bag. The chairs, held in suspended motion for the last few minutes, have resumed creaking. And the floor underneath creaks. And there's real emergency in the air.

Instead of walking back through the middle of the group, the widow begins to work her way behind the circle of rockers. She is noticing the cash register is unmanned and starts to look around. Freddie Moody bounds out of Hawaiian Sunset and heads for the register. The widow gives him a chilly smile. Once behind the register, Freddie balances the widow's cheese on his palm and tells her something about cheese. It's just a standard cheese joke, but the widow laughs right out at this . . . a kind of sweet hiccuppy laugh, which doesn't match her computerized FAXED and PAID IN FULL odor and cold smile.

Everyone shifts restlessly.

Once the BMW murmurs to life out beyond the curb and the rich widow is on her way, Arch Vandermast booms, "Well, he would hit her place eventually anyway."

Clarence Farrington's eyes rest on his folded hands slung between his thighs. "Shame to see him get an *invitation*."

"What difference does it make?" Arch wonders. "Invite or no invite."

"It's in his code of ethics," old Ray Dyer sniggers. "He'll get there eventually."

"But if I were in *her* position, I wouldn't rattle his cage. Just let nature take its course."

"*Que sera sera.*"

"I sell firewood too!" says one of the young guys along the lunch counter. "Our number is up there, too . . . up there beside the boat picture. Maybe I should've said something."

Arch Vandermast snarls, "She might as well stuff her fur coats and jewels and what-not in the wood stove as have Barrington and his bunch up there."

"She's probably got insurances up the yin-yang," says a young guy dismissively. "Doubt it would hurt her much."

Willie DeRoche cackles. "Wellllll, unless he does one of those . . . you know . . . scare the shit out-of-them routines . . . you know . . . the thing he does with the coffin."

A few knowing chuckles and head shakes.

One of the youngest guys along the counter gets big eyes. "He killin' 'em now?"

"No. Not exactly. It's just a coffin that appears in their yard with a . . . kind of a big doll in it. Has a face that looks just like the person. Remember that one of that real estate guy that bought up and subdivided the Freetchie land? They say the big doll in that coffin had some of Gaston's actual clothes on!"

"No shit."

Solemn nods.

Willie DeRoche cackles. "Yep. Somehow the old fox gets a set of clothes out of the person's house early on. Then when the body in the coffin appears . . . you know . . . having your *face*, it'll have your clothes on, too . . . your actual clothes!"

Clarence Farrington glowers. "Ain't nuthin' magical 'bout it so don't go gettin' all worked up. It's nuthin'. There's some explanation. Like Houdini. Houdini could be explained scientifically once they started looking deeper into the situation. This is probably along those lines."

Old Dick Ward leans with his elbows on his knees, looks into a few faces. "S'pose we shoulda warned her?"

"Nah!" Freddie Moody is settling back into Hawaiian Sunset, rubs his eyes tiredly.

"Where's your civic duty, Freddie!"

Freddie Moody smiles. "As rich as Mrs. Doyle is, I'm curious to see how it turns out . . . you know . . . she probably has the National Guard or something lookin' out for her . . . hundreds of electric eyes . . . TV cameras like they have at banks."

"Don't matter. I bet ol' Fox leaves her with nothing but the foundation of the house, her bathrobe and slippers," sniggers old Ray Dyer. "And a row of about twelve purple Murgatroids."

"Where's YOUR civic duty, Ray?! In your left foot?!" Old Rusty Pete gives old Ray's left foot a roughhousing kick.

Clarence Farrington raises his chin, similar to the raised-chin look he gets when discussing patriotic issues. Sometimes Clarence wonders if *all* these old loyals have turned . . . have joined up with Barrington . . . are *all* thieves. It's plain to see that his own sense of *civic duty* outweighs anyone else's in this room tonight.

PART TWO

Hot rubber stink on the air. Old Clarence Farrington's boots. He always gets them stretched out there too close to the stove. Clarence in Battleship Gray. Rusty Pete in Fandango. Albion Cole in Purple Ecstasy. Carroll Plummer in Spring Beauty.

A lot of coughing. Some bad colds. Some smokers' lung. One cough can set off three or four more.

Not all the chairs are going. But all are occupied. Marigold, Blue Boy, Tile Green, Pink Punch, Blue Moon, Gladiola, Limeade, Hawaiian Sunset, Lipstick, Pigeon Point, Standard Red. Willie DeRoche in Canary. Willie DeRoche who knows how to make a good rocking chair fly.

Carroll Plummer stone still. Carroll Plummer, keeping close to his uncle, Albion Cole. Only the smoke from Carroll Plummer's cigarette moves. Carroll Plummer, fresh out of prison. "Doing time" this last time was not for the hit-and-run. But for one of his many, *many* parole fuck-ups. Can't stay away from the drink, they say. Sooner or later it's bound to happen, Carroll Plummer's bound to become his party self.

But tonight no drink. No singing. No folly. Carroll Plummer who is not as old as the old wise men but not young anymore either.

Carroll Plummer *looks* like a con. The TV escaped type, hardened around the eyes. Dark-lashed green eyes, so unassertive a green they are more of a yellow. Hair like convicts get when they've been hiding in the TV woods for a few days with the TV hounds moving in. And on TV where cons escape routinely, and there are crafty cons and cons who work miracles of strategy and deviousness, the TV version of Carroll would have a scar and a crooked eye, or at least his eyes would have a more narrowed cunningish contempt. Eagle eyes. But the real Carroll, slouched in Spring Beauty, looks to be a very old and tired forty-six year old mixed in with the look of a very young man's misunderstandings, miscalculations, and bewilderment, a look always of just beginning . . . beginning again . . . the clean new start.

He ends one cigarette. Starts another.

The discussion at present is which year was it that the Coast Guard had an icebreaker in to open up Portland Harbor? And was it the same year Al Remmick got that bass for the derby, got pissed about the judge's decision, and stuffed it back down the hole?

"Sixty-seven" is Clarence Farrington's guess.

"Sixty-eight," Freddie Moody insists.

"Well, the ice storm wasn't the same year as the harbor freezing over," Ray Dyer says. "Ice storm was in seventy-seven. That was a whole other thing."

"Well, it depends on which ice storm you mean."

"*The* ice storm."

"Well, there's been hundreds of . . ."

"There's only one ice storm I'm meaning . . . the one where they had no parkin' in Lewiston or Portland for the whole goddam winter. *That* was seventy-seven."

"Well," Arch Vandermast says with cheek-sucking authority. "Al's bass was in the seventies 'cause there was no derby over to that pond till the seventies."

"Icebreaker in Portland Harbor was in the sixties. Same year they had that trouble with natural gas down there. Gas lines froze up. I had a niece down there in South Portland. They had to evacuate the whole street because everybody heated with natural gas. *Late* sixties." All eyes hang on Albion Cole's mouth saying this.

"*Cowslip*," says Ray Dyer.

All eyes hang on Ray Dyer's mouth saying this.

"That was the name of the icebreaker. *Cowslip*. You know, like a flower."

Clarence Farrington rubs his palms together, shakes his head. "I don't believe they'd do that."

"What's that, Clarence?"

"Name a miltary vessel after a . . . flower."

"Well, it 'twas. It surely was."

"I'm sorry . . . but I believe you've got something a little off on that one."

"Why Clarence, my man. Ain't you heard of the great aircraft carrier in the forties called the U.S.S. *Petunia?*"

A singular delirious howl of laughter made up of all the occupants of all the rockers except Clarence. And except Carroll Plummer.

Ray Dyer says, "But I ain't joking about the *Cowslip*. I swear on twenty Bibles."

Carroll Plummer is smiling vaguely. It's easy to tell when he has his hearing aids turned down. And with that one never-ending cigarette in his fingers, without the world of sound, his only council is smoke.

Sometimes he reads lips, they say. And he knows sign language, though nobody else on the planet seems to, so where would he get to use it? When he has his hearing aids shut off and his yellow eyes won't look at you, there's just no way to get through. Except to take him by the shoulder.

His uncle, Albion Cole, does this on occasion to get Carroll to tune in. And Carroll will fix his hearing back and a little discussion will take place between them out in the parking lot before they leave for the night . . . little discussion about their work for the next day . . . now that Carroll drives logs for Albion. It's plain to see Albion Cole is looking out for his wayward nephew. At least till Carroll becomes his party self again where he gets dragged off in handcuffs to the nearest cruiser.

PART THREE

The firewood. It shows up in a rumbling, and black, flexing stratas of smoke. A row of amber cab lights.

As the rich widow hurries into her jacket, she peeks through one low kitchen window. The truck is backing down off the hot top into the low limbs of an apple tree. Bird feeders bob and spin. She sees he is not alone.

She crosses the hot top briskly. Flat shoes and slacks. Security lamps make her belted jacket look sapphire blue.

She speaks to him through the open window of his truck, "Mr. Barrington! You certainly are prompt."

Moustache hangs heavy there. Like something dead in the claws of something else. The hairs of it are lavender and blood red and blue. Though of course that's just the lie of the security lamps.

He nods.

But why has he backed his truck off the hot top, to the farthest edge of light, truck facing the house? He is making a face like the light torments his eyes. Like he has come out from too long in a dark place into the light of day. He speaks in a voice that moves in and out of softness. "Where do you want it?"

She points to the wide-open barn door, her finger wagging as if to count off the seconds, a slightly impatient gesture. "Over there, please, Mr. Barrington. Thank you." She grips her collar together under her chin with both hands. Her breath freezes into a brilliant dough tumbling slowly toward his, which is tumbling slowly toward hers.

Truck engine sputters. Almost dies. Then roars when he mashes the pedal with his boot. He is looking hard at the house and barn. She knows what he must be thinking! How amazing the transformation! It is no longer the house it was . . . this house where a farmer died in his sleep. The house is now reclapboarded. Stained a solid dark brown. How high it sits on the apex of its many lawns. Fat trees. Several levels of decks with handsome lathe-worked rails and latticework arbors . . . a look-at-me house.

The wood man is making no move to deposit the wood . . . no move at all . . . and the others in his company seem equally ready to settle in for a while.

She has started to turn away, but turns back, looks once again into his face just as the heavy moustache flickers and he gives something in his mouth a couple of eager chews.

She looks to the faces of the others, also staring at her home, men that look so much like the driver, it's as if he has procreated himself amoeba fashion, dividing himself into three men with hat or cap, slightly hunched, thickly dressed. Except one sitting against the far door has a very British-looking briar pipe curved out over his jaw.

The driver at last stretches forward to shift into gear and so she backs away, hands deep in the pockets of her jacket.

The truck seesaws onto the frozen grass and starts backing slowly into the yawning barn. Now out of earshot of the rich widow, one of the men makes a low wolf whistle and Lloyd recites. " 'On life's vast ocean diversely we sail, Reason the card, but Passion is the gale.' "

The third man just whooshes air in and out of his unlit pipe. He bangs his door open, hits the hot top at a sideways run. The second man follows, also deft on his feet. One calls out, "YEPP! YEPP! YEPP!" running backward, hand signalling toward Lloyd's face in the side mirrors. The truck squeals duskily, lurches. Stops. The barn smells of paint. Barn has a couple new beams. Barn empty but for the BMW and a single cardboard box against the loft stairs.

One man unlatches the tailgate.

The rich widow appears now in the doorway that opens from the shedway to the house. In the incandescent lamps of the barn, her jacket is not a sizzling sapphire blue. It's only camel. She sees that the firewood is handsome, tiered high over the truck's stakes and slats. Like a monument. The proverbial "honest cord." Over the phone the wood man's odd raspy-soft voice had insisted "dry." Over the phone his local accent was so thick, the words kind of welded together out of feeling so at home with himself. Apparently never needing to communicate with anyone talking differently! Because of this accent she had expected a much older man. An *old* man. And here it is, the beautiful wood. No tricks like you expect with most businesses today. The bed of the truck rises in a hydraulic whine. There's the tumbling crash of the wood. One man reaches to flip a single chunk that is reluctant to let go of the raised bed.

The driver, Lloyd Barrington, chewing, ambles around to stand with the others.

Guy with the pipe spanks his gloves together.

None of them looks at the widow.

One guy pokes at the pile with a boot. His boots are something synthetic. A print of camouflage green-and-brown spots.

Now something has caught the eye of the man with the briar pipe. It's the cardboard box of old license plates. The last owners of the place had left them behind. After painstakingly removing them from the barn door and walls, with the idea that perhaps they would be a desired flea market item, they, the last owners, decided not to deal with the rusty old

things. They, the last owners, not owners for very long, had said what a
mess the place was when they bought it from the Town. "Uninhabitable."
They had had big hopes for a restoration. "Bringing it back." But after
only a year, they gave up, overwhelmed, heartbroken, in debt, having
done very little other than haul off all the old owner's "junk," stuff much
"worse" than the license plates. They had ripped down plaster, leaving
exposed water pipes and a stack of new windows still in their cardboard
and metal strapping. They were the wrong windows for a true restoration,
carpenters later told the widow.

The couple was from New Jersey. The widow had visited with them
after the sale. The widow, accompanied by a friend. There had been an
appointment made, but the owners were in the middle of making their
lunch, looking surprised, looking interrupted.

But the visit went well. The widow thought the couple sweet. Their
short barks of laughter were concurrent. Their sweaters bunched at the
elbows. Yes, sweet. How close they were!

The widow now gasps to realize how close Lloyd Barrington is standing next to her, his eyes on her face. He has strange eyes . . . one dark,
one light. He glances away quickly. Is he shy?

"I have your check right here, Mr. Barrington. You *do* take checks?"
She reaches into one pocket of her camel jacket.

He chuckles. "Kind of late for me to say no, 'less I go and pick up
all that wood."

She smiles. But she's embarrassed. She had written the check out last
night after she called him, now needs only to tear it with care along its
perforations. The ugliness of the truck exhaust and the sweetness of the
now-lighted briar pipe move this way from where the two other men pull
themselves back up onto the truck seat and slam the door. They seem to
be watching her now . . . though she can't be sure . . . the visor cap of
one and the brimmed crusher of the other make their eyes only shadow.

Lloyd Barrington tugs off his gloves, reaches for the check. He folds
and folds and folds the check down to a small triangle so that it fits into
a little leather drawstring pouch.

He sees she is watching his hands.

He sees that her eyes are dark, that she has a face and way about her
narrow shoulders that could cause you to make bad mistakes.

He jerks a yellow pad from his pocket, makes out her receipt slowly.
Tears it from the pad. Holds it out for her to take. Now he gives his

black watch cap a little chivalrous pull in front, jerks his body into just the suggestion of a chivalrous bow, says "Night now," all the while his eyes not quite being on her face.

Now his eyes slide across the freshly painted bare, bare walls of the barn. He turns on his heel.

She watches the truck rolling down the satin black pavement, out of the light into dark, the red taillights shrinking, squirming into the trees along the road.

PART FOUR

1 | Denise's Diner. White glossy sun on red Formica. Twelve-fifteen. Clangs and clanks of dinnerware. Heavy duty dinnerware. A cup in the hand weighs like a handgun. Needling gutturals of many voices, customers razzing each other tirelessly. Idling trucks along the road's edge. More arriving. Earthquakish tremor of trucks and of Anneka DiBias with a tray jouncing along heavily between tables. Big busted, big hipped Anneka DiBias. Big sneakers. Great big mouth. Hair in a short white wrist thick braid. Got to keep hair from appearing in a customer's plate It is the law of gravity. It is the law of good business. And insurance. Denise or Donnie. Routinely one of them must remind her of one thing or another . . . get her out back for a little talk. And amazingly Anneka abides.

Now she plunks two glasses of water down and booms, "So! What can I do for you two today! Anything special, Rick?" She reaches for the spoon by his elbow and gives his water a little stir, lays the spoon back easy-careful on his placemat. She smiles warmly.

Rick Dresser smiles warmly.

Some sort of bad blood here.

Carroll Plummer says, "I'll take a pepperburger and coffee with a tweak of milk." His dark-lashed yellow eyes move from her face back to Rick's water glass, water still spinning there.

"Fries with your pepperburger? Or chips?"

Rick Dresser snorts to himself at some thought.

Anneka DiBias glances toward the snorting and bats her eyelashes.

Rick glances away. Through the mesh of his billed cap, there's the hard oval shape of his balding head and sprigs of self-inflicted military cut. Patch on front. RED SOX.

Carroll Plummer says, "Fries."

Anneka turns to face Rick Dresser square on. "And you? More water?"

Rick glances at his water which has quieted down.

Anneka smiles big. Some of her white hair has come loose around her ears and temples. Hair that does not abide. Hair that objects. Hair with opinions.

Rick leans manfully onto one forearm. "I'll take a couple of BLT's. And chips. And coffee. Black. PLEEZE." He exaggerates his words as though she were of simple mind.

"Wheat? . . . you know, the brownish kind. White? The whitish kind," she explains as though he were of simple mind.

He says, "WHITE."

"It'll be just a minute!" Anneka says cheerily. Stomps off to the next order, two booths away.

Rick stares into Carroll Plummer's eyes a long moment, a look of enduring grief.

Carroll says deeply, "Well. We have ourselves food on the way." And he looks happy and sheepish, lifts his own billed cap, sets it on the seat on top of his jacket. He straightens, spreads both hands over his thickened middle. "Starved," he says into Rick's eyes, into Rick's steamy glare.

"You might not've heard. You know . . . because of your having been . . . you know . . . not around for the last few years . . . but that bitch is a bitch."

Carroll looks off toward where Anneka is rolling her eyes over whatever the three men she's now waiting on are saying. "Spirited," says Carroll. "A spirited person."

Rick eases back into the upholstery of the booth and crosses his arms slowly over the chest of his blaze orange vest. In this position, his red cap sits a little too high on his head, a little large for the shape of his head. Kind of basketish. He says low, "A year ago, she had every crazy woman for a hundred miles all ramming around in the woods with . . ." He pauses, again leans forward onto the Formica, sun streaking one shoulder. And he says momentously, *"white scarves."*

Carroll beams. "Funny thing, women. Huh?"

"Didn't you hear about that? It was on the television and in all the papers. There was a harassment charge put on those girls."

"Harassment."

"Law says you are not to interfere with a hunter. And believe me, this was major interference."

Carroll turns in his seat, sneaks a quickie appraising peek at Anneka who stands by the coffee maker. He turns back slow and easy, his yellow eyes twinkling mightily.

Rick fidgets with his spoon. Rick has significant eyebrows. Wiry. Red and gray. He has astounding control over his eyebrows. He can wiggle and wag them, make them almost jump off his face. Right now they are at ease. Like two fighting cocks held back until needed. "If it didn't get to court by this fall, we figured she and all the ladies would be back out again doing their thing. It hasn't got to court yet from what I've heard, *but* as you can see, Denise and Donnie solved our problem for us. Five-thirty A.M. to quarter to four every day. That don't leave many daylight hours for little bitch witch to be at large. And they work her ass off here . . . and with a job, you don't play hooky." He chuckles contentedly. "So things are pretty calmed down."

"It still seems to be an issue elsewhere . . . petitions and so forth," Carroll says. "I've seen a lot about nonhunters' alliances in the paper."

"That's what I pay my NRA dues for. Just for that reason. Keep them high-sterical women from doing damage. But it's just a lot of blah blah blah . . . that nonhunter bullshit. Won't come to nuthin'. You see, it's between two forces. Emotional hormones of women versus practical thinking of the hunter."

Carroll smiles quirkily.

Anneka passes their booth and Carroll glances over at the faces of the three truckers she's just waited on. The three are all straining their necks around each other to see out the window. There's a guy out there backing his septic tank pumper between a pickup truck and a telephone pole. Though the driver works deftly enough, there's something in the eyes of the onlookers, some unspoken shared point of reference, something like a tickle.

"Bucket on a basswood tree," says one trucker gravely and they all laugh like hell, falling away from the window back into their seats.

Carroll says, "The nonhunters' rights movement . . . mostly that's your yuppie element, I guess . . . nothing like *this* you had here, with all these regular people. Looks like what happened here was *real special* . . . real newsworthy. I saw it on the news back then. News had something about it a few nights running. You get a lot of hours of lock down, you get to see a lot of TV." He watches the pump truck driver bending to pick up a flat-looking cigarette pack in the grass around the telephone pole. "And one night I go, 'Hey! There's my town!' It really knocked me for a loop . . . you know . . . seeing ol' Egypt like that right there on the news. And it looked like there were a hundred thousand people with picket signs and flags . . . some uprising . . . the angry masses an' all."

"Bullshit. Weren't but twenty people. All women. Television exaggerates. 'Twarn't no hundred thousand. Believe you me. *That* woulda made a scent that would've drawn bear from ten states." He chuckles to himself. His tendrilled eyebrows jerk around.

Carroll sips a little water, smiles around at familiar faces. There's been something like déjà vu in this moment with the thin sweet watery autumn sun over the table. Sunlight strikes Rick's glass of water. Seems the glass explodes. Everything is water and light. And the buttons on Carroll's shirt cuffs are bright as eyes. Light on the walls. People stepping in and out of sheets of light. Light on a wristwatch. Light in spangles and little seas. Carroll sets his own glass back on the sunny Formica. Sun nearly burns the outside of his hand, while inside his hand, the glass is cold. Déjà vu, yes. The relived. How many times in forty-six years has he been witness to this small good thing? It is always there. But Carroll isn't. Why is it that sometimes the light sings? Another time it just lays there? He knows it has never been up to him. There is always the great gray hand that chooses the day.

"Just a little powder puff party was all," Rick goes on. "Like a big baby shower or Tupperware party. A nice bazaar. Only . . ." Rick sighs in frustration. "Only it 'twas in the *woods!*"

"Looked like a hundred thousand on the TV," Carroll teases. "Guys still back in Windham are gonna go on forever thinking it 'twas a hundred thousand women pushing you guys around. People everywhere far off . . . no way of finding out the truth . . . thinking you guys lost the battle."

Rick snorts. "Weren't no hundred thousand. That's for sure. Maybe twenty on a good day. It's just those guys use what they call a wide-angle lens. Blows 'em up bigger. Makes 'em stretch out. Fill up more space."

Carroll chuckles. "Well, it was something to make memories by."

Rick scowls. "You think it's funny. You better watch your pepperburger. She might put something in it. Did you hear her threaten me about my water? You know the type." Rick breathes hard once through his teeth.

"Powder puff," says Carroll.

"Well, the *rest* of them. They were the followers. What you got here is the leader. The instigator. Probably a dyke."

Carroll pulls off an outer shirt. Arranges it with his cap and jacket. Rolls up the sleeves of his chamois, a dark navy blue. New. But dusty on the seams. Like in a couple of short weeks it's already seen a year of wear. "Last time I was paroled, that little girl was a little girl. It was only a couple years ago. So she can't be very old." He looks down at his hands laying open on the table. "If it 'twern't for my trouble, I mighta got hooked up with one of those sisters . . . her aunts there. Ol' Merl and I used to run 'round to the fairs. Had us a camper on one truck . . . horses in the box truck. We had some wild times. Beautiful goddam teams around. I remember one matched pair of grays that came down from Canada . . . used to break my heart. Sweet. Sweet. An' *strong*. Smooth as any piston. I seen some nice things with Merlin."

The coffees appear and Anneka says into Rick's eyes, "Drink up!" then swishes away.

"Only tip she's gettin' out of me is the tip of my cap." Rick tips his cap to demonstrate.

Carroll holds his own cup of coffee close to his eyes. Then to his nose. Sniffs. Sets it down.

Rick makes the dismissive sound that is like spitting a speck from his teeth. "Of course she's not going to poison anybody. But Steve Bean says she salted his spaghetti beyond the beyond."

"Wouldn't she get fired?"

"Nah! Denise and Donnie must know she's safer here than at large."

Carroll laughs his deepest, gruffest. "If you say so. But your coffee does look . . . sludgy."

"That would mean it's just the usual stuff."

Carroll turns in his seat and sees Anneka many tables away loading empty plates into the crook of her arm. She is not the look-twice leggy beauty that her mother was. She's short-legged, short-bodied. Looks like it's drudgery for her to walk. Big sweater of the plainest brown hanging oversized off her neck and one collarbone. Short thick white braid has not one bit of sensuous swing and sway to it. On the scale of beauty, the girl could never live up to the Soule sisters. But . . . yes, fruit of the tree.

Carroll and Rick both work their coffees in silence. They watch a station wagon slowing at the lake, tailgated by a load of pulp chips that tilts on the crown.

"So," says Rick. "Cole's over there yarding up to Burgess Road."

"Yep."

"That's crazy. You got everybody coming off that hill doin' about fifty blind. Everybody says Cole is nuts."

"To load up over on the other side, you'd be skidding three miles . . . mostly bog. Building a skid road through that shit would cost a fortune. You've got to consider that."

"Well, you'll think so, you wind up piling up with somebody. You'll think so." Rick chortles. He leans forward and says, "It's no secret Al's been acting a little dingy these days." He taps one temple. His thick eyebrows jump. "Alzheimer's or something."

Carroll shakes his head. "That's not so. Al's the same."

Rick puts up both palms. "It's not just me talkin'. Lots of guys have noticed ol' Al's become . . . *strange*."

Two loaded plates plunk down. Plastic squeeze bottle of ketchup. Anneka swishes away, snaps somebody in the shoulder with her wipe-up rag four tables away. Guys in the booth behind Carroll burst into screaming laughter. "Why you wanta go and do that!!" one of them hollers around a solid mouthful of his burger.

"Somethin' to do," says another.

Rick calls over. "What's that?"

"You think Bernie ought to be shot out of a cannon?"

Rick shakes his head. "Sure."

"Somethin' to do. Right?" one of them says with a little snigger. "I says to him it's somethin' to do."

"You got plenty to do, Rodge," says another.

Carroll turns in his seat, glances among the faces, the back of the nearest man's head. Carroll nods to all, all of them being either related to his family, or familiar in their ways.

Nods are returned.

"HEY! CARROLL!" one of them shouts as so many will do, knowing of his hearing difficulty. "YOU KNOW WHAT THE HELL AL COLE'S GOT UPSTAIRS THESE DAYS? YARDIN' OFF THAT FRIGGIN' HILL??!"

Carroll says, "I just load and drive . . . just do as I'm told . . . load and drive. Decision's made by the Man."

"Well, he's gettin' old timer's disease," one of them says as Carroll is turning back to his plate.

Carroll gives his pepperburger a careful study.

"Open it," Rick suggests.

Carroll lifts the top.

Rick says, "Fergie's outfit's up there with Carp on Old Chase Boundary . . . chipping the friggin' b'jesus out of the south side clear down to the I.Q. stream. Nobody was allowed to strip like that before . . . nor chip so much . . . you know . . . like if they leave anything, they're leavin' only stuff like this." He shows the perimeter with his hands, fingertips touching. "Snip 'n' chip. Makes Steve and Rubie and Haney and you guys look like you're standin' still."

"Liquidation or whatever you want to call it," Carroll says. He chews. He swallows. He thinks. He says into Rick's silence, "Somebody out there in the world getting ready to pay off some bad debts, diversify, and gobbledygook. Stockholders are bored." He smiles sadly. "It's called hit-and-run. Only it's the big boys, so it's legal. They don't run over folks and kill 'em outright, you see. They just take everything there is to take and leave us standing around wondering what the hell happened."

Rick munches contentedly a minute, staring off. "I ain't sweatin' it. It'll straighten out."

Back behind Carroll, Anneka DiBias's voice. "Benny, you know what day this is, don't you?"

Silence in that booth, then a couple of low growling chuckles.

"Is this some sort of mental test?" a guy asks. "You going to ask me if I know my *name*, too?"

Anneka groans. "Naww. I won't strain you *that* hard."

The guys all cackle.

"Strain his brain," one of them declares.

Anneka forges on. "I'm talking about the holiday this is. You get a free dessert, compliments of the management. You want the frosted witch and black cat cookies or the cupcakes made to look like pumpkins? One cupcake or two cookies. Your choice."

"*Two* cookies must mean the cookies are very *thin*. Right?" one guy says in a toothless lisp.

"What day is this? What day is this?" Rick mimics squeakily. He scrinches his face.

"Be nice," Carroll scolds, his eyes merry.

Rick calls out, "Rodge! Benny! Duey! Bobby! You'd better get a close look at those cookies. Make sure what's-her-name here doesn't put a razor blade in one."

"Well, if I know Donnie and Denise with freebies, the cookies will be too thin to hold a razor," one guy calls over the short booth-back to Rick. Then to Anneka, "How big are the cupcakes, dear? Size of a tonic cap?"

Carroll turns. "Make her show you an example. Settle the question early on."

Anneka is rocking to and fro in her mashy loose-laced sneakers. "Okaaaay. I'll get some. But you guys are *all* going to be shot out of a cannon." She tromps away.

"Somethin' to do," someone says and they all hoot and howl.

Anneka returns with a tray loaded with the desserts.

Carroll turns in his seat and says, "I'll take one of those smiles before they get pawed."

Anneka arranges a cupcake on the edge of his ketchuppy plate.

"And you?" she wonders of Rick. "Compliments of the management. Whichever suits you."

Rick looks braced for danger, his eyes under the thickets of his eyebrows slide over to Carroll's smiling cupcake. He jerks his thumb toward the cupcake and says, "I'll take whatever it is there . . . the smile." Now he looks off dismissively through the window . . . pink and turquoise plastic flowers in the window box just beyond. He glances back. Anneka flashes him a wide smile, then says, "There's your smile. Anything else? More water, Rick?" She gives Carroll's cup a tap. "More coffee, Carroll?"

Rick sits up straight, shoulders squared. His eyebrows high-voltage.

Carroll says, "I'm all set, Anneka. Thanks." Covers his coffee cup with both hands.

Anneka turns to the next table with the tray.

Carroll strikes a pink-tipped match, fixes a cigarette solidly in one corner of his mouth, finds Rick's gray smoldering eyes.

Carroll swings around in his seat and snatches a cupcake off the tray that's in Anneka's grip, his reach brushing the shoulder of the man behind him. He lowers the cupcake to the edge of Rick's plate, and speaks around his jiggling cigarette. "Yours is biggest. Feel better?"

Rick's gray eyes won't leave Anneka's back as she tromps away down the length of the diner.

Carroll raises his chin, puts the smoke out toward the aisle. Smoke hunkers in the aisle around the waists and legs of passing people. "She's a kid. Remember being a kid? She's just goofin' around."

Rick cuts into his cupcake with his fork . . . pokes it and prods it. Tests a mouthful.

Carroll admires his own cupcake, hits an ash into his coffee saucer. "Halloween. I never gave it much thought."

"You mean you never waxed you some windows?" Rick wonders with a chuckle. "Never wung around a few pumpkins?"

"Well, yuh. But . . . I mean . . . I never really considered Halloween . . . you know . . . in comparison to the rest. Halloween . . . it's kind of pure. You know? No presents. No shopping. No shit. Halloween . . . is just . . . it's got just . . . this silliness about it."

"I'll say."

Anneka returns, scribbles up the tabs, mashes them between the salt and pepper. Then she's gone.

Rick says, "Aren't you going to eat *your* smiling cupcake, big shot?"

"Sure. I just want to watch you for a while and see what happens."

Rick wags his beastish eyebrows. "I switched 'em when you weren't looking." Now he grins, leans forward. "Hey! Let's go soap a few windows tonight . . . just for old times' sake. My mother-in-law . . . she's a good sport. Let's go do her storm door."

Carroll frowns. "Would. But I have to be real good for a long time. Anything to make a lawman look at me twice is . . . well . . . my parole people would get blood pressure problems."

Rick flushes. "Oh, yeah." He chomps directly into the remainder of his cupcake. "Eat yours," he says around stuffed cheek. "We definitely picked the right thing. These are pretty large. Cookies are shrimpy. This stuff's chocolate with peanut butter frosting. The orange part. It's really peanut butter but they dyed it. Kinda good. Kinda disgusting both. You just don't look at the orange part while you chew." He closes his eyes, chews happily . . . blissfully.

2 | Carroll Plummer coming down a straightaway, pushing and pulling into higher and higher gears, out of the black hills of early evening, sunset a mere thumbprint of a bitter rose in the split between Horne and Noble. This is his job. ALBION COLE & SONS on both doors. The sweet repetition of it. The back and forth of it. Empty and loaded of it. The stacking up of logs, and then again, go. Nineteen sixty-six Ford beast. Died and come back nine times. Nine engines. And everything else welded, soldered, jury-rigged, rebuilt, sweet-talked, and kicked. Exhumed. She's geared too low for paved roads really. You can just never get up to a real cruise.

He has no load on now. But with a load on a crowned road like this she rocks you. Rocks you on the curves. Rocks you like a mother. He often pulls out his hearing aids so the whining of the engine and the gritty pull of the transmission and the gritty pull of the road matter only to his skin. Like skin to skin. The skin of someone else's to his own. He drives longer and longer days, dreads home . . . home being the summer lake house of his brother, Dana Plummer, Navy man, soon-to-retire, now out to sea. Dana's family in another state. Texas this time. But here in Egypt, there's this big roomy place with a lot of glass and patio furniture. And the openness of the lake. And modern conveniences. And Dana's vacation clothes in the drawers. And the vacation clothes of the wife and two kids. Military people. They travel light. Carroll wants to feel heavy. Well stocked. He spends time at the shopping centers these days, sometimes borrowing his parents' car. He buys. He buys little things. Little junky things to set around and make Dana's home seem like his home. He never buys drink. But he thinks about it. He knows it's just a matter of time when one will come . . . one of those dark waves of desolation that has little to do with the dark. A wave. It has its own momentum, like food poisoning or a walloping flu. When you are struck by the wave, your face can't get any expression . . . your face is palsied. Death. You may not do it, but it's good to know death is there. Handy.

People tell you to snap out of it. To grow up. To look on the bright side. To consider people who are worse off. He knows that in olden times they called drink *medicine*. One of the guys in woodworking at the Corrections Center said "Yeah, drink is medicine," and he, this guy who looked sort of like Paul Newman only had a smaller face and was bald and had his top teeth missing, said that in the 1800s abortion was called *mercy*. "Everything is fashion," said the guy.

Everything.

There are no certainties. Only flexings and fluxings. Like this twisting black road. Just the rocking and the push against the back of your knees, shoulders against the seat. After such a good day, is there a wave coming now? Tonight? Tomorrow morning? Please, no.

Coming into the residential, he slows for trick-or-treaters and cars parked with flashers flashing and doors swinging open. White picket fence there fluttering amber. Little kids everywhere. Why are they *all* Teenage Mutant Ninja Turtles? He presses his hearing aids back into his ears and opens his window a crack to hear them. But they are silent. Determinedly pressing on from door to door. It is the young mothers he hears laughing.

Finally out of town, he gears down at a lake road, a one-vehicle-at-a-time road. Tree on the left bristling with name signs in the shapes of arrows. Most names he wouldn't know. Most of the lake properties are not *inhabited*. They are *vacationed*. Deserted in this season. But well-lighted. Pinkish purplish orangy green lights. Nowadays around the black, black space of the nighttime lake, the shore is just a sort of garish movie set. He takes this narrow gravel road slow, headlights sweeping across the camps, the low trees cracking and thudding against the high cab, against the top of the loader, rattling the stakes. And the chains sing metal to metal. Sweet. He is feeling good.

In the dooryard of his brother's lakeside split foyer, he checks all his gauges, shuts down the lights and the engine. Sits in the dark cab with a new cigarette, pulling in the good smoke, one pull after another, thinking about his uncle Albion Cole . . . now, yes, there has been something peculiar about the guy, but not a thing like *disease*. It isn't Alzheimer's, for godsakes. But what?

Stepping out, he balances on the running board while feeling for the right key to lock the truck. Even here in Egypt. Albion says lock up. Insurance company says so, Albion says, with a look in one eye like something is lighting his eye from within.

Carroll makes out three figures in the dark, moving in close to the truck. His limbs prickle with fright. He steps sideways. His short cigarette reddens hotly with his hard intake of breath. There are giggles. Girls. He steps off the running board to the ground. He strikes a clump of three matches, holds them like a torch. Two faces are warty, slashed, cratered. grayish and maroon, identical one-eyed rubber faces. And one very homemade-looking face. Looks like a lot of glue and spinach. "Jesus," he breathes.

"Trick or treat!" they sing out.

He raises his hands as he would to be frisked, turns, and flattens both hands to the truck's high bed. "I ain't got nuthin' on me. Honest. I'm a poor man."

Their giggles multiply into the great echoey space of the lake.

He turns, spits what's left of his cigarette on the ground. "I'd offer you guys a smoke . . . if you had mouths that opened." He tips his billed cap in a gentlemanly way with one hand, jams a fresh cigarette into the corner of his mouth with the other hand and lights up . . . shakes his match . . . drops it . . . scuffs it.

"My mouth opens," declares the spinach face. Anneka's voice. He stares disbelieving at that dark shape which is Anneka *here,* while only a few hours ago she was part of that other world. Ol' Anneka DiBias gets around.

"You kiddies like some dimes?" He chuckles. "I have plenty of change."

"We'll take whatever you got," says Anneka.

The rubber faces agree. "Right! Anything."

He grabs for his wallet. "You walked all the way down here to trick-or-treat?"

"Yep," says a rubber face.

Carroll's cigarette wags as he laughs a kind of quiet appreciative snigger, pressing a coin into each palm, discerning the faint grayness of each palm in the dark. Now he realizes two of the palms belong to the same girl. Way too many palms here! Full of tricks.

He knows Anneka DiBias knows everything about him. No secrets among Soules. And how many Soule sisters had he drunkenly sung and drooled in front of? The past is miles wide, while the present is only as wide as his slumped shoulders.

When they are gone, he trudges up the root and stone steps to the deck, then steps around the raccoons' supper bowls scattered about. Once inside with the kitchen light snapped on, he sees there on his brother's sliding glass doors great swipes and X's of soap and shaving cream.

3 | He meets up with his sister, Deb, around town, but there's no actual visits. She's not a conversationalist. There's nothing to say. At the IGA or PO, he'll stand by her car window and smoke and she might smoke with him unless her kids and dog are in the car. She won't smoke up the car with *them* in it. Then, after he puts his boot heel on the stub, he'll say, "Well." And Deb says, "Well." "Good to see ya," he'll say. "Take care," she'll say. That's as close as they get to a visit. Mostly they just pass on the road and flash headlights. And her husband if he's driving the family that day, probably a Sunday, he too gives the headlights a few hello blinks.

Carroll goes to his folks' place a lot. His mother is short and square and deep-voiced. His father, once tall like his sons, has a hump now . . . and a voice like a summer's low and distant thunder. Neither parent asks questions or offers much news. They mostly just stare at the TV during Carroll's visits. Used to be his mother kept busier at the farm . . . out in the kitchen . . . or working her quilts, handstitching them or working the chattering Singer in the cold poorly lighted and cluttery dining room . . . way too cluttered to be used for "dining." But now here in this trailer his parents sit like lovers on the couch, hip to hip, a mountain of jackets and gloves and junk mail on the couch's third pillow seat, stuff which nobody sees a need to move.

And in the spring rocker Carroll watches TV drowsily, arms crossed over his chest, knees apart. He can tell now and then that they snatch long glances at him. Like thieves. They have never touched him. In all his life he never remembers a hand, neither to secure him nor to harm him. Just the great soft work of their eyes. No touching his sister, Deb, or brother, Dana, either. He used to say they were like a family of lizards. "We just sit around together waiting for a fly to land." He'd say this and get a lot of laughs from those he told. But now he finds, as *he* steals glances at *them* while they are looking at the TV, that being near them like this, and being seldom more than ten miles away from the chunky deep-voiced gravity of them and this house trailer and that crowded couch, even when he doesn't visit them for days at a time, and his sister, if only for the flash of her lights, it's as much love as he could handle anyway. A big slobbery kiss and bear hug right now would be, to him, a kind of violence.

4 | She brings him coffee. He is alone in the booth. The diner is not busy. Carroll is late getting in for lunch. He is keeping an eye on some kids that are hanging around the loaded truck across the road. *The* truck. ALBION COLE & SONS/TRUCKING/LOGGING & PULP printed on the near door. The eloquence of business, white on blue. Anneka is looking off over her shoulder as she pulls the order pad from her pocket, seems she's checking the time. But she lays before him a snapshot . . . color . . . of himself with Rocket and Tommy in harness with a twitch of logs . . . he, Carroll, spread-legged, twenty-fourish, sober, riding that

twitch, traces slack, no sweat, good man with horses. He doesn't remember that picture being taken though he stares directly into the camera. It is not the fog of drink that fogs his memory. It's the fog of time.

"That really you?" she asks.

He chuckles. " 'Twas *once* me."

"You look different," she says.

He leans back, trying to gauge the intent here. Is she being cruel or what? Soules love to tease and torment. But how softly Anneka has spoken. She has the photo back in her hands now, squinting at it. "Do you wish you had horses?" she asks him.

He looks out at the truck, kids leaning against the grille, but only as they would prop themselves against a building to loiter and shoot the breeze. "Nah . . . not really."

"Me . . . I will always wish for one." She sighs, eyes still on the snapshot. He wonders whether she's looking at the team or him. Her silver-gray eyes seem filled with high regard.

"Gramp has that same Rocket but Tommy died. He has Dutch and Duke working . . . team he bought offa Funnel. Rocket just stands around mostly. You can't get on his back. He'll roll on you."

He closes his hands tight around the coffee, wants to ask her the news of Merlin, if he still cleans up at the pulls, and how many milkers does he have now . . . he heard Merlin has made a lot of changes, trying to keep up with the big guys, trying to get faster, bigger, better. More milk. More modern milk. High-finance-deep-debt farming. And not a cow to be seen from the road. But this is one of those times questions won't come out of him. His jaws only clench.

The diner door doesn't open. Nobody beckons Anneka. She just keeps on standing there, working her wide bright mouth around in deep thought.

"Where'd you get the picture?" he asks with a little croak in his throat.

"Grammie Dot," she says casually, slides it back into her pocket. "She'll skin me alive if she thinks I put even a little smudge on any of her pi'tures."

He looks into his coffee.

"So . . . you want a pepperburger, right?" Now once again there's pen and pad in her hands.

"*Two* pepperburgers, please," says he. "I started work at four-thirty this morning."

"Two pepperburgers," she repeats. "And chips or fries today?"

"Chips."

"Okeydoke," she says and pats him on the head as she swishes away. Kind of a rough pat. Like you'd do with a workhorse.

5 He sits at the lunch counter this noon, his back to the windows, unable to look at the truck waiting there, loaded with pulp today, bunched high up under the clam. Short runs to the chipper in New Hampshire today. His feelings are always fierce on the matter. Extreme pride. Or fear. His moods being like a symphony, swooping and abrupt, the private dark under the public light. They are killing these hills. They.

In prison he was touched.

Felt.

Probed.

Inspected.

Searched.

The untouchable private dark found out by the public's hand and eyes.

He drinks deeply of the coffee. Seven cups by noon. Medicine or mercy? Who names it?

They do.

Pepperburger on the way. Everyone up and down the counter and in the booths, coming in and out the door, all whooping, razzing, tickled pink. Sports and war . . . and the delicate fuzz between. And something about the "State boys," meaning the highway crew.

"That's nothing! You know that turn-off up by Nugents . . . well . . . there Tuesday I counted *eight* of them watchin' one guy fix a ruffle in the road."

HAWWWWWWWWWWW.

Anneka waits on tables along the wall, not the counter. The counter is Denise or Donnie's territory. Anneka tromps back and forth behind Carroll. Something in somebody's plate next to him smells like lemon meringue. He sighs. It's true that when one of your senses isn't up to snuff, the others inundate you. All of them. Sight. Smell. Kinesthetic sense. Sense of impending doom. Sense of . . . touch. *Don't touch me.* He is a 185-pound flesh bomb ticking.

He eats part of the pepperburger, can't finish. How did the cigarette get into the corner of his mouth? He sucks hard, harder. Nourished.

He steps off the stool, pushes into his green plaid wool overshirt.

Looks around. Into her silver eyes. She is by the door. As if just arriving. She hand signs to him. He is shocked. His face grows ash with the color of shock. Her signing is not deft. Nothing like the poetry of his sign language teachers' hands nor that of his friends at the deaf school. In Anneka's fingers, the finger spellings are wracked and squeezed. She is signing to him something about how he has to stay and eat the rest of his pepperburger . . . not to leave.

Mostly she finger spells. No sense of the true American Sign Language grammar. And she spells out every letter . . . so she takes forever.

He reaches back to get the cigarette off his plate, gets his collars straight and crosses the diner, maneuvering sideways between the pack of well drillers just coming in, all of them bright with the smell of the cold white day. Nearing Anneka, now with his right hand low against his chest for privacy, he signs, *"I can't."*

She solidly blocks the door. Very Souleish. He smiles thinly. Two women in long coats with vestibule-sized pocketbooks step in from the outside, so that Anneka hops to the left. The women stand between Anneka and Carroll. All Carroll can see of the girl now is the snowy fingers and wrist of her right hand up over their heads wrangling out a distinctive *"PLEASE!"*

The women move toward an empty booth still cluttered and ketchupped from its past meal, and now there's Anneka reappeared, sniggering mischievously into the knuckles of both hands. She hurries out through the back door to the pantry.

Carroll sees that some strangers in the near booth, two men and a woman in business dress, are staring after Anneka, too. The women are unadorned unhumorable-looking. The man has feathered hair. Blond. And a sunlamp tan . . . or a sunny-other-land tan. They are either whispering or their voices are lost in the din . . . which through Carroll's hearing aids in such a crowded room is *din ultimate*.

When Anneka returns, Carroll is back on his stool, his hands spread on the thighs of his wool work pants. He is between cigarettes. The betweens usually last only a minute. His billed cap which reads ALBION COLE & SONS TRUCKING is squashed down over his bristly TV-escaped-convict-looking brown hair. His expression looks . . . yes, escaped, hunted . . . and yes, in need of a drink . . . in need of a drink . . . in need of many many many drinks . . . in need of a high-hoopin' outburst of song.

Anneka storms up to the coffee machine, filling cups, snatching up forks, knives, spoons, ignoring Carroll. She hurtles away.

Guys on the left of Carroll say blah blah blah blah. Guys on the right blah blah blah blah ba ba ba baaaaaaaaaaa. All the world baaaaaaaaaaaaaaaa.

Anneka returns breathless, backs up against the coffee maker. She looks into his eyes. She raises her hand and the finger spellings are slow sturdy boxy and unmistakable. "*Will you marry me? Not joking. We can get the license started today if you meet me over Town Hall before four o'clock.*"

Guys on either side of Carroll stop talking. They are made wretchedly uncomfortable by Anneka's fingers probing and shaping out the spellings. And by the look in Carroll Plummer's yellow eyes.

Now Carroll Plummer's rubbing his eyes hard like he's trying to blind himself.

Anneka crosses her arms and frowns.

Carroll rests his elbows now on either side of his plate. Looks into Anneka's stormy eyes. Raises his hand.

Guys on both sides watch Carroll's hand spelling, "*Okay.*"

6 | At nearly four o'clock, there's not much business at Town Hall, just one station wagon in the weedy gravel lot. And wind.

The creaking rocking weight of the loaded truck turns hard, Carroll almost rising off the seat to work the stiff wheel and in his peripheral vision, Anneka is out there riding a white horse bareback. Balled up trash and leaves fly past the horse. Such a wind! And a *white horse for godsakes!* And Anneka's pale hair unbraided now, in a pandemonium around her wide face. The wind screeches. Anneka is out there, outside this hot cab, out of this world . . . Anneka, goddess of the wind . . . or something like that.

He steers the grunting chugging truck toward the recycling bins at the back of the lot, but she confuses him, confounds him, the old white draft horse keeping up with the old truck in low gear rolling slow and slower . . . Carroll leaning into the wheel harder, more desperately now, his eyes a bit bulged, veins and cords of his neck thick as fingers, wheel bearings grating. Wind slaps an oak leaf onto the glass. Truck grunts. Anneka's hair burns like magnesium, Anneka's hair hurtling, wrapping her face and head, then by the wind the hair is snapped away into rivulets pulled north and her face is so close to the glass . . . reins gathered into one hand . . . she bends away . . . tears a branch from sumac bushes. Carroll has no blueprint on this, no clue of the etiquette, of the good manners for this. In forty-six years of situations, he's never fallen into one this queer. He can't find a smile. But it seems that that would be the thing. His teeth lay thickly against the walls of his mouth, and something moves up over the bones of his face. But it's not a smile. It's a grimace. Like irritation. He can feel the whole skull shape beneath his face with its hot ache to do right . . . to smile for her. But his flesh face remains harsh.

Now against the truck's door and glass a CRACK! . . . snap! . . . squeeel of the sumac branch. Anneka is beating the truck!

Carroll downshifts and the truck snarls and snorts. He gives the window turner a few cranks, even as he is still bearing into the wheel for this tight not-wide-enough space to turn. One wheel rolls up into the weeds. And Anneka's sumac branch swats the glass. "ANNEKA! QUIT IT!" he bellers through the open part of the glass.

She knees the horse's sides and surges ahead, waving the branch, her white unpretty brows converged, her noble expression cast from some piano-accompanied fluttering melodrama. The old horse and the old truck in low gear, each with their burdens, move in tandem. CRACK! SNAP! SMACK! The girl goes to work with the sumac branch again . . . now beating a headlight.

"ANNEKA! QUIT IT FOR CHRISSAKES!"

Another SMACK!

He brings the truck to a stop alongside the cement half wall of the new handicap ramp built onto the back of the old yellow clapboard building. The white horse's big ass swings away, dirty burred white tail yanked to the far left by the wind.

Carroll realizes wearily that what he is about to do with the rest of his life boils down to this . . . THIS . . . his taking on into his life a difficult child.

7 | Where is she tonight? He has no idea. The thought of her makes him titillated . . . scared . . . tired.

He flicks the switches to the lights of his brother's home, lowers the six-pack to the counter. At the Town Hall, when she had signed the license he saw her handwriting was large and tumbling, transgressing into the small typed print of the form above and below it. Anneka's handwriting like coils of barbed wire. He considers how his parents are in their trailer across town this very minute . . . side by side on the couch, looking at the TV with their soft eyes. It will not be that way with Anneka. What will it be?

8 | *Dear Governor,*
I am writing to ask what is this I hear on the TV you want to give the government to corporations? Reform schools to start with, you said. And then it also was the President a while back who said he wanted to give PUBLIC SCHOOLS to companies. I read where he made a speech at Lewiston High that he wants to do this. He said TO SAVE MONEY. Something gives me the willies about this corporations idea. You ever MET a corporation? A corporation is nobody, just a thing. And listen, the people voting only goes with government. With corporations, it's something else. I don't know what. PRIVATE. This is something creepy and gives me the willies if you want to know. If after a while all different things of the government are corporations, would Maine still be called a "state"? What about the country? How does that work? I am VERY curious. Clue me.
    Sincerely,
    Anneka DiBias
    RR2 Egypt, Maine

9 | Back at the lake, Carroll Plummer turns to the counter and opens one of the Rolling Rocks. "To Anneka," he says deeply, and takes a swallow.

He slides open one of the glass doors, gathers up eight big stainless steel mixing bowls. He fills each bowl with dog chow from a fifty-pound bag slumped up against the side of the refrigerator. He carries the bowls back out onto the deck, arranging them with distance between, brings eight more bowls inside . . . very messy, very gooey, very gunked. He rinses them in the sink and fills each with water, one bowl of water to go with each bowl of chow. He arranges all the bowls with care along the sides of the deck. He shuts the deck lights off to give them some privacy. He sits at the kitchen table with his beer and waits.

Usually by now he's started supper. A few fried eggs or a frozen pizza . . . something to eat while *they* eat. But tonight. It should be a night to celebrate. What's a six-pack? It can't hurt. It takes *three* six-packs just to get him ready to drink whatever else comes along.

He knows they are out there, hanging on the sides of his brother's lakeside pines. In the dark. Waiting. Watching. He read or heard somewhere once that their vision isn't the best. But they know his habits. Probably the sound of the Ford rumbling and creaking down the lake road sets their mouths to watering. Since they are in the dark and he is in the light, they are watching him for sure, seeing his shape in their wavery watery dotted vision. He likes the feel of their eyes on him. They are one of the best things in his life . . . their gratitude, their approval, maybe even worship.

There is no such thing as *one* six-pack.

He closes his eyes, rams his tongue around against his teeth. He does not want to be drunk or hungover. He does not want to live. He does not want to die. He wants to be reverse-born . . . to recede to that size that would fit back in, to be swallowed back.

He gets up tiredly from his chair, carries his beer and the carton of five others out to the deck.

With a flourish, he twists off all the caps and sets all the bottles out, one beside each bowl of chow. He returns to the kitchen, fixes himself fried eggs and toast, opens a decorative jar of his sister's jam, which she makes with rhubarb and strawberry Jell-O.

They arrive. The first two of the evening. Bear-shaped, ready for winter, waddling to the dishes to take their routine positions. He can make them out dimly in the near-dark privacy of the deck. As they reach, dip, and munch, their black eyes regard only the distant trees now. Watching for competition. They seldom give Carroll a glance. Nor their meal. Only the trees.

A third arrives. There are many, many. Three mothers with three and four big kits apiece. And then the loners. They hold their heads up to crunch the chow in a kind of ecstasy. And yes, they eat without looking at what they eat. They know all there is to know in the palms of their hands. They gaze off toward the lake and woods and work their deft fingers over the eight bowls like playing something dreamy and fancy on eight pianos.

Carroll hears a beer bottle clink onto its side. He smiles.

More arrive. There's a grunt and many snarls. More beer bottles topple . . . clunk! . . . clunk! There's a shrilling, a keening. Someone is clobbering someone else. Biting. Shoving. Humpbacked. Pissed-off. No-body shares. A moment of silence. Then a screech. *Snort!* A big fight now. The works, a real tumble. Someone gets pushed off the edge of the deck. Carroll can see the white of his brother's flagpole . . . one of them shimmying up . . . one of them that wasn't able to stand his ground. Somebody is stepping into a bowl and dog chow clatters and rolls over the deck. Beer and water pours through the deck's cracks, splatters on rocks and roots below. Another brawl. A lot of thumps. Someone hurls an empty dish. Everyone stuffing themselves in the race to get it all, all of them celebrating in earnest Carroll's soon-to-be marriage in a big way.

10 | Anneka is late. They agreed to meet here at quarter of eight. A midmorning wedding. "Like opening up shop early!" Anneka had hooted.

He smokes four cigarettes, mashes each butt into the tuna can on the seat. The J.P.'s house looks too quiet. It crosses his mind that this is a set-up. A big Soule trick. Perhaps Francine's very own idea . . . ol' Francine . . . Anneka's mother, the brute of them all. And here he is about as conspicuous as you can get, parked here in the only vehicle he has regular access to since prison . . . ALBION COLE & SONS/TRUCKING/LOGGING & PULP splayed across the doors, clam spread wide across the back of the long, long bed. Albion Cole . . . his mother's brother. Al's been good to him. Everyone's been good to him. No remarks. No funny looks. No ridicule. Till now . . . maybe. And all because the Soules have always had such a power over him.

There is another wind coming up.

Without the heater running, the cab has chilled down. His feet are cold. He touches his nose. It feels like a very red nose. He glances over across the road at the J.P.'s house. Big gray place trimmed in white. Piazza across the ell. And a front door with its top half made up of colored glass squares. Smoke now bursts from the two chimneys at the same time. The wind grabs the smoke and tears it to smithereens.

His pocket watch has 8:12.

The trees wag and everything is cold and crazy out there. Like a day out of childhood. Those days when you colored Pilgrims and Indians and turkeys in school. The looks of his parents exchanged . . . wordless, but he knew it was Christmas secrets. And his grandmother coming around, she and his mother going off somewhere . . . the secret, secret Christmas missions. And his aunts whispering, rolling their eyes, acting nuts.

And his uncles in their red and red-plaid jackets.

Bulkheads and barn doors open. Everything a big rush. Like time running out, time running toward THE HOLIDAYS and the WINTER . . . mystery, miracle, wonder, wishes, and whisper, whisper, whisper . . .

But in those days *everyone* whispered *every* day. The teacher. The kids. Always the floating vowels, the half words out on the outermost edge of him. In those days before they figured out he was almost totally deaf. It was of their eyes and the musculature of their bodies that he understood them. Teachers complained to his parents that he goofed off, goofed around, acted "obstinate," "willful," "arrogant," "disruptive." And *dumb*, though that was not their exact word for it. But on the farm, even at age ten, he was skillful and adept, advanced. High-ranking. A man. He would watch a thing done. Then he would do it well and tirelessly. He was all back, arms, pitchfork, or wrench. Not that there weren't those ugly moments when his uncle Edmund or uncle Roger would grab him by the arm . . . as it would come to after perhaps hollering his name three or four times.

Now a little car pulls up behind. The flash of its windshield is caught in his side mirror before the whole car disappears behind the clam and bed.

And now she is here, kind of soaring upward, hangs off his door handle. He feels for one of his spare packs of cigarettes under the pile of wool shirts on the seat. She is out there dancing around, hyper as hell. He opens the door. She leaps again, hanging from the handle.

"Don't do that," he says. "Those hinges aren't the best."

She drops. She is wearing work boots and big slumped gray socks. But under one arm, all ready to go, she has some little slipperlike things . . . sparkling and fairy-talish. Over a white gauzy peasant dress hangs her everyday plaid poncho with yarn fringe. The dress yanks and churns smokily around her legs. Ring of white floppy cloth shasta daisies around her hair, her white hair scrambling and mixing with the white flowers, each nearly indistinguishable from the other. These flowers look like one of Francine's typical projects . . . which would mean she *knows* . . . that all the Soules know and there's been given, to his surprise, a kind of blessing.

A friend or some cousin . . . hard to keep track . . . accompanies Anneka. A girl with a grin and a look of amazement. She studies Carroll's face openly.

Anneka says, "This here is my lady of honor!"

The girl says, "Hi."

Carroll nods.

"And this here is *him*," Anneka says, looking now almost shy, a quickie look into his eyes, then back to her friend. Both girls giggle. Both have red noses. Eyes running with the cold. Anneka says in her deep commanding Soule voice, "HERE," and presses a ring into his hand. "It's for you to put on me."

Carroll's bristly hair squirms in the wind. He is glad he's tall so the friend won't see his bald spot. He is embarrassed about his age and about the ring. Everything about this wedding shames him.

Now Anneka bounds across the road, turns to beckon them, her halo of white flowers waggling crazily but staying fixed to her head, probably with a million bobby pins. "HURRY! HURRY! HURRY!"

11 So be it. His brother's kitchen. Modern. White walls. Clamshell trim. Trivets and small tiles picturing vegetables, herbs, and fish in that space between cupboards and countertop. A lot of stainless steel . . . ticking, beeping, very digital. It is noon. The sliding glass doors are sunshine extraordinaire. Carroll can't get his mind off the bed which he has made up very nicely this morning. He watches the backs of Anneka's bare calves as she swoops about, opening cupboards and drawers . . . laughing at what she finds . . . everything is a big joke. She calls his brother "The Chief." The wife is "Mrs. Chief." She calls Carroll "Old Sausage" and "Old Thing."

He says, "Don't talk dirty."

She laughs out. "It's not dirty! It's"—she hugs herself and twirls—"British!" She tries the radio . . . lets it blare a minute on the country music station it was fixed to . . . then shuts it off. She sets out a skillet. Her gauzy white dress slashes this way and that. She keeps her poncho on.

Carroll at the table leans on one forearm then the other. He smokes. Not just with lips and lungs . . . but with stomach muscles and back muscles, shoulders and arms . . . like climbing a wall. Whenever her eyes meet his, his own eyes lower to the cigarette in his hand . . . or his hand when it has no cigarette . . . therefore, he lights one.

She fries up onions awhile. Poking each one with a big fork. Onions seem to astound her.

She breaks eggs open on a plate.

"I *hate* those white string things in eggs, don't you?" she says with curling lip, cutting into the eggs with a chowder spoon. She uses a dish towel to dust off bottles of seasonings. She reads *all* the seasonings. She uses some. A dash of this. A dash of that. She announces, "I'm not eating. I'm too fat."

"You aren't fat," says he.

"One hundred percent Holstein," says she.

"So what's that make me? I have *this*." He kneads his middle.

"That, Old Sausage, is middle-aged spread."

He snorts. Smoke comes out of his mouth, nose . . . maybe ears, too. He quickly puts more smoke back into himself.

She is taking way more out of the cupboards and drawers than she needs, leaves everything about. Eventually off comes the heavy poncho. She stuffs it between a cupboard and the cookbooks and herb bottles and a gooey spatula on the countertop. His eyes seize upon the bodice of the peasant dress. He can't imagine eating. She rummages while things sizzle and ding-ding and tick-tick. More things are laid about. She swishes past him. He imagines grabbing a fistful of the plenty of her skirt, saying deeply, "Bed, baby." His eyes slide back to his cigarette. If he had a few beers, they'd be in the bed by now. Forget this what she's doing! Playing house. He pats his pocket for another cigarette, realizes he's not done with the one in his hand. There's the possibility that before this is over, he'll wind up with two lighted cigarettes in his mouth, looking like a lunatic.

She says, "You want some of this?" She holds out a box of tapioca mix that looks about six years old.

"Sure," says he. He can't imagine disappointing her. He understands how childish it is for him to be so impatient, that in good time, they'll make it in there to the bedroom. After all, it's not *he* that's the child. It's up to him to be the one who's disciplined.

"Well, Old Thing . . . we are going to see some tapioca! And . . . with this food coloring . . . I can make it lavender. Or blue. More partyish!" She makes a sound of jubilation, which upon entering Carroll's hearing aids gets reworked into a gargling-shrill like Godzilla makes when tumbling skyscrapers, flinging police cars, mashing armies with a heel. Carroll strokes his left temple.

Her cooking and fixing takes on a tempo, faster, and her motions have become adroit . . . beautiful . . . arms . . . legs . . . hair . . . the swirling dress.

Carroll crosses his arms over his shirt, jiggles one boot. Whatever happens will always be good now. Today has taken a funny turn, but it will right itself. There's the ding! and a beep! Now the hiss of tapioca falling to milk, sugar added . . . a few squirts of blue, a squirt of red.

12 | After he eats all the meal and all the purple tapioca, that she is not having any of, after he scrapes the bowl clean, lays his spoon down, she charges. She mashes her soft, too-large mouth onto his mouth. She pulls his shirt out from his dungarees, groans with desire to see his belly overcast with dark hair.

He goes nuts. He shoves his chair back.

She has her head at some strange angle, eyes focused on a thought . . . halo of cloth flowers still miraculously clinging . . . waggling crazily as he seizes bunches of the white dress at last.

He works to make the breasts bare.

But she is knocking him around, yanking at him, making funny noises that are now nothing like desire . . . more like an attack.

He can't manage any space for his arms and hands to operate for she has such a grip that keeps him too close.

They go around and around slowly, forehead to forehead, like two bulls.

Okay, he thinks, okay, okay . . . this is it . . . this is your way.

Just a rassle?

Just more play? Like the purple tapioca?

There's no mistaking it. Her head driving home into his chest. Knocks the breath from him. He hollers. Pushes her hard.

She pushes harder. She laughs.

Okay, he thinks and climbs up the front of her with all his weight.

She goes down.

She breaks.

It is in the knees that she buckles and a storm of white cloth flowers and pale hair fly at his face as he also drops to the floor. Too heavily. Painfully. Knees. Elbows. Back.

There on "The Chief's" kitchen floor, tiles of green dots, her fingers stained blue and red and yellow . . . and smelling yellow . . . turmeric? . . . and his mouth stained purple . . . they never make it to the bed.

She flings his belt across the floor.

The buckle ricochets off a chair leg with a clank.

He sees her mouth move and he's afraid she'll speak. But her mouth is just feeling the shape of some soft private thought. And he is grateful. For he thinks if she calls him "Old Sausage" while his pecker is in full view like this, his soul will die.

But she never does.

When it is done and she speaks, she calls him Carroll.

PART FIVE

It's not a sneaky theft.

Not like one of Lloyd's magic tricks.

This theft is showy. Official.

The swipes of blue cop light across the dark bedroom windows and the amber swipes of the tow and the shouts and beep-beeps and clangs of them fastening to the GMC, the bank-loan GMC, the behind-payments GMC . . . it is all, yes, official . . . a theft written into law.

It has come to this and Forest Johnson speaks softly without raising his head off the pillow. "I've never had anything taken back before . . . I've never had this."

And Peggy says, "Forest . . . it's not personal. So many people in trouble these days."

"It *feels* personal," says he. "I thought . . . you know . . . they'd give me those four more days."

In this past year, Peggy thinks he has become more like the younger Forest . . . watching time push his way. Obliging. Swept along. But was that the way young Forest was? Is memory like clouded glass? Perhaps this is a Forest who never was. A new Forest. Forest ruined. Forest dead in all his nerves. Peggy pushes this from thought. She clasps her toes and warm arches around his two-toed foot and the stumped ankle . . . happy to have him predictable, a good husband, a quiet friend. She holds fast to him till the clangs and beepings and revolving lights and the smooth-running official convoy move off into the night.

PART SIX

It is a summer day though not summer. Disquietingly reversed, falling back. Insects have come to life to creak in the high grasses beyond the high rock wall.

The rich widow is not the only one too heavily dressed. She looks and sees all their heavy blazers, heavy jersey dresses and a few long winter coats slung over their arms. She hardly knows these people. The druggist and his family. She has no memories to share. The dead child is just a name . . . and the repeated details of the child's slow death to cancer . . . the child's courage . . . and the courage of the druggist and his wife . . . all hearsay from the druggist himself told to the widow over the counter in the few months since she has become a patron there. The druggist . . . Gary. She would not name him as a friend. Nor is he really a neighbor. She has no friends or neighbors in this town. No relations. No servants or caretakers. This is why she is here! In Egypt. To be where no one knows her. To search the black tunnels of her mind, to create! To work, work, work, and nothing else. And yet now here it is, Nan and Gary Richards's bleary eyes and "courage." She feels attuned to this beautiful grief, more passionate than a love affair.

Off to the far left . . . dear God . . . she's not one bit surprised to see him, standing by his truck many yards away near the wood line . . . the gravedigger. The grave-digger is *him* . . . the wood man. Same man. Same truck. But instead of firewood the truck has . . . well . . . to be crudely put . . . shovels. He is, as before, chewing, the heavy moustache in quick eddies of dark and tawny and gray. Arms bare and folded across the chest. Boots apart in a kind of defiance. And of all things, a Civil War cap, faded and wrecked, as if stolen from a dead soldier in the midst of battle.

The dead. An ornately carved casket . . . dark like mahogany . . . but more likely maple stained to resemble mahogany. No flowers. Contributions to the American Cancer Society are requested.

As he, Lloyd Barrington, chews and now and then screws his cap on a little tighter, he is watching her.

She smiles to herself. Living in this town. It's like being in one of those off-off-off-off-off-Broadway plays, perhaps even a high-school play, where some of the actors take the roles of several characters. Where else will he turn up? Maybe he's also really the druggist but without a moustache in that role. She looks quickly at the druggist's face. She shouldn't be feeling silly now. Stop! She drops her eyes in shame.

The minister is telling the terribly silent group how children were especially loved by the Lord. The word "lamb" comes up again and again, although this child was nearly thirteen.

The rich widow sees the minister's hands raise over the casket and the parents' heads . . . and there, some people who must be the grand-parents, their faces twisted . . . and the minister's voice shrinking to a low tremble upon speaking the child's name. "Natalie."

The rich widow takes a breath. Seems she's about to faint . . . more stricken now than even the parents. But how is she stricken? She closes her eyes, trying to keep herself from rocking from foot to foot . . . faster and faster . . . like too many cups of coffee.

Death is the only frontier, the only unclaimed territory, the only adventure left. Or is it the place you need to get back to? Back to that pivot . . . death, life, death, life . . . that friction point, its rock-hard white chill. She tells such things to her psychoanalyst and the analyst narrows his eyes like a parent catching her in a lie. The analyst says, "You have a long way to go, Gwen."

Her feet ache. But she's not tired. She shifts and looks squarely into the gravedigger's face. No, not tired. She's ready.

PART SEVEN

1 | Anneka hears it coming down the lake road. Slack chains wran-
gling against the stakes. Gears gnashing. She hurries to find a clean fork and knife and spoon for him. She always fixes a little supper for him no matter what. No matter how long her day at the diner. No matter how many letters to politicians she's composed with pen in murderous grip. Mail spread out over rugs and chairs and the bed. And the news-letters. Her causes. No matter how many friends and relatives keep the phone ringing. No matter what. There is this ritual of the meal. The look on Anneka's face is indistinguishable from that look one wears anticipating

sex. What is the bed without the table? All essential. All life-giving. Both specifications of Anneka's love.

She rearranges mail and little notebooks to make him a space.

Zucchini in the pan frying up crisp.

Plenty of zucchinis. Big as blimps and seedy.

There's plenty of any and all things they grow over at the farm place . . . the plenteousness of Gramp Merlin and Grammie Dot and the aunts . . . fertility being some people's A-plus.

Anneka bangs open a few eggs. Dumps cornmeal from a cup. By the time the truck door smacks shut, she has found and rinsed and dried a fork, spoon, and butter knife, arranged them around Carroll's plate.

There are so many signs that his mood is bad, even before he reaches the door. The truck's engine going quiet, the exact way it gets so quiet. His boots scuffing on the deck. The air.

When he slides the glass door to one side, she runs at him to rub her face into his wool shirt with happy snorts. He is not an affectionate man. But he never says, "Don't."

Tonight he falls onto his meal without a word, without eye contact.

Zigzagging over the long countertops are serving bowls and glasses "soaking." Anneka is not much for a quick clean-up. She usually goes for the long "soak" method.

He empties his plate but says no to seconds.

She sits across from him and reads to herself from a hardcover text, turning pages and groaning. Now she says, "Ah-hah!" and "That's *just what I thought!*"

She gets up and reloads his plate. He leans back in his seat and watches her chunky arms, the fingers curled around the spatula and the openness of her collar. He says, "Anneka, I told you I didn't want any more."

She goes back to her chair across from him, turns a few pages. She scrutinizes something, then flips forward again and says breathlessly, "I've been reading about depression."

He skewers many many zucchini slices onto his fork, holds them up, gives the fork a shake so the slices flap. "As in the Great . . ."

"No," says she, wrinkling her nose. "As in . . . a person with it." She flips back pages, holds her finger to a line of print. "It says you have it."

He smiles. "Do they spell my name right? Two *r*'s?"

"*Please.*" She fixes him with a glare of her most silvery kind.

"I do not have depression," he says.

She reads silently for a moment. "Everything . . . all these symptoms but a couple are what you have."

He looks at his plate, forces a little smile, raises his eyes. "I wake up every morning with a smile on my face."

"You do not!" she booms. "You wake up very weird in the face."

"That's not depression."

"You know Betsy?"

"No."

"She's my friend from Lincoln . . . you seen her at Mum an' Dad's. She goes to this doctor . . ."

"A shrink."

"No . . . he's not. He's a regular doctor . . . you know . . . family practice . . . something like that. He cured her."

He pushes some of the spongy seedy part of the zucchini over to the edge of his plate. "Your grandfather has depression. Go work on him." He sneers. "I never seen anybody that ought to be as sad and blue and ready to kill himself as ol' Merlin must be."

"That's different."

"Just a little case of mortgage-itis, huh?" Carroll chuckles.

"What's so funny?"

"It ain't."

"You were laughing."

"No, I wasn't."

She reads on and on while his yellow hawklike eyes are zeroed in on her bent-down head. "Ah-hah!" she says again and again, as she follows the blocks of a chart with her fingers and thumb.

He stands up suddenlike, carries his plate of food to the sink. "A little soaking going on over here, huh?" he observes.

She turns a page, her eyes blazing with line after line of small print that does, to her, seem to hold in repetition Carroll Plummer's name. She says, "It has to do with what they call syn . . . ap . . . sing in your brain. You are under-synapsing."

"This bowl here with the pinkish stuff floating on the yellowish water . . ." He leans his ear to it. "It is depressed."

Anneka turns a page.

"Anneka . . . look . . ." He takes her by the shoulders from behind, gives the shoulders a soft shake. "I want you to settle down. Okay? You don't know where to stop, do you?"

"You have depression, Carroll."

"I'm forty-six years old, been in two different correctional facilities off and on for over twenty years . . . I'm an alcoholic . . . and"—pats his stomach—"lost my shape. That's life. Not depression. Anybody would wake up looking funny if they were me."

She turns a page.

He releases her shoulders, returns to his chair, straddles it, spits a piece of zucchini seed into his empty water glass, lights a cigarette, looks out at the dark lake through the glass doors. He pulls in the smoke, gets his chest very big with smoke, holds it till he's nearly dizzy. He reaches across the table, spreads a hand over the book as the smoke explodes from his teeth. And as soft as smoke, these words, "You don't really know me."

She gives him a hard level look. "I know *everything* about you."

His neck prickles.

She plucks the book out from under his hand.

He says, "If what you are getting at is . . . you are trying to say your family tells you stuff about ol' Carroll from the past, let's get one thing straight. There's nothing they *didn't* tell you. No sex in the back of a car or anything like that. I was never *close* to any of your aunts or your mother in any physical way . . . or in *any* way. I was always just around. I worked. Did milking, graining . . . helped with the calving . . . hayed. And we took out some logs one fall. Your aunts just happened to be out milking . . . or haying. There was always at least four feet between us. And then there were all those family occasions where I just lay down in my vomit singing. I used to sing a lot. I did not sing good. But I sang a lot."

Anneka licks a forefinger, thumbs back a page, reads squintily. Very very small print. She reads whisperishly as if only to herself. ". . . will self-medicate with alcohol, street drugs, nicotine, caffeine . . ." She whomps the book once with her open hand and utters a triumphant "Ah-hah!"

2 | Not many sales at Moody's Variety & Lunch this afternoon. Only one Coke. One bag of chips. Not much for wisdoms on the air. Only Hawaiian Sunset and Pink Punch occupied. Deep anguished wood-creaks match the cadence of the two men's words.

"Soon I'll need to sell off what I don't need to stand on, I expect.

Going to retire whether I want to or not." Old teamster chum of Merlin's that Carroll remembers from the old fair days, though he wouldn't recognize him if he hadn't looked twice. The guy has lost most of his hair. Used to have quite a head of hair. Now the bald head has a shape that wasn't noticeable back when it had hair. Teeth. The man does have a good solid mouthful of real teeth. "I always woulda said I'd 'spect to die in the harness. That's the way to go. No languishin'. I never would have predicted the way things would turn out these days. Who would have predicted it?" Shakes his head.

"What'cha got for a team now, Russ?" Carroll asks.

"Why? You want to buy 'em?"

Carroll laughs. "Not likely."

"Well, my boy isn't keeping his Durhams. It's just horses now . . . pair of five year olds . . . a lot of bluff really. Not the stuff those other cutters used to be. 'Member that one team I had that took the drag practically through the grandstand . . . in a curve!" He giggles. "That was all one ol' boy workin'. If they'd both done their job, I'd be rich now." He shrugs. Smooths his cap that rests on his knee. Smooths it again to the shape of his knee. A red print knit . . . along the idea of what small boys wear to play in snow. "Hughie's still at the fairs. And all those guys from Windham and that outfit with the kid that was in the fire. Well, they're usually on . . . the ones with the burned boy. Got Percherons now." He closes his eyes, shakes his head. This, Carroll knows, means the new Percherons are raking in some trophies. The old guy opens his hands, shows their emptiness. "Some say it won't last long. Peter out, don'tcha know . . . even though it's goin' like blazes far as you can tell to look. But it can't keep up like this. Tractor pulls maybe. Or Jeep pulls. Maybe Toyota sedan pulls!" He cackles over this. A bit too hysterically. "Can't have you a horse or an ox without you have a piece of field to put him in, don'tcha see . . . and some hayfield. Some fellers passed away . . . but you know some're getting in a bad way . . . havin' to sell. And banks, you know. Everyone around here's catchin' hell from the bank . . . and we got only *one* goddam bank now . . . less you go over to Conway. Everybody on the TV says banks're poor. These guys cry poverty when they don't make twice as much profit as they did six months ago. Used to be poor meant you didn't have shoes. Goddam 'em. Between them and the paper companies they own this whole region. I don't pity 'em. I'd like to see one of those Wall Street fellers walk in here now in his three-piece suit and look me steady in the eye for sixty seconds while he tells me he's not rich enough. I tell ya, Mister Man, he wouldn't walk outta here with his shoes on."

Carroll breaks the cellophane on a fresh pack of cigarettes, his hands steady, fingers deft. In most eras out of history, Carroll Plummer would be called a man in his prime, still strong, still able.

The old farmer squints at Carroll. "Well, I'm not going to give up on my team yet. I'll give up most anything else first . . . furniture or something. I figure I'll just work 'em for logs when I get a call . . . earn them their keep . . . call it good 'nough. I'll just get as practical as I can without selling 'em outright."

"Well, that's something anyway," says Carroll.

"Ayuh. 'Tis."

Carroll lights up, smokes hard and slow and deep.

Old guy says, "Merlin's place. I hear the bank's got that."

Carroll says, "Bank's got it in court or something as I understand it."

Old guy shakes his head. With a fingernail, he flicks something from between one of his good-looking teeth. He looks into Carroll's eyes. Looks like he's got tears, but it's most likely just that rheumy-gaze some old guys get. And there's the thickness of his glasses. You can't know shame and fear when you see it on these guys. It doesn't look any different than pride. He starts to tear open the bag of potato chips on his lap, but changes his mind. "You mortgage the homeplace to keep up, you see. The things you got to purchase to keep up. Ain't enough you can pro-duce 'nough milk to drown half the town. Whatever you produced this year . . . you got to produce more next year . . . and more after that. You need more gimmicks to produce more, and you need to produce more to pay for the gimmicks to produce more . . . and at some point you are snowballed right out of it, don'tcha see. And a cow ain't a cow. She's a wondercow. She needs to do better next year than last or there's a better cow comin'. She's expected to"—his wet eyes twinkle—"jump over the moon. Meanwhile, the government's in there . . . an' . . . well . . . dairyin' ain't farmin', don'tcha see?"

Carroll looks down at his hands.

Old guy lays his bag of chips on the rocker to his left. He pats it as if to make it comfy. "I can tell you about it. I'm speaking for Fred Phillips, too. He just said those same words Sunday. They've always talked about falling by the wayside is like, you see, a good thing . . . like it was for the best. The cream rises, they say. But what happens when everybody is at the wayside and a handful of agribusiness operations and other big fellas . . . big real estate companies . . . big chemical companies . . . automakers . . . plastic and energy . . . that . . . that global thing . . . now what happens to this world when you got that and the rest of us are just useless?" He leans toward Carroll. "You know they're going to have to tear-gas ol' Merlin out of there. It's going to be quite a show."

Carroll chuckles nervously. "Yeah . . . Fort Soule, huh?"

"Right!" The old farmer laughs heartily, fits his red knitted cap back on his balding head. "Fort Soule," says he and stands, snatching up his bag of chips from the rocker. His dark work pants show he's lost a lot of weight. He gives Carroll's shoulder a squeeze. "Good to see ya," he says, then heads for the door . . . a fairly quick effortless almost sneaky kind of walk . . . the walk of a man who, like Carroll Plummer, during any other time in history, any other era, would be considered a strong man, a good man.

3 | "Goddam lyin' sneaky son-of-a-bitch!" Anneka snarls from her deep chair in the living area . . . a chair, which quite possibly, is the Navy Chief's favorite when he and his family occupy this house. The forty-watt bulb of the nearest lamp is a little dim for reading. But Anneka's eyes blaze effortlessly along the page. *"Oh . . . 'thank you for your interest in my proposals to privatize some functions of state government.' "* She snorts. "Well, my INTEREST, Mr. Slime-head, is not like gee whiz!"

Carroll says, "What's wrong, Anneka? Who is it?"

"Oh . . . *him* . . . the governor . . . Governor Asshole." She reads along. "Here he says, *'For many services, such as state police, it is entirely necessary for state government to be the single provider of the service.' "* Of course of course of course. LOTS of police. Oh, yes, of course. You wouldn't believe how reasonable he's trying to make it sound! Looks like this letter was thought up by a baby lamb and not a goddam capitalist vampire shark! He says he's got no intention of hurting small business . . . that, after all, it's a freeeeeee market and may the best man win or some such shit. He's skipping over how the shithead in the White House has actually named three humongous corporations he wants to give the public schools over to. But of course, he's one shithead, the other guy's the other shithead . . . they just happen to be thinking along the same lines COINCIDENTALLY . . . there's no . . . you know . . . policy here." She sighs. " *'Feel free to contact me again with your concerns about this issue or any other issue of concern to you.'* " She sneers. "Carroll, we are ALL in DEEP SHIT."

4 | It is evening. They are in their bed. Well, they are in the Navy Chief's bed. But for now it is their time and place. Anneka is reading. Her hair, which may have some intention of being a ponytail, whooshes straight up. Her savage pre-history look.

Carroll has been lying on his back, eyes wide on the ceiling.

Anneka speaks.

He can't hear her.

She nudges him.

He looks at her.

She works her fingers and wrist to finger spell: *"Why do you have your ears off?"*

He turns completely. Face and body. And soul. Despairing. Hides his face against her neck.

5 | It's a surprise.

Gifts are wrapped in silver and pink and white paper, boxes the size of blenders, spatula sets, coffeepots. Some with no boxes. Soft bulkiness of towels and blankets, sheets and needlepoint couch pillows. And there is food, always the plenteous, the foil-wrapped breads, the casseroles of every potato or squash possibility. Apple crisps done five ways. The bounty. Everything in rectangles and squares, a patchwork resembling small acreages, resembling the source.

And Anneka. Plenteous in her way. Upswept fount of hair. Boisterous, goofy, and wisecracky and tender. So many ways for Anneka to be Anneka.

And Anneka's father, George DiBias, standing there with a rifle under his arm.

"My Marlin!" Anneka booms, snatches the rifle from his hands. She dances with the rifle, gives it a kiss, checks the action for its familiarity pushed along under the heel of her hand.

"Which *means* . . ." one of the Soule sisters shouts, "he wants you to go over and target shoot with him, not to forget who Daddy's little girl is!"

"Daddy's little crack shot," chortles Anneka's mother, Francine. "He needs her to go with him to the club, you see. His team needs her for points."

Two young boy cousins eye the rifle and step closer.

Anneka feels her father's bicep. "Man o' rock," she says, then spins away down the short hall to hide the rifle from the kids.

"Anneka probably don't have time for that ol' gun club now she's a married thing," says a Soule sister, wiping down the wall behind the stove with a wet dishcloth.

"But I thought she was on the shitlist of every hunter in town," says sister Faye.

"You get 'em in the black most of the time, you're hated and loved," observes one of the uncles, winking at George. "Poon has always made a lot of enemies," he adds, using one of the girl's nicknames from earlier times.

"Yeah, but that was *friendly* enemies," Francine explains. "What she made for herself last fall was *enemy* enemies."

"I only thought she'd like to have the rifle around," George DiBias says softly, a tide of a red flush rising over his large face.

Many Soules have converged out on the deck, though it's too cold to be sitting outside so near the windy gray chop of the lake, iced-over beach and rimy ledge. But the visitors seem to be getting such a kick out of the Chief's puffy-cushioned patio furniture. Beers and sodas go around. And coffee. And red punch. The glass doors glide open, then whomp shut, glide open, then whomp shut.

TV goes on.

"SHUT IT OFF!!" screams a Soule sister. "You kids go out! Go find some Indian relics. Probably tons of arrowheads and stuff around here."

"Indian relics." A kid rolls his eyes.

George DiBias and one of the other men say good-bye, headed over to the Kane place on the Emmons Road.

"What's at the Kanes'?" a sister asks.

"Burned out."

"No!"

"Yep. Nobody hurt but lost everything."

George DiBias tips his cap to Carroll as he turns to leave.

Sherry Barrington is carried in by a teenage boy. Sherry of the auburn hair . . . hair kept short for what the sisters call "sanitation purposes."

Sherry is the Soule sister that you can never leave alone or she'll fall out of her chair. There's a fuss now as the sisters arrange her, getting her comfy. She is beloved . . . so beloved . . . possessed, well, actually repossessed. Engulfed. Her green-gray eyes grope about, following voices, eyes like a kind of queer radar.

And Carroll's parents are here, his mother bundled up in her coat. She with her hair that never grays. Her round-shouldered readiness to take on the next bad surprise. Her lips flicker. A single-word remark meant only for Carroll's father to hear, his father, Marty Plummer, with those farmer's hands slack between his spread knees. Carroll nods to his father. And his father nods back. And there's his mother's little brief wave to him. How strange! His parents in this house where they never have visited before. For they seldom leave their own place. Here, out of context, like bears out of the woods, out in the open, like movie stars stepped off the screen, overly solid, dazzling. No need to force small talk upon them. Their decision to drive over here is to Carroll the honor of all honors. Best left in their true eminence untainted by the wishy-wash of conversation.

He turns away from them and steps out on the deck.

In the kitchen area Anneka and a couple of her cousins are fixing apple crisp in bowls of all sizes. Anneka totes bowls along the length of her arm in snazzy waitress fashion, stepping in and out the sliding glass doors to the deck crowd, then back inside for the big sweep around the living room area with its cathedral ceiling and fireplace made of vinyl-looking white rocks. She is stepping over outstretched legs, over kids, over the wrapped gifts and her heaps of newsletters and squinched revisions of revisions of letters and half-written letters . . . and clothes that have been tossed . . . all mixed together, a rubble. The Soule sisters, her aunts, take over as usual, picking up, rearranging, giving the Chief's house the final Soule touch.

"This room would look a lot better in yellow!" Anneka's mother decides.

"They callll me mello yellllo doo doo!" croons one of the others as she weaves through the various standing Soules and husbands of Soules. She carries her grandbaby on her hip. He is dressed like a miniature man. Baby-sized work boots. Baby-sized plaid shirt.

And close to Sherry Barrington sits Sherry's guardian angel, her youngest son, the one who carried her in from the car.

Anneka gives no apple crisp to Sherry. Only to the son. Anneka knows you never give Sherry a plate. The son, Joel, says "Yep, thanks" as he takes the bowl. This Joel, who is younger than Caleb . . . Joel and Caleb both born after Sherry's brain tumor operation. Anneka knows the story of these pregnancies. Anneka knows how Lloyd Barrington was beaten once because of making Caleb. Anneka knows Carroll's part in it. There are no secrets. None. She can look at Carroll's hands and see them in fists upon Lloyd's face. After Joel, they had Sherry's tubes tied, the story goes. There was no way to tie up the old fox. Family truths. Titillating.

Out on the deck . . . "How's Cole been treating you, Carroll?" one of the many husbands wonders as Carroll settles down at the umbrella table. "He's up on Burgess now, isn't he?"

Carroll smiles, not quite hearing every word, but understanding the gist of it. He replies, "We're about done there, but Hanley's opening up Raymond Pond . . . we've got a month in there . . . thereabouts." He sees among the feet and table legs the smeared, smudged, gooed, and battered aluminum dinnerware of his raccoon restaurant. He reaches for his cigarettes. There's possible news this weekend, but perhaps unmentionable . . . that yet-to-be-mentioned business of whether or not Merlin has sold the last of his herd. Unmentionable, touchy. For hasn't Merlin railed on and on that he will not "bend" for those "bank bastards"?

Very young boy, elevenish, towheaded as Anneka and having Anneka's ability to nearly knock over the Chief's patio table just by coming close to it, speaks. "You up to a wrist rassle?"

Carroll's dark-lashed yellow eyes move from the boy to the table. He stuffs his cigarettes back in his pocket. "Put it here." Pats the table.

"SHUT UP, BRENDA, ENOUGH OF THAT PLEEEEZ!!" roars one of the sisters somewhere beyond the glass doors.

Carroll smiles. He needn't ask about Merlin's dairy herd. Everything in the heart of a Soule is eventually shouted out.

Suddenly, next to Carroll's elbow, paper napkins explode in all directions at the same moment the icy wind is giving the boy's pale hair a ruffling and there's the snapping of the Chief's American flag above them. Kids chase the napkins. Everyone's nose is red. The lake rocks and sloshes. Carroll likes the feel of his own cold red nose and the boy's grip, getting ready. They stare into each other's eyes, then lower their heads.

Carroll sees one of the husbands pass by, sees him only from the waist down, sees the hand with the beer in it. Carroll's hand closes up harder around the boy's smaller hand.

"Ready?" the boy asks.

"Ayup."

"DON'T YOU THINK TO USE A LITTLE SALT IN THIS, ROBIN?!!" a Soule voice demands. "WE AREN'T THE HIGH BLOOD PRESSURE CROWD HERE YET!!"

"OH YESSS WE ARE!" another voice blares. "PUT ON YOUR OWN DAMN SALT 'N' SHUT UP!"

Carroll beats the kid three times in a row, then lets him win one. Carroll is starting to feel warm. He stands up, pulls off one of his chamois shirts. He says to the kid, "You got quite an arm."

The kid says, "You do, too."

Every time the sliding doors open, there's a blast of heat from the house. Sliding doors opening, shutting, opening. No supermarket could be busier. Carroll steps inside, pulls off another shirt and another, down to his black T-shirt and self-consciously thick waist. Oil heat rushes from the Chief's floor registers. Faces are getting a hot red bloat, especially Carroll's mother who won't part with her coat. Everywhere is the grinding jaws of Soules having apple crisp, those that aren't still working on the casseroles. And there's cakes and cookies and dip and chips and pickles . . . and Soule aunts ragging Anneka about housekeeping and Anneka ragging them about their "nerves."

"Where's Lloyd?" someone asks. Lloyd Barrington, the in-law who is now accepted among the fold after years of being their curse.

"Over to Emmons Road. It's them people that got burned out."

"No insurance, I heard."

"Well, I guess they had insurance . . . but you'd have to ask Randy or Merlin 'bout that. He was telling 'bout it this mornin'. Somethin' damn screwy."

Merlin finally arrives. He has gone light on the fairs this year. Anneka has said it's because of the bank thing, that Gramp Merlin is scared the cops will make a raid on his family while he's gone, that he'll come home to find them put out beside the road.

You wouldn't say Merlin is depressed these days over his finances. Seems more like he's emboldened.

Merlin Soule, a man who can make a footstool look like a throne. Ol' Merl teasing and grinning, giving orders. Big neck. Big head. Crew cut white and thick. Work uniform dark blue, buried by four outer shirts, all their collars in a clash of plaids. He has been over to the fire, he tells them. He smells like a fire, a burning house. A plate of zucchini casserole and cold buttered bread is shoved his way. "Insurance company says they won't cover because the shut-off to the oil furnace was too high for a short person. Damned buncha nonsense. You look at Gary and her, an' neither one is short. And besides the fire had nothing to do with the furnace in the first place. 'Twas wirin'." Merlin shakes his head, squeezes his nose, grins. "Nobody was home when the fire broke out so it 'twouldn'ta mattered if they were shrimps or giants." He again shakes his head, passes around a grim look. "Damned buncha nonsense."

Small grandchild stumbles over to look into Merlin's plate.

Carroll stares at Merlin. So many years. His previous releases from prison never brought him back this close to Merlin Soule, his friend.

Something jabs Carroll's back. He turns and sees Anneka. She looks to be fuming. "It's just the goddam big biz world playing hardball."

Carroll blinks.

"Insurance." She enounces this word clearly. "Insurance, Teddy." Teddy. Her name for him, which refers to his hairy body. Since marriage, he has had to live with many names that make him cringe. In prison, the worst he got tagged with was "Christmas Carroll."

Voices and the clash of silverware tear through his hearing aids. And there's too much dry heat. So hard to concentrate. Everyone, everything so astounding, paled and far off. He is scared someone will ask him a question or ask him to help out with a task, because he might just look into their eyes with a blank goofball expression and no speech.

A nearby child moans "Bubba" softly to himself. This child stands in the midst of the coming and going legs and feet, looking up to each face for the answer to his question. Soules are everywhere chewing, chewing, chewing. "Bubba," says the forgotten child again. Patient. Surely a trait inherited from a non-Soule father.

Cousin Sage leans against Anneka as if to waltz, then a *big hug*. "Come over and look at the presents. Come on!"

The small child rubs his eyes, dimples deep on his fat hands. He whispers ever so sadly to himself. "Bubba. Bubba. Bubba."

Sweat trickles down Carroll's neck.

Now Anneka leaps, mashes her wide bright mouth too close to one of Carroll's hearing aids for a kiss. The noise of this kiss, translated through metal and plastic technology, nearly cripples him. He throws one arm out. One knee buckles. Anneka trudges toward the gifts, and her girl cousins close in around her.

Carroll's parents watch all this as if on the screen of their color TV.

One of Lydia Soule's latest husbands stands next to Carroll and speaks a few words about the Civil War special they had on TV, which everybody in the country but Anneka and Carroll has seen.

Now, from the Soule women, an epidemic of high whiny fake Southern accents goes around mercilessly.

"Ya'll seen Mary Chesnut lookin' for her peen-sill sharr-piner?" Francine declares.

"Bubba."

Carroll stands with folded arms watching Anneka opening gifts . . . yes, a toaster . . . and yes, towels. She looks up from the struggle of white and silver paper to his face.

A toddler, not the one that is whispering "Bubba," this one with bare fat legs and a diaper, squats down and pats the lacings of Carroll's left boot.

Merlin Soule, done with the main course, is now working some apple crisp around in his mouth and telling one of his stories. It is the story of how the raccoons took care of his corn one year.

Piece of apple crisp crust sails through the air, tumbles down the front of Carroll's black T-shirt like kisses. He looks and sees it's his grandmother-in-law Dottie Soule across the room in one of the Chief's spring rockers. She pretends to pitch another, then laughs . . . and the daughter sitting heavily on the arm of her chair studies Carroll's T-shirt.

Carroll's not sure how to handle this. Dignity is important of course. Without alcohol, the laws of nature seem revised.

"These coons were professional," Merlin explains. "These coons schemed this haul for months. What they did was they stole some trucks . . ."

Many kids titter.

One says, "No way!"

"Yes, they did . . . they took dump trucks, tractor trailer rigs . . . whatever trucks was habitual to have their keys left in 'em. They got together in the trucks in a convoy and drove up over my field and backed the trucks up to my corn."

"NAW!" one kid objects.

"Trucks," says another kid grimly, rolling her eyes.

"And they had stolen corn pickers . . . not corn choppers. These was pickers for *ears,* you see . . . like coons like 'em. They loaded the trucks swiftly."

Carroll has heard this raccoon story before through the haze of a drunk . . . seems it was at a fair . . . and Merlin, even then, had his mouth full of some sweet dessert.

"Then they got back in the trucks, one coon at the wheel of each truck, and one coon each to ride shotgun. Coons don't use headlights a'tall. They don't even look to where they're drivin. Coons drive very well just lookin' out the side windows. They adjust their little masks and square their shoulders, tip their caps, let up the brakes, then ride away . . . clean. Just like everybody else, coons have had to keep up with mechanization. But they ain't dumb enough to borrow, you see. They *steal*."

Seems to Carroll this story has been revised.

Merlin fills up his mouth with the rest of his apple crisp.

"Dad! Do the story about Chief Krimple!" Francine calls from the kitchen area.

Carroll sees through the sliding glass doors that the young towhead boy there on the deck is wrist rassling with one of the younger Soule sisters, Cassandra.

Carroll takes a cigarette into his lips.

"OUTDOORS WITH THAT CIGARETTE!" sister Faye commands.

"Ya'll want to have a cup of coffee, sugar pie?" someone is drawling near his shoulder and he sees it's Francine . . . Francine from the Civil War . . . with her hand on his, pushing his fingers open. A mug of coffee just for him.

The wedding paper slashes and floats.

So these are his people now. Some by blood. Some by promise. This feels like the prelude to a good life, the newlyweds who raise a few children, who will make a little home on the back land . . . all of them and Merlin and Dottie and Carroll's parents, Marty and Grace, making "it" work . . . to bring about what? . . . a future of casseroles and apple crisps and warm rooms and knowledgeable hands? A future?

6 | With his left fingers, Carroll pokes his cigarette to the partly open window. In his right hand is the miracle drug still in its white paper bag. He and Anneka are still dumbstruck by the wonder, the light weight of this bag.

He shakes the bag. Little plastic container tumbles out. He places the container on the narrow ledge of the truck's dash.

Around the shopping center parking lot, other lives move clunkily and distant. From the great height of this logging truck, only Anneka and Carroll are true. From the same white bag, another bottle . . . the old and familiar . . . Anneka's usual medication for her heart trouble . . . occasional and violent episodes of tachycardia that she has had since childhood. Carroll presses that bottle into her hand. He looks at the container that is on the dash. "I feel like instead of swallowing them I should wear 'em around my neck or something. Maybe keep them in a vault."

Anneka says in low whisperish awe, "They will make you well."

"It's half your pay . . . or half of mine. Half a week of your running from table to table. *Half.*" He sucks hungrily on his cigarette. "More than half actually . . . *way* more than half."

"And you are my whole life, more than half . . . okay?" She glares at him.

"Not so. Only a little piece of your life, dear. You will outlive me by many many years and then remarry a younger man."

She looks through the window down into an open hatchback into which a pregnant woman is loading bags and bags and bags of groceries. "Maybe I'll die first. You never know. Then you'll have to marry a younger woman."

He laughs outright. "There is no younger woman. Younger than you, they are still playing jump rope." He keeps snorting over this, smoke chuffing out both nostrils. And Anneka, with her chunky crooked braids, is the picture of sweet unfledgery . . . if you didn't see the smoldering precocity of the silver eyes.

Now she looks down at the yellowy olive color of the dimpled cuffs of her home-dyed long johns top, longer than the cuffs of her sweater, though not nearly as long as her wrists. Homemade girl. Home-fed. Home. And this wedding ring . . . found in the family pile long ago . . . was she age eight? When she found it and stored it away, had she imagined Carroll? Maybe. Though she would not have been able to call him by name, how complete *was* her design at age eight? Now she thinks of it sweetly, how she provided the ring, how off guard he was caught by the wedding, how guarded he is now.

He taps his ash out onto the pavement. "Well, I guess, put simply . . . it's a lot to think about . . . the price of these. They better work, baby. And even if they do, I'll be redepressed from paying for them. There's so many places to put half a week's pay. Al says he could advance me the money so I can get a pickup. We need our own vehicle. You know . . . efficient on gasoline . . . and something that's not like a Stealth Bomber to park. Al's been pretty decent about me using this work rig for my own personal life, but I ain't going to milk it. And I'm not going to borrow my father's car again. It'll be the last car they'll ever be able to afford. So let's say Al advances me the cash. My check will be smaller than it is now. See? We're talking a bad money scene here. I'm way past trying to argue with you that I don't need medication to be a normal man . . . okay? You are probably right. I'm just saying I can't afford to be a normal man."

She taps her foot, watches the little hatchback with the pregnant woman whiz away.

Carroll snickers. "You'd think we'd just bought these dandies from a dope dealer in a barroom parkin' lot. It's a black-market price!"

She says softly, "It's worth it."

"Is it worth choosing between these and a truck . . . these and food?"

"I'll get another job," says she.

"Where?"

"I'll figure something."

"Think hard now. Where?"

"I don't know, but I will. I'll do anything for you. You are my . . . my whole life."

He chuckles. "You don't know how funny it is that you say that."

"Well, hurry up. Take a couple of the friggin' things. Let's get started. It's a proven fact that lookin' at pills doesn't do a thing to cure a person."

"It says here: 'Take in A.M.' This is P.M. we're in now. We'll have to wait till tomorrow."

"Shit!" Her eyes glitter with tears.

He looks at her. "In the long black tunnel of my life, twelve more hours is just a blip. So just settle down, Anneka. Okay?" He pats her arm.

They sit there till Carroll finishes his cigarette. They watch different cars pulling in and out of painted spaces. They nod or wave to those people they know. Carroll turns the container in his hand, the capsules tapping softly inside . . . tap tap tap tap tap.

7 | Cold cereal.
Black lake.

He wakes hard-faced to it.

She reminds him three times to take one of the capsules.

He swallows the damn thing without water. "WOW! I FEEL SO GOOD!" he jokes.

Now he hears her heavy trudging past the bathroom door as he shaves. He calls out, "Anneka! Where'd you learn signing, anyway?"

"In a book. That's all." Her words are mixed with munching. She carries food in her mouth as she gets ready for work, keeps running back to her bowl at the table to refill her mouth, then runs around some more.

"Why'd you learn it?" he asks as she again passes.

"To make you love me."

"You go to great trouble for what you want, don't you?"

She appears in the mirror, throws her arms around his middle, *squeezes,* rubs her nose on the back of his T-shirt. "Oh, Teddy . . . you say such oldish stuff."

"Jesus, Anneka! Careful of the razor." He leans forward to place it on the back of the sink.

8 | Carroll shows up for the afternoon milking, and yes, the stanchions are empty . . . no milkers anywhere . . . no heifers out along the hillside.

He has left the truck idling down at the end of the driveway, loaded sky high, rags of bark lifting along the sides of the logs to shake to the gray day's icy wind.

He drives his hands into his pockets and glances quickly, shyly, up at the Soules' kitchen door.

Without drink, the strategy is different. And without the routine of work that he and Merlin once had, there's no reason for him and Merlin to cross paths here today.

Merlin didn't have much to say to him at the wedding party. Barely a look. Carroll doubts that it's any sort of grudge or moral statement concerning Carroll's "mistakes." Not ol' Merl. But it was *something.*

Possibly Merlin is not home. Carroll is not familiar with what the man drives these days, so the old Chevy truck parked by one of the gates means nothing. But he suspects Merlin will not be gone long. He won't leave this place undefended for long.

Carroll looks out along the treeline, and the road curving out of the fields from town. THEM. THE LAW. There is an odd sense that THEY could spring upon this place any minute. This makes him feel *very* edgy. The wind burns his cheek. He turns, to stand another way, head bent.

He doesn't really have the time to stay long, but he figures he can give it five more minutes and into that five minutes a newish family-style Jeep chugs up into the yard. At the wheel, one of the sons-in-law. Stevie. There's always Stevie around. Stevie is head-to-foot blaze orange and shoulder patches for practically every make of firearm. Stevie, like every-body, has aged. He's heavier. But there's still the same look of no-compromise about his body, especially from the waist down. Stevie leans on the far side of the Jeep's hood, rubbing his jaw and squinting one eye at Carroll.

Merlin steps from the passenger's side, a revised assortment of plaid shirts piled on over his dark blue work uniform. He looks into Carroll's face. And grins.

Stevie spits into the weeds.

Merlin leans against this side of the Jeep and scratches his back like an old bear.

Carroll strides toward them, finding a way to lean against the Jeep to look settled in.

Merlin stands now with his arms folded, squinting down the road.

Carroll doesn't dare introduce *the* subject, but he knows it's coming.

It is not a silent moment. The idling of the logging truck is loud, and the wind groans.

" 'Twas a helicopter hoverin' over here before light this mornin'," Merlin says deeply.

Carroll looks up at the sky.

"Well, it weren't after you, Merl," Stevie says with an amused snicker. "It didn't care anything about you."

"Who knows?" Merlin says low.

"It was lookin' for grow lights," says Stevie. "Pot . . . You got a secret crop upstairs, Merl?" He snickers again.

Down on the tar road the wind throws some dry leaves around.

Merlin jerks a thumb toward a rusty gold pickup parked near one of the aluminum gates. "See that thirty-ott-six in the rack?"

Carroll nods.

"Ain't me started this trouble," Merlin says low, eyes sliding to Carroll's face, then back to the road, eyes bleary with age, bleary with cold. "You know how it goes along in the Constitution we got the right to bear arms, to form a militia if we have to . . . to protect our homes?" He winks. "I'm the militia."

Behind Merlin's back on the far side of the Jeep, Stevie shakes his head, taps his temple, shakes his head again, grinning at Carroll.

Carroll looks into Stevie's face a long moment.

Stevie straightens his shoulders, spits again into the weeds. Wind takes some of the spit back onto the gravel around Stevie's boots.

Carroll says, "*Their* militia's bigger, Merl."

"Ayuh! I counted on that!" Merlin booms. Big fantastic grin. Maybe Stevie is right. Maybe Merlin's lost it. Anneka has told of Merlin's big talk . . threats to set out booby traps . . . plenty of ammo . . . the works. But Anneka will also tell you that Merlin's just full of a lot of bluff. It won't come to anything, she insists.

Carroll lights up and smokes ferociously. "I doubt there's much pot still growing this late in the season," he says.

"That's what *I* say. I say it 'twas *me* they wanted. But Stevie, he doesn't want to believe that."

Stevie snickers. "Greenhouse pot. They got their minds on that."

"Maybe," Merlin says. Deeply.

"It's *grow* lights they see. They've got infrared to pick 'em up."

The three men stare into the open door of the near barn . . that whole area swept spotless. Everything in its place. It's always been a really clean operation here.

9 | With each day, it seems the marriage fills up more space. He and she, each filling the other with something . . . food and fluids, hands at work and glands shuddering.

The traveled way between her parents' apartment and the place on the lake, from there out again to Carroll's parents, from there to Merlin's and Dottie's, the way to Denise's Diner and back, the way to the mills and sometimes in another truck to the biomass plant, the rocking teetering loads and visits, visits, visits, these roads rhythmic and rising, falling, the sleepy way back home to the lake. It is a way polished smooth as an agate.

Tonight Anneka is not really asleep though her head bobs, her white ruffian topknot is tossed by the old truck's querulous suspension. Old thing.

Carroll smokes, tipping the ash out the vent window. The night is black and white. Smoke blue and alive, feeling its way around in the cab.

Anneka is plotting. Nothing about these recent weeks is a surprise to her. Everything is falling into place exactly as she has willed it, wished it. Her commitment to this hour, this night had begun when she found that old ring among the photos and war ribbons when she was not but eight years old. And then when she had become such a good shot . . . age twelve? . . . one morning of the shooting club, she and her father had gone over to New Hampshire to fetch John York, her father's shooting buddy, and John York answered the door. "Too early," said he, standing there in just his red union suit and socks. His eyes baggy with sleep. His thin hair. His farmer's hands. Her father laughed. "Caught you!" There was joking, something about a broken clock, their voices guttural in this grand collusion.

But Anneka is twelve and the tight-fitting union suit is red, and like never before, nothing like toddlers, dogs, and cattle, it is hung from the groin of this man, the bewitching fertility, fearsome and dear, the ripened apple, the promise, the "I will." She doesn't avert her eyes.

Then there was eighth grade, ninth grade, and junior year, seasons crackling through her, filling her out, and Forest Johnson taking her down, and then there was spring with hundreds of March birds . . . all nesting.

"Carroll?"

"Ayep."

She sits board straight now. "Can we get some horses . . . some day . . . not real soon . . . but pretty soon . . . you know . . . when we can afford them . . . you know . . . workhorses. We . . . you and me . . . can do woodlots for people. Some people want logs taken out but don't want the skidders. Well . . . a few people. We could advertise. I used to always stack brush with Gramp and them . . . some firewood. I got the basic idea there. I can do stuff, you know . . . with you. And we could have a garden. We could start a garden . . . maybe over to your mum and dad's. I bet they wouldn't care. Right there in that little open place. I had some pickling cukes win first at Fryeburg three years ago. You probably don't believe that. You want to see the ribbon?"

He is silent, smoking, cold smoke.

The truck crashes in and out of a pothole and they both bounce off the seat, shoulders jerking.

She says, "I have the names picked out. If they already have names, they can learn new ones. How do you like these names? Babe and Yogi . . . you know . . . like the baseball guys. I figured they'd give us good luck at the fairs."

He blinks.

She says, "Don't say we can't afford it. We'll get them to earn what they eat. And wouldn't it be sharp to get some ribbons at the pulls! I'll help you. I can learn to drive them. And I'm strong. I can handle the doubletree. We can do lots of stuff. Let's ask your folks about the garden. I bet they won't mind. I . . . you know . . . I just . . . you know . . . want to get started and . . . you know . . . make our life."

He is speechless.

She is looking hard at his hands on the wheel.

He is speechless.

She is looking at his hands like she's seeing the sun rise.

A black thing moves squirmingly upon his heart. He grunts. This voice that pours out from his throat is not his. "How can you be so smart sometimes and then turn out this dumb?"

10 | Crackling, snapping, squealing, the pine goes down. THWOMP! He wears a blaze orange vest over his shirts. Blaze cap. Blaze gloves.

She wears no blaze.

Every day she causes him a new worry. Her principles. Her playfulness. It's all the same to him.

She demands another lesson with the chain saw.

He says, "Not now. We're pressed for time."

Not much for good logs left on Merlin's land . . . Merlin already having a skidder crew in last year . . . making some fast bucks to please the bank. But this weekend, the family goes for the rest. Last chance. Last hope. And Merlin refuses to clear-cut.

This pine lays like a slain dragon at Carroll's feet. He knows Anneka is watching and this makes him feel proud. He kicks his left foot up against the tree and goes to work limbing with a flourish, saw howling and jangling. The limbs kick up, kick back, fly.

But Anneka doesn't stand for very long staring at Carroll with sweet regard. She is full of the devil, leaping on and off the sticky stump, which is broad enough to be a little stage for a jig. Her quick movements don't fluster the horses much. Being Merlin's team, they are used to the worst possible scares.

Now Carroll drives the team to align the twitch of two smaller pines with this prize. Carroll grunts as he works the log into a roll closer to the twitch. Working one end, then the other, he squats, face tortured. He throws his gloves down knowing he'll never find them again.

Anneka steps close. "Can't I help, Old Sausage?!!"

He cusses.

The light is going away fast . . . everything just a deceptive flat gray.

Anneka fetches his gloves. She tsks.

He needs friction of sweating hands to grip the peavey, he explains.

Anneka helps him chain up the twitch, strap the peavey and Jonesreds on. She squints at Carroll's face. "You think your medicine is working yet?"

"You have asked me that every hour for over a week now," he complains.

"Well, I can't tell. You seem the same."

"The doctor said it would take a while. It's not overnight."

"Well, the minute it works, you tell me, okay?"

He chuckles. "I will. Now just climb up on the top here and let's go."

"No way. It would be extra work for them. I weigh a thousand pounds."

"It's nothing to them," he says. "Get on."

"You don't know that for sure. Sometimes I think you're a little bit like Grampie . . . a little bit of a creep. Grampie drives them too hard."

"They are *work*horses, Anneka."

She rolls her eyes.

"And how do you think they win ribbons and trophies at the pulls? Pulling boxes of soda crackers?"

"Pulls are stupid."

"Anneka. You are inconsistent."

She covers her face with her mittened hands . . . *white* mittens of course.

"Jesus," he says. "Well, carry that gas can then. Be of some use."

She runs over to the ledge and climbs up to the treacherously steep overhang. She looks down over the valley to the last light, the pond, the roofs of Merlin's dairy buildings—some roofs dark, others metal—and the roof of the house, and the pinkish shorn fields. Her breath smolders white.

"Anneka, get back over here. I'm tired and I want to get back down and have time to help Stevie load."

"It's a beautiful evening! Look't that jet mark turning pink."

"I see it." He wraps the many traces around one hand, kneads at a chest pocket.

One horse shakes his head. Harness jangles prettily, almost sleepily.

Anneka smiles off into the distances, but on the edge of sight she sees the red bull's-eye of Carroll's Luckies pack moving into his free hand. And she sees his blaze vest. And the gray blotch of his tired face.

"It'll be pitch dark soon," he says deeply.

"It's nice up here, Old Thing. I'm going to spend the night."

"Anneka, let's go. *Now*. We've got a lot of work before we can even get out of Merlin's dooryard."

She plugs her ears. Hums.

He smokes for a minute.

She stops humming.

He asks, "What do you want, Anneka? I'll get you an ice-cream sandwich on the way home, okay?"

"Very funny."

"So what will it take?"

"I want you to be nice to horses."

"I *am* nice to horses. Jesus. I know when a team is getting tired or overheated. I'm paying attention to all that. I thought you had faith in me."

"You are just so . . . *cold* about it."

"I should kiss them on the lips?"

She covers her face.

"Do you want me to unchain the twitch?"

"No." She throws up her hands. "I just don't want you to be like Grampie. Grampie whips horses."

"Don't worry. I'll never be driving any teams at the fairs."

"You say that now. But if you get your own team someday, you'll turn weird."

"Anneka, come over here."

She goes to him. She stands close.

He says very, very softly. "Give up on that, okay? We are not going to be nice farmers or mean farmers. There just isn't such a thing any more as farmers. And workhorses . . . a thing of the past . . . like dinosaurs. Nowadays it's something else people have to find to be happy. I'm not sure exactly what . . . but I'm trying to figure it. I'm *trying*. The pills just aren't working yet. I still feel like getting shit-faced. I still feel sometimes like . . . like smacking somebody or something. But I'm trying very, very hard to be good. But I got nothing to give you pleasure . . . unless it would be a little pleasure to you that I give you a horseback ride on my goddam own back! That's the one thing that's not fucked up on me yet. My back. I got a good back. I guess I'll have that for a little while. Couple more years maybe." He grinds his half-smoked cigarette under his heel. "Come on now . . . let's get back down."

"Okay." She picks up the gas can and as the twitch gives a big lurch, crackling and hissing through young growth, she tromps along behind. The gas can sloshes.

11 | As always, there's the lamp by the bed glaring on and on into the night, the bed covers weighted with newsletters and newspaper clippings, scissors, pencils, notebooks, tape. Anneka charged by her causes, charged into action, scribbling off a note, an address, rereading certain fine print . . . "Those bastards!" she snarls . . . while Carroll has his head covered. His sleep is sweet. He has, over the past couple of nights, slept without waking. Whatever contest or trials the daytimes offer up, the nights come and pull him under. Anneka laps a stamp, affixes it. "There, you evil shits! Take that!"

12 | Carroll Plummer sits on the edge of the bed digging gum from the tread of one of his boots with a jackknife. The other boot rests on its side between his bare feet. He has long middle toes. Someone told him once, your having long middle toes means you're a warlock. Special powers. Ha! Also at his feet are his clothes in a dark pile.

Anneka is standing on the bed, grunting, working the last tack into a poster which shows the Statue of Liberty against a mass of black turbulent clouds. The words: ETERNAL VIGILANCE IS THE PRICE OF LIBERTY. Previously on this spot of the wall was a framed eleven-by-fourteen color photo of two rows of Navy officers in dress whites. Anneka jounces a bit, then leaps from the bed. She is wearing her lavender flannel gown. She refuses to let Carroll see her without it on. She says she's too "pudgy." She'll only take it off when the light is off, or after she's under the covers.

Carroll feels cruelly cheated. If only to smash out his eyes, get rid of the eyes that ask the impossible.

She stands by the closed bedroom door admiring the poster. Her arms are akimbo. Her lavender gown stands out around her legs in lampshade stiffness, which happens when you hang laundry to dry indoors.

The poster has a lumpiness. Could it be the Navy officers are still beneath it?

Anneka's eyes flick to the right to the window. What is it out there?

Lights flutter through the crisscross of limbs even as the croaks of hounds might still be confused with the "a-woooooooaow!" of an owl. But now separating into four throaty chants, dropping over ledges to the gravelly beach, they open out around the house.

Anneka flies at the window, cranks the window wide.

Carroll drops the boot and folds up the knife. Rises from the bed. "Anneka."

She moans.

He says, "Yes. Let me have your hand." He raises one foot, digs it into the bed . . . he goes straight across the bed . . . the shortest way to reach her.

"They are after raccoons," she says.

"Yep," says he. "Let me have your hand." He swipes out for her hand but she steps out of range.

She rushes to pull her rifle down from the closet. "I'm not stupid," she says. "I know what they do to coons. I know all the ways." She squats on the floor, fighting with twisted rawhide lacings, jamming a bare foot into each of her work boots . . . no time for socks, jackets . . . hindrances. The rifle lies juxtaposed with the lavender ruffle of her gown hem. One boot lacing is in an impossible knot. She calls it a "son-of-a-bitch."

The croaking of the hounds has swallowed this room. This room is no longer magnificent.

Carroll has bounded off the bed to squat in front of her, rocking on his haunches. "Anneka . . . *think.*"

She is smooth as a machine, the steel gears and pistons of rage taking over. Her silver eyes seem blind.

He grabs for her with both hands.

She hauls back out from the circle of his arms, the beloved darkly haired nakedness.

The tangled mess of her bootlaces drag.

With the heel of a bare foot, Carroll kicks the rifle under the bed.

He backs up to the closed bedroom door, flattens his shoulders to it.

She opens her mouth for a long hollow wail of grief.

She spins back upon the window, screams, "GET OUT OF HERE, YOU BASTARDS! GET OUT OF HERE!!!!"

"Anneka." His voice. Deep. Fatherly.

She turns and widens her eyes on him. He is tall. There's a lot of body between head and legs. She lowers her head and runs at him, driving her skull into his middle. He doubles over howling, grips her by the head. And smacks her. She bites his shoulder. And all over the room, all over the lavender gown and Carroll's body the coon hunter's lights, through the pines, jiggle. Everything jiggles. "I thought you loved raccoons, too!" She bawls, wide-mouthed. "How can you just . . . LET THEM??!! You ARE just like them after all. All along . . . ALL ALONG PRETENDING TO BE NICE. All along just a fucking jerk redneck asshole!!"

"You want me to go out there and break a guy's jaw, right? You forget, Anneka? You forget I'm on parole? You forget the law has me fucked? Remember? Remember?!!!"

"Well then, just get out of the fucking way and hide then . . . get out of my way . . . get OUT OF THE FUCKING WAY!!!"

When she's gone, he gets dressed. He smokes. He paces the whole house, smoking, smoking, smoking. He knows coon hunters well . . . as with bear hunters . . . coyote hunters . . . all the same . . . the gang hunt . . . their beery hilarity . . . their cool lusts. He pictures Anneka running toward them in her lavender gown. He pictures the possibilities. So this is the edge.

13 | Anneka Plummer is invisible in the black night. Only the hunters with their heads and hands like stars can be seen. There's new growth of popple slim as Anneka's own wrist. She feels her way along, taking each tree into her hand, screaming, "GET OUT OF HERE! GET OUT OF HERE! GETOUTOFHEREGETOUTOFHEREGETOUT-OFHERE!!" The hounds' hoarse chants seem to have no direction, nor do they seem to be moving away. They speak from the ground. They speak from the sky. They speak from every tree. While Anneka's voice grows hoarser and hoarser, turning to rags. Her voice in its new dimension warns from its hidden blackness, out of its lunacy clear as a bell: "I HAVE A LOADED MARLIN. I HAVE IT AIMED AT YOUR HEADS. TWO SHOTS FOR EACH OF YOU FUCKERS." But no gun. What *will* she do when she reaches them? Whatever it takes to stop them is the answer.

One of the men is calling to her. Gentlemanly. Almost apologetic. *Worried.* "Just let us get our dogs."

"I WILL KILL YOU! GETOUTOFHEREGETOUTOFHERE-GETOUTOFHERE!!!!"

"Just let me get my dogs," the same man says, or a different man. She can't know. They are interchangeable.

Suddenly her heart tickles, tumbles, knocks. She is starting to pass out. It's her little problem with the heart . . . the tachycardia, the arrhythmia . . . the white heat, the beating thing in the jaws, cheekbones, eyes, chest, and arms. She pulls herself along. Trembling trees. Trembling hands. Trembling lights. There's the sweep of dots of another near faint as she feels with her right foot over stumps, roots, slash . . . slash that resembles a human elbow or a cold open hand.

The lamps of the hunters ripple into deeper woods, dividing, multiplying, stretched. She hears just their faint tramping and the occasional disappointed croak of a hound being dragged away. They are heading west along the beach.

She crouches down. Her arteries are stretched by a kind of centrifugal force, the heart hurtling on and on at hundreds of miles per hour, while she, Anneka, remains.

The doctors had told her mother and her that she wouldn't die from this condition. She's young. Healthy in all other ways. Won't die. Don't worry. It's only pain.

14 | The raccoons wait it out, their patience imitative of the trees, for in coon religion, the trees and coons are one. But oh! the waiting vigil preceding the gesture that all is well, while there's this burning storm of the empty stomach, remembrances of chow. The unmoving coon might permit himself a little sigh. The minutes pass like centuries. In coon time, centuries are held against the hand. The hounds fade. Coons remain. Mother, son, daughter, daughter, and daughter, their masks fitted very well, their cheek-ruffs handsome. In the face of this common enemy, their patronage to all coonkind is momentarily warm and sentimental. Here! Another night you get to stay alive, to be beautiful, to party. Ah, life!

15 | Sunday. He arrives home from Merlin's where he has spent the day skidding out the last marketable logs. He brings with him the smell of horses and pine and gasoline and cigarettes.

Here at the lake, the Soule women have hit hard. The place is clean, the long Formica countertop vast and bare. Looks like the whole place has been lapped by a cat.

He finds Anneka hanging clothes everywhere to dry, over chairs and doors, all around the railings of the deck, Anneka being too principled to use the Chief's clothes drier. Right now she is in the big bathroom, pulling out another load from the washer.

On the supper table, a new project. What is it? A repeated phrase on strips of oaktag. COON HUNTERS HAVE SMALL PECKERS.

"Anneka."

She appears, her hair parted in the middle, scalp slightly whiter than the hair. Such pretty pewter barrettes shaped like little bows.

"Tell me something about these," he says.

Her voice is deep, broken, bruised, crackling. Strained from her screaming the night before. "These will be on cars everywhere. Every time you go out, a car will be ahead of you with this bumper sticker. Everywhere in parking lots. Rows of them. We got eight people already that Mum knows that want them."

He cocks one eyebrow, looks off toward the lake that is rocking gently beyond the glass doors. "The thing about you Soule women is you forget what a world outside the family is like. Most people aren't as . . ." He feels his pocket for his Luckies. ". . . as . . . as . . ." He lights a cigarette on a ring of the gas stove, sucks smoke desperately . . . once, twice. "Well, I guess I mean . . . most of the world is . . . is . . . more uptight."

Anneka squints. "Tough shit."

He reaches for her shoulders. It's such a short time together in this marriage. Nevertheless, she knows this is not affection. It's his being his firm fatherly self, that self that comes out through a funny look in his eyes, funny voice . . . capital *D* of discipline . . . capital *I H* of the Iron Hand. Ha! She pulls away. She says raspily, "Which means you won't let me put one on our truck."

He guffaws.

She reddens.

He says, "Anneka, to start with, it's not our truck. And besides . . . I know you don't see it this way but . . . that message is very difficult to wear around even if, like me, I think coon hunters are assholes."

"Ah-ha! So . . . you don't want one. *And* you don't have to say it . . . but I know you won't help in *any* way." She scoops the bumper stickers off the table into a grocery bag and carries them into the bedroom, reappears, begins to ram around fixing his supper . . . sets out his plate, fork, bread, saucer.

16 Carroll is down cellar shutting off the outside faucets. The meteorologists are predicting a deep freeze "just around the corner."

Above, Anneka is trudging back and forth over the floors.

Outside, the lake and sky both darken from silver to lead.

Anneka looks at the clock. The windows.

She warms some baked beans her mother brought. She makes corn muffins with a new box of cornmeal. She gets better at corn muffins every time. More golden. More swollen.

The windows darken.

Anneka's motions are stop and go. Her eyes flash from window to window, to clock, back to her busy hands. Her neck and back are hard, readied.

In the cellar, Carroll hears the sudden blare of the Chief's TV. Too loud for a viewer's pleasure. Loud enough to rattle unfixed objects.

Carroll heads up the cellar stairs, shuts the door. He gets a cigarette started.

Darkness bears upon the sliding glass doors.

Anneka is bent over the radio, giving its on-switch a hearty twist. Lights flicker across its panel. Together the radio and TV crash and jingle and chuckle and tootle like a kind of madness.

Carroll heads for the bedroom, reemerges pulling down the front of a clean black T-shirt. He watches Anneka as he presses the T-shirt in around his belt, cigarette now reduced to something barely as big as the bud of a daisy, yet hurtling great smoke up one side of his face so his staring is one-eyed . . . groping.

Anneka adjusts the oven.

Anneka adjusts the radio. Louder.

She arranges frozen french fries on a cookie sheet slowly, head bowed. She is not the same Anneka after dark that she was in the light of day. She sets out the hot muffins and some of the last of Merlin and Dottie's orange farm butter, pushes a stack of her newsletters around to make room for the pan of dark beans.

Beyond the glass doors the pink and yellow lights around the lake are fixed in the terriblest black.

Anneka sweeps past Carroll, past the Chief's yucca plants, to the living area, adjusts the TV louder.

Carroll leans into the doorframe to the bedroom, digs out both hearing aids.

When Anneka returns, he is at the table, feeling the table tremble against the palms of his hands.

He could say it a thousand times that there's no coon hunting on Sundays. But he knows and she knows they can train their hounds on Sundays. They can train any ol' time. They can run their croaking dogs and spill their light among the trees. And, with only one warden for hundreds of miles . . . who knows what else they really do? And all the times Anneka has heard it, at her father's shooting club, at school, at the diner . . . EVERYWHERE . . . it's no secret . . . *"Dropped outta that tree like a stone, by gawd. We let our dogs have her. Hee hee. Even the old lady hasn't got a scream on her that unholy. Then we got the kit. You know, he weren't so shot up as he put on. When I kicked him, the little bastard bit through my goddam boot! HAWWWWWW! Dickie kicked him into the dogs and they put him around like a tug rag."*

Carroll sees she has put on his hard hat with the ear protectors jammed against her ears. She looks so comical, stirring away at the stove like that . . . and yet, no, not comical. She stirs slowly, more slowly. Shuts off the flame, spoons out warm applesauce . . . slightly pink as the Soules' Macs often are. A little sugar, too. The way he likes it.

17 | Four times in the night he has uncovered his head and each time sees her lying awake on her back. She keeps one of her gooseneck reading lamps on, pointed out the window like a searchlight. Even with a pillow to each ear, she is listening keenly. Her thigh is to his thigh, hers oddly cool . . . sticky cool . . . nothing like her usual overheated rambunctiousness. It has been, he believes, a trauma for her . . . like war veterans. If he clapped his hands now, her heart might stop dead.

18 | The protector. This is now his job. He remembers how back in his parents' shed there's a fish tank bubbler and length of plastic hose. He uses up his lunch hour to fetch it.

Then while she fixes supper, he carries two box fans up from the Chief's cellar and arranges them to face the bedroom walls.

Supper on the table. Odors of smoky meat. The big ham being one of the many unforgettable but likely wedding presents from Soules. He is so eager for Anneka to see what he's done. He hollers close to one side of the hard hat and ear protectors: "ANNEKA! COME SEE IF THIS WORKS!!!" He points to the bedroom door.

On the night table there's a peanut-butter jar of water with the fish bubbler and hose making great lusty burbles . . . but kind of restful . . . like kettles of potatoes boiling. But the roar of the fans is another matter. They sound like small planes taking off.

He signs for her to take the helmet off.

She does.

"Sit on the bed!" he calls out.

She sits.

He says, "Take off your slippers!"

She kicks them off.

He crushes his cigarette into the saucer on top of the hall dresser. One of the fans has started rocking to and fro. He adjusts it a little, nearer to the wall.

It is not the weather for fans. Air sailing around the room is chilling even with the fans pointed at the walls.

"Lie down!" he says. He sits on the edge of the bed with his back to her, staring at his hands, one hand to each knee of his wool work pants. It's like he and she are listening to a radio program together. Anneka lies staring.

After supper, Anneka goes straight to bed and he turns on the bubbler and the fans. He drops his clothes in a pile and pushes down under the covers beside her. He leaves his hearing aids in his ears, adjusted to pick up whatever it is she hears . . . to see if this is working . . . this mighty effort.

In the night he's awakened by the sudden lurch of the bed. She's sitting up, in the light of her reading lamp, eyes wide with terror. He grabs her wrist. He will not let her out of this house again if the hunters come around. No matter what it takes to stop her. He will grip her wrist and lock his fingers as if hanging on to save his own life.

All around are these roars and gurgles, the thrumming and thumping of fans set on *HIGH*, and the water that has splattered itself out around the jar, and inside the jar the rest of the water is so frenzied, steadily frenzied . . . all these noises created to mask a more terrible sound. These noises, these kindly noises, are exhausting. And now also, in this association with the unspeakable terrible noise of the hounds, and this entrapment here, these sounds are not really a comfort. He considers masking these machines with the noise of something other, something of a GREATER NOISE.

With her left wrist in his grip, she works her right hand to arduously sign to him through the din. *"Maybe it was just in the fans. There is a funny hooting noise sometimes comes out over there. Do you hear it?"* She cocks her head. *"Hounds in the fans,"* she signs.

Her skin is cold as a corpse. And he is freezing. This room! It's churning little winds! The fans pushing, pushing, pushing . . .

She signs that there probably aren't really any hounds, that if she turned the fans off, she would know for sure.

He grips harder.

She signs that she meant that there probably would be no hounds *if* she shut off the fans, that she has no intention of shutting off the fans. She will never shut off the fans. In all the nights of Septembers, Octobers, Novembers, and Decembers of the rest of her life, there will have to be fans.

19 He can tell it's Rick Dresser who has just stepped up to the right side of him, Rick giving the vacant stool a one-handed spin. He need not see Rick's face, the bouncing scraggy eyebrows, or the NRA billed cap that sits on his head, the buck knife on his belt. For Carroll knows in his peripheral vision the familiar, cocky, short-legged bluster of ol' Rick Dresser, coon hunter, bear hunter, coydog hunter, moose hunter, deer hunter, squirrel hunter, goose, duck, partridge, turkey, and dove hunter . . . hunter prima perfector, Orion of the Ford Bronco

Brigade, hunter artiste, authorized and endowed, stalk 'em pursue 'em smash 'em bash 'em toast 'em trash 'em stuff 'em stuff 'em all.

Rick swings up onto the stool slow and easy, heaps his hands onto the red Formica counter and looks where Carroll is looking . . . at the three-pot coffee warmer.

Carroll listens to those on his left telling the old moose dung pie logging camp joke. How many times has he heard that joke in his life? Why is it always funny no matter how bad they tell it?

"So," says Rick.

"So," says Carroll. "Whatcha been up to?" Why ask?

Rick shakes his head vigorously as if to get water out of his ears. "Plummer . . . tell me the truthful rightful honest answer to this question. What have *you* been up to? I've heard an honest-to-god nasty rumor they are spreading around about you."

"Zat right?" Carroll feels for his Luckies. "What's that?"

Rick looks around, a quick scan of the many faces and profiles and backs-of-heads, tables, legs, boots, and sneakers and pants legs all in the alternate blocks of sun and the blue out-of-sun look between windows, smoke from ashtrays, steam from cups, and Anneka. He says, "You and *her*."

Carroll grins. "What'd they say about me and her? Somethin' kinky?"

"Worse." Rick sighs, picks a napkin from the chrome holder, opens it out, folds it back. He looks around again, fixing a hard unforgiving glare upon Anneka who is back-to, taking an order at the farthest end of the diner. "Married."

"I can't tell a lie. It's true," Carroll says, lighting up, drawing in the smoke. Like hot lead being poured into a mold, he fills and fills. The thick dear good smoke.

Rick is shaking his head again, wipes his face, jerks his cap from side to side by the bill—turns to study Carroll face on.

Denise does a hand-over-hand, a pepperburger to Carroll, a Welsh rarebit plate to the man at Carroll's left. Carroll leans forward, sniffs his food, squares his shoulders, knowing Rick's eyes are plastered all over him. Carroll takes a quickie last gulp of smoke, squeezes the end for later.

"I don't get it," says Rick, drumming his fingers. "But ain't none of my business. I'll just keep out of it."

Carroll chortles. "Jesus, Richard . . . where were you when the J.P.

got to the part about speak up now or forever hold your peace? Where in hell were you, my man?"

"I don't know," says Rick. "Could have been anywhere." His eyes under their bushy visorlike brows are wide on Carroll . . . the very picture of astoundedness.

Denise jabs Rick's shoulder, sloshes coffee into his cup with the other hand. "Hungry or what?!" she barks, pushes the coffee at him.

"BLT," Rick says softly. "Any old kind of bread you want to use, dear . . . and whatever you want to put on it. Surprise me."

In a sort of imitation of Rick's expression, Denise waggles her eyebrows and says deeply, "My pleasure," then pulls away, sticking her pencil in the hard dark netted bun of her hair, snatching a bowl heaped with balled-up napkins from the man at Rick's right.

Past Rick's shoulder, Carroll can see Anneka tromping along between the booths wearing the dark green sweater that's really her mother's but which goes back and forth between the two households. He sees she's finger spelling something to him, but he misses it as two ladies with canes and nearly matching long pleated coats bob along past to the restroom. He looks back at his plate, smiles, starts eating, jiggles one leg happily, a little inner bouncy beat.

Rick studies Carroll, then leans close and says low, "Is this why you seem like a new man these days? All that *exercise?*"

Anneka veers to the left of a group just arriving. As these newcomers get out of their jackets and coats, they blow on their hands.

Anneka's hand repeats the message with her boxy awkward rendition of the otherwise beautiful American Sign Language. *"Coon hunters have small . . ."*

Carroll's eyes slide away back onto Rick's face.

Rick is looking solemnly at the cup that's surrounded by his hands. He clears his throat. "You be careful ol' boy. You hear of it all the time. Guys dying in bed 'cause they can't handle it."

Anneka swishes by. Rick tips his cap to her . . . in honor of his old friend Carroll.

Behind the counter Anneka digs into crushed ice to fill three water glasses by the coffeepot warmer, turns and looks Carroll square in the face and with wet fingers laboriously finger spells: *"Coon hunters have small peckers."*

Rick chuckles uneasily. "What's that? That hand language for the deaf?"

Carroll smiles. "Yes, sir."

Anneka passes behind them with the glasses.

When she returns, she pokes a handful of orders down over the spike by the grill. She turns to Carroll and with an expression of the sweetest kind, clearly her love overflowing, eyes aflutter, her head coyly bowed, she signs again: "*Coon hunters have small peckers.*" How deeply into his dark-lashed yellow eyes her silver eyes plunge.

Rick shifts painfully.

At the grill, turning to drop handfuls of potato chips on three cheese-burger plates, the owner Donnie sees what's happening. He smiles.

Everyone is smiling at this beautiful thing happening, Anneka's snowy fingers, her bashful crooked smile to her man in this moment of intimacy. All up and down the lunch counter, heads bend forward to glimpse An-neka's hand . . . here it is happening, one of those little bits of the day you might carry home with you so that hours later, out of the blue you'll remember it . . . gives you a little lift, renews your faith in humankind.

20 | In the night, every night, it seems she never moves. She is just a cold body on its back. But keenly her hearing scans the uni-verse. The universe is all possible rumblings, burbles, croaks, and bizarre shrieks . . . wounded coon kits crying, "Mama! Mama! Mama!"

21 | Meanwhile each evening comes earlier and darker. Tonight Carroll spoons macaroni and cheese onto his plate. Some beets. Yeast bread that Anneka has gotten pretty good at. The riches of his plate.

She never fixes supper for herself, just watches his. A disconcerting thing.

The radio.

The TV.

All shaking the air, making the hairs on the nape of his neck tremble. He with his hearing aids in his pocket. She with her new earplugs.

She has started shutting all the drapes. None of the big glass doors show now. No pinkish constellations of lighted vacant camps around the lake, that space that Carroll cherishes.

Tonight after he has wiped his plate with bread, he stands, one cheek still full, leaves his plate where it's at, goes to her. He pulls her from her seat, nothing said. She presses her forehead to his work shirt.

He calls, "WITH ALL THIS MUSIC, WHY NOT DANCE?!!" He nudges her away from the table and begins that old waltz. Like in eighth grade. Nice slow churn to the far side of the house. He pulls back, reinserts his hearing aids and calls, "WE NEED TO MOVE FROM HERE!"

She pushes her forehead back into his chest, eyes squinched shut, pushes hard, trying to bully him back into that slow turn of the dance.

"WE NEED TO GET A PLACE IN THE VILLAGE, ANNEKA! MAYBE DOWN BACK BY THE MILL OR NEAR TOWN HALL!!"

She makes her eyelids tighter.

His voice booms through her rubber earplugs: "I DON'T MEAN RIGHT AWAY BECAUSE WE DON'T HAVE THE MONEY! BUT AS SOON AS WE CAN! SOMEHOW WE'VE GOT TO GET THE MONEY! MAYBE I CAN GET UP THE NERVE TO ASK SOMEBODY FOR A LOAN . . . EXCEPT EVERYBODY'S AS BROKE AS WE ARE! I HATE TO SAY IT . . . BUT ALBION . . . I DON'T THINK ALBION'S GOING TO HOLD OUT MUCH LONGER. HE'S JUST BEEN HIT WITH ANOTHER INSURANCE INCREASE AND SOME OTHER MESS. AND THE PAPER COMPANY . . . SOMETHING VERY WEIRD GOING ON WITH THE PAPER COMPANY. LIKE *SELLING OUT*. IT'S ALL COMING DOWN, BABY. BUT I LOVE YOU. GOD. THIS IS DRIVING ME NUTS. I CAN'T SEE THIS GOING ON AND ON WITH YOU, ANNEKA. IT'S JUST THE BASTARDS CALL THE SHOTS . . . BIG SECURITY DEPOSITS AND THREE WEEKS' PAY FOR RENT. BUT . . . IT'S GOING TO WORK OUT! HONEST TO GOD . . . WE JUST NEED TO MOVE TO SOLVE OUR PROBLEM. EVEN IF WE HAVE TO MOVE TO MIRACLE CITY . . . OR IN WITH SOMEBODY . . . NOT YOUR GRANDFOLKS 'CAUSE PRETTY SOON THEY'RE GOING TO NEED TO MOVE IN WITH SOMEBODY . . . BUT MAYBE THERE'S SOMEBODY WE CAN STAY WITH I HAVEN'T THOUGHT OF YET . . . EVEN IF JUST DURING COON SEASON!"

Anneka screams. "BIG FUCKING DEAL!!!! JUST BECAUSE WE'LL BE SOME PLACE WHERE WE WON'T HEAR IT, THEY'LL STILLLLLLL BE DOING IT!!!"

He is watching her mouth. He sighs. "WELL, THERE'S NOTHING

WE CAN DO ABOUT THAT, ANNEKA! NOT EVER!!!!!" he bellers.

She throws her head back as if into some seizure or devilish possession and she wails, a true keening.

In time, she wears out, and he resumes the dance.

22 Is he "out" for good now? Is this it? Is this his life? This scream of the loader, the signature of his frozen breath, the sweet glueyness of pine, the lugging-down rancor of cold exhaust, this bright day? Is this his new beginning, the rehabilitated new Carroll Plummer, normal man, gloved hands on the levers? He and the loader one combined fabulous creature, the might of the grim feeler, the clam's oversized halting grasp reaching on and on and on throughout the hours to make another load, another five loads, another fifteen loads . . . another day, another week . . . another hundred, another thousand. Is this delight? Is this home at last, scot-free, straining endlessly into this heart of thunder? While down out of the higher hills beyond Burgess Road come the chips from other operations, twenty-six tons a load, two trucks every fifteen minutes, grunting down along their perilous descent, brake . . . brake . . . brake . . .

Jays burst from low boughs, cursing.

Little plumpness of a squirrel out on the tar since early morning. Gone gradually to paste. Under the repeated harrumph! of dual tires and malediction, the squirrel complies.

While up on the far ridge Albion Cole's two patched-up skidders are bouncing, wrenching, battling through this sour poplar and mash of mud. Beast of the twitch against beast of the contraption. Is this war? This war that inevitably ends, ends all.

Is there anybody reverent?

Is the peace and quiet and goodness he has always longed for only going to happen within some future *void?*

23 He brings the old truck into the yard late, a little seesawing to get the old beast just so. How late? Only a little, a recurring problem with the truck's transmission linkage. It is only a little late.

He surveys the windows of the house as he jerks the keys from the switch. He knows she's in bed. Bed is refuge. Fans are blamming air around, roaring, rumbling, the bubbler bubbling, pillow over her head with just her eyes and nose wedged out through one side, open book in her line of sight. Or perhaps a letter from one of the congressmen she's started writing. The higher and higher authorities. Has she still not given up hope? Young Anneka.

He drops from the cab. The fine air sharp . . . cold . . . maybe snow soon. Maybe a nice thick sleet, slop and mess, yes, yes. Keep all this humanity at home with their TV's.

At first the sound from the hill behind the nearest neighbor's camp seems to be a hoot owl. But the next "awoooo-awoooooohowowwow" closer and clear, is of course, the deep muscular throats of hounds.

Why? Why now? Why tonight? Why this year? Why ever?

He sees now up along the ledge the wheedly scrambling unnatural progression of several six-volt lamps.

He looks toward the bedroom window, holds his breath against the flinty cold.

There's shouts from the hill. Seems the hounds have already veered southward, a little off toward the main road, that brainless chorusing of each other, hurtling on and on, pulled by the scent. Then stopped. Closing in. Hounds going nuts.

Carroll hurries up the Chief's railroad-tie steps. It would be best to be in front of that door if she comes out. He will never let her get out like that again.

There's a shot. Thin crack of a twenty-two. Not a killing shot. More like the shot that begins a race.

A shriek. Always eerie.

Now the gulpy eagerness of the hounds, and then the sudden quiet of them at their work, the object of this game being to pull the coon to the east, to the west, to the south, to the north, each dog getting a good shake . . . the loopy footage of coon intestine, still alive.

Now another shot. Another coon? The shriek of this coon more shrieky than the other . . . the prized bewitching cackle. The trophy of the night. Voices of men cheer and whistle and now low garbles of dogs at work again, long after the coon's pleas turn soft. Poor hounds. So dimly, earnestly believing in life after death. They will coax a ragged head and wet shreds to live on.

Another shot.

Carroll presses his back to the door.

More shots.

Coon won't let go of the treetop?

A shot.

A shot.

A shot.

Maybe twenty-five shots in all. How many shots can one coon take? Die! Die! Die!

24 He enters the bedroom of roars and whirling air.

"I heard hounds . . . I swear . . . and a twenty-two," she says on a half breath, her face chalky.

"'Twas in the fans," he assures her.

25 At the windows the light. Not sun. But an older, more courteous gray-white. Snow. Not much snow is expected today, but it doesn't take much snow to put Christmas in the air.

"What is it?"

"It's the Friendly Janitor." He chuckles. "Wait till you hear it."

"Friendly Janitor," she repeats, hands on hips.

"I stopped over to your grandfolks to look over some stuff in the loft. I knew Merl had some stuff like this around." He feels around behind the cedar chest for an outlet. Plugs in. Snaps the switch. The Friendly Janitor roars to life. "SOME SORT OF INDUSTRIAL VACUUM CLEANER OR BUFFER MOTOR!" he calls to her over the racket of this latest gadget . . . this latest monstrosity.

She holds her ears. She bends down and snaps it off.

He says, "It's louder than the fans, huh? Together with all the others, it should drown out all outdoor sound."

"Carroll, it's too loud. It's already given me a headache."

He studies it a minute, feels for his cigarettes, rocks his weight anxiously forward onto one leg, then back onto the other, to and fro, to and fro. He strikes a match on a dresser latch. He takes a drag, smiles. "We can put it out on the other side of the door. Let's try that."

"Okay," she says.

He unplugs the thing, then rolls it along with his foot. It goes with a ga-thunk over the threshhold and into the hall. He locates an outlet by the linen closet. She watches him squatted there, his broad back straining against his chamois shirt, the taut belt that affirms his bearlike middle, yet such effortlessness of his musculature. Farm boy. Nurtured by the good land, the good blood, the centuries of mastery over and fraternity with creature and furrow and tools. Now . . . the here and now . . . honor gone. The man . . . like fallow fields.

He snaps on the switch then pulls her by the hand back into the bedroom. He swings the door shut. They sit on the bed with the snowy white daytimeness at the windows. They look at the door, the wailing beyond the door.

"It sounds like a janitor all right," says she.

He looks down at the cigarette in one hand between his thighs. "It's kind of a nice thought, ain't it?"

"Yep."

"Like school."

She rolls her eyes.

He chuckles. "School . . . it was . . . it was all along just obedience training, wasn't it? You know . . . like 'sit!' 'heel!' 'come boy!' " He gives her hair a wild rubbing. "I can't imagine you were ever a very good puppy, Anneka. I bet you were a *bad* puppy, huh?"

"Yep, I was."

He looks away from her eyes. He can't stand her eyes anymore. And there's about her face a great age. A composure. Like Mrs. God. The manly white eyebrows. The way she laces her fingers together, hands on her lap. The way she has become so much less *fun*. Too much vigil. So much desolation. After dark this room is her life now. A cell. The cold winds of the fans with her in the center of it all, the eye of the storm.

He says, "Anneka, the pills are working, I think."

She looks at him.

He keeps his eyes on his smoldering cigarette. "It seems like . . . you know . . . before the pills . . . B.P., Before Pills . . ." He smiles. "Before the pills if things got like this, I'd . . . you know . . . get freaky . . . or pissy . . . or you know, I'd start drinking. I mean, I still want to get shit-faced. I really do. I think of it regularly. And I still feel foolish a lot . . . you know . . . like hiding in a log or something. I mean I still want to drink, but I don't. That point where I don't . . . that's what normal is, I guess."

She puts a narrow look on the closed bedroom door, beyond which the Friendly Janitor wails in a friendly way. "See. I saved you, didn't I? I am the princess on a white horse."

"Yep . . . you were." He gives her nearest bicep a squeeze. "But listen, Anneka. You gotta get something straight. You can't save the whole world."

She shrugs.

They both stare at the door.

The Friendly Janitor shrills on and on.

Suddenly Anneka's face crumbles into sobs and she pushes her face down into her hands. He reaches an arm out, hugs her to him.

"CARROLL! I'M NOT A PERVERT!!!"

He leans to push his cigarette into the ashtray on the Chief's modern bedside stand.

"Is it sicko of me to believe other animals besides HUMAN ONES have feelings?!! To believe that when they are tortured, they hurt?! Tortured or terrorized or separated from their mothers, or mothers from their young?! I suppose it's a real sicko reaction I have that I want to protect a smaller creature or helpless one from a gang of creatures that are hurting it . . . for . . . for SPORT!!! FUCKING SPORTS!!!"

"Anneka, you don't have to convince me. I'm not arguing."

"You know what the law says? You ever read the goddam hunting and trapping laws? Well, the laws have no gripe against mutilation or torture or terrorizing. After all, isn't that what coon hunting and bear hunting and coydog hunting is all about? It ain't got a thing to do with anybody's CORNFIELDS. There's NO corn in the woods! We are *MILES* from something like that. But the law book wants you to—while you are mutilating and terrorizing—to be sure you have your twenty-two firearm . . . *only* twenty-two . . . very specific, you see . . . and a six-volt light . . . very specific, you see . . . and a certain amount of time after sunset and before sunrise . . . certain number of minutes. Rules of the game. You see, the law says it's okay to do all that shit they do as long as they do those other little things. BUT . . . you see, meanwhile . . . the law says that what *I* do is illegal. If I am torn to pieces inside my very SOUL . . . if I get a heart attack . . . none of that matters . . . but if I go out there and *interfere,* try to stop the TORTURE, I'm an outlaw. Just like back when we did the white scarves thing after Courtney Gray was killed, for us to object in that way we did it . . . the ONLY way to REALLY get their attention . . . WE were the outlaws . . . the KILLER was let off!!! I read these laws a lot, okay? And actually a lot of laws expect a little restraint from these guys. But . . .

you know, Carroll, like I do . . . those guys got the law guys in the palm of their hands." She catches her breath. "You know, if I was going along and I saw somebody beating and terrorizing an old man or a little kid and I ran over and tackled the guy who was doing it . . . you know . . . and I saved the kid or old person, I'd get an award or something. Some sorta nice mention at least. But for this . . . this . . . THIS . . . if I went out there and *inconvenienced* these guys in any way . . . whoaaaaaah!!!!!" She laughs, then sighs. "Nothing makes sense, Carroll. Good is bad and bad is good."

"Promise me you won't ever go out there again."

"I can't promise that."

"Promise me now, Anneka."

"I promise to try not to hear it . . . but if I hear it . . . I . . . can't promise anything."

"Promise me now, Anneka . . . a *big fat* promise. I'm talking serious. It's not just the law part. It's what a gang of guys full of beer and good-timin' and lust for power over something . . . power to make or break life . . . you know? . . . the power to *kill* . . . this is what you need to know. If I go out there to keep them from you, I get in trouble. I go back to prison. See the position it puts me in? But then if I don't go out there, Anneka . . . Think! Think! You . . ." He draws up both her hands. "You got a gang bang just waiting out there for you. They could *rape* you."

She snickers, grins weirdly.

In time the Friendly Janitor has a bit of trouble. It shrieks like a live creature. Carroll slams out into the hall to yank the plug from the outlet, the hall smoky, paint chips settling daintily, stink of hot metal.

26 He dreams that it is a barn brightly lit from the inside in the old way, mostly darkness outside . . . the old way. And parked all around are cars and pickups of the many people inside the barn.

It is quite a crowd, all grouped around one box stall, the top half caged with heavy wire. The group is all men. It is smoky like a boxing ring. Business suits and farmers. A nice mix. Hand-over-fist cash. A lot of shouts. A man with a cigar, white short-sleeve shirt, rams his way among elbows. A lot of bright light beaming down into the stall, which is actually a pit of dirt sprinkled with wood shavings.

Carroll understands that he has walked in on a pitman fight. And there are the pitmen already embroiled. Down. Already one is winning. Carroll knows that this is not against the law. Pitmen. They are human in some way . . . yes. They are, in a manner of speaking, human. But humanness has degrees. This is so. The chests and bellies of pitmen are densely furred like bears. And, you know, their faces never vary. You can never tell one pitman from the other but by its brightly colored vinyl collar. And as everyone knows, pitmen are incapable of human speech or technology.

The winning pitman has broken the other pitman's back. There's cheers. More exchange of cash.

These pitmen are so identical that it seems they phase in and out from each other from time to time, both with long dark beards, both with slate gray eyes. But the loser is choking now from the broken things inside him, broken neck. One more punch, pull, and deft shake to completely paralyze him. That's the object of the game.

Now that the loser can't move again, the winner rises from his straddle.

Thunderous cheers of the winning bettors.

More exchange of money.

Somehow the money has filled every hand, more money than possible in this world, money deep as the wood shavings around the motionless pitman and the bettors' shoes.

The winner has been taken out of the stall. There's only the loser lying on his back in the pit, dying slowly. That is one of the legalities of the sport. Slow. Good and slow. If a sudden death happens, somebody will be fined.

Nobody looks at the dying pitman except the official timekeeper who wears some sort of badge on the patch pocket of his shirt.

Everyone else has turned away.

The dying pitman is completely paralyzed. Only full paralysis is legal. Even his face is paralyzed. But was there ever any human expression to start with? A smile? Outrage? Seems not.

Every one of the bettors is in good humor. Seems none of the bettors have lost.

The dying pitman's slate gray eyes are wide open, bubbling over with tears. The tears rivulate down over his cheeks into his beard and hair. With pitmen, of course, tears are just reflex.

27 | Around noon, Carroll Plummer parks on the East Dam Road to have his lunch. He can see for miles. The higher hills have snow. He's too broke this week for the diner . . . or Moody's where he also stops some days. Anneka has fixed him a mayonnaise sandwich and a Thermos of milky tea. What he wants more than food is a smoke. But he's fresh out. For a cigarette, he needs to work on his courage to borrow some change from one of the guys back at the landing.

What he sees as he eats is a speck moving from the woods below, out through a stone gapway. Merlin Soule. A dark blue cloth work cap is probably what covers the white crew cut. Blaze orange. That's the vest. Merlin. One horse. Old Rocket. One log. Silky-smooth strides of a well-bred, well-trained horse and one skilled man.

And around about, left and right are the fields and family garden, part snow, part tufted, humpy rocky old, old mean old land. And there are the buildings for milking and holding a milk herd. And the old Soule homeplace, which somehow along the way now belongs to the bank and the bank is backed by the law and the law is backed by the police and if need be, the police get back-up from the National Guard.

Could that one little speck of a man moving along down there cause enough commotion to have them bring in the National Guard?

Two horses, Merlin's young team, stare from their paddock across to the wood line as the old horse with a single log veers sharply down toward the little tin-roofed sawmill.

Carroll Plummer knows he could probably get home for Anneka's rifle and reach Merlin's position in less than half an hour.

How easily he could walk up across that field carrying the rifle and get within such close range of Merlin, Merlin thinking nothing of it . . . Carroll Plummer, his friend . . . being among those that are trusted. Though Merlin might frown slightly as Carroll set his feet apart for a solid aim, aiming for Merlin's face, Merlin would know in that split second of remaining life what it is that Carroll does, this act of courage, this mercy. Carroll would drop the old man in his field and it would be done with.

But Carroll is neither that courageous, nor that merciful. Thanks to medical technology, he is a normal man now.

He takes a little swig of milky tea and drums his fingers on the steering wheel.

PART EIGHT

1 | Gwen Doyle tugs off her argyle cap and her hair crackles. She clicks from room to room in her tall heels, snapping on light after light. In the living room she stops to fill one of the love seats with her handbag, leather-palmed gloves, and mail. This is the one room you would not call "countrified." The space of this room is like watery music. The furniture and drapes and carpet all creams and wheatens and whites and off-whites, mint and trailing-off yellows. It seems sometimes the dark faces, tails, and legs of her Siamese cats pace and fly about without bodies against this pale other. The many little sofas and love seats . . . they hug you. Almost a humid presence. Like a kiss on the back of the neck. And the carpet sucks you downward. And your voice disappears. All conversations you have in this room are simply a calming dreamy buzz.

Gwen adjusts thermostats.

Back in the kitchen, she checks the answering machine.

Message from her travel agent.

Message from her friend Ariel.

Messages from her mother, Phoebe.

Her mother had called every hour on the hour. A precision. A rhythm. A hammer's head. A beating heart. Her mother's voice over and over. "Couldn't reach you . . ." "Couldn't reach you . . ." Couldn't reach you . . ."

Gwen unplugs the phone and answering machine.

She feeds the cats. Apollo and Athena. She pokes their evening medications down the backs of their tongues while each one is zipped up to its neck in the veterinary-approved canvas bag that keeps them from gouging her.

Now she plugs the phone back into the outlet and with the receiver between her shoulder and jaw, she calls the phone weather.

She calls her travel agent, gets a recording saying the office is closed for the day.

She rips and chops up some veggies for a small but bright salad and munches as she dials the number of her friend Ariel.

No answer at Ariel's.

She dials another friend.

She chats with this friend for half an hour.

She finishes the salad, standing, still wearing her jacket. The old house is slow to warm.

She reaches another friend, this one at the paper where Gwen had had her job as photographer after college. She gets the update on newsroom gossip, always bigger news than the news that goes to print.

When they giggle their good-byes, Gwen unplugs the phone again.

2 He is thick-waisted and slow. He works in the wind. The day is darkening into night, on the verge of snow.

He is meticulous.

Thirty dollars for a grave.

A perfect grave. He squared it off using a coffee can.

Thirty dollars more if there's dynamite for ledge. Or a jackhammer for deep frost.

But if all goes well, just thirty dollars.

The dark wind grabs the sleeves of his jacket as his back is humped, this perfect grave still only knee-deep. The shovel scuffs on stone.

3 The bricklike chunk of mail lays on the hardwood and tiled breakfast bar. Of this day's mail, she has already checked for word from the galleries. Her dealer. And the Institute. But there's nothing from any of them. So many envelopes addressed Mrs. Earl Doyle, which means financial reports, letters from attorneys, accounting updates.

And then there's OCCUPANT.

Her jacket is put away. Her salad made, munched. Bowl washed by hand.

A letter from her mother reads:

> Dear Gwen,
> Received your lovely card from Turkey or wherever that was. I don't have it in front of me. Obviously if you are reading this, you are back!! I'm thankful for these trips you take and those you and Earl used to take. Otherwise, I'd never have any indication that you are all right. You'd think a person in Maine wouldn't need to go to Turkey to indicate to her loved ones in Connecticut that she's in good health. Dennis calls it "lifestyle." By the way, Judy is being difficult . . . AS USUAL. Dennis thinks she might leave. Ho-hum. What else is new? She's only left him so many

times nobody can count anymore. He'll be better off. He just doesn't think so now. When you get this letter, please call. There's mail here for you AS USUAL. People trying to track you down. You live like a spy. If you call, I can read the mail to you over the phone and that will save me from forwarding it.
   Love,
   Mother.

Gwen flips the pages of a magazine. The photos in this magazine always draw her. Like how we are all drawn to fire or deformity or death. So it is with unnatural glossy beauty.

She flips another page. Three long women in purples, reds, and yellows. This year's three big colors. The thing is to wear all three at once so that you explode before men's eyes. Gwen smiles. In Egypt, Maine, if you dressed like that, you'd be a leper. And anyway, if you struck some of those poses, you'd break your back. Yet on this page the three women are having such a blissful time. In the company of one another, heads flung back, teeth bared, perfect, slightly too-large teeth always the focal point. All that really matters gyrates around great teeth and the fantastic, almost orgasmic smile.

Such flowing pants legs and sleeves. A flowingness that exemplifies freedom. The sleeve of one woman merges with the sleeve of the next. And there a merging ear. Gwen leans closer. All these women have the same face. Not just similar faces . . . but the *same* face. Can she suspect this is the same woman?

So they aren't really together. It is just one woman. A trick of photography, the illusion of friendship.

4 | Several days and nights pass. The carpenters are behind schedule on the sun-room. Their zinging saws, their talk, their silences are both pleasant and intrusive. She keeps to her workroom, framing slides, matting some pieces for the upcoming exhibit. She drives up around the forks and parks on the high ridge, takes a few shots of her home just for the hell of it. The back of it still has the weathered black blotchy shingles of the original owner . . . the old man who died there. But for the sun porch edging out beyond the lilacs, this view could be 1950. Or even 1910. She squints one eye. She considers trying some black-and-white for this. Yes! Black-and-white! She will pick up a few rolls of Tri-X and shoot

the works. Just for her own pleasure. The experimentalness and off-handedness of this give her a wonderful rush.

When the carpenters are gone, she plugs in the phone, gabs with her friends Trish and Denise.

She unplugs the phone.

She writes a long letter to her friend Keith.

She sends her mother a thinking-of-you card, with one of those tacky but cute photos of one striped kitten, one spotted kitten in a basket of yarn balls. She writes that everything is fine. She signs it, not with her usual crabbed handwriting, but with a flourish!

She sits at the breakfast bar and scans the floor plans of the room the carpenters will start on next spring . . . a room off the kitchen to the left of the sun porch, which would be all windows and, but for that direction blocked by the barn, *three* superb views of the mountains and fields.

She finishes a smooth martini.

Cats yeowl from high places and low places. They glide over the sawhorses the carpenters have grouped around on the sun porch.

Gwen is not sleepy. Yes, too much travel can really screw up your system. Oh, well. A small price to pay when all is said and done. Now she reflects appreciatively upon her workroom upstairs and the large well-stocked darkroom within it, already cluttered as if she'd been busy in it for the last ten years. Such a lived-in set of rooms. Unlike the rest of the house, the workroom and darkroom are her private happy mess. She checks her watch. It's two A.M. Perfect time for darkroom work. She mixes another martini.

Cats yeowl from all directions.

Gwen crosses the room, rummages through a basket of messages and business cards. She locates the number with the three nines.

2:06 A.M. She plugs the phone in and dials.

The rings drag on and on but she waits.

"Yep . . . what?" The voice. Softer on *what* than *yep*.

"Hello. This is Gwen Doyle on Canal Road. I'm calling to order another load of firewood."

There's a murky silence. Then a chuckle. "Must be in a hurry," he says.

She says, "I have a lot to take care of here, Mr. Barrington. Heating this place . . . is . . . yes . . . impor . . . tant." She tips the phone's mouthpiece away as she sips from a too-full martini.

Another chuckle. "You burned that whole cord in six days?"

"Excuse me?"

"You burned that whole cord already?"

"No! Of course not!" she snaps.

"Well, it being a kind of emergency feel to it, ya know . . ."

"You are in the business to sell wood?"

A long pause. "Yes, you've reached the firewood hotline."

"Well, I would like you to deliver another cord, please . . . as soon as you can, please . . . thank you."

"I've sold all my dry. We're working up green now."

She nearly drains her glass, reaches across the counter to tone the drink down with a slosh of vermouth. "Um." She uses her finger as a stirrer. "Uh . . . how green would that be?" She sucks her finger.

"Well . . . what I could deliver you Tuesday is upright tonight . . . you know . . . as in vertically green . . . wind soughing through the boughs." He chuckles. Deeply.

She squats down on the floor, sets her glass against the mopboard, rubs the back of her neck with her free hand, fluffs her hair, sways to the chuff-tick chuff-tick chuff-tick of the entryway clock. "So what you are saying is you can't come up with *any* dry wood. Don't you . . . have . . . well, like some you might have forgotten you have, Mr. Barrington?"

Silence on both ends. Charged silences.

"You mean a few cords I might have misplaced?" he asks with a raspy easygoing laugh.

"You know what I mean." She speaks each word solidly and separately, trying to sound persuasive, but really sounding just a little drunk.

A silence on his end. An amused silence.

"Mr. Barrington. Are you still on the line?"

"Right here."

"Did you hear my question?"

"I did. You want preferred treatment, I suppose."

"I'll pay you fifty extra for your trouble. I'm not a beggar."

Silence. Big raw silence.

"Mr. Barrington . . . do you need this much time to think?"

"What kind of stove are you using? Are those twenty-one-inch pieces fitting in okay?"

"There are two little fireplaces here. I use one of them regularly and I have both of them fairly heaped when I have guests."

"Fireplaces."

"Yes."

"I suppose your chimneys are in good order. You've seen to that? Those old chimneys . . . you have to be careful . . . some aren't lined. Some are creosoted up so you couldn't even get a chain down through. Could turn into an ugly situation."

"The party I purchased the house from said they had a chimney sweep in before the house went on the market."

"Zat right?"

She presses the fingers of her free hand to an eye, rocks on her haunches, slower than the clock now. "So when could you deliver the wood if you located some that was dry?"

"I can tell you two other outfits where you still may be able to get seasoned hardwood this late in the year. Tibbetts in Porter and Steve Bean over to Holder Hill . . . and Albion Cole *might* have gotten into some . . . though I suspect he's just doing mill lots right now. But you could check."

"Mr. Barrington. You're in the firewood business aren't you?"

He snorts.

"Mr. Barrington. I'll pay you a hundred dollars extra if you could get me a load of wood here first thing tomorrow."

"Is *that* right?"

"That's correct."

5 | She has forgotten about the drink placed on the floor next to the mopboard. So she needs to start with a new glass to mix the next drink. As she reaches to shut off one of the kitchen lamps, the phone rings. She sometimes forgets to unplug it. It rings again and again.

The phone. Nice for calling out, but as it rings now, she pinches the adaptor to disconnect it. The ringing stops but it's worse now. Like a cry that is gagged. Or a staring secret eye.

Her mother, Phoebe. Pheeb.

What is the question tonight? What is the answer? Does she try to get through to Gwen all hours of every day, or does she just KNOW when Gwen is apt to slip up?

6 She comes to wakefulness in a struggle. She grasps out at something. What? A bottle of hand lotion plunks to the floor. She has overslept. Hung over. There's some appointment. What? It's her first real sleep in nearly a week and yet she feels misbehaved. Well, perhaps that's the martini aspect of the evening. And now these steel daggers in the eyes, steel rods in the temples. And the realization that somebody waits for her somewhere. Who? It's the women at the Peace Campaign Center . . . Are they calling her now? . . . *Gwen! Gwen! Can't reach you!* She pushes herself up. The waterbed sloshes, underfilled, lukewarm, nauseating bed of gentle waves.

She hangs one leg out over the edge of the bed moving her toes as into the sea, she is testing . . . testing.

Even her softest robe seems too abrasive. Its mild salmon color roars. The silence of the house roars. Her mouth . . . old hot dry crack. Passing each window, she whimpers for the pain the overcast day makes inside each eye. The cats are a thickness around her legs, pestering for their breakfast.

But the worst . . . the worst thing she finds down in the kitchen is an unnatural boundary of darkness . . . two windows, two views of the hills blocked. It is a monstrous thing. An aggression. It is as though, during the night, a gray building had been constructed nearly flush to this existing one.

She unlatches the door and steps out into the shedway.

So . . . it's a stack of trees *with limbs*. Some of the beech trees still have leaves, not summer leaves, not autumn leaves, but those blond veiny, whispering winter hangers-on . . . and all this . . . this pile of trees . . . precision close to the sheen of one fender of her BMW which is parked there.

She reenters the house, shivering, drinks water in gulps. She moans into the glass.

It is not unbelievable that he could unload those trees and not wake her. He doesn't need to be a genius to know she had had a "few" when she rambled on and on at two A.M. And yet the look of it now in its suddenness and entirety . . . *trees* . . . trees horizontal, with the arched spread of their limbs . . . filling out that tight space against the house . . . is beyond belief. She stands at the sink a long while in her pale robe, squeezing her fingers around the water glass.

Funny man.

7 She is sober tonight, therefore terrified. There are places and assemblages through which she would know her way, lovely and composed, her dark eyes, her professional nod, her quiet sweaters and suits, the twist of her wrist to check her watch. But this before her is a territory which is dim, faceless, bottomless. It is ten P.M. One of her hips delves into the warm recesses of the waterbed, which gives the bed a rocking rise and fall. The bedside phone has a lighted dial that glows huge as the face of a cathedral clock against her cheek. She dials the number that contains three nines. Phones in these hills don't ring prettily, but sound like well-spaced farts. Four farts. Five farts. On the eighth fart, he answers. "What?" His voice sinks softly into this single word so it sounds less like a word, more like a catching of breath.

She hangs up.

Does he guess it's her?

She dials again.

. . . nine farts, ten farts, eleven farts. The farts stop. Into the black abyss, his voice falls. "What?"

She hangs up, calls again, finds the line busy. Off the hook.

Downstairs there are thumps and clonks of the cats knocking baskets and vases from the tables and shelves . . . one of their episodes of friskiness. Or of *malice*. Gwen has never been fool enough to think her cats really love her.

8 Sometimes you get a smell here. At times it persists like a headache. Mostly on damp days, the consequences of choosing an older home, everyone tells her. It's because the walls and timbers get spongy, they say.

But she is suspicious of another thing.

The Putnams had lowered their voices into a near-fainting lament when describing "the condition we found this place in!" . . . how the old guy before he died "must have led his cattle through these rooms!!!! Everything so scarred, beat-up. Neglected! And a horrendous pink linoleum covering these beautiful pine floors! Layers of wallpaper. Those people don't know anything . . . they just plop another layer of wallpaper on top of another . . . layer upon layer! And junk! The *junk* that was kept! Stashed and crammed. No space in which to live! He didn't deserve this house!" they had agreed. "He'd have been happy in a hut!"

Gwen had asked which room he had died in. But the Putnams couldn't seem to remember if the real estate woman had ever mentioned anything like that. Probably not. "He wasn't . . . you know . . . dead long. There wasn't a decaying body or anything like that," the wife assured Gwen.

"Probably upstairs," the husband had suggested.

Earl would have found her question about the original owner odd. "Curious" would be his word, though he wouldn't be "curious" enough to ask her why she asked. Surely he would smile. Gwen made him smile often. He would have dismissed Gwen's interest as "existentialism" or even, with an amused chuckle, "Gwen's spiritualism." For Earl scorned even world and American history as "trivia." He had once explained that "The question is time, energy, and commitment. Considering our short lives . . . especially the very short time of productivity, we owe it to ourselves and to others to be selective."

At restaurants and banquet rooms and on the streets, his eyes would float over humanity as if it were empty sky. So much on his mind. A prisoner of his work. Forgive him! Forgive him! May his soul be at rest.

And his eyes were that blue as all time before creation.

She and Earl had some wonderful homes. She still keeps the Connecticut place. An unerring solemn old thing, fifteen rooms out of the eighteenth century. Brick. Brick house. Bricked pathways beneath old oaks and chestnuts and blue spruce. And around the back and side yards, brick walls to shut out the noise of the city, to shut in the peace. Walls choking in a stiff grid of old ivy where little birds nest and chatter and cheep.

And servants and caretakers. Though sometimes it seems lately like the house is really theirs. How they have settled in! And taken advantage.

Last year one of her brothers spent a winter there. Every time he called her from there, he was laughing. It seemed he was calling her from some foreign land where there were feasts and festivals and quaint costumes and a language unlike her own. A kind of sordid merriment had taken over that house.

She had had one of Earl's associates make arrangements to sell off the place in California, a place they kept purely for Earl's business needs. Gwen rarely spent time there, for the long trip and jet lag seemed hardly worth a fifteen-hour stay. Or even the occasional two days over. And although beautifully furnished in greens and yellows and warm woods, its dozens of glass doors and walls had an odd way of throwing your voice. Always that unwelcoming echo.

And then in Tokyo and Hong Kong, Australia, Mexico, South America, Milan, Canada there were apartments or homes, all necessary to Earl's business needs. Some of those places she never stepped foot into. And now in no way can she imagine them. Earl *never* took a camera. Not ever.

After his death, the first place Gwen had arranged to have put on the market was the place in Texas. She hated Texas. She couldn't seem to make a friend there. And all her photographs turned out cherry pink, like a kind of dyspepsia.

None of it mattered after Earl died. It was Earl who was her castle. It is people who matter, not the material goods of this world! A house is just a chunk of real estate . . . sometimes a work of art . . . sometimes a throwaway shell.

9 | It's 3:38 in the afternoon. An appropriate hour for calling. She stands in the doorway to the narrow front hall off the kitchen looking into the sapphire eyes of the Siamese who hunches on top of the sawhorses the carpenters have stacked near the attic door.

She is resolved to speak this time. She will.

What? . . . demand that he move the trees. Take them back? Cut them up? Does he expect payment for these trees?! For this inconvenience to her?! This disquieting thing? This scare? Ha!

The wood man is what Earl, with no expression in his eyes, would call "people." And then "End of discussion," Earl's eyes would say.

Gwen takes a swallow of her drink, tries to let it fall down her throat without swallowing. But you can't do that. The muscles of the throat grab.

She leans with her forehead to the doorframe, waiting while the fartlike rings reach twenty. And thirty.

Forty.

10 | Four o'clock she tries again. A child answers. A surprise and yet no surprise.

"Is your father at home?" Gwen asks, setting her drink on the edge of the counter.

"Daddy don't live here," the child tells her.

"Maybe I have the wrong number. Is this 9995?"

A long, long pause and heavy echoey openmouthed concentration, then, "Yuhn, it is."

"I'm calling about a purchase of firewood."

"Yuhn."

"Is your mother there?"

"*We* are just here . . . lookin' for somethin'," the child says.

"Who are we?" Gwen asks.

"Huh?"

"Are you Lloyd's child?" Gwen asks.

"Lloyd!" The child giggles, a great joke on the caller. "That's Grampa . . . Lloyd." A pause. "Are you my teacher?"

"No. Do I sound like her?" Gwen laughs.

"I guess not really."

"I'm calling for your grandfather . . . Grampa. I find it extraordinary that he has school-aged grandchildren."

"He's not here."

"What is your name?" Gwen asks.

"Angela."

"Why that's a beautiful name . . . Angela. Name of angels."

The child giggles.

Gwen sighs. "Oh, dear. I had hoped to find Grampa at home. Where is he?"

"Dumdie's."

"Where's that?"

The child snorts. "DUMMMdee's. You know! *Jim's*."

"Uh . . . a friend of his?"

The child groans with impatience. "You know HIM . . . with the saw. Fixes boards. You take logs there. He has the Doberman."

"I see," says Gwen with a sigh.

"MICHAEL!!! Get off the bed! You're messin' it up! GET OFF!" The child hollers this away from the phone. Then a long silence at both ends, just the sweet infinity of the dark unknown and the child's mouth so close . . . so close.

Gwen says, "Angela?"

"Yuhn?"

"What do you see there?"

"You mean . . . *here*?"

"Yes . . . what's it like at Grampa's?"

"Oh, kinda cold. Pretty cold."

"What else?"

"Oh . . . just, you know . . . the way it looks. His stuff. We walked down to find Beebee's leash. HEY! Quit it! QUIT IT!!!" There's a struggle. Grunts and giggles. "I could smunch you!! Get that off there!! Come on. Come ON! GET OUT!!!!!" Phone bangs. Feet run. Door slams. Angela returns gasping. "Hi."

Gwen is also breathless. "Where's Grand*ma*?"

"Who?"

"Grand-ma. Grampa's wife."

Angela giggles. "Grampa's not a wife! He's a *man*." Then she yells off away from the phone again. "Leave that alone! If you bust those, I'm tellin'!"

Gwen persists. "Where's Grampa's wife?"

Silence. Long silence.

"Angela. Does he have a wife?"

"I think so. Maybe he does. I'll ask him."

"No! Don't ask him. This is a secret talk, okay?"

The child makes her voice deep and very close. "Okay."

Gwen sighs. "If Grampa *had* a wife, you'd probably see her around, right?"

"Yuhn," the child says vaguely.

"How many children does Grampa have? His grown-up ones. The ones who call him Dad."

"Mumma calls him Daddeee," Angela says excitedly, realizing that they are on to something, the secret answer to this thing which feels like spying or police.

"Right. Okay. Who else?"

"Aunt Leighlah calls him Daddy, too. Some people call him *Dad* . . . Caleb. And Joel . . . I think. Sometimes it's Fox . . . people . . . around . . . and Caleb . . . call him Fox . . . I don't know . . . that's their joke. They like it. Fox."

"I see. Well . . . *who* is the nice lady your mom calls 'Mom?'"

"My mumma's mumma is called Mumma I guess."

"And where *is* your mumma's mumma?"

"Up to Gram's," says Angela.

"She *lives* at Gram's but Grampa lives where you are right now?"

"Yuhn."

"And where are *you?*"

"Right here!!" Angela chirps delightedly.

Gwen sighs. Exhausted.

11 Another day. Gray. Great for shooting. Six rolls of Tri-X black-and-white in their cans on the big kitchen table. All exposures are views of this house. Some from the distance, others close enough to glorify one irascible nail head.

Gwen in the bathroom, shower running like thunder.

Cat swipes at one of the film cans. It rolls around in a wide arc toward the table's edge. Now another swipe. Film can hits the floor, rolls around in a sensuous arc. Cat watches from above, blue eyes steady, engrossed . . . nota bene!

12 She comes slamming into the house through the series of shedway doors, hurried. The whole place still smells of new pine boards and stain . . . the morning work of the carpenters . . . Bill and Pete. She plucks off her cap, a knitted collapsed-looking silly but wonderfully soft creation that her friend Joey has sent her to "wear around the house" . . . it being a bit of a tickle with the old gang that she's gone up north to find seclusion . . . *way* up north . . . and Joey often sings out, "Mush! Mush! Wayyyyy up North!"

She sets the tea kettle on the burner. Chooses from an assortment of herbal teas. "Peach."

The cats, Apollo and Athena, bash themselves into her tall dress boots, purring, yeowling. Gwen hunts through the bag of groceries for a can of Seafood Platter.

Hearing the cats smacking and slisking on their suppers always makes Gwen feel good. She is a good person. Considerate. All of her life she has given off only the most gentle light. Solemn light. Her actions are the true Gwen. It is only in her dark eyes that she might appear severe. Something about the eyes. And maybe the voice. A cool cookie, her brother Dennis has called her.

She drives her letter opener into a fine piece of news . . . a clipping of a great review from the *Boston Globe* of her friend Pam's paintings and installations on the theme of Women Warriors.

She flips over a postcard of the "Connecticut Countryside."

November 12. Dear Gwen. Send word. Love, Mother.

"Send word" seems to match the Way Up North Frontier theme. Gwen smiles.

And here a postcard of the Swiss Alps from the Harrises forwarded from Connecticut by her brother Guy. Gwen misses the Harrises and the others at times. Few of Earl's executive friends have kept in touch with her since Earl's death. The "wheels" as Earl used to call them. The dinner parties always meant a lot of fuss. The caterers and maids and cook did all the hard work, of course. But hers was the territory of maintaining the impeccable. There were flexing rules and hazy boundaries. She never failed Earl Doyle. Not ever. Gracious, they told him. "Your wife is gracious."

The old life.

Before this seclusion.

The old life. Hadn't some of the "wheels" taken her out to dinner in that respectable time following Earl's death? Hadn't there been memos from Rudy Greer and John Hines? And that Texan?

The old life.

Before this seclusion.

This house, it has been understood, is her studio . . . for weeks of uninterrupted work and a sort of meditation. Her work. Her work in transition. Her last series is now completed with the feeling that a bright and shapely fruit has ripened, beyond which point it would just go bad.

She has already written a few friends about a party here . . . here where she has come to get away from them! The big distraction of them. The "old gang" . . . the dear ones, the true friends.

How nice it will be to set up the Rolleiflex and get a few group portraits and some of each beautiful face. These are her friends from college and some she met through the newspaper in her old photo lab days. Friends who call themselves "indigent bohemians." Not hardly are they indigent! But Gwen has seen them in their pajamas and in the thick of marital wrangles or in the hospital for appendectomies and in various limp or outraged stages of depression and hangovers. She has seen their kids grow. And kids of their second marriages. Their kids who she is certain will grow up to be the cream of humanity.

Earl always seemed pleased to see her friends stop by or come for a weekend of heart-to-heart talks. He told them hilarious anecdotes as he took their jackets.

But eventually, at some point in the visit, he'd say, "Excuse me, please," and go off to make calls in his alcove office. Sometimes, without the polite bowing out, he'd just vanish as if dissolved by the good air of that restful old high-ceilinged house. Who missed him? Not hardly the "old gang." Once he was out of the way, they came to life . . . rowdy or weepy . . . whatever they had come for. And Gwen's solemn eyes and tender light moved upon them.

Earl always spoke of Gwen's friends with respect. He never made cutting remarks about them. The "wheels" were the ones he had cutting remarks about, these princes of the corporate jungle. To diminish them? Why? None of them was more of a wheel, more of a prince than he. He owned everything! Most of them just helped him manage what he owned . . . or advised and plotted with him on the next big buyout or union bust. Yes, they were just . . . helpers.

Yes, it was Earl himself who often suggested Gwen have her dearest Kim or Nancy or Joey over for drinks. Yet, though it was never spoken, it was clearly one of the rules that there would be no mixing of the "old gang" with the "wheels." There was never a friend of hers present at Earl's dinner parties. Not ever. Why? Some of her friends are quite accomplished in their fields. And Joey, famous. What line did Earl draw here?

Taking a bar of unscented soap from the grocery bag, Gwen recalls those last years. Earl's delicate hair. White hair. His hair hadn't been much thicker or more colorful in his youth, his family told her. "Kind of reddish" were their words.

There were no old photographs of him available to her. They were not a "picture-crazy" family . . . their words.

Also there were very few clippings, although Earl's companies were mentioned in the news and in journals routinely. Heck, even the ever-changing labels of products were something for a scrapbook . . . these things that verified Earl's stamina, his finesse, his vigor, his derring-do! These things that still reflect his *life*.

Gwen had begun a secret stash of clippings when they had started to "date" . . . she in her twenties, he forty-nine for only a month after they married. She recalls the big commotion among the "wheels" when he turned fifty, a party at a private club. "A waste of time," he told her on the way home.

He had two wives before Gwen. No children. Neither woman was to be discussed . . . another rule. And there had been no pictures of them at all. At least none in his possession. But at age twenty-five, this pleased her, the fact that they were so unspeakably terrible while she never failed to make Earl smile.

Now she sets the cup of peach tea to steeping, then hurries upstairs to the bedroom. She snaps on a few lamps there, hunts down a pair of loose soft jeans. This room was two rooms once. The Putnams had torn out a wall, broke out plaster from the other walls and ceilings . . . and never got to the floor. Now there's a wallpaper of creamy roses on a mauve background, the exposed chimney painted white. Everything in the room is soft grays, mauves, creams, and sugars. The rugs are antique Persians, one in blues. The others are piled and overlapped, copper, red . . . but mostly the sweet pales. No bare floors up here. No knick-knacks, plants, or books. None of the handwoven baskets that make the rest of the house so cozy. Just a single large watercolor, a gift from her painter friend, Nancy . . . an image where human bodies look more like the rebounding shadows of silver fish.

She sits on the love seat that is loaded with striped pillows and three well-dressed white cloth polar bears. She changes into the jeans, a dark sweater over a white button-up blouse. Moccasins. She thinks of the women she has spent the day with in Portland . . . the Peace Campaign people. Already two good friends there. The new gang! She rushes back down for her tea and a little salad, scribbles off a few postcards . . . "A party!" she tells each one. "To celebrate my transition to black-and-white! I can't understand how I overlooked it for so long!!! Yes! Black-and-white! It's so compelling! So haunting! So dangerous!"

13 At Moody's Variety & Lunch, the counter is darkened, the configuration of wooden rockers around the barrel stove all tilted in various angles of evacuation and unattendedness.

Only signs of life are Dottie Soule and Louise Moody thumbing through catalogs on their low stools behind the register.

Outside there's the soft plunk of a car door shutting, the rich widow entering the store at a fast clip. The glass door slips shut behind her. She heads down one short aisle to the coolers.

Behind the register that is enmassed with baseball cards, Slim Jims, mint patties, and cheery snowman lapel pins are a couple of low whoops and a sniggle, the crinkle and snap of catalog pages being turned and Dottie Soule's pink and mighty bubble gum smell rising, a kindly welcoming, voluptuous smell, though Dottie herself is just an old and narrow wishbone of a woman.

Louise Moody's voice says, "What could a person possibly need with one of them?"

Dottie has no reply.

Catalogs, catalogs, catalogs. Two or three new catalogs in a day. The next day two more. Some just repeats of others. One with your middle initial. One without. If it's summer, you get what the new look is in fashions for fall. If it's winter, you get catalogs showing bare feet in the sand, gangs of people striding along wearing shorts in a weird otherworldly sunshine. Then there's the sales. The sell-outs. The last of the line. The last-chance sale. The next-to-last-chance sale. Another last-chance sale. The threat that since you haven't ordered in so long, this could be your last catalog. Then the next dozen catalogs they send you after that. Then the bonus sale. This week's sneak premiere. Next week's sneak premiere. The tall women's sizes. The tall men's sizes. Then wide women. Then wide men. And these are just the clothing catalogs. Then there are the household lovelies, gifts, and gimmicks. Pet needs, birdfeeder needs. Dial toll-free 1-800 so-'n'-so and your delivery will be in a week to ten days . . . hurry, hurry, hurry . . . charge card number, page number, net weight, sales tax, shipping, total. Now. Now. Now.

"Here's a seatbelt for your dog!" Dottie bellers.

"Notice they don't make cotton clothes anymore," Louise sighs sadly. "I always liked cotton blouses."

"I've seen some catalogs that specialize in cotton. But one of them cotton blouses costs as much as a car."

Dottie booms, "Trying to screw us! One I was looking at this morning said 'cool cotton comfort.' Then you read down through and it 'twern't but a speck of cotton mixed into the damn thing . . . 'twas some blend."

"You've got to read these guys like you're Sherlock Holmes."

"What's this? Look!" Dottie slaps a catalog into Louise's lap.

"Oh dear . . . it's a bat. Why would anybody want to wear a pi'ture of a *bat* on their T-shirt? Bats aren't that cute." She studies this page hard then hands it back.

Dottie smiles down at the bat T-shirt. "This one's cute. He's a doll."

"I don't care. I've never seen a bat in real life with a face that cute."

Two bottles of Poland Spring lemon-flavored water and a jar of gray gourmet mustard are lowered to the counter. It's the rich widow.

Louise grunts as she gets up. On her feet, Louise is still only head and shoulders above the counter.

The widow jerks a few bills from her tapestry change purse. Also she unfolds a name and number on lined paper . . . and the word FIRE-WOOD . . . all in a handwriting of small crabbed *o*'s and *a*'s and undotted *i*'s. She says, "Hello" as if over a phone. Her dark eyes have a grip on the area of flesh between Louise Moody's eyes. The widow asks, "Do either of you know this person? This is his notice which I copied from your wall over there."

Dottie Soule says yes she knows him and Louise Moody cackles.

The widow looks at the mouths of both women a bit expectantly now, but they are waiting for her. Perhaps it's something she wants to report missing . . . or worse, something that's appeared. Maybe a likeness of herself in an open coffin. It's just a matter of time, as everybody knows.

But the rich widow seems to have lost the thread of the subject . . . she packs the piece of paper back into the change purse. "Do you carry lettuce . . . ever?"

Louise says, "No, dear. We never carry lettuce out of season. We wouldn't sell enough of it and with that lettuce that's available nowadays, it's sent all the way out from California. Betwixt the time they cut 'em and the time we shelve 'em, they've nearly already got mushy middles. Nothing I want to mess with."

As the widow's gloved hands smooth bills onto Louise's palm, Louise calls out, "I have a one! I have a two! I have a two and a twenty-five!" This is Louise's usual jokey way of taking people's money that's supposed to sound like Beano.

Around the great pink gum wad, Dottie asks, "You got trouble with your well?"

The widow's eyes slant down across the counter to Dottie who is seated back there. "No," she says icily. "Why do you ask?"

Dottie points. "That bottled water. I just wondered. A lot of people having trouble with wells this year." Dottie tips her head toward Louise. "Her boy's in well drilling. We get it straight from the horse's mouth."

"My well is fine."

14 | As she edges the BMW in close to the barn and that monstrous barrier of trees, the limbs wag and wave, while the limbs of the live trees that surround the yard also wag and wave . . . beckoning.

As she hurries for the house, the cold wind screams out from the hills, snatches at her grocery bag and her hair. The metal chimes under the eave of the new sun porch sound like they are smashing to pieces. Her fingers scramble to guess which key goes to the kitchen door. What? The phone is ringing. How can this be? She remembers disconnecting it, unable to bear even the answering machine today.

Once inside in that dim zone between when the sky is radiant and when the security lamps check themselves on, she trips over the cats that stick to her legs, catches herself against the breakfast bar. The phone's ring is an alluring and coaxing tendril. She closes her hand on the receiver. The rings stop.

15 | Memories. One for each day, one day pulled from the other. The daughter, Gwen, is in her bed. The mother, Phoebe, will be singing down under the grate, slamming cupboard doors, stomping around. Her singing is of itself wildly pretty, but as it goes louder and louder, it gets too loud to be tuneful, just a screech. Now and then Phoebe drops a pan or can opener . . . or objects unknown . . . Gwen can only guess. Even stepping from bed and squatting over the heat grate, the view of the kitchen is only the square of floor and counter directly below. The rest, even as things happen, is no better than dream or memory. It is best to stay lying on the bed. It is best not to let the mother hear the scuff of a bare foot, the floor creak, the uneven breathing. It is best to *seem* unaffected. Every night into the girl's earliest remembering, the mother had reached her through the night this way. A few times the father William had said, "Phoebe. How do you expect Gwen to sleep?"

So Phoebe sang louder. Show tunes. Pop tunes. Rock and roll. Television jingles. And once a shattery tinkling splat! A glass thrown in the sink?

16 | In the night, wakened from sleep with a smile of mischief, she reaches to connect the phone and dials.

At his end, the phone is answered in half a ring as if it were pounced upon. "Okay," he says. "So, now . . . let's get down to basics. Is this a call about my underwear? . . . you know . . . like . . ." He does a fairly stirring rendition of heavy breathing. "A what-color-is-your-underwear kind of call? Or is this just for the sense of power . . . of privilege, that any rich hoity-toity bitch can reach out at will and get a grip on what she wants . . . whatever it is . . ."

She claps the receiver down, leaps from the bed with a small cry, shivering now, these upstairs rooms always cold, even with the electric heat constantly at work . . . *where* does the heat go?

Back in bed, she cranks up the electric blanket to what Earl used to call "Bar-B-Q'd Thigh." She lies with her eyes wide.

Something smashes downstairs in the front hall.

She leans over, snatches up the phone receiver, dials. The long sweeping nines seem to take weeks to revolve into place.

On the third ring, he picks up and says in his odd hard and soft voice, "I'm not naked. But I do have my boots off. Maybe you have a fetish for socks. These socks are . . . let me see . . . uh . . . let me get a light on here. Yep, red. They're red."

She lays suspended, floating on the bed while he talks. And his silences. She listens with reverence to those. His silence is different than her silence. His silence is a place, a *somewhere,* crammed with everything imaginable and answerable. Now he gets a little edge to his voice. "Anything else you want to know about me? Ask me now. You don't need to grill my family nor the neighbors. You can ask me direct. Ask me anything. *Anything*."

She floats, hand clutching the cord.

"Like . . ." he continues. "Let's see. You strike me as one of those women who insists upon credentials. Am I right? Yep. Rich bitch wants the file. Roll it out, run it over the screen. Name, dates, credit checks, references, degrees, awards, three forms of ID, passport, driver's license, library card . . . something with a face shot . . . and maybe a good frisking . . . just so the poor ass can deliver a couple of cords of wood."

The blanket is starting to really blaze. She fits the phone receiver more squarely against the bones of her cheek and temple, his voice boiling out into her ear. He says he should report her to the phone company. "Phone rape," he calls it. He says he's never felt so violated in his life, so nervous, so bothered. He chuckles. Then he says he's going to get a couple of Dobermans for protection and get his trailer wired for an alarm system and about fourteen mercury security lamps all aimed at his doors and windows so she won't try to sneak in and run off with his red socks. He says he doesn't dare hang them out on the line now. He raves on and on that his life has changed. It will never be the same after this. He snarls, "Leave me alone" and hangs up.

Gwen lies watching the hands of the illuminated clock squeeze together ever so slowly. Midnight.

When the phone dingles prettily on the nightstand, she raises the receiver but doesn't speak.

"This is your wood man."

Her chest thuds. "How'd you get my number? It's unlisted."

"How do you do *your* bloodhound work?"

She sighs.

He sighs. "Is this thing you are after me about . . . is it of a man-woman nature . . . or what?"

She tries to conjure his face, but only one thing presents itself . . . the moustache, a font of dark-edged lion-color and gray. She imagines he lies in the dark of his bed just as she lies in hers. "Man-woman nature," she admits.

He says deeply, "So we can chalk off the CIA possibility."

She pushes her wrist against her smiling mouth.

Silence.

She tells him how adorable his granddaughter Anglea was on the phone.

"Yes . . . adorable . . . the little wench. Thrives on turmoil."

Silence.

Gwen asks nervously, "So . . . how are you tonight?"

He tells her he's having a problem with his stomach.

She suggests ginger and water, that it's an old remedy and it works. That her father was a physician, but wasn't above "prescribing" ginger.

Lloyd agrees. It's a thing that's used with soda for calves with bloated bellies.

Gwen says that health and healing should be part of everyone's basic knowledge . . . especially healing. "It's mostly a matter of positive energy."

There's a rustle and some soft work of his mouth near the phone and Gwen now remembers the chewing tobacco and sighs.

She tells him some things about her father. Things that mattered. The puzzles and the certainties. She tells how she was not quite thirteen when she found him dead from a heart attack on the barn floor. She remembers his sprawl, his slightly clenched hand, his luster-faced wristwatch with its fine second hand sweeping, his head averted on his neck, cheek easy against the gravelly plank floor.

There's a groan, then only Lloyd's chewing, not like contented rumination . . . not like nervousness. Neither wet nor dry.

She tells more and more.

He makes tender, interested sounds.

After a time, she takes a deep breath and says, "Listen . . . on Friday I'm having a get-together of good friends, mostly artists exchanging the details of our miserable fates." She smiles at this thought, then shifts around under the blazing blanket. She reaches to set the temperature panel on low, but her hand just flops around in confusion. "I'd be honored if you'd come over"—she smiles—"without trees."

There's the clash, crumple, thump thump of the cats at work in the room below.

Gwen goes on to say, "It could be any time after . . . oh . . . I imagine the first ones will show up around six-thirty or seven. Just a smorgasbord . . . pot luck . . . and drinks. My friend Denise is bringing homemade pesto . . . yummy. If you come . . . I . . . would be honored. I . . . would be . . ." She closes her eyes to all the weird pink and interrogative lights at her windows. ". . . honored."

17 | Emerging from the chemicals the print is at first reluctant. Come out!

The house in the cleft of two hills as seen from nearly three miles from here, all the hillsides swelling forth, then falling away, dotted in rock, rocks everywhere, stone walled, tilted saplings strangled in stone. The house! The house! The house! Chimneys exalted. The blackened shingles. The iron sky. Single lighted window. And there's a boulder in the tough but perishable arms of tall weeds.

What is the lie?

She steps out of her darkroom, leaves the door standing open.

Downstairs she fixes a drink, stares out of a living-room window, gauging all details for their ability to answer to black-and-white film. Nothing else matters. Black-and-white . . . the nap, the weft of it, its reservedness, its boundaries, its grace.

Behind her something thwomps . . . rolls across the rug.

She hurries to the next window, and then the next. Each window is a different vignette.

Now she hurries to glimpse out of each window upstairs. Yes! Perhaps it is this! The inside looking out! Perhaps. But too late now, the sky draining out its life for night.

Tomorrow whatever the weather, she'll shoot. She can already imagine the soft cobwebby A.M. light on clean glass. And these virile headstrong hills dissected by the bars between panes.

18 Most of the morning, she shoots. Then she runs the films through the chemical baths and rinses, fixer, and tap, does a few contacts . . . squints at the results, drumming her fingers on the darkroom sink. She works up several prints. She trots down to the kitchen to mix a drink. She calls a friend. "Come up Friday! Yes! Yes! And tell Becky. I need you all. I miss you. Yes! Oh, yes!" She laughs her most abandoning hiccuppy laugh. "Yes, right. I'll roast up some blubber. There's so much of it! It'll just spoil." And she swings around and around, teary-eyed with laughter. The phone cord winds around and around her waist.

19 The food is in a jumble on the tables and countertops. Glass and porcelain servers of sauces and jams. Cutting boards with crusty breads. Dark crackers. Cheeses, both runny and solid. The cold remains of four roasted ducks . . . duck being for those who eat "animal." Hummus and pesto and tabbouleh and raw veggies for those who don't. Pleasant-looking raw veggies everywhere. Plastic storage bowls, pretty plates, platters. Veggies arranged in patterns of texture and color like an exhibit of new-age art. Wines, teas, fortune cookies. Dips with ham . . . dips with lobster. Green dips. And here comes more hummus and some macaroni salads arriving in deli cartons. More breads. Unopened wine bottles bristling on the small entry table. A cat gives the sealed cork of one of these a tentative poke. Bottle jiggles. Everywhere are empty wine bottles or wines half gone. And cloth napkins for those that object to the use of paper. And paper napkins for those who don't.

And in the vortex of every eye are the bright fireplaces.

This house, they say, *is* Gwen. "It's so Gwenish!" one friend shrills. Softly lighted areas, dim cozy shy corners, faces seen across space. Clouds of scent. Something minty, something vanilla. Next to a candle, a dark-faced Siamese licks her paw.

"Hey, Gwen. This is the actual town you grew up in? Am I correct?" someone asks . . . husband of one of her old friends from the newspaper . . . so many friends from those days . . . when she was Gwen Curry, staff photographer . . . the newspaper which Earl Doyle's corporation bought out while she was there. How in tarnation does a photographer hook up with the chairman of the board? . . . on the elevator, of course . . . although the elevator was crowded and nobody spoke. But later that week, a message arrived at the photo lab. He had, through the powers that be under him, tracked her down.

Gwen tells her friend's husband that yes, this is the town, and that the house she grew up in is less than two miles away. "But all built up around it, of course," she sighs woefully. "Development on all sides." She takes up another armload of coats, jackets, and gloves.

As her friend Joey, just arriving, empties a grocery bag of more deli cartons, more wine, he asks Gwen, "How are the Eskimos?"

Gwen tells him the Eskimos are fine and she hugs him and he kisses her hair.

Next he paces. His body is so fretful. But his radio-television-trained voice is, as ever, inflectionless and well-projected and calm.

There's not enough seats in the living room for those that like to sit. There's a little group of them converged on the rug around the fireplace, arms around their knees, the wheaten carpeting soaking them up, pulling them in. Others stand against doorways with their drinks. Joey paces.

When Lloyd appears out in the kitchen, Gwen plunks her drink down too suddenly and goes to him, wiping the spilled bourbon from her hand. She looks composed. But in her stocking feet, though she's a tall woman, she seems truly harmless now. She asks if she can get him anything. She waves her hand over the array of pretty foods.

He says, no.

What would he like to drink?

He says, nothing thank you.

He hasn't brought a house gift or food. She asks for his jacket. His hat.

He says he'll just hang on to them, thank you.

His face is fuller than she remembers and she had forgotten that one mottled eye. And shorter. Gosh, he seems even shorter than before. This can't be the same man she has been so intimate with over the phone in the floating darkness of her bed.

He has such a grip on his green felt crusher hat. He pulls off his jacket. His hair is combed with water in a way that seems against his will . . . like it is with some small boys. Sweet. And a very new-looking gray plaid shirt buttoned right up to his neck . . . some effort to be formal. Can she believe what she sees? That he almost trembles? Fear? His eyes avoid her face. She asks if he'd like to come in and sit in the living room. His eyes are fixed so earnestly on the china closet behind her where she keeps the little Danish tea service Earl bought for her on their honeymoon trip . . . silver so fine it looks soft and takes on a pink look at times . . . when pink is in the air.

He says, "Okay," and she sees that his teeth are stained, sees the graying dark effusion of his moustache against the short beard, the cheek that moves. How had she forgotten that ugly business of his mouth!! She wonders how long he can hold the stuff without spitting. He is nothing like the man on the phone. This man in her kitchen is solider, thicker, harder, standing heavily with his feet apart. She had pictured someone nobler, some long-bodied heroic Admiral Perry or Civil War general with sword and gold braid. Even a William Faulkner or Mark Twain. She is crazy. She has become so compulsive. She has become indecently and irresponsibly romantic. How protected she was all those years by Earl . . . and those unyielding, precise circumstances . . . protected from herself!

Lloyd Barrington's eyes are back on the cabinet and as she turns, keeping discreet, she sees it's not the tea service he's looking at. It's that set of Blue Willows.

He squats now to pet one of the Siamese cats that has come to sniff his pants legs.

Then Gwen leads Lloyd by the arm into the living room, introduces him as "my friend and neighbor" and tells him a few things about those standing near . . . as they all look into each others' eyes, nodding, smiling . . . Gwen gracious, patting Lloyd's arm, patting the arm of one of the others . . . like priming pumps . . . coaxing the flow.

Gwen wants Lloyd to have a chair. She sees someone leaving a straight-backed oak and she works her way with him toward it between people standing with their drinks. She wants him to have this chair, or an even nicer chair. She wants him to leave. She wants him to eat and have a nice time, to adore her friends. She wants him to fade. She wishes he had never come. She wishes to hang on to his arm forever. She hopes he'll never come back here again. She wishes him dead. She wants to float on his beautiful voice, his squalid old-fashioned accent, the heaviness of his voice, the omen, the warning, his humor, his chuckle, the secrets she and he have together.

But what is this smell from his clothes and hair? Where has she smelled it before?

Nearby Joey is flipping the thick glamoury pages of a fashion magazine. He handles magazines like some men handle a deck of cards, a prettyish purry th-th-th-th-th-th-th-th. Joey's tortoiseshell glasses make everything he does look like such serious business. He nods at one of the other guests who brushes his elbow on the way to the bookcase where Gwen keeps many rare books and along the bottom, the impressive spread of brand-new not-yet-perused Britannicas.

At the oak chair, Gwen releases Lloyd's arm and smiles. "Sit here." He does. He sits with knees apart, still gripping his jacket and crusher. He watches the cats slink around. One really likes him, keeps hanging out with him near his boots or on the bookshelf next to his head.

The room hums with Lloyd Barrington, hums *to* him. His eyes raise to Gwen's and he moves the thing in his mouth from left to right.

Someone asks him, "You a childhood buddy of Gwen's? Did you live around here, too, when she used to?"

Gwen doesn't hear his answer because some of them from the Women's Peace Campaign are arriving late and she hurries to greet them. Turns out these women already know the women of the environmental group. "Mary Wright!" one of the new arrivals exclaims. And there's hugs and squeezes and compliments firmly forthright. And there's the svelte and tireless, yet tired-looking state senator who insists she can't stay long.

But she keeps on staying, sharing her elation over some recent legislative victories . . . and blessings to those who worked hard, not giving up when it was evident that the victories on this important issue would be small. "We have been fortunate to have had such commitment throughout this long, long term," the senator says with a wonderful smile. And here, so many jackets with padded shoulders. Shoulders played up. Hair played down. Every part of one's self being worked like a rudder. Only the lightest murmurs of perfume. Subliminal only. These vigorous good women! Something shifts. Gwen feels righted. Back on course.

Once again in the living room, she introduces and reintroduces all. Her friend Keith gives up his seat, shaking a few hands before he slumps into the deep rug, exhausted from his long drive up from New York.

And Joey never sits. He flits from person to person, bookshelf to bookshelf, window to window. Now he is saying, "This fireplace isn't large, but it's got character."

Gwen smiles. "The couple who tried fixing the place up discovered these fireplaces. The owners before them had boarded them up!"

Gwen's old friend Suzette gasps. "Criminal!"

A few others hiss and boo.

Gwen notes that Lloyd's eyes are fixed on either the aligned profiles of the three women from the peace group or a certain title among the spines of her small collection of rare eighteenth century novels.

Joey is telling jokes, none of them very funny, his strong point being that he's such an attentive listener as he would be with guests on his talk show. Except that on camera he's apt to cut people off for "purposes of time." Joey Minetti. Celebrity. And although he is wearing his tortoise-shell glasses instead of his contacts, one of the women from the environmental group recognizes him and shakes his hand hard. "So good. So good," says she.

Now Lloyd is looking hard at Gwen, not just at her face. She has a defenseless-looking way of sitting on a chair arm, a little hunched. So narrow-shouldered, long legs loosely crossed, the big sleeves of her fashionable russet top float and flounce like her hair also floats and flounces. This week she had had her hair trimmed. Special for this night. And a little more blond streaking through the dark. Just in case another few grays have come. The shaped eyebrows and light makeup, slim hands cupping the top knee of her crossed legs, her little easy rocking from side to side. He beholds her. He doesn't even try to hide the fact that she bewitches him.

There's a flash. Friend Becky taking Polaroids randomly, passing the finished snapshots around for the squeals and cussings they cause.

Someone asks Lloyd if he paints or writes. ". . . or . . ." and they put out a hand for him to finish the sentence. But he just says he doesn't do any of that.

Gwen says she hopes that in the morning she can get some nice shots of those who are spending the night. Some of the old gang groans. Gwen tells Keith who is also a photographer how she's rediscovered black-and-white. "And I want to go with it awhile. Explore. Newspaper photography got me in a bad mood over black-and-white . . . but I'm at a stage in my work where . . . oh, I don't know . . . maturity, I guess . . ." Her fingers touch her lips and she laughs. Luminous, almost trilling. "Life looks different now. You want to hone down and make the photo answer some questions. It can't just titillate. It's got to account for itself."

Keith asks if she's familiar with Olive Pierce, Cedric Chatterley and Tonee Harbert who have done some really important work on people here in Maine.

She admits she's still mostly into landscapes, architecture, and sky. "And some of the stonework around here! It's really something!"

Fortune cookies go around.

"Who brought these?" someone asks resentfully as they squint at a fortune that must be unpromising.

"Me," Gwen confesses. "We all need to be prepared for the future."

Keith grunts.

To make a good example, Gwen picks a fortune cookie from the bowl. She munches on the cookie, puzzled by the message which reads *Imagination without education is like a bird without feet.* "They must mean a bird without *wings*," she says to herself testily. "I don't think they put a lot of thought into these."

There's the flash of Becky's Polaroid.

Beside Gwen, her old friend Denise reads aloud: "*Someone from your past will seek reconciliation.* Jeepers! I hope not." She looks up at Gwen. "Here! Let's switch 'em."

Becky is flapping a snapshot to dry it.

"Gwen! I really love your space!" hoots one of the old gang over by the kitchen doorway.

Gwen says, "I do, too!"

Two heated conversations happening on either side of the room. Heated agreement. Sexual harassment in the workplace and colleges is unacceptable. Global warming is unacceptable.

And somewhere in between is Becky's husband saying, "Well, it's also the light . . . well, the lack of it. The short days."

"Same here," says another.

With his well-projected television voice, Joey suggests, "Maybe what you both need are miners' caps . . . but made with the light to point at yourselves."

Now Joey remembers a great story about the old days . . . the old-days Keith and the old-days Bill. And from this, one story leads to another.

Gwen knows that Joey will probably sleep with her tonight. Like at the Connecticut house a year or so after Earl died, Joey was a kind of "stabilizer," she had told the others. He would bring food to bed and eat and talk and yes, listen. And his dog . . . the housekeepers *hated* that dog . . . a golden retriever who would scratch all night, his leg thwonking on the rug over there on Joey's side of the bed.

She is sure Joey has packed a couple of condoms in the gym bag he has with him tonight, there with his toothbrush and floss and battery shaver, Shower-to-Shower powder, deodorant, change of clothes . . . and maybe that copy of *Anna Karenina* he borrowed from her many months before. Joey is good about returning books.

Her precisely groomed dark eyes move over onto Lloyd.

Who could guess what the twinkle in *his* eyes means? It's not friendliness, she's sure of that.

She washes the remains of the fortune cookie down with the remains of her drink and the two sweetnesses clash, turn to bitter. She circulates the rooms with a full bottle of Bordeaux with which to refill all the glasses of the red wine drinkers. A few smokers have gone outside. The activists from Portland and the senator are now departing, their cars whining away into the night. Returning to the kitchen with the empty bottle, Gwen looks back to see Lloyd. His profile. He looks so meek, so hurt, so confused. He stares into the fire. Someone is dutifully exclaiming, "The mountains here are different from those in Vermont and New York . . . different from the Rockies . . . different from any I've seen. They're so close, aren't they? Almost cloistered. Cozy. Very nice."

Lloyd says yes it is nice.

Gwen grits her teeth. What's the matter with him? He is not a man who has trouble with words. On the phone he has *personality*. Why doesn't he just leave? Why does he keep sitting there if he's not enjoying the company? She realizes she's already begun to avoid him, hoping to chill him out. She doesn't check to see if there's anything he needs. There's nothing he needs. He's like a piece of the wall.

Finally he does leave. It is while she's upstairs with Suzette having a private heart-to-heart about how vicious Suzette's supervisor is at her company.

When Gwen returns to the living room, no Lloyd.

Her old friend Chuck Morse is giggling. "So, Gwen. That was one of your . . . your neighbors?"

"An Eskimo," says Joey.

Gwen says that he, the neighbor, is a grandfather of school-aged children. "Imagine that!"

"How quaint," Suzette says.

"Authentic," says Chuck Morse.

"Well," says Becky. "I thought he seemed shy . . . but nice."

"Pitiful," says Chuck Morse.

"I thought he was something Gwen got at an auction to go with the colonial decor . . . some chipped but still serviceable antique." This is Pam with her husky quiet dry wit.

There's snickers and guffaws.

"Jeee-zussss. Have some heart," Joey says evenly. "The guy's probably got a rough time of it. The lives that some of these kinds of people lead would bring you or I to our knees."

"You're right, Joey," Becky says solemnly. "We're just teasing Gwen."

Someone notices Nancy has fallen asleep curled up in one of the love seats.

Becky takes a snapshot of Nancy sleeping.

Becky gets snapshots of the lazy, satiated expressions of those in conversation about Washington, D.C., scandals, which turns into conversation about the hi-tech highways of the near future with their fast all-pervasive information . . . kind of scary, kind of wonderful . . . which somehow turns back into a conversation about sexual harassment in the workplace . . . then Suzette bursts into tears. Then there's some stories of the things Biff used to do . . . Biff being the nickname of a beloved member of the old gang who was killed in a car crash three years back.

Out in the kitchen Denise and Gwen talk in low tones before the other fireplace. Denise's eyes eddy with tears. "It's pretty amazing how we've all hung together over the years. We've all gone in so many directions and yet always manage to be friends. Things have changed a lot for me. I tell you, I just don't know my head from my ass sometimes. And the kids . . . they are like meter readers . . . they *know*. And they'll push me to my limits. My work has taken a backseat. There are times when I think it's all lost. It's so good to know I'll always see you all again. I can always count on you guys to know exactly what I'm trying to say. I just wish I could see your faces . . ." She blinks her eyes rapidly, tears on the lashes, "more often."

Gwen reaches to hug Denise and coos, "Yes, yes, yesssss . . . I know."

20 | Gwen eases down into the gentle rise and fall of the waterbed.

She tells Joey about Pam's review that was in the *Boston Globe* and he says he's not surprised, that Pam's work has so much power. They talk a little bit about the subject of women warriors.

When the light is out, they talk some more in the dark that is really pink and not dark at all. So good to hear Joey's voice from the next pillow . . . his trained broadcaster's voice, the calmingness of it, its lack of inflections . . . just the riveting razor-sharp consonants and disowned vowels, like a voice speaking from a realm where people are always in the same mood, a fine mood, are always polite . . . people in the pink . . . people who have never been encumbered by the terrible weight of life's whites, blacks, and grays.

21 | The following days are hectic . . . back and forth to Portland with her peace and environment work, back and forth to Augusta. A new friend in the legislature urged her to come up and see the exhibit of a Russian photographer whose images of the hurting environment burn with light. No sludge. No murkiness. No cliché Russian gloom. Just mesmerizing devilish light. And there was a lot of yakking. A little wine. A lot of driving. Through the short nights Gwen's dreams are splintered with voices and faces that turn into other faces, none familiar, but all of them flaccid with good will . . . and dedication.

On Thursday she is left alone with *it* . . . her work. She sits in the morris chair in her workroom, a stack of prints on her knee. What is the lie?

By midnight she is drunk. She dials the number with three nines.

No answer.

She calls at 12:15.

She calls at 12:30.

Again at 12:35.

She can't remember where she left her drink. In the bathroom? No, not there. She makes another drink, then can't find that for there's her pacing from window to window, staring out to the gauzy edge of the security light, at the black unseeable presence of the hills beyond. Where is he? Is he refusing to answer his phone? Is he unplugged? Ha! Another person who unplugs? Unlikely. And what if *everyone* unplugged? Ha! Well, would he be out? Of course he could be out . . . a party? . . . a lover? . . . an emergency? . . . a new night job? . . . where? . . . north, south, east, west?

She calls at 1:00 A.M. No answer.

She calls again and again throughout the night. No answer.

There's a smash of glass in the downstairs bathroom.

22 | Now in this day the clouds are tough as the organs of animals and the light on stone and shingle and spotty maple is stern. She shoots over a hundred exposures of Tri-X. She has no meals. She only drinks. Bourbon. At 8:10 in the evening she calls him. She sits at the breakfast bar with a bag of paper trash burning in the kitchen fireplace and nothing else for light.

He answers and his voice is hard and soft on the single syllable. "What?"

She informs him that the trees heaped in her driveway upset her. That she is becoming a nervous wreck over those trees. Her voice shakes.

He says, "I'll come over with a saw."

"Oh! I wasn't hinting that you come over for that. I realize it's a lot of work. I intend to pay you. I wasn't hinting at anything. I was . . . n't taking advantage of our friendship. I intend to pay you, Lloyd." All this on the shivering pauses and gulps of gentle weeping.

And on his end, a mountainous silence. After a while he says, "It's okay."

"But I wasn't really meaning to even bring up the subject of the trees! Oh . . . I don't know . . . it just popped out. It's not why I called you."

"It's okay. I'll just take care of it."

She asks, "Did you like my other friends?"

No answer.

The remains of the trash bag in the fireplace make barely a gleam now and there's a stink like something plastic must have gotten into the bag by error.

He says with a chuckle, "So . . . I overheard that you used to be Lois Lane in your other life."

She laughs out. She tosses a magazine toward the fireplace. It falls short. She slings another one. It lands right, but tumbles over and lays quietly in the dark. "I was a photographer, not a reporter."

"Well, I like to picture you as Lois Lane. Secret mission person."

She smiles. "I wish . . . you were here. Now."

He chuckles deeply. "I am. I am there now. I'm right there."

What a weird thing to say! It chills her. For an instant the ridiculous thought that maybe he is on the upstairs extension, stretched out on her bed. "You mean," she corrects him. "We are . . . together in our souls . . . our most inner beings connected."

He recites, *"Name me no names for my disease with uninforming breath; I tell you I am none of these, But homesick unto death."*

She jerks away from the phone receiver. She leans against the bar now, pushing the phone back hard against her ear. Who is he? She imagines herself pulled into the spiraling dark center of his body by his voice, by that remembered musty odor.

"When do you want the work done on your firewood, Gwen?"

"Now."

He laughs. "How about Tuesday? Till then I'm tied up with other work."

She says Tuesday will be fine. She can't bear to hang up.

He can't bear to hang up either, can he? He asks her about her day. She tells him how she climbed over ledges to get the best shots and once crawled up on top of her car! He seems impressed. His chuckling and mouth against the phone are warm, heating the plastic against her own ear and temple.

She asks about his day.

He tells about how he and his older son and father-in-law took a bull to Windham. He tells how he and his son argued over the volume of the radio. He tells how he gave in to his son. He tells how he and his father-in-law and the bull, not any one of them could relax. He tells how this was a bull who had spent the summer a bit wild in the woods and would have been sold earlier if he'd showed his face when the milk herd went. He tells her he can't seem to shake the stomach trouble. He tells her how he almost had a head-on with a guy passing on a hill and then a chips truck, which was passing four cars on a curve. Too much life, he tells her. Humanity is like a garbage can of maggots and the lid is quivering, getting ready to pop off. He tells this like prayer. She listens gratefully with bowed head.

23 | She reaches out into the pale crackling new day for the phone. "Hello?"

"You are home!" Phoebe sings out. And Gwen can hear the smoke slisk out from Phoebe's teeth and nose. And Gwen can *smell* the smoke! She wishes more than anything for a glass of water. And what if someone could see her now this hung over, her eyes looking like rotten fruit, her hair deflated, her tongue wooden against the wooden walls of her mouth . . . wooden lips . . . monstrous face.

Phoebe jokes that Gwen's darkroom must be soundproof.

Gwen insists that the phone is not usually plugged in.

Phoebe states that that is a really peculiar thing.

Gwen insists it goes with the job.

Phoebe chatters about the family. Gwen keeps one palm mashed against one eye. Some of the things Phoebe says make Gwen laugh. Phoebe tells all about a play Lawrence took her to off-Broadway . . . and then the high-school play she went to at Kristina's school, which was lots better. Phoebe wonders if Gwen has been okay, has she been happy? And Gwen tells her about everything . . . the peace and environment women, the trips to the cities . . . her change to black-and-white. And how she has fallen in love! Phoebe really perks up at this in-love news. "Who?" is the question. Gwen promises to send some photos. Phoebe asks if he is American. Gwen breaks into hysterics. What a delight, her mother! It is never so terrible once Phoebe reaches her. Nothing like she imagines between calls. The real Phoebe is so . . . so *cute*. Gwen tells Phoebe that Lloyd is a farmer. Phoebe is speechless. But then she snaps out of it, makes such cooing little delighted noises and presses for more details. And Gwen tells so much. About the spiritual bond. She rambles on and on, her ramblings accelerating . . . faster, faster . . . she can't believe she's doing this . . . and yet isn't this what she's always done? Isn't that what mothers are for? Gwen says she'll send the photos soon.

Phoebe asks if Gwen is planning to bring this man home for Thanksgiving.

Gwen says probably not. She says she'll send the photos. She'll send some beautiful photos.

Phoebe is so lighthearted.

When they say good-bye, Gwen lies with her long arms outstretched on the swinging swaying bed of water, eyes shut.

Late morning she makes oatmeal for breakfast.

24 It is Tuesday. He is here. Out there with the pile of trees. He works with a peavey and chain saw . . . and a gas wood splitter hauled in behind his truck.

She doesn't greet him. She is drunk. Not slightly drunk, nor smashed. She is perfectly drunk. She watches him be taken into the rhythm of his work, pulling white chunks from the splitter, giving them a toss, hefting another whole piece behind the ram, hefting, tossing, kicking, reaching for more . . . while above him the remaining trees are still a wall, and beyond that the barn which is a dark crown upon the blond fields, then the back fields rising up to the gray woods and the sky. There inside the house, she presses herself to an upstairs window and squeezes the shutter, advances, squeezes, advances. She hugs up to three different windows, forty exposures. Then once, after another change of film, he looks up to the window and sees her. He turns slowly away, adjusts his old felt crusher, reaches for another chunk of wood.

At noontime, he leaves his wood splitter and saw and gas cans and peavey there and moseys over to his truck. She watches the old truck braking down the drive, moving by mere inches, turning onto the road now, a left turn toward the east.

She changes out of her sandals into sneakers, throws on a jacket and warm cap, loads two cameras, hangs them from her shoulders, hurries up the field toward the ledges and woods above. At this angle, she settles in . . . waits, scooched against a boulder. When he returns she works the telescopic lens to bring him in at every possible degree of closeness. Only visible are these grand and swollen hills, the barn, the wood, the truck, and the tiny figure at work. No sign of the BMW behind the stack of trees.

In the darkroom, she holds her breath as each negative comes true in the washes, each contact sheet, each print. Wonderful. Wonderful. Wonderful.

25 No sleep. No need for sleep. She is racy. She fixes oatmeal for breakfast, tosses raisins into it. Coffee with cream. Looks like rain today. Maybe he won't come over. There's that odor of dampness, that reek of age . . . old house . . . old walls. It seems especially strong this morning. Yes. Very strong. When she washes out her bowl and spoon, the smell is so strong, she swears it comes from the faucet. She sniffs the bowl. No, it's not in the water. She dries her hands. So what we have now is a game of Hot and Cold. She moves away from the sink. The smell gets stronger, warmer. She moves toward the shedway door. It fades. She steps into the narrow hall that connects to the small back room. It seems to be worse in this hall.

The rain begins.

He doesn't show up this day.

She grieves.

26 The next day is bitter cold and gusty. He shows up to work on the wood. He climbs around on the remaining pile of trees, lopping off the limbs with the whining, jangling saw. He hee-haws certain four-foot lengths into a roll with the peavey or gives them a nudge with the heel of his boot. Strewn all about are four-foot lengths and stove lengths. The wind sets the mounds of sawdust into pale explosions around his pants legs.

The old house moans.

At noon, Lloyd seems to have vanished, but his truck is still out there. Gwen bundles up in a smock-waisted herringbone and her heaviest gloves. One camera. One lens.

She roams the yard awhile before catching sight of a spot of orange out across the little pond. Hardly the degree of orange that you see most men around here wearing in this season. *His* quilted vest a grimy washed-out orange. Not showy. Not a bother to the eyes. Its duty diminished.

He sits on a stone wall with his back to her. A long walk to reach him. She beholds the various ways he fills space, at varying degrees of distance. She squats every few yards to get a few shots, then trudges on up the last stretch of uneven fallow field.

When she arrives, his crusher is so low over his eyes, seems he doesn't see her. He is drinking coffee from a Thermos, looking down over a steep wooded embankment to a dry streambed. Under the vest, he wears about four shirts, all their collars wobbed together at his neck. His face and neck are again a little fatter than she pictures while on the phone with him, and the great brown, tawny, and gray falls of his moustache and short peltlike beard are yes . . . no . . . yes . . . unbearably beautiful . . . her hand tightens on the camera. This motion of her hand catches his eye.

She says, "Hi."

He says, "Hi."

She settles on the wall beside him facing the dark ravine. She crosses her legs, swings a foot. This morning she fixed her streaked blond and brown willowy hair into a frothy topknot with a peach-colored silk scarf. Her hair jounces and her foot swings.

He holds the plastic Thermos cup out to her.

She stares at it too long.

He starts to draw it back to himself, but her hand folds around it and his hand lets go.

She takes a few swallows. Coffee that is heavy with cream and not especially hot. Her breath explodes white around the cup as she drinks.

They both stare down at the ravine.

He pulls off his crusher, pushes his hand into his hair.

The woods are dark here even with the leaves down . . . pine and hemlock, some married, trunks twisted together into obliging figures as if from a single root. Boughs toss and whistle above, while down here on the rock wall, there is peace.

Gwen asks, "Would you mind if I photographed you here?"

He keeps his eyes down, shrugs. Places his crusher on the wall beside him. "Break your camera."

She laughs though it is such an old and silly line.

He keeps his eyes down, his strange eyes, one brown and spotty, one green . . . how strange, too, his shyness, when on the phone he is so bold. She might doubt he's the same guy, but for the voice . . . that gritty soft rasp that makes every conversation with him a kind of sanctification.

Gwen puts the cup back into his hand.

He looks down into the cup.

She stands and moves around him, setting her camera, checking the light. Something sticky about her light meter today. She checks shadows and reflections. The treetops hiss and boil. Ragged bits of punk and live limb smack to earth close by. Nothing stays in place. She's crazy to expect anything good to come from this furious windy contest with nature.

"These are going to be very close shots," she tells him.

His shoulders shift. He finishes with the coffee. His eyes meet hers before she raises the camera. By the time the shutter snaps, his eyes are down on the cup in his hands again. She edges back and forth, shooting up the rest of the film. She loads again, asks, "Do you mind this?"

He shrugs and smiles easily. "It's okay."

Many of the frames will show the house below . . . house dinky, while in the foreground, cup in his hands, eyes on the cup, Lloyd Barrington is a titan. But there are profiles of him that don't include the house. In these he seems monkish, his frozen breath rimming his brown hair, a creature so resolved in this frugality of light.

When she is finished, she says, "Thank you. Thank you so much. I'll make you up some prints of the best ones." Finally reaching down, the wind tugs some of her curly topknot across her eyes.

He says, "You're welcome" softly. And he smiles.

27 | It is not even a memory anymore. It is more like a motion in the corner of her eye. Life here and now takes on the shape of it, the mystery.

Gwen had moved toward the toaster. It had happened that night before. The blood. She had gone to the back hall and the box was there. She had managed to get the whole box to her room without getting caught by the others. She had managed everything. It had all gone smoothly.

Her father is chewing, lost in his fine print, his eyes running along the page. But Phoebe is smiling such a smile! Not showing her teeth at all. Not a grin. Just a little twisted bud of a smile, a shriek of red lipstick, screaming eyes on the good doctor, savior of lives.

Gwen carries her plate of toast to the table.

Phoebe suddenly seems to be working against a sharp pain, the smile and her fluttering eyes tightening down against the pain. "What stinks?"

William looks up from his reading. "What?" He sniffs in one direction, then another. "I don't know. I don't seem to smell anything."

"Oh, yes," Phoebe insists, smiling more hugely within the hard red knot of her mouth. "It's pretty strong and getting stronger. Ikk!" She holds her nose. "I'll have to get out the air freshener," she says tiredly.

William looks up at the daughter, Gwen. "Do *you* smell anything?"

Gwen shrugs.

William shrugs.

Phoebe is up lightly on her feet, headed for the cupboard where the air fresheners stand, snatches the nearest can. Colonial Spice. She sprays and sprays and sprays. The air is turning yellow even as she sprays, turning to memory.

28 | As it so happens, the carpenters and Lloyd are all here on Friday, the dooryard full of vehicles, the wail and shrill of every sort of saw and rotor. The cats gallop about, energized and wicked.

She decides against shooting today. She has plenty of work in the darkroom. The close-ups of him in the woods come out strange. In some it seems his darker eye is an empty socket . . . in others it's a kind of otherworldly eye, wider, and frighteningly perceptive. There are fifteen of these where he is staring directly into the camera! And yet as she had snapped the shutter, wasn't he looking down at his cup?

And those with his eyes on the cup, the house sprawling in the background could have been so beautiful, had she set the lens right. Or was it the wind?

"Break your camera," he'd said and she had laughed.

She swears that with most of those frames she had set both aperture and lens perfectly and shot in the quiet between gusts of wind. She *swears* this. But how crazy and dazed she was that afternoon. How can you trust your memory to be lucid when that "present time" wasn't?

She selects a few contacts to work with. To compensate for the over- and underexposures, she dodges and burns and winds up with three hauntingly beautiful prints of Lloyd and the house . . . and one of him in profile. She works up an eight-by-ten of each and several five-by-sevens, all on glossy. Every hair of his head and beard, each eyelash . . . every thread of the pale quilted hunting vest . . . every droplet of frozen breath . . . is hers to keep.

She makes up a packet of five-by-sevens and writes out her mother's name and address on the label.

Now she works up a few that she took from the windows. He wears a helmet with ear protection. That hunch of his body, his slight squat with the heavy saw, his kicking away lengths of wood with his heel, then laying a measuring rod down as he backs along that topmost tree, a pale-skin beech, precariously crisscrossing another . . . this is all hers to keep.

At noon, the noise of saws and hammers dies.

Gwen hurries down and finds the carpenters' vehicles are gone. The cats stride around the small back bedroom, checking out this latest set of developments.

Lloyd Barrington eats a sandwich in his truck, running the motor for warmth. He stares into the open barn doorway.

With nothing over her thin jersey and swishy skirt, arms folded across her narrow chest to warm her, she goes out to invite him in for tea, then dashes back in ahead of him to fill the kettle.

Now he is again here inside this house!

He stands in the middle of the kitchen and again she's surprised that his legs are shorter than she imagines on the phone. He is not at all tall but a medium-sized man. Now his reticence again irritates her.

"You want Red Rose or herbal?" she asks a bit snappishly.

"Red Rose." He sees her ears are pierced. He sees her butter-color jersey with satin appliqué bodice. But now his eyes drop away.

She points out the breakfast bar. "Have a seat."

He does. And once again, he studies the Blue Willows and as he does, there's something so sly about his body.

The Blue Willows are not valuable. Most of them chipped. They were among the few things the Putnams hadn't thrown out when they cleaned the place up. She herself would not have kept them if something in her intuition hadn't forced her hand. Like living creatures, the Blue Willows had pleaded for mercy! And now in the cherrywood cabinet, the old plates and cups and saucers and one broad platter are the soul of the kitchen . . . the little blue rugs, blue bottles, and tapestries, and all the blue tilework around the sink and bar . . . everything here now to accommodate those old dishes. And some days, there from that near window, there is a consummate blue light.

She prepares his tea.

He raises a leg to get astraddle one of the bar stools. Lays his hat . . . today a brimmed red-and-black checked wool . . . on the stool to the right. On the lefthand stool, a Siamese appears, merowling loudly, stretches a paw out to hook the man's sleeve.

"Stop that, Apollo!" Gwen scolds.

"It's okay," says Lloyd.

"Siamese cats are aggressive," she sighs.

"It's okay."

He is so accommodating, so meek, so without fight. She imagines herself putting cayenne pepper in his tea . . . a chunky dose. She sees herself saying a cruel thing.

She sets the tea before him. A peach print mug out of a set she brought from Connecticut.

He says, thank you. He smiles. His teeth are stained. She wants to climb into that smile and, as small as Tinkerbell, melt in that dark beginning. No. She wants to kick his teeth. She sees the sun move softly over the shoulder of his plaid shirt and hunting vest and his hair. A few hairs among the dark brown are red. Under each eye are the V-shaped gathers of skin most men in their forties have, especially when the sun strikes his face from the periphery of a darkish room.

She says, "Would you mind if I bothered you for a few more pictures?"

"That camera still work?"

She doesn't laugh. For it is more frightening than funny now. "Yes. It still works."

She hurries up the stairs to collect her cameras, leaving him alone in the kitchen. Something about his being alone there bothers her. For it seems that his presence there is expanding, spilling out of itself, crawling, climbing, covering the walls.

She stumbles around her workroom, drunk, though she has had no drink today. She returns with a wide-angle lens and a portrait lens. She leans back against the living room wall and snaps several frames showing the two open doors with the kitchen beyond . . . then once she's in the kitchen, she takes another three . . . this dark-edged quiet kitchen with a figure drinking from a cup in the sun . . . and what's that?!! . . . a cat on the bar drinking from her cup! "Apollo! Get out of my tea! Lloyd, please just shoo him off the bar."

Lloyd stands, reaches for the cat.

Gwen strolls around and around, whisking off a few more shots with the wide-angle.

Now she settles across from him and places both cameras on the bar.

The sun is sliding away. Lloyd's hair and shoulder and forearms no longer rage with light. It has all gone to ashiness.

With her hands folded on the bar, she shuts her eyes and thinks. She hears him swallow. She *hates* the sound. She opens her eyes, her eyes with their most dark, unfriendly questions. "Would it be uncomfortable for you if I took some *quite* close?"

His eyes slide away to the darkest part of the kitchen . . . a cat edging along the mopboard there. He says, "You are like a dentist."

She laughs. "Yes . . . it's kind of like that, isn't it?"

She leans toward him with the light meter, clucks to herself happily, leans back. Now moving in close again with the camera, she gives the lens a delicate twist, and with steady hands snaps several pictures of his face, and the throat with wobbed-up collars. His face. Half his face. His dark uncanny eye. Closer. The eye. What does it see? When he leaves here, will the eye remain and surround this house?

On the last exposure of each film, she lays that camera aside. Now she drinks from the tea that the cat had tasted. She has trouble looking into Lloyd's face now. She sneaks glimpses when he's looking out the window or down at his hands. And when she is up pulling out the dishwasher drawer to find a certain plate for Oreos, she knows *he* stares at *her*.

When he stands to go back out to his work, she wants to cry, "No! How dangerous those crisscrossed logs are! And your truck . . . it looks held together with glue! Stay! Stay! Stay!" And yet, he is making her feel frightened. With him in this house, she's in danger. The house . . . it is coming alive . . . even now, it is starting to put off that sweet damp stink! . . . and *this* is a sunny day! Not a drop of rainy dampness in the air!

He goes back to work. And she kind of roams the big house, distractedly . . . sitting, standing, rearranging things out of place . . . and for her cats she has sweet talk. In time, Lloyd leaves for the day. What is that thing he's left out by the barn door . . . what is it? . . . not a tool for cutting and splitting firewood. It looks like some kind of augur.

Now she turns, hugging herself with her long arms and sees there is something standing against the cabinet of Blue Willows. A worn shorthandled broom . . . that broom she has seen poked into the pipe that's wired to the wooden dump body of his truck. He wasn't carrying that broom when he came in for tea! She feels violated. She feels good. She eats a good meal, two helpings. She goes to bed early. She is buried alive by a dreamless sleep.

29 | Four o'clock in the morning she dials the number. He answers brightly as though he were already up and ready for his day. For sure, he is.

She asks, "What are you wearing?"

He laughs.

"What are you doing, Lloyd?"

"Reading."

"What kind of things do you read?"

"A spy getting ready to crack Moscow."

How sweet. It's just what she expected. So easy to picture him this way. "Where is your wife?" She bunches her pillow, tries to get comfortable, but there's no comfort.

582

"Her folks take care of her. She has a disability. Big family there . . . lotta sisters . . . twenty-four-hour surveillance . . ." He chuckles to himself. Some private joke.

"What are you wearing?"

"Everything. Nothing good shows." He chuckles.

"If you were here, I'd do anything for you," says she.

"Zat right?"

"I'm getting crazy."

He says, "I'm trying to remember if we ever met back when you used to live over on Weber Road."

"We never mixed."

"Therefore you never existed," says he.

She covers her face with her free hand. "I *existed*. I was skinny and ugly."

"I was fat and eccentric."

"We may have seen each other as we passed each other riding with our parents," she says, sniffing, wiping both eyes with the cuff of the sheet.

"We are about the same age."

"Yes . . . we saw the same moon . . ." She sighs.

"We sweated out the same summers. Got stuck in the same blizzards. Remember the blizzard of fifty-eight?"

"Not really. But my mother has pictures of us all sitting on various snow bankings, squinting into the sun. We were a family of terrific squinters."

"My uncle . . . Walty . . . he made the best snowmen. It was like he carved them out of marble. A lot of detail."

"What house were you living in, Lloyd? Was it over near where you are living now?"

He is quiet a moment. "The house I grew up in no longer exists."

"I'm sorry."

He snorts.

"Please don't laugh at me."

"Okay. I won't."

"I wish you were here. I'd give anything for you to be here, for you to love me. You would be safe here."

"Safe?"

"Yes. You wouldn't have to do so much of . . . that murderous kind of work."

He grunts. "Then who would cut our firewood?"

"We'd hire someone else!"

"Gwen . . . listen . . . *you* are not safe." His voice accentuates a kind of threat.

She feels the ice. From the walls the odor slides in strata toward her bed that is washed in pinkish security lamplight. She slams the receiver down. Unplugs. Outraged.

But then at dawn, he is back at the woodpile again.

She dresses for her trip to Portland where she'll work with the women of the Peace Campaign. As she passes him on her way to her car, he's on the tailgate of his truck filing his saw. The dump body of the truck is high, so his feet dangle. He is hatless, for his orange hard hat is over on the woodpile, slung over an upright chunk of oak. But he tips a pretend cap to her. Chivalrous.

30 When she returns home before evening, she finds all is well. No more horizontal trees. The last of them are sawed into a heap of two-foot lengths. Small limbs heaped into the dump body of Lloyd's truck, and in meticulous brush piles down near the culvert. And in the barn, the split wood is tiered handsomely, just as she has expected.

But in the kitchen, on the floor beside the china closet, added to the short-handled broom, are a pile of heavy chains, a can of creosote, an old rifle. And on the breakfast bar, folded with care, is a stained delapidated quilt. From this quilt, THE SMELL pours, the sweet taunting dampness. And matching it, there's that which emanates from the walls . . . especially in the narrow back hall. She stands there in her coat, cats bashing her legs. Cats crying, *Merrowl! Merrowl! Merrrrowwwwwwwlll!*

31 For many days, no Lloyd. There are gray days with skies like steel. A spit of snow. And then abruptly, deep snow. And the whole house reeks of its sweet fearsome walls, especially in the back hall. And then a week of melting snow. Days of distractions. Her new friends in Augusta put so many demands on her. So much yet to be done to save the air, save the water, save the endangered species, stop the bombs. There are meetings, calls, little get-togethers at the homes of legislators and lunch with senators. Her head whirrs with this good work.

She gets home just at dark on Wednesday and Lloyd's truck is in the yard. He has cleaned up the last of the firewood , , , but what is this?!! . . . this!! . . . this other vehicle parked alongside the barn, a wheel high on a patch of unmelted snow. The thing's not even registered.

She doesn't question it.

32 | Even after dark, he's still out there in the barn . . . some sort of dull light spreading in an oily way from the wide-open doors.

She throws a jacket over her shoulders and steps out through the series of pantryway and shed doors, finds him on his knees, fiddling with some sort of . . . of pump or motor . . . whatever. He has installed an incandescent bulb which hangs directly over his work.

She asks him to come in. "Please," she insists. "I want you to see something."

He enters the house.

He climbs the narrow attic stairs ahead of her. She says, "Turn right at the top. It's that door with the statice wreath."

Her photos are everywhere in this slant-ceilinged well-lighted room. Photos tacked to homosote partitions. Photos in boxes and curly-edged piles. While some of this is her recent work, most are framed photos from her old exhibits . . . an older theme, nothing familiar to this place and time.

The black-and-whites of this house and Lloyd Barrington are nowhere to be seen.

Torn up or burned in a rage? Or quietly hidden?

A couple of large color prints are matted behind glass on the gable wall. Some matted without glass. The colors are muted and grainy so they seem black-and-white at first glance. Lloyd stares at the largest framed photo across the worktable.

This is a photo of his heart, his life . . . that hill behind the house, prickly, curvaceous fields, spires of its dark firs, rock wall . . . earth pale, skies darkened by a rust-colored storm. The sun in the east is a glob of palest lemon yellow. Colors that look like they are done in crayon with the lightest pressure . . . hand of a hurt child . . . crabbed and hesitant. He grips his crusher hat to his chest. His eyes ease over onto other prints, variations of one naked apple tree with splotches and sparkles beneath which are caused by certain light striking certain liquids on certain leaves of grass. And here and there is a dangling apple, almost black against the bark of the thick-trunked tree, and the sky black, while the grasses whipped by wind are a ghostly lavender mixed in a watery blood red.

He has nothing to say.

Down in the kitchen he refuses her offer for a snack or a mixed drink or tea. "Anything," says she. "Water?"

"Naw," says he. But he doesn't leave, just hangs around looking at things, feeling this or that, squatting to rub the cats' heads. Now and then he looks over at Gwen, but then he looks away.

She asks, "So . . . what *do* you think of my work?"

A man with so much moustache and beard has all gesture in the eyes. He looks at her and says, "It's nice."

She blinks.

He looks away.

She crosses the room to the little antique desk and twists the switch to the glass-shade lamp. Removes an envelope from a basket. "Here you go!" she says brightly. "The check for . . . the . . . the trees."

He opens his hand for it. Folds the envelope down small. "Even-steven," he says.

33 He whispers this. *"I hate and I love. Perhaps you ask why I do so. I do not know, but I feel it, and I am in torment."*

He shuts his eyes and turns onto his side. The darkness here at his trailer, without such things as security lamps, is complete and kind.

There are so many old sayings of the old sayers, the old truly wise ones who have said it all. He has memorized so much. There is always an occasion. Funny how one will pop into mind when perhaps he only lives to relive the sorrows of past men. Alone here to whisper to himself, another word would only choke him.

34 In the passing days, it seems the smell from the hallway is actually twinged with the smell of death. How disturbing. She mentions it to friends long distance. The old gang. The old gang suggests she shouldn't be up there alone "on the frozen tundra" anyway. Denise says maybe it's a dead rat. Joey throws out the Big Foot possibility. According to Big Foot trivia, Big Foot sightings are always accompanied by a tremendously ripe smell. She laughs. Joey. So funny. She calls everyone for their opinion, even some of her new friends.

And she calls the carpenters. Bill says, if it's a dead rat, she must also have "lotsa live rats." He suggests she set out poison. The other carpenter, Pete, says not to worry. It is probably a dead red squirrel. In time the smell will fade.

While these men are there on Friday to finish the ceiling in the little back bedroom, she asks if they would would please tear open the hallway wall.

Standing in the hall, Bill says, "I don't seem to smell it."

She says, "It's worse at times. Then at times it fades."

He says, "I smell . . . you know . . . that old house kind of smell . . . but that's not a dead smell. It's just a kind of woody smell. Campy."

"Yeah, campy," agrees the other carpenter. "In the summer you probably get it worse."

"It's not summer," Gwen says impatiently.

So after lunchtime, they take wrecking bars and begin prying and smashing away the wall that the Putnams had finished so lovingly in new Sheetrock and antique wainscoting of wide pine boards from some other old house.

Hugging herself, her narrow shoulders a bit hunched, Gwen watches. Nails shriek. The Sheetrock pops and crumbles.

Wide-eyed cats circulate.

What they find behind the wall is an old cupboard painted white and an inner wall of plaster painted with a dark olive color that was popular in the 1950s. Bill explains, "Looks like whoever renovated here just wanted a deeper partition here to go flush with the closet behind that doorway. They just left all this as it 'twas underneath."

She can smell it . . . what is it? Sweet. Death? Life? Her head pounds.

She steps up to the little cupboard as Bill is pulling the doors of it open. The shelves are loaded. Cans. Jars. Tin boxes. Shoe boxes. Some empty. Jar of fishhooks. Jar with a piece of candle. Scissors. Christmas cards. Hairpins. Hat pins. A photo.

"What's that?" Gwen starts to grab the photo.

Bill puts it in her hand.

The photo trembles with life in Gwen's hands. There stands a young beardless man, dark-haired. Lloyd.

"Well," says Bill cheerfully. "No rats. Not even a mouse nest. No sign of any rodents."

"Campy," says the other carpenter. "You want this wall put back exactly like it was, Mrs. Doyle?"

Gwen's voice kind of squeaks as she wonders, "This is him, isn't it? Lloyd Barrington. The man who has been doing my firewood."

Bill and Pete both lean in to get a good look.

Bill chuckles. "How can that be Lloyd? Look at the plate on that old Dodge. It's only got a letter and three digits on it. Musta been in the late thirties, early forties. That would make Lloyd pretty old. Seventy at least."

She tips the photo toward better light. "Well, then . . . it's *some-body . . .*"

"Yeah, probably his father." Bill leans in again and squints at the photo. "I never actually knew him."

"Well," says Pete. "We did. And I'd say that's Ed . . . or, you know . . . one of those others. See the eyes. Yeah . . . I'd say that's Ed. No big deal. The good news is there's nothing in this wall that's . . . you know . . . gooshy." He stands back, pushes some Sheetrock clumps around with the toe of his work boot. "Just a false alarm." He snickers.

Gwen blinks. "But don't you think it's odd there's a picture of Lloyd Barrington's father in this wall? Or is it just because everyone in this town is so related . . . that it . . . just all . . . crisscrosses." She sounds jokey, but her dark eyes are humorless.

"How much did you look at your deed, Mrs. Doyle?"

Gwen lowers the photo. Both Pete and Bill are chuckling. Bill says, "This was Barrington's house."

"No, it was not!" Gwen snaps. "There was no Barrington on that deed!"

"Oh, well. Maybe it 'twas in Fogg's name. Come to think of it . . . since the others were Foggs."

"Foggs, yes," says Gwen.

"Well," says Pete. "You got Foggs. You got Barringtons. Anyway, believe me, I've known this place for years, known Ed, and this was their place. And Lloyd always lived here."

"I see," says Gwen, smiling a chilly smile. "Of course. Well . . ."

Pete interrupts. "While we're on the subject . . . you might've already heard . . . about Barrington being a little shady." He doesn't get a response from Gwen so he turns to Bill. "You heard that, didn't you? Him and some of that Turnbull bunch and some others . . . some ring of some kind. Not drugs. Maybe drugs. Who knows? I just heard it was some-thing."

Bill says, "Yeah, I heard something." He looks at Gwen. "It was that they give some people a hard time."

Pete nods.

Bill looks to the left and right quickly, then back to Gwen's face. "You might want to keep your eye on any valuables. Barrington's quite a fox."

"Well, yes!" says Gwen almost cheerily, almost in song. "Thank you! Thank you for helping me with this. I really appreciate it." She turns away.

"We can re-Sheetrock this, but not till . . . oh . . . probably Tuesday."

"Yes, fine."

"I smell that smell now," Bill says. "It's dampness, I'd say. You got wetness in the cellar, Mrs. Doyle?"

"I don't think so."

"Want us to check the sills out? Wetness can cause all kinds of trouble. Ants . . . dry rot . . . it would only take a minute to check."

"If you wouldn't mind. I'd appreciate it."

Pete says, "It's just these old places . . . you know . . . it's that way. I like the smell myself. Reminds me of my uncle's old place up to Nor-ridgewock. It's all a matter of what you like. Some like it. Some don't."

35 | A letter from Phoebe. Pink scalloped envelope. Gwen doesn't open it immediately. She spends the day guessing what Phoebe has to say.

36 | Weeks pass. It's a cold winter. But little snow. Gwen tells the carpenters she prefers to have them wait till spring to complete the work. And she's having some reservations about the idea of building the addition. She really has enough space already.

When she dials the number with three nines, there's never an answer. Sometimes she can go for a week without trying. Some nights she tries every fifteen minutes all the night through.

She keeps the photo handy . . . the one the carpenters found that might be Lloyd's father. At times she feels more attracted to the father, Edmund, than to Lloyd. Edmund with that cocky set of the mouth, the motley light of trees on his folded arms.

She works with zest on the black-and-whites of Lloyd and the house, enlargements and bigger enlargements. With paper that isn't glossy, she applies watercolors . . . no crayons . . . light as a fairy's touch . . . colors that are not of the natural world.

Meanwhile more magic out in the real yard. More things appear. Another old car with no doors. A row of rimless tires, leaning like dominoes. Four drums. Industrial pails . . . gray and blue and white. In the barn, tools she has no name for. Used and unused rolls of flagging tape. Fuzzy turquoise work gloves, dirty on the palms. But Gwen never sees Lloyd nor his hand in these deliveries. Sometimes, while outside, she'll pull off her gloves and lay a hand on the cold crusty lid of a drum. And she photographs the drum. To her collection she adds poster-sized prints of the drums. In real life they are an industrial gray, but when she is done . . . the landscape is gray, the drums yellow, as obliterating as four suns.

Months pass. Gwen does some work with another women's group, these concerned with reproductive choice. There's a march planned and she helps with the mailings and meets more people, many of them artists, and many of these photographers. They are fine and successful photographers and the conversations they have always inspire her. She puts in long hours in her darkroom. Through the winter she does nearly fifty 11 × 14s and poster-sized prints from the shots of Lloyd in the kitchen . . . all manipulated and touched up in sepias and blues. These prints are the best. Splotchy and eerie, that warm and cold look of light. One day she brings them to Portland to show her new friends of the prochoice committee. There's a hush as the women stand around, while Gwen, wearing white cotton gloves so as not to mar the surfaces, picks the prints up one by one to view.

37 | A letter every day from Phoebe. Thick cream vellum monogrammed in navy . . . P.R.C.

Phoebe's letters pile up. Here's a day in which two arrive.

Must have run out of the cream vellum. Now lilac . . . a chain of them . . . stretching out from one to the next. "Dear Gwen . . ." "Dear Gwen . . ." "Dear Gwen . . ."

38 | The winter and early spring are lost to time.
T-shirt weather, the locals call it.

But . . . Tennis weather! Sailing weather! These are the ways in which Gwen's friends describe it.

She wears a silk kimono . . . a pattern of twisted trees and rising suns, silver against cream and plum and black. Pleat-waisted pale rose pants. And Birkenstocks. Her hair has a new shorter sharper-angled cut. Dyed back to her true dark brown . . . just minus the few grays. Her woven handbag is old. Her favorite. Turning from locking up her car, she has a distracted hurry-up stride, quickly passing into the shadow of the IGA entrance. She makes her few purchases quickly, then moves through the checkout, writing her check in her tight crabbed handwriting.

It's the first time she's seen his real-life face in months. Strange how this actual face beyond the glass doors seems so softly deteriorated, as if he were in another century into which she can't call to him. But he gets closer and closer. He wears sneakers and ratty work clothes. A billed blue cap that reads: MACHINISTS UNION and features a large gear. The supermarket door purrs open for him but she is already out the OUT door that has opened and now squeezes shut behind her. When their eyes had met, he had tipped his visored cap, but that was it.

Outside in the heavy odorous heat of near noon, she is agitated to a wildness.

She looks out across the lot and sees that someone is waiting in the cab of his old truck. Who is it? One of his cohorts in the ring of outlaws the carpenters told of? Or his father-in-law? Or a child? His wife? *Them*. His people. Any or all. They are his. Not hers. They have nothing to do with her life, her being.

She turns back and reenters the store, the air-conditioned cool. But Lloyd has disappeared already.

Where? She rushes down the first aisle, then strides along parallel with the meat cases, glimpsing down each near-empty stretch of aisle. She finds him in PET FOODS. Loading a wagon with what must already be thirty cans of Alpo. His T-shirt isn't really black, but a dark green wetted to black from the heat and his unimaginably unendurable lifting, pushing, swinging, squatting, pitching, and bearing-down backbreaking work. Upon realizing she's approaching, he snatches off his cap and his hair is drenched into dark ribbons and cowlicks.

"I've been meaning to call you," she says pleasantly, shifting her small bag of groceries.

A young woman with a thick-legged baby passes, stops to bend for a few cans of cat tuna just beyond Lloyd's cart.

Lloyd's eyes flick over the length of Gwen. He slaps his cap back on. His bare arms are browned, sticky-looking, gritty. Along the protruding arteries there's darkness like shadows, but it's really grime, while his nails are yellowy like feldspar, thick, nothing like you'd trim with clippers, more like a substance that has to be chipped away. His moustache doesn't flicker. No smile. No hello. But this is not a dismissal. His expression is changing slowly to kindliness, a welcome.

Gwen steps closer, clasps her long fingers around the mesh of his grocery cart.

The young woman with the baby wheels farther up the aisle, stops again, then moves on, disappears.

Now an old man passes with a carry-basket. He is hunched and weak-shouldered but his bare arms are as robust as Lloyd's. The old man studies every shelf as if on a search for something lost.

Gwen says, "I need someone to come over and do a few odd jobs . . . yard work mostly. Some dead tree limbs that I'm afraid might hurt someone if they break off in a wind. They could hit someone on the head or smash a windshield. It has to be someone who can get up into a tree and do that kind of thing. And there's some little trees up back that need to be cut down. Why that's happening . . . is . . . someone told me the fields need to be mowed . . . like with a tractor. At least once every other year is what I was told." She watches him hard as she names each thing, watches his eyes that are turned away from her now as he imagines the house and its yards and fields and woods. "And I have an idea. Swings. Out on that big maple. Some of my friends have children. A swing is nice, don't you think?"

"Swings . . . always a big hit," he agrees in his soft dark eddying voice. And his eyes flick over her again and again between glimpses of the far end of the empty aisle.

"I was thinking one could be painted red, one yellow, one blue. Crayon colors," she says with a smile. Her smile is suspended in this fluorescent brightness, this humming cool.

"Are these swings for short-legged kids or long-legged kids?" he asks.

"Three heights!" She speaks breathlessly. "In fact, I'd like one high enough for me. It would be a kind of healing to go out and sit under that old tree some evenings this summer . . . to read . . . or meditate . . . or to . . . to *swing*."

His eyes slide to her hand gripping his grocery cart, then up the front of her silk kimono. "Okay," says he.

"When?" Urgency.

"Real soon," says he.

She tries to back up now, but can't seem to let go of the cart. She flushes. "Well . . ."

He doesn't take hold of his cart in a dismissive gesture. He just stands there waiting. Docile. Sweet. And yet, she doesn't doubt one bit what people say . . . she knows within every alerted intuitive nerve that he is, yes . . . a fox . . . yes, going to steal from her . . . or worse . . .

Now she sees his jaw move slightly with the tobacco. She imagines what that would be like. To be crushed by his spaced yellowy teeth, warmed and ruined by his saliva. She imagines all the ways.

39 | Having expected a call from a gallery in New York while she was out for the groceries, Gwen had plugged in the answering machine.

But the tape overflows with Phoebe's smoky voice. "Eleven-fifteen. Trying to reach you." Click. Click.

"Eleven-thirty-five. Trying to reach you." Click. Click.

"Twelve-ten. *Tryingggg.*" Click. Click.

"Twelve-forty-five. GWENNNNNNN. Pleeeez call when you can. Are you really there? Come on, Gwen. Just pick up. Okay. Okay. I'll try again." Click. Click.

"One-twenty. Can't reach you. Yoooo hoooo! Gwennnnnn!" Click. Click.

40 | She steps out from her darkroom to find the rest of the house dark, too. Where did the time go? She stares into the pinkish security light at one window, that unyielding glow. But then as she strides through the house, snapping on a few table lamps, she hums. Sweat shirt pushed to her elbows. Her hair gathered up into a tiny dark tuft on top of her head. She is thrilled with her latest work. All day has been HIGH VOLTAGE. The colors of the world and universe had exploded from her hands. She had only to stand there and stare at Lloyd Barrington's face slowly forming in the chemicals and all that must be done was racing ahead of her. She is exhausted now. Eleven-thirty-four P.M.

Apollo and Athena have knocked two rows of books from the hallway shelves. Now Athena claws into the new wainscoting. "Stop that!" Gwen scolds. "I'm not going to feed you faster when you act that way if that's what you think you're doing. Maybe I'll go slower! See!" She moves in slow motion to the kitchen, clamps the can opener to the can in slow motion. The can opener's whirr gets the cats into a worse frenzy. They writhe tight as pythons around her legs. They yowl. Gwen stumbles to get out two plates. Athena clamps onto one of Gwen's legs and bites hard.

"Stop!" Gwen shakes the cat from her leg. She sets out the plates with distance between so they won't dish-switch. She pours herself just one small celebration drink. Just a pretty little rosé . . . nothing serious. She snaps off the lights, heads up to bed, stopping in the upstairs bath to shower and change.

In the bedroom there is the queer security light pouring in at every window. And there on the little wheaten love seat with the white polar bears and striped pillows, there's a man's head and shoulders. Gwen strikes the wall switch. Two leaded glass wall lamps come to life. It is, of course, Lloyd Barrington. Billed advertisement cap dangling from one hand.

She stands there in her nightshirt, which has a print of cartoon Pogos. In this soft-edged light, she looks like a tall skinny kid. "How did you get up here!" she cries. "Every door is locked!"

He looks down at his hands, fingering the cap's little adjustable strap. He looks sheepish. He looks sorry. He looks sweet.

"I have the phone number of the State Police memorized," she hisses. "In fact, I memorized it since I first heard about your reputation. I've been expecting to need their services."

He turns the cap in his hands, raises his face, the brown-spotted gentle eye and yes . . . that green eye . . . pale and scrutinizing as the eye of a fox. He says, "My father was born in this room."

She places the glass of rosé on the nearest nightstand and rubs her face hard, all the Pogos of her nightshirt rippling and jittering.

"My father *died* in this room, too. Right about there." He jerks a thumb toward the far edge of the king-sized waterbed. "My father was sixty-four when he died. He was a strong son-of-a-bitch. Could crush a Revereware saucepan in one hand. Could make a field rise green and high as your chest. Could make cattle fat. Treated 'em good. And kept 'em clean. He was clean . . . clean inside and out." He narrows his eyes on her. "He did right. But his abilities are no longer the fashion. How is it you goddam white yuppie trash people say it? An unfortunate thing. But part of progress. He fell by the wayside. Well, the wayside seemed to kinda kill him, you know? Mrs. Doyle . . . he shrank and he died there . . . at the wayside."

Gwen is still rubbing her face hard, but slow, like a face massage.

He says, "So, I see you made this all one room. That over there used to be a wall and beyond that, my room."

She drops her hands, face left looking chafed . . . and angry. "Why am I feeling guilty? I didn't steal this house. I bought it!"

"There's many, many kinds of stealing."

"Your family owed back taxes for twelve years . . . that's not anything I had to do with. The *Town* took the house."

"Seeing as you are from a class of people equipped with more ways to effect laws, what have you done to change that bit of unfairness?" A little extra breath is spat out between his teeth.

She steps toward him. "Why didn't *you* pay the taxes if you wanted this place so badly?"

His gaze shifts from the waterbed made up in its wheaten spread and heap of print pillows. He looks down at his empty left hand and the right hand, which clasps nothing but a cap. Need the question be answered? He says nothing.

"You could have *stolen* the money for your father!" She cackles.

He looks at her. "There's many ways to make a little booty well-spent when there's so many bigger thieves leaving so many in need of a small-time thief's services."

She blinks. She blinks again. She says warily, "So . . . you have some of your band out there in the shadows waiting for you to make some signal, I suppose. Tonight was scheduled as your big raid, am I correct?"

He glances out into the pinkish night, then smiles, again sheepish. "There are no shadows here."

Gwen goes over to the bed and slumps on the edge, folds her arms around herself. The Pogos flatten out and lay still.

Lloyd watches Gwen hard as she reaches for the wineglass, thrusts the drink high and chirps, "To our house!" She sips. Then she says cheerily, "Please have some, too!" She stands.

He stands.

She crosses the layered profusion of helter-skelter rugs.

He jerks a colored rag from his dungarees pocket and spits into it, wipes his moustache . . . slowly.

She is certain of one thing . . . and this room . . . these close quarters are now drumming with that fact . . . that he is wild with wanting her . . . that he is hot.

She presses the glass into his hand.

He doesn't sniff the bouquet of the wine first. He just glugs it down.

"To our house!" Gwen says again brightly with a show of her perfect teeth. She plucks the glass from his hand.

He draws the rag from his pocket again to touch up his moustache and she sees the distinctive assemblage of white stars on a blue field and the red stripes and the white stripes.

She says, "That was a bit dry for a Tavel. But I know you like milky coffee better anyway. I know *that* about you." She says this in singsong. Pleased with herself. Girlish. She bounces on her toes. She reaches for his bare forearm. Forearm goes rigid. She giggles. She gives his arm a hard shake, trying to get him to be playful. She gets a hold on his cap. "Let me put your cap up for you." He won't let go of the cap. Now his eyes are fixed on the door.

He says deeply, "I've never been an impulsive person. Everything I've done in my life has had a plan . . . a major plan . . . with . . . with belief . . . and deep conviction, you might call it."

Her hands flop to her sides. "So what is the major plan here?"

He looks around at the wallpaper and at the chimney painted white. "I'm married, you see. Twenty-seven years to the same woman. No complaints."

She squints one eye.

He fits his cap back onto his head.

"So why were you waiting here in the bedroom of a woman at bed-time, Mr. Convictions? Why are you here?!!" She folds her arms around her narrow rib cage, shrinks a little, shoulders slumped.

"Maybe I just came to see what you people did to my family's house. Okay?" He moves around her.

She says, "And where do you come by such liberty?"

He says, "Where do you come by your self-assurance?"

"I'm not self-assured," she insists. "If you knew me well, you'd know I'm not."

"You are used to having things . . . work out for you," he insists, still facing the door.

She blinks. "That is a stupid thing to say. You know that just being alive, one has to face daily trials. Some people just pretend well, Lloyd." Her voice softens. "Believe me, please. All people aren't what they seem."

He turns and his moustache flickers. "Which means somewhere deeeep inside people like you is a shred of something decent."

She closes her eyes.

He says, "Earl Doyle's money came and went into interests I'm familiar with. I have . . . familiarized myself with the man's influences . . . and his knacks . . . and his friends . . . like his union-busting attorneys, hostile buyouts, all kinds of buyouts, take 'em bleed 'em throw 'em away."

She keeps her eyes shut, while his eyes grow wider. "But mostly hearsay of course, since private enterprise is so *private* . . . since private books are so malleable. But his political influences are mostly on record for those few who have the knack for and curiosity to explore them. I'm not saying he was a *complete* crook. He played by the laws for the most part. So I guess my biggest worry is with those old laws and new laws that allow people with no accountability, no conscience, no obligations to *my* people, to have such free rein. So maybe old Earl was a huggable dumpling with little heartaches and disappointments and good deeds when he was home with *you* . . . but out in the world . . ." He draws air slowly through his teeth, fills his chest. "Mrs. Doyle, listen hard here. Crud like Earl Doyle is ravaging everyone I love."

"I am not Earl Doyle," she whispers, eyes still closed.

"YES YOU ARE!!" He shifts from foot to foot, prizefighter-style. He moves around from her left elbow to her right.

She keeps her eyes scrinched tight.

He says, "*My* people are expected to be patriots. We go to fight wars for corporations . . . excuse me . . . *American interests.*" He chuckles. "We punch time-clocks for corporations. We go to schools that try to teach us to aspire to corporations. We work our maximum output or we are told we haven't enough work ethic . . . which is tied in somehow with . . . *patriotism.* That's because America *is* the corporations. The flag is a corporate banner. Lately, *anything* that's not big and corporate falls by the wayside. We are totally dependent on corporations." He smiles, his spaced yellow-stained teeth like bars against darkness. "Forgetting little ol' Earl Doyle, now . . . have you ever seen the *face,* held the *hand* of a corporation? Heard its heart beat? Shit! The big machine. And now . . . there's not enough profit left in America so they're all picking up and going elsewhere to where people don't realize yet that the life of conveniences and corporate dependency is *poison,* where people will work for sixty-five cents an hour. Which leaves all my people here with nothing and if one of us complains, the corporation boys will get that little thin smile and say, 'But *we're* just using good business sense' and then they get out the really big question. 'Are you suggesting that restrictions be put on the *private* sector? Are you intending to weaken *free* enterprise?' You know what *I* say, Gwen? I say fuck 'em. Fuck their goddam eyes! How much can they go on doing in the name of good business sense and free enterprise? Put us in camps, Gwen? Experiment on us? Bury us in piles? I mean . . . men like Earl Doyle are admired so much nobody expects them to be distracted by abstract notions like ethics, patriotism, and common decency. Earl Doyle was the goddam devil and you know it! I tell you what . . ." He leans in close. She covers her eyes with both hands. There's the sharp ugly stink of his tobacco mouth. How much longer can he rail on? She never imagined that he was this full of talk. *This* talk. What happened to the spy who cracks Moscow?

"I had a dream recently," he is telling her. "There was this new law passed. All new infants to welfare mothers would have to be taken away. This was a stiff law to make those welfare mothers shape up . . . you see. The army and police would bust in and get the babies. If you tried to have the baby in secret, someone might know and call on the welfare hotline to report you. So they come and get that baby while it's still wet with mucus. And some nice people suspected that the crack babies and various undernourished babies or deformed babies were being landfill material. Nobody knew. How could they? The states hired *private* enterprise to do the job. Police and army were all tied in with private sector in slick ways. Concerned people—"

"Stop it! Shut up! Jesus. Jesus. Jesus."

"Concerned people wrote the governor but the letters were answered in clever ways. And the people called the governor but he was a recording with a nice voice. And the people marched to Augusta. But the governor wasn't there. And the people marched to Washington but nobody could find the President!!! And you know . . . they rammed the doors . . . and the police and army killed most of us . . . but some of us got inside . . . and when we got to the President's desk . . . there was just an answering machine clicking on and off with the nice voice of the President. There was no President. There was nobody."

Silence.

She opens her eyes. With his face next to hers, he whispers, "You know, Mrs. Doyle. I'm *not* a good man. If I'd really been a decent man, a good man, I'd never have made my sons and daughters. I'd have thought twice, wouldn't I? I should've ripped my goddam pecker out by the root." He grabs himself between the legs and it does seem his hand works to crush himself.

Again Gwen closes her eyes.

But he gets her by the wrist and her eyes fly open and she sinks a little, pulling back.

He is turning her ringless hand, giving it a close study, the long nails, the very long fingers. He says, "*Will all great Neptune's ocean wash this blood Clean from my hand? No; this my hand will rather The multitudinous seas incarnadine, Making the green one red.*" And he draws her hand up into the wiry smotherishness of his moustache, kisses along the topmost ridge of knuckles.

He doesn't hang around for anything else.

After he's gone, Gwen sits on the edge of the bed listening for the sound of his sneakers, the sounds of doors. Or his truck starting. But he's like fog. She considers a more hi-tech security system . . . electric eyes and alarms.

But as she makes breakfast down in the kitchen in the morning, it seems there are cameras and eyes watching *her!*

She hurries to her darkroom, shuts the door, straddles the high stool, oatmeal still packed along the sides of her molars. She clenches her hands, head bowed, weeping. "My god. My god."

41 It is 2:26 A.M. on a hot night with open windows.

No security lamps. No pink. She has had them disconnected. No locks. Nothing to keep danger out. She wakes and wakes. Restless with the heat. She thinks of the air-conditioner . . . but the sweetnesses of Egypt, fields and woods and warm tar has its way with her. And the miring odors of the house these days is total. So many things have appeared. More tools. Pig iron. Plow blades. Chicken wire. Toys.

Now under this single sheet, her own nakedness seems part of the sweetness of this house . . . and a distendedness inside her that grows and recedes, grows and recedes as the moon bears across the windows on certain nights while other nights the sky comes back empty.

Tonight she dials the number with three nines and when he answers, she says, "I'm not like you think."

There's something he does. Sounds like a swallow. It's not a word.

"I'm not like you think. You don't have *any* idea."

"Okay," he says.

She says, "I'll give you everything I own. I don't even know how much that really is. But I can reach people who could find out, could estimate. There's so much invested . . . it's not like cash . . . but there *is* cash I could get. Soon. Some I could get my hands on within days. Some tomorrow of course. I would give it all to you to do whatever you want with . . . help your people . . . anything. And of course, this house. You can have your house back! Just come here and live with me and know me . . . that's all."

He chuckles. "No thanks."

42 | The light through the maple twitters and giggles down onto her hair and long arms and the smell of paint rises up. There are the three swings he's put up for her, using a stepladder on the bed of his truck. One swing is yellow. One is blue. One red. She has picked the red as her favorite, its height perfect. Sometimes she swings high. But now it's just this slow spin-around. Digging her sandal heels into the dirt.

Every fifteen minutes a chips truck growls heavily down from the hills, building speed on the grade, gears gnashing. Many, many chips trucks. But what interests her most about that road is that possibility of Lloyd's truck. He has refused to accept her offer of his old homeplace. And yet somehow he edges closer every day. Last week he spent whole days in the barn. He has set up a workbench out there. Everything he does has such a cunning and weird twist.

Going into the kitchen for lunch, she checks her answering machine . . . there's Helen from the environmental group, two of the pro-choice people, and yes! . . . the gallery in New York!!! All of those voices stating time and number where they can be reached all crammed onto one slim recording tape . . . a thing you can hold in your hand. Such a day! She can tell by their promptness in returning her morning calls that she is in their high regard. It has come to be the most productive time of her life. She is moving up.

PART NINE

1 | Eight P.M. They walk with the farmer between them, moving away from the passenger door of his box truck from which he has just stepped down.

He is handcuffed but not roughed up in any way.

He had stepped down from the cab of his truck toward them and they were ready for the worst. Their automatics and .38 specials were already drawn.

But he had simply stepped down, one boot at a time to the sand . . . like he was shaky and infirm in his age . . . though they knew he wasn't. And he just stood there, blue revolving cruiser lights smashing into his eyes while they read him his rights.

For there had been a warrant for his arrest, reports by nameless callers . . . and certain evidence that was misconstrued . . . this he supposes. They urge him to admit that he fired with a high-powered rifle at a National Guard helicopter . . . these helicopters working in conjunction with the Maine Drug Enforcement Agency. But he is silent. Truth has no value in this. Only their eagerness has value. "You were under the belief that the helicopters were watching you?"

And surely there are now statements by the bank officers involved that he had threatened to booby-trap the property with homemade land mines, therefore there is also a warrant to search the woods and fields for booby traps.

The firearm found in the rack of his truck is loaded and is confiscated.

He has not shown any attempt to use this firearm tonight. He seems confused. His replies are that of a sweet old man.

In the back of the truck stands one Belgian workhorse. The truck rises and settles upon its springs whenever the animal shifts its great weight.

Women rushing from the house are swearing at the cops and crying and one of these officers tries to contain the situation while the other cops get edgy and the night gets darker outside the edges of the headlights and between the brisk sweeps of the hypnotic pale blue.

The farmer is being walked to the nearest cruiser, quite close to the back of the box truck, when the old horse shifts its weight again and its harness jangles and the farmer just drops.

The cops who have a grip on him, being ready for the worst, grab harder, but keep hold of only a sleeve of his shirt and this action pulls his shirt from his belt and partway up his back. The farmer is sort of down on one knee, now rising enough to put one cheek against an iron hinge of the ramp doors . . . an awkward position with cops yanking to get him back on his feet.

Old horse turns its head and the blue light whisks across its face, its eyes. Horse shifts. The truck rises and settles lissomely against the farmer's cheek.

2 It is morning. In another town, half hour's drive from Egypt, a bank manager sorting through his keys at the door of his car sees something unexpected on the driver's seat. Turns out to be a plastic half gallon milk jug. Filled. But not with milk. Filled with blood. There's a note attached, typewritten in a very common typeface. Note reads: DRINK TO GOOD BUSINESS SENSE.

The statement given by the bank manager says also that his car locks looked tampered with. Attached statements by police and Ted Allen of Allen's Exxon had differed from that. According to these reports, there seemed to be no tampering of the locks.

3 State reports that the blood is human but of mixed types. Blood contains no alcohol but certain medications . . . one which is often used for arthritis . . . another for underactive thyroid.

4 On Saturday a young bride wearing a gown festooned with every beauteous crinkle and fringe, a whisper of makeup, mock pearls, and a new haircut, unwraps the gift of a microwave oven to the ebullient *ahh*'s of her friends.

PART TEN

1 Another year. Another late summer.

Kit Turnbull. Even in weather made for bundling, she wears shirts that are too deeply V-necked or only partly buttoned. Or it may be a sleeveless denim Harley vest worn over bareness. And held together in front with only a single rhinestone pin. Big breasts. It is always these breasts that make people swallow hard at the pharmacy, at the PO, wherever she is sighted dragging one of her sisters-in-law's kids along by the hand . . . or her grandchild Lulu . . . maybe one child to each hand. Everything about the Turnbulls is vivid and terrifying and handsome. Even the many Turnbull dogs with their rippling clover-color tongues in big heads. All Scottish terriers with no necks, broad chests, claws like badgers. And unlike most dogs, they can outstare you . . . their dark eyes prickling with deduces and deductions.

Even Kit's mother-in-law and the boyfriend of the mother-in-law, Billy Sargent, are vivid creatures, so brightly fused onto the beige plainness of the modern day. Mother, father, child, or child of child, like the thunder of their Harleys, there is thunder in their genes.

David Turnbull is late getting home from the mill. Kit feeds the kids and dogs. She nibbles.

She knows what has just happened at the mill.

The kids and the TV clamor. The dogs lie about on piles of rags, which are their beds. And they are under the table where it is cool or by the stove where it is hot. Like planets, dogs everywhere you look, rotating, orderly.

Kit is pregnant. The dark below the navel that shows beneath the shrunken T-shirt is like some mark of the devil, like sin. And clearly visible through the tissuey thinness of this old T-shirt are two tattoos. The one on the right breast is an apple blossom and leaves. The blossom is pink and intricately veined. The leaves gleam. While high on a shoulder is a poorly done homemade black cross.

Kit fears looking at David's empty chair at the table. She fears its impendingness. She fears David. She knows that when he sits there tonight how his face will look. She has already gotten the call from her pal Marcie who works in the carding room and Marcie has told her everything.

Kit sways, a left-right rhythm. Beaded braided rope of her black hair sways. Fear. Her arms. Fear. Hands fidget. Her arms . . . such skin you could never put an age to . . . nor a race . . . her race being some farfetched mix, nearly nobody else as dark as she in Egypt, Maine.

Her shift at the mill is night. His is day. There is always somebody in the bed, always somebody away. Though never far. The mill is only a few hundred yards downriver. And always the thrum-bum-bum-bum-bum-bum-bum of the mill's compressor. It is with them in the bed.

She now hears his truck up above, this not being a completed house but a capped cellar hole made cozy. She moves toward the door and around her ankles the terriers hurry, too . . . rolling along in a dignified manner together.

When he enters the kitchen, Thermos under one arm, the dogs leap at him, dig at his boots, bound around, pivoting on their weirdly adept hind legs.

He is a giant in this cellar home . . . a six-foot-three man under six-foot-six ceilings. His eyes are on Kit. "No warning," he murmurs. "Shut down." Now he places the Thermos on the drainboard and goes to his chair at the table. Even with only his wrists revealed, the tattoos tumble out: barbed tail of a small devil and, all the way to the knuckles of the other hand, a flame that licks.

She wants to hide her belly from his sight, not to remind him of this newest province of obligation.

"No severance pay, no bonuses . . . *the* bonuses . . . no retirement, no more insurance," he explains as if reading her mind and indeed, yes, he is looking directly at her distended middle. And then he raises his fist and smashes it upon the table. Dishes leap. Dogs duck away. One dog hurtles toward him. Three of them bark.

The unborn infant patiently considers.

2 | There's so few that have shown up for this protest, so few that they can all sit at the same time on the tailgates of two trucks and rest now and then.

Anneka Plummer's idea, this protest. None of the organized efficiency you would get with a union shop. Just this . . .

"Can't take this lying down!" she booms.

Anneka Plummer, even more pregnant than Kit. Where pregnancy makes Kit especially vivid, Anneka seems especially pastel. No motherly glow for Anneka.

Anneka has made all the placards. One reads: WHERE'S MY BONUS YOU PROMISED?

Another reads: IS THIS HOW YOU TREAT THOSE WHO GIVE THEIR LIVES?

Another: LIARS!!! PIRATES!!! SNAKES!!!

Also on hand are some of Anneka's aunts and cousins and a cousin-in-law, these people being Anneka's only connection to the mill, her only obvious reason to be here other than her usual unfettered blustery outrage.

David Turnbull stands sullenly with a group of smokers, placard over his shoulder.

Artie Bean lounges in the weeds, wiggling a placard distractedly over his knees, watching an ant.

From the passing cars there's the blare of a horn.

Everyone hoists their placards up and yells.

The silver stack of the mill looks delicate today against the sky that is hot, glutted, yellow-gold.

3 | The following day it rains hard.
"What good does this do?" some ask.

4 | Next day Anneka Plummer shows up, driving her truck, which has a camper. She parks it snug against the curb, windshield wipers slashing against a rain that sounds like bullets on the glass and cab roof.

No one else has shown up.

It's just Anneka. She has made a new sign: THE FUTURE OF MAINE'S CHILDREN WAS DECIDED HERE. She waddles pregnantly through the rain.

Unlike the white-scarves-in-the-woods march, this issue does not seem to be much of a draw. "Not cute enough for the media," she snarls. "Not cute at all."

And so the next day, not even Anneka shows up.

5 | Moody's Variety & Lunch. Lights are shut off over the horseshoe counter, countertop wiped clean, napkins in their dispensers, and beyond and below are the mousetraps all set and ready.

Around the barrel stove the many bright rocking chairs bend inward toward the discussion of the moment: moose.

Dottie Soule and Louise Moody thumb through catalogs on their low stools behind the register, the counter that is stacked high with Slim Jims and *TV Guide*s, mint patties, Chap Sticks, and what's left of today's papers. Louise calls this her "fort." Outside the fort, over by the barrel stove, Louise calls that "enemy territory."

How many shots did it take Danny Merrill to drop his moose last year?

Four in the face, two in the neck, one in the haunch, six in the shoulder.

Out in the back room, the well drilling Reverend David Moody sorts through returnables. What shows of him is just the back of his shirt with its embroidered lettering.

Someone pulls open the glass door to come in, and heads turn. It's David Turnbull and his next oldest boy Shawn Turnbull . . . Shawn who is newly married and has worked most of this summer at Kool Kone making ice creams. But now like many he has no work, lost his job to the Kool Kone owner's sister who *was* at the mill. The young man has close-set eyes like his father, significant nose, significant hands, tall . . . tall as his father . . . but a clean shave. Looking for work "into the city," Shawn has been advised by many to keep shaved clean as a whistle. Shawn is pressing his back to the door to hold it wide for five black Scottish terriers who are entering the store in a bunch . . . dogs with broad chests, short thick-clawed badgerlike legs, weird big collie-shaped heads, and massive moustaches . . . not what the Egypt wise men and young bucks would call a man's dog. Not hardly.

Clarence Farrington, Arch Vandermast, and Rick Dresser exchange glances.

Shawn Turnbull gets a grip on the Canary rocker, drags it away from the hot stove, settles in among some of the younger men. Dale Lamont is now onto the subject of the new rules at Beechridge . . . and how Jimmy Douglas and them are getting out. And so begins a little talk on the stock car races.

As David Turnbull strokes a five-dollar bill out flat into Louise Moody's hand, his dogs huddle around his legs. They shift from foot to foot like small prizefighters. One nose jabs David in the calf. Then another. And another. The Scottish terrier way of "touching bases."

Now David Turnbull trudges over to the bulletin wall and the five scotties bustle over there to stand with him. They watch David's hands as he wrestles open a Slim Jim, breaks it into five equal pieces. He squats. All the heads open up to reveal white and yellow-white bear-sized teeth. In go the beef jerky pieces. Now the teeth and jaws work and the eyes glitter.

Clarence gives a little tsk.

Old Willie DeRoche asks, "Say, Turnbull . . . what'd you say those things are? Scotties?"

"Naw. Baby bears. These are my sweet baby bears." David Turnbull speaks in a baby voice, scratching his short beard, cocking his head, smiling warmly. And tonight, being a heavy August evening after a humid, on-and-off rain, way too warm for the barrel stove to be loaded, there's the flies, dragons, wizards, devils, and skulls coursing vibrantly down both brawny arms of David Turnbull. "You're Daddy's baby bears, aren'tcha?"

Shifting from foot to foot, the scotties stare into his eyes and he smiles.

"Those are rat dogs," explains the son of David Turnbull. "Mean sons-a-bitches. They could take on a half a barn fulla rats all at once. Or a badger. Not many dogs could take a badger. Scottish terriers got a special way they pivot on their hind legs. Mean fighters. Teeth like alligators."

"Not *my* baby bears," says David Turnbull in his baritone. "Not my little girls. They don't kill anything or Daddy would scold. Huh?"

The dogs' gleamy eyes all look hardest at David's mouth when he is saying the word "Daddy."

Shawn Turnbull flushes.

Clarence Farrington, Arch Vandermast, Rick Dresser, and old Rusty Pete exchange *The Look.*

Young Dale Lamont says, "Hey, Dave. What do *these* dogs have to say about the world situation? Didn't you used to have another one of them that used to snarl an' stuff?"

"King wasn't a Scottish terrier. He was a Schnoodle," David says softly. "Never be another guy like him."

"He had opinions," Albion Cole tells them with a chuckle.

"These dogs got any opinions?" wonders young Dale Lamont.

David Turnbull draws a red ragged bandanna from his jacket pocket, works it into his nose, seems to be stalling. Nobody's really seen any of these new dogs do any tricks. David drives the bandanna back into his pocket, stares down into the many gleamy eyes. "Louise? Kathleen? Mary? Margaret? Helen? Listen to Daddy. I'm asking you an important question so you can take a few minutes to answer." He sighs. "What can we do to undo the damage the politicians and their unregulated big biz pals have done to us . . . and what about all those voters that had their heads up their asses who think they are such hot shits when they voted for these kinds . . . how can we undo this what they've done? The workin' people's kids got nothing but wiped-out resources, part-time jobs or no jobs, no place to live . . . no good feelin' in the world but a drink or a drug"—his big voice shakes—"and now all over the country riots and violence . . . and despair. What . . . what do you think?"

The dogs are looking hard at David's mouth. One of them hops from foot to foot, jabs at his left shin. Another one jabs his right shin . . . jabs hard. Another looks off to the far left as if to hear a ticking clock.

"Well," Clarence Farrington says with a little sniff of triumph. "*That* certainly was a flop." He smiles into Arch Vandermast's eyes and then to some of the others.

David says, "But Clarence. What if somebody asked *you* the question?"

"Jesus!" old Rusty Pete hoots. "Don't ask Clarence any questions on politics or we'll be here for a week."

"This sounds like another long night. I need a beer bad for this," complains one guy, pushing himself up out of Rootie Kazootie.

"I could be seeing that special on Sass-squatch," another man says grimly.

David Turnbull steps between two rockers, closer to Clarence and the old man looks up into David Turnbull's face with a sleepy, satisfied smile.

The laid-off David Turnbull seems less patient than the foreman-at-the-mill David Turnbull. His eyes are way too steamy.

Albion Cole shifts, places his hands on the chair arms, getting ready to rise. "David. Let it go."

David looks around, sees the little dogs waddling over to stand close to him, except for the two that are sniffing Dale Lamont's pants legs. David Turnbull says to his son, "Shawn, call 'em."

Shawn stands up, claps his palms together. "Come! Come! Come!" He backs away toward the register, calling the dog's names, and they all charge him, their eyes gleaming with excitement, and he scoots them out the door and then he goes out after them and the door squeezes shut.

David wonders, "Clarence. What *is* your plan for saving us all?"

Clarence keeps smiling his satisfied smile, his bring-back-the-paddle-to-the-schools, throw-'em-in-the-camps, strap-'em-in-the-electric-chair smile.

The reverend well driller David Moody has stopped rattling cans out back, now stands in the shedway door, very quiet.

David Turnbull fills out his whole brawny height with a look of fight, all the while looking into Clarence's eyes and he knees into Clarence's rocking chair and then a nudge with his work boot. Clarence is jarred to and fro. The chair arm clatters against that of the next man. And among them all there is such embarrassment and fright and sorrow in the silent aftermath of this move.

6 | Now they walk along Rummery Road on the dirt shoulder. A single set of headlights expands around the hiss on wet pavement, then gone . . . now again darkness.

It is the two Davids walking there. David Turnbull who is tall. And the Reverend well driller David who is short, but a thick-backed, strong-looking short.

"That was bad," says the reverend.

"You are right," says David Turnbull.

"Once . . ."

"No. Please. It's the mole story, right? Please . . . no. I don't want to hear about any more goddam moles. I'm sorry, Dave . . . but you know . . . I've taken that mole story to heart . . . I get hawk nightmares now because of you. Please . . . no more of that friggin' shit."

"Amen," says the reverend.

They cross the road and the town is below them, squares and dazzles and soft blips of light . . . mainly the mill. Mill quiet now, but never dark.

The reverend says, "We knew it was coming, didn't we? We knew they'd shut down. It's happening everywhere else. We're not special here."

David Turnbull grunts.

The reverend says, "You know, I'm nowhere near elderly yet, but I tend to think the good ol' days are over. Maybe there never were any good ol' days . . . but there was a *belief*, you see, that the good ol' days were ahead. Hard to think that way now." The reverend, in his hurry, has left his jacket behind at the store . . . and there's David Turnbull with bare arms . . . neither guy expecting this growing chill. The reverend hunches a bit. The other David punches a road sign that shows a large + for crossroads, black on yellow. THONNNGGGGGGG!

Reverend says, "Of course you're fed up with Clarence and them. Of course." He glances back in the direction of the store. "You know . . . all this big government, big business . . . so faceless." He lapses into a silence, though it's clear that this is the beginning of a gentle tirade.

Another car approaches, passes. They watch the taillights, the head of the driver silhouetted there. Then gone.

"God? Or Satan? Some believe it is one. Some believe it's another. If you can't even identify your god or your devil, can't get a consensus even among your own people . . . it's . . . it's . . . there's no unity."

"No shit."

"What will become of us?" the reverend wonders.

"The chair!" snarls David Turnbull. He bends for a rock, turns and throwing a leg out, pitches hard . . . the road sign in the distance speaks again. CHCKKK—THWANGGG! And he says, "If Clarence had his way, we'd all wind up in the chair sooner or later. The chair or gas . . . whichever's cheaper."

The reverend's low weary voice says, "Or the chains." He closes his eyes. "I have never *seen* God. I've never *felt* the presence of the Trinity. In my understanding, worship is only the belief in and complete submission to a perfect being so that the worshiper can dump all responsibilities onto that being. Look closely at the words of most hymns. People don't want the responsibility of each other's lives. With worship, it's so easy. You just fall down on your knees and you don't have to do another damn thing. Such a cinch!"

He opens his eyes and begins walking again. He hunches more and more into the chill.

The other David lights up a cigarette, walks backwards, smoking, watching Moody's store grow smaller. He has a bitter smile.

The reverend says, "A big god is a bad thing anyway. A big anything is bad. Nothing has ever gotten better by getting larger. Bigger businesses, bigger labor unions . . . what does it all come to? Bigger schools. Bigger towns. The earth is infested with humans . . . while the varied other creatures of the planet are being massacred . . . and now more than ever the human population massacres itself. Isaiah wrote, 'Woe to those who add house to house and join field to field until everywhere belongs to them and they are the sole inhabitants of the land.' " He is walking with one foot in the wet weeds again, deeply distracted. "I guess there's nothing we can do about the mill getting shut down, Dave. And we can't stop our country from soon becoming owned and governed by some global board of directors. There's nothing for us but to *see* it coming like Isaiah and *those* fellers did. But I know one thing that we've *got* to work harder at than we've ever done before . . . you know? . . . we . . . we *can't* fight amongst ourselves, Dave. We gotta keep cool."

7 | Moody's Variety & Lunch. Afternoon of another day. Slant of sun. Old man's hand has a grip on a rocker arm . . . Fandango. And the sun on the bars of the back of the chair and between the bars on the old man's jacket is a stout benediction. A quiet time.

Over by the magazines, two kids whisper.

And the two old men in the rockers talk low, not in secrecy, but with the sleepy feel of the stove and the sun.

Clarence Farrington says, "If we had the electric chair in Maine, he'd a thought twice about trying to do me in."

"Aw . . . he wa'n't going to do nuthin' anyways."

"He wanted to kill me. I know when a guy can't handle it . . . his temper. I can tell a thing like that. I could see he wanted to kill me . . . in his eyes. Nothing better for deterrin' a crime like that than fear of the chair . . . or the gas chamber . . . whichever is cheaper."

8 Big moon. Broad river. Music from three radios and a tape deck mixing. Along the guardrails and up into the woods are cars, pickups, dressed-out choppers, full dress and half dress. And a truck with a ramp, no load, reads: LETOURNEAU'S USED AUTO PARTS / EGYPT, MAINE on both doors.

Entrance to the covered bridge has its moony-blue haunted-house look tonight. No teenagers inside there cannonballing it out through the one staved-out side. No firecrackers and girlish giggles.

But there are people in the water. They make quiet slisping sounds, wading and bobbing . . . no serious swims . . . just there getting wet, coming out clean. The river isn't much fun this near to September. River is high and cold and has a little hurry-up to it. The fun is out on the road. A few guffaws inside that sweet, sweet illegal smoke. And those deep swallows of cold beer. And somebody teasing Kit Turnbull and Shell Turnbull about this summer's garden . . . something about zucchinis that needed to be sliced with a cutting torch. Kit's not a good one to tease. She doesn't squeal or argue. She just gives you that level look. But Shell, she squeals very well.

From the tunnel of trees on the Egypt side, headlights sweep, then jerk away as a newish van eases down into the sandy shoulder against the guardrail behind the line of parked rigs. Headlights are cut.

"Out-of-state plates," Macky Turnbull harrumphs. Macky who is as big and bull-built a biker as his brother David. Only with Macky there's even *more* of an anger . . . like cut glass in his eyes. Even when he grins. And at intervals, there's his crawly right-out-of-a-horror-flick laugh. Though at the moment, he's pretty well settled into just his steady pissed-off thin grin.

"Tourists," sighs Chucky Hubbard, whose frothy blond hair is cut short these days for purposes of job hunting.

"Must be lost," Macky sneers. "Looking for the outlets, tracking down the moccasin malls."

Sniggers.

"No shopping here!" asserts another.

Albion Cole, nearly shoulder-to-shoulder with Chucky Hubbard, has settled into a nervous silence.

They all listen for the van's doors to open. But for a while the van just hunkers there, moonlit windshield blank and omniscient.

Moon on the river is soft and familiar as a neighbor lady's face. Moon up in the black night is rock.

Macky Turnbull has never had patience. He heads for the strange van, his head bent, biker hardware clanking, his left leg pulled along with effort . . . his most recent injury . . . slower to heal than those of his youth.

The van doors swing open and three figures step out around him. He reads the plate by moonlight. *West Virginia*. Now the three people introduce themselves. And there's a question and another question.

Macky squints, nods, looks back toward the riverbank. "Yep" and "Yep," he answers.

Now he leads these people across the tar, between the opposite line of parked vehicles. The path down to the water is all rock and root and often a surprise banana peel. Or a nasty tissue tossed there near something else that is nasty. You have to take this way slow.

Down where the current shakes tall grasses, divides around high bush blueberry and alder, the strangers find who they are looking for among others. A lot of bareness and beards here.

If there was ever a question of whether or not David Turnbull's tattoos exist below the beltline, this is one of those nights which will answer that question. Meanwhile, the other men's nakednesses are less colorific. Just moon blue and the dark of hair . . . little weaselish Norman Letourneau, the reverend well driller, Joel Barrington, and his father, Lloyd Barrington.

From the trio of intruders, all dressed in flannels and denims, a woman's voice is solemnly raised. "Good evening, Reverend."

The reverend grins. "Jewel Grissom." He trudges to the edge of the water and the woman kneels down on one knee and reaches. He places one wet hand into one of hers, which is dry, then he brings up his other hand, folding both hands around her one. And now she applies her left hand and the clasp between them looks like some sort of pact. The woman laughs gently. Shakes her short dark perm. She has that Scotch-Indian Appalachian face . . . the mouth, the eyes, the shoulders all moving with such peace and good humor that it would seem that all fears and sorrows of everyone in her company here tonight would be erased.

She speaks to the reverend as she releases his hands and stands. "My brothers Francis Grissom and John Grissom."

The two brothers nod. Both men wear billed advertisement caps. One man is taller than the other by a head and has a black man's nose and mouth and a black man's musculature. Their hellos, like their sister's words, are that of the West Virginia hills.

Jewel Grissom glances around to some of the Maine men. "Heard you like picketing mills."

A few real hoots of laughter are raised to this.

David Turnbull says grumpily, "Which paper did you read this in? Or was it the world and national on six o'clock TV?"

Titters.

The woman turns back to the shorter David down in the water and speaks gravely. "No, but your good friend David here . . . he writes swell letters."

Big biker David Turnbull slides his eyes accusingly over toward the Reverend Moody.

The Reverend Moody is now climbing up onto the rocks to claim his shirt and pants.

Lloyd Barrington hangs *way* back, remaining ankle deep in the cold river. Looks like he might turn to the river and make a quick escape. He keeps glancing that way, eyes scanning the opposite shore. But his son Joel, who has the Soule family's gregarious bright face, steps closer to the conversation on the riverbank and folds his arms across his chest.

The tall black-featured brother speaks in his hill country drawl. "We heard y'all have a *type* of union here."

"You heard that," Macky Turnbull states flatly.

Again many eyes accusingly find the Reverend Moody.

Norman Letourneau, often so full of hell, hangs back with Lloyd, shivering, teeth chattering, St. Christopher's medal spinning before his chest, a blue glint. With cleft pallet and doctored harelip, Norman's speech would be thick and hard to understand . . . *if* he had speech tonight.

And also uncharacteristically silent, scooched on a mossy log and dressed in dark work clothes, is Walt Fogg's lover and friend, Morelli. You never see Walt Fogg himself at these spontaneous social gatherings at the bridge. But Morelli, skilled machinist, master electrician . . . light step. Always near.

Soles and heels of boots strike rock. Merlin Soule and Albion Cole appear on the path, arms folded across the chests of their work shirts, neither man too old to look menacing in moonlight.

"Well," the woman says gently, assuagingly. "At some point all little bitty unions got to get to know each other."

Albion Cole says, "I missed something."

Merlin has nothing to say. He has not been part of this little gang for very long, but he *senses* something is wrong . . . and since jail, he trusts all his senses.

Now Shell and Kit and Chucky appear on the path . . . quietly . . . just listening to Norman Letourneau's teeth chattering and the slap and slisk of the river as it blunders past and the Reverend David Moody's belt buckle and the chuckling and thumping and lamenting of all the radios and tape deck in the parked vehicles up on the road.

Norman Letourneau's chattering teeth keep drawing the West Virginian woman's eyes his way.

Her tall black brother says, "People back where we're from . . . we got grandaddies that remember what a company was like before the unions . . . especially when it was the *only company*. That's nearly what you have here now. Mill's gone. What you got left? Paper company land? A little work in the woods?"

"Yep," says Albion Cole in a most gritty way.

"Well . . . back home," the West Virginia man continues. "You got your land taken out from under you by the company a long time ago. You got promises by the company. You loaded coal for the company. You sometimes got paid. But sometimes you just owed . . . owed *them* . . . 'cause they owned the store, too. Your kids were sick and hungry. *That* was the easy part. The hard part was when you decided you wanted to get the workers some consideration, which was to get 'em unionized. This was hard for you to do, you see, with the company finding a union card on you and opening up the furnace door and stuffing you in. Companies drove down through the coal camps and shot into the doors and windows." He pauses, waits for a response, but only the river speaks; only the river is not suspicious. But the man smiles, persists . . . "Where we're from, we get a little union history course every time one of us sets down with a grandaddy or granmomma. And you know people died bad to organize. You know that when you start from scratch, you die bad . . . because it was bad before you started when everything was going the company's way. You think things get easier when they are *upset???* You best not wait till it's *that* bad, my friends. It's all uphill when you start from scratch."

The sister Jewel says, "You all have had some labor unions around here . . . maybe not in this town . . . but in this state. You people here in Maine aren't under some impression that they were handed to you on a silver platter, are you? You don't think it was something some nice lawmakers thought up, do you?"

Everyone is pretty quiet.

The black-featured brother says, "I'll tell you my granmomma's brother had his eyes put out by the company . . . one eye at a time. With a tire iron." His West Virginian pronunciation of the last two words sounds like "tar'n" but everybody understands it clearly.

The other brother says, "And that was what you'd call a company. What we have nowadays to deal with is these humongified corporations. They got technology and psychology. They got everybody in the trance of their TV psychology. And their pet puppy is the government. They can clean us up neater now. No mess. No fuss." He takes a folded white handkerchief from his shirt pocket and presses it to his sweating top lip. And then he says slowly, "Funny thing about people. All people. They aren't in a fighting mood till they've lost everything. Only when there's nothing left to lose do they feel frisky enough to raise a hand."

Another laid-off foreman from the mill, Mark Finley, standing near Morelli speaks up, "You people sent here by some kind of union?"

"No sir," replies Jewel Grissom. "We were not *sent.*"

The Reverend Moody, finishing with tying his boots, steps up alongside his friend and with his hand on her shoulder says, "This is the Reverend Jewel Grissom . . . she . . . she was *invited* by me. She's West Virginia. We here . . . we're Maine. Time we had a little talk."

Now the Reverend Jewel Grissom speaks as if she is under the impression that this introduction means she is now welcomed. "But let me tell y'all, we're hardly a speck of grit in the shoe of these giants. Just a bitty nuisance factor. But . . ." Her twinkling eyes pick out Lloyd's face across the moonlighted few yards of water. She clasps her hands. "I guess it's just some of us don't like to take a thing lying down. It just feels damn good to stand up to the thing that has you in its claws . . . to bite its toe, to give it an itch . . . and always with that hope that our people will endure and win out . . . just because there's more of us. There are many more of us working class folks than there's them. Yes. *Yes!* Why, we're thick as fleas!!"

Merlin booms, "Ministers ain't like they used to be. I thought Dave was the only minister that was . . . odd . . . you know . . . he doesn't preach in a church and . . . you know, doesn't behave himself."

The Reverend Jewel Grissom lowers her eyes to Merlin's boots and wide stance and the few inches of crooked rooty path between him and Albion's wide stance.

Now David Turnbull heaves up onto the bank and passes behind Jewel and David Moody. With his head down, pawing through a pile of clothes, he asks, "So what *do* you want us for?"

And Merlin says under his breath, "This feels like some kinda communist conspiracy . . . just jokin' . . . but you know . . ."

The Reverend Grissom looks off toward the far bank of the river and at the pieces of ragged moon riding fast water, and then up at the pale shape of Merlin's face. She smiles shyly. "And all that y'all been up to up here . . . sneaking around and giving the well-to-do folks and greedy folks hell, stealing and setting up caskets with papier-mâché likenesses in their yards and goat stink in their cellars and milk cartons of blood in their cars . . . ya'll been thinking of *yourselves* as communists?"

The shorter of her brothers grins broadly and drawls, "Why that blood in the milk carton was mighty impressive."

Shrugging into his denim Harley vest, David Turnbull is chortling, mostly to himself.

"We all gave to that," brags the other mill foreman, Mark Finley.

"And we run the knife through bleach every time," Macky Turnbull tells them. "You know . . . in case one of us has the nasties." He now breaks out into one of his lusty heinous laughs.

Joel Barrington says with a little teasing bob of the head, "We almost lost Norm . . . cuttin' him an artery. Main channel, was it Norm?"

"Yep," Norman replies and now at last laughs his own heinous laugh. "But I lived."

Shell Turnbull tsks. "It *did* look bad at the time, you guys . . . you know . . . Norman bleedin' that bad. It's only funny now."

"Can I say another word about communism?" the black brother wonders.

"Yes, comrade!" Macky Turnbull jokes.

"Well, the thing about communism," the man explains, "is it has always been welcome among populations that have been ravaged by capitalism. The best way to prevent communism is to maintain a system where there's no masses of oppressed or neglected people. I can tell you that hour by hour this country is no longer yours. You stand here right now on this spot of American soil. But hear my grandaddy's wisdom . . . it isn't beyond a company's means to take that ground right out from under you."

A few faces glance over at Merlin Soule to try and see how he's taking this.

"So," says Macky. "I don't get it. You want us to help overthrow the government?"

"Heck no," says the tall black brother.

"Time for the pledge of allegiance!" Macky Turnbull hollers. "Hey! Lloyd-o! Give us a flag!"

Lloyd's eyes are steamy on the strangers, arms at his sides. He's not moving. Just the river moves, grabbing at his ankles, moving on. Night. It is always his friend.

Joel squats down to his and his father's clothes bundled between mossed rocks. He tugs something from a pocket of a pair of dungarees. A striped rag, blotched and torn. Joel raises his fist with the rag.

Macky groans a few bars of the national anthem.

Through all this the black brother has been staring at the shadowy face of Lloyd and finally says, "Lloyd Barrington. Mastermind. Houdini. The legendary. I'm honored."

Lloyd's hair and heavy moustache still drizzling with water, body goose-bumped and locked into a motionless full-blown terror . . . forever the shy, once-fat boy . . . he, a man whose deeds put him in true peril . . . finding equal peril in ordinary introductions to new friends. He barely nods hello.

Now the Reverend Jewel Grissom is also trying to make out Lloyd's face, the glowing white-blue parts of his face that aren't whiskered. She whispers to her friend, David, "It is . . . that's him, isn't it?"

"Our fearless leader," David whispers back with a snort.

"I wasn't sure if he was here tonight. I can't really tell who is who. My brother John . . . eagle eyes. He's right good." She touches David's arm. "Your fox is not what I expected."

"What did you expect?"

She leans closer. "Someone more like *you*."

The shorter brother speaks low and the gulping, shlishing river steals some of his words. "In the old days . . . the old old old very old days, robbing from the rich and tackling a bad government was possible. You could always find a way to scale those castle walls. But in the 1990s, y'all ain't going to get anywhere near the power figures . . . not ever. The 1990s royal folks are hi-tech and that's that. Just for instance, y'all heard of the *A*-pache helicopter?"

"Yessir!" Morelli calls out.

Jewel Grissom speaks out in her fetching preacher's voice, "There's nothing we can do about our government! Nobody's going to overthrow it . . . not ever! It may fall economically into the complete ownership of a global corporate entity . . . but *we* are not going to lay a finger on that government! Our only hope . . . and this is just my observation . . . is interdependence. We need to start saying 'no' to jobs with big businesses and their products . . . whenever there's a choice. We need to rely on each other. We need only to eat, stay warm, stay well, and love!" She closes her eyes. Seems an Amen would be called out from her congregation now. But of course . . . nothing . . . just this terrible and unwelcoming silence. She looks around from face to face to face, says, "We need to relearn how to move softly and with dignity like the Indians. We need to support each other . . . whatever's left of your small businesses and farms, your tradesmen. To hell with buying American. Buy or trade with your *neighbor!* Buy from that *face* not the brand name! Do this whenever there's a choice, even when it costs a little more. What price can we put on our freedom?"

Nobody says anything.

Jewel looks down into her hands . . . hands learned in prayer. She says, "Interdependence. Community. Families. A whole new concept dredged up from death. Think about it. For thousands of years we grew our own food. In two or three generations those skills have been stripped from us. Schooling has done this. And we condoned it . . . this reverence for the white shirt, the desk, the clean hands, the books, the computers, the bucks, the conveniences, the 'good' job somewhere else! How many survival skills do your children have? How many kids today can provide for themselves food, tools, clothing, warmth . . . from the elements? Please, please, please, in the *name of God,* pass along any skills you have . . . any of the old skills . . . *teach* . . . teach your sons and daughters . . . whisper your secrets to your neighbor's child! Get them ready! Please! This is serious! They are in danger!"

Silence, but for the river and the glibberish of the distant radios.

The Reverend Jewel Grissom turns on David Moody in a sudden and says sharply, "Your friends don't . . ."

David takes her hands. He grins. "Well . . . it's just . . . they aren't . . ." He squeezes her hands. "They aren't feeling presentable, madame."

She takes a deep breath, becomes once again composed and ministerly. "You are right. This isn't a very well-planned visit." She glances around quickly, then shrugs. "The enemy's board of directors are never expected to plan their strategies in the nude. I'm going back to the van and give your people here a chance to . . . to . . . get their dignity back. I'm sorry. I just get so . . . so carried away! We just got in and then Shirl said you were over here, David . . . and I was so anxious to see you. I truly am sorry." She glances up at Kit and Shell Turnbull and Chucky Hubbard and Merlin and Albion all on the path, blocking the way out . . . which is a good sign. This group that is synchronized, so much common tie, tied by blood and the common roots . . . the truest passion . . . the only real love.

Joel Barrington tosses his father his pants.

9 | Saturday. Midday. In this small home that Shirl Moody keeps snug as a feathered nest, this place where she keeps her heart . . . they have come.

Here it is, Aspect Street, near enough to the mill that you would still miss that thrumm-bm-bm-bm-bm-bm-bm-bm-bm of the compressors and the high noon whistle. Mostly silence outside. And the ticking of the two clocks inside.

Shirl wipes her hands on her jeans. Hands that not only make a home, but make music. Sufficient music. Nothing that would make her world-renowned. But music that guides the voices of her beloved small circle . . . hymns and songbook favorites like "Red River Valley," "On Top of Old Smokey," and "Let Me Call You Sweetheart." Shirl's hands aren't really made for playing. Her hands sweat. Her hands actually drip. Causes the fingers to slip on the keys. But the way the family tells it, Shirl's dripping hands heal. They can name half a dozen occasions when people and pets, even automobiles recovered from maladies when Shirl touched them. The faith in Shirl's family is your old day-in-and-day-out never languishing faith, part of every thought, every cry, every swallow, every word. They worship. They wail. They belong. They are not so sure about David . . . Shirl's husband . . . but they forgive him and love him. It is their job to forgive. It will be *God's* job to take vengeance.

Whenever Shirl plays the piano, she wears dress gloves.

Shirl is quiet with these guests. Not a cold shoulder. Nothing like that. She has welcomed them. But their talk is incessant. They are like hounds onto something, hurrying along on a scent. They are up all night with David . . . and some of David's friends from around town . . . talk, talk, talk, talk. Then their talking begins again at breakfast. The West Virginians have wonderful manners. The men call her ma'am or Miss Shirley. But then there's the talk. Convoluted and questioning. They seem to press for a commitment to something that isn't clear to Shirl. But she knows it's not *God*. She hates them. She starts another pot of coffee. She wipes her hands on her jeans.

Wearing reading glasses, the Reverend Jewel Grissom walks forward on the rug on hands and knees, spreads a hand on one newspaper. So this is Jewel. David's old friend from seminary. There have always been the letters . . . typed letters running ten and twenty pages . . . sometimes weekly. But this is the first visit.

Jewel says, "Now look at this. You got these state employees here, social workers in this picket. Then here"—slides her hand to an overlapping section of *State & Local*—"You got these paper mill men here . . . and then over on this previous week, these machinists here at this place . . . all union boys there, too . . ." She raises up onto her knees, pulls a section of paper toward her. "These people here . . . people getting mad about poison waste being dumped in their neighborhood." Jewel smiles up at Shirl who stands near with her hands in the pockets of her jeans. Jewel laughs. "Why look at that ol' boy! All those message buttons. I can't make out what they read, but there's his T-shirt . . . reads DON'T UNDERESTIMATE MAINE'S PEOPLE. Don't he look *mean* pointing there with accusation across that microphone . . . hard ol' farmer is what he looks like . . . ol' boy standing up to those waste management committee folks." She rises to her feet, places this section of paper in Shirl's arms delicately as though it were a spray of flowers.

David stares around his wife's shoulder at the picture.

The tall black-featured Grissom brother whose name is John leans in and chuckles, "Hey . . . *that* boy, I like. Looks like a little wet hornet."

There's a clomp in the close-by room. The baby waking up too early from her nap. Her signal for help is to pitch out her bottle of juice.

The Reverend Jewel Grissom says of the picture, "Gottem festerin'." She looks over Shirl's shoulder to David's face. Her eyes a dark muddy green there behind her reading glasses. And her overshirt is that camouflage print of varied greens and beiges, this worn over a shirt of an almost revolting green-yellow. Now she kneels again, returning to her examination of the stacks of recent papers, nudging and nudging the nosepiece of her glasses. Her motions could fool you, and that expression on her face like some sweet half-remembered good thing . . . this is not the full truth . . . David Moody knows . . . it is part of his friendship with this woman . . . her pigheadedness.

Shirl steps away to open the door and then inside that little room, there's her voice and the baby's giggle.

Jewel says, "Now here's this with the group objecting to an ash dump . . . and here's some men . . . what's this? . . . Kiwanis rebuilding a burned covered bridge . . . nice, very nice." She sighs, both hands now spread on the thighs of her jeans, head down, eyes shut. She drums with the fingers of one hand.

David squats next to her and studies a headline. The movement of him so near her "reawakens" Jewel so that she pulls a heap of papers toward her from the far left. "Then over here"—she nods toward a tabloid-sized paper—"nice people picketing outside an agribusiness operation that's importing and abusing Mexicans . . . some nice cheap labor there, you see. One placard here calls it 'servitude.' "

Another paper. "You have an especially big problem around here with helicopter surveillance . . . hmmm. A few good souls getting irritated with that. Bless them." She squints toward the foot pedals of Shirl's piano. Not much of a house, but *a lot* of piano . . . and now Shirl's feet and legs reappearing, stepping around the newspapers. She carries the baby. Going to the kitchen with the baby.

Jewel returns to the picture of the placard that reads SERVITUDE. "Law on that's pretty sludgy-goin'. Can't do much. Maybe catch a few workers with fake papers. Immigration'll send them home so fast they won't have time to grab a coat. And . . . you know . . . that satisfies a lot."

Now Zachary appears from another doorway, too excited by the guests to even get started on his nap. On his face no sign of sleep. No bloat, no creases, nothing like disorientation. He runs a beeline over the newspapers, muckles onto his father's legs and looks up to say "Hi!" as if David were the guest . . . long-time-no-see. David grins. He pulls the boy up over his shoulder and turns to the couch. David says, "*I* need a nap." True . . . such darkness around the eyes . . . a darkness emphasized by the dark blue of his work shirt . . . not a well-drilling shirt today. This is one of his weekend shirts. No penny-color embroidered lettering, but otherwise the same. He's never looked so tired. He lowers himself to the couch gratefully and shuts his eyes. On his lap, the boy jounces. The boy is towhead. David's hair is more of a yellow . . . but no doubt a towhead of the past.

The Grissom brother named Francis calls from another seat. "Hey boy! Ate all that popcorn already?"

Zachary bails out of David's lap and rushes for the kitchen.

Jewel is saying, "What you got is fifteen people on a curb with twenty to a hundred miles between each curb." She gets to her feet, backs up and settles on the piano stool, arms crossed over her thighs. "And in all those miles that are between the curbs are folks that are watching scandals on the TV . . . or complaining . . . but just complaining to themselves . . . about the big bad stuff that's happening to them and their families. But you see, all these folks' problems have a common denominator . . . capitalism—consumerism—and impractical schooling . . . the thing that has been so holy for so long that even now . . . here, you see, they don't question it. Not as a whole. Only their little particular grievances."

The brother John says, "The big picture is too big."

Shirl carries the baby around the outer edge of the newspapers and asks David, "Can you hang on to her a sec?"

He takes the baby, tips her upside down, roughs her up, mashes his mouth against her stomach and makes a fart noise there. Baby giggles and gags and her cheeks get redder and redder.

Zachary comes back, carrying a cup of popcorn, stands a few feet from Francis's chair, stares at Francis and crunches up a few unpopped kernels.

Jewel is scowling at another paper. "I don't see one single placard that tells us: This business is behaving in a fashion that is unpatriotic and un-American. Wouldn't I love to see a little Thomas Jefferson quote about it being impossible for an industrialized nation to be a true democracy.

All you see here"—she nods toward the array on the rug—"State employee here with a placard that reads: My property taxes up $100/My pay down $1,800." Jewel shuts her eyes tight. Silence. Is this prayer? Condemnation? Unconditional love? She ruffles her dark curly hairdo, eyes sweeping over the various headlines and photos and photo captions.

David says, "Well, you see those ash-dump-people don't care about that manufacturer over there bustin' the local machinists' union . . . and these machinists don't give a damn about the Mexicans . . . in fact, probably somebody's blaming the Mexicans for taking up jobs."

Jewel sighs.

Shirl sinks to the couch alongside David, Shirl with her chipped front tooth, short chestnut hair, gray eyes, yellow turtleneck jersey. Shirl's yellow isn't anything like the ghastly yellow of Jewel's shirt. Shirl's yellow is like buttercups.

The baby crawls back and forth between David's and Shirl's laps.

Jewel says, "You are right, David. The people protesting there for the Mexicans aren't working class, I'll bet. I see it looks like a little bitty group of your usual god-blessed oldish hippie element. Whoooooooo-eeeeeee! Nice." She stands, collects a few papers, shapes them into a chunky even-edged pile. She hefts the pile. She opens her hands and the pile smacking the floor makes David jump . . . for he had, in these few seconds, closed his eyes again and drifted.

Jewel's laugh is an easy one. "Now *that* would have broken my foot if it landed there." She smiles as if at something secret, then glances from one child's face to the other. "To get the people together as a power . . . it's a little like Dr. Frankenstein's homemade man . . . named Legion . . . made of many. The doctor used the arms of one body, the head of another, the heart of another . . . and for these differences, the creation was empowered." She pushes at the sleeves of her shirts and looks at her forearms. They are beautiful nearly hairless dark arms that look to have known more hard work than prayer. "But things didn't go right for Dr. Frankenstein in the end. His creation kept spoiling on him. Little spots of spoil kept cropping up on the skin. And the creature couldn't get its breath at times. Had to keep jolting the creature's chest . . . trying to bring life back. Its brain kept spoiling. Its heart kept losing interest." She stares at David's face. "What do you think? It's got to be local, huh? It's always gotta be small."

David says, "Right."

Jewel looks at Shirl. "And we've got to consider the schools. Schools are where it's at. Big business is moving in. Getting more of a hand in education policies. They say students are not showing enough 'excellence,' their scores not as high as students in some other countries. Got to keep up with those other countries! Got to win! Win! Win! Rah! Rah! Rah! Big Biz says if they own the schools, or if they can help us out with policies, our kids will win win win. There's been no interest thus far on the part of educators to teach our kids *self*-discipline, interdependence, and a sense of responsibility to others . . . certainly not any working together. Only competition. And now Big Biz insists, if they are given the chance, they can create the ultimate competitive society. And I believe they can. And everyone will be entirely dependent on big business, and entirely created in the image of big business. Many will fail at the competitive part, but they'll certainly be dependent! They will not make the grade at the fast and funny new hi-tech life. They will fall by the wayside. But there will be a place for those kind! The military. The prisons. And executions like you never saw before." Now she speaks into Shirl's slight glower, "Yes, it's the children we've got to educate *our* way. We can't let the business world get its claws on America's last unexploited unspoiled resource."

10 David Moody takes his friend for a drive in the family wagon. Shows her a lot of Egypt. Shows her some of the places where he has drilled wells. He shows her where his boss lives, old farmplace in tall grass close to the curvy narrow uphill road. There are no working drill rigs on the premises, all three of them having been set up somewhere, waiting on water. He tells her of some of his days, the five-hundred-feet days with nothing but sand. He tells her about the last conversation the crew had on Friday. And then how the Johnson boy and Vic Landry burst into howls . . . then there was a falling into silence, like prayer. This often happens he tells her. The holy damn awful wonderness of water that *never* comes . . . of equipment that breaks down every time you look at it wrong . . . of the great patience of his boss Omar Wicks whose glasses have black frames and the lenses are thick and because his name is Omar some of the crew have, over the years, always called him The Sheik. But Omar has never been married, is a dyed-in-the-wool hermit . . . but there's no evidence that he dislikes being called The Sheik . . . and the holy wonderness of water when it *does* come, the relief of water when it comes, the slap on the back, the giddy whoooooooooosh, the mess, the hustle. The particular way ledge cuttings will lodge, blocking veins. Air pressure. Water pressure. Keeping drill bits cool. The tophead, the carousel, and drill rods. Then he tells her about "Hydro-Frac," the latest big gadget in the well-drilling biz.

"Hydro-Frac," he repeats, his mouth feeling good around the good word.

He asks Jewel if she'd like him to drive her over to Silver Heights to see a well rig set up.

She says she would like that very much.

He beams. It is like he is taking her, his friend, to see a monument to his soul.

Out across a clipped lawn, up among the high branches of trees, the iron cage of the rotor, cables, and hoses soar. A tower. And above that only sky.

He tells her how Omar still has a "pounder" . . . a slow, but more efficient rig . . . the old way. Though not as old a way as driving a point. Or digging with a shovel, then lowering down the tiles or granite with chains or rope.

He tells her how one of the guys, St. Cyr, dowses. But that St. Cyr doesn't like to talk about it. He just does it. "Try and explain dowsing," David says with a grin, shaking his head. "Just don't ask St. Cyr to explain. You'd think you'd asked him to explain masturbation."

At Bean's Variety, David stops and picks out ice-cream sandwiches, one for Jewel and one for himself.

Headed back toward East Egypt, they talk about the seminary days and the few others they've kept in touch with over the years.

They talk about her and her brothers' trip home to West Virginia that begins tomorrow at dawn. He insists she try Route 81 to avoid the worst cities.

He tells her how good it has been to see her after all these years.

He tells her of the responsibility he feels here, that somehow . . . he feels responsible . . .

He gives the wheel a yank as if to avoid striking something in the road. But the road is empty. He steers the little car to the shoulder of the road. He crosses his arms over the wheel. His blond hair is thick and shaggy over his collar. Only the top is thinning . . . a small crescent as pink and vulnerable as his face.

He lays his head back, working his jaws, so close to tears. But this is okay. A best friend always understands. A best friend has cried many times for the same reasons. A best friend who, like yourself, a disappointed child of God, had once believed light and truth, when you found them, would be synonyms for joy.

11 | Word of the good mission is passed on.
     Out on the porch of Bean's Variety where old men slouch, a lone five year old happens along and the old men's eyes widen upon him.

This kid is no stranger . . . he's Hal's great nephew, ain't he?

They hustle him out to that resilient tall grass that grows up around the propane tanks.

"Hold it like this," they explain.

The hasp of this scythe is worn to fit the shape of a larger hand, but the little boy seems earnest.

These old guys look into each other's eyes.

Some want to tease the little boy.

Others praise.

Depends on one's style.

The mother bursts around the corner. She wears a snappy blue jacket that matches her eyes exactly. "Jason!"

Her eyes travel around over the figures and faces of the old men as if there were something here . . . something *going on* . . . something lecherous.

She brushes off the boy's pants and sleeves, his new school clothes. "Come on, Jason. Let's go." She looks up to meet the eyes of the closest man. She laughs nervously. "You just can't imagine how quickly kids can get into things."

The old men watch her lead the boy to the white car, where the boy is fastened in, door shut and locked. Safe.

The mother shifts into drive.

And away they go.

PART ELEVEN

1 | In Miracle City, your neighbors are close. You hear their coughing
     up and down the lane. Different kinds of coughs. Some coughs are like chuckles. Some croupy and deep. Sherry Barrington's cough is

like a bucket gone down a well, coming up in that way you have to heave-ho with both arms.

Merlin Soule's cough comes mostly from next door where he spends his time these days. Merlin's "other woman" with the floppy flannel shirts and that mole they used to call a "beauty mark" beside her mouth. Her hair is styled like Elvis's. She calls it wash 'n' wear. Dottie Soule, who would usually have a lot of high-hoopin' opinions on a thing, has nothing to say on this, even when through these thin Miracle City walls, the other woman's deep and even drone of conversation seems fairly nonstop, a fairly constant reminder. Since the night Merlin fell down on his knees, since the night of cops and Merlin's arrest, the jail, the pictures of him in the newspapers, his face miserable with confusion, hands handcuffed, just hanging . . . and the plea bargain, and the talk, talk, talk . . . and now, Dottie knows she can no longer handle Merlin . . . the big job of Merlin Soule . . . the big job of Merlin's Soule's shame . . . the big job of seeing his face and all the bluff that amounted to nothing.

Merlin has never smoked cigarettes or anything. His cough is a mystery.

Nor did Sherry smoke, and yet Sherry's cough is the eye of the storm of all Miracle City coughs.

Sisters and daughters of the sisters and the husbands of these take turns driving Sherry to different doctors. Some doctors say Sherry's cough is nothing. One doctor says Sherry's cough is a mystery. Tests on Sherry's blood show nothing. Doctors and tests costing the sisters and their families all the money they have. What about Lloyd? It's Lloyd's turn. After all, Sherry is *his* wife.

But all Lloyd says is, "Let her be."

"Hospital is free," some say. So now the sisters and daughters of the sisters and the husbands of these take turns at the phone booth at the IGA or at the homes of the sisters who still have phones . . . hospital emergency number written in ink on the tops of their hands. And the story of Sherry's cough is a long one. Hospital isn't interested in any long stories. For a cough "you just need to have her see her doctor," the voice informs.

Three times they take Sherry to three different hospitals. "A cough is not an emergency," said three different ways.

Back at the farmplace, which the bank took, the distance from the sofa to the opposite wall was several ferns of the fern-print linoleum. But here in Miracle City, no space. The sofa where Sherry lies now in her hard fetallike ball shape serves as her bed, but also a place for those who need to sit down . . . a sister with her knitting or a child with its own kind of cough.

Everyone knows Lloyd has *ways* of coming up with money. At *least* another hundred. The sisters and nieces bully and curse him, but all he says is, "Let her be."

Eventually, the sisters, and the neighbors they are closest to, collect another hundred dollars.

Hundred dollar doctor writes a prescription which costs sixty-eight dollars to have filled. So there's a scramble for this money, but then ol' Sherry . . . she just couldn't swallow those capsules anyway.

Meanwhile, Lloyd is out behind the Soule camp, laying board to board for a fir casket. In his "business," he knows by feel the dimensions for a good casket.

Merlin and his other woman hang around with Lloyd, looking on.

Merlin tsks. "Is this legal? Is this something you can just go ahead and *do*?"

Lloyd says yes. According to Maine law, you can be buried in a sheet. He looks into Merlin's eyes. "Unless you are near a water table or well."

"Buried in a sheet," the woman repeats with a trace of a smile.

Merlin roams off and returns with a ratty shred of sandpaper.

Lloyd is grateful for the sandpaper, slides it into a pocket of his stained washed-out old blue chambray shirt. He listens to Merlin's woman talking. Her voice is so clear and low and emollient.

Merlin keeps his hands at his sides, except to jerk a fist to his mouth to cover one more cough.

Out on the tar road past Miracle City the chips trucks come every ten minutes. Twenty-six tons a load. Unlike the rhythm of the tides, these truck runs bear in tighter. And tighter still. Ten minutes between. Now six. And there's the howl of the chippers on the edge of morning to the falling off of dark, on and on and on and on. The old forests *will* succumb. And the trucks come and come and come and the tar roads are broken to pieces.

Sherry's hair is red and gray, kept short for easy care. Her freckled arms, cheeks, and temples sparkle, damp. A sister rests her hand on Sherry's shoulder. The sister stares out the open door into the hot weeds and sand. The sister is trying to keep a grip on Sherry's life, the life that isn't even worth another hundred dollars. And from the apartment-sized propane stove next to the sofa, there's the contented gurglings of boiling potatoes. And under the hand of her sister, with no understanding of the brake, brake, brake of chips trucks on the hill or the crack, crack, crack of that nearby hammer, Sherry finds her own rhythm . . . a breath, a breath, a breath . . .

2 | Funny about hospitals. Funny about laws and the ways of the world of official doings. Soules wish now the hospital would leave them alone, just let them keep Sherry, make her place of peace their own way . . . the direct no-nonsense way . . . the quiet early-morning chuff chuff of the shovel. But oh no . . . now the hospital and the law demand they turn Sherry's body over and no Soule bullying or bluffing can stop them.

3 | Two weeks and still the hospital keeps the body. So much "paperwork," the hospital voice complains. "With an undertaker, the process is much faster."

"We can't be the only people without a big wad!" Francine DiBias bellers into the phone.

The nephews that have accompanied Francine are racing in and out of the IGA's automatic doors.

The hospital voice reminds Francine that the body will be in a plastic bag, that whoever picks up the body should be prepared for that.

"Oh, thank you for that important reminder!"

Now inside the store, Francine squats to compare the prices of three brands of tuna.

While outside the chips trucks come roaring through the middle of town, bearing down on the bumpers of slower vehicles.

4 | From the sofa Dottie Soule looks up as Lloyd Barrington steps through the door, looking large, as everyone does in such close quarters. Crusher hat in his hands.

And Dottie, also large . . . big and skinny. Ponytail, skinny, nearly all white. Lenses of her glasses scratched and cloudy. Too expensive to replace.

Lloyd sits at the other end of the sofa with a respectable space between them. A whistling tea kettle goes off in a nearby trailer. A chips truck shakes the earth and air. And there are coughs all up and down the lane.

And TV with soap operas with big music and commercials that shriek.

With no land, no real kitchen, and a husband who falls on his knees, Dottie has no more busy days. These losses are greater than losing Sherry, the grief insurmountable.

Sherry is now at last buried over at the big cemetery on Rummery Road.

Lloyd and Dottie get into a conversation about all the ways your stomach can give you trouble. According to Lloyd, the worst is that which runs like a torch up to your throat at night . . . or maybe the worst is the kind that sounds like World War II movies in your lower stomach. He fusses with one side of his moustache throughout these considerations.

"Well *that* . . . there's no need of that, Lloyd. You just have to stay away from cabbage and turnips. God almighty!" Behind her glasses, Dottie's eyes become narrowed. Prickly. "Stay away from cabbage and turnips!" she commands.

He says he will.

And now they discuss the rumor that in order to pay his taxes, old Eldon Shaw has a marijuana patch with plants as big as elms. "It's because he used to sell whiskey with his brothers in the twenties and got away with that, so he probably figures this will blow over, too," Dottie supposes.

"Yep," says Lloyd, who supposes the same thing.

Now they talk on other subjects, both there on the couch with the space between them. They look out through the open door or at each other, but mostly through the open door, and on all subjects they suppose the same thing, and the afternoon wears on gently.

PART TWELVE

In Portland, Maine, the Bureau of Manpower Affairs puts out notice of a machinist's job at a local company. Two thousand, two hundred applicants show up.

PART THIRTEEN

In Portland, Maine, hotel banquet rooms are hired to accommodate the elongated unemployment lines. Some of the Egypt wise men say that this is the government trying to keep these ranks less visible. Some Egypt wise men are uncharacteristically silent. One will shift his boots. Another pretends he is sleepy.

PART FOURTEEN

1 Contractions. Labor pains. It has its own brain. It is an eye other than your eye. It has its eye on you. It is smarter than you or anybody. It lives, it moves, it crawls. When Anneka is resting from the last time it ripped through her, her hand now dangling from the sleeve of her purple robe, she is listening for its next move, as it whispers to itself and among its selves. For Anneka, there's no rhythm, no way to predict. She can't figure out a way to brace against it. Most times it's an ambush.

While out on the tar road the chips trucks grind past five minutes apart, then three minutes apart, then two minutes, fierce and deliberate, a river of crushed trees, pouring out of Egypt.

2 It is the third day of Anneka's labor, three days, three nights since the hospital said no. Hospital said admittance is only when it's an emergency. An emergency is labor. What Anneka is having is not labor. The hospital also mentions that when she returns with real labor, she should have either a health insurance card or a deposit of a thousand dollars. They ask if she and Carroll own their own home or other real estate. What is the value of their car? The hospital explains that they will not turn away an emergency, money or no money. To Anneka, these words ricochet in and out of meaning. There's something she hasn't heard right. She doesn't trust herself. Carroll says that *he* is always mishearing things. Join the club!

So what Anneka has is not real labor. It is something that will go away. "Lie on your left side. That helps," the hospital suggests.

Chips trucks out on the hill. Coming down harder, faster. Brake. Brake. Brake.

"Home" for Anneka and Carroll Plummer these days is a camper on a pickup truck, camper with a bunk and little door. This is Turnbull land. Turnbulls are bikers. There's the river with its buggy swampish tall grasses. View of the silent mill and its thin silver stack . . . stack is very pretty and slim . . . like a ladies' cigarette.

And off to the left are alder and partridgeberry.

And up and over all is the flaccid white hot early September sky.

There's no going back to the Chief's house on the lake with the Chief's family settled in there now . . . with the wife . . . the wife who says "no way." And home is where you are wanted, isn't it? And the Turnbulls have never minded a crowd.

It is now dawn. Between contractions, Anneka lies quietly. Spent. Her purple flannel robe is twisted around her like she's been caught in a big wind.

The phone. So far to get to a phone. Seems like ten miles to David Turnbull's mother's place . . . the nearest phone. Across the field and packed dirt yard, beyond the garage and biker clutter, and bikers in the distance working on Harleys or stock cars of their own or for customers, beyond the capped cellar where David and Kit and their kids and dogs make constant door-slamming, pan-clattering, rummaging, rapturous never-ending noise; along the path to the sweet white house where the mother Turnbull lives with her boyfriend Billy . . . that's where the phone is.

To walk this path alone, Anneka risks a contraction that will ambush her part way to the house.

Like yesterday. Right there, alone on the path, she had to squat. And she keened in her pain. And there, directly over her, a green National Guard helicopter chomp-chomp-chomped.

The trees swooned and wagged.

She could see the heads of the operators, headphones and coiled wires, the mirror-look of the sunglasses of one of these heads. And the terrifying inner chamber of this aircraft. And the chomp-chomp-chomp made a pressure she thought might explode in her head. But worse . . . her shame . . . to be squatted there . . . to be *viewed* . . . the overhead surveillance of her squat.

It swung away . . . circled again . . . swung away, circling.

She knows that all open fields and woods are suspect.

So today Anneka has started out long before noon, long before the surveillance usually begins, sunny noontimes being prime time for the "drug warriors."

It turns out that the mother Turnbull isn't home. But she has always insisted that Anneka feel free to help herself. The mother Turnbull calls her little white clapboard house "Headquarters."

Anneka dials the number and talks to one of the clinic doctors whose voice sounds familiar though she doesn't catch his name. Doctor says that what Anneka has is not real labor. He tells her to lie on her left side and it will go away. The doctor seems vexed. "This is Anneka Plummer, right?" he sighs.

She says yes.

He says, "And this is the same thing as before . . . when you were in here."

She says, "Yes, it goes on all night real bad, but in the day it comes and goes . . . but it's really awful." She says, "Maybe the baby needs to come out like my cousin's. She had to have C-sections."

He says if it would make her happy, she could come to the hospital and be checked, but that she'll only be sent home again if it's not *progressive* labor. He sighs again. And she says thank you and hangs up.

Another contraction that begins with a whisper now brings her to a squat on the mother Turnbull's kitchen floor.

3 | Night brings the worst . . . the great fight to the finish . . . the contractions that mean business . . . five minutes apart, then four minutes apart, then circling her, they recede to six minutes, ten minutes. But then, high-pitched and fiery . . . five and five and five.

And Carroll, her dear one, her soul, disappears beyond the wall of flame . . . out there saying, "Anneka. Jesus . . ." and she is there inside the pain where he can't enter.

By morning, when he's gone with one of the Turnbulls job hunting, after she grinds up a cracker in her teeth, her medication, a cup of water, the contractions subside. That one and only night Anneka had gotten inside the hospital, the sonogram said the baby is breech, backwards breech—feet down, face out. Doctor said not to worry. And Anneka wasn't worried. No, not worried.

She slides off the bunk again and steps over to the peeing pail. She sees one of Carroll's chamois shirts wound into a ball at one end of the wheelwell bench . . . and there is his prescription bottle in it. She reads the label, the date of expiration, the date of last refill. He has not refilled this bottle for several months.

Anneka climbs back up on the bunk.

The birth canal walls are like bare live electric wires on the verge of the next ZAP! Feels like something wrong there. A short circuit, a cheap make. But nothing is wrong! Everything is routine! The doctors know all the ways. The doctors are not worried. Anneka is not worried. Just tired.

The chips trucks coming in through town are glutted, racing against time and money.

And then at noon, there's the advancing CHOMP-CHOMP-CHOMP-CHOMP of the drug war helicopter. It swings down and around. Seems a pressure builds inside the little camper. The CHOMP-CHOMP-CHOMP-CHOMP is sucking out the air.

How deep and lusty all these engines of progress. And how their gears so efficiently comply.

4 | It was a nasty scene this past spring with his uncle Albion Cole when Carroll lost his job. This evening the subject of jobs is in the air.

"Biting the hand that feeds you," Anneka snorts.

Carroll narrows his dark-lashed yellow eyes on the middle of her face and she suddenly fears him. And she wonders if in some way Albion had also feared him . . . Albion Cole who has been so good to Carroll . . . there is no counting the ways. And so now, all this summer, there's been days and days with no money but for Anneka's little pay and tips from the diner . . . till the contractions started. Now it's all up to Carroll. And what is there out there for Carroll? A Saturday now and then at the salvage yard. And cutting for Del Jackman's crew till Del's brother got off his drunk. Then a little sawmill work up to Jim Fogg's. But not *much* sawmill work. Most loads are leaving Egypt. Biomass and pulp. Fall it, chip it, truck it. After that you haven't got a hand in it.

He smokes and smokes and smokes. He's not good to be near right now . . . and yet he is so good . . . his yellowy eyes filled with apologies even as his mouth is hard and smoke scrawls in an ugly way across his face and stained T-shirt.

"Well, I have work tomorrow," he tells her. "Billy's letting me take his van even if he doesn't go. He might not go. Depends."

This is Carroll's mystery work, the job he won't answer her questions about. So now she's stopped asking. It is the work of death. Death by his hand. Cattle? Turkeys? Sheep?

"You take what you can get," says he, looking away from her, pitching his crushed cigarette butt out through the open door of the camper. She watches him hard for signs of depression. She would think these were the signs, but nothing is clear anymore. *Everybody's* depressed.

The night is one of those September nights with a good bite of frost in it, but Anneka is running hot, twisted in a lather from the endless work of endless labor.

In the morning before light, Carroll fixes a Thermos of water and some crackers to take with him to his mystery job.

After a contraction, Anneka returns to clarity to find him gone and she grieves. Then just as suddenly, in the middle of the next contraction, he materializes, hunched over the little cabinet, then turns, reaches up to the bunk to get a grip on her, saying, "Jesus . . . this isn't right. I've *never* heard of a baby coming this way."

He steps outside to get her a cup of cool water poured from the row of plastic milk jugs stored along one of the truck's rear tires. He gives her a tablet of her heart medication. "Take this. And I'll make you a bowl of cereal." She swallows the medication with the water, has another contraction . . . then finds him standing there with a bowl of oatmeal made just a little too gluey. She swallows some oatmeal. Has another contraction. It's so hard to swallow, so very gluey. And she's so tired. But she is obedient. She can barely remember the old Anneka, the unruly one . . . the person with cause and effect.

5 | Before noon the distant chomp-chomp-chomp-chomp wakes her like a washing machine that spins to rinse, a bad stammer in the walls. Each day she has a bigger and bigger flash of fear. She has heard how the drug warriors can bust in on you screaming FREEZE! and PO-LICE! and SEARCH WARRANT! Black SWAT outfits and National Guard greens. They frisk you. They stand by the beds in the rooms of your home and hold rifles to your kids' heads while they tear your rooms apart looking for marijuana or marijuana seeds or paraphernalia or some sort of records. And they take your belongings, take your kids, and eventually claim your home. Carroll has told her about the Drug Hotline where anyone can call leaving no name to say there's something fishy about your big field, your garden, your trees, your friends, your habits. The government need only suspect you have pot to observe you inces-santly, then make their raid. There were the people in the news who had had only alfalfa seeds. There was the man on the island with the little oriental maple trees and the maple leaves had tested out as marijuana in the government labs. Then after a time they tested again and got it right.

At one time Anneka would have dashed off letters in red ink, complaining what this must cost the taxpayers! And why all this fuss over a relaxant herb?!!!

But now she just lies here against the shaking tin wall, imagining them busting in while she is squatted on the peeing pail. They would enter this space . . . which is not much larger than the space of her womb . . . to stare at the peeing pail, to stare at *her*, grim and bossy with their need for evidence.

6 | It is the fifth day after a long night of what *seemed* like progressive labor . . . ten minutes apart . . . then eight minutes apart . . . then three minutes apart. And now the dawn, sun a big mushy yellow-white. And warm wind. Carroll urges her to eat. She shakes her head. He tips out a tablet of her heart medication, offers it to her with water. She swallows it while looking over the cup rim into his eyes. She hands him the cup. "You've been sneaky, Old Thing. You have been secret with your plan to go off the antidepressant."

He says, "We are friggin' lucky to have the money for *these*." He shakes the bottle of her heart medication. He plunks the bottle onto the rim of the teeny stove. "Let's not get into a wrangle over this subject, Anneka. We are getting low on friendly subjects, aren't we?"

Anneka is hit with a contraction, three minutes since the last, thereabouts. When it subsides, she says tiredly, "Maybe this is it." Her mouth is bloated against her bloated face. Her rabbit-white hair is a little darkish . . . dirty.

Carroll has slumped to the wheel-well bench, massaging his knees. "It's a long drive to the hospital. We might as well head out now."

"No . . . the doctor said wait till it is two minutes and *stays* two minutes."

Carroll snorts. "I don't get it. It doesn't sound right."

"Things are different these days. They're kind of easygoing about it, you know. In the old days, people thought of having babies as a . . . an illness. Nowadays, it's nothing."

He stands up, opens and closes both hands. His uneven hair, his television-escaped-convict look never leaves him.

"Carroll . . . do you think you're getting your depression back? Are you starting to think about . . . you know . . . drinking?"

He doesn't answer . . . which is as good as an answer.

Not even true daylight yet and already there's the good roar of a Turnbull out messing with his Harley.

Carroll says, "I've got more work coming up with Jackman. Big lot over to Harrison . . . some guy over there died. They're setting up to yard Thursday morning and I can go over anytime after that."

Another contraction. Anneka grips the sides of the bunk, her face scrinched into a pale unpretty knot. She whines.

Carroll slumps back onto the bench.

When she is finished, Carroll says, "That was about two minutes from the last, I'd say."

Tears run over Anneka's face.

"Look, Anneka. If this keeps up, I'm taking you in again . . . progressive or not. I'll drive this fucking truck right through the fucking hospital doors."

She speaks with no inflection, no expression. "They said they'll just send me home if it's not progressive. It has to be progressive or it's not real."

"Bullshit."

The vrummmmmm-bm bm bm bmbmbmbmbmbmbmmmm of the Harley is so gloriously rhythmic. No error.

And now the first chips truck of the day, barreling toward the crossroads. No error.

Anneka says, "I don't want to go all the way in there unless they keep me. I had to walk through all those halls, across the parking lot, clinging to parking meters, hanging off of car fenders because of those pains. Remember! It hurts so bad. And all for nothing. And they act like . . . like I'm nuts. I felt pretty foolish. It's not worth it." Anneka stares at the camper ceiling which is only inches from her face . . . this coffinlike space, cold at night, breathless heat by day.

Carroll sighs. "So when I'm at work, why can't you just go over and stay by the phone. They can look after you over there."

"Because I have to be polite there. *Here* I can scream."

"They don't care if you scream. They are . . . people who are used to anything. They've seen it all."

"I don't like to scream in front of people. Not even *you*."

Her next contraction wavers . . . peters out. Then there's not another for fifteen minutes . . . just a little twinge of a contraction . . . an on-the-verge whisperish thing.

Carroll shakes his head, pushes open the camper door and steps down, shuts the door behind him.

Anneka tries to imagine the baby's face. On the sonogram the clinic doctor had pointed out where the proof was that the baby is a boy.

All this hell will be over soon and all the Soules will be passing the baby around and Carroll will walk like a peacock and everything will be nice.

7 | Sixth day of labor. Hard cold rain bangs the roof of the camper. Gray plastic cement sealer pail by the wheel-well bench to catch the leak. Ploink. Ploink. Ploink.

Anneka writhes on the bunk. The clamping, bright, sinewy thing deep between her legs attacks every ten minutes, then eight, then five, then twenty, then five, then three, then fifteen. She doesn't cry out. She never cries out in the presence of others.

Little camper shudders. Little camper can't handle Anneka's mother Francine and Aunt Alberta, their outrage, their shoulders, their hips, their shifting this way and that. The truck's springs bray. Francine booms: "I'm going over to one of them Turnbull places and call the hospital NOW. I'm bringing you in and I'm not leaving till they induce."

"With a baby backwards and feet-first, they'll do a cesarean!" Aunt Alberta booms.

"They ain't doing a goddam thing! Look at her! What we gotta do? Fight our way in there with a goddam machine gun?!!"

Anneka goes limp, very very quiet.

"You been taking your heart medicine?" Francine asks.

"I can't remember," Anneka sighs.

"Jesus . . . where is it?"

"On the back of the sink."

Now at the sink window, Francine gasps. "Holy shit! Who's that gorgeous thing out there in that shop doorway? He's workin' on that . . . what the hell is it? . . . looks like a fire engine . . . old truck or something. Who *is* he?"

Anneka says with a giggle, "Ma, how should I know? I can't see them from this bed. Could be anybody. There's a bunch of them."

"Well, this one has a sweet face and short curly dark blond hair. A Florida type shirt . . . flowers or pineapples or monkeys . . . tropical."

Anneka laughs. "Ma, you should live here. You'd like it. There's hundreds of them. I don't keep track. Carroll's enough work for me."

Aunt Alberta narrows her eyes. "Make Carroll wait on you hand and foot at a time like this."

Anneka says, "He's trying."

Francine hunts down a cup, gives it a rinse with water from a plastic jug. "Here . . . have one of these. We don't need you to die of a heart attack or something."

Anneka opens her hand for the tablet.

Aunt Alberta says, "The offer still holds if you guys want to come over. Our couch folds out. We lost the phone . . . but we might get it back after the weekend. At least you'd be near a tub. And there's people to keep an eye on you. We're in and out all day."

Anneka smiles. "You're so nice, Al. But it's okay here. Really. It's okay."

The contraction comes first as a little flickering warning twitch, then the works. Anneka grips one side of the bunk with both hands.

"Where's the keys to this truck!" Francine snarls. "I'm going to drive you in now. You can just lay there where you are. Is there gas in the tank?"

Alberta says to Francine, "They have all kinds of stuff settin' around outside . . . their water and cooler and stuff. Better take her in the car."

"No!" Anneka insists. "They say they won't keep me unless it's progressive labor."

"Fuck the progressive! You been like this for almost a week! And nearly three weeks past your due date! I've never heard of such a thing! Unless you wanna count Sherry! And look what happened there!"

Anneka struggles through the next contraction, gripping the bunk while Francine and Aunt Alberta both breathe like bulls.

At last Anneka is quiet, staring at the ceiling a few inches from her face. "They do things different now than when you guys had kids. They're not as . . . they don't seem as . . . nervous. They do babies all the time. They must know what they're talking about. Ma . . . Sherry was wicked sick with something. Havin' a baby is not an illness, you know."

The rain drums harder and harder.

Something like a fire engine starts up nearby, somebody squashing the gas pedal enthusiastically, making it roar.

Aunt Alberta accidentally bonks her cup against the sink and Anneka's baby jumps.

Francine gets a grip on Anneka's closest hand. "Promise me, Anneka, that if you still are having these weird pains tomorrow, you'll have Carroll call the bastards and say you're coming in."

"Carroll doesn't do well on the phone . . . you know . . . his hearing aids."

Francine looks like she's growing two feet taller, eyes narrow. "In a case like this, it isn't important what the bastard likes. You let that guy walk all over you, Anneka. I can't believe it either. It makes me sick. If he ain't man enough to tackle the goddam hospital shitheads, get that cute little blond out there to do it for you . . ." She pivots to get another look out the wee camper window. "He's right out there . . . handy. You listen to me, okay?" She turns and smiles. "This is your mother speaking."

8 | Watching bats. They pirouette across a neighbor's porch light. Always a good show.

Lloyd Barrington and the old man from three doors down sit transfixed. A queer night. Foggy. Soft. A night with a veil.

Old man again offers Lloyd one of his beers.

And again Lloyd says, "Naw. You keep 'em, John."

Lloyd's porch is made of a stack of three forklift pallets set on level ground against the trailer door.

Since Lloyd has had his trailer moved to Miracle City, he's boxed himself in pretty well. Stacks of forklift pallets on three sides, while the backyard has a clothesline, always loaded. Privacy is all-important to Lloyd Barrington. A place to crab up into and be out of the public eye.

To get into Lloyd's little yard, there's a space in the forklift pallets facing the lane with a gate made from pallet slats and barn hinges and a blacksmith-made hook and eye.

Old John swigs off his beer now and then and chuckles. Contented.

Lloyd chews in a way that *looks* like contentment.

They slap mosquitoes, mosquitoes bigger and meaner and later in the season than any of the Egypt wise men can remember. But Lloyd and old John don't discuss this. They just watch the bats with gratefulness . . . bats gobbling, gobbling, gobbling.

Whir of an engine beyond the soft edge of fog. Now a car easing up to park flush along the pallet pile. A BMW fender shows between slats of the gate.

Old John tips the last of the beer into his mouth with his skeletonish but steady hand.

Lloyd stares at the gate.

Car door slams.

"It's a lady," John whispers.

The woman appears wearing a bright slisky ski jacket. Her hair, backlit by the across-neighbor's porch light, is cut shorter on one side for a saucy effect.

Lloyd gets to his feet. He leans into the gate, pops the heavy hook from the eye. He shows Gwen a place to sit, a shorter stack of pallets between his right thigh and the outside pallet wall.

She scooches down, gets comfy, keeping her knees together, her narrow shoulders halfway between worried slouch and dogged courage.

Old John says, "Nice night."

"A little foggy for driving," Gwen reports. "But it's nice once you've reached your destination." She glances at Lloyd. He is opening and closing his hands between his knees, as though his hands ache, keeps his head down, short visor of his Civil War kepi low for privacy.

They wait out the silence of nearby TV's and slamming doors and coughs and an owl ooo-wow-ing up on the ledges.

Lloyd spits.

Gwen says, "You don't make introductions?"

Lloyd says, "Gwen, John."

Gwen tells John it's good to meet him.

He grins.

Gwen asks Lloyd, "Why did you get your phone disconnected?"

Lloyd chuckles. "Corporate policy."

"Oh."

"And then I moved off the land I was on . . . that also being a corporate policy. And besides . . . there's nobody a person needs to call here. Everyone's here." Lloyd's moustache flickers.

Old John is giving the rich widow a thorough scrutiny.

Gwen says, "I brought a little something for your wife, Lloyd. Will you see her tonight?" She raises a hand to show off a little crinkly gift-shop bag.

Lloyd fussily adjusts his kepi, settles it on the back of his head. "She's at Beano or something."

John giggles. "Beano!" John has just two fanglike front teeth.

Lloyd says, "So you were on a trip or something, I heard."

Gwen gives a wan smile. "You heard."

He smiles off toward the woods, then he looks back at her, shrugs, and looks sheepish.

Gwen says, "I'm having trouble with my work. I thought a little travel with my good friends would give me a fresh perspective."

Lloyd says gravely, "Kind of like a few spins on the Flying Bobs."

"Flying Bobs!" Johns snickers, knowingly.

"The Italian countryside this time of year is healing. The colors! The glorious odors that make you . . . make you ache. Everything is so old there. So veritable. So permanent." She sighs. "You would have loved it, Lloyd. You would have loved the people. Someday . . ." She sighs. "Lloyd, it's *important* to see the Old World . . . to . . . to believe in humanity's ability to endure. For me, it's always been a kind of growth."

Lloyd stands up in a sudden.

Gwen does, too. Seems like a fistfight is about to take place.

The old man pushes up from the porch. "Come on, folks. Be nice," he commands.

Lloyd says, "John . . . excuse me a sec." He reaches with both arms and hugs Gwen to him, then backs up along the edge of the trailer, around to the little side alley there.

This is not exactly a surprise to Gwen . . . the hard push against the trailer wall, the shoulder and body of the man giving no excuses, no courtesy, no compromise . . . and his mouth against her hair.

He says, "Hey! Listen! If you want this here . . ." He steps back to point at his chest with a thumb. "If you want ol' Lloyd, you gotta take what comes with ol' Lloyd . . . a fucked-up heavy load, big goddam ton of worry."

She grimaces. "But . . . you *know* that my offer still holds . . . about my holdings, about everything, including your house."

He cocks his head.

She rests her head back against the trailer.

He says, "Being a yuppie, uneducated in most ways, you may or may not have had any idea what you'd find when you came out here tonight. This . . ." Waves a hand to indicate the crowded V's and forks of the settlement. "This is homeroom. You want to go with me tonight and get your classes?" He gives her shoulder a seductive little rub. "Night school," he chuckles. Then says thoughtfully, "I just need to load a few things into my truck first."

"Lloyd? Is what you want me to go with you to do . . . is it . . . illegal?"

He squints. Lets his hands drop, steps back, pulls his kepi low again, soldierlike. "Never ask me if it's legal or illegal. Ask me if it's right or wrong. Right?" He laughs. Pokes her playfully in the ribs.

"I'm scared of police."

He says grimly, "Me, too." Then he whispers, "It's just you and me now, okay? No Earl." He leans in close again. His hands move through her jacket and shirt, from pocket to pocket, and she lets him, keeps her eyes closed. He finds four keys on a ring with beaded tassles. He hurls the keys out into the foggy dark behind the trailer and there's no jangle striking earth. It's as if the keys just cease to exist.

9 | Across from her on the frazzled high seat of the truck is Lloyd Barrington, shifting gears, piloting them through the fog with care. Lloyd Barrington . . . worse than a whore. Body and soul, he is dispersed among so many.

She asks, "Do you keep Tylenols or aspirin in this truck?"

"Aspirins at times. Take a look." He nods toward the glove compartment and pats the flashlight on the seat.

The jammed-full but somehow neat glove compartment turns up no aspirins. Just copper wire, tools, soft-looking pencils, and rags . . . rags that were once flags. One is balled up and blotched with blood. Forget the aspirins. She snaps off the flashlight, bangs the compartment door closed.

Out of the fog two mailboxes materialize. Lloyd turns in here. The mumbling truck jostles along under heavy old trees and leggy upstarts of birch. Up ahead are two sources of light. To one side is a lavish home of floor-to-ceiling glass and cathedral ceilings with enormous reddish beams . . . surely the work of a fine architect. So much light. And the sloping lawn . . . ablaze with the confounding pinkish orangy glare of security. But no sign of the residents. People engaged elsewhere or in unseen rooms.

There's a forking in the road and there in the curve, another house . . . small, shingled on one side, slumped porch on front, windows dimly lit. And lights outside, hard high-wattage white light, light for working. And headlights which undulate with the legs of active over-excited kids. Here and there a cigarette's dark red . . . waxing and waning.

Signs of life.

Gwen sees Lloyd reach to downshift, turning up into the yard behind the other trucks and cars. She looks past his face at the floodlight fixed to a logging truck's boom, the great arm and jaws of it at rest, the light aimed into the open hood of a second logging truck. Bats snatch in and out of the light's blinding core. Squatted in the motor cavity, working a wrench, working with strain on something that won't give, is a man with a crusher hat, dark work shirt. Like Lloyd, the man has a full moustache that crawls along to the jaws. She is coming more and more to understand this oldest kind of dignity. That no matter how many aristocracies overtake the common man, no matter how they denude and molest him, there are always men like these who can never be gelded, who will always have this pageantry, this covenant, this fierce high rank, the faces of kings.

And it seems that as she looks at this other man's face, she knows Lloyd better. Gently, things are becoming clearer.

And all around the open hood of the lighted truck, men and women cluster, watching the wrench finally break the grip of rust, and a couple of young men gesticulate triumphantly . . . a fist in the air . . . and a war whoop.

"Who are these people, Lloyd?"

"Nothing illegal," says he. "Just my friends . . . a nice visit. You can relax." He pulls an envelope of Day's Work from his pants pocket, fills one cheek. "Well, I mean . . ." He works the tobacco around lustily, getting it set. There's a little soft whistle through his nose. "That there working on that piece of equipment is our locally infamous Reuben Bean. Your people ever heard of him?"

"No," Gwen says grimly. "My *people* haven't heard of him. We've been too distracted by the local infamy of *you.*"

Kids clamor around outside Lloyd's truck. As he steps out, they make a tight knot around him. They touch him. He touches them. He hugs them, he jabs them, he tousles their hair.

"Dad says you weren't coming!" one of them hollers.

"Well, here I is," says he.

One little girl wears a plaid dress. Sash drags. Sneaker lacings drag. She hugs Lloyd's left leg, then starts up one side of him like a cat climbing a tree, up and up. He settles her on his shoulders. She hugs his head. She gives the top of his Civil War kepi a kiss.

From the dark screened porch there's cooing whistles like a couple of mourning doves. Lloyd turns, cups his mouth, and answers with the same haunting call. Now he goes to the back of his truck and fetches faded flags still stapled to their sticks. Hands grab at these from every direction. Girl on his shoulders reaches across his face.

Lloyd says with a snarl, "You impale yourselves on these or poke out your eyes, you don't get any more."

One boy, wearing only gym shorts and sneakers with no lacings, bounds up onto the truck bed. "What else you got here?"

Lloyd says, "Out."

The boy climbs the boarded up sides of the bed, spreads his arms, leaps, lands deftly on all fours.

Close by stand two men, both in dark work shirts, one with WICKS WELL DRILLING across his back . . . the other with LETOURNEAU'S USED AUTO PARTS. Both of these guys are smoking. One reaches into the open door of a car and snaps in a tape . . . set low . . . country western, the new modern kind that has no twang and not much "country." The other guy turns to Lloyd and they exchange hello nods.

Two girls, early twenties, stroll across the busy light toward Lloyd. One girl is chubby, wears shorts and a white eyelet blouse. Glasses. Beautiful hair. Hair you'd have to call "brown absolute" . . . no red highlights, no blond highlights. She has the sides of that hair gathered back in a clip. So much hair. It flashes behind her, reaching the backs of her knees. Gwen's feminist friends would call this kind of hair a symptom of submission. When Gwen is with her friends, they make perfect sense, but here and now, all those great conversations become just static and garble.

Without warning, the two girls throw their combined weights upon Lloyd, catch him off guard so that his kepi flops to the ground and the little girl on his shoulders shrieks and waves her legs. The girl with the beautiful hair feels into the pockets of Lloyd's dungarees. The familiar leather drawstring pouch is confiscated, opened. The girl holds a dime up to the light. "Figures!" she snarls.

Lloyd stares into the girl's eyes.

Gwen stoops for the kepi, then steps back, looking breathless, a dot of light on each of her dark eyes.

The girl pokes the dime back into the pouch, stuffs the pouch back into Lloyd's dungarees. Then she pats his arm. The two girls turn away.

"Leighlah. Look here. I want to introduce you to someone . . . my friend, Gwen." With his annoying reticence he avoids Gwen's eyes. But he is trying. He is learning how much courtesy means to her.

The two girls . . . gosh, yes . . . it's just the way friends so often are . . . dressed similar . . . the second girl's blouse is also white . . . her hair also fairly long, but more thick, a black and surly rigamarole of hair.

"My younger daughter, Leighlah," Lloyd says, indicating the first girl. "And this is her all-time best friend, Cookie."

Cookie of the black crazy hair lowers her eyes, blushes. Gwen reaches for her hand to shake it. "A pleasure to meet you," Gwen tells her. Then to Leighlah, "A pleasure to meet you, Leighlah." And Gwen falls in love with Leighlah, the eyes, the slope of the shoulders, so suddenly and disturbingly dear, that fifty percent of Leighlah that is Lloyd.

A wordless few moments passes between them all until Leighlah tells Gwen she loves her haircut.

"Thank you. But don't ever cut yours, Leighlah. You'll be sorry. *You* have beautiful hair."

Cookie snickers. "Once my mother cut Lloyd's hair when it was long as Leighlah's."

"It was *never* as long as Leighlah's," Lloyd says quickly.

Gwen hands him his kepi and he slaps it back on his head.

"Well, Mumma says it was long and they kept 'it' around to show people for a few years. Mumma says I kept 'it' in the toy box." She blushes. "I don't remember doing that."

Leighlah hoots. "That sounds like something you'd do, though."

"Cold storage packing?" Lloyd asks, changing the subject.

Leighlah says, "Yeah. We've already sealed one room. Come to see me, Dad . . . I want to show you the new way they are set up to wash 'em. Come at noon. You can have half my sandwich."

"Might," he says.

Might means yes.

Leighlah says, "See you guys later," as she and Cookie turn and head up to the screened porch . . . something going on behind the screen . . . something teenagerish . . . lots of whispers, thumps, moans, and screams.

The child riding Lloyd's shoulders says, "Yites moranes impy" and points toward a gang of small kids playing war with the flags. Flags make great swords.

One of the women is breaking it up, snatches away a few flags. She strikes one of them across the shoulder with a flag. "*See* how it feels, buddy!"

As they trudge up toward the house, Gwen asks about the child riding on his shoulders. "Is this little girl one of your grandchildren?"

"This is Mary," he answers. "No relation." He turns and looks about. "My daughter Sage is around here somewhere. She's my grandbaby-maker. She's married to this little gal's big brother . . . half brother. They are living here till times get better." He speaks the word *better* with an ugly inflection.

"I thought you said she was no relation . . . this little one here."

"Well . . . if you want to be picky, yeah. And my father's sister, my aunt Hoover . . . real name of Marjorie, married this little gal's father's mother's brother . . . so we're related that way, too. And Mary here, her father is him . . ." He nods toward the glare of light and Reuben Bean's humped-over back. "And then there's that guy there that's just said hi to us . . . drills wells . . . he is the son of a guy who is my half-brother, last name Johnson. This guy, Jeff Johnson, he was married once to Amy Bean, Rubie's brother's girl and now Jeff's being cozy with Amy's cousin Jessica, one of Rosie's kids, Rosie being Reuben's and Ernest's baby sister." He glances at Gwen with twinkly eyes. "Got that all straight?"

A woman breaks free of the gang of smokers. She tosses a cigarette butt into the dirt, mashes it with her sandal. Smallish woman. Dark blonde braided knot of hair. Stern mouth. Sweet ways. Fortyish. Very pregnant. She says, "Gosh Lloyd . . . we're having supper late tonight . . . it's almost ready. Gonna eat?"

"Yesssss," Gwen says and tucks her arm through Lloyd's. "We'd love to."

10 | To Gwen, there's a feeling to this kitchen of impending uneasy thrill . . . like waiting out a hurricane or holding hands for a séance. All these faces lit by trembly lamplight, Coleman and kerosene. The voices cross and crisscross the table, with each throat and tongue and walls of the mouth pushing out the words of a plump, almost glutinous pitch and inflection, just like Lloyd's . . . just like Gwen's father . . . the good man, the savior of lives . . . voice of the hills, all one flowing river of voices, a mastery, a proficiency enviable and the even more enviable association of their clan.

Oh . . . she is sure . . . they see this as only an ordinary Sunday night!

There's the meal. Flat pie-sized meat loaf, no sauce. Big waxy plastic bowl of boiled potatoes. There is a blind warp of darkness beyond the faces while the hands pass the food along. Two skillets of scrambled eggs are emptied fast. Eggs a big hit here, it's plain to see. The dim walls are close, hung with tools, framed school pictures of the boy they call Loren . . . Loren in three different grades . . . some paper plate Pilgrim faces, left from a long-ago November . . . a slapdash job . . . most likely Loren's.

A pan of small round overdone biscuits is passed along. Jars of dark preserves. Lots of bread-and-butter pickles, quite yellow and candy-sweet. And now a pan of stewed tomatoes.

Lloyd's oldest daughter, Sage, big freckled gal, hair chemically frizzed. Looks like Lloyd when she's got her head cocked and that grimace, glaring at all the pans and bowls and skillets going around. But then turning full-face toward Gwen, to tell her to "Help yourself! Dig right in! It don't bite!" she has the face of somebody else . . . Lloyd's wife . . . the disabled . . . at Beano? Don't ask. Gwen is starting to wonder if the wife might be *here*. But as she learns each woman's place, she sees that Lloyd's wife has still turned up missing.

Tight fit here between Lloyd and the young well driller Jeff Johnson . . . the table not large enough for so many people . . . those that live here, and those that have just stopped by . . . it's hard to know which are which with people who don't make introductions.

Gwen tries to guess which young man is Sage's husband. She glimpses the well driller Jeff Johnson's profile and almost weeps . . . for across the eyes, he looks like Lloyd. She tries to recall the tangled explanation Lloyd gave her . . . this Jeff was included. She sighs. She breaks open a biscuit with her butter knife.

Sage is plainly in charge. The blond Earlene Bean seems more like a shadow. Just a small hand and wrist appearing now and then with a tub of margarine, another Ball jar of dark preserves.

Sage booms, "You almost done, Artie?! Make room!"

"Ain't done," says Artie Bean, rolls his eyes.

Sage herself doesn't eat, just huffs all around . . . watching plates, the boss of people's plates

The next round of eaters still waits out on the front porch. Now and then Sage steers someone to the table as another from the first round stands, freeing up a seat. There are a lot of coughs. Croupy. Deep.

With his back to the wall and window, Reuben Bean is silent . . . glum. A man in his early sixties, gaunt around the eyes . . . powerful build . . . a body that labors, a head that worries. Seems like this might not be the first meal he's dawdled over. Dark and gray welter of moustache shows through his fingers as he holds his chin. Gwen's eyes fix on that hand, a thumb, two short fingers, and a claw. She looks away fast. To stare outright is not appropriate in *any* society. And what did Lloyd mean by "infamous"?

Little Mary shortcuts under the table and appears next to Reuben, leans against him, waves three flags to get his attention. Someone has retied her sash. A pretty bow.

All the men are talking about "the Ford." They ask Reuben questions about "the Ford." He answers with "Yep," "Ayep," and a sniff of disgust. He watches what's left of the meat loaf coming his way, his eyes that color brown that changes to amber in daylight. He is one of the coughers. He jerks to the side and bows his head whenever it takes him.

There's a confusion in one of the unlighted bedrooms . . . the boy Loren using one of the beds as a trampoline and Sage's twins and another kid trying to knock him dead with pillows and spear him with their flags. These flags are confiscated. Many, many flag-related infractions here.

"Have more biscuits, Artie!" Sage commands. "Hurry up and free up that seat! Eat! Eat! Stop yakking. Plenty of biscuits. What's left of them tonight's goin' out to the pigs."

"Good," says Artie Bean. "You been reheatin' them marbles for three days."

Sage's elbows fly as she moves a pretty scalloped serving dish one way, pan of biscuits the other. Such great vigor inside those blue flowered sleeves.

"Rubeeee Rubeee Rubeeee," Mary sings and sighs her father's name, whacks the table with her three flags. Reuben closes a hand around the flags. "Go out," he says.

"Rubeeeee Rubeeeee Rubie!" she sings, tugging at the flags.

Reuben gets up, places the flags up on the top of a cabinet of rifles, loaded cartridge belts, and gun magazines. When he returns, she's on his chair. He lifts her off the chair. "Go," he says. She stands beside him now, flagless, but holding her ground.

Not many women seated at the table yet. Out on the porch, that's where there's women. Liz, Lydia, Dib, and Ellen. Leighlah and Cookie and Jessica and Trish. And teen boys. And tired kids. And cigarette smoke. And talk which is like code . . . half a word . . . piece of a sentence . . . a sniggle . . . always understood.

Gwen asks Earlene Bean if she can help.

Earlene says, "Just enjoy yourself." Earlene dressed too dressy for cooking and serving. A summerweight maternity sweater top, off-white with wheat specks in the weave and scalloped cuffs. Sweater top stretched tight. There are certain ways that she'll stand that you can make out the distended dollop of her navel.

Sage gives Gwen's shoulder a brutal squeeze. "NO WAY!! You are our special guest tonight! Take it easy. Have some more biscuit and preserve."

Uneasily, a lot of faces turn to look at Gwen . . . sizing up what is obviously Lloyd's "date."

"Too many cooks spoil the broth," Artie Bean reminds them. This Artie, Gwen is starting to figure, is Sage's man. He is the tall Hercules type. His green-and-black plaid flannel shirt is strained at the buttons. Seems like practically all the men in this place are the Hercules type . . . while there's Earlene Bean, so fairylike and dainty, even in full-flower pregnancy. But she moves among them undaunted, at home.

Gwen learns the preserves are strawberry-rhubarb. So good. She tries a little of everything to show courtesy, but the preserves are her most favorite. She realizes Jeff Johnson at her right side might be a little drunk. He sways. Not like he's losing control and will fall off his chair. It's just a happy sway. She envies him.

A little boy wearing a dressy white shirt and dressy pants but barefoot, very quietly slips between Lloyd and Gwen, leans into Lloyd and stares at Gwen.

Lloyd ruffs the boy's hair. This makes the boy sigh, then turn and bury his face in Lloyd.

A guy across the table stands up.

Sage hollers, "Leighlah! You and Cookie hungry?! Get that hassock from the back bedroom! You can both probably squeeze in!!"

As Earlene brushes close to Gwen, Gwen smiles and asks, "When are you due, Earlene?"

"Saturday," she answers. "Feels like twenty years on this one."

Sage snorts. "It's *twins*."

Earlene speaks a little testily. "No, it's not. I *told* you."

"A sonogram means nothing. One could be hiding behind the other," Sage twitters. She swings the water pitcher hard to the right to get it started around the table again, keeping her eyes sharp on everyone's water tumblers.

Things are getting *wild* in the near bedroom.

"Loren! Please stop!" Earlene calls out in that direction. "We'll have no beds left."

Little Mary scoots off to join the other kids out on the porch.

"I see you finished that room," Lloyd observes. Little boy peeks out at Gwen, keeping his face mostly covered with a fistful of Lloyd's shirt. The little boy has the cough.

Sage says, "I wouldn't call it finished, Dad. And I'm tellin' you, it's going to be cold with no cellar under it and not closed in under there."

Artie says, "Baby, we do what we can do."

Sage turns to Lloyd with tears. "I'm not ungrateful, Daddy. You know I'm not like that. Since Lydia and her kids came over Easter, we've all been on the floor. It's time for me and Artie and the kids to get out of the way some. I'm not complaining. I thank my lucky stars for that room."

"Thank me!" Artie crows. "And the old man." He points at Reuben with his fork.

Space is made for Leighlah and Cookie and so the bowls and skillets and pans of food go around once more.

Lloyd hoists the little boy onto his lap and says, "I heard Chris might need to be putting his family up somewhere. He coming over here?"

Artie pushes his plate away. "He might find more room at Steve's, but . . ."

"Darleen is a bitch and Judy's a bitch," Reuben says with a snort. "They won't get along."

Earlene raises her voice over theirs. "I'd rather they come here if Steve and Darleen don't work out. Otherwise . . . they mentioned going out of state."

Jeff Johnson tsks over this. "Nothing out of state but more of the same. *Worse*. More w-e-i-r-d."

Earlene glances at Lloyd. "And I'd rather have them here than Miracle City. Everyone says the Town or somebody is going to go in there soon and run everybody out. *Everybody*." She looks long into Lloyd's eyes. "I figured if we had a separate building up back . . . make it look like a garage . . . or a little gambrel barn . . . so's from the road you couldn't make out it 'twas people living in it . . . that might work."

"Don't be dumb," says Reuben. "Yuppie assholes overway are just itchin' to catch us at another broken law."

"But if Chris stayed here," Earlene insists, "at least Judy and Jamie would have a ride with Sage to Westbrook. This is what they've been wanting, Reuben. Remember?" She pulls Jeff Johnson's dish away as Jeff stands.

Reuben watches Earlene's back as she hurries to the sink.

Sage booms in the direction of the porch. "Dib! You wanna *eat?!* Meat loaf's gone . . . but there's stuff!"

"Yeah, yeah," from the porch. "I'm coming."

"What about the rest of you out there?!!!" Sage calls. "Any of ya keelin' over yet?"

"SEND FOOD!" a teen boy's voice bawls, which is swallowed by giggles and whoops of the others. Something dazzling out there in the dark . . . that on-and-off playful brawl of them with their secret beers . . . so full on beer that food hardly matters. Nothing matters but the dazzle.

Sage calls to them. "Well . . . we'll send something out!" She rushes to draw another pan from the oven, pokes into it with a fork.

Artie mutters, "Lock 'em out."

The little boy's fingers are inside the chest pocket of Lloyd's faded chambray shirt. The fingers find just an emptiness there. So he takes a bit of biscuit from Lloyd's plate and fits it into the pocket and pats it and looks dreamily into Lloyd's eyes.

"Thanks," says Lloyd.

Earlene squeezes along behind the chairs and leans toward her Reuben to flip him a piece of toasted bread . . . bread with a cinnamon swirl . . . something special . . . some sort of "gift" . . . has a slathering of perhaps *real* butter? . . . by lamplight, it's hard to tell. But in her hurry, the toast skids over his plate, flips onto the table near Artie's hand.

Artie picks it up. He says, "I know how that goes. She's saying 'Here's your suppah! Eat it and shut up!' Kinda . . . you know . . . like they throw you a bone . . . 'Here, here ol' boy. Shut up and lay down!' " He does a high and growling mean-woman imitation, then scales the toast back onto his father's plate.

Now up and leaning against a closed wooden door out of the warm zone of lamplight, Jeff Johnson wonders, "Earlene! You talk like that to *Rubie?!*"

Artie chuckles. "Them two always talk nice to each other."

"Nice 'n' nasty," says Sage.

"We have our occasions," admits Earlene, glancing toward Reuben, glancing away.

Something smashes in the back bedroom. There's a yell and several accusing gasps.

Reuben says thickly, "Earlene . . . go see what them kids are up to. Enough's enough." He leans back to the wall, not yet having touched his special toast. "Kids ought to be fed. Bog 'em down some," he says deeply.

Sage says, "They've been snackin' all day. You give 'em this food and it'll just get left on their plates."

Earlene has disappeared into the dark bedroom.

The boy on Lloyd's lap churns around, screams, "ANGELA!" then slips down and runs like hell after Earlene.

Sage bullies Gwen into another biscuit. More preserves . . . these being black raspberry. "Our guest must eat!" she roars.

From the direction of the porch, two kids appear on the soft yellowy edge of the kerosene and gas light. Reuben's eyes turn onto them and they give their flags little involuntary nervous wiggles . . . something that resembles a salute.

A fresh steaming pan of stewed tomatoes is plunked down on the table. A tear of sweat moves down Sage's stout neck. In the near distance is the whisperish complaint of Earlene's voice, trying to get her boy Loren under control.

Sage groans. "Kids . . . I'm getting so I can't stand 'em."

Earlene returns, followed by the boy that wears only gym shorts. And Sage's twin girls, gleamy-eyed and fat-cheeked. Earlene fixes Loren a plate and settles him across from Gwen. Gwen and Loren very briefly stare into each other's eyes. The boy has beautiful eyes. Eyes that both damn you and cherish you. Eyes that say he knows something about you.

Eyes with no humor. Yet they are eyes that "ain't seen nuthin' yet" as the old saying goes.

Reuben pushes his chair back slowly, achingly, caught in one of his coughs, fetches his crusher hat off the sideboard, then trudges out. And Artie follows. And it is understood that they have returned to work on the motor of "the Ford" . . . may go through the night. The special toast is gone from Reuben's plate, too suddenly for him to have eaten it. Probably in his pocket . . . will be a treasure at three in the morning after many more turns of the wrench and finger-tightening of hose clamps.

The empty seats fill up fast with small kids and their flags.

Earlene spoons tomatoes into cups for them, fries up some of the cold potatoes the way kids like best.

"Can you let your flags go half-mast awhile, guys?!!" Sage demands.

They all lower their flags.

"Flags are stupid," Loren says.

"You'd've kept yours if you'd have behaved with it!" Sage roars. Now Sage turns to Earlene. "See why I had my tubes tied?! I figured I was lucky with my three. It was knowing Loren that gave me the incentive to have the thing done." She turns to Loren. "What a business you are! What a trial!!"

Earlene bristles noticeably, but says nothing, just wipes her hands on a towel, and steps back out of the light.

With both hands, Lloyd gives his moustache and eyes a hard rubbing, squeezes his eyes shut, bows his head. Like grace before a meal. Only his meal is already eaten.

11 While one of the flag-waving kids escorts Gwen to the woods to show her where the outhouse is, Earlene Bean has a word with Lloyd. Her voice is thin and weary.

Lloyd is wetting up a new chunk of tobacco, his jaw tensed, squinting into the light of the logging truck's boom across the yard . . . he, too, quite tired . . . yes, everyone tired.

Earlene explains, "It's our turn to do it. But you can see Reuben's going all night on this thing and I can't handle her alone. It shouldn't take long. I hate to bug you tonight. I know you already did her Thursday. Irene said you've been doing Thursdays."

Works his tongue against the tobacco. Nods toward his truck. "I've got chow I was taking over to the dogs anyway . . . but if you've got her dress and stuff, just give them to me . . . and a little more water. You just stay here and take care of these people. How'd you wind up with her on Sundays anyway? You've always got so much going on here Sundays."

Earlene sighs.

He says, "Just go on in and get me that dress and stuff and let Gwen and me take care of it ourselves tonight."

Earlene looks toward the house, then back into his eyes. "I need a break from *this here*. I *want* to go."

Lloyd chortles, gives her thin bicep a poke. "Pretty bad here when going up to rassle with Helen is thought to be a break."

"Sometimes just going for a ride is . . . all I want." She turns from him. "I'll go change. There's filled water jugs over against the shed ready to go."

Gwen returns from the woods, her ski jacket carried over one arm, flag-waving kid hanging on to her other arm, kid keeping her in the loose grip of his long convoluted story of what is probably from a TV movie, Gwen's dark eyes two spots of light . . . and Lloyd turning to face her has written all over his face that he loves her. He will get to the heart of things soon, she is certain. It's just a matter of hours . . . maybe minutes.

Lloyd tells her there's a job a mile down the road. He mashes his tobaccoey hot mouth to her ear and whispers, "It's legal."

Little kid taps Gwen's elbow. "Wanna hear the other one?"

Lloyd says, "Wait till next Sunday. She'll love to hear it *next* Sunday. You can wear a person out telling them too much at one time. You need to work on practicing your strong silent side."

The kid scrinches his face. He makes a fart noise with his mouth. Just a small one. Pokes the ground with his flag. Embarrassed.

Earlene calls from the house toward the lighted logging trucks. "Nick! Jason! Can you help out here?!!"

After a minute various young people come marching down with plastic milk jugs of water, and load them onto the back of Lloyd's truck along with the water jugs already there.

Now, alone with Lloyd in the truck, Gwen asks, "Who was the young man who sat beside me at the meal? You told me before but . . ."

"Jeff Johnson. My half-brother's boy. Wicks laid him off Friday. You know . . . it seemed to me . . . I know him pretty well . . . he was acting a little stunned tonight."

Next she asks, "What makes Reuben Bean 'infamous'?"

"His temperament."

She scowls.

He watches her face hard.

She asks more questions and he answers with a twinkle in the eye or a grin. But there are questions she doesn't dare ask. Questions that will anger him. She is quite clear on which questions are safe and which are not. But these unasked questions smolder. And this divides her from him. So perhaps the deeper into his world she travels, the further from him she gets.

With a grunt, Earlene climbs aboard. Paper bag in her arms, big baby in her belly.

Out on the road again the fog is worse. Lloyd steers the creaking truck up onto the paved stretch of Seavey Road, down a dirt strip of town road toward Jupiter Hill, a straight-up hill . . . truck going up, up, up, and up like a small plane boring through clouds.

Where they turn in, there's no mailbox, no sign of light beyond the trees. Ruts and washouts. Loose rock. At one place, the truck rises up on one side, putting Earlene high, Lloyd down low, Gwen in the middle. Earlene grips the door. Gwen grips the dash. Low limbs bash the windshield, hiss over the cab.

Beyond the fog there's the roars and bellers of many large dogs. What looks like a big loaf of bread is really a trailer sealed in one vast sheet of plastic. And there's cyclone fencing all around it, which gives it the appearance of officiality.

Lloyd leaves the truck running with headlights beamed into the fog. He steps out. When Gwen and Earlene come around to the back of the truck, he has his back to them, one hand spread open against the flatbed. The racket of the dogs makes what Lloyd is doing soundless. Gwen realizes when she sees his shoulders shift that he is pissing on the ground. Earlene reaches for a jug of water to carry with her free hand.

The cyclone fencing shakes and twangs with the weight of dogs . . . Dobermans and Doberman-mix . . . their oily-looking black physiques and dartlike heads looking like the sure work of the devil.

Now Lloyd hauls a sack of dog chow from the truck bed and Gwen asks, "Are these the dogs that eat the dog food you buy so much of?"

"There are many swell dogs in many locations," he says evenly, shouldering the sack. He spits off into the grass, wipes his moustache on a sleeve and recites, "Dogs in the street. Dogs with feet. Dogs in the air. Dogs in your hair. Dogs. Nice to you. Everywhere. Help yourself. There's plenty. Dogs on the ocean. Sailing in boats. Big hats. Once a yellow hungry dog at my school. Yooo hooo! Yooo hooo! Open up the door. Open up the door. Let one in. Doggiedoggiedoggiedooroo dooroo!"

Gwen blinks.

Earlene smiles. "He's quoting himself now. You can always tell."

They head up along the weedy path, Lloyd aiming a flashlight into various dog faces. "Heigh ho there!"

The dogs beat harder against the fence.

"Lloyd's happy!" Earlene shouts to Gwen over the dogs' barking. "It must be you!"

Lloyd jabs the latch, opens the gate.

Tails are like iron whips. Noses jab into all the most private places. But all in the name of welcome.

Lloyd doesn't knock on the trailer door. He just sallies forth. But there, standing to block him, just inside, is a man-sized old lady with hair like spiderweb, eyes lost under the drooping frills and bunches of what were once eyelids.

Bad, bad smell.

The old woman doesn't hesitate. Doesn't need to see. Seems to know where Lloyd is by radar. She smacks him in the shoulder, knocks him sideways and the dogs churn and worry and whine and glower. Earlene scoots in around Lloyd, pulls a chain to an electric light, sets her jug of water by the sink, goes to work with her head down, using rags and a wood stove ash shovel to clean up where dogs made mistakes.

Seems like the old woman is looking at Lloyd's hands.

Gwen hangs back by the door but the old woman doesn't seem to register her anyway. Old woman cocks her head, aware of the presence of people who aren't here now . . . but perhaps once were . . . people of another time, the layers of time existing over this time.

Earlene bustles off through a door into another part of the trailer.

Lloyd keeps his back to the old woman as he works the sack open, dogs pushing and ramming.

"ROB SHIPLEY FELL THROUGH THE ICE!" the old women booms. Dark folds of her dress are ripped at the waist and dark dirty folds of bare belly push out between the missing buttons.

Lloyd dumps the whole sack of chow into an aluminum sap vat by the picture window. He empties many water jugs into bowls along the wall.

Old woman catches sight of Lloyd's moving hands. But when the hands are still, she seems to lose track of him again.

Dogs crunch and slurp, tails hung with businesslike concentration.

Gwen says, "What can I do to help?"

Lloyd's eyes widen on her.

Old woman cocks her head.

Lloyd says, "What the job entails next is we just got to get the shit off of Helen here 'cause she doesn't know anymore how to wipe herself after a shit and she can get pretty chafed if we let it go. And as you can see, she's feeling her oats. Her husband . . . he makes three of me . . . when she hits *him,* he hits her back. We don't."

The old woman goes from foot to foot now, squintily aware of Gwen's fidgeting hands. Old woman murrs like a cow.

Earlene reappears, tosses some rags into a line of paper bags.

Old woman swings right, hunches menacingly, bellers at Earlene. "BEEN DOWN ON THE BRIDGE STOPPING NEIGHBORS?! BLOW YOU TO THE SKY."

Earlene laughs.

Gwen smiles wanly.

Lloyd takes the old woman's wrist. Old woman howls as if Lloyd's touch were electric shock. She jounces, the belly spewing forth more of its dirty dark dough between the open front of the dress. But she doesn't jerk her hand away. She lets Lloyd rub the wrist with his thumb.

"So where is her husband now?" Gwen asks.

Earlene mouths the word JAIL. The soundlessness of the word seems not for secretness, more for the sake of emphasis.

Gwen has a couple of bigger questions to ask. But she knows not to ask. These would be on the list of unsafe questions. Instead she asks again, "What can I do?" Lloyd's eyes slide her way and she knows that this has been the right question, the A-plus question.

12 | Back in the Beans' kitchen, there's only one kerosene lamp lit. There's coffee and the cold remains of a popcorn feed in the bottoms of several greasy bowls.

Gwen has very little to say. Just a wide-eyed sleepiness. Her makeup must surely be worn away but in this forgiving dark-light, she cares not.

Many people are gone. But still there are many. Coffee, coffee, coffee, and much talk . . . mostly teasing . . . not anything Gwen would call a true conversation.

It seems that maybe the laid-off well driller, Jeff Johnson, lives here . . . but in time Gwen understands that he doesn't. It's just that he can't tear himself from Jessica . . . Jessica who has a distant knowing smile, chin raised, nicely freshened makeup, handsome dark looks, one normal arm, one arm small, curled close to her body, a Tyrannosaurus Rex arm.

Meanwhile, outside, work on the logging truck engine keeps on and on . . . mist drifting across the glare . . . and Lloyd goes out to help . . . leaving Gwen.

She wants to follow him, but he's given her a look that means no. She is mad, refuses Sage's offer for more coffee, but it is a courteous refusal. With heated water she has washed to her elbows in the Beans' deep kitchen sink, but still can't get rid of the smell of that battle with the old woman.

Earlene has vanished.

Sage tells Gwen she's fixed a pallet for her in one of the bedrooms and leads the way, stepping over sleeping children and a few sleepers that are adult-sized, some with faces covered with blankets like you see bodies in newspapers or on TV after a disaster.

Gwen is *so* courteous. She thanks Sage, then sinks slowly to her knees. The pallet is made of musty blankets and old wool jackets.

There's a cough . . . deep, croupy, insistent, in the other bedroom beyond the wall.

At last there's this chance to sleep, but no sleep. All around her are children sleeping well.

Out of her bedding the odors explode against her cheek and nose. She can label each one. Kerosene. Humid summers. Wet and sour babies.

When he finally comes to her, stepping over the others, he kneels beside her and rests his hand on her back as if to feel for signs of life. He sorts through the blankets, easing under, curls up against her, his knees to the backs of her knees, his moustache and short beard burrowing into the back of her neck. He locks his arms around her. Half hour passes, his breathing uneven, breathing that is *awake* and agonized. And she, too, is very awake, too much caffeine, and her anger with this night that he owns, that has been her submission to his laws of rightness. On and on his arms remain locked around her. Angry yes. She can't quite shake the anger. But beyond the anger, it is there, that which she has coveted even before memory. It is this. Security. She has never in her life felt safe.

13 Anneka is seated in a pretty maple captain's chair with quilted seat cushion while Carroll dials. Phone is turquoise. Everything in the mother of Turnbulls' kitchen is turquoise or complements turquoise. This mother of Turnbulls . . . Anneka is nuts over her. Shivering on the woman's flaccid bicep is a tattoo of a turquoise winged horse.

Now she and two other Turnbull women all stand around the kitchen and watch in silence . . . Turnbull women so flashy of body, but conservative with words.

Anneka is having a small contraction, head bent slightly, eyes half shut, like someone waiting at a station for a very late train. Carroll waits with his finger in the hole of the last number.

When Anneka comes out of the contraction, she laughs. "Can you believe this? This whole thing is kinda funny, isn't it?"

Kit Turnbull grunts, folds her arms over her own pregnant belly. Kit's "maternity top" is nothing Anneka would *dare* wear. It's obviously an old red slip, cut off at the hips and hemmed.

Carroll pulls his hand away and the dial spins, the last number engaged.

Anneka gets one of the clinic doctors whose name she recognizes and a voice she recognizes from her past check-ups over the months and who upon hearing her voice as she begins to describe her situation, recognizes *her* voice and stops her with vexation. "Is this you *again*? Is this Anneka Plummer? Weren't you just in for your appointment a few days ago?"

"Yes," she admits. "But . . . the pains let up in the daytime . . . mostly. They let up for an hour or so at a time. And that doctor who examined me said she couldn't find the cervix. Guess I'm too chubby." She giggles. "That's what she said, that it was because I'm too chubby. But since she couldn't find the cervix, wouldn't it mean *maybe* I'm ready and she couldn't tell?"

"Is what you are having now . . . is it *progressive* labor?" He enunciates the last two words to be sure she is hearing them.

"It is . . . but then it isn't," she says with a bit of tremble to her voice. "But it's been seven nights of it. I'm kind of . . . tired."

The doctor sighs. "As it has been explained to you already, you can come in if you want and we'll check you, but we *will not* admit you unless it is *pro-gressive la bor* . . . five minutes apart, then three minutes apart . . . and then two, and then it stays at two. Okay?"

"I live about an hour and a half from the hospital, do you think . . ."

"Look, Anneka . . . if you want to, you can come in now. We'll examine you, but we will not keep you unless you are ready. It's *your* decision. But what I suggest is you lie on your left side. That often helps . . ."

14 On the drive over to the "elderly-housing" complex, Lloyd announces that his wife died three weeks ago. It is spoken out of the blue, out of a worn-out silence, not as an answer to one of her many questions. And as he utters his wife's name, "Sherry," he takes his right hand from the wheel and opens his fingers to the windshield's panorama of sun and hunkered-up closed-in green hills.

Gwen frowns, looks down at her hands. She doesn't give condolences, nor scold him for his lie about Beano. This whole matter of his marriage is a sad, unspeakable ball of fire. She turns her face away.

He speaks with that voice that diffuses into softness on every other word. " *'There the wicked cease from troubling, and there the weary be at rest.'* "

She turns from the waist and faces him, placing her left hand open on the seat and she recites, " *'No one is so accursed by fate, no one so utterly desolate, but some heart, though unknown, responds unto his own.'* " She expects him to smile at her cleverness, but no.

She wears a casual sweater and jeans. A woven hat with yellow silk daisies wreathing the crown. She can wear hats. Some people can't. But Gwen, with her long neck! Her striking face. Yes, she has a face that turns heads. If a beautiful face only mattered, she'd have nothing to fear. If grace or courtesy only mattered. If a pretty hat mattered. But he is only staring at the narrowing road ahead. And chewing. And his lower stomach is noisy. It growls. It trills.

As the truck clanks into a pothole of broken tar outside the housing project, Gwen searches through her shoulder bag for the little house gift she has brought for his uncle. The little bag rustles. And Lloyd glances at her hand.

There are plenty of empty parking spots here at the "elderly housing." And the old people in lawn chairs clustered on the little lawn near the main door . . . they know Lloyd's truck . . . and they stare expectantly.

Lloyd twists the key and the motor dies. Beyond the steep bank there's the river and falls and the mill. The falls roar. Lloyd opens his door, without getting out, just leans over the seat, and spits into the grass. He slams the door. He tugs a striped rag from a pocket and wipes his mouth, drives the rag back into his pants pocket. He leans back against the door, flattening and fussing with his moustache with thumb and forefinger, and he is looking at her. It's that look that comes and goes, the look that says, yes, sometimes a beautiful face, grace and courtesy, and a pretty hat . . . they matter.

15 | The man that Lloyd introduces her to as Unk Walty despairs over kettles and bowls and pans and jars of live yeasty sourdough all over his little apartment. Walty calls it "Amish Friendship Bread" with a roll of his eyes and an exhausted sigh. "If you take some of it when you go, dear, I'll kiss your feet! It's taking over my life!" he tells her.

Gwen says she'll certainly take some off his hands. It'll be fun to make some bread like that. She takes off her pretty hat and Walty takes it and fusses over how fine a hat it is.

This man, Unk Walty, shocks her. What a looker! A man in his mid-sixties, but hair still mostly black. Perhaps he dyes it? The white streak looks shamelessly contrived. Big green eyes. Serene, reptilish, thin smile. He leans on a roughly carved cane-head . . . for "there is *something* with my knees," he complains. He is dressed in a black turtleneck and jeans, leather slippers . . . not the uncle that Gwen imagined Lloyd would have. But then there's Morelli, Walty's housemate . . . wearing work clothes. But he doesn't have the local accent. It's what Walty calls "the Portland waterfront" and Lloyd calls "Italian." And all the while one conversation is turning into another, Morelli speaks from under the sink, mostly just his legs and waist showing as he works a wrench and applies sealer. Once he sticks his head out to make a disparaging face at some "wisdom" of Walty's, but then he is quickly back into the dark cavity of the sink doors.

Gwen is impressed. Both men so handsome. Both charming. Lloyd has informed her earlier that Walty can't see much without glasses but probably won't be wearing them in front of a guest. Lloyd also mentioned that Walty almost never leaves his apartment. Morelli, who still works, even though he is near seventy, runs all the errands and makes family appearances, and still squeezes time in for Walty . . . celebrates Walty, thrills over him, has given Walty in these late years a lifetime's worth of high regard.

Lloyd straddles a chair at the little table, cleaning mackerels into two pails and a pan.

Unk Walty sets out helpings of gingerbread and whipped cream on plates of a leafy, delicate green-and-white pattern . . . perhaps expensive? Other "nice" things show from a glass cabinet, end tables and catty-corner shelves. Walty uses a careful hand to position each plate, saucer, cup, napkin, and spoon. Seems he has odd knuckles. Arthritis, Gwen surmises.

Walty keeps patting Gwen's shoulder, fussing to be sure she has everything she needs. Between Gwen and Walty there's immeasurable courtesy. And a kind of gratitude. And Gwen thinks, yes, this is a part of Lloyd's world, too! . . . this . . . this! While the night of Beans overwhelmed her, this . . . this is sweet.

Walty gets a few yogurt cartons of bread starter ready, sets them by the door to be sure Gwen doesn't leave without them. "And anyone else you know who would like some . . . I have enough here for the *world*."

Morelli says, "Just throw it out. Don't be a slave to bread dough, Walt." This from under the sink.

Walty folds his hands like prayer. "It feels too much like killing."

A groan from under the sink. "Well, you kill it when you bake it."

"But they die for a good cause . . . not waste. Just shut up and keep your head in there, pleeeeeze." Walty arranges a few more paper napkins on the table.

Hung on hangers from clamps on the walls all around the kitchen-living-room combo are items of formal wear, wheaten tuxes, floor-length satin gowns, one cream, five emerald, gowns of darker wheatens, one black and brown, quite rich. And there are bolts of fabric in plums and blues. And burgundy. And something tweedy. And a jacquard of red and black. No sewing machine in sight. Gwen glances at two closed doors.

Even with every window closed, there's the din of the falls by the closed mill.

Unk Walty tells her that Indians used to call this area around the falls "The Land of the Little Dog." And he says, "They didn't mean beagle. They meant *fox*."

Gwen sees that Walty and Lloyd don't exchange glances upon the word "fox," but there's a cessation of movement that chills her.

Gwen understands that Lloyd and his uncle are close in some way other than words . . . in that way that ballet dancers or football players are attuned, practiced . . . muscle, heart rate, and thought . . . some vigil of the soul.

Gwen glances at Lloyd's untouched gingerbread, at his hands and the dark knife blade opening up the fish's streamlined middle. Seems the fish's stomach, lungs, and lustrous heart leap gladly to the pail.

Unk Walty leans onto his cane close to Lloyd, watching the fish cleaning and watching Gwen . . . like these are two projects that need an uncle's guidance. He says, "They've been around you know, Lloyd. They've been *after* me. They wait till they see Morelli leave . . . then . . . they pounce."

Lloyd smiles. "Oh yes, *them*."

Gwen cocks her head, touching the paper napkin to her lips.

Lloyd says, "Some neighbors who do a lot of church want Walt to join up with them." He swings around to look up into Walty's wide eyes. "So why aren't you in church for heaven's sake, Unk?"

Walty touches his temple as if near fainting and leans in close to Gwen. "Lloyd teases me all the time. It's not what I need. I need an *ally*." Now Walty gives Gwen's narrow shoulder a little good-feeling rub. "And what do you do, dear? You look like a career woman to me."

"I'm a photographer."

Morelli hops to his feet, raises the knob on the faucet, strides out of the apartment without explanation.

Gwen tells Walty how she has been doing photos for organizational pamphlets lately. She tells that she's had many exhibits but not in any major galleries. She hopes to do a book of photos at some point, a collaboration with a poet. She has several friends who are fine poets, "though none would have poetry compatible with the subject matter of my work."

Walty has moved away, has brought more half-and-half for their tea. "So dear, you were in the newspaper biz. My gosh," he says reverently. "My favorite TV person was always Lois Lane."

"Well." Gwen laughs. Glances at Lloyd. "Lois Lane was a reporter. I was with the photo lab. Seems you and Lloyd think alike."

"Maybe it was Jimmy who did the photos," Lloyd says.

Walty waves this away with a hand. "Lloyd . . . don't be nitpicky. It's beauty of soul I speak of. There's something about Gwen here who reminds me of the *person*, Lois Lane."

Gwen insists, "Lois Lane was nothing like me. She was brave. I'm not a brave person. I was always uncomfortable in newspaper work. I've always been a meek person. I hate myself for it. It's a thing I've tried to work on, but I'm in my forties, too old to change now, I guess."

"Just a dyed-in-the-wool sweet meek person!" Walty cries, and gives Gwen a fierce hug and Gwen is startled by the strength of the arm, and then as the hug lasts and lasts, she starts to feel claustrophobic, but then the hug is finished and Walty is circling away again, to dig waxed paper out from a low drawer and she can still smell the smell of Walty on her neck . . . some perfectly right after-shave fragrance.

And Walty now speaks with his back to Lloyd and Gwen, and the voice is different . . . deeper, with an edge that's almost like accusation. "Well, you know, Lloyd, who Gwen reminds me of?"

"No . . . who?"

Walty keeps fussing in the drawer. "Your mother. Her bearing, her voice . . . her . . . her meekness!" He giggles and pivots on his cane. "I'm not surprised." He giggles. "Your lingering interlude into the Soule hub-bub was . . . is . . . what surprises me."

Lloyd narrows his eyes on what's left of the fish in the pail of ice.

Walty persists. "Gwen, dear, if you have won my nephew's heart, you are now in a rare position. I beg you to make Lloyd do something with himself, *make* something of himself. He has a wonderful mind."

"Unk wants me to be a schoolteacher," Lloyd tells her. "Right, Unk?"

"Well, at least! But maybe even a professor."

Lloyd works the knife along the underside of another mackerel

Water from the faucet suddenly smashes into the sink.

Walty thwonks the floor with his cane three times, then steps over to shut the faucet off.

Gwen says to Lloyd, "You are well-read, Lloyd. Some self-educated people have the greatest minds."

Walty sniggers. "Wellll . . . Lloyd does have a master's degree in Sociology . . . and he majored in Social Welfare for his B.A."

Gwen looks at Lloyd. She pales. She speaks after a moment. "Lloyd, you never told me that."

Lloyd shrugs.

Walty snorts. "He could have picked law instead of all that social smoshal. He could be a lawyer now!" Walty sighs. "Lloyd loves to argue. Perfect lawyer kind of guy."

Gwen's face, snow white. Eyes, dark and glistening. "I guess it's just a funny thing not to mention."

"He could make a better living for himself," Walty laments. "Sawmill, odd jobs . . . all that mess . . ." Walty tsks. "Why Lloyd! You could have made us all so proud!"

Lloyd glances into Walty's eyes.

Walty continues gravely, "Gwen, dear. Have you seen Lloyd's home?"

"Yes." She lowers her eyes.

"I would think he'd be too ashamed to show you!" Walty fumes.

Gwen looks at Lloyd. "It's really okay."

"Have you seen the inside?" Walty asks with narrowed eyes.

"No." Her mouth works into a knot.

"Well, Gwen," Lloyd's voice gets low. "You want to see it? I figured if you were curious, you'd speak up. It's not like you give up easily. Actually, I thought it was *you* that was ashamed."

"See!" Walty crows. "He argues all the time . . . a great lawyer. It's in the Dougherty blood. Fighting Irish, my mother used to say."

Gwen hunches a bit.

Lloyd lays the last black striped filet down with a flourish.

Walt says sadly, "Lloyd's got brains. He could use his brains for other things besides complaining all the time about our country! He could be more . . . well . . . you know . . . uplifting. He's just such a crank!" Walty prances away, poking a drawer shut with his cane, then swerving back to the table . . . so straight-shouldered, expanded chest, head up . . . such flair . . . Gwen can barely take her eyes off him.

And Gwen is certain that Walty's diatribe has been tongue-in-cheek. Is Walty bringing Gwen to the edge of their confidence? She is almost certain of this.

Lloyd stands up, backs away from the pails, works green dish soap over his hands and forearms at the sink, runs the water hard. When he turns back, working a towel between his fingers, he looks into Gwen's eyes.

"You are a very private man," Gwen says.

"Shy," says Walty.

"Bullshit!" cries Gwen. "Shy is not what it is!"

Walty hoots. "You Irish, too?!!"

"Yes," says Gwen with a laugh. "My grandfather was a Sheehy."

Walty giggles.

Gwen stands, asks to use the bathroom.

"That door, dear." Walty points.

She opens a door. Wrong door. It is a room with a double bed made up neatly in blue pastel. A sewing machine heaped with red fabric. A worktable of fine brushes bristles-up in cans. Canisters and tins. Though there's no sign of what his work there might be. No paintings on the walls. The walls are bare. The closet doors tight. How much is hidden?

"No, dear, not that door." Walty is quite good-natured about her error.

And then there's Gwen's own "Oops." And her look of apology. She tries the next door, which is the bathroom, shuts the door behind her. Small bathroom. Lots of mirror the way new apartments are, gives the illusion of space. The countertop and floor and tub look virtually unused. Though everything necessary is here. Nothing is missing. Nothing hidden? This visit. It has been like audience-participation theater with costumes hung all around. Like backstage. Yet somehow very much center-stage. Well, yes, Lloyd had told her earlier that his uncle sews for a living, mainly for wedding parties and proms.

And the rest is really no mystery, even that which he doesn't tell her. So many around town have *warned* her . . . told of the caskets with papier-mâché likenesses in them, the wizardry of Walt Fogg's hands to make a face true. *This* is not the surprise here. The surprise is how kindly and classy Walt Fogg turned out to be. A joy.

16 | Walt's voice goes deep and ugly. He leans onto the back of Lloyd's chair. "What's the matter with you, Lloyd? Our fearless fox. Can't you make up your mind when to strike? You going to drag this on forever with her? Like a crucifixion?"

17 | "Hi . . . this is Anneka Plummer. Is there one of the clinic doctors around I can talk with a minute?"

She has a long wait.

She doesn't look at Carroll where he stands a few feet away. She thinks looking into his eyes right now would be the worst thing. Hard to see his eyes anyway, just that trailing-off yellowy wreath of smoke. How crazy he looks! His cigarette going in and out. His eyes jumping from face to face of the passing people. Now there are none of the "conveniences" there were at Turnbulls'. The convenience of water for one thing. The convenience of that same blue eye of the sky at the camper window every day. Some call a beard a thing you "raise," you "cultivate," you "choose." But Carroll's three-day beard looks like spoilage. His dirty maroon chamois shirt hangs out one side of his belt, bunched up on the other side. He looks like a loser.

Here it's the IGA parking lot. There've been other parking lots. They try a new one each night. Carroll got fed up with Turnbulls. Anneka argues that Turnbulls are nice, that David Turnbull walks all the way up the mountain on the Chase Boundary to a cellar hole . . . carrying the bodies of unknown cats he finds killed by cars, and some squirrels and raccoons when they aren't too squashed. This is called the Chapel of Creatures, a Turnbull kid had confided. It's got an archway of fieldstone and different kinds of wildflowers. Carroll accuses the Turnbulls of exhibitionism. And with even greater disgust, he had said, "You think these people make sense when they set a gasoline fire to a Honda as a sacrifice to the gods?" When she argued that millions across the nation cut and decorate perfectly nice trees as a sort of god-sacrifice every Christmas, he looked like he was going to hit her. But it was just a look. So she pressed on. "That Honda wasn't running. It wasn't . . . any good. And besides it was Snail Arsenault's idea to do it. And it doesn't have anything to do with anything, Carroll. It doesn't have anything to do with us. What is it? . . . you afraid they'll do something to *us*? Set *us* on fire?" He said no that wasn't it. Nowadays Carroll has short patience with everyone for this or that and suspects treachery everywhere. It is only Anneka he loves. The only things he trusts are Anneka and the tinny inside dimensions of the camper.

Voice comes onto the line and asks Anneka, "So what *seems* to be the problem?" The voice explains that she is the supervising nurse and that the doctors are all busy.

"Well, I've been in labor for I think it's *two weeks* now and I was wondering if . . . you think I should come in now." The words "two weeks" spring from Anneka's mouth with a kind of jubilance, like crossing a finish line, ending some prescribed number of endurance tests.

The nurse sighs. "Anneka Plummer, right? Is it progressive labor, Anneka?"

"Well, no but . . ."

"It *has* to be progressive labor . . ."

Anneka laughs a little. "I'm *over* three weeks overdue. They told me when my labor started up . . . you know . . . over two weeks ago . . . that it was up to me about whether or not I had the baby regular or cesarean and . . ." She laughs again. ". . . well, I didn't have any idea. I told them I don't know about these things . . . but now . . . I think I'd really like to just go ahead . . ."

"Have you tried lying on your left side?"

Anneka laughs softly. Just a little friendly laugh, nothing to challenge. Perhaps she's already laughed a kind of laugh limit, beyond which they will write her off as a wise guy. "I've done that *a lot*." Some stress on "a lot" but not too much stress . . . nothing to badger, nothing to seem too aggressive.

"When your contractions are ten minutes apart, then three . . . and they *stay* that way . . . then you . . ."

"Even for cesarean?"

The nurse sounds as though she is lifting something very heavy as she speaks. "When . . . the . . . contractions . . . are . . . progressive . . ."

"Probably a foot hanging out?" Anneka suggests, a little bit on edge, a little harshness, a little twinge of bad temper . . . but she covers it with a little jokey laugh . . . no offense, no offense, no offense! You do not offend the gods in these matters, these matters that matter, nothing like school, school was nothing like this, rape was nothing like this, none of those things could ever truly rule ol' Anneka DiBias, none of that had her heart, body, and soul over the jaws of this chasm. Now in Anneka's throat something large. In her eyes, tears . . . large. She says timidly, "I'm just so tired. And there's a weird discharge. And . . ."

"You can come in if you insist, Anneka, but unless your labor is progressive, we will only send you home again."

"So you think this discharge business is okay?"

"Of course! It's normal. We are busy here, Anneka. What color is the discharge? Does it . . ." Nurse sighs, a sigh of greater exhaustion than Anneka's, and greater anxiety . . . but also something a little like pomp. "Does it have a color?"

"Well, brownish tan. Like that brown mustard." Anneka laughs another little nervous jokey laugh.

"It's perfectly normal. I suggest you walk around a little, then lie on your left side awhile if the walking has no effect. Lie on your left side and stop worrying. The *left* side. It often helps."

"I've done that . . ."

Silence at the other end.

"Well, okay . . . bye," Anneka says.

But at the other end there's no good-bye.

Anneka leans against the brick wall of the IGA. She feels foolish, how they talk to her like she's a pest. Like she's a *nut*. But she is not an expert and these things that seem odd are not odd at all to them, the experts. When the time comes, they will know what to do. Right this very minute at the end of the dead line, babies by the dozens are being born in a nice way.

18 | In the night, during the worst part of the night when Anneka's groans overlap themselves like a quartet of Annekas singing alto in rounds, Carroll gets down off the bunk. He scooches on the wheel-well bench to lace up his boots. Bright lacings . . . the newest thing in this "household," bought to replace the others that rotted and broke into six pieces. These are *so* yellow! Like chrysanthemums. When Carroll laces his boots these nights, his shoulders are stiff, looks like he's winning a boot-lacing race. Then he bursts out of the camper and out there in the dark parking lot of whatever parking lot they've landed in, he smokes if he has cigarettes. And with or without cigarettes, he paces. He has stopped smoking near Anneka these days. She has nagged that his insomnia is back because he's stopped taking his pills. "De—pressionnn!" she has hissed.

He has argued that it is only reality that keeps him sleepless. "Some state cop is going to come along . . . he is going to come to get us out of this parking lot. Some cop is going to start something." He has insisted it's not depression at all, but a condition that begins with *P* called "parole."

Anneka has argued, "We aren't doing anything wrong. We can't help it if we have no real home. We can't help if there's no jobs!"

"There are laws against loitering, Anneka. There're laws against camp-ers. *Wrong* is what a cop finds in the fine print of *the law*. And what do you think they're doing every day at the legislature, Anneka? And in Washington? Making more fine print!!"

She had said yes, yes, yes, yes.

He said, "Remember how some lawmakers in Washington tried to pass laws last year to make punishable by death *fifty* more crimes than what they already have? Remember that? And to pass a federal law that overrides all state laws so they can have capital punishment in EVERY STATE??"

Anneka said she had written one of the senators about that.

Carroll just looked at her when she said that, thoughtfully scratching one side of his face, the loser beard.

"Remember, Anneka . . . how one of those laws was that if you get caught with a firearm and an illegal drug on you at the same time . . . and you get convicted for it . . . *you get death*. Think about it."

She had said okay, okay, okay.

He said, "Listen to your prison expert here. Prisons are crowded. For lesser offenses, like . . . oh . . . say . . . loitering . . . in time . . . given the . . . you know . . . evolution of our laws . . . you know . . . it will be prison for loiterers . . . given that drug dealers and drug users will get the gas chamber. Anneka, isn't there something awfully *similar* between drug use, drug dealing, and loitering???"

"Yes, yes, yes, yes, yes," she said.

And then he had smiled at her. He had even winked!

She looked away.

But he persisted, "Anneka . . . you ever heard this term before? It's a word the government uses when they do nuclear testing upwind of ranches and little schoolhouses . . . when they shackle prisoners into chain link pens near ground zero or venting areas to test the effects of bombs on *skin* . . . and when all the people living for miles and miles around become as bunchy with tumors as a sack of apples and their kids are born with chests shaped like turkey's chests . . . know the term for these Americans? Guess. Guess, Anneka."

She had no guess.

He had shaken the bunk to be sure of her attention. "The term is 'the low-use segment of the population.' " Then he had gone outside to pace.

He always has Anneka in a corner these days with his arguments. Seems he's right about everything and she is wrong, wrong, wrong. It used to be she was smart. And spunky. Name the injustice and Anneka would have a letter written for it. She doesn't even know where her Constant Vigilance poster is anymore. Stuffed in the trash at the Chief's place by the Chief's housecleaning wife? The old Anneka. Now she is starting to think she could never live without Carroll out of her sight for more than a minute. He is everything.

Tonight when he clumps back up into the camper and clanks the thin door shut, Anneka tells him, "I'm getting cold or something . . . wicked chilled." Then she grips his hand through the next nonprogressive contraction.

When she comes out of the contraction, the mother of Turnbulls' kitchen flashes before her eyes, its turquoise blue radiance so far away.

Carroll says, "If you're still sick in the morning, we need to call the hospital and ask if having a flu will hurt the baby."

Anneka laughs at this. She laughs high and witchy and with great abandon.

19 | Another day, another parking lot. The contractions pick up. Hot machinery that grates on itself. But the rest of Anneka is chilled. The pains go from four minutes apart to ten to fifteen to two to ten to twenty to three. Now the unborn baby slings himself from side to side. The big belly is sometimes not in front of Anneka but on her right side, then on the left. The baby is burning in his bed of ice. The pains stop, then come again, stuttering . . . joke pains . . . the don't-call-us-pains, the don't-be-a-pest pains. Baby flexing. Belly flexing. Baby flying. Rebounding. Side to side to side. Getting hotter. Getting hotter. Getting hotter.

20 | The rescuers are all around with their flashing lights and their radios that squawk from every belt . . . the orange jacket rescuers, one state cop in his gray-blue uniform and his huge stiff Smoky hat . . . and a very very very young-looking sheriff in brown. It's like we all were once led to believe, that the army always shows up in the nick of time.

The state cop dials the number for her.

Orange jacket rescuer says to Anneka, "Tell them that you are coming in, that your temperature is a hundred and four and if they say no this time, hand the phone to me."

The cops and rescuers watch the phone's dial rotate back into place.

The camper, Anneka's world, parked in the IGA's fire lane, close to the pay phone where she stands in shame in her dirty and torn purple flannel robe. Her cheeks flame. Her eyes are coals. The belly quiet. All is watchful. Even the people passing by who stare don't make much sound.

It seems Carroll Plummer is not part of this scene, but is part of a Find the Hidden Face picture. He is only there beyond the faces and shoulders of others. As Anneka is taken by a contraction, it is the state cop's hand she hangs onto for dear life. The phone receiver drops, swings away from her, clatters against the brick wall of the store. A rescuer grabs it, finds nobody at the other end.

"Whoa," says the cop softly to Anneka.

"Don't worry," the young sheriff tells the others. "I've delivered babies before. It's a cinch."

Anneka on her feet again. Anneka waits for the state cop to dial. Anneka hears a familiar doctor's voice, the familiar pained indulgence. "Is this progressive labor, Anneka . . . or is it just the same thing?"

"Please let me come in . . . please take the baby . . . please! I'm burning up! *Please!*"

Silence. Is the phone dead?

Anneka persists, "And the rescue people said . . ."

"Anneka!" the doctor's voice a true scolding. "Why have you called the rescue? This is *not* an emergency."

"They say I should come in. They say with the fever and the brown stuff . . . that I should come in."

"You can come in . . . but if it's not progressive labor, we'll just have to send you home. But come in if you want. We are *very* busy. There will be a wait. But we will check you if you feel it's necessary . . ."

"Thank you!" Anneka says breathlessly.

Over by the store's automatic doors, Carroll has gone to get even farther away, keeping the cops in his periphery. Seems like he's trying very hard not to look part of this. But the cops seem hardly interested in him. If anything, as they shuffle and hover about, they seem demure and shy and shaky. And warmhearted. Like favorite aunts. Nothing like the evil forces that would give you the gas chamber for breaking some senseless law.

21 Anneka notices that Carroll doesn't have his hearing aids in his ears. Probably in a pocket of his work pants. His ears. Such perfect-looking ears. Thick-lobed the way a lot of older guy's ears get, bulwarks into his brown willful misbehaved spiky hair. His eyes, more green in certain light, but in this light they are absolutely *yellow*, dark-lashed, and ringed below in tired bunches. And the age lines are more like fissures . . . these eyes are raised to meet hers and she finger spells to him, *"Do you think we can name him anyway?"*

He looks away. He shrugs.

The hospital people have brought the baby in for them to hold for a few minutes. Be quick! Well, actually they don't *say* there's a time limit, but the young nurse keeps leaning toward Anneka to urge her on with it. The nurse is talky talky talky talky. Even when she steps out away from Anneka's face, she never leaves the doorway. Just once. To reappear with another warmed-up baby blanket. She takes the cooled-off blanket away. Then she returns breathless. "They treat babies extra special in Heaven!" she exclaims, mad with gaiety. "So cute, isn't he? In Heaven, God and the angels will say 'heeeeere comes a cute one . . . more cute than most!' A lotta hair. Lookit that hair! God wanted that cute baby for himself! They always look cuter with lots of hair, don't they?"

Carroll gets to his feet, looking disoriented. The gray on the chin of his short beard surprises Anneka. Was he this gray this morning? Well, it's just that gray is more absolute in the fluorescent absoluteness of this little room. There's no way here to hide what's here . . . that Carroll Plummer is an old graying man and the baby is gray with his never-meant-to-be. If only. If only Anneka could be alone with her husband and child. How she had begged to get in this hospital! Three and a half weeks of yearning to be here. And now, if only she could escape. The nurse wants the baby. The nurse wants to take the baby away forever. He is no longer Anneka's baby, never was. He always belonged to them . . . the officials . . . the experts. Always he was out of her reach. Part of the mystery. Part of what they knew that Anneka didn't know and which they would never tell her, never will, for even now they insist that the baby's death is a mystery to them all. What happened? What happened? Anneka doesn't press it.

How thin this baby is. How disquietingly old. His eyes shine a little between his nearly closed lashes. Living babies always have such blank eyes. But this baby's eyes *see*. Anneka shifts him. His weight, though light, is breathtaking. Here he is. Real at last. Dead, but real. There were times that even *she* questioned that her labor was real. Am I making this up? Is this baby made up? Why don't they believe me?

She looks up at Carroll. What does this glaring horror hospital seem like to him from his soundless seclusion? Perhaps a few stark degrees brighter? Anneka stares at Carroll even though it's the baby's pale hair she strokes. The nurse makes a quick move. Going to grab the baby! But no, she's only leaning in again, squealing. "God's reasons are not always understandable! But they are his reasons! We don't have to understand him. Just trust him. His wisdom is something we can all find comfort in!!"

The nurse is getting bigger and bigger and louder while Carroll standing next to the nurse . . . Carroll who is six feet tall and bear-built . . . is getting smaller, shrinking . . .

It's Anneka herself who says, "I guess I'm done."

The nurse closes in. She chirps with delight. Lifts the baby. Starts toward the door . . .

"HEY!" Carroll bellers tonelessly.

The nurse pivots on her soft soles.

Carroll extends his hand. Jerks his thumb toward the rocker he has just risen from . . . a very homey varnished maple rocker.

Anneka's chair is straight backed . . . utility.

The nurse trills. "Oh! I'm sorry! I'm really sorry! Yoooooo want another turn! Yesss! Yesss! I understand. We can arrange that! Heeeere you go!"

Carroll sits in the rocker, legs apart, looking braced. The nurse settles the loose-limbed child in his arms. Carroll opens the blanket. His eyes fix first on the wasted thin shred of umbilical cord that has remained at the baby's center. Then the Pamper that is tightly tabbed. Baby's waist. Wouldn't it seem a little perverted for him to undo the Pamper right now, to look at the genitals and all that part of the child that is, though no one says it, off-limits. He will never see this baby again after tonight, as he has never seen this baby before tonight. You must give a lifetime of love in twenty minutes. And this Pamper is *them* again, standing between him and his son, this likeness of himself who was a different soul . . . could have made him, Carroll, a much larger man. The fingers of his right hand slip along the baby's tapered chest toward the Pamper. He looks up. The nurse's eyes are targeted on his hand.

Carroll jerks his weight back in the glossy rocker, bellers tonelessly, "WELL, BY GAWD. YOU'RE DEAD." As he has spoken, his eyes grow wide on the nurse's face and the nurse's gaiety vanishes. Her chin draws in. Alarm going off in her that there's a problem.

Carroll begins a slow arduous rock to and fro with the baby's sightless face pushed against the front of his shirt. The baby is cooling down. The warmed blanket is cooling down. But Carroll's chamois shirt is sodden. This hot work of grief, this fire of his rage.

He rocks deeply. And so unhurried. Death is forever. Carroll is getting larger and larger, regaining. The nurse is shrinking now. Carroll and the ominous creak of the chair are utter and measureless.

"Dead," he says to Anneka.

Anneka nods. For the first time in weeks, she is energized. Erect. Wide-eyed. The room is charged, fizzing with life.

Carroll hollers, "DAMN HOT IN THIS PLACE!!! THEY SURE LIKE THEIR HEAT!!!!" He gives the baby a few little sportive jounces with his leg like you do to keep a live baby sleeping.

The nurse. Gone.

Long, long minutes pass. Anneka stares wide-eyed at her husband's face. He stares back at her, jounces the baby.

Anneka finger spells to him. *"He does have nice hair, doesn't he? Usually fair babies are bald. Usually you only see dark babies with that much hair."*

Carroll says loud and clear, "THEY KILLED HIM."

A hospital employee with white pants, loose green tunic, shoulders of a barroom bouncer, and a deliberate, wide stance fills up the doorway. He says firmly, "Time to get your wife to bed, Carroll. Anneka has been very sick. She needs her rest."

Anneka stands obediently, forgets about the IV . . . almost tips the IV stand over . . . everything rattling, jangling, clonking. She slumps back into the chair. Wide-eyed.

The man with white pants says, "We almost lost Anneka, too. What happened to her was *serious*, Carroll." His voice has a baby-talk ring to it. Hospital people are filled with love now . . . joyous love and this loving sternness.

Carroll doesn't seem to notice this man. Carroll just keeps his vigilant gaze on the noteworthy thick hair of the baby, the bony shoulders. The ribs. He kneads the baby's loose left hand . . . the newborn littleness of that hand . . . its masterpiece perfection. He gives the chair a few especially deep, lusty rocks.

Anneka says, "He's deaf."

The fellow in white pants turns to her . . . his bushy brows, bright eyes. "Dead, yes . . ." he says and steps three steps into the room.

"*Deaf*. My husband is DEAF," she repeats. "He can't hear you."

"I see." The fellow nods. He makes a motion with both hands to catch Carroll's attention.

Two more men appear in the doorway. One in all white. One in a security uniform. The green tunic bouncer-built guy reaches toward the baby . . . just a little tentative test. Carroll's rocking chair freezes. His yellow eyes recessed in dark fatigue fly to the man's face. Carroll squints. With something nearly like the kick of a horse . . . thump! . . . Carroll starts the chair rocking again, two lunges backward, close to smashing into the stainless steel cabinet behind.

The head of the child fits exactly into Carroll's hand. Carroll hollers out tonelessly, "ROCKIN' THE BABY!!!" He closes his eyes, rocking.

The security man pushes around the others, steps within kicking range of Carroll's chair, stares down at the baby . . . loose like a dead kitten . . . arms and head lolling to and fro, to and fro on its father's chest. "Sir. You are worrying people here. Do you realize that?"

Anneka says, "My husband doesn't hear you. He's almost deaf. Next thing to it."

Two more people appear. A nurse. Not the original young jubilant nurse. This is a different young and jubilant nurse . . . her voice floating and trilling with assurances and comforts. And now in the doorway, a soldierly face, blousy yellow garb . . . this man nudges a wheelchair into the room. "Ready for some rest, Anneka?" No one waits for an answer. They load Anneka aboard deftly, wasting no time, this time that seems to be ticking away fast. They wheel her out and push the IV stand along. Long, long hallway. Elevator doors. They pass these elevators, but find another pair to stop at. Down the hall beyond a lighted station there's a security man who is speaking urgently into a walkie-talkie.

22 | Back in the recovery room, Carroll Plummer rocks the baby.

23 | On the elevator the new jubilant nurse exclaims over the new paint job that has changed the walls from an aged smudged green to "this nice new cream."

Anneka watches the numbers flickering over the elevator doors. Carroll will give them the baby any minute now. He wouldn't do anything to get his parole guys mad. He is so good. Mr. Right. Old bossy boss. Old Thing.

24 | Carroll moves his yellow eyes over the faces of the two city police who have just arrived. Carroll tells them in a darker, more guttural tone, "Rockin' the kid."

25 | On an elevator four city police stand, legs apart, feeling the whizzing lurch and pull of their approach to the maternity floor.

26 | On another floor now, Anneka asks what kind of floor this is. Seems from what they answer, there's a lot of bladder patients.

The room they wheel her into is dark but for a low cold light over one of the four beds. Anneka peers over at the three filled beds. Patients who sleep. While she is fast, fast, fast.

The nurses who help her onto the lighted bed are bladder floor nurses, not at all jubilant. They speak evenly and businesslike. One has a voice nearly deep as a man's. They have pulled a chain to make a brighter, even *more* businesslike light. In no time they are finished with her. One. Two. Three. Done. They shut off the light and off they go.

27 | More cops come jamming in through the doorway to gauge the situation . . . and these cops have no doubt done some checking on the name *Carroll Plummer* . . . their expressions are like those expressions he has known.

Cops in the hallway murmuring strategies. Cops everywhere. The baby is cold. Carroll kneads the baby's cold right hand. How important the hands! Hands of his people. Hands deft upon truck, tool, and beast . . . the goddam rightness of a goddam right Yankee farmer, hands that ensure your indomitability had you worked hard enough.

Had Carroll Plummer worked hard enough?

A cop barks, "MISTER PLUMMER!" Cop's right hand on the doorframe. Left thumb in the belt of his holster. "What is the problem here? Are we having a showdown?"

But of course, Carroll never hears the question.

28 | Across the hall from Anneka at the nurse's station, a printout machine creaks like a nuthatch. Anneka is wild. Sociable. She wiggles her knees under the thin sheet. The IV apparatus clangs against the high aluminum sides of her bed. She looks into its supple faces of hanging plastic bags of solutions and tells them, "Sorry about that."

---

29 "Mister Plummer." A newly arrived gray-haired officer speaks. "We understand this is upsetting to you . . . but people here need to tend to the baby. Be reasonable."

Carroll tightens and raises his knee, drawing it close to himself, as if protecting the child from danger.

All the cops and hospital people regard the raised knee, the yellow-laced boot.

30 From her high bed, Anneka watches the cold dawn whiten Port-land Harbor. Her head is echoey with the shouts and voices of the preceding hours, the preceding years, the seashell roar of it all . . . and someone guffaws, perhaps her grandfather "Et by a bear! Et by a bear!" . . . meaningless and meshed with a woman's voice, "this nice new cream."

Anneka is beginning to sink. A great sorrow pulls on her blood. But she holds back the sounds that climb up her throat. Grunts. Bleatings. A screech. How can you grieve in the company of so many? She longs for the sweat-rank, vault-sized camper, sees herself there freely keening. She turns her face away from these many sleeping forms. She gives herself an expression of immense dignity, her wide mouth made thin.

31 Carroll Plummer rocks the baby.

32 Morning light like a promise. One of the other patients opens her eyes, looks at Anneka. Anneka waves and says, "Hi." In another bed, a shoulder shifts, a magazine falls from the blankets, flops to the floor. Anneka watches the third bed expectantly.

33 There are only three things he wants to remember about last night . . . the look of that place dead center between the shoulder blades of the man walking away with his baby. And the strength of his own legs . . . a strength like ecstasy. And then his palms, his fingers around the neck of that man . . . gray-haired cop . . . the windpipe's stiff and woody breaking point.

34 At the honk of his truck's horn, she is dressed and down to the dooryard gasping. As she hurries toward the truck, he says, "Don't rush. I just came by to see you."

Gwen rolls her eyes. Sighs. "You ever try ringing a doorbell?"

Lloyd's graying moustache quivers slightly. So be it, a smile for her.

"Come inside." She hugs herself. Fresh from bed, she feels the night chill bone deep.

"I'm not stopping that long," says he. "I tried calling you. Just to say nightie-night . . . but as usual, you were just a bunch of rings into infinity."

She puts her hand on the doorframe of his truck. "But you said you had no phone." Seems she's trying to catch him at a little lie?

"I called from the IGA pay phone."

"How romantic."

He chuckles deeply. He looks down at the steering wheel and blinks. He looks at her. He covers her hand with one of his.

She leans in close and possesses his hand with her two. "Come in the house and do what normal people do." So close to his face. Her words smell of wine. "Lloyd . . . it's . . . kind of cosmic, don't you think? That we should come together given our differences?"

Lloyd grins . . . many tobacco-stained teeth . . . and on one side, an eyetooth missing. "Us social workers have a different kind of outlook. Not cosmic exactly."

"I spent all day in my darkroom wondering who I am . . . and why I'm back here in Maine. I made an error. I can see that now." Her eyes narrow. "My work is dead. You killed it."

He raises his right hand like a traffic cop.

But she insists, "At first I believed I was in a transition with my work. Now I realize . . . it was just . . . in its final throes. I'm a fine photographer technically . . . but . . . oh, I don't know . . . maybe I'm just depressed."

Lloyd says softly, "It's natural. It takes so long to get through the grieving process. Your husband has only been gone now . . . what? . . . three years?"

"You bastard! You will not let go of that, will you?!" She jerks her hands away, goes back to hugging herself against the cold. Shifting from foot to foot.

"Us social workers have a keen eye. My eye says you . . . you had a dysfunctional childhood . . ."

"That's crap!"

He bats his eyelashes. "My eye says . . . it's been rough in ways, but you will do better in a year or two. My eyes . . ." He bats his lashes again. "Know."

She laughs, shakes her head, makes a dismissive gesture with a flick of the wrist. "Lloyd. Once and for all, this has nothing to do with Earl. This has to do with me, here and *now*. I am withering up! Everything I do has less meaning every day. I've quit the peace campaign work. What good is any of it?!! Just my tongue on a few envelopes . . . my hand shaking the hand of some senator who with the rest of Creation has turned a simple thing like *peace* into a complicated mess, *so* complicated that war and peace are no longer separate entities, no longer a fight and the absence of fight but a science, a calculated but clogged-up system beyond any hope of making sense . . . of being logical ever ever again. I just want to . . ."

Lloyd reaches, gets a hold on her forearm. She leans against his hand. He looks past the barn to the darkness beyond which is the mowed field, the hill, and pond. "Tide with a teacup," he says grimly. "Whichever way you look. A lot of goddam futility."

She is shivering against his hand, hugging closer.

He says, "But Gwen . . . you're just past forty. That's young. For *you*. You'll live till you're eighty or ninety. You will grow more and more purposeful. Energized. You will grow more and more beautiful. You will have many admirers and friendships and so forth. You will be embraced by the wheel of time." He stares at the lighted three-over-three panes of the kitchen door. He straightens his shoulders, which sometimes tend to slouch. "I'll die young. It's my lot. Nothing cosmic. Just part of corporate policy. But . . ." He kneads her forearm, rubbing and rubbing into the thickness of her jacket sleeve. Her arm is stiffening beneath. "You know, Gwen, I planted all these maples along the front of this house . . . all but that old monster there with your swings. I planted them when I was a kid. It was my mission. Did I tell you this already?"

"No."

"There are ways to live beyond the grave."

She leans into the window and hugs him, pressing her forehead down upon his shoulder. "I hate the way your mind works," she says into the sleeve. "I hate everything about you."

They both laugh, little nervous snickers.

"Can't you come in the house now and make progress on this relationship? I just want a little company, a good friend, warm arms at night, and other *normal* activities . . ."

"All right," he says.

She raises her head.

"But first," he says, pulling at his moustache thoughtfully. "A few more days . . . if you will. I . . ." He grins sheepishly. "Just need more time to sort this out."

Gwen says okay. She believes him.

In a few more moments, she is stepping back reluctantly, heading for the house.

He taps the horn once.

She turns.

He gives her a little friendly wave.

Then he sits for a while, filling his cheek with tobacco and watching her lights go out . . . each set of lights blanking out in succession the direct route to her bed.

35 | Cosmic? Her word.

So many new lights along this ridge, splattering and blinking through the trees . . . such glowering pinky-orangy-purple-green things where once this old mountain road knew only blackness and stars.

He downshifts at the forks, heading west now toward Miracle City.

Dear one. Dear Gwen. Gwen who slept with the devil and looked fondly into the devil's eyes, worked to do right by him and gave him grace when he had none. Earl Doyle. The hand that culled and deduced. Hand of fire.

But does Lloyd really see in Gwen's solemn face the corporate regime that is smashing his people? Does he really see *them*?

He can never really get to *them*. Not ever. Even just to play a dazzling clever trick. And therefore, he will never ever be able to get back from *them* what they have taken. There is no touching *them*. You can't even *know them*. There would be ways you could know one or two of these guys. But *each* one of them is not the same as *them*. Because THEM is the whole, the corporate conscienceless IT. And IT is the true evil.

But he knows Gwen. He has been touched by her. Touched. Nerved-up. Hornied-up. Torn. There is only Gwen.

Now he glances into the truck's side mirrors at the lights spotting the black mountain, a bright mire of security lights, corporate garbage, the slag of their inventiveness.

36 | Another Saturday. Another bride. Cars and pickups line both sides of the road by the Mason Hall. Everyone is grateful for the weather. "A perfect day."

Lots of egg and tuna rolls, peanut-butter bars, chips, dip, and cake. Music. Not much dancing. Shy people.

The bride, one of the Vandermast girls, pulls the white-and-yellow wrapping from a box. "I DON'T BELIEVE THIS!" she cries out.

But yes, it is, another microwave oven. The *third* one she has unwrapped.

"Better too many than none," her older sister tells her sagely.

37 | He paces his trailer. He chews hard, harder, spits into the trash. Even with the windows closed, he can hear the coughs of his neighbors along the lane.

He sits on his bed.

He gets up. He stands at the sink and stares into the drain. Dishes all done, put away. Meticulous for a man.

When was it decided that he would save the world? And how many major plans have had to be scrapped? So much for Plan 9,992. Go to Plan 9,993. And when was it he realized that all the ways of the world overlapped? They washed over him, a million-million cries, taking his breath away.

In time he edges toward his bed. Afraid.

This thing that he beds down with! He lies quietly outstretched for a while, staring into nothing. But it is master of Lloyd and eventually he has to give in. He closes his eyes.

MATRIX BANKCORP ENERGY INTERNATIONAL and ANSCOT-DUOTRON FOODS. The final and nearly singular global corporate regimes. The future. Too near.

This is what he sees.

38 | And so the next day, in the chain drugstore, under the vibrant meretricious light, he buys a soft-bristled toothbrush. This average man doing this small good thing.

39 | Then night again. What is there to do but to face square-on this grinning black angel of no sleep? Flat on his back. Palms out.

What is this MATRIX BANKCORP ENERGY INTERNATIONAL? What is this squirming speck of the future, the thousands upon thousands of people who will not make it, will not keep up with hi-tech . . . the people not made for hi-tech . . . these people made by God to farm, to hunt, to fish . . . people of the earth and air?

He sees the answer.

He sees it is a love story. A story of love. He sees their hair, the backs of their necks, accommodating squats, a hand reaching through the terrible all-encompassing light to comfort. Some will still tell the stories of the land. The hills. What he sees in the eyes of the men and women is their deep blush of shame that practically the only thing they know how to do anymore is suck.

Like newborns. Nothing in the hands.

The land heaves up, running muck and suckers with leaves enough to only pretend at shade. Certain flies glitter gold in the sun . . . crawl into your mouth and nose flaming. So many flies. Flies that favor shade. You are the only true shade.

He sees those of his people that still run free, hiding. But mostly he sees the shoulder-to-shoulderness of the camps, the claustrophobic broken hearts.

Where is the pretty row of tomatoes, their overzealous ripe slump?

The helicopters. They see only your skin, your spoiled shirt. But what it feels like is that they see all.

The law you must never break is TRESPASS.

Yet how can our people float in the air above all that is owned by the MATRIX which is all?

Lloyd sees this is the land of blackberry and sumac and panicked deer.

And chain link fence for miles and miles along the valley.

Not a single tuber's vine. No apple.

The helicopters. They see your skin, your wedding ring, your splintered nails.

When the helicopters come, the deer zigzag and drive hard to get nowhere. Since their shelter of dark hemlock went to harvest and loopers, deer have learned a thing that looks like square dance.

Lloyd sees there are many of us who died before this, so we need not die now.

In this future time, you can only be one of two possibilities. A success. Or a lawbreaker.

The helicopters. They can see only your bug-bitten skin, your swollen eyes. Your frozen feet. Your TRESPASS.

How to measure grief? Can you weigh it? By the size of the police cruisers? By the size of an army truck? Eight tons of sons and daughters? Twenty tons? Shall we measure in millions?

So much separation. Lost brothers. Lost fathers. Lost lovers. Lost to success. Or lost to the law. Gone.

The helicopters. They can see your fingerprints. They see with infrared and other devices. They hear. Open up wide! They see down your throat.

Beyond so many cheap doors, how will we imagine the source of our food? Our terrible dependency! Our yearning! Whose hand gets to fondle the grain, the fruit, the egg, the hen, the hog? Who has this grip on the most intimate hollows of our mouths? What stranger? Friend or foe?

Camps provided by the government, though the word "government" isn't like the word "public" anymore. Since privatization, it's a real chuckle to hear them on the fiber hi-way screens calling them "public housing."

It's hard to follow things in this future time. That fusion to make a solidly sealed hive.

Camps come in varieties. Variety as in CHOICE. Ha! Ha!

But listen, our government is good. You are not jailed or tortured for dissent here. In this country you can complain to your heart's content. Everyone complains. Complaining is not against the law.

You are jailed only for failure. But that's life. The hard facts. Hardball. Complaining is not against the law.

In this future time, drugs are against the law. Not all drugs. Just the drugs they call street drugs. Like sports. The shots have been called. They set up some of the first camps to put the people in who committed drug crimes. Dealers. Users.

Shortly after drug camps came "opportunity centers" where the millions of untrained get trained to keep up. Mandatory job training.

Next "shelters for the homeless."

Camps and shelters of all varieties. But nobody has actually ever seen one. Well, at least nobody has come back from one to tell. Of course, they are shown on the fiber hi-way screens in many American homes. But everything just mixes and fizzes in and out of truth.

The fiber hi-way screens tell Americans that in the "homeless shelters" it is warm in winter. And there is food and medical treatment for all.

But Lloyd Barrington, old man in future time . . . why does he run from promised food and warmth? Why does he stay this way in the sorrow of his freedom?

Run. Run. This land. These hills. The curvaceous bitter rock and fallow.

This land became too valuable for him to call "home."

Land must be corporate for its most "efficient use," it is said.

On the fiber hi-way screens, they tell of the glamour and rewards of the hi-tech life. The corporate village complexes are vibrant. Fun places. A world of convenience and style.

Sure, many people in America have an address and of course, a job. Millions of them. And their kids go to the "friendly privatized schools." Even here in the new Egypt there are still a few homey looking homes that belong to the "successful."

And there is traffic. Though not your old come and go of friends and family . . . nothing like that. Clean air laws are strict. Only the very successful can afford to break the clean air laws.

The new gleamy trains run between the cities where most people must live, *by law*.

And the old way: tractor trailers, delivery trucks, and service vans. They seem inclined these days to run with blank sides and no registration plates, no company name, no fuss. Business is streamlined. Simplified. Clean? As a whistle.

MATRIX BANKCORP ENERGY INTERNATIONAL is what we call it.

But of course, it has changed many many times, evolving into a corporate power that is globally intertwined into three or four massive warlike beasts. What does it matter to Lloyd's people, those clunky multi-language ever-changing names?

Fiber hi-way screens tell viewers that America's children are its most valuable resource.

They lowered the age for "co-adoption" to the day of the baby's birth if you, the parent, aren't settled solidly into a high-aspirations situation with the MATRIX. This is to give all American children the same opportunity to become "successful."

Some say eventually the power structure will crumble. It is too top-heavy. The hi-tech network will snarl, go blank. Total darkness will paralyze the great system and into this darkness millions of people will revolt. Maybe.

Some say, but before that happens the flat bad orange sun will crisp the land and boil the dirty sea. Maybe.

But Lloyd lies in the darkness of present time, taste of toothpaste cool on his teeth. "Maybe," he says softly, hoarsely, mockingly, assuredly.

40 | Anneka Plummer places her prescription bottle on the high counter and says, "Could I please have two dollars and seventy-five cents worth of these . . . or . . ." She smiles. "You know . . . whatever it comes to just under that. Three or four of those will get me by for now."

The pharmacist moves his eyes up from his work, steps toward her. "Our minimum is five dollars. You have to purchase five dollars worth. Even if all you wanted was one tablet, I'd have to charge you five dollars just to fill the prescription."

"I don't have five dollars . . . but I need this medicine. You have this little sticker on here that says 'Discontinuation of this medication can be dangerous.'"

He takes the bottle into his hand, looks down at the bottle quietly, then replaces it on the counter. "You don't have five dollars?"

Anneka snatches the bottle, runs, works her way among the maze of aisles of greeting cards, beauty needs, and camping equipment, reaches the car where her mother is waiting.

Even as Anneka drops to the seat, the tachycardia begins and she cries out as she starts to faint. Then she raises her head, eyes dulled. "It's doing it."

"Couldn't you take one in there . . . with water? I bet they had water."

"He wouldn't sell me any pills. He says I have to pay a minimum of five dollars."

"WHAT?!!"

A long silence, both women knowing the grave meaning of this.

"Did you tell him you've already missed two days?"

Anneka shakes her head.

"Before you started taking this stuff, those attacks would go on for seven hours at a time. Then . . . you'd get it stopped and a few hours later . . . bang! . . . you'd start up with another one. You couldn't eat. You would just get all worn out! You could die!"

Anneka smiles crookedly. "No, Ma. The doctor said I won't die. It's just pain."

Francine looks hard at Anneka's chest that visibly flutters with the crazily beating heart. She flutters all over. Skin flutters. Hair flutters. The fabric of her clothes flutters. "That's what they said about your baby."

Anneka says, "Yuh, I know . . . and then there's this little label on the bottle that says something about going off the pills could be dangerous . . . so maybe that's another thing . . . maybe the *condition* doesn't kill . . . maybe the *pills kill*. But who knows? I'm so tired of trying to figure it all out." She closes her eyes. Her eyelids tremble in her trembling head.

Francine says, "So I suppose he said it wasn't his fault, that it's the rules."

Anneka shakes her head . . . her face whiter than usual, not that sweet melancholy pallor, but a bad pallor . . . cadaver white.

"We are fucked!" Francine yells. "In the old days you could wheel and deal with old Harold . . . the pharmacist we used to have when we were allowed to call 'em *druggist* and he was in the *drugstore* . . . over there by Mertie's. Now it's this *chain* store shit . . ." Francine drops her hands onto her lap. A look on her face of prayer. This is Francine's prayer: "Goddam them fuckin' shitheads. What they need is a goddam fuckin' bomb up the fuckin' ass and I'd like to do it personally."

41 In the night, under the overhang of the IGA, Lloyd Barrington pushes a quarter into the slot. He waits, leaning on brick. Gwen's voice is froggy, tired, tender. "Lloyd?"

He hears his name. Hears it twice. Hangs up. Gently.

42 Another night. Another quarter. Another succession of rings. She answers. "Lloyd?"

"I'm coming," he tells her. "Pretty soon. I guess not tonight. But pretty soon."

43 Hawaiian Sunset: "You talked with Raymond today? He's tellin' around that the paper company sold off. All sixteen thousand acres that they own in Egypt. Sold."

A hard, incredulous silence.

Then, Spring Beauty: "To who?"

"Nobody knows."

Pigeon Point. "Sixteen thousand acres . . . that's most of the town . . . more 'n half."

Silence . . . like the void between two claps of thunder.

Hawaiian Sunset: "Well, you know how they been up there, Sargent and Cole and Beans. And then there was Days over on the Boundary. Bull 'n' thrash since last winter. All that equipment Day had in there, really tearin' up . . . chippin' everything but themselves. Quite a sight. 'Twarn't leavin' nothing. And no let-up. Then today these guys come in from out of the blue and told everybody to pull out. To stop everything right that minute and go. They said the paper company sold and now nothing is to be cut. They said to get everybody out. And they went to all the crews and said the same thing. Stop now, go home. And Cole, he asked 'em who bought the land. And they said they couldn't say. It's a secret. So Cole goes home and calls up one of the selectmen and the selectman says he heard what happened but the buyer is *unknown*. He told Cole that the whole works was sold as one piece. And get this, they sold it for only one thousand dollars an acre! But all hush-hush so none of us had no bid, no chance at it . . . and of course they wanted to hawk it as all one piece. Haney comes over afore noon with the mail and he says it's probably Japan."

Canary: "I don't get it. Somethin's fishy."

Pink Punch: "I bet it's a utility. Everything utilities do is fishy."

Spring Beauty: "Nuke dump."

Marigold: "They wouldn't do that. We've got people here."

Pink Punch: "Well, I bet it's *some* utility."

Fandango: "Developer. Some hotshot developer."

Hawaiian Sunset: "Like how's that? A shoppin' mall on the side of a mountain?"

Canary: "Well, it ain't houses. Nobody can afford one of those anymore. Ain't houses."

"Well . . . ," the wise man in Fandango says quietly. "They'll develop it all right. It's the big rage among your outer-staters . . . nothing new . . . no big secret 'bout it. It's probably that thing that doesn't make sense, but ya know it twitterpates them outer-staters no end. You all know *exactly* what I'm talkin' about. It's when they carry an outer-stater to the top of the mountain and then the outer-stater does this special thing *all the way* till he gets to the bottom." He grins.

It's just another dig at the skiers, but fear and tension are set aside a moment for howls of laughter and many chairs creaking in and out, in and out, in and out of shadow.

44 After a couple of weeks of "paperwork" the hospital releases the baby's body.

There is no funeral, no fuss.

Before Lloyd takes the little casket from the back of George DiBias's truck, there's a paper for Lloyd . . . permit to move a body. He folds it to fit his empty tin coffee cup on the dash of his own truck. The cup sets between two novels with covers that show mystery and intrigue.

Meanwhile, Lloyd's son Caleb ties a piece of rawhide around the casket. The rawhide has a clump of blue jay and hawk feathers and an acorn. This casket is just a little box the size of what might hold a few tools. Caleb explains that the feathers are what Indians used to call "good medicine." Caleb is tall with streaky blond hair and spotty soft dark whiskers.

"You okay, baby?" George DiBias asks Anneka.

Anneka says, "Yep." She is wearing a pair of stylish sunglasses with pink tinted lenses. Her eyes are just sparks behind the purply secretish plastic.

"Pine . . . nothing like pine," says Caleb, feeling the box with the flat of his hand.

The grave is waiting. Covered with boards, though it is only three feet deep.

George DiBias says, "Well, he was a nice baby. Nothing wrong with him. Doctor told us he was perfect." George looks at Lloyd. "Doctor told us it's a mystery what happened to him."

Lloyd's eyes drift over to Anneka's profile . . . then back to the pine box in the back of George DiBias's truck. Lloyd makes no move to rush this. This feels like the power of a glacier, dragging over the continents . . . an inch in a thousand years . . . this is the summation of so many lives. No rush. No red lights or green lights here.

Caleb says, "Named him Richard, huh?"

"Yes," says Anneka. "Richard after Carroll's grandfather . . . the one he never knew."

"That's a nice way to do it . . . grandfathers and such."

"Yes," says Anneka.

George DiBias says, "Good medicine, huh?"

"Yep," says Caleb, nodding, stuffing his thumbs into the pockets of his jeans.

Anneka says, "That means like good spirits. Not as in *cure*."

"Right," says Caleb. "Good spirits."

Anneka is looking very hard at the box. Very hard. She says, "Well, it's all right. It's okay he died. You know? I'm glad. He's . . . you know . . . *safe*."

Her father frowns.

After another minute, Anneka says, "I love these sunglasses. Pink makes you feel nice."

Caleb chuckles. "Really?"

"Sure. Try them on."

Caleb tries them on. "I see what you mean."

"They should be standard issue," Lloyd says with a disgusted grunt.

"Yep," Anneka agrees, sliding them back on her face. "It helps."

45 Lloyd at home in Miracle City reads by his Coleman lamp . . . reads a few investment articles. Reads an article on the latest in hi-tech. Reads some editorials. He shuts down the hissing mantle. Paces in the dark. He fears the bed. He would go out and drive around awhile, but the truck's nearly out of gas. He stares at his bed, made up meticulously in its bright plaid and dark wools.

46 Another night. Noisy wind. Wind screams. Quarter in the slot. A hello that comes from that wavering easy place of too many gin and vermouths . . . a paralysis he can gauge . . . as with all things on earth, there is good and bad timing, gravity, wax and wane, ebb and flow.

He decides on tonight.

He can't imagine her face. He has summoned the devices to blank her face out. No face. No pretty hat. No forehead pressed against his shoulder. No hiccuppy laugh. Nothing to cherish.

47 The constable, Erroll Anderson, parks his jeep under the trees.
Everyone seems to have just arrived. And *everyone* is here . . . marked cruisers and unmarked. Hearse. State cop he knows, named Bob.

Down on the road neighbors are braking but there's a state cop ordering them to move on.

Morning sun breaks clear of the trees, everything in its uproarious amber autumnals, long shadows of purple, frost burning, steam.

The constable, Erroll Anderson, takes his time stepping from his jeep.

Everyone is in motion. Everyone with a purpose. Only this constable stands here with a look of puzzlement.

He is not surprised to hear that the house has been robbed . . . Grand larceny, a *big* haul. But the woman is in shock so there's no getting her to be as clear as they'd like. And of course, they want things clear. Her people in Connecticut are having fits. State cop's voice sounds a little sassy as he tells this part, "These people are richer than they look here. Billionaires. This house, according to Mrs. Doyle's attorney, is just her *studio*." He flutters his eyes on the last word.

They speak now of a body.

The constable is not surprised . . . this is part of Lloyd Barrington's style. He glances toward the barn door . . . cops and technicians moving in and out. There is often this with the casket. Casket open to reveal the likeness of the person who Barrington wants to make his point with. There will be the hands folded across the middle and that unmistakable blankness of nonlife, when a person is no longer a person, but an object, a weight, vibrationless as if he were a kitchen chair. And this which is not death will impress the constable. For somehow the papier-mâché creation of death always seems more horrific.

But why the hearse? And now there's mention of the State's medical examiner soon to arrive.

He looks up toward the windows of the house for a sign of *her*, the rich widow.

But now there's mention of her being in the hospital . . . oh, yes . . . in shock. And she will go later to stay with friends.

Constable starts for the barn door. He can already make out a wall of stacked firewood . . . and there's the BMW, and its registration plate that reads: Maine and in smaller print Vacationland.

But what is this with the casket . . . yes, there is a casket . . . or one might suppose it is a casket . . . one who was *expecting* a casket.

But this is not a new casket . . . not a trick casket . . . not a fun casket. This casket is soft, spoiled, loamy, crushed in on one side. And there is soil. Soil and dark chunks fan out from the casket, like a black star, the casket which is the vortex.

The body is not in the casket. Head. Turned to one side, averted on its long neck. Cheek easy against the gravelly plank floor. And what would have been a face decades ago is now gone to soft web, like the wieldy work of spiders filling in time. And what would have been a suit jacket seems gentler now. More comfy. But there are no pants. This, of course, because pants are not included in your usual funeral package. Pinned to the back of the jacket is a note with words slashed with paint . . . IS THERE A DOCTOR IN THE HOUSE?

The constable sighs, steps back from the professionals who have the means to solve this mystery without him. The constable is chilling down . . . rubs his hands together briskly, reaches into a pocket of his bowling jacket to find an Atomic Hotball there . . . peels off the paper, pops the ball into his mouth. He can see his breath . . . brrrrrrr. He is, as ever, not dressed warmly enough.

He glances back into the barn. Sees that one arm of the corpse has been arranged . . . outstretched, the velvety bony framework of a hand that once clasped, prodded, found pleasure . . . reaching now toward an intact pair of glasses. And on the grisly wrist are the rusted remains of a watch . . . loose on one skeletal finger, a wedding ring . . . still gold.

48 | Two towns out of Egypt, granite monument of a pink cast, near a river, on the dark afternoon hillside of a large treeless cemetery, this grave of Dr. William Curry . . . seems the turf has known no recent visitation, no shovel, nothing abrupt or violent. Doesn't it *appear* seamless?

So it is cold here. The humility of a cold day weighted upon cold grass. Cold is your covenant, inside or outside this grave. Wherever you are, cold is your promise, rest is not.

PART FIFTEEN

In midwinter comes the expected. Realty sign at the foot of the drive. The most elaborate kind of sign, of course. One to draw the eye of the financially able. Post made of beveled pine with an arm of the same from which the sign hangs tastefully.

PART SIXTEEN

This. The checkpoints, the corridors, the frosted windows on and on, the double locked doors and windowless cells, six by eight feet in which

Carroll Plummer and Bobby Wright are in lock down which is sixteen hours, you see . . . sixteen hours every day.

Off in another cell there is singing.

Some people don't like singing. They take turns telling the guy to "Shut up." A lot of people get pissy over any racket above and beyond the unavoidable hollow and constant din. And when you hear it's crowded up there in maximum security these days, believe it.

The guy's singing isn't at all bad. He's a kid. He sings about a dancing bear, a chimney sweep, a ship at sea, a gypsy. His voice is a high trill of revolving words down through the endlessly lighted, never dark nights of the endless formidable grids, of thuds and clangs and chuckling TV's.

Carroll Plummer hears none of this. And with his eyes shut he can block out all but the feeling of his skin and the solidness of his body. It is a rigamarole here you have to go through to die by your own hand. In the world of punishment the two things they intransigently deny you are *life* and *death*.

But the drugs will always move from hand to hand and the bedding is supple enough to knot.

Carroll pulls off his shirt, regards the weave. The length of the sleeves. The quality of the seams. He pulls off his T-shirt. He looks over at the bunks, Bobby's back . . . the back of Bobby's graying head. He looks to the row of bars, their paint peeling delicately . . . like scales of a perch. He looks at the windowless wall. He looks at the ceiling. Then back at the bars, where the horizontal meets the vertical, a junction of iron taller than himself.

PART SEVENTEEN

Anneka with her jacket over her waitress clothes slumps on the couch, while others yak and run about, getting ready for Easter.

Anneka preoccupied with a monster movie. Black-and-white. Foreign. People's mouths are not in sync with their cries and shouts. Big thing in a cage in a city. People selling tickets to crowds coming to look at the big thing. Big thing is at least two stories tall. The big thing roars. It is your standard Tyranosaurus Rex type creature . . . a lot of teeth, little arms.

Conversation of the aunts and Anneka's mother and Grammie Dot is boisterous. They seem almost to be their old selves.

Now from out of the ocean trudges a monster like the first one only this one is FIFTY stories tall.

It is night in this seaside city. Weird tinny creepy music accompanies this monster's every move. This hugest of monsters rips the city apart. There are fires, explosions, sirens, wee screams. The thing picks up cars and flicks them away. It leaves what looks like a hospital and a major office complex in just a smoldering pile of bricks and steel girders.

The army tries to kill the big thing with bazookas, machine guns, rocket launchers, flamethrowers. But bullets just bounce off. Flames roll away. Big thing's skin is not flammable . . . kind of metallic-looking . . . but probably green . . . though with black-and-white film you can only wonder.

Searchlights crisscross, illuminate, pick out the big face . . . makes the big face squint. Makes the big thing roar in anger.

Nothing can stop the big thing.

This big, most humongous of monsters arrives at the cage where the smaller one is, tears at the wire. The wire is electric. It sparks and hisses. ZAP! But the big thing opens it right up. Small monster steps out. The small monster that is only the size of a two-story house. It is plain . . . this is a mother and child. Mother and child step along over the ruin and rubble . . . a few sirens, single searchlight, everything in flames.

The sea hisses as the giant mother's foot touches water, her metallic skin heated by so much assault. The baby treads along, beady-eyed, monsterific . . . nothing the human race could call adorable, but to its mother, he is everything.

Now he is stepping into the sea, too . . . hip deep, chest deep, chin deep. The water folds around them.

So this is a story with a happy ending. Anneka stares with an unreadable expression, watching the credits play over the black nighttime sea, the waves rolling, foaming onto the beach . . . the tinny creepy music . . . the film very old, spotty, snowy. Just another cheap Saturday afternoon filler. Probably bowling is next.

HARVEST AMERICAN WRITING

Diana Abu-Jaber
Arabian Jazz

Tina McElroy Ansa
Baby of the Family
Ugly Ways

Carolyn Chute
The Beans of Egypt, Maine
Letourneau's Used Auto Parts
Merry Men

Harriet Doerr
Consider This, Señora

Donald Harington
The Choiring of the Trees
Ekaterina

Randall Kenan
Let the Dead Bury Their Dead

Dan McCall
Messenger Bird

Lawrence Naumoff
Silk Hope, NC
Taller Women: A Cautionary Tale

Karen Osborn
Patchwork

Jim Shepard
Kiss of the Wolf

Brooke Stevens
The Circus of the Earth and the Air

Oxford Stroud
Marbles

Sandra Tyler
Blue Glass